C000260585

About the author

Don left school at the age of fourteen and started to work for the Manchester Ship Canal Company. He serves a seven year apprenticeship in the Company's main engineering works, Mode Wheel Workshops at Weaste, Salford.

He was apprenticed as a locomotive fitter and was then called up for National Service. He worked on all manner of machines and equipment which gave him a good grounding in engineering. During his service in the Royal electrical and Mechanical Engineers regiment (R.E.M.E.) he was introduced to other skills and experiences which broadened his horizons even more. After twenty years with the M.S.C, he took up a position with the University of Manchester as a technician at the laboratory of the Aeronautics Department, later moving to the departmental drawing office. There he was involved in the design of such things as wind tunnels and small experimental models.

Due to his early years, Don was inspired to write the history of the *Railways of the Manchester Ship Canal* and during the research for that book he came across a great many stories connected with the building of the canal which prompted him to write this novel

People of the Cut

Acknowledgments

I wish to thank Elaine Lowe, Freda Sykes, Louise Meldon and David Roberts for offering their services in typing the manuscript. Their offers of help and their subsequent efforts gave me the impetus to start the book, as I could not at that time use the word processor.

Also I thank my brother John, Ian and Elaine Lowe, Craig Edwards and others for their help in surmounting the difficulties I was having with the computer.

Dedication

This book is dedicated to my dear wife Pat; she certainly suffers for my art!

Don Thorpe

People of the Cut

Vanguard Press

VANGUARD PAPERBACK

A CIP catalogue record for this title is
available from the British Library.

ISBN 978 1 84386 710 4

Vanguard Press is an imprint of
Pegasus Elliot MacKenzie Publishers Ltd.
www.pegasuspublishers.com

First Published in 2011

Vanguard Press
Sheraton House Castle Park
Cambridge England

Printed & Bound in Great Britain

Disclaimer

With the exception of people like Thomas Andrew Walker, Lord Egerton of Tatton, Daniel Adamson, Councillor Bosdin Leach and the named engineers, the characters in the book are all the product of my imagination.

At no point in the narrative are there any words or passages which imply any criticism of any of the named personages. Nor are there any words or passage designed to sully the reputation of those personages.

Contents

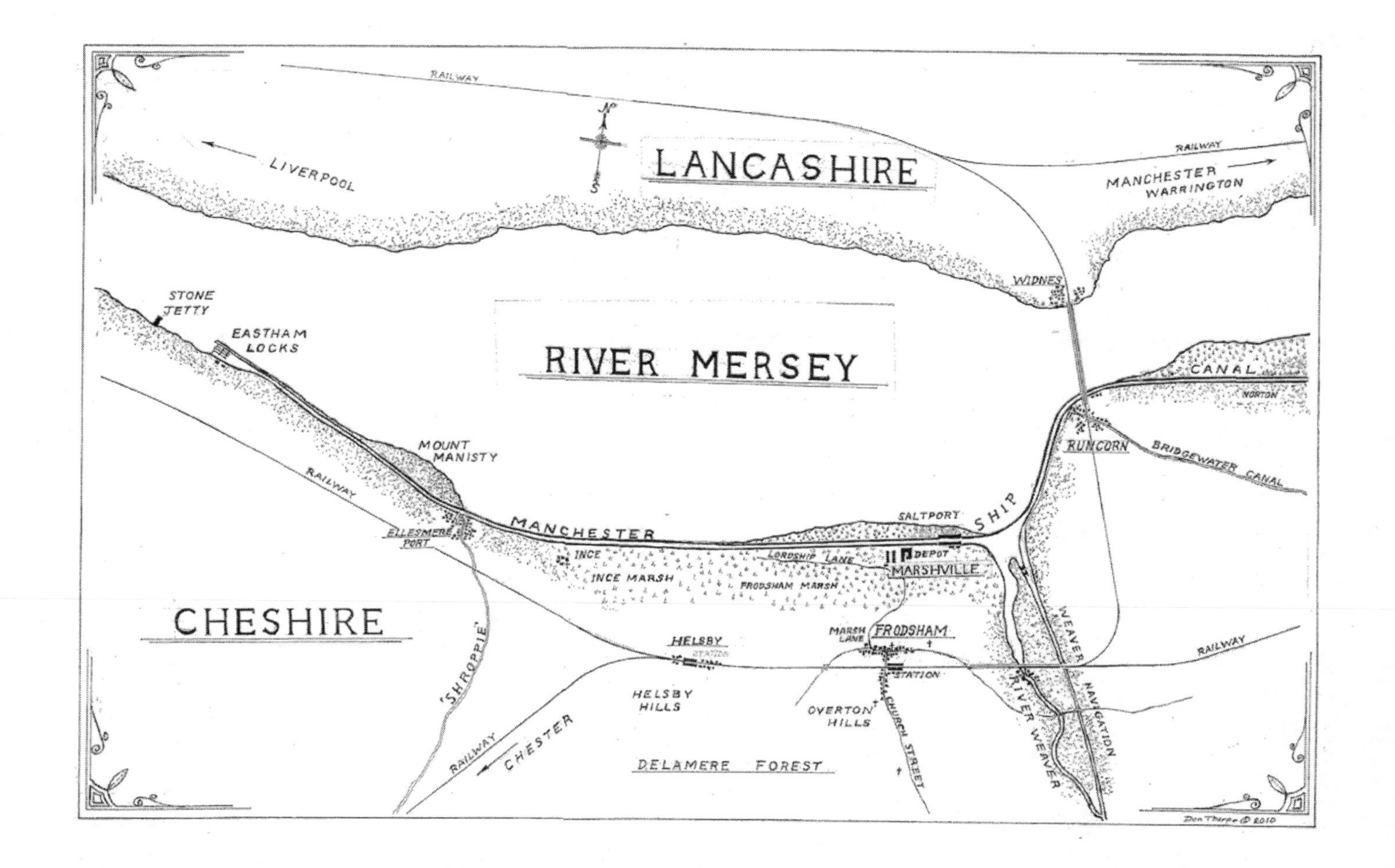
LANCASHIRE
RIVER MERSEY
CHESHIRE
RAILWAY
LIVERPOOL
MANCHESTER
WARRINGTON
WIDNES
STONE
JETTY
EASTHAM
LOCKS
CANAL
NORTON
RUNCORN
BRIDGEWATER CANAL
MOUNT
MANISTY
MANCHESTER
SHIP
SALTPORT
ELLESMERE
PORT
INCE
INCE MARSH
LORDSHIP LANE
DEPOT
MARSHVILLE
FRODSHAM MARSH
MARSH
LANE
FRODSHAM
STATION
HELSBY
HELSBY
HILLS
OVERTON
HILLS
CHURCH STREET
WEAVER NAVIGATION
RIVER WEAVER
'SHROPPIE'
CHESTER
DELAMERE FOREST
Don Thorpe © 2010

Chapter 1

Norfolk. Autumn, 1888

Unusually warm for the time of year, the air outside was only slightly cooler than that inside the cottage. Such air as passed through the tiny casement window was heavy with the scents of a dry and dusty day just ending. Very little light entered the room, for the heat haze which had dulled the sun's brilliance during the day now did the same to the starlight.

The wakeful man lying in his bed was used to the lack of light; even in good light the overhanging thatch made the room a little dull. However, it was neither the light nor the oppressive heat which was stopping Thomas Banham, Yard Foreman, from sleeping. Indeed, with the worried state of mind he was in, he was hardly aware of the discomfort engendered by such minor irritations. There had been many nights of troubled sleep these last few months and if he judged the situation correctly, there would be many more before things were settled one way or another. Life had been, if not idyllic, certainly more settled when Mr. Serle owned Longfields Estate, but since his late employer had sold up and moved to Norwich, events had shown that the estate employees, the Banham family in particular, had much to be unsettled about.

Even with his thoughts ranging over the unpleasant changes brought about with the advent of Captain Rodgerson into their relatively peaceful lives, Thomas was still aware of the various sounds associated with the cottage at night, and his mind was assailed by his main worries, those concerning his family.

Lying beside him his wife Beth breathed evenly as one in a deep untroubled sleep, undisturbed by the sudden cricks and creaks from the woodwork, together with the occasional noises coming from the fields as nocturnal creatures fought their survival battles.

As yet, Beth had no idea how bad things were between her husband and Captain Rodgerson, and knew nothing about the man's provocative goading. Thomas had so far managed not to rise to the man's baiting; he was determined to keep a firm grip on his temper as he had done for over twenty-five years, ever since one particularly reprehensible episode when, in a rage, he had narrowly missed killing another youth.

Being possessed of such a temper was all the more surprising when considering the temperament of his parents. Thomas's mother, a gentle Norfolk-born woman of indifferent health, had never in her son's memory displayed any anger, her forbearance with his father being sufficient to make her a saint in her son's eyes. His father, a Cambridgeshire man, was a good-humoured, bookish person who, although adoring his wife, at times caused her a great deal of worry with his schemes for making money (something which rarely happened). But even when his latest scheme had failed, he would receive only the mildest of reproof from her.

They were aware of their son's temper and did their best to get him to control it, but it was the incident which occurred when he was a seventeen-year-old apprentice which finally shocked him into doing something about it himself.

At the time he was working for the firm of Thomas Burrell, engineers and traction-engine makers, of Thetford. What started as a silly prank nearly ended in tragedy.

A fellow apprentice had thrown a paraffin-soaked cleaning rag at him which caught him full in the face. In a blind fury, with his eyes smarting from the paraffin, Thomas had picked up the first thing on the bench his fingers touched, and hurled it with all his might towards his tormentor. The object was a large file without the handle, and the pointed tang buried itself into the timber baulk behind which the other boy had been hidden.

Both boys were shocked and it was sufficient to make them put aside their differences as they wrestled to wrench the file out of the baulk before anybody else saw it, for such a stupid bit of horseplay would have earned them both the sack and without a reference.

Beth knew about his temper, not that she had ever seen any evidence of it, for from the earliest days of their courtship he had been completely honest with her. But fortunately, in all those years he had never had to contend with anybody as vindictive as Captain Rodgerson

For his family's sake he knew that he must not allow himself to be provoked; they would be in a very desperate position if he lost his job. He knew that one single rash word was all it would take, and that would lead to the loss of their home, for the cottage they lived in was tied to his job.

His thoughts shifted to the early days in his life and the time when he first met Beth. The year was Eighteen Sixty-eight. At that time he was working as a journeyman fitter with the firm of Henry Maudslay & Company at their London works, and Thomas had been very thankful to have been taken on, as the company were very choosy about whom they would employ.

Thomas's superintendant, a Mr. Rigby, and his wife were old friends of Mr. and Mrs. Serle, and they had arranged a visit during the early summer of that year. A joking reference by Mr. Serle to an 'ailing windpump' and an exhortation to 'bring your tools' had resulted in Mr. Rigby bringing Thomas and *his* tools to Longfields Estate. To get Thomas away from Maudslay's, Mr. Rigby had suggested that he treat it as his annual holiday (unpaid of course), but with the chance of earning a little remuneration.

Thomas knew that he was being manipulated, but the chance of escaping the soot-laden air of the capital and to breathe the pure air of his native Norfolk was too good a chance to miss.

Travelling to Norwich by train was done according to Mr. Rigby's dictates, and he and his wife travelled first class whilst Thomas was put in a third-class carriage, but the journey from Norwich to Wroxing was completed using the Norwich to Cromer stagecoach. This meant that Thomas had to ride inside with the Rigbys, and Mrs. Rigby had chatted with Thomas most of the journey, much to her husband's exasperation.

They arrived at Reeve House in a certain Mr. Timms's trap, but a message from Mr. Serle sent Thomas back to Wroxing village where he was to lodge with Mrs. Pugh, the Postmistress. Apparently Thomas was supposed to have slept in the stable block, but two of the stable hands had succumbed to some sort of sickness and it had been decided that it would be unfair to subject him to the chance of falling victim of whatever was troubling the men.

Within an hour of settling in at the Post Office with Mrs. Pugh, Thomas had come face to face with one of the young housemaids from Reeve House, and he thought his heart would stop. With her beautiful chestnut brown hair and her greenish grey eyes, she affected him like no other girl he had ever met. Many months later Thomas was to learn that he had affected her in exactly the same way.

None of this was missed by the voluble but sharp-eyed Mrs. Pugh and she let him know in no uncertain terms that he would be closely watched with regard to the girl. She told him that she and many others in the village were 'powerful fond' of Elizabeth Jane Grice and wouldn't take kindly to any 'smart young man from London' trifling with her.

Thomas had no intention of 'trifling' with the girl; he had made up his mind that she was going to be his for good, but how he was to get past this army of self-elected guardians and set his cap at her in the one week that he had at his disposal, he did not know.

In fact it was the vociferous Mrs. Pugh who managed the whole business for him. The truth was that when Thomas had come to the Post Office about the room, Mrs. Pugh, whatever she had said to his face, had been taken with the open-faced and well-spoken young man, and saw him as the perfect match for young Beth, but she wanted to make sure about him before she poked her nose into such a delicate business.

As the week went by, Thomas even managed to share a pot of tea with Beth and the cook (another of the girl's guardians) in the kitchen at Reeve House. He was convinced that the beautiful young maid at least found him interesting, if no more than that.

Mrs. Pugh told him something about the girl's early years, about Beth's affection-starved life with her cheerless parents, a lovely and lovable child in poor clothing who obtained her affection and care from others in the village. And she told him how Mrs. Serle had more or less 'bought' the child from the Grices and took her to the House, ostensibly as a maid, although the little girl was not yet ten years of age. She told him of the difference in the girl from that day on; clean and properly dressed, she had been nurtured by the Serles, given an education that she would never have got with her own parents, and turned into a 'real lady', as Mrs. Pugh would proudly have it.

At the end of the week, which Thomas had really enjoyed, with the job successfully completed and his 'remuneration' almost matching his normal week's wage, regretfully he had to return to London. However, he left a letter with Mrs. Pugh to be given to Mr. and Mrs. Serle. In it he had requested permission to write to Miss Grice.

A few days after he was back at his work, he received a reply from Mr. Serle which, whilst reminding him that they had no jurisdiction over Miss Grice's correspondence, they were quite satisfied that he was in no way unsuitable to exchange letters with her. Furthermore, they informed him, as Miss Grice herself had expressed a desire to correspond with him, coupled with a recommendation from Mrs. Pugh, they put up no objection.

Thomas was overjoyed and as soon as possible he wrote back thanking them for what he saw as a compliment to his character. The following day Beth received her very first letter and Thomas would have been gratified if he could have seen her reaction to it. She read and reread it several times, then gave it to Mrs. Serle to read. Her mistress was only too pleased to read it, and check whether the contents bore out the high opinion that they had formed of the young man. Satisfied at the tone of the letter, she then gently told her maid that any letters in the future had to be treated as Beth's alone to read.

That night Beth slept with the letter under her pillow, and indeed did so with each letter she received from that day on.

It was something special to look forward to for Thomas also, but about seven weeks after his visit, he received another very welcome letter, this one from Mrs. Pugh. She informed him that Mr. Timms's son, Billy, and a man from Longfields Estate, had left to join the Yeomanry, and in consequence there were now two jobs to be had at Wroxing.

She urged him to write and apply for one of them and added that his room at the Post Office was still available. It did not take much deliberation on Thomas's part, and he applied for the job at Longfields Estate.

It surprised him at just how smoothly everything went. Mr. Serle, having met him and seen examples of his work, was very quick to offer him the job. Mr. Rigby, a good-hearted man, ruefully wished him much luck for the future, the gentleman having realised his folly at using Thomas the way he had done, reflecting that he alone was to blame for losing a good tradesman.

Later Thomas was to wonder whether Mr. Serle and Mrs. Pugh had put their heads together and brought him to Wroxing. As the lady herself confided in him some time after, both she and the Serles had been rather concerned at some of the unsuitable young men (and some not-so-young men) in the village who had begun to take an interest in Beth. Foremost amongst them was Simon Andern, the blacksmith's son and apprentice, who, although a sound young man, was in many people's opinion much too rough and ready for a girl of Beth's sensitive nature.

Within a few months Thomas and Beth were walking out together. Over the next year Thomas had proved himself again and again in his work with the result that when Mr. Serle promoted him to yard foreman, most of the men accepted the new situation without a murmur. With more money in his pocket Thomas felt that he could afford to ask Beth to be his wife, and on the twelfth of May, Eighteen Seventy, he and Elizabeth Jane Grice were married.

A wonderful gesture on Mr. Serle's part was to let them have the tenancy of the old cottage which belonged to the estate.

As he lay there recalling the events of the past years, Thomas could not bring to mind any really unhappy times except those when first Mrs. Pugh, the family's adopted 'aunt', had died and in the last year when Mrs. Serle had died. He could not see such happiness prevailing at Longfields Estate again with Captain Rodgerson at the helm.

The gentle snoring from the next room he knew to be coming from his eldest son, Will, whilst the slight wheezing coming from the same room told him that Peter, the youngest member of the family was suffering the effects of the present dry, dusty weather. The little boy was subject to asthma and had been examined by the Serle's own doctor, a kindness that had been very much appreciated by the Banhams. It was the doctor's opinion that Peter would grow out of it and he had told them that they should not, as he put it, 'mollycoddle' him too much.

Only a thin partition separated the boys from their parents. Even so it was much better than it had been when the newly wedded Banhams had moved in over eighteen years earlier. Since taking the tenancy of the two-hundred-year-old cottage, they had made alterations and carried out repairs to the near derelict property with the blessing and practical assistance of the owner. Mr. Serle had supplied all the materials on the understanding that Thomas did the work himself, a task the owner judged him easily capable of, and in truth the cottage was in far better condition than it had been in the last two hundred years or so.

When he and Beth moved in, the rooms were much as they were when the cottage was built, two rooms downstairs and a large open platform above. It now boasted three bedrooms upstairs, admittedly small, giving a degree of privacy, something that, at Victoria's age, was much appreciated by their daughter.

Victoria was approaching seventeen and was as beautiful in nature as she was in appearance. In looks she was just like her mother had been when Thomas had first met her. These God-given gifts had given them so much joy and contentment over the years, but were now a source of worry, particularly to Thomas, since the new owners had moved into Reeve House.

Both mother and daughter worked at the House, Beth having been in service since she was twelve years of age when she started as a scullery maid, although she had been with the Serles much longer than that. Thomas had been taken on when Beth was just eighteen.

Life had been good with Mr. Serle as master of the estate, and as the years went by, Thomas and Beth had both improved their respective positions. Beth, by then married to Thomas, worked as a parlour maid. With the arrival of their children, her job had remained safe and eventually she had been offered the position of cook, a job she had been delighted to accept.

Mr. and Mrs. Serle, having no children of their own, had taken the Banham children to their hearts, Mrs. Serle lending support to the Banhams in their efforts to improve their family's education beyond that given by the small ill-equipped village school. She had given them access to her modest library, told them about the countries and seas beyond Britain with the aid of a large rotating globe of the world, and of her and her husband's travels in Europe and Egypt. A favourite with the children was her collection of Mr. Francis Frith's photographs of places all over Britain. The reward for the Serles was the affection and devotion showed by the Banham children.

Nostalgic memories of those happier days intruded into Thomas's troubled mind but only served to aggravate his worries about their future, but even more worrying was their daughter's behaviour these last few days. Victoria had been unusually quiet and seemed reluctant to go to work each morning. This was all the more disturbing, for she had very quickly formed a strong bond of loyalty with her new mistress, to whom she was personal maid, as she had been previously to the late Mrs. Serle.

Beth had also commented on their daughter's behaviour but had shrugged it off as being 'something to do with her age', a view not shared by her husband. Whilst he bowed to her superior knowledge on many things, he was deeply worried that the problem might have stemmed from something either said or done by Captain Rodgerson.

Thomas, in his capacity of yard foreman, was more often in contact with their employer than Beth was, and he had very early on sized up the man as a bullying brute, but one who liked to look well in the eyes of the society he aspired to. The yard foreman, like many others, saw his attentions to Mrs. Rodger son's sister, Mrs. Howard, as downright scandalous, and he had formed the opinion that the man was nothing better than a philanderer.

This last trait was the reason for the gnawing suspicion in Thomas's mind concerning Victoria. 'As God is my witness,' thought Thomas savagely, 'I'll strangle the cur with my bare hands if I find he has interfered with my sweet, innocent girl.'

His thoughts ranged back to the day when Mrs. Serle had died suddenly leaving a very anguished husband and a distressed staff, her death draining the joy from the household. Victoria had been particularly devastated, having never before lost anyone so close to her, and she had loved Mrs. Serle dearly.

That terrible day, thought Thomas drearily, was the first of many unhappy days that followed. After the loss of his beloved wife, Mr. Serle, whose health had been indifferent for some years, had begun to feel the burden of the estate more than he could bear, whereupon, following advice from his doctor and his friends, he had decided to sell up and buy a modest house in Norwich.

When everything had been set in train, he gathered his estate workers and house staff together and broke the news. Apart from those present who had been privy to Mr. Serle's decisions, the assembly was shocked almost to silence. All that was heard was the muffled sound of one of the maids sobbing. Before anyone could speak, Mr. Serle held up his hand and began to tell them of the future for the estate and their jobs.

He informed them that Longfields Estate had been bought by a member of one of the county's best known and respected families. Mr. Serle went on to state that he had been assured that there would no dismissals as it had been noted with approval that the estate was known to be well run and in excellent shape. At this he gave a nod of acknowledgement to Thomas.

After the gathering broke up, the men, sad but relieved at Mr. Serle's assurances, went back to work, whilst the rest of the staff returned indoors. As

Beth and Victoria were about to enter the house, Mr. Serle asked Beth to come to his study. Once there he broached the subject of staff at his new house.

He explained that his own staff would be of necessity a small one; his manservant, whom everyone was aware would be going with him, whilst he already had the name of one lady who would be able to take on the housekeeper's post, but the position of cook was one which had not been filled. Although, he stressed, he realised the likelihood of Beth being able to move to Norwich was remote, the position was hers if she wanted it, but sadly he could not offer any employment for Thomas or Victoria.

Although Beth was pleased that Mr. Serle valued her skills enough to want to retain her services, she was rather taken aback by the uncharacteristic thoughtlessness of her employer as regards the splitting up of the Banham family. Even if an arrangement could be reached so that they could have time together at intervals, Beth was both shocked and hurt at Mr. Serle's lack of concern for her family.

Mr. Serle was obviously uncomfortable with his handling of the situation and hastily added that he understood how close the family was. He then said encouragingly that a man as experienced as Thomas would have no difficulty in obtaining a position in the Norwich area if circumstances dictated such a course of action.

Even to Beth's innocent mind, the last bit seemed to hint at something rather ominous.

There was however one thing clear in her mind; the Banham family would stay together. She thanked Mr. Serle for the offer but declined the position. Just as she was about to leave the room, her employer, conscious of the clumsy way in which he was ending their close, almost family association, said, "Beth, I want to thank you for all you have done for me and Mrs. Serle, and for the joy you have brought into this house over the years." Then he said, with a return to his more businesslike tone, "Remember, Beth, should events not turn out for the best, my offer still stands." With that rather ambiguous end to his little speech, Mr. Serle wished her and her family well and let her go.

Beth was so overcome that she was hard put not to burst into tears, but she managed a whispered "thank you, Sir," before making her escape to the kitchen where she did break down.

Beth's mind was in a whirl; whatever was Mr. Serle hinting at, surely he would not want Thomas to give up his position just because the estate was to have new owners? She was quite bewildered by the episode and resolved to talk it over with her husband when the family were in bed.

For a few moments after Beth had left the room. Mr. Serle sat unmoving at his desk, then leaned back wearily in his chair, his eyes closed as if trying to blot out the whole sorry business. "Oh, Mary, my dear," he whispered sadly, "why has it all gone so badly wrong, without you here I do not want to stay, I miss you so."

He felt spent and useless. The business of selling the estate had been a mistake, at least as far as selling to the Rodgersons. Mrs. Rodgerson was a fine lady and she did come from an excellent family. Initially he had dealt with the buyer, Mrs. Phoebe Prentice, and had been aware from the beginning that she was presenting the estate to her great-niece and her husband. Only after the completion of the sale had he met Mrs. Rodgerson and had gained the impression that the lady, for some reason, was not exactly overjoyed at being the recipient of the gift.

Whilst he found Mrs. Rodgerson a very charming lady, it was only lately, after meeting her husband, Captain Rodgerson, that his doubts had set in about the wisdom of selling to that particular couple.

Mr. Serle was a gentle, thoughtful man but he was very shrewd, and could read a person's character quite well. He saw the man as a vain and arrogant scoundrel and unless he was very much mistaken, a cruel man as well. By speaking to Beth about the position in his new home, he was desperately trying to give the Banham family a lifeline if things went badly for them. He was positive that they would need one. It was just that he felt that he had handled his attempt quite badly.

As Thomas lay wakeful in their bed he once again recalled Beth's interview with Mr. Serle and came to the conclusion that their late employer had been more far-sighted than anybody had realised.

As time went by there had been many instances where Captain Rodgerson's arrogance and military attitude had been displayed to the farm workers or yard labourers, but it was not until a few days ago that Thomas had borne the brunt of the owner's foul temper.

It had all started with sacking of a labourer for taking a few potatoes, something that the previous owner had never considered a crime. Agricultural workers were on such low rates of pay that the loss of a small amount of vegetables, providing that the privilege was not abused, had always been ignored by Mr. Serle.

The dismissal of Caleb the labourer had angered the rest of the men but it had also served to make them uneasy as to who would be the next to lose their job through some minor transgression, real or imaginary.

On approaching Captain Rodgerson for permission to take on a new man as a replacement, Thomas, who already had a man in mind, was greeted first with sarcasm, followed by a display of arrogant bad temper. The man's hateful voice still rang in Thomas's ears, the tirade etched in his memory.

"So, Banham, you have it in mind to employ a new man eh?" He then raised his hand in mock resignation. "No, don't tell me the man's name or any other dreary details, no doubt you consider his abilities sufficiently useful to employ the wretch." He went on in the same sneering voice that had the foreman longing to punch the man on the nose. "I have no doubt that you have other schemes in that head of yours to bring changes to the estate, yes, eh?"

The last part was delivered in a gentle, almost reproachful manner, but was then followed with an outburst of sheer bad-tempered invective about Thomas and his role on the estate. For the life of him, the foreman could not understand what he had said or done to have made his employer dislike him so much, but he realised in those few moments that it would not be long before he too would be out of a job or perhaps demoted to a labourer's position.

He realised also that from that moment on, he would have to be even more careful for his family's sake and keep a still tongue in his head.

Chapter 2

The Ploughing

From the cottage, Woods Field, the area due to go under the plough could not be seen, but the smoke from both traction engines was clearly visible rising in the still air. The boiler fires had been lit earlier by the farm boys, who should have started at five o'clock to ensure they had full working pressure in time for the start of ploughing. It was going to be a long day's work, and this was one of the few times when Thomas was out of the cottage at the same time as his wife and daughter. *Their* normal day had to start early in order that everything would be ready for the owners and their guests when they arose from their beds.

Thomas felt unwell and was suffering from a dull but persistent headache, and was uncharacteristically sharp with the men when he arrived at the field to find them lounging around one of the ploughing engines. Although the men looked surprised, there was no comment apart from one man. It was Seth, the 'man-boy' as some called him, who had been taken on by Captain Rodgerson against his foreman's advice. Seth called out cheekily to Thomas, "Aw, Mizer Banham, we ain' gonna' spoil the field 'afore you came, eh, boys."

John, one of the older hands, put his hand on Seth's arm and said, "Come on, Seth boy, we'll get over to the other engine and you can work by me." Thomas looked on and his irritability evaporated as he beheld the pathetic human being whose body was larger than any of the men present but whose eyes mirrored the small boy's mind trapped inside.

Gently he said, "That's right, Seth, you help John, but mind yourself near the wire rope and the belts, boy," and to the other, "mind out now, John." The older man nodded his understanding and answered, "Right, Mr. Banham," before turning away, taking Seth with him to the other side of the field. The farm boys had done their jobs reasonably well and both boilers had a good head of steam even if there was rather too much dirty smoke for Thomas's liking.

Steam ploughing was mostly done using two traction engines fitted with large cable winches which were slung under the boilers. The road wheels were unpinned allowing the winches to be operated without the traction engine moving. From the winch drum came a wire rope which spanned the field and connected with the winch drum of the second traction engine. One rope was fastened to the balanced plough, a contraption which looked rather like a large see-saw on wheels. Each end of the 'see-saw' held a seat and a steering wheel and below were the two sets of plough shares. The pull of the cable had the effect of pulling the end with the seated driver downward then forward, causing the ploughshares to dig into the soil.

At the end of each run the driver would change seats on the plough and the manoeuvre would be repeated to cut the next furrow back towards the first ploughing engine. Both engines would be repositioned one furrow width after each cut.

Many farmers did not have their own equipment for steam ploughing, and if they did not do the work using horses, they would employ contractors who moved from farm to farm during the ploughing months. However, under Thomas's hand, the Longfields ploughing gang could hold their own against most contractors, but the new owner had promised that if, in his opinion, the job took longer than he thought it should, he would bring in contractors the next time. Thomas had no means of knowing how much experience Captain Rodgerson possessed about the subject, but he reasoned that the man would make a judgement on the matter purely on the basis of like or dislike, and the yard foreman had realised that his employer did not appear to like many people at all. His exact words aimed at Thomas left him in no doubt as to his chances of keeping his job. Captain Rodgerson's closing remark after his talk of using contractors was to observe, "Well, I wouldn't need a mechanic, would I?" By taking poor Seth on, he had handicapped the ploughing gang enormously. Thomas thought bitterly that it would not come as a surprise if they learned that the man had done it deliberately.

At the far side of the field from Thomas, John Wilson signalled that all was correct and ready for the signal to start. His foreman checked with the plough steersman and on receiving the word that he too was ready, climbed aboard *Horatio* the traction engine. Both engines were named after battle heroes, the far engine being named *Wellington*.

A blast on the whistle and the rope went taught as *Wellington*'s winch took up the tow, and the plough dug in then started across the field. As it closed on the far engine Thomas began to relax. With his mind on his work he came into his element and all other thoughts were thrust to one side. The whistle blast from John Wilson's engine announced the arrival of the plough at the far side, which meant a repositioning of both engines. This was soon done, and the plough was quickly dispatched on its way back to Thomas. Whilst cutting the third furrow, rapid shrieks from *Wellington*'s whistle signalled stop and reverse, which Thomas obeyed instantly."What the devil's gone wrong now," he grumbled, as he clambered down from the engine.

Then he heard the screaming, and the foreman broke into a run towards the group of men clustered round somebody lying on the ground. He knew at once from the size of the injured man who it was. Seth had passed out and his dead weight was giving them a great deal of difficulty as they tried to move him away from the steel rope. Thomas was almost sick as he saw the state of the crushed and bloodied hand.

One of the labourers was not able to contain himself and was vomiting by the traction engine. As Thomas shouted to the farm boy with the order to 'run like the devil' to Doctor Porby's house, the safety valve on the traction engine lifted, the shrieking noise adding to the bedlam. "Shut off the blower," he yelled to John, and then to the second farm boy, who had just arrived, he gave the task of bringing the cart over so that the unfortunate Seth could be carried away.

Gingerly he lifted Seth's arm and steeled himself to look at the mess that was the man-boy's hand. He could see immediately that the poor wretch would lose at least two of his fingers and maybe even more. Carefully he wrapped his handkerchief around the hand but grimaced as the blood continued to pour onto the ground. All his knowledge was to no avail; he simply did not know how to deal with this situation.

John Wilson, kneeling holding Seth's head clear of the soil, spoke. "He needs a tourniquet around his arm, Thomas, that will stop the blood coming." Thomas, clearly relieved, let John take over and soon the flow was stemmed. While this was being done Seth was beginning to moan, showing signs of regaining consciousness. Both men tensed themselves, for they knew that if poor Seth saw his hand and started thrashing around, they would be hard put to restrain him.

"I knew something would go wrong with Seth around," groaned Thomas. "I just knew it was asking for trouble and I tried to tell the Captain so. In God's name, why did the man not listen?"

John nodded his agreement and said apologetically, "I'm sorry, Thomas, had him moving the coal up the field a bit but suddenly he was there, excited and laughing a bit wild, and then, as the plough was moving towards us, he suddenly jumped forward and started banging on the wire and, well you know what happened." He shook his head as though to shake the scene from his mind. "You were quick, Thomas, no sooner was he in the winch than he was out again."

Suddenly he stopped as he noticed that his companion was looking beyond him, then he too heard the fast approaching horses. Looking round he saw two horse riders bearing down on them at a smart pace. The leading rider was Mrs. Howard, closely followed by Captain Rodgerson, and they could see he was in a towering rage.

"Banham!" he yelled. "What the devil's going on? I don't employ you to be loafing around with the men. Get back to your work or by God I'll make you regret you ever worked on this estate."

He was roaring at the foreman in the same arrogant manner that he had formally used on his army subordinates, and Thomas's eyes narrowed in anger, but before he could reply, Mrs. Howard exclaimed, "Gavin, here comes Doctor Porby. What is going on !"

A terrible cry came from the giant on the ground and as all eyes turned to him, he attempted to rise then fell back, wailing as his damaged hand struck the ground. Thomas and John dropped to their knees to hold him but Seth just lay there sobbing.

Doctor Porby leaped down from his trap but instead of making straight for the injured Seth, went up to the mounted riders. "Morning, Mrs. Howard, morning, Captain Rodgerson," he said jocularly. "Bad business, hey!"

Thomas had had enough. "Doctor, the talk can wait, the sick man is on the ground, not on the horse!" and he practically pulled the doctor over to face the group clustered round the weeping giant, which to Thomas's surprise now included Seth's mother, who was kneeling by her son and making soothing sounds to the now quietly weeping Seth. Before any of the shocked onlookers could open their mouths he continued, “John has put on a tourniquet, Doctor, so can we get the poor fool down to your house quick as quick.” By this time the cart had been emptied of coal and sacks had been spread ready to receive Seth. The men then prepared themselves to lift him on the cart.

All this was in a few seconds, then suddenly Mrs. Howard burst out loudly, “Gavin, are you going to take that from this, this – insolent fool,” pointing at Thomas. The foreman, by now in a cold rage, spoke to the Captain, seated high above him on the massive hunter, but kept his voice level and clear. “Yes, Captain, are you going to take that from me, hey? Well I’ll tell you and the world this, poor Seth was crippled in his mind before but he was whole in his body, but now through you, he might lose his hand,” and he added in a rising tone, “I told you what might happen. Now are you convinced, man?” For a few seconds everyone was silent, the men and farm boys looking aghast at the outburst, then Mrs. Howard’s shrill voice shattered the silence. “How dare you speak to your employer in that tone? Gavin, use your whip on the scoundrel,” then stopped as she beheld her companion’s face. He was smiling. The look that he gave her was one of triumph mixed with malice.

“Oh no, Mrs. Howard, that would be the wrong thing to do, would it not,” he said. “No,”, he continued, in his silky voice, “Banham is a free man and he can have his say.” He paused, then said in a deliberate manner, obviously enjoying every word, “Even if he does lose his job and the cottage which goes with it.” Before it had properly sunk in with the listening group he carried on. “So get your belongings and your mealy-mouthed family and get off my land before nightfall. Do you hear, Banham, lock stock and barrel, out before nightfall.”

——— ——— ———

Icy despair gripped Thomas and like a man in a trance he turned away from the flushed triumphant face of his late employer, to begin the walk back to the cottage, the last time he would ever do so. His mind was in turmoil and he felt sick in his stomach. All those years ago, as a single man, and without a job, he had started out into the wider world of London to look for and eventually find work at Maudslay’s. At that time he had done so with a light step and a spirit of adventure in his heart, but now, with his family to support, and no job, his heart felt as leaden as his feet. “Oh God above,” he cried silently to himself, “why has this happened to us, to my Beth and my children, what have we done which is so wrong, how could I have allowed myself to lose my temper after all these years.” He could have kicked himself over and over again for allowing himself to be outmanoeuvred by the man.

As he stumbled on he became aware that somebody was following, the sound of boots striking the hard ground, the sound of a man in a hurry. Looking back he saw John the labourer trotting towards him, his face grim.

John had been on the estate almost as long as Thomas and held him in very high regard. “Thomas, boy,” he panted, “I’ve been told to make sure that you’ve moved out before nightfall.” He paused to get his breath, his eyes beseeching

Thomas to forgive him, then he burst out, "I don't want to do this, Thomas, you and me have been friends too long for me to go against you."

"That's all right, John," said Thomas heavily. "I'll be glad of your help but where we are going to end up, only the Lord knows." Both men fell silent and started once again towards the cottage.

As the heartbreaking task of moving everything out of the cottage and into the lane began, Thomas's practical nature reasserted itself, and he blessed the fact that at least the warm dry weather still prevailed which would ensure that none of their furniture would be damaged before it was moved into a place of shelter.

As he worked, his mind was ranging over the problem of where Beth and his family were to sleep the coming night; he was not too bothered about himself in that respect. In this weather he would simply find a secluded spot by the hedgerow and near a stream where he could drink and wash himself. For a moment he was not even contemplating the future, but he was certain of one thing: the family must stick together. Not for them was the grim prospect of the poorhouse with the chance of being split up. Beth and the family could possibly stay with her parents if nothing else could be found, although he knew that his family would hate the idea. His in-laws were not hard or cruel in any way; they were just plain miseries, and their cottage was dreary, damp and in truth, not too clean.

Still, thought Thomas, beggars cannot be choosers, and he ruefully recognised that they would be uncomfortably close to being beggars if he couldn't find work quickly.

It took but a short while too clear the lower rooms of the cottage and both men were wet with sweat when Thomas called a halt to their labours. Suddenly there were Beth and Victoria at the gate, both weeping, his daughter's arm protectively round her mother's shoulder. Beth was almost distraught and Thomas sprang forward as his wife appeared about to collapse. He helped her into one of the chairs, where she sat crouched whilst her husband kneeled by her, his arms holding her close. Victoria, silently weeping, could not bear to watch and rushed into the almost bare cottage, her home for as long as she could remember, in a few hours to be her home no more.

Outside, John stood uncertainly wondering where to put himself, his eyes filled with compassion and a lump in his throat. He would gladly have taken the Banham family into his own home if he had been able to, but he lived with his elderly mother in a cottage even smaller than this one, and neither had they storage space for the Banham furniture. His rage at his employer coursed through his body and he wished him and all landowners like him in purgatory.

Meanwhile Thomas had gently calmed his wife down and was assuring her in a confident manner that 'they would soon get things right with the Lord's help'. Beth knew he was, in fact, extremely worried himself but found herself comforted by his words; she had always regarded her husband as one who, once making his mind up to do something, always succeeded.

From the cottage came a more composed Victoria carrying a wooden tray on which was a teapot and crockery. "There," she said in a tremulous voice, "a cup of tea is just what everyone wants." Turning to John who was hovering uncertainly at the edge of the little garden, she said, "Mr. Wilson, would you care for a cup of tea?" He nodded and then smiled as she said in her best drawing-room manner, "Would you like a chair, Sir?"

Suddenly there was an odd sort of noise and all eyes fixed with concern on Beth. She was laughing. It was a quiet sound and Thomas, who could not see her downturned face, leaned forward anxiously. "Steady on, girl," he said quietly, but then his wife looked up and laughed out even louder. "Oh, Thomas, that was so funny, our Victoria serving tea," and tears of laughter came to her eyes. "That was so funny," she gasped again and wiped her eyes with the hem of her apron. Then everyone joined in, the tension broken. If the gale of laughter was a touch high-strung, it was just what was needed.

Heeding Victoria's invitation, John sat down by Thomas and Beth, all of them now ready for a cup of tea. At first an awkward silence hung over them, nobody knowing what to say, until Thomas turned to his friend and said, "Now, John, if..." and at that point he hesitated, not wanting to use profanity in front of his family. "If that man wants you to become yard foreman, I would only wish you well." Again he stopped as John appeared to be about to protest. "No, boy, you must look after yourself. I would say that you are the most fitted to take the position."

"I believe Thomas is right," said Beth a trifle tremulously. "We..." Her voice trailed away, then she sprang up, brushing down the folds of her apron, curtsied and in a faint tone said, "Mistress Rodgerson, what must you think of us." There at the gate stood Captain Rodgerson's wife. "May I speak to your wife, Mr. Banham," she whispered.

Thomas replied civilly but with no warmth. "Please come in and take a chair, Ma'am," then was immediately ashamed of himself as his wife's late employer cried out, "This is none of my doing," and rushing towards Beth, burst into tears.

Beth took over completely. "Thomas, bring the best chair, Victoria make a fresh pot of tea," and as everyone moved to comply, took Mrs. Rodgerson in her arms and said lovingly as if to her own chid, "There now, my dear, we don't hold you to blame for this, we know that a man has to run his house his own way," Then she added, before the sobbing woman could speak, "We will be fine, just you see, Mr. Banham is powerful clever with his hands and his brain, and I am sure there is many an employer who would be glad of him in their service."

As the sobbing gradually subsided, Beth was about to offer her own handkerchief to Mrs. Rodgerson, then just in time remembered that her own weeping had probably saturated the thing. Instead she signalled to Victoria the need, and her daughter rushed inside and up to her room where she found a sensible handkerchief, after which she quickly returned to where the two women, both now weeping, were holding on to each other. The men were nowhere to be seen.

Mrs. Rodgerson looked up, sniffed, very much like a little girl, and thanked Victoria, saying, "Mrs. Banham, Victoria, ask the men to put back your furniture, for you are not to leave your home, not for a few days at least." 'Was it distaste in her voice,' thought Victoria, as a former suspicion became a certainty in her mind? "My husband," said Mrs. Rodgerson coldly, "has decided to give you a chance to find a new place to live before you go." She came to a stop, her face working, then buried her head on Beth's shoulder, weeping like a child. "What will you do and what will I do when you are gone?" she cried. "I rely on you both so much." Her agonised cry lanced through both mother and daughter but Beth put on her best face and said stoutly, "Nonsense, if you don't mind my saying so, Ma'am, there are many who would serve you just as well and just as willingly," but was interrupted by her late employer. "But you are not simply my employees, you have become very dear to me. Who else in that house have I got to turn to?"

Beth and Victoria were so overwhelmed that they could not put in the words which would adequately answer that heartfelt plea. Victoria crouched down by Mrs. Rodgerson and tentatively put her hand on her late employer's arm. Then the three women of different ages were held for a few moments, sisters in their shared distress, and Victoria knew then what she had long suspected, that her dear lady had no love in her marriage and nobody close to confide in. The young girl felt a wave of pity for the other woman, comparing Mrs. Rodgerson with her own mother, who so obviously still loved her husband.

After a while, a calmer Mrs. Rodgerson left them and returned to her own home, although by then she hardly thought of it as home. The old brick and flint Hall, with its lovely outlook, the beautiful furniture and fine carpets, seemed to close in on her, and she felt caged. Running upstairs, she stifled the tears that threatened again, until she reached her bedroom, locked the door and flung herself on her bed where she wept, calling silently for the one man she truly loved, and had done since she had first met him as a child. "Oh, my love, where are you, I need you by me so badly this day." She did not know how to deal with this nightmare situation. After the earlier furious row she had conducted with her husband, a row which had absolutely devastated her but had also shaken the complacent Captain Rodgerson and her sister, she had threatened him with exposure to the other members of their social circle.

Once she had drawn out of him his contemptible activities regarding the poor wretch Seth and his use of the man as a device to lure his foreman into a state of anger, his lack of concern for the injuries Seth had sustained, and finally his treatment of the Banhams, she had turned from a well bred, dutiful wife into a raging tigress.

She had lashed him with her tongue, and her sister also, as Cecelia coolly attempted to pour scorn on Kate's beliefs concerning the 'lower classes', as Cecelia put it. The older sister had languidly walked away from the still raging scene with a bored expression on her face, but in reality she was very badly shaken; she had not seen Kate in such a rage since she was a child. 'Gavin had better watch his step,' thought Cecelia, for he was still fairly dependent on the allowance his wife gave him, and he did tend to be extravagant.

Downstairs, husband and wife faced each other, the atmosphere icy, he outwardly cool, almost derisive but inwardly raging. He was still shocked and taken aback by his wife's strength of feeling and the manner in which she had verbally attacked him and the ease with which she had dispatched her sister.

Angry as he was at being made to look less than masterful in front of Cecelia, he was even more angry at his wife's use of the one weapon which she knew would hurt him, and that was to reduce his position in the sight of others in their social circle, the Norfolk county society, a standing that he would do almost anything to maintain.

But he had flatly refused to reinstate Thomas Banham; the loss of face before his workmen was something else he could not bear, and he knew that whatever happened, the farm workers would most certainly talk. 'That would be damnably awkward,' he thought, 'if some of our crowd learned of his employment of the idiot. Still, he could always say he was 'giving the wretch a chance'. Not a particularly clever man, the more he considered what he had done, the more he realised the problems he had created for himself.

Eventually he was forced to grant a stay of eviction and his dogged wife got him to agree a payment of relief money of ten guineas above wages owed, they amounting to no more than one pound nineteen shillings and seven pence, little in total to keep a family for more than a few weeks. She told him nothing of her own plans for helping the Banhams. She did tell him that with regard to poor Seth, she was having her family physician take care of the young man; she had little faith in Dr. Porby, as he was another with an envy of the county society, and was forever fawning around her and her husband. No, she decided, it was to be her father's doctor and whoever else was needed to look after Seth. Actually, Captain Rodgerson thought that the last gesture was a wise move. It would reflect favourably on himself in the eyes of others if he let it be known that he had suggested it.

The following day at the cottage, Beth, her eyes swollen with her bouts of weeping, was hard at work doing as much washing as she could before they had to leave their old home, reasoning that at least they would have clean clothes to last them a few days once they were out.

Thomas was at the back of the cottage nailing odds and ends of wood together making storage chests and crates, for although the Banhams had very little of the world's goods, he had to consider the fact that wherever the family ended up, there was always the possibility that their bulkier belongings might be scattered about in the houses of family or benevolent neighbours. 'Lord knows where it will all go,' thought Thomas glumly.

His precious tools gathered over a lifetime would have to be boxed, but he decided that they must be immediately accessible in case he found work that involved his skills. Reluctantly he looked at his best wood stock. Some new, but most of it saved from old agricultural equipment, damaged furniture, and other pieces from the time when Mr. and Mrs. Serle were having alterations done in the house some years ago. Thomas had reluctantly come to the conclusion that whether the wood was oak, beech, mahogany or ash, or for that matter, just plain pine, it would have to be used to make the cases. Apart from any other consideration, it was going to be difficult to store a dusty stack of old timber when, as yet, they had no place to live.

Sighing at the waste of such beautiful wood, he buckled down to his task. An hour later he had worked out just how far his timber would go, and which of their possessions were to be boxed. However, before he had set saw to wood, he was interrupted by the sight of Beth, very much more controlled, coming towards him followed by, of all people, Simon Andern, the blacksmith, accompanied by his wife, Nora. To say that Thomas was surprised was to understate his feelings, for the two men had never been on good terms; in fact it would be nearer the truth to say that there was a great deal of animosity on the side of the smith.

Beth halted and said in a steady voice which held no trace of unfriendliness, "Thomas, Simon would like to have a word with you." As the other man stepped forward to face him, Nora impulsively moved to Beth and then placed her hand on her one-time friend's arm, murmuring an almost inaudible "Beth love". The next moment it was as if the years had been swept away as both women clung to each other.

Nora, the blacksmith's wife, had been Beth's closest friend throughout their childhood years but had fallen out with her when Simon started to show an interest in Beth. Even though Beth had made it plain that she had no interest in the young blacksmith's apprentice, he single-mindedly badgered her with repeated offers of marriage. Nora, who had also set her mind on whom she wanted to marry, resented her intended's interest in Beth, and refused to bother with her again. After all their early years of companionship, the sudden change to outright hostility had upset Beth greatly, for with her sunny nature she had never come up against really active dislike.

Simon Andern was, for all his infatuation, an intelligent young man and realised that unless a miracle occurred, Beth would never be his wife and eventually began courting Nora, albeit half-heartedly. With the arrival at Longfields Estate of the more articulate and well read Thomas, he had seen even his faintest hopes vanish, and on Beth's marriage to Thomas had proposed to Nora. With such shaky foundations it was amazing that the couple's marriage could survive, but it did and what is more, it was just as successful a union as that of the Banhams.

As time went by, there might have been a chance of reconciliation between the two women except for one stumbling block. With Thomas having had such a broad experience, his skills meant that much of the work which had formerly been done by the village blacksmith was being dealt with in the estate's own workshop. Only a few jobs, including the shoeing of horses, one of the things that Thomas was not happy with, went to the smith. This set the seal against any chance of a friendship between the two men, and in consequence, the chance of a renewal of friendship between the two women was also lost.

Thomas's bemused gaze went from the small powerfully built man to the two women as they turned and went arm in arm into the cottage. He faced the smith, who for some reason seemed to be ill at ease, yet he was sure that the man had come as a friend.

"Mr. Banham," the smith began, then, "er Thomas, we have never seen eye to eye, but I think, we think," he amended, "that what you done for young Seth was fine, and we came to offer what help we can give you, boy." He stopped and kicked lightly at a stone in an embarrassed manner. "Seems like you need all the friends you can get right now, boy." To the astonished Thomas it was if he was facing a guilty small boy who had come to own up for some mischievous deed, yet the ungrammatically phrased speech told him one heartening thing quite plainly: the breach was healed. He moved gladly forward, his hand outstretched and with only the slightest hesitation, Simon Andern grasped it and both men sealed a new bond of friendship.

Thomas was very moved and said, his voice husky, “Thank you, Simon, for the kind offer of help, we will value that always, but,” he added, his voice concerned, “we could not impose on you; just think what such an offer would mean to you if Captain Rodgerson at the House heard of it.” He halted at that point, for on the smith’s face had appeared a look of real anger, then the man burst out, “Me worry about him,” he roared, “I don’t worry about him. He will need me before I need him, why he is responsible for ruining my poor nephew’s hand,” then in a less ferocious manner, “The Lord protect our Seth, he is but half a man without any more burdens.”

Then it dawned on Thomas. Seth was the son of Nora’s older sister and the young man had spent a lot of his years hanging around the smithy ‘helping’ his uncle, who had been extremely kind to him all through his growing-up years. “How is Seth,” asked Thomas a little guiltily. “You know, Simon, my mind has been terribly occupied with our own troubles, I haven’t been thinking of much else.” Then he asked, “Is there a chance for his hand?”

The smaller man shook his head, saying, “The boy will lose two fingers for certain but the rest, well…” then in a different tone he said, “Did you not hear, Mrs. Rodgerson had her father’s physician look at him and he says that there is a mite of a chance that the rest of his hand might be put right.” He continued in a wondering tone. “Now that is the sort of thing that the old owners would have done. Mrs. Rodgerson is a fine lady.” Thomas wholeheartedly agreed with the sentiment and was telling Simon how good she had been to the Banham family since the trouble started, when from the doorway Beth called out to ask Simon if he would like tea. He thanked her but said that he had to return very soon to the smithy as he was particularly busy this week, and turning back to face Thomas he said, “We didn’t come just to waste your time with words, Thomas, boy, it might help you to know that my shed is there for your furniture,” and then he added rather hesitantly, “and somewhere to sleep if you are not able to find room anywhere else.” He seemed unsure as to whether his old adversary would feel offended by the latter part of his offer, but he need not have concerned himself on that score. Thomas was certainly not offended, he was in fact overwhelmed by this unexpected act of kindness.

After the blacksmith and his wife had gone, Beth and Thomas sat companionably on the wooden bench outside the cottage finishing the pot of tea meant for their late visitors. The difference in Beth’s demeanour from the time before Simon and Nora had called was remarkable; she was almost radiant. Thomas himself felt more at ease just fondly watching and listening to his wife. For all that has happened lately, he thought, ‘I still think that I am a lucky man.’

Chapter 3

Out of the Cottage

As soon as was possible the Banhams moved out of the cottage, Beth, Victoria and Peter going to Beth's parents' cottage, Thomas and Will to Simon Andern's shed behind the smithy. Of the two abodes Will thought he and his father had come off best, for he had never enjoyed the company of his grandparents. The change in his demeanour when in their presence could not fail to be noticed. He became stiff and very formal, answering in a polite manner but volunteering nothing. It was not that he had ever experienced any deliberate cruelty from his grandparents either in deed or in speech, but there had never been a single sign of affection shown to any of the children. In particular he did not like the way his mother was treated; any act of kindness or helpfulness on Beth's part was received at best as though it was expected of her, and at worst with complaint or critical comment. Will's father was bitterly resented; after all, he had taken away their daughter, or to put it more plainly, their skivvy. 'Yes,' Will decided, 'he and his father were much better off in Mr. Andern's shed.' If he had been easier in his mind concerning the situation which the rest of the family had fallen into, he would have settled down quite happily, the gypsy style of living appealing to him very much. Also Mr. Andern, with Thomas's approval, had let him help in the smithy, even showing him the art of welding two pieces of iron together by heating them in the forge to a white heat then beating them on the anvil with the hammer. His first attempt did not look very pretty but Mr. Andern said that it had 'taken' and that it was a good weld. Will was enormously pleased with it and kept it by his bed in the hut, showing it to everyone who came in.

His father meanwhile was out tramping the countryside looking for work. He was well aware of the difficulties that lay in store for him, but he felt confident that with his wide range of experience in all manner of farm machinery and equipment, together with his knowledge of handling workmen, he would have a better chance of getting a job.

It therefore came as a shock to realise how difficult it was going to be to find somebody local who was prepared to take him on.

One thing he hadn't taken into account was the hidden hand of his late employer. Whilst talking to a carpenter in the next village, he was quietly given the information that Captain Rodgerson had let it be known that the estate was to be more selective of its local suppliers from now on, with a special eye on the people employed by the businesses concerned, and local folk were in very little doubt about which person in particular was not a suitable employee.

Whilst being angered by this vindictive display of power, he was realistic enough to realise how dependent many local people were on the estate owners, and Longfields Estate was the largest employer in that particular part of Norfolk. In consequence Thomas returned to his temporary lodgings in a very despondent state of mind that night.

Another prick to his self-esteem, and one which brought him face to face with the less attractive side of his own class, occurred when he went looking for work at Doves Farm some three miles south of Wroxing. By cutting through a wooded area which formed part of an estate adjacent to Longfields Estate, he could save a long walk round the lanes to reach his objective. When Thomas was about halfway through the wood, he was confronted by two men; one, Lawrence by name, was a gamekeeper and known to him. It was he that Thomas addressed. "Hello, Lawrence," he began, "I hope you will forgive me tramping through your master's land but..." He was interrupted roughly by the second man, who snapped shut his shotgun which he had been carrying broken over his arm, and raising it slightly told the startled Thomas, "I am head gamekeeper here, Banham and I order you to go back the way you came, and," he added, "you just thank your luck I'm not taking you up to the house and having you prosecuted for trespassing." There was a brief silence, then Thomas, by now inwardly raging, turned and started back down the path he had just trodden. In that moment of time he had looked into the eyes of a man who would not hesitate to pull the trigger. It was an extremely uneasy trudge back through the woods with the man's dogs skulking at his heels and the sound of both men following. He was, however, slightly easier in his mind knowing that the still-silent Lawrence was behind him, for he had the strongest feeling that without his presence, the head gamekeeper would have peppered him! To end an exceedingly trying day, when he did reach the farm, he had just missed the job.

That night he slept hardly at all, reliving the dreary events of the day, his spirits lower than they had been for a long time.

Throughout his life Thomas had faced many adversities but with a great deal of determination, a faith in his own abilities and some luck, he had usually overcome them; but with the situation he now found himself in, he was increasingly aware of the nightmare possibility of not being able to support his family. His mood ranged from impotent anger to deep despair, a cold fear clutching his heart as his thoughts kept dwelling on the future should he not find work. He had seen the workhouses in London and had looked on with deep compassion at the cowed, helpless wretches whose fortunes had led them to those grim and pitiless places. In rural areas there was even less help to be had. Throwing yourself at the mercy of the parish was unthinkable, and even so, in Wroxing there was not even a parish poorhouse. In other places where there were such establishments they were not much better than the city workhouses.

The change in Thomas was noticed by all who knew him, but to Beth and Victoria the thing which shocked them most was the helpless look, that of a small lost boy, a look of one who had suddenly come face to face with his own lack of control over events which affected his life. Thomas would try to talk encouragingly to his family but as time went by he found it more difficult to do so and would often have little to say to anyone, and when Beth attempted to rally him round she would notice more and more the defeated look on her husband's face.

There were times when he would be away for days as he tramped further afield looking for work, sleeping more often than not behind the hedgerows. To his family, used to the fine, upstanding, confident and kindly man which was Thomas Banham, it was a heartbreaking spectacle. What the approach of winter would do to him, without a job and with their meagre savings ebbing away, was something they tried not to think about.

On the other side of the coin were the many acts of kindness which uplifted them, helping them in renewing their faith in human nature.

There had been gifts, usually vegetables or fruit, left on the doorstep at Beth's parents' or at the smithy. Also there had been invitations to share a meal with people and there had been the odd parcel brought to them by Mrs. Rodgerson's maid, a small bagful of their favourite tea being one such luxury.

The Banhams were amazed but exceedingly touched by each kindly gesture, for most of the gifts came from people who were themselves very poor and struggling to make ends meet.

Time was hurrying by and the urgent question of finding a permanent place of abode appeared increasingly difficult to answer. From the earliest days of their eviction, Beth and Thomas had agreed that when they did find a dwelling, it had not to be tied to a job, and naturally, roomy enough for all the family to live together. They realised that in a few years' time Victoria could possibly be married and Will himself could have found a job, but for the present they were determined to have a family home for the five of them. It was a natural but emotional reaction to the perilous and frightening situation they now found themselves in.

The first part of their resolve had taken on something of the nature of a slowly fading dream, the inescapable fact being that all the dwellings in the area were either tied or rented. What aggravated Thomas was that with his skills he could have easily built a cottage himself but of course that needed land and money for materials, and he had neither. Two years previously a derelict cottage on land belonging to Mr. Taggins at Down Fields Farm had been let for a pittance to a destitute family by the name of Bleggs on the understanding that the husband made it habitable, in some ways similar to the agreement between Mr. Searle and Thomas Banham.

In fact the old cottage at Down Fields was only slightly less derelict than it had been before the Bleggs had moved in. Bleggs himself (nobody knew his Christian name) was shiftless and idle, his wife being no better. Thomas had experience of their slovenly and dishonest ways when Mrs. Searle, a few months before her death, had asked him if he could find some casual work around the estate for Bleggs, whilst she took on Mrs. Bleggs and her oldest daughter as extra kitchen staff during an annual family gathering. It had turned out extremely unsatisfactorily, with all three Bleggs being dismissed and narrowly avoiding arrest for theft.

Although Thomas did not begrudge Bleggs his good fortune at having the old cottage, he wished that such a chance would come his way; it would have been turned into a very snug dwelling if it had.

As to the second part of their resolve, they were together for at least one meal each day even if they lived apart, and although Thomas fretted constantly about Beth's situation, he accepted the blessing, flawed as it was, of his wife, daughter and young Peter having a roof over their heads.

However, when the offer of a job came, so fraught had the situation become that both of their resolutions were sadly abandoned and Thomas decided there was nothing left but to accept it. It was a heartbreaking decision but Beth put on her bravest face and agreed that it was inevitable that the family would be split up.

About the same time, over two hundred miles away in Manchester, events were shaping up which, as a consequence, would send another man, equally desperate, but for a different reason, to the same town on the banks of the River Mersey.

Chapter 4

Clarence

The young man people referred to as One Eye was a misfit even in the slums of Manchester where he was born. His name was Clarence Lumb, but whether his surname was that of his real father, he did not know, for his slatternly mother had many men stay in their two-roomed dwelling. Her openly promiscuous habits, coupled with her indifference to the violent behaviour towards him by some of her men, imbued in him contempt for all women. To survive he developed a low cunning, an extraordinary talent as a pickpocket and a very necessary fleetness of foot.

The nickname One Eye was in itself a misnomer as he really did have the use of both eyes, but the damaged area around his left eye, the result of being kicked by a horse, did indeed give him the appearance of having lost the use of that eye. A blacksmith in Ancoats would let him help out when he was shoeing a horse and that is where he had his accident. However, it was as a result of seeing too well which caused him to quit Manchester, and led him eventually to end up working on the 'Cut' at Frodsham.

How this came about was as follows. On that fateful day he had set out early to see what he could pick up around Blackfriars Bridge quay. However, he was disappointed: no boats there, so no passengers coming ashore, and these were often good for loaded purses and were innocent of the likes of Clarence.

He wandered off towards the Cathedral, then along to Market Street. He became increasingly uneasy as he moved through the early morning throngs on their way to work or shopping, for the street seemed to be stiff with police. As two constables strode towards him he casually turned to look into a cutler's shop window as though studying the display.

Their voices reached him as they passed by and he heard one say, "…must have got the safe away on a four-wheeled cart, a weight like that would be too much…" the rest being lost to him as they moved out of earshot.

Drifting over to a street vendor who was as nervous as himself, Clarence muttered, "Wot's up with this lot, somebody bin' robbed?" The vendor jerked his head indicating a nearby ginnel. "Moneylender," he answered.

The frustrated pickpocket decided that things were too hot in this area and moved off towards Piccadilly but was further put out when he spotted a group of yet more constables and a sergeant marching towards him from the London Road direction.

He had only gone a short way down the narrow street when he passed the entrance to a yard. Hearing a voice with a rich Irish accent, he turned and found himself staring into the eyes of a very large, powerfully built man. Whilst only seconds passed, it seemed a lot longer than that but even in that brief time, Clarence saw enough, and as the big Irishman leaped down, the terrified pickpocket took off like a startled rabbit. He did not stop until he was back home.

For the rest of the day he kept himself hidden, only venturing to peep between the rags of curtains to see if anybody was hanging round near his door. The hawker had muttered the word moneylender, but that particular one was no ordinary moneylender, he was a man who, it was said, had a lot of influence in places that mattered. 'No wonder the Law was out in such numbers,' he thought gloomily.

As the day wore on and his panic slowly subsided, he mulled over the idea of going out in the evening when it got a bit darker, and try his luck with the theatre crowds. Clarence was not down to his last farthing but he liked to have a bit put by in case his pickings were meagre.

Finally he decided that he would go out, but before he had got his coat on there came a knock on the door, the sudden sound making his legs turn to jelly, and it was a moment before he could creep to the window. He almost collapsed with relief when he recognised the caller as Abe, the striker who worked at Joe's smithy. He was alone.

Cautiously, Clarence inched open the door and beckoned Abe inside. The striker burst out as soon as he was inside; he was obviously dying to let Clarence know all he had to say.

"'Ere, One Eye, wot yer bin up ter," he whispered in an excited tone, "big Irish fellah bin askin' of yer, said he owed yer summat." He then said proudly in a more normal voice, "Joe said he seemed ter remember someone like 'e was asked about, and then after he'd pretended to puzzle it out like, 'e then said 'e 'ad a mind that a lad like that lived 'Anging Ditch way."

Abe chuckled as he recalled the smith's cleverness, but then a worried look crossed his face and he said urgently to the quaking young pickpocket, "Look One Eye, yer want ter clear out, that Irish fellah looked really nasty and it looked ter Joe and me, that wot 'e owed yer wasn't goin' ter do yer 'ealth much good." Then a thought struck him and he said in an awestruck voice, "'e might even be one of them Fenians, blimey."

But he need not have bothered to tell Clarence that, for the now terrified young man was frantically throwing what he thought he would need into a sack, and meant to quit the city as soon as the daylight faded. He would put as many miles as he could between him and the Irishman before the day was done.

Eventually Abe decided to leave but as he reached the door he stopped; with his thumb on the latch he asked Clarence if he knew about the moneylender being burgled. 'I know about that,' thought the pickpocket, 'and I think I know them that's done it, and that's why I'm clearing off.' All this went though his mind as he visualised the scene in the yard off Dale Street.

Once again he saw the big man standing on the cart, bales of straw behind him and on the ground, by the two other men, more bales of straw, but more importantly, a large, shiny safe with a sort of iron-wheeled cradle clamped around it.

Abe was just finishing off his tale and with a gleeful laugh he said, "An' then the police found the safe in a yard near Dale Street but the gang 'as got away."

At that, Clarence shivered afresh. 'No wonder the Irish fellah was looking for him,' he said to himself; the thwarted burglar probably thought Clarence had informed on him.

When Abe had gone, Clarence pulled out his secret cache of money and other things which he carefully stowed around his person in his special pockets. He was very aware how to protect his valuables from other pickpockets!

He then, as an afterthought, took a little of his mother's money, then making sure that there was nobody lurking outside, he slipped out into the gathering darkness.

Carefully avoiding the brighter lit streets, Clarence worked his way round to the area at the rear of Deansgate to end up in Knott Mill where he joined Chester Road. Each yard towards Old Trafford and Stretford beyond made him feel a mite safer.

By the time he reached Stretford he was less fearful but very weary. As he was crossing over a canal bridge he thought that a good place to sleep would be under the bridge on the towpath. Unfortunately for him, two vagrants had the same idea and he was forced to look somewhere else.

Eventually he came across a crane under which was stacked several stout planks. He hung his sack high up on the crane so that rats could not get at the bits of food he had thrown in there, then lay on the stack to rest.

Before dawn he was trudging wearily on his way, having been awake most of the night and cold to his very bones. His senses were suddenly sharpened by the smell of frying bacon. The delicious aroma made him aware just how hungry he was. He slowed down as he neared the source of the mouth-watering smell.

Two narrowboats were moored up; a woman stood on the deck of the second boat whilst ahead on the leading boat a man was seated on the boatman's cabin. A horse was contentedly cropping the grass alongside the towpath.

Clarence touched his cap to the woman, who stared back at him in a suspicious way, her expression not altering as he moved off towards the seated man. Touching his cap again, he said simply, "Could yer spare a bit 'o bread and bacon, mister? I'll pay for it."

For a few moments the boatman did not reply; they themselves were often treated as inferior and subjected to abuse so he had a certain sympathy for the bedraggled undersized creature who stood before him. On the other hand there were some about who were prepared to take advantage of a lone man and his wife if they were given half the chance.

Even so, he and his missus had a problem; their little lad was down in the cabin fast asleep, having been up all night with some childish ailment, which left them nobody to work the horse, but he had some questions of his own before he made up his mind as to how he dealt with the man.

"What puts you on the towpath at this hour, lad?" he asked in a neutral tone of voice. To which the famished Clarence replied, "I'm looking for work, mister, come from Manchester yesterday," then could have bitten his tongue off. Lying about looking for work was alright but telling the truth about where he had come from was a bad mistake.

"Can you work with horses?" was the boatman's next question, to which Clarence nodded his head. At that the boatman shouted to his wife that she should make the lad a bit of breakfast. Without a word she went below to do as she was bid. For one of the few times in his life Clarence felt a surge of gratitude towards someone who showed kindness.

When the woman handed him the hot bacon between two thick rounds of bread, he tried not to grab it and stuff it into his mouth, and even with his lack of upbringing he realised that he had to show some sort of manners if he was to get more food.

Clarence even managed a 'thank you', then tentatively offered the boatman's wife sixpence, which she took without a change of expression. She must have been satisfied, for after he had wolfed down the first lot, the woman, still not smiling, gave him a second helping. When all three had eaten their fill, steaming mugs of tea were produced. Never had Clarence tasted anything so good as that which he ate in the cold morning air on the canal towpath.

By the time the sun was up, the boats were on the move, Clarence having helped with harnessing the horse. Without much being said, he seemed to have been accepted, and was now walking the horse westwards, further away from his enemy, and although he did not know it, away from his old life forever.

Within the hour they were clear of works, warehouses and coal yards, and had entered a world which Clarence had not even dreamed of. As far as the eye could see stretched fields greener than any grass he had ever seen, with copses and whole forests of trees, and the occasional house just nestling there. Then there appeared on his left a large grand house set in a park of meadows and yet more trees. Clarence's head was swivelling this way and that as each new sight presented itself to him.

The thud of the horse's hooves on the towpath and the sound of birds was all that disturbed the early morning peace. A sky, bluer than any ever experienced by the young city man, the fresh untainted air, and a warm sun on his back had combined to work such a magic on Clarence that his weariness had left him and he was striding out more purposefully than he ever normally did.

A hail from the boatman made Clarence turn around. The leading boat had been steered close to the bank and the boatman was holding up a steaming mug. Also standing by his father and poised ready to jump was the little lad.

Casually the boy leaped ashore, took the mug from his father and carried it back to the second boat where his mother was ready to receive it. A few moments later he took a second mug off his father and without spilling too much brought it to Clarence.

All this was accomplished without the boats stopping and in no time at all they were back on course gliding silently through the tranquil waters of the canal. Within half an hour of the little boy joining him, he knew that his name was Charlie, and that he was seven years of age and learning to read and write. He also asked what Clarence's name was and how he had hurt his eye, and told the bemused and amused young man that he came from a place called Leigh.

It all was said in what, at times seemed to Clarence, like a foreign language. That the boy was intelligent was not to be denied, and he was very knowledgeable about all things connected with the canal and the countryside.

As they neared what appeared to be a small town, a large grey bird took flight ahead of them and with slow beats of its huge wings flew a few hundred yards up the canal, then settled itself on the bank on long spindly legs.

Clarence exclaimed in wonder at the sight; why, the wings must be six foot across, he thought, he had never seen a bird as big as this in his life.

"Heron," said Charlie airily, "they stand in the shallow waters and catch fish with their long beaks." He went on, seeing that Clarence was really taken with the bird. "In a bit it will get fed up with moving up the canal and then it will fly back, maybe over our heads if we are lucky." Before they reached the first building of the town the heron did as Charlie said it would but sadly not over their heads.

As the pair of narrowboats with their loads of coal entered the built-up area, Charlie said, "Lymm, that's the name of this place," then he became quite excited, much more like a little boy than he had been previously. "Me Mam might want to stop in the village if the market's on."

The excited boy's wishes were soon granted, for as they approached a humpbacked bridge, the boatman called out to Clarence and Charlie to slow the horse. By the time the village centre had been reached both boats had been skilfully brought to a stop alongside the bank. Mooring lines were secured, the horse tethered with nosebag on, and the boatman's wife was all set to go shopping in no time at all.

Charlie entreated his mother to let him go with her and she agreed to let him come providing that he did not dawdle. Whilst a cargo was being moved, boat people could not linger unnecessarily, for time was money.

The woman spoke to Clarence for the first time since he had met up with them all. "There is a second-hand clothes stall on the market, lad, he might have a stronger pair of boots for you, them you have on don't look as if they'll last much longer." Then she added, frowning, "That's if you have any money, lad."

Clarence nodded in agreement; his lightweight boots had been alright for city pavements, especially as their very lightness had been a boon in making his quick escapes. He did a quick calculation of how much loose money he had handy, then satisfied he would have enough without delving into his secret pockets, he said he would accompany them to the market. The boatman stayed with the vessels to do other jobs whilst he had a chance.

To reach the village from the towpath side of the canal, it was necessary to either walk to the humpback bridge and cross over to the opposite side of the canal, or to do that by going down the canal embankment and then walking through a short road tunnel under the canal, a route which Charlie's mother chose to take.

Off they went, Charlie in front blithely swinging the empty milk cans. Emerging from the tunnel Clarence was quite taken with the view of the village street, but the couple ahead were hurrying on towards the market, the business in hand leaving no time for gazing around.

Whilst mother and son shopped for bread, milk, eggs and bacon, Clarence found the stall he wanted. Some of the boots and shoes were very cheap but not much better than the pair he wore, but then he spotted a pair of heavy boots which looked almost new. The price was much more than he wanted to pay, so disconsolately he wandered off looking for another stall selling second-hand boots.

As he meandered about pondering whether to pay the extra coppers and get the good boots, he found himself weighing up the type of persons which thronged the market, just as he did back in the city. Certainly there were plenty of pickings to be had here and they looked so easy to be taken, but for some reason which he could not explain right there and then, he could not bring himself to dip into anybody's pocket. He normally did not differentiate between right and wrong as those two words had little meaning to him, yet here he was unwilling to do something which in the past had kept him and his mother from the workhouse.

Charlie and his mother appeared and with a sharp look at his feet the woman enquired, "Nothing to fit?" to which Clarence replied, "Aye, but too dear." She swung round and beckoning to Clarence to follow, charged off towards the second-hand clothes stall.

Still puzzling why he had jibbed at taking a purse or two, Clarence pushed through the crowd and arrived at the stall where Charlie's mother was already haggling over the boots. She was obviously enjoying herself and without raising her voice much she beat the hard-eyed woman down in price so much that when the amazed Clarence walked away, he was carrying not only the boots but a pair of socks without a single darn in them, and a very presentable shirt, all for little more than the original price of the boots.

Nearby was a homemade cake and jam stall and as the three of them made their way to leave the market, Clarence darted back and enquired about the jars of jam. "Two pence a jar, my dear," said the lady at the stall. With the boatlady's persuasive manner still fresh in his mind, Clarence decided to see if he could do the same.

Putting on his most pleasant face Clarence asked, "How much for two, lady?" The stallholder laughed. "Well, my arithmetic tells me that two and two make four, but seeing as I'm nearly sold out you can have both for three and a half pence." Clarence remembered to say thank you then said with a blush, "They are for the lady with the little lad, they have been very kind to me."

The stallholder looked towards Charlie and his mother, the latter obviously anxious to get away, and noting her clean apron and white lace-trimmed shawl, she recognised her as a boatman's wife, and said with a smile, "And for a good deed another half pence off," adding that the boat people could not waste too much time, so he had better be off.

When he told Charlie's mother what had happened she laughed, then with a wave to the stallholder they hurried back to the boats.

Their delayed midday meal of bread, cheese and pickle was eaten as they moved on towards Runcorn. To the young man (could it be said, 'late pickpocket?') the food was of the same mouth-watering quality as the bacon and bread of the morning.

As Clarence strode along leading the horse, he marvelled at the events of the last two days, especially the present day. With so many new experiences, sights and impressions printed on his mind, his old life seemed to have happened years ago. He thought back on the quiet boat people who could have turned their backs on him, accepting him without question, feeding him and letting him share their world. Charlie calling him Clarence, telling him about the ice-breaking boat living in its own tunnel at Lymm, the heron, the small bright blue bird they might see if they were lucky, a bird, said Charlie, that his dad called the 'Flying Jewel'. There was so much more that the scarred young man had learned today which made it impossible to pick out the part he liked the most.

His daydreaming was interrupted by a call from Charlie, who was taking a rest by riding the horse. "Another pair coming, Clarence, I'll get down," which he proceeded to do without help.

During the day they had passed several pairs of boats coming from the opposite direction, some loaded, others returning empty. The latter, sitting high in the water, were the easiest to pass, for their towing rope could be passed over the horse then over the boat's top plank without much effort, but a loaded pair meant that their towing rope would be a few feet lower so being more likely to catch everything on the cabin top.

As it was, the manoeuvre was as faultless as the others had been, with the same banter between the crews as they passed.

Long before they reached Preston Brook, the boatman had decided to stop there for the night, as the sun was low in the sky and there would be no chance of reaching Runcorn in daylight.

During the latter part of the journey, the boatman's wife had walked the horse, to stretch her legs she said, which allowed a grateful, leg-weary Clarence to rest in the stern of the second narrowboat whilst Charlie took the tiller.

Much of the impressions etched indelibly on the young man's consciousness were enhanced by the pleasantness of the weather. After the chill of the morning, the sun's gentle warmth had acted like balm on Clarence, and the sky, donning its dress of becoming blue had given the day a sense of something clean and unsullied.

Towards the end of the day, the sky changed as though to let the entranced city lad see what it really could do. The blue of its gown deepened in hue and with the setting of the sun, a hem of glorious red appeared edged with gold and turquoise, a spectacle to fill any person's heart with wonder, never mind that of an ignorant city dweller.

With his restricted vocabulary, Clarence had difficulty in expressing himself as to the wonders he was witnessing, but the boatman and his wife understood only too well how he felt; it showed by the expression on his face, and despite seeing many such sunsets, they also had not lost the sensibility to enjoy them.

As the narrowboats glided silently into Preston Brook, there was still enough light to enable them to moor up and prepare for the night. Clarence attended to the horse whilst Charlie and his father made a 'nest' on top of the coal to give Clarence a place to sleep. With pieces of canvas, some sacks and a thick blanket, the delighted young man then had a place to lay his head other than on the towpath. He was scared of rats and the thought of sleeping on the ground had been troubling him.

After a wash and a warm meal he climbed into his bed, which was surprisingly comfortable. With so many new experiences crowding his mind, at first he had difficulty in falling asleep. Spurning the canvas sheet over the top planks he gazed out in wonder at another sky which he had never seen in his life, one which was carpeted with countless stars. His heart was so full it took his breath away.

It was not until a long time after that Clarence realised that the time spent with the boatman, his wife and Charlie was the turning point in his life.

Sounds of activity woke Clarence, who promptly heaved himself out of his 'berth'. Although he ached all over from his previous day's walking and he certainly knew he had been lying on lumps of coal, he had slept soundly enough.

Following the example of the boatman, he swilled himself down with water from the bucket, but before he could put back his shirt Charlie's mother took it from him and handed him his newly acquired shirt, now with the missing buttons sewn on, and told the speechless Clarence that he would get it back when she had, as she put it, 'seen to it'.

By the time the boats were moving, dawn had broken and the sky showed a promise of repeating the previous day's weather, and it did not disappoint, and before Runcorn came into view, the washing which had been hung out over the 'butty boat,' as Charlie called it, was dry. However, as they approached the town, Clarence was dismayed to see a grey smoky haze over everything, the sun being dimmed, much like Manchester.

After experiencing the clean air and beauties of yesterday and this morning, he had not expected their final destination to be as grim as that which he beheld. He then realised why the boatman's wife was dressed in dark clothing and why she had swiftly put the washed clothes into the cabin.

Runcorn Gasworks was spewing out a dark, noxious miasma, the lack of wind causing it to settle over the boats awaiting unloading. Apart from pairs of narrowboats, there were two large broad-beamed barges, the bulk of the almost empty one dwarfing their much narrower cousins.

On the towpath there were children running about or playing games. There were also some of the boatwomen chatting and as Charlie called to his friends, the women waved to the couple and their son. Clarence saw the curious glances that were cast his way but was comforted to see no signs of hostility.

Charlie, after getting permission to join his friends, dashed off, leaving his father and Clarence to moor the boats and see to the horse. The boatman then showed the eager young man how the side cloths and top planks were removed in readiness for the unloading of the boats.

When all was ready the kindly boatman said, "Before you go off looking for a job, stop and take food with us, lad." He then nodded and strolled over to a group of other boatmen who were taking their ease leaning against the towpath rails whilst smoking their clay pipes.

Whilst Clarence did not feel left out, for he knew they could not have him with them any longer, he nevertheless experienced a yearning for the sort of camaraderie he was witnessing.

Just then a little girl came up to him and said, "Charlie said you're his friend and your name is Clarence. My name is Daisy and I'm Charlie's friend." With that she ran off giggling, and Clarence grinned with amusement at the short conversation, all delivered without stopping for breath. Also, he felt touched at what she had said: Charlie had told Daisy that he, Clarence, was his friend!

Their midday meal was the same as the previous day's but with the addition of a piece of fruit cake with his tea. Those simple meals would remain in his memory as long as he lived.

Before he left the kind-hearted family and started his search for work and shelter, the boatwoman put some apples and slices of bread and jam wrapped up in paper in his sack, and also some pieces of fruit cake. Then she handed back his clothing which she had washed and mended.

At this Clarence felt choked with emotion; never in his life could he recall anybody treating him so kindly.

He thrust his hand into his coat pocket and pulled out several coins which he offered to the boatman's wife. She smiled at him and then spoke to him in a sympathetic manner. Her Lancashire accent was even more marked than her husband's, but Clarence understood her to say that he would need his money if he was tramping looking for work, but he was even more affected when she used his name.

Blinking back the tears which threatened to spill he could only manage a whisper as he thanked her, words he had rarely used in his life. The woman herself turned her head away and Clarence knew that she too was upset.

Turning to the kind-eyed boatman he touched the neb of his cap, at which the man held out his hand and said, "Good luck, lad, look after yourself." Charlie followed his father's example, an act which in spite of his upset state made Clarence grin.

He shouldered his sack and quickly walked away before he lost what was left of his self-control. Before he passed out of sight he turned and raised his hand towards the family and was rewarded by three waving hands, no, there were four hands. He thought he recognised the diminutive figure of Daisy waving. The tears then did flow in earnest, his face wet as he walked unsteadily on his way. It was as if something was released from him that had been bottled up for years and afterwards he marvelled at how changed he felt.

By the time he reached the end of the canal (which he had been informed by Charlie was the Bridgewater Canal) he was much more in control of himself. Thus when confronted by the view from the top of a staircase of locks, his spirits lifted again as he gazed at what he saw before him.

Where the locks finished, there were docks crowded with sailing ships which were much bigger than any he had seen on the River Irwell, whilst on the river (and such an immense width of water it was), a much larger sailing vessel with three masts was being slowly towed from the docks by a steam paddle tug. But also he could see a great many ant-like figures at one side of the opening to the docks, swarming over an embankment, digging the soil, trains of trucks hauled by small steam locomotives, and other steam-powered machines.

However, what Clarence wanted to see more than anything was where the broad river flowed. With that in mind he crossed over the lock gates and made his way through the streets until he came to an area of houses with one side of the road bounded by iron railings.

Pausing, he gazed down once more at the river. Being past noon, the sun was then towards the west, giving the now much wider river the appearance of a huge sheet of glass. Scattered on it were several vessels, both sail and steam. The sight took Clarence's breath away.

He was disturbed from his reverie by the voice of an old man who had come across from his house on the other side of the road.

"Grand sight, eh, lad?" he began. "See that ship there, eh? Well, that's the schooner *Adventurer* and I've sailed on her a few times to South America, fine vessel, aye." His eyes had taken on a faraway look and he seemed to be lost in his memories. Then suddenly he changed subject, asking the younger man if he was looking for work, and when Clarence nodded, the old man became very heated in his words.

He growled fiercely and told the startled young man that it would not be wise to even think of employment in Runcorn, adding that even if Clarence was lucky enough to get a job, "For that lot down there with their picks and shovels and machines is diggin' a big ditch right up to Manchester and when it's done, Runcorn will be finished," he bellowed angrily. "Mind you," he said in less forceful manner, "them Liverpool shippin' folks they do say as 'ow it won't get finished, for sure as eggs is eggs, that daft lot in Manchester will run out of money." With a happier look on his face the old man nodded sagely and said, "Aye, that might 'appen."

Then turning back to the secretly amused Clarence he concluded by repeating that there were no jobs in Runcorn and then stamped across to his front door, disappearing within.

He need not have bothered warning Clarence; the young man had already made up his mind. The grime-coated buildings he had passed were too like Manchester for his newly awakened senses; he wanted to work all right but he yearned for the fresh open skies and clean smells he had experienced, so he decided to go on towards the hilly area he had seen in the near distance, and shouldering his sack again he marched on his way.

He arrived at noon the following day in the small but bustling town of Frodsham, and he liked what he saw. The main street, which was very broad, was lined with a mixture of very old timber-framed buildings with others built of stone or a mellow brick, and they were not grimed with soot!

His first enquiry concerning work brought an instant response: there might be a job on the Marsh, he was told, for down there they were digging out a new canal.

The man who gave him the information had sized Clarence up as a 'navvy', if somewhat of an undersized one, and was not really that welcoming, for the townspeople had been plagued by a lot of rowdiness and drunken behaviour since the arrival of the canal construction workers.

However, Clarence was not put off by the man's attitude; after all, he had pointed out the place where he might find work, and gruffly thanking his informant, something that the one-time pickpocket had learned lately, made people better disposed towards him.

One of the biggest blessings which had helped Clarence since his flight from Manchester had been the warm dry weather and this helped him in another way, for the farmers locally, anxious to get as much work done in the fields before the good weather ended, had managed to lure some of the contractors' labourers away from the site. It was not uncommon for this to happen elsewhere.

The young man from the slums of Manchester was not a particularly muscular specimen and he was quite aware of the fact; therefore he was relieved when, after presenting himself at the hut which served as the Agent's office, he was taken at his word and given the job of a horse handler, though he was warned he would be on trial.

On being asked whether he had lodgings and admitting he had not, Clarence was told to go to the workshop and ask for Albert Tarleton. The young man did as instructed and on meeting the man was overjoyed to learn that there was indeed a spare bunk in his hut. He would have to make sure he was clean and stay sober otherwise Mrs. Tarleton would not let him stay. He would share the room with one other man and the rent would be eight shillings a week. Clarence could not read or write but where money was concerned he had no trouble adding and subtracting. When he was told hours would be at least ten hours, five and a half days a week, sometimes more, he knew he would be well off. Two hundred and forty pence (a pound) would leave him one hundred and forty four pence to live on.

The foreman fitter directed Clarence to ask the driver of the locomotive standing near the water tank if he would oblige him with a bucket of warm water for an all-over wash. So the young man, understanding the unspoken message, did as he was told and the driver filled the bucket by the simple expedient of opening both boiler feed steam valve and water valve at the same time, and in seconds Clarence had a bucket of warm water.

After the unheard of luxury of a warm washdown instead of his usual cold wash, Clarence felt ready to confront a dozen Mrs. Tarletons. The effort was worth it and Clarence was grudgingly allowed to stay by the foreman's wife, but only after he had handed over his eight shillings. The young man's purse was by then getting much lighter.

The man sharing the room with Clarence was a fitter, aged about thirty and very sure of himself; he did not have a lot of time for someone like Clarence, who with his background could spot another shifty fellow a mile off.

Mrs. Tarleton was not a woman to over-exert herself in the feeding of her lodgers but to Clarence, his evening meal was not as bad as those he had eaten when he lived with his mother so he was quite content with his lot.

He was down in the excavation before seven the following morning. As he reported to the foreman ganger for orders, he was met by a stream of foul-mouthed invective from the man, seemingly for no reason whatsoever. Clarence found out later from others that it was a typical morning greeting from McDonald and most people tended to keep clear of the man early in the day.

He was told to get over to where the other horse shunters were preparing for the day's work. Their job was to move the railway wagons to and from the digging area. For the major moves such as whole trains of wagons carrying the spoil, that is, excavated soil or rock, steam locomotives were used.

Amazingly for somebody who had never been fully in a proper job, the transformed Clarence began to really enjoy himself. The dirt and mud of the excavation was not the grime and squalor of his life in city of his birth, it was clean dirt!

He was also becoming more sociable, and was less tongue-tied when in the company of others. He was a good listener for he was eager to soak up information on any subject. However, Clarence was very conscious of his inability to read; he vowed that one day he too would be able to understand things with words printed on them, and he would learn to write as well.

The late city petty criminal had entered another phase of his transformation.

Chapter 5

Captain Howard

"Here you are, sir, compartment to yourself," said the porter, a slight elderly man who, despite his appearance, had handled the trunks as if they were filled with feathers and who now held open the door of the carriage with the air of one who has just done the impossible. The erstwhile passenger smiled in spite of himself, for there were a good number of empty compartments on the train, but the porter had been very helpful and cheerfully polite, not servile, and one of Captain Howard's dislikes was servility. After just over sixteen years in the Army of Her Majesty Queen Victoria, he had long recognised the value of people who were respectful without being servile. He dug into his pocket and handed the porter a one shilling piece and the man beamed his delight. "Thank you, sir," he said, "I 'opes you 'as a good, safe journey, sir."

Richard Howard settled back contentedly into the seat, ignoring the dusty state of the compartment, his thoughts more concerned with what, or to be more precise, whom would be waiting for him when he finally reached Wroxing. His wife had been down there for over two months now and showed no signs of wanting to move nearer to where his business kept him or even to their own house near Winchester. Admittedly there was little to keep his wife entertained at their own home, if home was the right word to use, for she was not one to keep herself busy, being a woman who needed the stimulus of smart, light-hearted company, especially, as he was all too well aware, the company of men.

However, at that moment the Captain, late of the Royal Engineers, was not particularly thinking of his wife; it was her younger sister whose image he had in his mind's eye. He had been trying unsuccessfully for eight years to stop thoughts of Kate intruding into his mind, for he was an honourable man and he could see no future in daydreaming of life shared with his sister-in-law.

By the standards of the day her beauty would go unremarked, but to be in her presence for but a short time was sufficient to impress on the beholder that here indeed was true beauty in face and in nature. In startling contrast her sister Cecelia, seven years her senior, was in so many ways her exact opposite. The impact of her beauty was felt immediately by all who met her, and she could, when it suited her, be as charming, as witty and as enjoyable a companion with both women and men as anybody could wish for.

That was how the young inexperienced Lieutenant Richard Howard saw her fifteen years before, and nobody had been more amazed than he when she had agreed to his offer of marriage two years later. Her sister Katrina, or as everybody called her, Kate, was fourteen years old when she became her sister's chief bridal attendant and at that age she was already devoted to her brother-in-law. Captain

Howard loved the gangly shy child as a young sister but as years sped by, she developed into an elegant, willowy young woman of character, and her brother-in-law found his older brother feelings of affection changing into something much deeper. His marriage was by then effectively dead, but being a man of principle, allowed nobody, not even Kate, to see how he felt.

When his regiment sent another company to India, Captain Howard went with them. He was determined to bury himself in his work with the vain hope that in time his feelings for Kate would diminish. In that he was singularly unsuccessful.

His thoughts went back to his time in India and the events which had wrought such changes to his life.

Much of the work there involved the strengthening or, in one instance, the rebuilding of the garrisons in the area between Jaipur and Agra. Due to the effects of the monsoon, there were times when the work was halted and other problems required their attention.

When he and his company were ordered to build a temporary bridge over a gully swept by floods, little did he realise that it was a start to events which were to end his army career and send him back to England.

The torrential rain had caused the normally dry gully to be turned into a raging torrent which had swept away the abutments supporting the single line railway bridge and effectively halted all railway movement between Jaipur and Agra.

After temporary supports had been built, not an easy task with the water still flowing, the bridge spans were ready to be manoeuvred into place, when the three-legged gantry tilted over slightly, causing one of the sections to swing violently sideways.

At that moment Captain Howard's attention was directed elsewhere and he was totally unprepared when he was suddenly knocked to the ground by a sepoy who ended up on top of him.

That the Indian soldier had saved his officer's life there was no doubt, but at a cost to the man's hand, which was badly injured.

When the bridge section had been carefully lifted and both men removed, it was soon obvious that Captain Howard's leg was broken. There was also an injury to the back of his head where he had struck the stony ground.

Even as he mulled over the events of that day six years earlier, he could not recall much of what happened, including the journey back to Agra; even the time spent in hospital, where he was also affected by a weakening fever, was a bit hazy. Eventually he was sent to a hill station to recuperate.

Whilst still at Agra, he enquired after the sepoy and asked that when the man was well enough, he be brought to him. The native soldier's name was made known to him as Revi Gupra, a name that Captain Howard knew he would never forget.

Ensconced in his invalid chair with his leg propped up before him, the officer felt somewhat at a disadvantage when the smart young sepoy corporal was brought to him. He was given a very correct salute which he returned as best he could in his sitting position, out of uniform and in a hospital gown!

"At ease, Corporal," he said and then pointing to a chair near him he asked the sepoy to sit. The corporal did so but rather reluctantly and ended up sitting to attention.

His commanding officer asked him how his hand was healing and received a reply that it was 'very good', a reply that seemed to be at odds with the wealth of surgical dressings hiding the injury. Although Captain Howard knew the answer to his next question, he feigned ignorance and asked the corporal whether he would still be able to serve in the army. To this the sepoy sadly replied that he would be given an honourable discharge, which meant he would leave with a good name but no extra money.

Asked what he would do when he was discharged, the young man said optimistically that he would return to his family village and work with his uncle who was a well digger.

Captain Howard leaned forward and said, "Corporal Revi Gupra, you have saved my life and that is something I will never forget, and I will make sure that you will not return to your village a poor man." At this the young sepoy corporal, his eyes shining with pride, said, "It was my duty, Captain sahib, I do not need a reward to do my duty sahib."

At that Captain Howard smiled and said, "It is to your credit, Corporal Gupra, but none of us can buy food and support our families on duty well done. I too will probably leave the army but I will not return to England a man without money to live on and you will not return to your home without money either."

With those words the officer gave the reluctant sepoy a bag, and holding out his other hand for the young man to shake said, "I wish you a good life for the future and thank you," then added with a twinkle in his eye, "for doing your duty." After a moment's hesitation, for it was unheard of for any ordinary soldier, especially a sepoy, to shake hands with an officer, Revi Gupra shook hands with Captain Howard, then went down on his knees and salaamed to his officer. As the conversation was now concluded, he got to his feet and although visibly in a very emotional state, gave a very smart salute and marched away.

Even after all this time, Richard Howard, sitting in a railway carriage, travelling through the English countryside on a cold wintry day, could picture it, feel the sultry Indian heat and smell the flowers in the hospital gardens. He sighed and hoped that the young sepoy was prospering.

His thoughts drifted back to the time when he first received the letter from Kate telling of her forthcoming marriage. As a married man himself he could never have any claims on his sister-in-law's affections; he had nevertheless experienced such a feeling of desolation that he had to mentally take himself to task for entertaining such selfish thoughts. After all, she was not his, she had been unattached, and at nineteen, or was it twenty years of age, Kate was eligible for marriage. If she had found someone whom she loved, one who would love her and make her happy, then what was he thinking of, acting in this dog-in-a-manger way, and so his thoughts had gone first one way and then another. He had hoped with all his heart that she had found true love, but then the same anguished heart cried, "But I have lost her."

Kate had written of her engagement to a Captain Rodgerson and enquired if her brother-in-law knew him, as her fiancé was in the same regiment, but Captain Howard had not known him.

They had met at a hunt ball held at her parent's home in Norfolk which he and a fellow officer had attended. They both seemed to have a slight friendship with her sister Cecelia. At this piece of information his mood of depression had deepened; any man who had a 'slight friendship' with Captain Howard's wife was, he had judged, not to be recommended as a candidate for Kate's hand in marriage!

The date on the letter had shown that it had been posted nearly three months previously, a not unusual state of affairs in India, for mail tended to trail around from place to place as the army units moved about, which meant that by then the wedding would have taken place.

Although he had felt much better physically by then, he had come to the conclusion that there would have been no point in rushing off home, for the only strong reason for going back to England had then lost its attraction. To be honest with himself, he had been worried that on meeting Kate, he would find that he had lost even the luxury of her sisterly affection.

As he sat there in the carriage lost in his memories he hardly noticed the little villages the train passed through, only coming out of his reverie when they pulled up at some busy station where all was bustle.

He had in the past written several difficult letters to relatives of his men when he had to inform them of injury or death in service, but the letter he had written to Kate and her husband had been just as difficult. In his attempt to congratulate the pair on their union with the hopes of a happy and successful future, yet not revealing the slightest hint of his feelings for Kate, he managed to pen a letter which was so devoid of warmth that it might almost be a lawyer's missive. Once it had been dispatched on its way to England, he had almost immediately begun to worry himself about the lack of warmth or feeling in the wording: would Kate read into the words of one who was merely being polite, one who was indifferent to her and her affairs? How he had wished then that he had not sent it. He recalled the dreary state which he had sunk into, the mood of despondency staying with him until, on his return home, he had plucked up enough courage to visit her at her parents' home, where he had learned she and her husband were staying.

His convalescence at the hill station lasted several weeks but eventually he was allowed to travel down to the coast where he had taken his discharge from the army, then was forced to while away the time whilst he waited for a ship that would take him home.

During that time Captain Howard would dine in the officers' club where sometimes he would meet old friends and fellow officers.

It was on one such occasion that he heard talk of a Royal Engineers captain by the name of Rodgerson, and he had not liked what had been said of the man. Of course, he had reasoned, it was not to say that it was the same Captain Rodgerson.

He well remembered his feelings at that time, the horror at the thought that his beloved, gentle Kate had married a bullying, vindictive, womanising gambler. As he sat in the railway carriage, Captain Howard could still recall the terrible despair and sense of helplessness which had gripped him, thousands of miles from Kate, and he could do nothing to show his support for her, that is, if it was the same man, and if he had treated her dishonourably.

One thing he was going to do, he had vowed, when he reached England, was to go to Norfolk and see Kate. What he would do if she was in distress he had not decided; in true army fashion he would act in a way which suited whatever situation he found when there.

Captain Howard looked out of the window and on recognising something of the countryside through which he was passing, checked his watch. Not long now, he murmured to himself. He smiled as he thought of Kate, for by now he knew that, if he did not have her love, he had never lost that warm friendship he had always enjoyed with his sister-in-law.

He once again let his thoughts drift back to the day when he had paid her the first visit soon after reaching his country's shores. He had been surprised but absolutely delighted to come face to face with the same lovely young woman he had left so many months ago. Although later he detected subtle changes in Kate, the initial reaction on seeing him in the entrance hall of her parents' home had allayed his fears immensely. With a joyful cry Kate had flung herself at him with tears in her eyes.

"Oh, Richard, how wonderful to have you here," she said, laughing through her tears, "we hardly thought you would be back in England so soon." Then more seriously she said, "We have been so worried about you with not having news these last weeks. Come inside out of the chill air." She loosened her arms from around him but tucked one arm through his and led him into her sitting room where a tall good-looking man stood with his back to the fireplace.

Reflecting on that first meeting with Kate's husband, Captain Gavin Rodgerson, he recalled the tremendous sensation of relief which washed over him. Obviously he would not be met with a fellow with a vicious mouth and cruel eyes; Kate would never have become involved with a man like that, never mind marry him, but he had been expecting somebody, not exactly with horns, but certainly with overt signs of his devilish nature.

When Kate had introduced them she merely said, "Gavin, may I introduce you to my brother-in-law, Captain Richard Howard," then followed by saying quietly, "Richard, may I introduce you to my husband, Captain Gavin Rodgerson." With that her husband leaned forward and both men shook hands.

By then he had made up his mind; this man was surely not the same Rodgerson whose unsavoury exploits had reached his ears those many weeks ago in India? The friendly dark-haired, blue-eyed man with his firm handshake had impressed Captain Howard very much and he felt as if a great weight had lifted off his shoulders.

Later Kate took him along to see her parents, a pleasure that he had been looking forward to, for he was on very affectionate terms with Mr. and Mrs. Prentice. The whole party was then summoned to dinner. They were joined by

Captain Howard's wife Cecelia, who came in on the arm of Captain Rodgerson, followed by Kate's brother, James, escorting a comfortable-looking young woman whom he introduced to Richard as his fiancée, Miss Charlotte Kingsley. Kate had informed Richard that Aunt Phoebe would be dining with them so he had elected to escort her into the dining room. As it was, the lady, who was in fact Great-Aunt Phoebe, was helped to her chair by Kate holding one arm and Richard taking the other.

Captain Howard was gladdened to see that Aunt Phoebe was still as spirited as ever even if she was having difficulty with gout. It came and went, she explained briefly, but told the concerned younger couple that she did not intend to let it interfere with her life.

As was her normal mode of dress, she wore all black clothing and had done since her husband had passed away, thus emulating Her Majesty Queen Victoria. Making her way slowly and obviously in some pain she nevertheless managed a beaming smile for everybody present, for she was not too old to have her little vanities, and to be escorted into the room by one of her favourite young men and her favourite great-niece filled her with satisfaction.

The ladies were helped to their seats by the men who then took their own, Mr. Prentice at the head of the table, Mrs. Prentice to his right and Aunt Phoebe to his left. Seated next to Aunt Phoebe, much to her delight, was Richard facing his wife. Next to Richard was Kate, which caused him as much pleasure as his company had given her. Across from Kate sat her husband, which, unknown to most of those present, gave her no pleasure at all. The chair next to Kate was occupied by James with Charlotte facing him.

How well he remembered that meal; it had started off so well. Captain Howard recalled the almost euphoric state of his mind at the realisation that his beloved Kate had not married a villain. However, as the evening progressed he had begun to notice almost imperceptible cracks in Captain Rodgerson's carefully constructed façade, and his depression had gradually returned.

It had started on a light-hearted note as James and Kate got involved with one of their conversations of malapropisms and misunderstandings. They were particularly good at it and sparked each other off. That night they surpassed themselves, creating gales of laughter such that even the servant Florence was hard put to keep her face straight. As always Cecelia found the whole thing too puerile for words, at one point scathingly commenting that, "It was just like a common music-hall act," to which the quicksilver-minded James riposted, "Well, we are not familiar with such places of entertainment, Cissy, perhaps you would be so kind as to elucidate."

His elder sister had flushed and told him not to be so ridiculous and to stop calling her Cissy.

Kate had turned to Richard and asked in mock seriousness if they were being childish, and he had replied, "Kate, my dear, laughter is a wonderful medicine and I am feeling much better already." He laughed and then remarked, "You know, I have not heard James and yourself do that for a long time and tonight you both excelled yourselves."

Kate had smiled happily, giving his poor heart another jolt, then noticing that the food was before everyone, picked up her knife and fork and started to eat.

Three things stood out in his memories of that night. The first was the uninhibited laughter of Charlotte and the transformation of her face. He had seen in those few minutes what an attractive woman she was, and thought how fortunate James was in his choice.

The second memory was that Captain Rodgerson never exhibited one single expression of enjoyment at his wife's part in the entertainment, simply disinterest. Indeed, he had whispered something to Cecelia at which she shrugged her shoulders unsmilingly.

The third was the way the controlled expression of a decent, hearty young man had almost disappeared as he drank more wine. During a triumphant story told by Cecelia concerning her part in the dismissal of a waitress from a top London restaurant, Captain Rodgerson's face had registered an expression of amusement and he kept nodding his approval.

Richard could not let this go without comment; after all, however things were between them, Cecelia was still his wife, and he felt he could hardly be seen to agree with her.

"I hardly find your actions at all amusing or clever, Cecelia; the woman you caused to lose her employment was possibly a main or even, the only breadwinner for her family. Does it not occur to you that by being dismissed from a good place of employment, she might have had difficulty finding work of that class again?"

The sharp tone of his voice had silenced everyone and he noted that Kate and her mother had been just about to remonstrate with his wife, but had held back, then nodded their agreement at his sentiments.

Cecelia was obviously taken aback but all she could muster up by way of a reply was, "Oh, not the poor downtrodden servants again," whilst Captain Rodgerson said in a bored tone, "Really, old fellow, she was only a waitress, you know."

Richard, by now thoroughly disgusted with both of them, answered in a quieter tone, "Yes, Captain Rodgerson, but remember, there but for the grace of God go any of us here."

With that the now sober party broke up. Richard was then wishing he had held his tongue, and was glad of the chance to buttonhole his host before he went up to his room. He need not have worried, as his father-in-law was also angry at Cecelia's attitude and had agreed with his stance in the matter.

That night he had lain in his bed unable to sleep; the feeling of having a knot in his stomach had returned. He was confused by his sister-in-law's demeanour; she had been just like the Kate of old, happy affectionate and so full of fun, not at all the picture of a woman who had married badly. And yet he was by the end of the evening convinced that her husband and the infamous Captain Rodgerson were one and the same man.

Daybreak had brought him little relief; his aching leg and aching head scarcely made him a happy breakfast companion. The family were very solicitous and forbore to ask him about India and in particular, his accident.

His wife and Captain Rodgerson were not present, having gone out early with the local Hunt. One of the few things which Captain Howard admired about Cecelia was her skill on horseback; he and many others considered her to be equal to any man and better than most riders.

Later during the morning James, Kate and Richard had gone out to the courtyard to view Aunt Phoebe's latest carriage. It was every bit as elegant as she had described during the previous evening's dinner. With its mirror-like paintwork of deep crimson and black lined with yellow, it was a triumph of the carriage-maker's art.

Aunt Phoebe's late husband had made and lost several fortunes in his lifetime and on his death had left his widow an exceedingly wealthy woman. She had never been a spendthrift, only giving to worthy causes, when she thought that her gifts would be properly administered, but her one personal extravagance was her carriage, or to be more precise, carriages, as Aunt Phoebe always owned at least two.

Richard had declined a ride in it, for even when well wrapped up, he was at that time still feeling the chill of the English air after the hot humid weather of India. Nevertheless he had been sorry to disappoint her; he was very fond of Aunt Phoebe and admired her enthusiastic approach to life. Her health, though, was giving her family a great deal of concern, which was not so surprising given her age, and they worried about her 'jaunts' (as she called her carriage rides), particularly in the wintertimes.

In turn she was extremely fond of her family; therefore it was all the more sad that her last, and largest gift, unknown to anyone at the time, was to create such misery for Kate, her favourite niece.

Captain Howard and James stayed outside chatting after the rest of the group had moved back indoors and inevitably the conversation turned to the events of the previous evening. James dismissed his older sister's snobbish ways with the dry comment that, "Well, we know Cecelia's ways, don't we?" but proceeded to fuel his brother-in-law's worries over Kate, by bringing up the subject of her husband.

As Captain Howard recalled the conversation he remembered the almost casual way in which James had introduced Captain Rodgerson's name into it.

"Ever met Kate's husband before, Richard, same regiment and all that?" he queried. "We know he's a fine horseman, oh yes, and he comes from Ireland but other than those facts I don't know anything about the man."

It was just what had been needed to relieve Captain Howard of his mental burden; the fact that Kate's brother was letting him know that he was not too happy with the man in question was sufficient to let all his fears spill out. He judged James to be trusted to hold his tongue, so he repeated all he had learned concerning a certain Captain Rodgerson, concluding with his suspicion that Kate's husband was the same man.

His young brother-in-law, so often the clown of the party, was more of a thinker than people outside the family were aware of, and his companion realised that he had been quietly observing Gavin Rodgerson for some time.

"I'll tell you the main facts as I know them. Young Kate hasn't told you how she came to meet the fellow, has she?" At this Captain Howard shook his head and asked James to carry on.

"The whole affair started at the Hunt Ball; no, it was on the day of the Hunt itself. Old Hulse had agreed to let Cecelia bring one of her friends to ride to hounds with her. Rodgerson is a very good horseman and such was his manner that when he was invited to attend the Hunt Ball he was made welcome by everybody. He marked Kate's card for several dances, so what with his gentlemanly manners, his skill in dancing and the fact that we, I am now ashamed to say, approved of him, set poor Kate up for the courting of her." He said sadly, "You know, Richard, she seemed so happy those days."

His brother-in-law could very well picture it all. Hunt Balls were looked-forward-to events in the country and most of the top people attended them; they were also events where the eligible young people could meet.

James took up his narrative, telling of the man's decorous attentions culminating in him proposing to Kate and with her parents' blessing, she had accepted.

"It was within hours of the wedding ceremony that we got an inkling of what sort of a fellow he really was, and you know what sickens me, Richard," he said bitterly, "I'm sure that my sister, your wife, knew more about the scoundrel than she let on, and still let it happen. I simply can never forgive her for such treachery." He was silent for a moment, his face hardened in anger.

Then he carried on with his tale. "Later on at the reception the effects of the wine loosened his guard and the cad's true nature asserted itself, and I could see that people around him were starting to look uncomfortable. Poor young Kate, she simply did not know how to deal with it and it was one of her friends who rescued her when two of Rodgerson's fellow officer guests took him in hand." He shook his head as if to rid himself of the embarrassing spectacle and continued. "Luckily our parents witnessed very little of his worst behaviour."

Captain Howard sat in the train carriage oblivious to the countryside he was travelling through, his imagination once again picturing his beloved Kate and the humiliation she must have endured through the actions of Rodgerson, aided by Captain Howard's own wife, and he cursed the day he married Cecelia. However, from what James had told him that day standing by Aunt Phoebe's new carriage, Kate had outwardly maintained her role as a married woman, believing that divorce would have reflected shame on the family name, but simply treated him with a courtesy borne of good manners and carried on her life as a single woman.

Her parents were bewildered at the way things had turned out but had not heard a single word of complaint from their youngest daughter and so had no reason to act against Captain Rodgerson.

He remembered his young brother-in-law's words as he had concluded his tale. "The morning after the reception, that oaf was found at the bottom of the wrong flight of stairs, still in his wedding suit, still drunk and sporting a large egg-sized lump on his head. Never knew what happened there but it was a grand sight to me." He grinned at that.

"And there was a further mystery that day. Rodgerson received a letter by the first post, told everyone that he had been called to his regiment, apologised to everyone and before we knew it, was off to the station." James paused as though to create a dramatic effect, and in truth Captain Howard found himself hugely interested in the next part. James did not disappoint him. "The next day, two very large uncouth fellows called and asked for Captain Gavin Rodgerson, and were informed that he had rejoined his regiment and was now, according to what Rodgerson told Father, on the ship bound for South Africa. Well," James said, "we had been told of the regiment's move, but had understood that it was a matter of months, not days, you know." Here he told his rapt listener, "Then, would you believe it, as soon as they were told the news, they jumped into the waiting trap cursing, and rushed off down the drive, and to add to the mystery," he added with obvious relish, "a few days later, two of his fellow officer friends, uncouth devils they were, had been seen at an inn in Beccles. And now he's arrived back here saying that they have been stood down for a few more months."

Captain Howard, thoroughly entertained by James's dramatic telling of the saga, momentarily diverted from Kate's problems, joined in his brother-in-law's laughter.

Then James became serious again and told Richard how things stood in the family with regard to Captain Rodgerson. With the exception of Aunt Phoebe and Cecelia, nobody quite trusted him anymore, and Albert, the elder of the four siblings, had urged James to look out for young Kate, as he thought her husband was, as he put it, "a wrong 'un."

Dear Aunt Phoebe, for all her astuteness, had her weak spot for young personable men who played up to her vanity, and according to James he never let his mask slip when in her company. She seemed unaware of any coolness between Kate and her dubious husband.

As the two men had strolled back for lunch, James had turned to Captain Howard and said lightly, "You know, Richard, it's such a pity that you didn't marry Kate," then seeing the startled look on his companion's face, he said, "Well, you both hit it off so well, you know you do," then he laughed disarmingly and led the way indoors.

Captain Howard hoped his face did not show his true feelings at James's words; he almost gave himself away, feeling the urge to blurt out his love for Kate to his sympathetic brother-in-law, but managed to still his tongue.

During the remaining few days of his visit, he had noticed several odd traits in Captain Rodgerson's behaviour, and afterwards, when comparing notes with James, they both agreed that the man was always on the alert for some threat or other connected with visitors calling. It was noticed that on occasions when his wife's parents were not present he would subtly adopt some of his father-in-law's mannerisms whilst in the presence of other guests.

James was the first to voice his suspicions when he said sagely to Captain Howard, "I'll wager you that the fellow has dunned someone for money, and I would say a lot of money if those bailiffs or whatever have been paid to get it back, and you know, Richard, I think the cad married my sister to raise his position in society. "Poor Kate," he said bitterly, "she is just a rung in his ladder."

Captain Howard had been inclined to agree, and indeed James was right on both counts, but as regards to the man's debts, it was years after before he learned that her husband's creditors had been paid off by Kate herself.

Over the years, Captain Howard had often cast his mind back to that weekend, the first family gathering he had attended since arriving back in England. So many images would appear in his mind's eye, but always Kate through it, Kate and James in their light hearted clowning, with her parents whilst the others were out riding, and the poised, elegant Kate whose mature and dignified behaviour so excited his admiration for the way she had dealt with the humiliating position she had been put in.

He had felt so spent and dull, still recovering from his problems in India, yet Kate had made him feel alive again. "Oh, Kate," he would sigh to himself, "I was born too early for you."

Soon after that week, Captain Rodgerson's regiment had gone to South Africa taking the man with it, and those who had pledged themselves to 'keeping an eye open for her' were able to visit her in a more relaxed atmosphere. Her husband eventually came back to England but after a year or so, suddenly resigned his commission. Those who had him weighed up suspected some misdemeanour, and they were right, but again, it was to be some time before Captain Howard learned the reasons.

The slowing down of the train brought Captain Howard back to the present, and on realising that it was drawing into Wroxing station he set about getting his small luggage down from the rack.

By the time he was stepping down to the platform, he had managed to push the less happy of his thoughts out of his mind, his eager thoughts at seeing his sister-in-law overriding everything else. With the odd-sounding cry of 'Rorksin' from the porter ringing in his ears, he carried his bags towards the exit, his heavier luggage being brought on the porter's truck. As he surrendered his ticket he saw that the well-used trap with its driver Billy Timms was in its usual place, so he motioned to the porter and walked across the station yard towards it. He thanked his lucky stars the day was dry even if it was cold, for after such an exceptionally warm autumn, the weather had reverted to its normal seasonal mixture of cold misty days alternating with heavy rain and the odd dry day.

The driver, having served in the army for a (few) years, was usually well disposed to Captain Howard. Normally an amiable and courteous man, he surprised the late Royal Engineers officer by averting his eyes from him whilst stowing the luggage in the trap.

After the trap was in motion for a few minutes and still no attempt on the part of Billy to pass as much as the time of day, it became obvious to the puzzled engineer that something was bothering the driver, so he decided to draw him out.

"Well, Billy, I must say the weather is better for us today than it was the last time you carried me, wouldn't you agree?" When the only reply he got was a muffled "argh," the Captain decided that he had to speak his mind. A courteous man himself, he expected nothing more than courtesy in return.

"Mr. Timms," he said, "you obviously have a troubled mind and your manner shows it, but I strongly advise you not to let it affect your dealings with your patrons." After a pause during which Billy uttered not a word, the Captain went on quietly, "otherwise you will surely lose their custom."

Almost before the speaker had finished, Billy Timms burst out fiercely, but still keeping his eyes forward, "Thomas Banham is out of a job and his family as well, and they are to be thrown out of their home," and turning to glare at his startled passenger, he finished his outburst by saying angrily, "and that's the work of the other Captain." He then added in a slightly heated tone, "People round here feel badly 'bout the Banhams, aye, and they don't look kindly on them as was once in the army and can't forget it." The last was almost spat out, and was accompanied with a flick of the whip over the ambling horse. As the animal smartened up its pace, the now angry captain replied as if he too had felt the touch of the whip. "And you too once a soldier, Billy Timms," to which the driver had replied angrily, "Not an 'orfficer," repeating it twice.

Captain Howard was really angry but not so much with Billy Timms as he was with Kate's husband, for his treatment of the unfortunate Banham family bore out what he had heard of the man that day in India. He had been told that Captain Rodgerson enjoyed his power over his subordinates and wielded it vindictively.

He said quietly to the silent driver, "Mr. Timms, tell me, what are the Banhams doing now, where are they living?"

Billy had had time to think over his outburst and was now regretting it, therefore he felt heartened by his passenger's tone of voice, and replied more soberly, "Thomas and his eldest boy are living in the shed behind the smithy, Beth and the other two are staying in her Mam and Dad's poky cottage." He then added gloomily, "Thomas 'as tramped for miles in all sorts of weather and can't find work."

Both men fell silent, busy with their thoughts, Captain Howard appalled at the cruel way that they had been treated. What of Kate, he thought, she had grown very fond of Mrs. Banham and Victoria, what was her part in all this? He could not bring himself to believe that his gentle sister-in-law was capable of such an act. Then it struck him: he had received no letter from Kate for some time and that was unusual. The fact that he had received a letter from his wife was also unusual, for the only times when she bothered to write to him was when she needed extra money. He was actually meeting her at her sister's home at her request; not that he minded, for he had not been able to fit in a visit to Reeve House for some time due to him being so busy in his work.

His thoughts reverted back to the plight of the Banham family, and he felt another surge of anger at the system of tied cottages which gave the occupants no security of tenure, and condemned whole families to a life of destitution if a man lost his job.

As they entered the drive leading to Reeve House, Billy spoke up, his voice holding a pleading note. "Captain Howard, sir, I hope you don't hold it against me for what I said. I didn't mean to speak out so bold, but I'm that angry about the Banhams, sir, I let my tongue run away with itself." Then he added, "I'd like to say I'm sorry, sir."

Captain Howard's eyes were by then drawn to the house as he caught sight of movement in one of the windows. Kate, he thought, then turned to the anxious driver and told him, "Mr. Timms, I understand and share your concern for Thomas Banham and his family, but you surely cannot blame all and sundry for these events; it would be better for your business if you keep your anger under control." Then, as Kate appeared on the step of the house, he turned back to the chastened driver and handed him his fare plus a little extra and said, "I do not hold grudges, Billy."

As he turned to mount the steps, his sister-in-law called out, "Good afternoon, Mr. Timms," to the mollified and slightly guilty driver who had just started to deposit his late passenger's baggage by the steps. To Captain Howard's amazement, Billy doffed his cap and replied very effusively, "Good afternoon, Mrs. Rodgerson," then with a touch of forehead, he mounted the trap and moved off.

Whilst his luggage was being dealt with, Kate took his arm and led him into the house where she asked with a smile, "Why the look of wonderment at Mr. Timm's civilities, Richard? He is a natural gentleman; do you not find him so yourself?"

Although her tone was light and she was smiling, Captain Howard sensed the tension in her. His sister-in-law's arm linked to his was trembling perceptibly, and he felt a rising sense of alarm.

No sooner had they entered her sitting room, than she let go of his arm, thrust the door shut and with her back to it, burst into tears.

In an instant, the appalled Captain Howard had taken her into his arms. "Kate, my dear, what is wrong, what has happened?" As the sobbing girl clung to him he was overwhelmed by a feeling of such tenderness for his young sister-in-law, his lovely Kate, crying like a child, the only love of his life and she was in deep distress.

Through her sobbing she jerked out, "Oh, Richard, I have needed you so and you weren't there, what could I do with nobody to turn to?" and with a fresh paroxysm of weeping she cried, "And when you did not reply to my letter I thought that you too had abandoned me. Oh how I have prayed and prayed for you to come, thank God you have come," she cried. "Oh, Richard, help me, help me."

Holding Kate to him, the thoroughly distressed Captain Howard found himself stroking her hair and murmuring comforting words as one would to a child, but when her tear-stained face was turned upward, he could not restrain himself any longer; he kissed her cheek then before he could control himself, her lips fiercely.

Shocked at his own actions, he jerked his head back, but before his faltering words of apology could leave his lips, he was drawn back to her, Kate's arms around his neck and her eyes beseeching him to kiss her once more.

Gently they kissed and clung to each other. Kate's voice softly, lovingly, whispered, "Richard, is it possible?" then as if she feared that she would not hear the words she wanted to hear, "Is it possible that you have the same love for me as I have, as I have always had for you?" Richard Howard's senses reeled; Kate loved him. He wanted to shout out to the world, 'Love you, Kate, I love only you,' but all he could manage at that moment was an emotional but simple, "Yes, Kate, my dear, yes."

It was as if everything around them receded; they were the only persons in the universe as they gazed at each other so intimately close, their fingertips brushing each other's features.

Then her brother-in-law, realising suddenly the awkward situation they would be in if any other person entered the room, gently disentangled himself from Kate and reluctantly set himself down on a chair at a decorous distance away from her and asked her to tell him exactly what happened regarding the Banham family.

"But I have explained the whole sorry tale in the letter I wrote to you," she said. "It was written and posted on the same day that Cecelia wrote to you, did you not receive them, Richard?" To which he answered that he was here as requested by his wife and was only too pleased to use the excuse to come and see his sister-in-law, but, he added, as she made to move over to him, he had not received a letter from Kate.

At that, the expression of puzzlement returned to her face and she sat back in her chair. "But, Richard, I gave my letter to my sister, she told me she would make sure that both letters would go by the next post."

Both of them sat silent for a few moments as they digested the implications of the situation. Richard forbore to point out the fact that it was utterly foreign to his wife's nature to volunteer to do anything for anybody else. Kate said without conviction, "It must have got lost in the post."

Captain Howard persuaded Kate to tell him what had happened to cause the Banham family to lose their jobs and home. As the whole story was revealed to him by a very angry and frustrated Kate, his anger mounted and he bitterly regretted the fact that she had been on her own to deal with it all. Her staunchest ally James had been in Italy with Charlotte enjoying their honeymoon and her sister had supported Captain Rodgerson against her all the way.

Captain Howard was amazed and delighted when Kate recounted the way she had routed her husband and her sister, his already high opinion of her rose even higher.

After gaining a stay of eviction for the family, Kate had learned from Beth that her husband had known before the event that it had been only a matter of time before he was sacked, but he had not spoken of his convictions to anyone. Beth also gave her late employer the message that he would have been proud to serve Mrs. Rodgerson if that was ever possible but never Captain Rodgerson.

During Kate's anguished outpouring Captain Howard realised that he had not given a single thought as to where his wife or Captain Rodgerson were, and although it suited him very well, he was irritated when he learned that they had both gone to London, Cecelia to see her dressmaker and Captain Rodgerson on business. Kate had been informed that they would be back in a day or so.

But for the wonderful realisation of his and Kate's love for each other, he would have been furious with his wife. As his contractor's business was involved in a very large scheme in the north-west of England at that time, the only way he could spare the time to absent himself from his work was to delegate much of the work to his assistant. However, with what had happened on this momentous afternoon, he was almost prepared to forgive Cecelia.

What Kate could not bring herself to do was to speak of her certainty that her sister and her husband were conducting an affair. Even now, with knowledge that her most precious dream had become reality, she felt that to speak of such sordid behaviour would tarnish the day for both of them.

Another matter which was worrying her was the suspicion that her husband had done something in the last few days before the eviction which had badly upset her maid. The thoughts that dear sweet Victoria had been despoiled by the vile beast she was married to made her feel physically sick. Oh, how she hated him!

Later, as he enjoyed dinner with just Kate and himself for company, Richard told the contented girl that he could not recall a time when he had been happier, and her answering look of love had sent his heart soaring. Kate's maid, Mary, thought her mistress seemed so different, and somehow prettier than she had ever seen her before.

"I think that Mrs. Rodgerson is in love with Captain Howard," she said to herself, happily. Although Mary thought him a bit old, she liked him very much. What a pity they were both married. She thought it would please Victoria if she knew, for her friend had said once that Mrs. Rodgerson always shone when her brother-in-law visited.

During the evening Kate was suddenly moved to ask Richard if he would be able to offer Thomas Banham work of any kind or if it was possible that he knew of anybody who could take him on.

Captain Howard smiled at the naivety; she knew he was engaged in a big civil engineering scheme, and that he employed a good number of men, but she was innocent of the cut-throat business of labour costs. To not have enough men was almost as costly as having too many men and a good employer was one who judged his labour needs wisely.

However, unknown to Kate he had already toyed with the thought of offering Thomas Banham a job, for the way the man had been treated had angered him; he hated despotism and for the despot to have been Kate's husband made him wish it was still legal to take pistols at dawn with the hound.

Captain Howard had only met Thomas Banham on two occasions but had liked what he saw, and the way the estate equipment was maintained showed that the man was interested in his job. The engineer would have been only too glad to have him on his payroll if he had a position to offer him.

The scheme he was involved in at the present was the building of a canal, the widest in Great Britain which would, on completion, take the largest ships from the sea to the city of Manchester.

To construct something of that size needed a contractor of great experience, and such a man was Thomas Andrew Walker. He was not only a first-rate contractor, he was also a man who cared for the welfare of his men. Captain Howard was one of his specialist subcontractors.

The task was mammoth and was expected to last five years. As progress had been good, there were high hopes that the contract could be fulfilled within the specified time.

Captain Howard gave considerable thought to the matter of employing Thomas on the canal site but he could not see how he could employ him in his rightful position in an engineering or supervisory capacity; there were simply no openings in that direction. Even in the event of such a job becoming vacant, he had men who had worked for him on previous contracts, and who were eligible for promotion if such a chance came their way. The good Captain did not feel it right to upset his present labour force just to fit Thomas Banham in.

The following day during a stroll around the garden with Kate, leaving a decorous two feet distance between them, he voiced his thoughts on the matter, and whilst Kate saw the situation much as he did, he thought she looked very thoughtful and he asked her to tell him what else was worrying her.

Kate hesitated for a moment, then turning to him asked, "Richard, could not they be together if you could employ Thomas?" and then went on with a rush, "You see, my dear, they are such a close and loving family, I do not know how they would take to being torn apart like that." Then she went on almost in tears, "Beth told me that she and Thomas had made a pact not to be parted no matter what happened. Oh, Richard," she cried, "why have they been served so cruelly?" Tears flowed freely now and Kate found herself in the arms of her love. Oblivious to the chance of watchers, Captain Howard tenderly held Kate to his breast, his other hand stroking her hair until the slender figure ceased to shake and the weeping subsided. Suddenly Kate pulled away, and with a quick glance around, she said tremulously, "We must not give Captain Rodgerson any reason to make difficulties for you, Richard," and with that she offered her arm to link as they continued with their stroll.

The third day of his visit dawned and still his wife and Captain Rodgerson had failed to return, and he had to admit to himself that he was now only mildly curious as to what she wanted of him. However, during the afternoon, a telegram was delivered to him informing him that his assistant Ian Blake had been struck down with some kind of fever and was under the doctor.

Richard Howard was like a man torn in two; his concern for Ian jostled with the wanting to be near his new-found love but he simply had no choice. He made arrangements to return to Frodsham. As for his wife's affairs, he was not concerned at all; treating people casually was her usual way and this time she outsmarted herself.

It was a very subdued Kate who saw him to Billy Timm's trap, a woman in love and unable to show it, but she knew now that from then on, she had the knowledge that Richard loved her and that he now knew that she felt the same for him. It was a different man who set out on the return journey north than the one who had stepped up into Billy Timm's trap three days previously. Gone was the resigned look, the heavy walk. This new man was more brisk, more purposeful and he looked younger, yes, even boyish with a bright alert glance. Here was a man in love. Even so, the plight of the Banhams was firmly fixed in his mind; after all, as has been mentioned before, he was a humane person with a strong sense of justice, and he would have done something to help if it had been in his power. In fact he was quite willing to keep eyes and ears open for any hint of a job for Thomas, but there was little he could do locally and he was not sure that such a close family as the Banhams would be prepared to live apart in the event that Thomas was offered work outside Norfolk. Especially he wanted to help because that is what Kate, his sweet love, had asked of him, and he would have done anything to show her the devotion he felt for her.

He was at the same time concerned by the illness which had put Ian Blake in his sick bed. His assistant was a singularly healthy young man, one who was not likely to give way to any ailment; therefore the fever stated in the telegram must be an exceptionally serious one. He vowed to see him as soon as he could, following his return to Frodsham.

Billy Timms must have done some thinking during the last few days and soon after leaving Reeve House, he apologised sincerely, an apology which the Captain accepted in the same spirit. On impulse Richard told Billy that he would look out for a chance of employment for Thomas, but then realising how, if word got back to the Banhams it could raise false hopes, he added, "Jobs for men like Thomas are scarce everywhere, Billy."

Chapter 6

Captain Howard at Frodsham

Alighting from the train at the end of his journey, Captain Howard elected to walk the short distance from Frodsham station to the Bear's Paw, the inn at which he had a room. His bags were to follow by porter.

He was looking forward to a hot tub and a change of linen after several hours of travel in a somewhat mixed bag of carriages in terms of cleanliness, ranging from the fairly acceptable to the truly appalling. However, hardly a few minutes had elapsed after he had completed his ablutions, when he was asked if he was prepared to accept a visitor.

The man was Jacob Morrison, one of his foremen, a steady and capable man but one who was at that moment obviously ill at ease.

"Sorry to come mithering you, sir, especially as you've only just come back, but we've had a bit of trouble down at the depot," then seeing the apprehensive look, he added quickly, "No, sir, not an accident or anything like that, I'm glad to say that, I'm just sorry to say it's a case of thieving and the like, that's what." Jacob handed a bundle of letters and papers for Captain Howard's attention. "I was asked to give you these, sir."

Amongst the navvies, fighting was not that uncommon, especially after consuming strong drink, but thieving was less so. Amongst the engineering workers employed by Captain Howard, it was exceedingly rare, but for it to be brought to his attention and so quickly indicated that it was quite serious.

"Well, Mr. Morrison, I must say this is not the sort of welcome to gladden the heart, but for you to be in such haste to impart the news, I take it that it is not a small matter of a few lumps of coal or such."

"No, sir," said Jacob gravely. "It's more than a few lumps, it's more like a few wagon loads of coal and of other things as well, and, sir, it's not one of our men but two of them, what's worse," he added, "is that one of them is someone who I would have trusted with my wages, sir." Here Jacob hesitated, for he had worked with this man many a time and it grieved him to have to tell Captain Howard his name.

Then his employer said heavily, "Who is it that's been involved, Jacob?" and when he was told that one was Joe Clayburn the fitter, he felt just as shocked as Jacob obviously was. Clayburn was a tradesman who was so talented and with a gift of being able to work with any type of machinery as to be considered for a more senior position. It was indeed hard to credit.

After the initial shock, there came a feeling of anger but then, conscious of the now silent figure by the door, he restrained himself, then being a fair-minded man, he started to look at the possibility that there could have been a terrible mistake. He would hate to see men branded as criminals for the rest of their lives.

The Captain broke the silence by saying, "I take it there is no shadow of a doubt that both these men are involved in this criminal activity, there is no possibility of some mistake." Even as he heard himself utter the words he realised just how naïve he sounded.

"I beg your pardon, Mr. Morrison," he said wearily, "you would not have come to me in such haste had you not been certain of the facts, you are not a man who jumps easily to conclusions."

Jacob was not offended by the Captain's questioning of Clayburn's part in the affair; he recognised this for what it was, a vain hope that the man whom the Captain had such trust in had not played him false.

Contract workers by the very nature of their work tend to form close-knit groups. Moving from place to place led them to be treated with suspicion by the local inhabitants, and blamed for every instance of theft or damage. With a large number of casual labourers employed, there was some grounds for this type of attitude. However, with a small specialised firm like Captain Howard's, there was very little casual labour and this resulted in the formation of a group of men bonded together by loyalty and trust.

Just like the army, any man who betrayed that trust had to be got rid of, and that is why Captain Howard was making sure they were justified in labelling the men without positive proof.

"Right, Jacob, I must speak to these men and get to the bottom of the matter before the police become involved," then stopped from continuing by the worried look on his foreman's face. "Sir, the police are already involved, they are hoping to see you as soon as they can."

His employer became really angry, but still keeping his voice down, he demanded, "By whose authority was the constabulary called in?" To this, Jacob answered that nobody had sent for them, the police were, in fact, already on the Marsh in connection with another matter altogether, but one which involved the labourer employed as a coal heaver, who as it came out was involved in the theft of the coal

Captain Howard rose to his feet, saying to his foreman, "I'll go straight to the police station now and see what I can do to sort things out. Oh, Jacob, this is a sorry business," he said wearily. "I will be down to the depot when I've done with the police and had a meal, and mind you, do not talk of this matter to any person not connected with the affair, although," he said almost to himself, "news travels fast on the site."

Jacob touched his cap and left Captain Howard to ready himself for a visit to the police station.

Before he left the inn, he asked the boy to prepare his horse ready to ride to the depot after he had eaten. By then he was feeling much fresher, less angry and quite hungry.

When he reached the police station he was lucky in meeting the Inspector just as he was about to leave the building. The man smiled at Captain Howard, whom he had met before on several occasions, and turned to re-enter the station.

After shaking hands with the Inspector, he was shown into an office where a sergeant was writing something on a sheet of foolscap paper.

The Inspector thanked him for coming in so promptly, then said, "I'm glad you caught me before I left. I take it you are here on account of the trouble on the Marsh, or should I say more correctly at your depot?" When the engineer agreed that he was, the policeman continued, "Why I say that, is that we have other problems on the canal site, the investigation of which has led us to your depot where we discovered the organised theft of coal; do you know about that, sir?" The engineer admitted he had been given the unwelcome news but added that he was in possession of just the barest of details. He told the Inspector of his hopes that the charges against his men would be found to be without substance, but the sight of the policeman sympathetically shaking his head told him that the evidence against them was very firm.

The Inspector spoke first. "Captain Howard, sir, I do realise that you entertain your hopes that your men are trustworthy and are guilty of no wrongdoing, but I'm afraid there is ample proof that at least two are involved to some extent in the theft of considerable amounts of coal and for all we know, other things as well. You see, we have one immediate confession and we found evidence to connect your fitter Clayburn with a known criminal."

Richard Howard said nothing but waited for the Inspector's next pronouncement. "I will explain how we more or less stumbled upon the shady goings on at your depot, but first I will remind you of something that no doubt you already know. With a large-scale works such as this, it acts like a magnet to all sorts of shady characters, hucksters and tricksters." He looked at the captain, who nodded in agreement but sat silently waiting for the police Inspector to continue.

The Inspector went on, "The contractors themselves do have their own rules I know concerning drunkenness, fighting, and also to some extent, the problems of men losing their wages through gambling. Well, that's all very fine but that only concerns us, the police force, when a crime is committed through any of those three, and what we are concerned about is the involvement in gambling on the canal site of a certain Mr. Joseph Sheehy; he and his gang are real bad villains."

Captain Howard looked up with interest but also with a look of enquiry, but he motioned for the policeman to continue with his narrative and the Inspector did so with the dramatic statement, "Mr. Sheehy had a man planted at your depot, a man who formerly worked at Birkenhead as a fitter on ships, but an ordinary working man who owns, not rents, a house in that town where he lives with his wife and lodgers. He also owns at least two more houses managed by members of his family who also take lodgers." The Inspector paused for dramatic effect, and was pleased to see that he had his visitor's full attention. "Not bad for a man on fitter's pay, wouldn't you agree, sir?"

The engineer was really intrigued and despite his sadness at the man's betrayal was curious to know whether the activities of Clayburn had brought the police to the depot. At this the policeman had looked a bit sheepish, and admitted that their quarry had, in fact, been the coal heaver who they knew acted as a runner for the criminal bookie. When the police called at the depot to question the man, he had, as the Inspector put it, 'sung like a tame linnet'.

If the policeman had laid out the details of his story to cause an effect, he certainly succeeded and he could see by Captain Howard's face that he had shaken the man, but was only asked one question. Did the Inspector know whether there were any others of his men involved? The policeman shook his head, almost regretfully it seemed, then told the engineer that Clayburn had gone on the run but that they were confident he would be found at one or the other of his houses in Birkenhead.

By now the weary engineer was thoroughly famished and within a further ten minutes left the police station and made his way back to the hotel and his evening meal, after which he rode down through the darkened lane to the depot, but with a less heavy heart.

The reason for the lift in his spirits was that whilst eating his meal, the realisation came to him that he could now fulfil his promise to Kate by offering Thomas Banham a job here on the construction site. If Clayburn was involved in the theft, and there now seemed to be no doubts in the matter, then the depot was short of a machine fitter and he thought Thomas would be the right man.

The thoughts of Kate's reaction made him as happy as a small boy given a treat. Then the reality of communicating the proposition to the man himself made him realise that involving Kate would create an embarrassing situation for his loved one, should the matter become known to her husband. The situation looked rather complicated.

As the noises from the site machinery became more distinct, so did the sight of moving locomotives and trains of spoil wagons, steam excavators and swarms of navvies show up in the glare of the flares and Wells lights. These wonderful pieces of equipment turned parts of the excavation almost as bright as daylight.

After having a few words with Jacob Morrison he went to the workshops to discuss the affair with the foreman fitter, Albert Tarleton. He found him in the building which was used as a fitting shop. There he came upon the man struggling to assemble the brake gear on the locomotive named *Frodsham*, aided by a willing but unskilled youth whom he referred to as Robbie. The boy was immediately dispatched to brew some tea whilst the foreman and his employer talked.

The captain was shocked to see how changed his employee was since the last time he had spoken to him. The foreman seemed to have aged and he didn't seem to be able to meet his employer's eyes easily. It bothered Richard Howard for he had known Albert Tarleton many years and his demeanour was totally different from his usual easy manner. The engineer put it down to the fact that a criminal scheme had been in operation under his nose and he had not spotted what was going on.

Captain Howard discussed the matter at some length with him and whilst not letting him think that he was blameless, dealt with the problem in a practical way but not coming down heavily on the dejected man.

The matter was then raised concerning a replacement fitter, much to Tarleton's relief, and the engineer outlined his plan to try and get Thomas

Banham to take up the post. The worried-looking foreman seemed only too eager to accept the solution whatever it involved.

As Captain Howard rode back to the Bear's Paw and bed, he did so with mixed feelings. One part of his mind was pleased that he could put into action his plan to offer Banham a job, but he was uneasy as to why his foreman fitter was so changed. One thing he was not going to do was ignore the problem, for although he was willing to give Albert Tarleton a bit more time to unburden himself, he was not willing to allow any problems to interfere with the working relationship which had been built up over several years.

After an unsettled night's sleep, but with much of the problems dealt with, he managed to pay a visit to Ian Blake's lodgings where he was greeted not by the landlady, Mrs. Joyce, but by a young woman he vaguely remembered meeting somewhere a few weeks ago. She was not a pretty woman but had an attractive, intelligent face and an air of assurance and humour which had appealed to Captain Howard. Then he recalled the event where he had seen her. Ian had introduced her to Richard at a garden party given by one of the town's two doctors. Sarah something, and yes, he began to remember details of that afternoon. The young lady was the doctor's daughter and if he was not very much mistaken, Ian Blake was rather attentive to her on that occasion.

It was immediately obvious from the cool attitude of the young woman before him that she was not pleased to see him; Captain Howard introduced himself, reminding her that he had previously made her acquaintance at her father's garden party. Her answer was just as cool as her demeanour.

"How do you do, Captain Howard?" she said. "I do remember Mr. Blake introducing us; he had mentioned previously how pleasant and thoughtful an employer you were. I had the notion that you would have called yesterday evening, but of course you would probably be tired after your journey." He felt a flash of irritation at her censure, though he knew what was behind it; at the same time he was angry at her presumptuousness.

Just in time he remembered her surname and speaking as coolly as she said, "Miss Mills, I do understand your strong feelings concerning my seemingly tardy attitude in not visiting Mr. Blake sooner. I would have called much earlier but I must remind you that I am responsible to my main contractor and many men." He continued in a firm but pleasant tone. "There have been events on the site which I have had to settle without delay. Some of these events will no doubt be public news in the town; bad news does travel fast," he concluded a little wryly as he had the previous day.

The girl before him had gone a little pink about the face and the angry look had been replaced by a look of uncertainty. Sarah realised that the cold-hearted employer was simply a man who was in need of a rest himself. She was swept by a feeling of shame and almost reached out to touch his hand, but remembered herself in time and contented herself with a few words of apology.

"Perhaps you would take a seat, Captain Howard, and I will bring you some refreshments," she went on. "Ian, er, Mr. Blake, is asleep but he is a little better now that the crisis has passed." Her eyes beseeched him to forgive her, and he had to smile; she was not like his Kate but he could detect something of the same qualities about her. He recognised the olive branch offered and, thanking the contrite young woman, he took a seat whilst she went off to make a pot of tea.

'Lord,' he thought, 'I am weary.' The break he needed, which was partly the reason for the visit to his sister-in-law, whilst wonderfully revealing, had been so short. Hopefully, if Thomas Banham did take the job, things would soon settle down; the man had an air of dependability about him.

On the return of Sarah, carrying the tea things, followed by Mrs. Joyce bearing some scones and butter, he willed himself to be attentive and listen to a session of sick-room details and small talk, but after a short while he found that he was in the company of two well-informed but warm and witty women, and also that the feeling of weariness had eased. True, he was given the details of Ian Blake's illness and what had been done for him, but also of their concern over the young man's return to work. The Captain reassured both anxious women that Mr. Blake would only be accepted back on the site when he was strong enough, but not at the same pace as previously.

He noticed with amusement how often Sarah dropped the title 'Mr. Blake' in her conversation and simply used his Christian name. Richard's heart warmed to both women but particularly to the younger one, having a shared feeling for another, for he could see how deep her feelings were for his younger assistant. It was all he could do to stop himself from telling them of Kate and how much he cared for her. Captain Howard could not speak of his feelings but was sure the lady's reaction would be as he imagined James's would have been.

He stayed a lot longer than he had intended and whilst he had not been able to see Ian Blake, he felt much more reassured, for he liked and respected the young man.

As he walked back to the Bear's Paw he marvelled at the uplifting effect that good company and lively conversation had on a man. How he wished he had Kate with him to share such conversations. Well, he consoled himself, that will probably never be, but at least they now knew of their feelings for each other.

Before he had reached the Bear's Paw, he had put the matter firmly at the back of his mind and was considering the matter of informing Thomas Banham of the fitter's job and the urgency of filling the post. Of course, if the man declined to take up the offer he must take urgent steps to find a man locally.

Within half an hour of entering his room he had drafted out the wording of the telegram then went thankfully to bed.

Early the following morning he went to the telegraph office and sent the following message "To T Banham, c/o Smithy. Wroxing. Norfolk. Fitter needed Urgent. Ches Stop. Reply Captain Howard stop Bears Paw stop Frodsham Cheshire stop."

With that sent off he rode down to the excavation site for the day's work.

After the dramatic revelations of the previous evening Captain Howard was primarily concerned with making sure that the depot would be able to function with two men short. The coal heaver would probably be replaced without any difficulty, for labourers were always turning up looking for work. Jacob Morrison even then might have found a replacement. He also needed to work with Mr. Robbins in putting in place a better system of keeping a check on goods and equipment passing in or out of the depot. The recent spate of large-scale thefts had shown up many weaknesses in their present system.

A few days later, affairs at the depot were back to something like normal, though the loss of the fitter was putting a lot of jobs behind. Albert Tarleton was working all hours to keep everything going but his behaviour was still concerning the other foreman and Captain Howard, who was worried about the man but was still convinced that eventually he would divulge what was bothering him.

The engineer was on his way down to the depot, and as he rode down, letting his horse pick its own pace, he mulled over the events of the previous days. He was more content now that he had received a telegram from Thomas Banham accepting his offer of a job. What was just as pleasing, or possibly more pleasing, was the letter he had received from Kate, expressing her pleasure at having him at Reeve House for the few days he had stayed. She also sent her wishes that his workforce problem would be now resolved.

He chuckled to himself as he thought once again of her careful wording. Good girl, Kate; she knows that Thomas was coming to work for him. There was also her invitation to visit again whenever he could. Innocent words and phrases took on a new meaning now that he could read between the lines of her feelings for him. The situation was not ideal but he felt like a man who had come into possession of a most precious jewel.

Chapter 7

Thomas Receives the Telegram

When the telegram arrived at the smithy, Thomas was just getting back on his feet after being bed-bound with a severe chill. The combination of weeks tramping the countryside looking for work, bad weather and not enough to eat had sapped his resistance and he had been laid up in his bed for several days. Beth and Victoria had taken turns to nurse him through the worst days and, not being used to him being ill, had been worried sick. Their imaginations had conjured up all kinds of terrible fevers, their fears only being banished with the surprise arrival of Mrs. Rodgerson and her family's physician, the latter pronouncing, after giving Thomas an examination, that the patient needed rest, nourishing food, and little more.

Mrs. Rodgerson was horrified at the little food the family were managing on, for even with help from people in the village, it was still short fare all round. To see them all once more, after so many weeks since their eviction and looking so much thinner and paler, pierced her heart. She was so angry at what was happening to the Banhams that she decided there and then that whatever temper it put her husband in, her late employees would have sufficient food from now on.

When Kate was informed of Richard's offer of work for Thomas, the news gave rise to a real mix of emotions: pleasure that her love had kept his promise to her, pleasure for Thomas, but upset that there was no place for the whole Banham family at Frodsham.

Her emotions were as nothing compared with those of the Banhams. The womenfolk were very affected. Beth and Victoria were fearful as to what would happen to the family if Thomas went north to work, but individually they realised that to get back the man who was a husband and father they had to let him go.

Obviously both the boys were upset, Peter being particularly so. He was very worried about the family's situation if his dad would not be there to protect them all, for although he had seen Thomas brought low with illness and the problems of finding employment, he still saw his father as a tower of strength for all of them. Peter was a very frightened boy.

Will was affected in much the same way, except that at fifteen years of age he saw himself as the man of the family should his dad have to leave them to find work, but like everyone else, he wanted his father to lose the beaten look that came over his face when he dropped his guard.

The situation at Beth's parents' cottage offered no room for the family to hear Thomas say what would happen if he took up the offer of the job, so he had them all down at Simon Andern's shed. Apart from any other consideration, it would be better without the mutterings of his father-in-law, echoed by Beth's mother, going on to anybody who would listen, that their son-in-law was too choosy about what job he would take, their oft-repeated dig that he was too high and mighty to take any work in order to support his family. This was not so, as Beth was often pointing out: her husband had applied for work at a brickworks, a pig farm and a job of ditch cleaning amongst others, but to no avail. The Grices, Beth's parents, simply had no good words for her husband.

After the evening meal at the Grice's cottage, the family made their way to the smithy hut. The two boys had raced on ahead, glad to be free of their grandparents. Beth and Victoria followed on at a more sedate pace, and were just in time to meet Mary, one of the maids from Reeve House, accompanied by one of the gardener's boys.

It was usually Mary who brought extra food for the Banhams from Mrs. Rodgerson's kitchen, Mary being fiercely loyal to her mistress. The gardener's boy, being an old school friend of Will, was also utterly trustworthy. Although Kate was completely indifferent to Captain Rodgerson's feelings in helping out the Banham family, she did, for appearances sake, try to do it discreetly. The deliveries were usually at dusk and for that reason Mary was always accompanied by the boy. The handover was aided by the fact that the smithy was not near any cottages, therefore the whole business could be done without the prying eyes of others.

Once inside the hut Mary handed over a package to Thomas whispering, "Open it after," then she added, "from Mrs. Rodgerson, Thomas." After collecting the previous day's basins and dishes, the pair left to return to the House.

Although the hut was fairly large, much of the space was taken up with their furniture and Thomas's wooden boxes containing the smaller items. However, the dining table was able to be used, also two simple wooden chairs, so by making do with two of the boxes, and with one of the boys sitting on his dad's bed, they were all able to enjoy a meal together. The blacksmith and Will had installed an old stove set on a flat stone at one wall of the hut. Patched and rusty as it was, on that dreary cold day its welcoming heat, together with the glow of the hurricane lamp and the luxury of two candles, made the hut far more homely than Beth's parents' cottage would ever be.

After their plates were empty and everything washed the family sat with their cups of tea in front of them and listened whilst Thomas explained what he was going to do. Both his wife and his daughter knew what course he had decided upon; they had seen the change in him, there was a spring in his step now and gone was that defeated look, and words were not needed to tell them which way the wind blew.

Thomas began by reminding them of his determined attempts to find work and a place to live, telling of his failure to find either, with the added problems which might come if the coming winter turned out to be a bad one. He did not say how bad their position was as regards money, for apart from Peter, the family knew full well how things stood in that direction. It had not escaped his attention how quiet his youngest child had become lately and he was racking his brains as to how he was going to break the news to the boy that he was taking the job up north, when Peter said in a steady voice, "Dad, if you go away to work how long will it be before you take me, 'er and Mam and Victoria, and Will," he added, including the others almost as an afterthought.

His father looked at the others and smiled. It seemed his youngest child was a lot more aware than he had realised.

Gently he spoke directly to Peter. "The first task I have set myself when I have earned some money to send back to your Mam is to look for a house for all of us." Here he stopped and turned to the others, and in the same quiet voice continued, "There is no other way," and added fiercely, "I will not see my family in the poorhouse." They now knew without him saying the actual words, "I'm leaving", that Thomas would soon be away.

The first one to speak was Will, attempting to sound grown-up to disguise his upset, asking whether there would be work for him up there. The question jolted Thomas as all he had been concentrating his thoughts on was getting a job to support his family, but Will was right, he was now fifteen years of age and would have been working, but for Thomas's preoccupation with his own troubles.

True, Will had been helping Simon at the smithy and his father was easier in his mind about using the smith's shed, for the cost of housing so much of the Banham family's possessions would have probably run away with their money by now.

"You know, son, I do believe there would be work on such a big job as that; it's said there are over ten thousand men and boys working there." In spite of his worry at being left as the man (as he saw himself) of the family when his dad went away, Will felt the stirring of excitement at what they would see when the family moved north, for he was convinced that it would not be too long before they all moved.

Meanwhile, Beth was hiding her dread at what was to come of all this with remarkable composure, but Victoria could feel her mother trembling as she sat close with her arm through hers.

Beth picked up the package which Mary had slipped to her before returning to the House. Handing it over to her husband she asked him to cut the string and break the seal. "I'm sure, Thomas, that this will have something to do with Captain Howard's offer of work."

When Thomas opened the package the first item to emerge was a letter for Beth, and the second item was a letter for her husband. Beth, who was a slow reader, was only part way through her letter when Thomas exclaimed, "Just listen to this, girl. Captain Howard has asked Mrs. Rodgerson to act on his behalf in the matter of expenses incurred through train tickets and such to make my way to Frodsham in Cheshire. Furthermore, he instructs me that there will be a place for me to stay!" It was if another weight had been lifted off his shoulders, for one of the things that had worried him was how much money Beth would be left with once his fares had been paid

Apart from the train fare, there was Billy Timms to pay for the journey to Wroxing Station, which was situated some distance away from the village. His tools were obviously the heaviest part of his luggage, but his clothes and other items he could not manage without Billy's trap.

Then Beth, with tears running down her cheeks, handed her letter to Thomas saying, "Read that, husband, and you will be affected too. Mrs. Rodgerson is a lady and a saint, just see what she has written." Her husband scanned the pages and he felt a lump form in his throat, and at that moment he experienced a shocking feeling of hatred for the vicious monster that Mrs. Rodgerson was tied to in marriage.

'Dear Beth and Victoria, (it began)

'This has been the most difficult letter I have ever written in my life and I ask your forbearance with my attempt to keep the contents free from what could descend into mawkishness. The truth is that there could be an element of that but I sincerely hope you will see that to express my feelings in regard to both of you equally, there cannot help being some emotion shown. To explain further, when Captain Rodgerson and I moved to Reeve House, for various reasons my life was not a particularly settled one, but within a very short space of time I found myself happier than at any time since I forsook my single status. I beg both your pardons if I shock you but I merely state the facts.

'The reason for my new found happiness was the genuine affection shown to myself by each member of our staff at Reeve House, but in particular the affection and, I am humbled to hope, the feeling of friendship which comes from you, Beth, and you, Victoria. A friendship such as this transcends every social boundary and is more valuable than mere gold.

'If the Banham family does move away for Mr. Banham to obtain work, I send you on your way with all the best wishes from my heart and hope the move will help you regain your happiness and contentment.

'I close my letter with the hope that when happier times come, and they surely will, we may all meet again.

God Bless you all,

Yours affectionately,

Kate'

When Victoria read Mrs. Rodgerson's letter it was her turn to weep; the two boys sitting there in an uncomfortable silence were also affected by the emotional display even if the contents of the letter were not known to them. However, they fervently agreed with their mother and Victoria. Mrs. Rodgerson was a real lady.

Thomas and Will walked back through the darkened village to Beth's parents', with Beth, Peter and Victoria, then having made their rather subdued farewells, returned to Simon's shed.

Before they retired to sleep, which to be truthful, eluded both father and son for some time, Thomas spoke to Will about the part he had to play in looking after things, especially with regard to Peter. At this Will felt very proud, but also just a bit apprehensive at the measure of responsibility. Just as they were about to take to their beds, his father stressed once again a warning he had given to both of his sons many weeks earlier, not to get involved with anything that involved Longfields Estate, or even any other property, which could incur the wrath of Captain Rodgerson.

The following day passed in a whirl of activity for the Banham family; a telegram to be sent to Captain Howard accepting the job, seeing Billy Timms concerning the trap, choosing which tools he would most likely need and booking the train tickets. Both of the womenfolk set to sorting Thomas's clothes: washing, darning, patching and sewing buttons on. It served to distract their minds from the fact of Thomas's leaving.

Much as they tried not to talk about the effects of his going, Beth and Victoria found themselves coming back to the subject again and again, and also that of the rather sad letter from Mrs. Rodgerson, and once again they expressed their upset at the loneliness of their dear lady. One other matter which mother and daughter agreed on: they were very touched by the knowledge that their late mistress regarded them as friends and not just as servants, but they could not bring themselves to address Mrs. Rodgerson as Kate, that would be going too far. One thing Victoria was glad of was that Mrs. Rodgerson had a fiercely staunch ally in their friend Mary, and Beth heartily agreed with her.

Thomas had called to thank Simon and Nora Andern for all they had done for him and his family. They told him that they had been only too glad to help and assured him that they would look out for Beth, Victoria and the boys. He vowed to himself that one day he would make it up to the smith and his wife.

None of the family slept well that night. Thomas's imminent departure weighed heavily on them all; Peter was particularly affected and during the following day he played out for just a short time then kept dashing back indoors to make sure his mother and sister were still there. They in turn were keeping themselves busy in the vain hope that they would put the following morning's leave-taking out of their minds.

Meanwhile, Thomas, following instructions passed on to him from Captain Howard, purchased his train tickets and arranged for him and his bags and boxes to be picked up and taken to the railway station. Apart from his clothing and effects, he had collected together the bare necessity of tools. Even so, when packed in the wooden case they still added up to a considerable weight, and he then began to worry about getting it all in the trap. As it turned out, Billy Timms brought a four-wheeled cart round to the shed early on the morning of his departure and his luggage caused them no problem.

He was up at five o'clock the following morning and by half past was eating his breakfast, which had been prepared by Beth on the hut stove. It was pitch black outside, but still without rain which was something they were thankful for.

The train he had booked to travel on called at Wroxing at twenty minutes past seven; therefore he needed to be on his way to the station by ten minutes to seven by the clock.

The leave-taking was even worse than he had envisaged; his own heart felt that it was being torn in two as young Peter clung to him, sobbing. The child had to be more or less pulled from him by the weeping womenfolk. Will was trying to act as grown-up as he could, but even he could not stem the tears that flowed as his father hugged him.

The carter Billy Timms turned away from the distressing scene with a lump in his throat and a rising anger in his heart. One man, he thought, one man to cause such misery. As God was his witness he wished Captain Rodgerson in hell.

When eventually the cart started on its way up the village street a few cottages were lit and the occupants came to their doors to see him on his way. Some people were still abed and those who had appeared to wish him well did so with quiet voices. The postmistress and her husband called quietly, "Best of luck, Thomas, boy, we'll keep an eye open for your folks," and in the darkness, Thomas, tears running freely, could not answer for the huge lump in his throat. He kept looking round until his family could be seen no more.

Once out of the village Billy Timms could contain himself no longer. "The swine should be shot," he said savagely. "I've seen some real nasty 'orfficers but I never seen one as vicious as that one." He kept on in this vein for another few minutes then, as his companion had not uttered a word, relapsed into silence. Thomas could not manage a single word; he was so choked with emotion and his mind's eye kept conjuring his beloved family forlornly waving him off. In the darkness of the morning he had not actually been able to see their faces, but he could picture each one clearly. At one point he had to use all his willpower to stop himself from jumping off the cart and running back, but he knew only too well that there was no chance of being able to find work in Wroxing; it had to be that he took the job at Frodsham.

He realised that his friend was still on the subject of officers. "Now that other one, Captain Howard, now he's a real gentleman, I would have been proud to serve under him, a real gentleman," and on a different note he commented, "And Mrs. Rodgerson, she is a lovely lady, not like Captain Howard's wife. I'm sorry for the Captain, married to that one," he concluded.

Thomas surreptitiously wiped his eyes and face, glad of the darkness which hid his tears.

"I'll keep an eye on things for you, boy, and others will as well," said Billy as they came into the station yard, and Thomas, now in control of himself, nodded his thanks.

The boxes and bags were soon deposited on the platform and the carter prepared to set off back to the village and his breakfast. He shook hands with his friend and wished him luck, then turned and disappeared into the darkness.

Two of the porters whom he knew quite well came over to him and asked him about the job he was going to. It always amazed Thomas how people in the village seemed to know what was going on in other people's lives without being told. He replied quite frankly that he knew very little about the actual job but understood it was part of a contract to build a canal, and they wished him luck and hoped he would soon have his family with him.

Within minutes of the train arriving, they had him and his luggage aboard and he was off. In the early morning light it seemed that every one of the station staff had assembled on the platform to wish him luck.

In years to come, Thomas would say that he remembered nothing of that miserable journey between Wroxing and London, but would never forget the short journey between King's Cross Station and Euston Station.

The train from Norwich would normally terminate at the Great Eastern Railways terminal at Liverpool Street Station, but due to problems on the line, the

London train was diverted onto Great Northern Railways lines which meant that the train arrived in London at King's Cross Station.

Although this was an advantage for Thomas because of the shorter distance between that station and Euston, the behaviour of his cab driver created nothing but trouble for Thomas.

The behaviour of the cab drivers in London at that time was legendary. There were admittedly many who were to be trusted to take their fare by the most direct route to the desired destination, but there were others who would take a more circuitous route to fool the innocent traveller into paying much more. Thomas, however, had lived for a few years in London and therefore by subtle use of words let the cab driver know in advance that he realised the distance between King's Cross Station and Euston Station was quite short, but he needed a cab simply to save him carrying all his luggage between the two terminals.

Whether the cab driver took exception to his fare's apparent knowledge of the ways of London cab drivers is not known, but the man prevaricated to such lengths about whether or not the boxes constituted personal luggage or whether they would be classed as goods that Thomas realised that he was cutting it fine if he wanted to catch the Manchester train, and was forced to offer the man extra to get moving.

It took very little time to reach Euston, but by the time a trolley was found, the luggage transferred and the breathless Thomas arrived at the platform, his train was just departing.

Suddenly he was engulfed in a towering rage. For weeks his emotions had been held in check lest the family were upset by any loss of temper, but the events of the last fifteen minutes had been the last straw.

He swung round and rushed back to where the cab had dropped him and his luggage, with the intention of venting his fury on the driver, and in his haste narrowly missed a nearby man. But the cab driver had left the station a lot faster than he had arrived, and was nowhere in sight.

As Thomas stood there panting, his hands clenched, he was approached by a railway constable, followed by the well-dressed man he nearly bumped into. The latter was haranguing the policeman in a blaring voice to do something about the 'low-class hooligans' running unchecked about the station!

"Now then, my man," said the constable to Thomas, "this gentleman has complained to me about your unruly behaviour and says you nearly knocked him flying." The complainant butted in almost before the policeman had finished his sentence, at which the officer held up his hand and continued as if he had not been interrupted. "And I must remind you that it is an offence under the Companies Regulations that no person should act in such a way as to interfere with other persons' safety or comfort."

Thomas, his rage cooling, became conscious of the people slowing down to enjoy a 'hooligan' being arrested, realised that if he did not calm things down quickly he would be in danger of missing the next train, or even being charged and appearing in court.

Putting on his best accent he said to the irate complainant, "My dear Sir, I do apologise most profusely. I was in such haste to catch the cabbie before he left, I quite forgot myself." He smiled, something that cost him a great deal of effort, and bowed slightly. The polite tone and the well-bred manner of the 'hooligan' took the wind out of the man's sails, and with that he stalked away grumbling, much to the disappointment of a few of the onlookers.

As the small crowd dispersed, the constable grinned at the worried Thomas and said, "Well done, mister, that action of yours saved us both a lot of bother, but he was right to report your rushing about like that, the Company don't allow that sort of thing." Then he asked him, "What made you go after the cabbie like a mad bull." He laughed. "You weren't going to give him a bigger tip, were you?"

The now relieved Thomas told him what had happened and before he knew it he was spilling out the story of his troubles, though not every detail. Whether it was the almost fatherly attitude of the policeman, which was odd because he looked only a few years older than himself, or whether it was because he had bottled up his feelings for so long, but by the time he had finished he felt a lot less angry.

The constable shook his head sadly at such villainous doings and remarked in a confidential tone, "Like the gentleman, if I may use the title loosely, we have just had dealings with, they don't concern themselves with the plight of them they put into trouble. Why," he said, warming to his theme, "that one is a regular in Euston and he is always finding fault; if it's not the Manager he's mithering, it's the stationmaster, and if not, it's us lot. Our lads," he went on gloomily, "say that if he used another station, we could manage with one less of us."

They had been walking back towards the trolley which held Thomas's luggage, and the policeman said kindly, "Take your small bags and go and get yourself a hot, sweet drink; I'll make sure your boxes are put on the right platform." Then he added, "Good luck with your new job, lad," then walked off to get a porter.

Later, sitting on a form on the platform, Thomas mulled over the events of the last hour. What a fool he had been, losing his temper again. He would not be in this position and his family would still have a home if he had not lost his temper with Captain Rodgerson, and if he had caught up with the cab driver, what trouble would he have brought on himself. He shuddered at the thoughts of his family's predicament if he had ended up in prison.

When at last he boarded the train, confident that his boxes and bags were in the luggage van, he began to relax a little. Indifferent to the dusty state of the carriage, he was glad to see the back of London.

Alighting at Crewe, he had enough time on his hands to refresh himself before taking the Chester train, and he had just congratulated himself on having a compartment to himself when, at the last moment, the door was wrenched open and a large ruddy-faced man hurtled in with the words, "Only just made it," in a strong but pleasant voice.

During the run to Chester, the man, who turned out to be a farmer, proved a genial talkative type and very soon had Thomas involved in the subject of horse ploughing as against steam ploughing. It was a subject on which he could hold his own with anybody and for a while the arguments took his mind off his family.

There was also another subject on which the farmer had strong views on, and that concerned the policies of Mr. Gladstone; he did not agree with any of them.

At this point Thomas retired from the discussion. He had always avoided arguments concerning politics or religion, so he simply let the man have his head, just making noncommittal noises here and there. Actually he agreed with many of Mr. Gladstone's policies.

The train halted at a small station displaying the name 'Waverton' and with a cheery wave the man left the carriage as lively as he had arrived. For a short time he had succeeded in lifting Thomas's spirits and in truth he was feeling a bit more his usual optimistic self when he finally got off the train at Chester.

Although the light was fading he had glimpsed enough of the countryside from the train to feel that he liked Cheshire; how glad he would be if only Beth and the children were here to share it all with him.

It was dusk when he finally arrived at Frodsham. The town or village seemed much bigger than he had imagined it to be and he had high hopes that he would have little trouble finding a carter willing to take him and his luggage to the house where he was to be billeted.

As it turned out, it was a lot more difficult than he had imagined. The trap drivers were not keen on taking the heavy luggage, saying that their springs would suffer if they went down to Marshville, as they called the place. Thomas felt the familiar feeling of frustration sweeping over him, but this time he managed to hold his temper. One of the drivers pointed over to a young man, little more than a youth really, and suggested that he might be persuaded to go on the Marsh.

The young man did not raise a single objection and he asked almost apologetically for a sum which, to Thomas's mind, did not seem too steep at all.

As his luggage was being loaded on the cart, it was noticeable even by the dim light shed from the station gas lamps that the paintwork and lettering of the cart gleamed. It all looked new.

As they eventually turned into what the young man said was Marsh Lane, Thomas had learned that he had lately started up as a carrier and the cart was indeed new, and it obviously was a source of great pride to him.

Once they were in the lanes which ran off Marsh Lane, there were no gas lamps and they would have been in total darkness except for two or three patches of light in the distance. "What's happening over where the lights are?" asked Thomas. He wondered at so much light over the fields; it was something outside his experience.

The young man did not express surprise at his fare's ignorance as to what was going on. He merely said, "Oh that, it's the navvies working late, they're digging a canal to Manchester." Then warming to his theme, he told his astonished listener, "Sometimes they work night and day and you can hear them at it all night, and feel it too! When they get going with their piledrivers, 'Long Toms' they call 'em, you can feel the ground shake. People round here aren't pleased, I can tell you, what with that and some of the navvies getting drunk and fighting outside the pubs."

Thomas felt a vague feeling of apprehension about what lay ahead for him and once again questioned himself as to whether he had done the right thing in taking the job. He drew comfort with the thought that at least his family would be away from all that once he had found a cottage to rent in Frodsham.

As they progressed down one lane and then another, the road surface seemed to get more and more uneven; the young carter, now holding the horse's bridle, walked holding a storm lantern.

Suddenly they entered an area where there seemed to be large structures on each side of the lane, which he then realised were huge stacks of timber. Then just as suddenly an odd lighted window appeared. They were in 'Marshville', the contractor's hutted village.

Two figures materialised out of the darkness, each carrying a hurricane lamp. Thomas was taken by surprise when one of them called out his name. "Hello, is that Mister Banham?" When Thomas affirmed who he was, the taller of the two, Robbie as he said he was called, told Thomas that he had waited at the station for over an hour to meet him on the orders of Captain Howard, but when he did not show up he had gone back to the Depot, as he called the place.

The carter said he would not enter the 'street'; he said it was too difficult to turn round, so three of them took his luggage down to Mr. Tarleton's house whilst the smaller lad held the horse.

As they carefully made their way over the uneven ground of the street Thomas could see quite a lot of the huts, as they appeared to be, showed light and he was surprised at how many dwellings there were.

At Robbie's knock, the door was opened by an unsmiling woman who motioned them inside. Thomas felt his heart sink as he surveyed the bare cheerless interior, bare unadorned walls, bare floors and drab curtain material. He thought back to Simon Andern's shed which Beth and Victoria had made so comfortable and his spirits plummeted.

Mrs. Tarleton showed him into a small room which held two bunk beds and some cupboards, and told him to put his things in there. One of the two tall wooden cupboards was empty; the other one, she informed him, was used by Clarence, then followed up by saying that the man was supposed to have been back before now, for his meal.

Thomas had just finished stowing his clothes away when he heard the creak of somebody descending the stairs, then the sound of a man's voice enquiring 'if the person who had just come in was Clarence or the new fitter'. At this Thomas left his room and introduced himself to the man, who turned out to be Albert Tarleton.

He saw a sad, tired-looking man and he also noticed the softening of Mrs. Tarleton's features as she glanced at her husband.

Soon after, Clarence Lumb came in from work and Albert introduced the two men, almost disinterestedly it seemed to Thomas. Some men associate a firm handshake with somebody to be relied on but in his experience this was not always so. Certainly with the man's marred facial appearance, Clarence did look a bit villainous, and his grip was not firm, but the young man did look as if he wanted to be friends, so Thomas was contented to meet him halfway on that score.

The meal was both welcome and tasty, and Thomas felt himself relaxing a little. Even so, as the meal progressed he noticed that apart from the lack of conversation between man and wife, there was an air of despondency about them.

At the end of the meal, while his wife cleared the table, the foreman told Thomas what his job would normally involve, what hours he would be expected to work, and other related details. He then said, "Captain Howard wants to see you tomorrow and he will tell you how much an hour you will get paid and things like that." He then went silent for a few moments as if thinking of something else, then he said quietly, not looking at this new fitter, "He's a good man to work for is Captain Howard, none better, but he expects you to give him your best." His voice seemed to waver at the end of his sentence, and once again Thomas was conscious of that air of melancholy about the man.

Albert Tarleton recommenced his instructions for the morrow. "The Captain comes early unless he's got other arrangements, usually about eight o'clock, so we normally start about seven." He stopped and then told Thomas about the arrangements for ablutions.

With a simple screen arrangement set up, Thomas was given first choice at washing himself in a galvanised metal bowl placed near the slopstone. He felt somewhat better after his wash, and he was glad to climb into his bunk.

The experiences of the day and the people he had met had served to push the heartbreaking leave-taking of his family to the back of his mind, but once alone in his bunk, it all swept over him again and he could have wept. But mercifully he had not been under the blankets for more than a few minutes when weariness overcame his grief and he slept.

The following morning he was awake even before the creaking of the floorboards above told him that the Tarletons were up. Within a short time he was dressed in his working clothes and ready for his breakfast.

To his surprise, Clarence, who had risen even earlier, was sitting at the table with a slate in from of him, writing in an unpractised hand the letters of the alphabet. At Thomas's entrance, he glanced round with a sheepish look and grinned at him. He said with a touch of embarrassment, "I'm learning me letters. I never learned ter read nor write an' I want ter." In answer, Thomas, who was really moved by this rough-sounding young man's eagerness to learn, said, "Well, Clarence, I don't mind helping you, if you want me to." The young man's face lit up at that and he said, "Would yer, ta."

Breakfast was a repeat of last night's meal, good food but very little conversation, but Thomas sensed a less apathetic air about the couple, as though they had come to a decision about something that had been weighing heavily on them and was now resolved. 'Perhaps it is on account of my arrival,' he thought, 'he may have been hard pressed with one fitter less.' Little did Thomas know that the loss of one man was the least of the foreman's woes.

It was still dark when he and Albert Tarleton walked to the depot, or more correctly, the workshops, which was where Thomas would be working. Oil lamps illuminated the interior, whilst on one side there came a glow through the open doors of a smaller building, which Thomas guessed came from a blacksmith's forge.

As soon as he stepped through the doorway of the workshop he was transported back to his apprenticeship days at Burrels. The nostalgic sights and smells associated with heavy steam engineering assailed his senses. Along each side of the barn-like wooden building were benches, racks containing steel bars, and sheets of metal. Near the door, standing like soldiers to attention, was a row of screw jacks, whilst hung on the walls were all manner of paraphernalia associated with engineering maintenance. It had a dirt floor with a few areas of brick paving. Down the full length of the workshop were laid two railway tracks, but what interested him more than any other object in the place was a six-wheeled locomotive. Below it was an inspection pit. He now knew what sort of work he would be doing, for up to that moment he had no inkling of what was expected of him.

He and Mr. Tarleton were almost up to the small glass-windowed office when a hidden voice called out, "Ready for switch on," and an answering voice shouted, "ready we are." Then came the sighing-noise of a steam engine coming to life, followed by the rapidly increasing slap slap slap of flat belts driving the machine shop line shaft.

All familiar sounds to Thomas, but then came a phenomenon never before experienced by him.

Albert Tarleton entered his office and touched something on the wall, and a yellow glow lit the interior. Thomas had learned about Michael Faraday's earlier experiments on electricity when he worked at Maudsleys and had taken a lot of interest in the subject ever since. He had read about Mr. Edison's light bulb, but this was the first time he had actually seen one, and he felt the first stirring of excitement since coming to Frodsham.

The foreman, noticing his reaction to the light bulb, said rather wistfully it seemed to Thomas, "Oh, yes, we have all the most up-to-date devices to aid us: you may be familiar with some of them, but I think you find will much to interest you here."

He was taken on a tour round the workshops and other parts of the depot. As he had already worked out, the steam engine which drove the line-shafting also drove a large dynamo, which he found very interesting. In the other workshop were two lathes, a large drilling machine and small one, together with a grindstone and other pieces of equipment, all driven off the line-shafting.

When they had finished the tour and returned to the fitting shop, several more men and boys had arrived and some of the benches were now lit by the electric light bulbs. Altogether, the place impressed Thomas favourably, but he found the foreman's melancholic demeanour puzzling, much as if he was proud of his workshop but on the other hand was distancing himself from it all.

As the day went on and he was told what work was expected of him, he was surprised and further puzzled by the amount of detail he was being given about the running of the place, information that as a fitter, he would not need to know.

Eventually he started work on his first job; as he expected, it was the locomotive which needed attention. It needed new brake blocks, attention to the injectors and to a damaged 'dumb' buffer. (That was a block of hardwood in place of the normal spring buffer.)

The loco, which bore the name *Bromborough*, had apparently been involved in a collision, a not unusual occurrence according to Robbie, but at least nobody was hurt, he added. He told Thomas that the navvies called the loco drivers navvy crackers but he wasn't sure why they were so named.

Although Robbie, who was one of the two apprentices, had not yet developed the muscles necessary for the type of heavy engineering the workshops dealt with, he was a willing lad, but even more importantly, he was a fountain of knowledge for which Thomas was extremely grateful.

Just before the midday meal break, Captain Howard arrived and made straight for the foreman's office. After a quick nod to Thomas, he and Albert Tarleton moved outside, ostensibly to look at another job awaiting attention, but in fact, the engineer wanted to know his workshop foreman's opinion about Thomas Banham. He was also hoping that Albert would come out in the open as to what was troubling him.

On that score he was to be disappointed, but the man himself seemed to be a trifle more at ease with himself and Captain Howard decided to let sleeping dogs lie for a little longer.

The foreman told his employer that in his opinion Thomas Banham would turn out to be an asset to the workshop, and certainly easier to work with than the recalcitrant Joe Clayburn.

By the time the two men moved back into the workshop, Thomas and Robbie were out from under the loco and had just finished cleaning their hands. With a smile Captain Howard went to Thomas and shook hands with him. His employer did not make the mistake of asking him about his family; instead he welcomed him to the 'Marshville' Depot as he called it, and added that he was grateful to Thomas for responding so swiftly to his urgent need of a fitter.

Turning to the foreman, who was standing at one side during the exchange of pleasantries, Captain Howard asked him would he mind if they used his office whilst he went over the terms of employment with the new fitter. At this Albert acquiesced and excused himself, then went off for his meal.

The engineer opened the discussion by outlining the work he was contracted to do and the length of time which the contract was expected to last, which at that time would be in the region of a further four years. He then came on to the rate of pay and the normal hours of work.

"Contract work of this nature, Mr. Banham, is subject to weather and natural disasters, on top of the more normal problems of sickness, supply hold-ups and all the other nuisance things and because of that we are forced, whilst the weather is in our favour, to work more than our ten-hour day." Here he stopped while he tried to get his pipe drawing. When at last it was to his satisfaction, he continued. "And sometimes we have to work on through the night, which can be quite exhausting." He paused for a moment whilst he drew on his pipe, then told Thomas the rate of pay that applied to skilled artisans.

"As a fitter you would be paid sixpence an hour for ten hours with a further two pence per hour for each hour over your normal working day; we also pay extra per hour for overnight working." Then in a less businesslike tone he said, "Mr. Banham, if you find the situation not to your liking, I quite understand, and in view of the exceptional circumstances, I will pay your train fares both coming here and returning to Norfolk. Having said that, Mr. Banham," he added, "it is my sincere wish that you will stay and with a bit of luck, manage to find a place here in Frodsham for your family."

Sitting quietly listening to what Captain Howard was saying had only served to reinforce his opinion that he was doing the right thing. Apart from the pay, which was much more than he had ever received at Longfields Estate, since coming here he had been conscious of a new enthusiasm, a feeling of being a useful part of a grand scheme. He felt more optimistic than he had done for over twelve months. Apart from that, he had observed the engineer and the way he had acted with Albert Tarleton. Whatever the problem was which made the foreman so melancholy was possibly known to their employer and when they had stood talking together, Thomas could see that Captain Howard had treated the foreman in a gentle and sympathetic manner.

"Well, sir," said Thomas, "before I give you the answer in reply to your generous offer, I would like to thank you, and Mrs. Rodgerson," he added, "for giving me and my family a chance of a fresh start. We will never forget your kindness, and as for the other matter, sir," he went on, "I will stay and do my best to give satisfaction. Thank you once again, sir."

Captain Howard smiled at Thomas, held out his hand and said, "Thank you, Mr. Banham, I'm glad you have joined us, I do not think you will regret it."

With those words he left the workshop and rode back to the Bear's Paw for his midday meal, leaving a wonderfully invigorated Thomas ready to take on anything that the job threw at him!

Chapter 8

Thomas at Frodsham

Two days after Thomas Banham had started in the workshop, Captain Howard was on his way down to the depot. As he rode, letting the mare pick her own pace, he mulled over the events of the last two days. He was particularly pleased at the way his new fitter had reduced the list of small but important jobs that had been building up over the last week. Thomas Banham was certainly making the mark in the workshop. In retrospect he realised that Albert, though a first-class boilermaker, was out of his depth when faced with some of the jobs they were having to deal with. One of the reasons why he had taken on Joe Clayburn was to bolster up the weakness in the fitting side of things and he had done so in spite of misgivings concerning the man's attitude.

That brought his mind back to the worrying problem of Albert Tarleton. He was still not his usual easy-going self, but on reflection, his workshop foreman had not been his usual self for a few weeks. Surely he was not troubled by a problem with his health? The engineer decided that today he would make a determined effort to reach the truth of the matter. He knew that Thomas Banham was working over near the Weaver sluices this morning, so he reasoned that this would be a good time to have a serious talk with Albert without interruption.

On reaching the workshop and in the act of tethering his horse, he was surprised to see Ged Pimblot, the boilermaker, who was also supposed to be working out, coming towards him in a state of great excitement. He was holding an envelope which, by the grubby state it was in, looked as though he had been handling it all morning.

The boilermaker, who was inclined to stutter when he had something important to impart, obviously had a lot to say, for he was hardly intelligible when he gabbled out his news.

Captain Howard held up his hand to halt the rush of words, and with a raised voice said, "Slow down, man, slow down and start again." Ged thrust the envelope towards him, gulped and said at a slightly slower speed, "Sorry, sir, but he's gone, er, Albert, er, Mr. Tarleton's gone, sir, and he's given me this letter for you, sir, and he's taken all his tools, sir." Ged was twisting his cap between his hands in his agitation and could scarcely stand still.

So this is how I find out what is troubling Albert, thought Captain Howard glumly, and telling Ged to stay for a few moments, he walked a few yards from the man then opened the envelope. He had no idea what he was going to learn when he read the letter but he was totally unprepared for what his workshop foreman had written, and he was overwhelmed by a feeling of sadness. The fact that he also felt angry did not lessen his feelings of pity for the Tarletons.

Albert Tarleton, a thoroughly decent man, had fallen into debt through gambling and he had become entangled, by the look of it, with the same criminal bookmaker that the police inspector was trying to trap. Apparently the interest on money owed went up each day and Tarleton had realised that he could not possibly pay his debt. This was when the author of all his troubles, Joe Clayburn, has suggested he turned a blind eye to a few hundredweights of coal going missing. Mr. Shee (or some name like that) would probably not press him too much. Albert Tarleton realised now that he should have come to his employer and thrown himself on his mercy, but he felt he had let the deception go on too long and rather than face Captain Howard, he had decided to leave. He concluded by hoping that his late employer would one day find it in his heart to forgive him, for he could never forgive himself for his breach of trust. He added that he had waited until he was satisfied that this new fitter was right for the job and when he noted how competent he was, decided that it was time to go.

Why on earth did he not come to me when he was first propositioned, thought Captain Howard wearily. We could have stopped it before it got out of hand. He felt desperately sorry for both Albert and Mrs. Tarleton.

He decided there and then that there was only one thing he could do if the vicious Mr. Sheehy was to be stopped, and that was to show Albert's letter to the police.

He walked over to the waiting boilermaker and told him to tell Mr. Banham that he wanted to speak to him when he returned to the workshop. As with most boilermakers, Ged was quite hard of hearing due to the noise of riveting he had endured over the years, so Captain Howard had to raise his voice to make himself heard, and he was not surprised when somebody popped their head round the smithy door to see what was going on, then quickly ducked back when he saw it was his employer.

When he reached his hotel, he left his horse with the stable lad and walked up to the police station. He was unlucky as the Inspector was not there. There was nothing to do but leave a message with the desk sergeant, mentioning the name Sheehy. This produced a very alert glance from the policeman, but he merely said that he would make sure the Inspector received the message.

The engineer felt a bit deflated by the man's absence but consoled himself that at least the bookmaker might possibly be stopped with the contents of the letter in his hand.

He was undecided whether to return to 'Marshville' and call in on Mr. Robbins, or whether to seize the moment and visit Ian Blake, whom he now knew was not bedridden, but it was very important that he see his bookkeeper to talk over details of an improved system to check everything that passed into the depot and also what went out, but he also was anxious to see Ian.

The dilemma was resolved with the appearance of Miss Sarah Mills, who immediately came over to him, smiling. He touched his hat and said how coincidental it was to see her. After the usual pleasantries, he told her she had made up his mind for him; he would visit Mr. Blake now rather than later. At this the young lady said she just happened to be passing by and she also would take the opportunity to call on Ian, er, Mr. Blake. Captain Howard, charmed at the young lady's blush on the use of his assistant's Christian name, smiled and offered his arm. With her arm linked through his, they crossed the street and made their way to Mrs. Joyce's house.

As they reached the house, Captain Howard realised that the man walking along the pavement just ahead of them was the police Inspector. As Miss Mills knocked on the door the engineer excused himself and hurried to catch the policeman. The Inspector, surprised at the sudden arrival of Captain Howard, laughed, then held out his hand. "Not many people chase after me, sir, it's usually the other way round." Then noticing the grubby envelope in Captain Howard's hand he said, "Wouldn't be something for me, sir, would it?"

The engineer turned to check whether the young woman had been admitted to the house, saw that Mrs. Joyce was looking their way, and held up his hand to indicate he would be along in a few minutes.

Turning to face the waiting Inspector, Captain Howard answered the question with a question of his own.

"Inspector, this letter is, in effect, a confession concerning the stolen coal, not of actual theft or profit from the theft, but of turning a blind eye to what was happening, under duress. I must add, I do not intend to bring charges against the man; therefore I ask you, would the police need to take any action against him?" Then he added, "A certain Mr. Shee is mentioned."

At that the policeman smiled. "Captain Howard, we are after a very nasty criminal gang and we are working hard to gather evidence which will put him and his bully boys inside for a long time. I give you my word that your man," pointing to the envelope, "is of no interest to the police except that he provides us with useful evidence." Almost as an aside he added, "By the way, the Birkenhead police have nabbed Clayburn but as yet they can't connect him to Sheehy."

At that Captain Howard handed him the envelope. As the Inspector read the letter he started to grin, and at the finish said jubilantly, "This is capital stuff, sir, the names of Sheehy and Clayburn linked together. This will close the net even more." Then he added in a more sober tone, "This is a very sad letter, sir, I feel sorry for the man. It's this trail of human misery that Sheehy and his sort leave which goads me on to get them behind bars."

He asked permission to hold on to the letter, and with that granted, went back to the police station.

The engineer retraced his steps to Mrs. Joyce's house, and was admitted almost immediately, then ushered to the same room where he had spent such a pleasant evening one week ago. Ian Blake was sitting by the fire, whilst opposite was sitting Miss Mills, and they had obviously been enjoying a cosy chat. Ian was looking relaxed and happy, whilst the young woman looked positively radiant. Thinking of his dear Kate, Captain Howard's affectionate smile brought an answering smile from both of them and Sarah jumped up to let him be seated so that he and his assistant could talk.

The engineer assured her that he would be quite happy to sit anywhere but the young woman insisted he take the chair, then informed him that Mrs. Joyce was hoping that he would stay and share a light meal with them. His initial reaction was to graciously refuse but when Mrs. Joyce popped her head in and implored him to say yes, he gave way, and he had to admit he did feel hungry.

Ian grinned at him and said, "Wait till you see Mrs. Joyce's sandwiches, Captain Howard, none of those drawing room paper-thin offerings, but real bread and real fillings. I don't think I will ever leave this house, I am too well fed." Everyone laughed and Mrs. Joyce, who was just entering the room carrying a large plate heaped with sandwiches, beamed. Sarah, closely following, was just in time to hear the amused Captain Howard asking his assistant, "And what might a future Mrs. Blake make of that, Ian, that is if any lady would want to be saddled with a man owning such a large appetite." This sally was greeted by Mrs. Joyce saying, "Oh, I don't think Mr. Blake will be left on the shelf, appetite or no appetite." Again they laughed but poor Sarah blushed bright red, but managed to hand out plates quite composedly. Ian's eyes followed her around the room, smiling contentedly.

After a while, Captain Howard begged to be excused and somewhat reluctantly made his leave. As before, the company of these people raised his spirits and, heaven knows, lately he had had trials enough to dampen anybody's spirits. Had it not been for his knowledge of Kate's feelings for him, he thought that he would have descended into a state of melancholy. Albert Tarleton's problems bothered him more even than his loss of a foreman and diligent worker. He sincerely hoped that he and his wife would be able to make a new life for themselves.

He collected his horse from the hotel stables and rode down to the 'village' to fulfil the other tasks he had set for himself, that of working through the necessary papers, memos and receipts with Mr. Robbins. Even in normal times he loathed that side of the business and he had never regretted enrolling Ted Robbins to take the burden off his shoulders.

The huts, or rather houses, which had been allotted to the Tarletons and to Mr. and Mrs. Robbins were built originally as lodging houses but with rooms for offices, two in the bookkeeper's house actually being used for that purpose. One office was reserved for the sole use of Captain Howard, whilst a third room was simply furnished as a bedroom in case a visitor to the depot needed emergency accommodation.

When he presented himself at the bookkeeper's house, he was admitted by Mrs. Robbins who, not knowing whether their employer was aware of the events of the previous afternoon, asked him if any arrangements had been made with regard to the feeding of the two men in the house next door.

At this, Captain Howard gave a start; with all the problems raised by the defection of Albert Tarleton, he had not yet given a thought to the domestic upheaval which would ensue. Apologetically, he confessed as much to Mrs. Robbins and her husband. The engineer had naturally assumed that Mrs. Tarleton had left with her husband, but had forgotten about her lodgers.

It was Mrs. Robbins who gave him what details they knew of Mrs. Tarleton's departure, not that they had been aware she had actually left until mid-morning of this day.

The previous day, one of the other women in the 'village' had asked to accompany her to the Moore contractor's settlement where her sister and her family were lodged. Her sister had not long ago given birth to a baby girl, and she was anxious to see them both. The reason she wanted a companion with her was because the Moore settlement was frighteningly large and the woman was rather timid.

They had taken a train to Moore and walked down to the settlement. Briefly, the visit had been a success but had lasted longer than they had planned, and resulted in a return to 'Marshville' in the darkness. So it was, that when the trap they had hired at Frodsham station passed another hooded cart coming away from their village, they had not been able to see anybody on the vehicle, never mind recognise them. Mrs. Robbins said, a trifle guiltily, that she was so glad to be home, she had not even noticed whether the lamps were lit next door.

Mr. Robbins took up the story then, and said that he had heard noises next door suggesting that furniture was being moved about but was so busy that he did not take much notice of it. It was only when he began to be really worried about his wife's lateness that he looked out through the door in time to see a cart moving up the lane towards the town. He pointed out that all he could see was the tail lamp swinging from the back of the cart.

With that Captain Howard and Mr. Robbins went to the Tarleton's late abode and, finding the door not locked, entered the darkened house.

Mrs. Robbins followed carrying a lamp. They located another lamp and lit it. The glow from both showed the simple table and chairs and not much more, then Mrs. Robbins pointed towards one wall and said, "The box has gone, sir, the one they used as a sideboard. Mrs. Tarleton told me once that they have two of them which they pack all their things in when they move to another contract," she went on, "they empty them and use them as furniture."

The small room used by Thomas and Clarence was as left by the men that morning and the engineer closed the door quietly as though by doing so it would serve as an apology for not respecting the absent men's privacy. He looked at the simple furniture, picked up cheaply at some second-hand shop and noted the scrubbed top of the table. Some of the people did have pieces of furniture which they took with them from one job to another, but others preferred to buy cheap second-hand furniture at each new contract, and resell it when they moved on. We are rather like nomads really, he thought wryly.

His thoughts were interrupted by Mrs. Robbins observing aloud that Albert had left the fire banked so at least the place would be warm when the men came in from work. She then said suddenly, "I was just thinking, sir, if it's all right by you, sir, I could make sure they are fed, that is until you make other arrangements, about the house, sir."

Before Mrs. Robbins had even finished what she had to say, Captain Howard had thought of a solution, that is, if Thomas Banham agreed with his proposals. He had brought to mind what Kate had asked of him, namely that the Banham family be kept together.

He was suddenly buoyed up and smiling at the bookkeeper's wife, he said, "Thank you for your offer, Mrs. Robbins, it is very good of you. I will make sure you are not out of pocket with it." As she shook her head, saying that it was not a trouble, he then finished by telling her that he might have a solution to the problem.

With daylight fading so early he knew that his new fitter would be back at the workshop before four o'clock, so the engineer decided that today he would cut short his discussion on the new ordering and issuing of stores, and make haste to the workshops.

Leaving Mrs. Robbins to make out her list of things she needed for the men, Captain Howard and Mr. Robbins returned to the office and spent about three-quarters of an hour on the new proposals. The system was certainly better than the one then in use and the bookkeeper was pleased and also relieved to get his employer's approval of his scheme.

Richard Howard was eager to get Thomas Banham's reaction to his proposal, but as he rode between the rows of dwellings, he found he was looking around him with a more critical eye. Would Mrs. Banham want to stay in a place like this, he wondered. It was a typical contractor's hutted settlement with no pleasant flower-filled gardens, bushes or trees to soften it; in fact, in this half-light it looked depressing. Still, he thought, if the arrangement was of short duration until they found a house for rent, it would be a step in the right direction.

By the time he reached the workshops he had ceased to be sure his idea was a good one; in fact, when he came face to face with Thomas he almost left his thoughts unspoken.

Thomas spoke first with, "Good afternoon, sir." He was just finishing drying his hands, and he looked enquiringly at his employer but waited for him to broach the subject of the foreman's departure.

"Mr. Banham, you will by now, I am sure, be aware that Albert Tarleton has sacked himself," he said, and Thomas affirmed that he was. Whereupon Captain Howard went straight to the heart of the matter and said, "We are now in need of a workshop foreman, and I am convinced that you are the man most suited for the position," then he said with a smile, observing Thomas's astounded expression, "I really would be obliged if you would accept the job."

At first Thomas was taken aback at the directness of his employer's approach but then his brain began working at top speed. He could hardly believe how much his situation had changed in so short a time. From a near destitute unemployed man to fitter, and now workshop foreman, it was all happening too fast for him to answer immediately. Another thought suddenly occurred to him; his wages were now much more than he had ever earned, and with the extra money from the new position, he would be able to pay back that which Captain Howard had loaned him very much sooner. He was gratified by the engineer's faith in him but was worried about the effect his promotion would have on the other skilled tradesmen in the workshops.

As he voiced his concerns to Captain Howard, his employer shook his head and then explained the position to him.

"I'll explain my position to you plainly, Mr. Banham," he began. "I have built up a sound reputation over the years in the contracting business and have maintained that status until a few months ago when my original foreman retired and my fitter left me to take a job nearer his home. We struggled for some weeks until a fitter called Joe Clayburn turned up and from an account of his all-round experience we took him on. I had made Albert Tarleton up to foreman with the intention of having a senior man whom the others could turn to when necessary. Unfortunately Albert proved unable to cope with the responsibility and we now know what that led to." He shook his head sadly, and went on. "Joe Clayburn was a fairly good all round fitter but he turned out to be all-round at other things we could have done without," he said dryly. "As for the other men, I believe they will be only too glad that there will be somebody there with the necessary knowledge who they can turn to."

To Thomas, what he had just heard was the final balm which was needed to lift his self-esteem after the nightmare experience from which he had just emerged, and now he now had no hesitation in accepting the position.

His voice was husky with emotion as he gave Captain Howard his answer, and he added, "I will endeavour with all my being to give satisfaction, sir, thank you for giving me this chance."

They shook hands at that, then his employer broached the subject of the house. He started off by explaining how he had made enquiries in Frodsham regarding houses to rent. There were two types of house owner in the town, he said; one group was quite happy to rent rooms or even houses, often premises totally unsuited for the purpose, eager to make as much money as they could whilst the contractors were there. The other group were house owners who objected, quite naturally, to the troublemakers who invaded the town on paydays, starting fights and damaging property. This second group of owners would not rent or sell their houses to anybody connected to the canal scheme. The result is that finding a place to stay, in or around the town, had become very difficult

"Mr. Banham," the engineer continued, "I know that your family are used to many of the finer things in life." Here he paused as he composed his words so as not to cause offence. "If I offered you the chance to take on the tenancy of the Tarleton's house would you take up my offer?" Observing that his newly-promoted foreman was about to answer the question, he held up his hand to indicate he had more to say, then explained to Thomas what the tenancy would involve.

"There would obviously be conditions attached to the tenancy, I regret to say, but I have at the moment no alternative but to impose them." Here he looked at Thomas and smiled. "You yourself are at this time the recipient of one of these conditions, and in one word that means lodgers."

Thomas was at once delighted then deflated. Of course, he thought, we cannot simply tell Clarence to go, he would have to let him stay until the young man decided to go himself, but he had no idea how many rooms there were in the place for his family, and he was not sure whether Beth would want to live in a place like Marshville.

As if he could read Thomas's mind, Captain Howard said, "If you were wishing to bring your family here, Mr. Banham, there are three rooms upstairs which would house your family, but the room you presently occupy is for two men, and remember, when you take on a fitter, he might not have lodgings, so the man would have to be offered the second bed." He looked understandingly at Thomas and concluded by saying, "I know it is not the perfect solution to your problem, Mr. Banham, but it is the best I can offer." He added, "Give yourself time to think it over and when you come to a decision let me know, then we can discuss such matters as rent and coal, oil and candle allowance."

Almost as soon as Captain Howard had finished speaking Thomas had made his mind up; after all, it was only until they could find a house to rent. He began by thanking his employer for the offer of the house and told him he would take on the tenancy of the house with conditions attached. "I will write to my wife this evening, sir," he said, "but with your permission, I would like to put some paint on the walls and generally strive to make the rooms more homely before my family come here." He hesitated before carrying on voicing his thoughts, then he said slowly, "As you said yourself, sir, Mrs. Banham and my daughter have over the years got used to finer things and to come here and, er, well…" Thomas was floundering, not sure how to phrase the things he had to say, but Captain Howard came to his rescue and with an understanding smile put it in plain words for him.

"Yes, I understand what you mean," he said, "the village can be a very dreary place to live in at times, mud during the wet weather and dust everywhere in the fine weather. It takes a degree of fortitude to cope with it all, I have to admit, but," he said in a quiet voice, "the majority of people here are decent enough, honest and helpful, and I believe that makes up for a lot of the drawbacks."

At that he stood up and Thomas did likewise. "Thank you, sir, for helping me out there," he said gratefully. "I will set to as soon as possible, and get things moving."

With the business concluded, Captain Howard left the workshop, and Thomas searched out the man who was responsible for the steam engine and dynamo. He had to learn a lot before he considered himself a proper workshop foreman.

Afterwards, when he was satisfied that he had grasped the important details of what was needed to shut down for the night, Thomas and the men walked to the village, the boilerman insisting on repeating all he had told his new foreman about the boiler house, a lecture he bore with good humour. Thomas felt exhilarated, his mind full of all that occurred during the afternoon, and he now understood why poor Albert Tarleton had given him such a thorough grounding on everything in the workshops. He suddenly felt very sorry for his late foreman and his wife. Thomas wondered if he would ever learn why the man had flown in such a secretive manner.

As the men walked up the street, the only light to be seen was that which showed from the windows of the huts, but such was the low power of these lights that they did nothing to illuminate the outside. Thomas kept near to a central course between the huts, for he did not wish to stumble into either of the two rainwater ditches. These ran on both sides of the rough lane the full length of the village. The ditch was spanned at intervals by the simple expedient of laying two or three rough planks in line with each hut doorway.

As each man said goodnight and made for their own front doors, Thomas marvelled to himself that none of them missed stepping onto the little bridges. He had previously seen that the bridges to the two-storey houses were of a much better construction, and with the additional blessing of having the edge boards painted in a white or cream colour

He made it to his own front door and on opening it was greeted by a wonderful smell of cooking. The woman attending to the pan on the hob must be Mrs. Robbins, he thought, and as she turned and smiled a welcome, he was conscious of a feeling of relief. If this lady is our next door neighbour, he thought, I am sure Beth will settle easier in the place.

"Hello," she said, "it's Mr. Banham, isn't it? I'm Mrs. Robbins from next door. Captain Howard has agreed for me to feed you both until the new tenant moves in," then a trifle hesitatingly, "that is, unless you would prefer to manage on your own." On that score Thomas was quick to reassure her; his cooking skills were somewhat sketchy, and besides, after a full day at work he did not want to set to and make a meal.

Clarence was already sitting at the table, and in front of him was a slate. He grinned shyly at Thomas and told him he was learning his letters. After hanging his coat up he sat down by the younger man and asked whether he minded having his work looked at.

Clarence eagerly pushed his slate in front of Thomas, and pointed to the ill-formed but legible letters and proudly recited the alphabet.

As he listened to the young man, Thomas experienced a surge of admiration. He saw that the rough-spoken, rather uncouth Clarence was striving to elevate himself in life. Lord knows what sort of conditions he had been brought up in. He thought of his own life and that of his family and offered up a silent prayer of thanks for all their blessings.

Clarence finished his slow, halting recital and looked at the older man anxiously, but his familiar grin replaced his uncertain expression when Thomas praised his efforts.

He then turned to Mrs. Robbins, who appeared to be about to set out the plates, and asked her if she was aware of Captain Howard's intentions with regard to the house, and she replied that he had not confided in either her or Mr. Robbins.

"In that case, I think it would be proper if I spoke to yourself and Mr. Robbins at the same time, so if it is not inconvenient, do you think your husband would come in later and learn what has been decided on by Captain Howard?"

"That will be all right, Mr. Banham," she replied. "I don't believe that Mr. Robbins knows any more about the Captain's plans than I do, so we will pop back in about three-quarters of an hour's time." Mrs. Robbins was eager to know what was going on, and not only with regard to the house but with other matters, for she sensed there was something else Mr. Banham wanted to tell them.

Thomas and Clarence had just finished washing the pots and pans when Mr. and Mrs. Robbins knocked on the door. He asked them to sit down, then motioned to Clarence, who seemed to think the conversation did not concern him and was about to go into the lodger's room.

When everyone was seated, he opened the conversation by telling them of his promotion, at which Mr. Robbins, showing relief, congratulated him and told Thomas that he was sure that they would work together very well.

Thomas could sense that the others, and particularly Mrs. Robbins, were keyed up for what else he had to say and when he told them that the tenancy was now his, he was convinced that his neighbours became more relaxed.

Whilst the bookkeeper was quite curious about his new neighbour, it was his wife who asked all the questions concerning his family, which he was quite happy to answer.

With her obvious air of relief, he wondered whether she had been worried at the house becoming a lodging house outright. In later years he was to learn that he was correct in his surmise.

As Mr. and Mrs. Robbins rose to leave, Thomas said, "Thank you for coming in to hear what I had to say, and when I get a reply to the letter I will shortly write, I will let you know what the outcome will be." With that his neighbours wished him and his family well, said their goodnights and left.

Once the couple had gone, Clarence, who had heard only part of the conversation, said in a worried tone, "Will I have to go, Mister Banham? I mean, if yer family all want a room there'll be no room fer me."

"There's no need to worry, boy, I will still be obliged to take in lodgers and I have no reason or intention of asking you to go. However," he added, "when I get a fitter he might need a bed so you probably will have to share the room again."

Clarence's face brightened. "That's alright by me, Mr. Banham, too," he said.

Later, after Thomas had written his letter to Beth, he moved his belongings from the bunk room into the largest of the three rooms upstairs. He could scarcely sleep that night, mindful of what he had to do if he was to make the house more welcoming for his family.

Chapter 9

Michael Rourke

The hordes of children playing their various games or just rushing up and down making a lot of noise was just as it had been over the years, but to the twenty-one year old Michael Rourke, who had some years back played in much the same noisy way, it seemed like Bedlam.

Since his sister had moved back to the family home, bringing with her a husband and a baby, he thought gloomily that the only peace he got was when he was out in search for a job.

Some weeks earlier he had completed his seven years as an apprentice fitter and had been laid off in the usual way to complete his one year as a journeyman.

The previous evening when he had returned home, his mother had told him that Tom, one of his friends, had called in to let him know that the fitter's job at their yard had been taken. It had come as a blow to Michael as he had thought he stood a good chance of the position.

Michael's father had suggested that he write a letter to his brother Luke in England explaining the situation and asking him whether he knew of any firm which required a mechanical fitter. His son seized on the idea and very quickly put a letter together and posted it off that same night.

A few days later, Luke had replied and had kindly invited his younger brother to come to Liverpool and stay with him and his wife whilst he searched for a job. He explained that in their capacity as teachers, they were not in contact with any people in industry, therefore they were unable to say whether there any such jobs available.

Michael blessed the insistence of his parents that he and his siblings had been made to put a few pence away each month and not spend any of it unless they really needed to. He could easily afford to cross the Irish Sea without having to borrow from anyone. Even so, his father insisted he accept something from him, in case he had to return to Belfast, but he vowed that was not going to spend his father's gift unless he had no other choice.

On arrival at Liverpool he had been met by his brother and his English wife. They were obviously pleased to see him and it pleased Michael also to observe how contented they were with each other, for none of the family had set eyes on Tess, as she was called.

The first evening was probably the most pleasant one of all in the weeks he spent there, for they spent the time swapping news of everyone's goings on, both there and back in Belfast. By the time he got to bed, Michael was tired but happy and looking forward to the following day's adventures.

He was not too disappointed when, after a day walking around the area nearest to his brother's home, he had not been lucky. There is always another day, he thought sagely. However, as time went on it became increasingly clear that the move to Liverpool was not proving to be a success.

He could not find any work in his trade, and such work he did find was of an unskilled nature and was badly paid; it was most disheartening. Added to these miseries was the lack of light-hearted company in the house. His brother and his wife and their occasional visitors seemed only to talk of gloomy subjects; they positively revelled in the perceived incompetence of the government and the scandalous behaviour of people of position and wealth.

Whilst he loved his brother, and admired his cleverness, and that of his sister-in-law, he found that his usual sunny nature was beginning to desert him, so he decided to go before he descended into a state of melancholy.

Using the excuse that he might find a job easier to come by on the other side of the Mersey, he told them of his intention to leave and to try his luck at Birkenhead. His brother generously refused any money from him for his stay with them and invited him back if he was unsuccessful in his search.

He left early the following morning after receiving a hug from Luke and a kiss from a tearful Tess, who also handed him a bag containing 'something to eat,' she told him. Michael felt really guilty and was very touched by their generosity but still considered he was doing the right thing by leaving.

It was another cold day, the overcast sky lending a dull colourless appearance to the rows of terraced houses, and though he was still out of a job, he felt he was on top of the world. His optimism had returned and he felt in his bones that his luck was about to turn.

As he reached Pier Head he was just in time to see the Birkenhead ferry leave the landing stage. One of the men who had helped cast off the vessel turned, and seeing the disappointed young man standing there, shouted that the other boat would be here soon.

He walked over to Michael and, noticing the sack of tools, said to him, "Looking for work, son?" At a nod from the young Irishman he carried on to say, "There's not a lot of jobs over there either, son, but then you might be lucky." He then said with a grin, and pointing to another steamer tied up further along the pontoon, "They say there's plenty of work where that ship is going."

Michael, his interest aroused, asked the amused man where it was bound, and he was answered with a hearty series of chuckles and the information that it was going to Eastham and the Big Ditch, "the Manchester Big Ditch, as we Liverpool folk call it."

Somewhere in the back of his mind something surfaced. "Oh yes, I seem to remember the talk in the newspaper of a new canal to Manchester. I didn't realise the scheme had started." Then he asked the hugely amused man, "Why do you call it a big ditch?"

"I'll tell you why, son," the man said. "See that ship?" He pointed across to a large steamship being manoeuvred into position by two tugs, "Them Manchester softheads are telling everyone that ships like that are going to sail all the way to their town," and he laughed again. "To get them there, they will have to drag them across the fields 'cause them lot will never finish the digging of it, they'll run out of money first." He ended his mocking tirade with a self-satisfied guffaw.

Then, as a new thought struck him, he said gleefully to Michael, "Mind you, if you can get a job over there you might as well take the money they are throwing away; the job might not last that long but I'm told they pay well."

Michael suddenly made up his mind. If the successful firms did not want him, he might as well try one of the failures. He shouted his thanks to the still-grinning man and made his way to the Eastham-bound vessel and booked a one-way ticket.

Shortly before the next Birkenhead ferry arrived at Pier Head, the Eastham ferry cast off.

An odd thing happened as they sailed upstream. Michael experienced a feeling of giddiness and he felt for the nearest stanchion, closing his eyes and taking gulps of air. A voice came to him and he perceived a small and very elderly lady eyeing him with concern.

"If you are feeling seasick, young man," she said in a very upper-class English voice, "just stand on the stern deck, face backwards and keep your eyes on the horizon. Oh, and breathe naturally." She said sympathetically, "Even the most experienced sailors suffer from mal-de-mer on the river," and then added, "Shall I take you by the arm and steady you?"

Michael mumbled his thanks and tottered aft to follow the lady's instructions, completely abandoning his bags, and took his stance in the centre of the stern deck. Gradually his feeling of sickness eased and he started to take an interest in the pleasing shoreline.

He was amazed when he considered the crossing of the Irish Sea some weeks back. He had not suffered the slightest discomfort yet here he was on the river and he had almost been unable to stand upright.

Just before the steamship reached the small pier at Eastham, he made his way back to where he had left his bags and found the genteel old lady chatting happily to one of the crew, who was standing by ready with the mooring warps. Catching sight of him, she called in a gentle voice, "Are you recovered, young man? You appear to be so much better."

The young Irishman replied rather shamefacedly that he was indeed feeling much recovered thanks to her advice, then he said, "Thank you, ma'am, for looking after my bags, I am most grateful."

On the road near the end of the pier stood a carriage and pair. Standing by was a man dressed in an attire that was formal but not really a uniform, and as the steamship gently touched the landing stage, the man moved towards the point where the gangplank was to be placed.

The first passenger to be helped ashore was the old lady, who was met by the man from the carriage. He touched his hat respectfully and then as she made her way towards the end of the pier, her carriage driver followed, carrying the lady's bags.

"Who is that lady?" one woman asked the crewmember standing by the gangplank. "That is Mrs. Tillotson, lady, her late husband was a shipowner," came the answer.

Michael did not hear the rest of the conversation, for he was carefully negotiating the gangplank whilst carrying his bags, but as he passed the carriage in which the lady now sat he was surprised when she asked him to speak for a moment.

He put down his sack of tools and tipped his bowler, and said, "Can I be of any assistance, ma'am?" She shook her head and replied with a smile, "No, I think not, young man, but thank you," then she said a trifle hesitantly, "I do not wish to seem inquisitive, but seeing you carrying your bag of tools… they are tools, are they not?" Then when the curious Michael had confirmed his guess, she carried on. "I was wondering if you were to be employed on the construction of the Manchester Ship Canal."

Michael was wondering about her interest in the matter and was also surprised at her giving the scheme its full title, but he then answered her by telling her of his aim to find employment there.

The lady then said to him, "Whatever some people say, I do believe in the scheme and I am sure it will be of great benefit not just to Manchester, but for the whole of the North, and," she added, "when you see it finished and ships sailing to Manchester from all the countries of the world, I think, young man, you will be very proud." She smiled at him and finished by saying, "I do believe you will be lucky in your search for employment." Then she nodded to the carriage driver and as a smiling Michael tipped his bowler again, the lady was borne away.

"Well, what do you make of that, Michael Rourke?" he said aloud. "She certainly makes me believe that miracles can happen; my luck could be turning." So saying, he picked up his bag of tools and marched off towards the plumes of smoke and sounds of activity that told him he was near the site of the 'Big Ditch'.

When he reached the top of the embankment he was halted in his tracks by the immensity of the excavation. Beyond the embankment which was holding back the tidal waters of the River Mersey was a deep, wide channel. In there were scores of men working on the construction of the huge lock piers. By the depth and the dimensions between the stone-built piers, he could well imagine the very same ship he had seen being shepherded by the tugs at Liverpool passing through into the canal.

By the lock area on the same embankment he was standing on was a tall building attached to a boiler house and as he walked past it, he could see the rods and beams which he recognised as a Cornish pumping engine. Below him was an even deeper pit to which pipes were led from the pump house.

Beyond the lock area the cutting was being worked on by what seemed like hundreds of men. Excavators were also to be seen, their huge toothed buckets biting away at the sides of the cutting and depositing the spoil into the railway wagons which were lined up behind a locomotive.

There were more locomotives and steam cranes on top of each embankment. A number of wagons containing coal had been brought in to stock up the supply for the boiler house, and the driver and his fireman were talking to another pair of railwaymen.

Michael, his sack of tools weighing heavily on him now, trudged over to the group of men near the loco. They stopped talking as he came near, but as he said hello, one of them said, “You’re from Belfast, then, looking for work?” Michael grinned; he too recognised the familiar Belfast accent.

The fireman asked him what trade he was in and the talk then turned to reminiscences, places where they had played as children, places where they used to go in their youth, and such normal subjects that people from the same home town talk about. That’s how it seemed to the disinterested onlookers, but to Michael and the fireman, it was part of a ritual which could either join people together and bring forth a helping hand, or it could divide people and bring no help at all. This was the way life was conducted in Belfast and possibly in other towns in Ireland; the invisible religious boundary followed a man even here in England, Michael reflected philosophically.

Eventually the fireman was satisfied that the young man attended the ‘right’ church and the ritual was ended with the offer of help.

The fireman said to Michael, “That’s a coincidence, so it is; I hear that it is a fitter they are in need of at Frodsham, Michael Rourke,” and turning to the others he asked, “Is that not right?”

“Aye, that’s right, the other fitter ran away with the police after him.” They all laughed at that remark, which puzzled Michael, but he was not put off by the reference to the police. All he wanted to know was how far he had to walk to get to this place called Frodsham.

The fireman, Clancy, as the others called him, said, “Now what would you be wanting to walk all that way for, when we, by another coincidence, are off to the very place as soon as that lot,” nodding his head in the direction of the pump house, “have the last wagon emptied?” Then, turning to the driver, he said, “Can you fit another one in, Bill?”

The engine driver explained to Michael that as soon as the empty wagons were ready, they were off to Ellesmere Port with them, and they were running along to the Frodsham depot with the other driver and fireman, who would be driving another engine, *Bromborough*, back to Ellesmere Port. That meant accommodating five men on the footplate. The driver said Michael could come along but warned him that he might have to ride outside the cab.

Eventually they were on their way towards Ellesmere Port which, according to the second engine driver, was once called Whitby Locks and was now the connection to the River Mersey for the Shroppie, whatever that was. To allow vessels to enter the port via the locks, a gap had been left between the two sections of the excavation, the ends of the cutting being sealed off by earth dams. Michael shuddered to think what would happen to the men working down below them if the dams were breached.

To cross the entrance to the port, a temporary swing bridge had been constructed by the contractors and although it looked a bit fragile to the young engineering fitter, the other four men evinced not the slightest interest in it as the short train rattled across it.

Michael was very impressed with the railway track they were travelling on. Being a contractor’s line, he fully expected to be bounced up and down every few seconds but he was pleasantly surprised to find that the ride was fairly smooth.

As they left Ellesmere Port he was surprised to find the line was now running alongside the river shore. At a distance of two or three hundred yards into the river was a long line of huge timber posts showing above the surface of the water. These stretched for miles and when Michael questioned the knowledgeable driver as to their purpose, he was told that a sea wall was being constructed by driving piles into the river bed when the tide permitted, and when completed the whole length would be filled in with boulder clay to form an embankment. This stretched all the way to Frodsham Marsh. Thereon, to the River Weaver, the excavation would be dug out in the usual way.

They soon came to the marsh and eventually arrived at the Frodsham depot. As they were slowing to a halt, Clancy sang out, "Marshville, all change," which caused a bit of a laugh.

The spare driver and fireman clambered down from the cab and, after a few words with their counterparts, strolled over to the locomotive bearing the polished brass nameplate which told Michael that this was *Bromborough*. A faint wisp of steam from the whistle showed that all was ready for the return journey.

Michael stopped for a few moments to thank Clancy and Bill, then turned to make for the workshop, but was stopped by the driver who told him that they would wait a short while to see how he went on.

The young fitter was very touched by the gesture and told them he would be back to them as quickly as possible. Both men just waved and wished him "good luck", and he made his way to the open doorway through which two sets of railway lines ran.

As he humped his bag of tools into the workshop he was met by a youth clad in dirty overalls. "If you are looking for Mr. Banham, he's in the machine shop. I'll take you to him if you want."

"I am here about a fitter's job," said the now very nervous Michael. "Oh, good," said the youth. "I'm Robbie, one of the apprentices. I'll take you through straight away." With that he set off at a fast walk towards the back part of the building. They were met in the doorway by a man of about forty years of age, who on spotting the familiar weighty sack of tools over his visitor's shoulder, started to smile.

"Oh, here's Mr. Banham now," said Robbie, and with a quick grin set off back to where he was working. Thomas held out his hand and said, "What can I do for you, young man?"

Michael felt instantly at ease with the man before him, and was heartened by the fact that he was not instantly informed that there were no jobs available.

After shaking hands, Michael thought it wise to ask if a fitter was still needed, then he could let Bill and his fireman know what he was going to do with himself.

"Hello, Mr. Banham," he began, "I'm a fitter, well, a journeyman actually, and I heard there was a vacancy here," then he added nervously, "do you still need a man?"

Thomas answered kindly, "We do need a man, son, but first, what's your name and would you care to give me details of your experience? Oh, and have you ever worked on steam engines?" Michael gave his name, but being realistic and honest as well, knew that his reply to the final question could scupper his chances of the job. "No, Mr. Banham, I have no experience of those." He then gave the foreman a quick verbal list of what he had done and when he mentioned pumps and, wonder on wonder, electrical dynamos, Thomas decided he had got the right man.

Michael was getting anxious about the waiting driver and fireman and told Thomas the story. "Right, Michael," said the foreman, "I'll have a quick word with Bill before he goes. Oh, and by the way, the job's yours, boy!"

As Thomas walked over to the engine, the young Irishman felt the urge to dance a jig and how he managed to stop himself doing so was a miracle of self-control. The huge grin on his face said everything.

Eventually Thomas returned, and as the engine started on its way back to Ellesmere Port, took Michael through the workshop, explaining what sort of work they had to deal with and the skills of the other men that were employed there. He then told Michael which bench and vice was to be his, and where to store his tools. Before he showed him around the depot, Thomas said to him, "We might as well go back to the house and tell Mrs. Robbins she will have one more to feed tonight and," he added, "I had better show you where you are going to sleep, that is, if you have not made your own arrangements." Michael expressed relief at having a place to stay.

When Thomas knocked on the door it was opened by her husband who told them that Mrs. Robbins had gone to Mr. Roberts's shop and should only be about ten minutes.

The new fitter was introduced to the bookkeeper who, after shaking hands with Michael, asked the two men whether they were intending to have their mid-day meal there or down at the workshop. He explained that if they were staying he would put more water in the kettle for tea.

Michael, on hearing that they were staying to have their meal at the house, brightened even more and showed them the little bag of food provided by his sister-in-law but said he would be glad of a brew of tea.

As they left Mr. Robbins, Thomas let themselves into the house of which he was now the tenant. Mrs. Robbins had been in, Thomas could tell, and she had banked up the fire so the room was warm and welcoming even though it looked rather bare.

Michael was shown his bunk, and although he was a little disappointed in having to share a room, reasoned that it was better than having no room at all.

A short time later they were tucking into a bowl of soup each which had been made by Mrs. Robbins, Thomas afterwards sharing Michael's somewhat delicate sandwiches.

A tour around the depot and an introduction to the other men occupied the first part of the afternoon, then he settled himself into his working area. He was just being shown the job he was to start on the following morning when Captain Howard arrived.

When earlier he had been told that the final decision as to his employment rested with a Captain Howard, his spirits had sunk; he did not like the idea of having orders barked at him or being subject to army-style discipline. However, on being presented to their employer, his spirits revived. True, the upright carriage and the brisk way of walking spoke of his military background, but a glance at his face showed him as a man of intelligence, with kindly eyes and a mouth shaped by humour.

Michael thought he would be happy to work for the man. When Captain Howard had bid them goodnight and left, Thomas returned to the job he had been working on when Michael arrived earlier, and with help from the new fitter and Robbie, managed to finish the last part of it.

Later, when Thomas and Michael had gone to the house for the night, the young Irishman, like Thomas a few days earlier, was surprised to find Clarence sitting at the table with slate and chalk, working at his letters. As soon as Michael set eyes on Clarence he took a dislike to the man. He knew he was being unfair but, more importantly, realised that he would have to bury his feelings if he was to share a room with the other man.

Mrs. Robbins had done them proud with their evening meal and later, when replete and warm, he snuggled into his bunk and mused that things could be a lot worse. He was quite happily looking forward to whatever the job would bring.

Chapter 10

Letter from Thomas to Beth

The lane lying between Mr, Cragg's garden and the hedge bordering the farmer's field was a little overgrown, whilst here and there were small puddles of muddy water. Victoria was carefully picking her way, trying not to get her shoes and the hem of her skirt dirty whilst at the same time keeping an eye on the dog which was now in the lane behind her. The animal looked as though it was a stray, and had started to follow her soon after she had left the village. Usually Victoria felt at ease with dogs, but this particular one had skulked behind her in a very menacing manner from the moment it had appeared.

Since her father had left Wroxing to work in Cheshire, Victoria had taken it upon herself to help her mother by earning a few pence a day towards the housekeeping. The Wroxing postmistress employed her for a few hours, work that Victoria enjoyed very much, and Mr. Cragg also let her earn a few pence more by letting her collect eggs for him, selling eggs being his livelihood.

His problem was that one hen was not laying on his property but was laying in the lane outside. Ethel, as he called the hen, was an outcast and was living in the hedgerow where Victoria was searching that day.

Although the hen had hardly any tail feathers, the poor bullied bird was a good layer, hence Victoria's daily walk in the lane. She mused that one day poor Ethel would be taken by a fox, and that would be the end of her and of Victoria's few extra pence each week.

She became aware of the sound of a horse being ridden on the road that led to the village, and she turned ready to wave to the rider. Then when she recognised who it was, her blood seemed to turn to ice.

Captain Rodgerson had already noticed her and seeing that nobody else was with her, brought the horse's head round and entered the small lane.

The terrified girl stood there frozen to the spot, her brain telling her to run and to scream out, but her legs seemed to have lost their power of movement and she was unable to make more than a thin whisper of sound. It was the same as it had been when he had cornered her near Mrs. Rodgerson's bedroom door whilst his wife was out of the house.

But here, in this lonely lane, there was no Mary to come along, dusters in hand, as she had that day in the corridor, before Captain Rodgerson could even put a finger on her. Mary had made it her job after the incident to keep an eye open for her friend.

The rider slid to the ground with almost insolent ease, his hated face wearing a triumphant smile, and walking up to her said, "Well now here we are again, the fair Victoria, and all snugly wrapped up against the cold." He moved his hand as though to undo the buttons on her coat, at the same time saying softly, "You don't need these layers to keep you warm, my lovely, I can do that."

As a scream rose in her throat, he clamped his other hand over her mouth, then all hell broke loose behind him. The stray dog that had been prowling round the hind legs of the horse set up a ferocious round of snarling and barking. The thoroughly unsettled horse started rearing and twisting, trying to rid itself of its tormentor.

With an oath, the enraged Captain let go of Victoria as he attempted to catch the reins whilst dodging the flailing hooves.

The physical force just used on the girl had broken the bonds of fear that had held her, and Victoria ran past the struggling man and fled sobbing back to the village.

The smithy was unoccupied when she got there and she rushed straight down to the shed where Will had his bed. All she wanted was somewhere private where she could hide her humiliation.

She had not been there for more than two minutes before Will burst in. Alarm showed on his face and he went over to her as she lay face down on his bed, her muffled crying tearing at his heart.

"Victoria," he cried, "what has happened, is it Mam, or," here his voice faltered, "nothing's happened to Dad, has it?" His sister shook her head slightly but would not turn her face towards him.

He gently stroked her hair until the sobbing subsided, then patiently coaxed her to put her feet on the floor and sit beside him. With his arm round her shoulders he felt her gradually relax, but the boy himself was wound up like a clock spring, and he was not going to let her go until he had wormed out of her the cause of her distress.

Ever since that first time when Captain Rodgerson had forced his unwelcome attention on her, Victoria had wanted to unburden herself, and after this latest and more frightening episode, she felt that she could not keep it to herself any longer.

"Will," she said in a tremulous voice, "promise me you will not speak of this to anybody else, especially to Mam or Dad. I could not bear the shame if others knew of it." She stopped, her eyes entreating him to respect her plea.

Her brother hesitantly nodded his acquiescence, but he felt sick inside at what he was about to hear.

Victoria told him of both incidents, but could not bring herself to reveal the man's words or of his fumbling with her coat buttons.

Her brother's reaction was far worse than she had imagined it would be, for with a hoarse cry Will leaped to his feet and rushed out of the shed. For a moment his sister was too surprised at the suddenness of his actions to do anything but stare at the open doorway, then realisation dawned on her. "Will," she screamed, "no," and jumped up to go after him.

Victoria rushed after him, but was too late to stop him diving into the smithy and snatching up a long-handled striking hammer. Fast as she was, hampered by her long skirt she had no chance of catching her enraged brother.

She was struggling for breath so her exhortations to make him come back went largely unheard.

Her eyes streaming with tears and with a pain in her side from a stitch, Victoria reached the little lane in time to bar her brother's exit as the thwarted boy made as though to run up the road towards Reeve House.

He tried to shake her off, but she clung on to him with all of her strength until suddenly he stopped, tears of frustration wetting his cheeks.

Then it was her turn to administer comfort. Will dropped the hammer and allowed Victoria to calm him sufficiently to listen to reason.

"Will, I don't want you to ever do that again," she said sternly. "If you had caught up with that hateful man, think what could have happened, think what would become of us if you had been hurt or sent to prison, and," she went on, "think what it would be like for our Dad." Then Victoria said soberly, "Thanks to the good Lord and," she said with an attempt to make Will smile, "a stray dog, I was not harmed." Her brother showed signs of returning agitation but Victoria stopped him and said, "Soon we will be away from Wroxing, then we will start a new life, but only if we go as a family so, my impetuous brother, do not do anything that will bring us trouble."

She let go of him and said, "Well, seeing as you are here, Will, help me find Ethel's eggs." Heaving a sigh, her brother picked Mr. Andern's striking hammer and joined her in her search. In that they were lucky, one egg in each of two places.

As they walked back to the smithy, having given Mr. Cragg the results of Ethel's labours, Victoria felt much more at ease with herself than she had done in months. By speaking of the matter to Will, she had shed some of the load that had oppressed her. She knew her brother would never divulge her secret to anybody without her agreement.

Impulsively she squeezed his arm and said, "Thank you, Will, for letting me get that off my chest; I needed to tell someone." He gave her a watery smile and said, "I'm glad you chose me to tell it to, Victoria, and I am glad it made you feel better. I will never say anything to anybody about it."

The following morning the postmistress handed Victoria a thick package, saying to her, "Here you are, a letter from your dad," and added indulgently, "Better take it to your mam now, so off you go girl." Victoria thanked her and then sped down the street to her grandparents' cottage. Her mother was hanging out the washing in the back garden when the girl arrived.

"Hello, Victoria," said Beth with a rare smile that made the girl glad she had been able to bring the package across so quickly, for her mother had very little to smile about these days.

Beth said to her daughter, "Don't rush back for a minute or two, let me read it out to you, there might be some news to cheer us up."

The girl was only too willing to tarry and hear what her Dad had to tell them, and the way her mother's face was transformed when she had read but a few lines told her that there was some very special tidings indeed to be told about.

"Victoria," her mother said breathlessly, "your dad tells me that he is now the tenant of the hut he has been staying in, and there is room for all of us."

Her jubilant daughter began to dance up and down, clapping her hands and laughing joyously, and Beth, affected by her excitement, could not help but join in laughing.

"Oh, Mam, when do we go to Dad? I am really glad we are going," said Victoria. Her mother answered in a more sober tone and warned her daughter that there was a lot to do before they would be able to go.

With that she shooed Victoria back to the post office, then sat down to read the rest of Thomas's letter.

Beth was a slow reader but she was quick to comprehend what was in store for them at the hutted village, which her husband said was locally referred to as Marshville, for reasons he had not enlarged on. However, he did tell her it was a bleak place at this time of the year, that some of those living there appeared a bit uncouth, but from what he had witnessed up to the present day, seemed quite decent.

He had written nothing that would make any sensible woman want to go there, but even with the information that he also housed two lodgers, Beth wanted nothing more than to join him as soon as possible.

Thomas had ended his letter pointing out that when the family moved to Frodsham, they would be able to look around for a house to rent.

As was their wont, all four of them settled themselves comfortably in Simon Andern's shed and Beth read the letter to them. They were all in the same mind; they wanted to leave Wroxing as soon as they could, and move to this place which sounded so inhospitable. Will and Victoria exchanged a secret smile, both of them thinking the same thing: 'we are getting away from that man'.

Beth told them that their father had sent enough money to pay for all their travel needs and enough to pay for the boxes to be transported by the railway company. Unfortunately, for the time being their furniture would have to remain in Mr. Andern's shed, that was, if the blacksmith would still allow them to leave it there. It was a very excited family which went to their beds that night, only Beth beset by worries about what they would have to put up with, living in a rough-and-ready workmen's settlement.

The amount of work involved in making sure that her husband was well equipped for his move north, was as nothing compared to what had to be done this time. The day had started well enough for Beth, but by mid-morning her temper was starting to fray. Whilst she and Victoria were each occupied with their respective tasks and Will had taken it upon himself to pack the wooden boxes, the excited younger member of the family was bustling about getting under everyone's feet as he dragged in various items of playthings and toys which he wanted to take with him.

Eventually Will, seeing how short-tempered his mother was becoming, took Peter down to the smithy shed so that he could, as Will phrased it, 'help him with the man's job'. Actually he had very little more to do as most of his effects had been packed in the boxes when they had left the cottage. There was also the pressing question of what toy Peter needed to have with him on the journey! Will had explained that there was no room in railway carriages to play with a toy train, so Peter had settled for a clown on cords between two sticks as the best one to take.

After a visit to the post office, where Peter was given a small cheap notebook, they called on Billy Timms to let him know about their need of a cart sometime in the near future. The driver was taking a trap to the station ready to meet the next train, and he invited the boys to have a free ride.

At the station, Will enquired about the train times and the cost of tickets, noting it all down in Peter's new notebook. He also made arrangements for the wooden boxes to be collected from the shed and sent on their journey to Frodsham station.

Billy Timms had picked up a fare, so the boys walked back to the village. Victoria was standing outside the post office talking and as they drew near, she told Will that there was a meal ready for them both, so the boys, who were by now very hungry, followed her back to the cottage. Carrying the covered bowls of soup, Will made his way back to the shed, Peter following with a few slices of bread and cheese.

After they had eaten, Peter flopped down on Will's bed and almost immediately fell asleep. Thankfully his brother draped a blanket over him and got on with finishing the boxes ready for the railway carrier.

In her grandparents' cottage, Victoria had descended into a most uncharacteristic mood. For a while her mother ignored it, for she also was still wound up with the burden of responsibility, but after noticing her daughter once again picking up items of clothing, holding them up, looking at them, then flinging them back on the bed, she remonstrated with her.

To Beth's consternation, Victoria burst into tears and rushed out of the room. Her mother left her for a few minutes to let her cry it out, but when after a while her daughter had not returned, she went out to see if she could talk about what was bothering the girl.

She found her sitting miserably in the garden, her arms wrapped around herself to keep warm. Victoria raised her woebegone face towards her mother and Beth's heart flinched. She sat down beside her, and putting her arms round her said, "Victoria, girl, whatever is the matter? Surely it would be better if you would tell me," then trying to conjure up a smile said, "a trouble shared is a trouble halved, you know."

Victoria suddenly burst into a fresh bout of weeping and cried out, "I have nothing to wear and we are going to London." Her hands went to her face and she cried afresh.

Beth stared at her daughter in exasperation. 'Here I am,' she thought, 'thinking that something terrible had beset Victoria, and all it was about was what the silly girl is going to wear.'

Mixed with her annoyance was a feeling of relief; at least it was not a problem that could not be solved.

"Come inside, child, it is too cold to think straight out here." So saying she persuaded Victoria to go back inside.

Beth suddenly decided what to do. Telling her daughter to make a pot of tea, she went to the bedroom and removed her everyday shoes and her working skirt.

Quickly she donned her best skirt and her lace boots, put on her most colourful scarf and her best coat. To finish the ensemble, Beth chose a hat and gloves, then went into the other room.

Victoria looked at her mother in alarm, but Beth merely said, "Pour out the tea and I will tell you why I am dressed like this."

Beth remained standing whilst a perplexed Victoria did as she was bid.

Her mother began, "You see me now as you will see me when we travel to join your father. I will be walking through the throngs of people in London, a dirty town your father tells me, and I will pass some elegantly dressed people and I will also pass many more who will be dressed far, far worse than me. I am a decent woman and I will be accompanied by my lovely daughter and my two fine sons. Victoria," she said quietly, "I am not ashamed of what other people think of my clothes. I am happy with myself and proud of my family." Then she said, taking off her hat and gloves, "Now I will have my cup of tea, girl."

Her daughter jumped up and flung her arms round her mother's neck, saying in a happier voice, "Oh, Mam. I'm sorry, I don't know why I was getting so worked up about it all; you are right, we will appear as elegant as the best of them." In a return to her more usual manner she said, "I will pour your tea, and may I have a jam tart with mine, please?" Beth laughed and said she may, but somehow she felt a little sad. Oh yes, she knew why her daughter had had her tantrum; her little girl was suddenly a grown-up.

The following day everything went a lot easier. Peter spent much of his time with one of his playmates, allowing Will to complete the task of screwing the lids on the boxes, nailing the labels on, and arranging for the railway company's cart to collect them.

By early afternoon everything was done, their baggage was down at the smithy shed, and only a few personal items were left to be dealt with on the following morning. The boxes had been taken to the goods yard and all they had to do then was make a quick visit to their friends and bid them farewell. The most difficult of them all was that to Nora and Simon Andern. Even Will felt a bit choked up as he shook hands with the blacksmith. The women clung to each other and vowed never to lose touch again.

The parting from Beth's parents was also very upsetting, but only for their daughter. The Grices were more aggrieved than sad; no tears were shed except in Beth's heart for the lack of love and affection from them all through her life. She reflected sadly but not bitterly that they had not had the son that they had wanted, but they had been blessed with a good servant.

They followed Thomas's footsteps the next morning at exactly the same time of the day as he had, and were soon away from Wroxing and off to a fresh start. Perhaps they would come back to the village one day, even if it was only for a visit, but both Victoria and Beth were hoping that there would come a time when they could meet dear Mrs. Rodgerson again. Each of them had received a letter from their late mistress wishing them much luck in their new life and adding that she hoped they would write to her from time to time.

Chapter 11

The Family Travel to Frodsham

It was the first time that Peter had been on a train, and he thought it was wonderful. Beth, Victoria and Will had travelled before, but only once. Thomas had taken them to Norwich some years back and none of them had ever forgotten the experience.

On that occasion, however, it had been an exciting family day out, but this time it was a much more emotionally charged journey. At the end of the train ride, Peter knew that he would be with his father; it was what he wanted more than anything.

Beth also felt the same, although she was apprehensive about what the hut was like which Thomas was renting, and what sort of men he had taken in as lodgers. Since the contents of the letter had sunk into her brain, she had consoled herself with the comforting thought that they would only be there until they found a proper house.

Another emotion which was bothering her was the feeling that they were turning their backs on Mrs. Rodgerson. She knew it was illogical but after all their late mistress had done for them, she felt sad that they would not be there if Mrs. Rodgerson had a need of them.

Victoria felt just as bad about it as did her mother, and since the two terrifying approaches by Mrs. Rodgerson's husband, she had developed a deep sadness for the lonely young woman she had grown to love.

The incident in the lane, together with the other which his sister had told him about, had profoundly unsettled Will, and in his bed that night he found himself experiencing the frightening cold rage again and again. He realised what terrible things he could have done to the man if he had met up with him. Will was only too glad to be leaving Wroxing. He felt really sorry for Mrs. Rodgerson though; he thought she was a lovely lady.

However, he was looking forward to their new life and was desperately hoping that there would be a job for him.

The run into Norwich was accomplished in good time, but about twenty minutes after leaving the city, the train began to slow, then the brakes came on quite violently, almost bringing them off their seats.

Peter started to cry and Beth, who was also feeling deeply shocked, pulled him to her and attempted to calm him. Will jumped up and opened the window, then stuck his head out to see what had caused them to stop. He could see nothing on that side of the train as the line curved away from him, so he crossed the compartment to the other side. In the near distance he could see the reason for the sudden halt; a loaded farm wagon appeared to have suffered a broken axle by the looks of things. It was halfway across the level crossing and men were attempting to unload the wagon to make it easier for the horse to drag it off the line.

The crossing keeper, the engine fireman, and another man joined the wagon driver and his mate to speed things up. In no time at all they managed to accomplish the unloading sufficiently for the line to be cleared, the fireman climbed back on the engine and soon they were on their way. Presently they approached a signal and they beheld the Norwich-bound train just starting to pull away. They shuddered to think what could have happened on the level crossing if the two trains had hit the farm wagon.

Of course the delay cost valuable time which caused them to miss the Manchester train. However, it was to prove a blessing or rather, two blessings in disguise.

What they had seen of the street in their short journey between King's Cross Station and Euston Station had confirmed Thomas's disparaging remarks concerning the dirty state of everything, but they had not been prepared for the number of carts, cabs and horse-drawn buses which packed the thoroughfare. Pushing their way through all this were pedestrians. It was amazing that anything moved at all. Will found it very exciting, unlike the rest of the family, who were appalled by it all.

When their train drew in at the platform, they were delighted to discover that it was made up of a much better type of rolling stock. By the general appearance and the dust free state of the upholstery, it looked as if it had not been in service very long. Then Will saw that there was a corridor on one side, running the full length of the carriage.

The guard, obviously very proud of his train, popped his head in their compartment and informed them that the washroom was at the end of the corridor.

Beth thanked the kindly guard for his courtesy and found herself telling him of their morning's adventures and the subsequent failure to catch their intended train. The guard laughed and said, "I don't mean to make fun of their misfortune, lady, but you are now seated in the better train of the two; these carriages have only just come into service." He smiled as he withdrew and then added, "I wish you a comfortable journey, ladies and gentlemen."

When he had gone, Will and Peter dashed up the corridor to look at the washroom, returning almost immediately when Peter burst out, "Mam, it's got a privy!"

Beth, embarrassed by the fact that the compartment door was still open to the platform, said, "Shush, Peter, you will have everyone looking at us." Victoria was trying to stifle her giggles whilst Peter insisted in a slightly lower tone that there was indeed a privy.

Just then the platform staff came along closing the doors after the whistle was heard, and the train glided smoothly out of Euston Station, taking them on the next stage of their journey.

In just under three hours the train pulled in at Crewe, and as it was an important interchange station, a good many people disembarked. With his newly acquired air of gravity, Will got a porter to direct them to the platform where the Chester train was standing.

Whilst Beth stayed on the platform guarding their bags, Victoria took Peter to a small kiosk where she was to treat him to a few sweets. Will wandered over to look at a smart six-wheeled carriage which was at that moment being coupled onto the train. Two men were working in between the buffers, lifting the coupling links onto the draw hook.

He was however more interested in seeing the inside of the coach and as he peered through the spotlessly clean window, he was surprised to see that instead of being divided into compartments with long seats, it was like a large well-decorated room with comfortable armchairs grouped around a polished table.

Suddenly a belligerent voice bellowed in his ear. Startled, he swung round to find himself facing a tall good-looking young porter. "Keep away from that coach, lad, it's only just been cleaned, so shift yerself." The loud-mouthed youth was glaring at Will in such an arrogant manner that he was tempted to argue with him, but realising that there would be no chance of winning an argument with that type of person he mustered up his dignity and walked away, contenting himself with a muttered, "Keep your rotten carriage then."

The porter swaggered over to where another porter was standing and they stood there, talking and grinning like silly youths do when they think they have done something clever. Even so they were keeping their eyes open for a prospective customer, or rather the possible large-tipping customer. They had seen Beth surrounded by luggage but had gauged her as one who would not be good for a big tip.

Just then Peter came rushing across to show his mother what his sister had bought him. Beth, seeing Victoria following slowly behind him whilst she fastened her bag, picked up one of the larger bags and made ready to go and seek a compartment on the train.

The two young porters, on seeing Victoria, nudged each other, then the loud-mouthed one broke away from the other, dashed towards her with his hand raised, and shouted, "Carry your bag, Miss?" In his eagerness to get to Victoria he blundered into Beth's bag and caused her to stagger to one side. Her cry of surprise alerted Will, who had returned his attention to the men who were just finishing the task of coupling up the carriage, and at first he did not comprehend just what had made his mother cry out.

He then noticed that the arrogant young porter was trying to take his sister's small personal bag, and that Victoria was not letting go of it.

Just as he was about to go to his sister's aid, a loud authoritative voice rang out, causing more people to turn and stare.

"You clumsy oaf, what do you think you are doing, you have nearly knocked this lady flying." Then turning to Beth, the man asked in a more solicitous tone, "I do apologise on behalf of the Company, Ma'am. I trust you have not suffered any injury from the over-enthusiastic actions of this stupid boy?"

Beth, who was now actually embarrassed at all the attention she was receiving, assured the well-dressed elderly gentleman that she was indeed uninjured and thanked him for his concern.

The gentleman then turned to the wretched youth, who had now recognised the person who stood before him as one of the directors of the railway company. The Great Person spoke to him. "I want you to apologise to this lady, porter, and before this train leaves, I want a word with you in the stationmaster's office."

The nervous lad made his apology to Beth, then stood back uncertainly, waiting for his next orders. His fellow porter had somehow melted away.

With a kindly smile the gentleman turned to Beth and asked her whether it was her intention to take the train to Chester, and when she answered that she and her family, her gesture encompassing Victoria and the boys, were going to Chester, he held out his hand towards the smart carriage and said, "Madam, would you do me the honour of sharing my coach? It would in some small measure go towards repairing the damage done to my company's reputation," and he added with a twinkle in his eye, "I am sure your youngest gentleman would be pleased to oblige me in that aim." It was true, Peter was hopping from one foot to the other in his excitement. As Will put it to his father when later they described their adventures, "If Peter had grown a tail, he would have wagged it!"

Beth had been very embarrassed at all the attention they were attracting, but at this latest good-humoured observation she laughed and accepted gracefully.

The carriage attendant had appeared at the door and the director said to him, "George, would you please make the ladies and gentleman comfortable whilst I finish my business here," then turning back to Beth, he added, "I'm sure you would be ready for a little light refreshment." He touched his hat, then turned to the anxious porter and told him to carry the luggage into the carriage, and when he had done so, to report to the stationmaster's office.

The thoroughly deflated young porter hurried to do as he was instructed, passing Will but avoiding his eyes. Will would have been justified in feeling triumphant at the bullying braggart's humiliation, but instead felt sorry for the youth. He was worried that the lad would end up losing his job.

George the attendant ushered them into the carriage and before they seated themselves, quietly informed Beth and Victoria that they were welcome to use the washroom if they so wished, then asked whether they required tea or coffee.

As George disappeared into his little kitchen, Beth took Peter, who had been hanging on to every word, to one side and whispered, "Just remember, Peter, not a word about the privy, you understand?" Her youngest son solemnly promised not to say the word, but under his breath he added, "Not until I see my dad."

No sooner had the director returned and settled in the carriage than the train started on its way.

After enquiring whether their needs had been attended to the director introduced himself as Mr. Edmunds. Beth returned the compliment by introducing herself and her family to him. When he was not looking stern as he had been with the clumsy porter, Mr. Edmunds appeared to her as a really benevolent gentleman; with his full head of snowy white hair and his neat beard, his was a fatherly mien. However, she knew he would have to be quite hard when the need arose to have reached his present position.

Mr. Edmunds spoke easily, and his guests found themselves relaxing as he explained the function of the carriage in which they were travelling. There were cleverly devised sleeping arrangements and a beautiful mahogany writing bureau, everything finished in a most luxurious fashion.

Beth succumbed to his fatherly manner and told him, without going into too much detail, about Captain Rodgerson, and why they were moving to Frodsham. Mr. Edmunds was most sympathetic and mentioned the Company's railway workshops, adding that there was always a possibility of employment for Mr. Banham should his present position prove not suitable.

Both Victoria and Will told him of their hopes of finding suitable work, whilst Peter, not to be outdone, told him about the little train which his father had made for Will, but was now his.

Altogether, it was a very pleasant journey for each of them and in no time at all it seemed they arrived at Chester. As they were donning their outdoor clothing, Peter suddenly astounded them all and, much to Beth's embarrassment, said to Mr. Edmunds, "I wish you were our grandfather."

Victoria and Will could not think of a single word to say which would excuse their younger brother's cheeky pronouncement, whilst Beth, scarlet face looking at the director with agonised eyes, could only murmur weakly, "Oh, Peter."

Mr. Edmunds, as befitted a man of his standing, handled the situation beautifully by answering Peter in a gentle voice and said, "Well, I must say young man that if you and your brother and sister were my grandchildren, I would be a very proud man indeed."

Will looked at Victoria and rolled his eyes whilst she shook her head ruefully. Beth experienced a rush of mixed emotions: love for her innocent youngest son and gratitude for the way in which Mr. Edmunds had handled the situation. She felt the urge to hug the elderly gentleman but contented herself by saying softly to him, "Thank you, sir, that was a kind thing to say."

George had brought out the bags ready to place them on the platform, but Mr. Edmunds told him that he would arrange to have the porters move everything over to the platform serving the Frodsham train. He added to Beth, "I am sure you will find that our station staff will give you no cause to complain." Then he said, "And I do not think the foolish young man at Crewe station will give much trouble to future passengers; he is to be instructed afresh."

Each of the Banham family felt happier at this piece of information; they had all been feeling rather guilty at being the indirect reason why he might be dismissed.

Mr. Edmunds had gone to see the stationmaster and within minutes he returned with a veritable army of station staff, or so it seemed to the embarrassed Beth, consisting of a frock-coated gentleman wearing a top hat, a man who could have been his assistant, the head porter and two ordinary porters.

The kindly director shook hands with the slightly bemused family, only Peter seeing nothing odd about all the fuss. He gravely shook hands with Mr. Edmunds who, after touching his hat to Beth and Victoria, returned to his carriage.

It was a sight to behold and many of the of the other station users paused to watch and wonder as the pink-faced Beth and her family were escorted to their train by their retinue just like nobility, then to cap it all, installed in a first-class compartment.

Once the train moved out of the station, the babble of voices and laughter erupted as they recalled some of the events of the day, but in the end, they all agreed that Mr. Edmunds was a grand gentleman.

However, when they reached Frodsham it was a different story altogether. For a start there was nobody at the station to meet them; the harassed stationmaster had not been informed by anyone of any arrangement to get them down to 'Marshville', as he called it.

By now Beth was at the end of her emotional reserves, and Will, recognising by the rising note in his mother's voice that she was getting upset, told her that he would get hold of somebody who would take them there, 'wherever there is', he muttered to himself.

In the station yard there were just two vehicles, a four-wheeled cart and a trap. He decided to try the driver of the trap first, but although the man knew exactly where they wanted to go, he seemed unwilling to take them and their luggage, so Will walked across to the four-wheeled cart. He told the young driver of his situation. The young man said, "I'll take you and your luggage quite willingly but my cart is not suitable for ladies to travel on." He seemed anxious to please and as Will was turning the choices over in his mind, the rest of the family drew near.

He explained the dilemma, but for Beth there was no dilemma; she turned to the driver of the cart and asked him if he would take their luggage and when he agreed to do it, she walked over to the trap and requested that he take them to Marshville, as she thought it was called. He grumpily agreed to take them but not all four at once.

Beth was getting more worked up by the minute, so Will told her to get in the trap and said he would ride on the cart with the bags, and that was decided upon.

Once the little cavalcade had descended the sloping station approach and entered the street, Beth's and Victoria's interest was awakened by what they were seeing. There were a good number of shops, their windows glowing from the lights within. The street itself was lit by gas lanterns, the greenish-yellow light giving it a slightly eerie atmosphere, but nevertheless welcome to people like the Banhams, who had never seen a street light in their lives.

They turned a corner and entered what they assumed was the main street, and they were entranced. The street was wider than any they had seen before and was a hive of activity. Down one side was a row of market stalls, some of them in the process of being dismantled, but even so there were many more that were still busy. Each stall had its own oil lamps, which gave the picture and air of cheerfulness. Beth decided she liked Frodsham.

Various carts and vans were being manoeuvred in the street, which slowed them down, but eventually they reached Marsh Lane. On entering the lane they lost the light and it was some time before their eyes adjusted to the gloom.

Before they had travelled more than a quarter of a mile they were suddenly aware of a figure hurrying towards them. It was a youth dressed in overalls and by the way he was puffing and panting, he had obviously been running.

He signalled for the trap to stop, then when the surly driver complied, he asked the occupants if they were the Banham family. On hearing that he had the right family, he explained that Mr. Banham was out on a serious breakdown and he, Robbie he said his name was, had been instructed to meet the train from Chester. When he found that they were not on it, he had gone back to the depot hoping that Mr. Banham or Michael had returned. When he realised they were still not back, he waited at the workshop for a while then decided that he would be better employed by waiting at Frodsham Station.

Will had hopped off the cart when the trap had stopped and had heard some of the tale, so he suggested that Robbie ride back on the cart. The young apprentice was only too glad to take advantage of the offer and hauled himself onto the back, and with that the cavalcade proceeded again.

The family had no idea what to expect when they reached the hutted village, so they were relieved to see what looked like a shop at the beginning of the street. They could just about make out the line of the huts by the faint glow from some of the windows. The trap driver said that this was as far as he was prepared to go, so his three passengers thankfully removed themselves from his trap. Beth could not make out what change she gave him due to the darkness, but she hoped that the tip was very small.

Robbie, Will and the cheerful cart driver were preparing to take the bags along to the hut, and Robbie was telling Beth about all that was available at the shop, when the shop door opened and a couple came out. The man was carrying a large storm lamp and as they passed Beth and Victoria, bidding them good evening, the light briefly illuminated Victoria's face, but in that short space of time the shopkeeper, standing in his doorway seeing his customers out, felt his heart do very strange things. Victoria was unaware of his features as the bright lamp light shining behind him dazzled her. She turned away so as not to appear to be staring, her thoughts more on the fact that at least they had a shop nearby.

They were all surprised when Robbie, after only walking about fifty yards, stopped at the first hut and tapped on the door. It was opened almost immediately and a woman was framed in the cheerful light from the room.

At the sight of the woman, Beth drew back: "I'm sorry, I was expecting this to be the house where Mr. Banham lives." But before she could go any further, the woman laughed and said, "But Mrs. Banham, you are at the right house, my dear, come in," and so saying she stepped aside to allow them to enter.

"I am Mrs. Robbins," she announced after they had all trooped in, and then called after Robbie as he melted into the darkness, "Don't forget to call for your parcel before you go home." An unintelligible reply came faintly back.

Mrs. Robbins closed the door and said, "You will find some hooks for your coats over there," pointing, "and before we go any further, would you all like a cup of tea before your meal?"

"That would be most welcome, Mrs. Robbins," said Beth rather formally, for she was still puzzled as to why the lady was in the house at all. Thomas had mentioned in his letter that he had to take in lodgers, but she had assumed that he meant men who worked on the contract.

Perhaps it was Beth's manner or a hint of her puzzlement which prompted Mrs. Robbins to explain her presence, for she carried on by saying, "I live next door, but I promised Mr. Banham I would have everything ready for you when you arrived." Beth smiled properly for the first time and answered, "Well, you have certainly succeeded in making everything truly welcoming indeed, Mrs. Robbins, thank you."

As everyone had now shed their outdoor clothing, they were then taken upstairs to see their rooms before they settled down with their cups of tea. Beth was pleased to see that the double bed had been made up with freshly cleaned sheets and pillowcases, probably, she guessed, due to the labours of Mrs. Robbins. She had already noticed how well scrubbed everything was downstairs.

She popped her head into the next room to find Will and Peter both lying full length on two palliasses which were laid directly on the floor. Both boys were grinning hugely, and Beth reflected on the fact that to them, now that they were with their father, they would treat everything as an adventure.

"I'm really sorry, Mrs. Banham," said the other woman ruefully, "we only had one bed to spare, and we put that in your daughter's room." Victoria was sitting on the edge of the bed and said happily to her mother, "I've got a room of my own again, Mam," then she turned to their gratified neighbour, and thanked her for her kindness.

Something which had struck Beth immediately on entering the house was the number of oil lamps which had been lit. Three of them in the one room was much more than they ever used even in their own cottage, as the price of oil, or for that matter, the price of candles, forced people to limit the amount of light they could enjoy or how long they could stay up before they retired to their beds. Shrewdly, Beth had guessed that the extra lamps had been lit to make the Spartan room more welcoming. What with the light and warmth from the glowing fire, the house already felt like home.

Contentedly they went downstairs to the main room to enjoy their cups of tea. No sooner had they taken their seats than the front door opened and in came a very strangely-dressed person with a truly villainous appearance.

Each of the Banham family was shocked at this apparition, but Mrs. Robbins did not turn a hair. "Hello, Clarence," she said pleasantly enough, you are just in time for a cup of tea before you clean yourself up."

As for Clarence, coming face to face with Mr. Banham's family sent his fragile confidence crashing down. He felt completely out of place with people of this type and he was also painfully aware of their consternation at his appearance.

As was his habit when the weather looked unfavourable, he had taken to wearing a long and badly used overcoat he had found, a cape made from a piece of old tarpaulin held together with string ties, and a very disreputable bowler hat. The whole ensemble was rendered even less elegant by the fact that it was liberally coated with mud.

Mrs. Robbins moved over to him and volunteered to take his outdoor clothing off him whilst he removed his muddy boots. Gratefully he surrendered the garments, which were then carried away into the scullery area.

Poor Clarence scuttled after her, carrying the boots and trying not to drop loose bits of soil on the clean floor. He then set about the task of making himself look more presentable before he would venture over to the bedroom where he could sort out some clean clothes and shoes. Thoroughly uncomfortable, he decided that once he had gone into the room he shared with Michael, he would have his drink then stay in there until he was called out for his meal.

Clarence's appearance had put a real dampener on the conversation in the main room, and Mrs. Robbins sighed inwardly as she, aided by Beth, prepared the table for the meal. She sympathised both with the Banhams and with Clarence; it was a very unfortunate introduction to the place which from now on was to be their home, and as for the unfortunate young man, he most obviously felt himself to be the odd one out.

The family had gone very quiet, just now and again speaking of their day's adventures to each other in subdued voices. The desultory conversation was only interrupted by Clarence as he shot from the scullery area to his and Michael's room.

As they all looked at each other a trifle uncertainly, Mrs. Robbins asked Beth if she would excuse her whilst she went to get her husband's meal ready. Beth, glad to be able to take charge of her own establishment, was nevertheless sorry that her neighbour would not be there to deal with the rough-looking young man, answered by thanking Mrs. Robbins for all she had done to provide such a warm welcome for them.

Mrs. Robbins, her face wreathed in smiles, was just about to reply when the door was flung open and two more equally disreputable figures strode into the room. There was a moment of silence, then a little bundle that was Peter came flying across the room and locked onto the older of the two men and yelled, "Dad, we've come to live with you."

Then they were all on their feet, joy written on their faces, but they hung back as Thomas laughingly disentangled himself from his youngest child, and then, smiling happily he said, "Let me get out of these muddy boots, and I'll greet you all properly. Oh, and by the way, this is Michael," he added as the smiling Irishman stood waiting to take his boots off. Both men also carried their share of mud, the results of wallowing about in it whilst attending to the breakdown.

Mrs. Robbins announced that she was off to feed her husband, but before she went, Beth gave her an involuntary hug, and her new neighbour then left, contented that she had been able to help.

When Thomas came out after his ablutions he was immediately enveloped in his wife's arms, mud or no mud; she had not travelled all this way to stand around and wait while he 'prettified' himself, as Beth put it. Michael watched the happy reunion and was warmed by the family's obvious affection for his foreman. Even so, now he had seen the family, he wondered what Mr. Banham was thinking about when he had decided to bring his family to this place. They did not seem the class of people who would be comfortable with contractor's workers and their families.

By coincidence, the same thoughts were being aired right then by Mrs. Robbins to her husband.

Beth thought it only fair that the men were fed before themselves, but her husband decided to wait until Clarence and Michael had eaten, then enjoy his meal with his family this first evening. In spite of Thomas trying to include Clarence in the general conversation, the tongue-tied young man bolted his food down and retreated early to his bed. Michael stayed talking only a short time longer then he too retired. He realised that the family would have a lot to talk about, and although everyone was quite pleasant to him, he knew that they were anxious to be left alone to swap their news, so he went off to bed.

Once the family were on their own, there was such a babble of voices, there was so much to talk about. Thomas listened contentedly as they described their journey, especially the kindness of Mr. Edmunds. Of course, Peter was simply bursting to tell his father about his special carriages and the fact that each had a privy. Beth and Victoria tried to get him to keep his voice down as they both glanced at the closed door of the men's bedroom. Peter could certainly cause them to feel embarrassed without much effort.

Eventually tiredness forced them all to bed, and before Thomas and Beth retired they made everything ready for the next day's early start.

Thomas was soon fast asleep, but Beth lay a long time as her troubled mind wrestled with a new worry, the good-looking young Irishman.

The day just ending had been a revelation to her; she had seen Victoria, not as a daughter but as others might see her, a lovely young woman. Beth could not help but notice the admiring glances cast in her daughter's direction as she walked with a natural elegance when they were in the large open area of the stations.

Before today her daughter had rarely been in a situation where she would be seen by people she had not known throughout her life, and in consequence it was as if she had not seen any man she regarded other than a friend or a fellow employee. Beth could only hope that her daughter's innate good sense would not desert her. Living in such close quarters with a personable young man like Michael Rourke could play havoc with even the most sensible of women.

The man who was causing Beth so much anxiety was also having trouble sleeping. Michael had been hard put to stop himself looking at Victoria. There was such an air of innocence about her, and her loveliness was beyond anything he could remember. He wondered afresh at Mr. Banham's wisdom in bringing his family here amongst such rough and ready men, some of whom he had noticed had no idea how to behave decently. Such were the thoughts of the young gallant. 'Well,' he thought, 'I will do my best to shield her from the worst element and in time I hope she will come to look on me as a good friend.'

Clarence was another who saw her as someone special and already he had placed her on a pedestal. His mind went back to his childhood days before he had come to the conclusion that innocence and purity could not possibly exist in the world he lived in.

Little children believed in beings called angels, and know that they are not like ordinary people; they did not throw stones at windows, or go larking about on the canal and getting into trouble generally. They came to teach to be good and lead a better life. He had, very early in his life, lost his faith in angels.

Miraculously some months ago he had discovered that there was indeed a better life, and he was determined that he would be part of it. To have an angel living so close to him was just wonderful.

Victoria was the cause of another man's sleepless state, even though he did not know her name. Dafyd Hughes, grocer, was still reliving the effects of just one glance at the girl in the darkened street. Whoever she was, he was determined to get to know her.

He had heard that Mr. Banham was bringing his family here, so perhaps the girl was his daughter. 'Mind you, a lovely face did not mean that she would be a lovely person,' he mused. The itinerant nature of the men and women, decent as most of them seemed, who travelled wherever the contracts took them, did not lend itself to nurturing delicate-minded children. Even so he was hoping for another glimpse of the girl.

Meanwhile the girl at the centre of all this male interest was herself having difficulty in sleeping. The events of the last few days and, in particular, those of this day, had left her decidedly unsettled. Victoria had never experienced such attention before, not just attention but admiration. Or was she making too much of the looks she had attracted today? She had become quite embarrassed at some of the more obvious admiring glances directed her way. Victoria hoped her mother had not noticed any of it. The whole experience had left her with a strange exciting sensation. Even the unlikeable porter at Crewe had looked at her in a different way than any boy had done before. The young Irishman had also been studying her when he thought she was not looking. He did seem very nice though. It was all quite unsettling.

The next morning the whole household was awakened by the sound of heavy rain driven by strong winds, hammering on the roof. As the day grew lighter it revealed a street flanked by two trenches running with water, whilst on either side were the rows of tar-covered wooden huts. The whole outlook was so bleak and depressing that Beth was gripped by a terrible feeling of despair. 'Oh, Thomas,' she cried to herself, 'what have you brought us to?'

Chapter 12

Marshville

The men had breakfasted and left for work, and Beth sat alone by the fire trying to summon up some enthusiasm for the day ahead. She had let her family sleep on whilst the men ate and although she knew that soon they would have to be roused if they too were to be fed, Beth was too depressed to do anything about it. In fact she was having a struggle not to break down and weep. The truth was the place was nothing like that which she had expected.

Ever since she had received Thomas's letter concerning his tenancy of the hut, she had carried the image in her mind of a place a bit like Simon Andern's weatherboarded shed, but this ugly black building had none of the cosiness of the one back in Wroxing. For a start, there was no greenery and no trees growing near this miserable collection of huts, and there was not one sign of colour to alleviate the drabness. Her spirits felt as heavy as the leaden sky.

Beth, alerted by a series of creaks from the floor above, got to her feet and, forcing her face into a semblance of a smile, greeted a tousle-haired Will followed by Peter who, before he was halfway down the stairs, whined, "Mam, I'm hungry." Before she could stop herself Beth snapped back, "Well, you will just have to wait, won't you," then instantly regretted it.

The unexpected sharp tone of his mother's voice upset Peter and he started crying. Will, who had also been shocked by his mother's uncharacteristic bad-tempered retort, tried to ease the situation by sitting his sobbing brother down and holding him close whilst trying to calm him. He was sensible enough to realise that what was an adventure for Peter and himself was not something that his mother, or for that matter, Victoria, would find easy to cope with.

Racking his brain, he thought of something that he could do to help his mother. "Do you want me to go to the shop, Mam?"

Poor Beth; she knew she had been wrong in taking it out on Peter when the problem was in her own head, and her lips started to quiver. Victoria, awakened by the sound of Peter's crying, came down the stairs clad in her nightdress, just in time to see her mother drop into a chair and burst out weeping.

Victoria took control immediately, and told Will to take Peter upstairs and see that he got dressed. Her relieved brother was only too willing to escape upstairs. She then knelt by her mother and held her close until her paroxysms of weeping subsided.

"It's the best thing you could have done, Mam," she said stoutly. "I do not know how you have kept going all this time, I really don't, and I know how you feel about this place, Mam, but when we have got things here the way you want it, then it will feel more homely." Then Victoria, who was herself feeling like crying, kissed her mother on her cheek, arose and said briskly, "I'll make a cup of tea for us all, then afterwards we will go to the shop and get what we need for breakfast."

Beth was amazed at the way her daughter had taken charge of everything. This new maturity was again making her realise that Victoria was now a young woman, and at that moment, she was grateful for the fact. She now did not feel quite as overwhelmed by everything.

When Will and Peter came downstairs again, Beth had managed to pull herself together, but the sight of her youngest son's woebegone face was almost enough to start her off again. She put her arms round both boys and gave them a hug, saying, "I'm sorry I was a bit sharp with you; your Mam is a bit tired, you see."

As soon as they had all had a drink, Beth and Victoria put on their outdoor clothing in readiness to do the shopping. Of course, both boys wanted to accompany them to see what might be on sale which would interest them. Eventually all four of them emerged from the hut and dashed through the pouring rain to the shop. Just as they arrived, the door opened and a slightly-built young woman came out carrying a large basket with a cover pulled over its contents. "Hello," she called cheerfully, "Mr. Banham's family, isn't it? I'm Sally, can't stop, got to see to the twins." With that she dashed away down the street.

Beth was amazed. How did the young woman know who they were. But it certainly felt nice having someone young and cheerful living here in this dreadful place.

Once inside they were very surprised to discover just how much was stocked in the deceptively small building. One set of shelves was almost full of loaves of bread, and she was suddenly struck with the awful thought that it was only there for those who had ordered it previously.

The dark-haired young man behind the counter smiled politely at them as they turned to face him after their perusal of his stock. His wife (Beth and her daughter had both, like most women, noticed the girl's wedding ring) stood impassively waiting to serve them.

"Good morning," said the shopkeeper "Am I correct in thinking that I am addressing Mrs. Banham?" His voice was as pleasant as his demeanour, but his accent was one which none of the Banham family had ever heard before. Rather melodious, Beth thought, and wondered what part of the country he came from or even if it was the local accent. Once again she was surprised by the fact that they were known and also that they were less cautious of strangers than the people of Wroxing; a person had to live in the village for years before they were accepted. Beth had always been thankful that Thomas had so easily come to be accepted all those years ago.

Beth acknowledged that she was indeed Mrs. Banham, then enquired whether the bread and milk had to be ordered in advance.

"Well, Mrs. Banham," the shopkeeper replied, "it is certainly wiser to order those items and also eggs in advance, but in fact I have got you marked down for all those items. Mrs. Robbins informed me yesterday of your imminent arrival, and asked me to order extra for you," he added easily. "If you do not need what I have set aside for you, it is quite alright."

Beth breathed a sigh of relief. 'Bless Mrs. Robbins,' she thought, when at that very moment, the subject of her blessings entered the shop. In her hand she carried a large jug.

"Good morning, Mr. Hughes," she said, then turning to Beth she said, "Good morning, Mrs. Banham, I just caught sight of you making your way here and I realised that you would have nothing at the house to carry the milk in, so if you would like to borrow my spare jug, you are welcome to do so."

A relieved smile spread over Beth's face; such was the state of her mind this morning that she was not thinking of such mundane things as milk jugs. The problem was that all her household items were packed in the boxes which were still somewhere on the railway system. She could have hugged her neighbour but contented herself by warmly thanking her. As Mrs. Robbins left the shop, she was immediately replaced by two other women. This made the shop seem overcrowded, and Beth became acutely conscious of the space that she and her family were taking up.

She felt this morning's panic coming over her, and Victoria, seeing her mother becoming agitated again, said to her, "Shall we just take what we need immediately, Mam, and come back later for everything else?" Beth felt a sense of relief as her daughter took command of the situation, and she readily agreed that it would be the best way of doing things.

Whilst they were being served, Mr. Hughes suggested that they leave their list with him and he would make up the order for them to pick up at their leisure. Beth just wanted to get out of the shop, so this was arranged and she escaped back to their hut.

Once they were back at the hut, Beth relaxed and then confessed to Victoria that she had felt rather overwhelmed whilst in the shop. Her daughter could see that her mother would need a lot of extra help with everything if she was to settle into life at Marshville.

After breakfast the boys were sent upstairs to sort out their room whilst Victoria cajoled her mother into making a list of what they would need to make the place more comfortable. They could start to make the rooms appear less bare when the boxes were delivered, for apart from pots, pans and other necessities, there were also ornaments, pictures and cushions.

They would also need some different outdoor wear. There were several things they had noticed during the morning. Most of the people that they had seen passing wore clogs, which seemed to Beth and Victoria much more sensible than shoes, especially in the wet weather they were now experiencing. Even Mrs. Robbins had worn clogs that morning. "I will ask Mrs. Robbins where she bought them from, and how much they cost," said Beth. As it happened it was her husband who broached the subject later in the evening and suggested that they consider wearing clogs whilst in the village.

Another item of apparel which seemed to be in fashion here in Marshville was the cape similar to the one worn by Clarence on the previous day. However,

Victoria and her mother agreed that they would prefer the oilskin coats worn by some of the women.

Will and Peter volunteered to go over to Mr. Hughes's shop and bring over the groceries and vegetables, but before they could carry out their self-imposed task, there came a knock on the door and on opening it, they found the grocer himself standing there and he was carrying two sacks containing their vegetables.

Beth was taken by surprise at the visit, and was not too happy at the thought that people, even those as pleasant as Mr. Hughes, would see her poorly furnished home.

Reluctantly she invited him in and as a matter of courtesy asked him if he would like a cup of tea. The grocer declined regretfully, and said that as he left the shop, Clara was just putting the kettle on to brew a pot for both of them, but thanked her for the offer.

Beth told him that the boys would go back with him to bring back the rest of the groceries. After the grocer and the boys had left the hut, Beth, her embarrassment dispelled by Mr. Hughes's friendly manner, said to Victoria, "He really is a nice young man, Mr. Hughes, nothing seems too much trouble for him."

Her daughter answered agreeably enough, but inwardly she was fuming. A nice man indeed, she thought, such a man who would casually refer to his wife by her Christian name to virtual strangers instead of her correct title of Mrs. Hughes, that was not a true gentleman's way. Another black mark against him was the way he looked at me, she thought angrily. She had only too recently seen that sort of look in men's eyes, and she was affronted that he, a married man, should think that she was the sort of girl whom would welcome attention of that nature. So ran Victoria's outraged thoughts. 'I will certainly show him by my demeanour that I have no regard for him.'

Soon the boys returned with the rest of Beth's purchases, but also carrying a fruit cake which the grocer had sent over with his compliments.

Beth was charmed by the gesture and looked so pleased that Victoria decided to keep her thoughts to herself as to why the man had sent the gift.

Midday saw mother and daughter preparing everything for the evening meal; luckily the fireplace with its oven was a particularly good one and Beth was feeling a lot better now she was getting familiar with everything. Living in Marshville had two other advantages over living at her parents' cottage: one was the generous allowance of coal, the second was the equally generous allowance of lamp oil. It helped enormously to dispel the dreariness of the day when lamps and fire were glowing and the door shut for the night.

The first of the men to return was again Clarence, and he looked in much the same dishevelled state. Soon after Thomas and Michael walked in, but this time they looked quite respectable.

After they had all taken their turn at having their evening meal, Thomas, noticing that Clarence was going to shut himself in his room, told him that he was welcome to sit at the table for half an hour if he wanted to work on his letters.

Clarence was grateful for Mr. Banham's offer but not yet confident enough to let others look at his efforts. He did, however, stay for a while before finally going to his bunk. He found it difficult to join in with general conversation, being unused to normal family life, and with Victoria in the same room, he became really tongue-tied.

Michael, on the other hand, could talk enough for two, and had no difficulty holding a conversation with anybody. He also could be very funny, which was just what was needed given the unhappy state of the family. Peter had latched on to Michael and after a while he was back to his normal happy self, listening to the young Irishman's tales of life in Belfast.

When Peter went to bed, Beth followed and gave him an extra hug, for she was still feeling upset over her loss of control earlier in the day.

Downstairs her husband was discussing what might be done to make the hut more comfortable, and as Beth rejoined them, Michael made as if to go to his bunk but was waved to his seat again. It seemed to Beth that her husband had started to include Michael in the family circle, and found herself to be quite happy with that.

Eventually everything was done in readiness for the night and they all went to their beds. Beth, although still upset by the events of the morning, was nevertheless feeling not quite as depressed, and had very little trouble falling asleep.

Thomas lay awake longer, for he was well aware that his wife was really unhappy, and he knew that whatever he did, it was not going to be enough to get to the root of the trouble. He cursed the terrible weather for making a difficult situation worse. Even when the hut began to feel like a home, the winter would have to be over before everyone began to feel better. Eventually he too slept.

That night was one of the worst Victoria could ever remember. After witnessing the near breakdown of her mother, she saw now only too clearly that the burden of keeping everything going in the household would probably fall on her shoulders. Now that they had got their father back from that terrible state he had sunk to, their mother appeared to be heading for that same place. The poor girl wept silent tears whilst she prayed that she be granted enough strength for her and her mother. One glimmer of light in all this gloom was Michael. Victoria liked him very much.

The following morning, just before ten o'clock, Peter dashed to the door and peeped out. "Mam, there is a cart outside and it's got," here he hesitated, "it's got letters on the side." He slowly pronounced, "LNWR: what does it spell, Mam?" As he was reciting the strangely spelled word to his mother, the carter got down and looked at the doors of the huts, then said something to someone else hidden under the canvas still covering the cart. Before Beth could answer Peter's question, Will pushed past his younger brother and ran over to the carter. "Excuse me," said Will, "have you come to deliver three boxes to Mr. Banham?"

The carter nodded and grinned at Peter, answering that he and his mate would bring them into the house. "No use you getting wet, son," he said cheerfully.

It was not raining quite as heavily as the previous day and the sky was lighter, making it a much less depressing day. Beth was overjoyed at receiving her possessions and decided to put the kettle on in case the railway delivery men would accept a cup of tea. The carter and his mate were so careful with the boxes that Beth decided that they deserved a good tip.

Both men were very friendly and gratefully accepted the offer of a cup of tea. "Just moved in, Mrs. Banham?" said the older of the two men. "Well, they are not a bad bunch down here, not like some on the digging."

As soon as the kindly carters had gone, Will found the screwdriver and commenced to remove the screws which secured each lid. Mother and daughter were just as excited as Peter when the boxes yielded up their contents. Beth kept dashing in and out of the scullery with various dishes, pans and cutlery, whilst Peter whooped with delight when he found his wooden train. When they drew out the wall mirror and the pictures, Will bemoaned their lack of hooks on which to hang them. He was disappointed that he could not put them up straight away. His father had told them all not to venture into the depot unless there was something very important that he needed to be informed about, so Will had to accept that he would have to wait until his father came home to finish hanging the pictures.

Altogether they enjoyed the day very much more than the previous one; even Victoria, who had woken with a bad headache, ended up feeling happier.

When Thomas arrived at the hut later, he was delighted to see the difference in his family, and to note the changes in the main room. The boxes were empty and waiting to be put away or to be dismantled, although one of them, which had been placed against one wall, was now being used by Will and Peter as a seat. He decided that before they started on their meal, the two remaining boxes would be taken upstairs, one to go in his and Beth's bedroom to be used as a makeshift dressing table and storage, the other to be used for the same purpose in Victoria's room.

There was certainly a more cheerful atmosphere in the hut that night. After a good meal they were all sitting comfortably letting their food settle when Peter suddenly burst out, "Dad, what word does LNWR spell?" Before Thomas had grasped what his son was asking, Clarence, who was sitting on his bunk said, "London and North West Railways, that's what it means." Everyone was silenced, then Peter said, "I thought you were only just learning your letters." Clarence turned scarlet on finding himself the centre of attention, and muttered, "I just know what the letters mean, but I can't write the full words down, nor read 'em."

Beth was instantly sorry for Clarence and told Peter to apologise for his rudeness. He did as he was ordered but was quite puzzled as to what he had done wrong. Michael, who had been deeply affected by the other man's sadly voiced admission, chimed in, saying, "I will help you with your letters, Clarence, that is, if you want me to." Clarence was really pleased that there was somebody else who would help him, and accepted Michael's offer, saying, "Oh yeah, I'll be glad of your help, ta."

Thomas soon had some screws in the wall. The pictures and the mirror transformed the place. He looked at Beth's smiling face and felt a surge of hope. Perhaps she would begin to find the hut more homely from now on.

Saturday dawned bright, dry and cold. After Will had been to the shop for the usual daily fare, he returned to find Mrs. Robbins talking to his mother. They were planning to go into Frodsham, and wanted Victoria and the boys to go with them. Mrs. Robbins was going to show them where the clog and boot repair shop was situated. Apart from that, Beth and Victoria were dying to see what the shops had to offer.

To reach Frodsham Main Street, they had to walk about a mile and a quarter, which took them just over twenty minutes, and by the time they arrived they were comfortably warm. After a look round the shops, Mrs. Robbins led them into Church Street and the clog shop. The sign above the window proclaimed the proprietor to be J. Moss, Clogger and Boot Repairer.

From the way Mrs. Robbins had been greeted when they had visited the various shops, she was obviously a regular customer and it was the same at the cloggers. Quickly the Banham family had their feet measured and feet shape matched to the wooden soles. Victoria plumped for brass nails fastening the leather uppers to the soles, which she thought made them look less like working footwear. The clogger asked Beth if she and her family could come back on Tuesday for a final fitting before the uppers were nailed to the soles.

Afterwards they looked at the remaining shops, then set off back to the hutted village. They were all in a happy frame of mind and Mrs. Robbins silently congratulated herself for suggesting they visited the town. Her plan to make them feel less isolated from civilisation seemed to have succeeded.

That first morning in the shop had shown her that the family were deeply unhappy. They were certainly not the same people she had welcomed to the hut the previous evening. Peter, the youngest boy, had obviously been crying, and unless she had been very much mistaken, Mrs. Banham had also done a lot of weeping, whilst Victoria and Will had been watching their mother with anxious eyes. Mrs. Robbins fervently hoped they would survive whatever problems they were troubled by.

At one side of Main Street stood Bourne Methodist Chapel, and as they approached it Beth slowed down to see if there was a board giving the times of services for the following day. Two women, who were standing by the gate talking, smiled and asked her whether they could help them in any way. Once the times of the services had been established, Beth thanked them, and promised that they would attend on the morrow. 'Now that is another step in the right direction,' thought their neighbour. To meet fellow churchgoers and make more friends would help them feel more at home.

They were all relieved the next morning to find that the cool dry weather was still holding. The thoughts of trudging up the exposed lane in the rain whilst dressed in their Sunday best clothes gave them no pleasure at all. Spread out along the lane were other groups of people wending their way towards the town and, by the way they were dressed, were also making their way to church or chapel.

Once at the chapel, the Banhams were greeted by one of the same women that Beth had spoken to the previous day. After introductions had been performed, they were welcomed to the chapel then shown to a pew.

They had not been seated long before they noticed a well-dressed man and woman pass the end of their pew, making their way towards the front row. Beth touched her husband's arm and whispered, "Thomas, I do believe that the young man from the shop is sitting near the front. I wonder if the lady with him is his wife."

Before her husband could reply, the minister came in and the congregation arose. As the service progressed, they noticed one voice which stood out during the hymn singing. It was the rich baritone of the man Beth thought of as Mr. Hughes.

After the service they were waiting whilst the congregation filed out past the minister, when they espied Mr. Hughes making his way towards them, a smile of recognition on his face. Of the woman who had accompanied him earlier there was no sign.

"Good morning, Mr. Banham, Mrs. Banham," he greeted them, then turning to Victoria he dipped his head and wished her a good morning also. Beth was very pleased that he had acknowledged them and introduced her family to him. Thomas, who had also taken a liking to the young man, shook him warmly by his hand. Beth and the boys expressed their pleasure at seeing him, Peter once again thanking him for the fruit cake. Mr. Hughes laughed at that and said, "I can see how much taller you have grown, young man, so I take it you have eaten all of it." Peter protested that they had all had a share, so he concluded quite seriously that it must have been something else he had eaten which had made him grow. Will just rolled his eyes at the grocer and shook his head.

Victoria, however, expressed no delight in meeting Mr. Hughes. Her response to his overtures was cool to a point where they could be interpreted as a snub.

Her mother was surprised at her daughter's coldness, but decided not to make an embarrassing scene here in the chapel. Even so, she vowed that she would take Victoria to task when they were alone.

Mr. Hughes, however, did not appear to have noticed anything out of the ordinary in Victoria's behaviour and carried on the conversation in an equable manner.

Beth expressed her admiration for his wonderful singing, which brought a blush to his cheeks and he said, "Well, you see, Mrs. Banham, like most Welshmen, I have sung in a choir since I was small; it is something which gives me a great deal of pleasure."

Over near the doorway stood a woman of middle age, and she was obviously waiting to speak to Mr. Hughes, so Thomas and Beth bid him goodbye and left the chapel. Beth was furious at her daughter's behaviour towards Mr. Hughes, and it had cost her a lot of effort to maintain a smiling countenance in front of her husband and the young Welshman. Once they were on their own, she vowed to remind Victoria of the good manners she had been taught.

Beth was wrong in thinking that the grocer had not noticed Victoria's coldness. Mr. Hughes was still shocked at the naked dislike in the girl's face. 'What on earth had I said or done to inspire such a look?' thought the disconsolate young man. 'I am not sure now that she is as nice as she looks,' and he felt sadly disappointed.

Once they were in Moorditch Lane, as they then knew it was called, Beth quietly told her husband to walk on whilst she had a word with their daughter. Thomas, unaware of any trouble between his wife and Victoria, happily walked on, holding Peter's hand and chatting to both boys.

When the three of them were far enough ahead to be out of earshot, Beth asked her daughter what was her reason for putting on such a display of bad manners to Mr. Hughes. Victoria, almost in tears at her chastisement, burst out in a voice that trembled. "But, Mam, I dislike that man intensely," she said, trying not to cry. "I am sorry, Mam, and I will try and hide my feelings in future, but it is no use, I just do not think the man is the gentleman everyone seems to think he is."

Beth felt sorry for her daughter, but she had to tell her that from this day on, she must never again behave in such a way that she showed herself or her family to be lacking in good manners.

With that said she took Victoria's trembling arm and they walked after the rest of the family.

Once they were back at the hut, Beth set to and brewed a cup of tea for everyone, although Victoria had gone to her room as soon as they got in. Wisely, her mother decided to let her come round in her own time. She herself was feeling upset with all that had occurred.

Thomas was taking the boys down to the depot for a quick visit before they had their midday meal. That Sunday, no work was being done in the depot, so there was no danger of accidents through the movement of trains. Clarence had gone down to look after the horses whilst Michael had not yet returned from church.

Victoria sat on the edge of the bed feeling very sorry for herself. She knew she had been guilty of an appalling display of childish bad manners. She could see that quite plainly now, but it seemed that whenever she was in the company of that man, she felt her hackles rise. It made things worse when everyone went out of their way to praise him. 'Oh yes,' she thought, 'he is good looking, his manners are perfect, and his clothing is all in good taste. Oh yes, and now he has a marvellous singing voice. It's sickening,' she thought childishly, 'just how perfect the man is.'

She felt the hot tears roll down her cheeks and she lay back on her bed, ending curled up in a ball. Victoria had never felt so alone and miserable in her life. When her tears had stopped, she began to think about her attitude towards men. She had felt complimented on her journey to Frodsham when men looked at her admiringly, but here in Marshville, the look affronted her. Before, it did not matter, for she was not involved closely with any of those men; she knew that she would probably never see any of them again. It did not matter if they were all married, they were just passers by. She suddenly had an awful thought. 'Had those frightening encounters with Captain Rodgerson caused her to have a dislike of men for the rest of her life, and would she ever meet a man she could trust enough to marry?' Her dreary thoughts were interrupted by a gentle knock on her door and the voice of her mother asking if she could come in.

Beth came in carrying a jug of warm water. "Here you are, girl," she said briskly, "something to freshen you up. You will feel much better afterwards, and when you come down I'll make you a fresh cup of tea." She gave her daughter a hug and a kiss on the cheek, then went sadly back downstairs. Her heart had constricted when she had seen the sorrowful look on Victoria's face; it was like looking at a stranger. That guileless innocence had gone and had been replaced by a sad martyred expression. Beth did not know whether to laugh or to cry. She sighed, 'Was this another sign of her daughter's transition from childhood to woman?

The boys came back full of the wondrous things that they had seen at the workshops. Over the years they had heard their father talk about lathes, shapers and other such metal-cutting machines, but until this day they had no idea what those machines looked like or how they worked. Peter earnestly told Victoria and his mother that when he grew up, he too would work in engineering.

Will, on the other hand, wanted to talk about the sailing ships they had witnessed moving up river towards Runcorn. He seemed to be more interested in ships than workshops.

With the absence of their lodgers, the flow of conversation was reminiscent of such family mealtimes at their cottage at Longfields Estate.

Far from making Beth feel upset at the reminder of happier times, she sat listening to her sons and their father with something approaching contentment. Victoria did not have a lot to say, but Beth recognised that her daughter was exerting herself to appear interested in the conversation, even if she did not understand one word of it.

Later, after the last meal of the day, Michael kept his promise to Clarence, and helped him with his letters. As his 'pupil' eagerly copied everything the young Irishman showed him, he found that he was enjoying himself. Clarence surprised him with the quickness with which he grasped what he was supposed to do. 'Perhaps,' he mused, 'I have some of my brother's traits in regard to teaching.'

By the time they were ready for bed that night, even Victoria, under the influence of the happy buzz of conversation around her, felt more like her old self.

Chapter 13

Sheehy's Bully Boys Visit

Monday had always been the day that Beth washed the clothes and bed linen, and this day was no exception. As usual the water had to be boiled kettle by kettle on the fire. The large galvanised bowl, which was also used as a stand-up bath, was to be used to ponch the washing in, and Victoria had just brought it in when a knock came at the door. And there stood Sally, mother of the twins.

"Hello, Mrs. Banham," she began, a little nervously. "Me and Mrs. Guest take it in turns to take the boys to Frodsham Infants School, and we wondered if you wanted to come up to the town with us?" At that point, she paused, then explained quickly, "You see, Mrs. Banham, the contractor, Mr. Walker, provided schools for us but the nearest to us is at Ince or Ellesmere Port, and that's too far to go." Sally continued seriously, "Frodsham Infants School is a good school, and we thought you might want your youngest boy to go there."

Once again Beth was touched by the kindness of the people she had met in the hutted village. She thanked Sally and asked what time they were going to Frodsham. The young woman told her when, gave her a smile, and dashed off to get her boys ready for school.

Victoria, having heard the conversation, said to her mother, "Would you like me to walk up to the school, Mam, or do you want me to see to the washing while you go out?" Beth thought for a moment, then said, "I think it would be better if I went up to the school myself." Then she had another thought. "Mind you, Victoria, they might not be able to take Peter, but still, we will just have to cross that bridge when we come to it."

At the agreed time Beth set off with Sally, who was taking another boy as well as the twins, whilst Victoria, aided by Will, carried on in preparation for the washing.

Meanwhile, in the fitting shop, Michael was happily working at the bench. A particularly difficult job had been dealt with, and he and Robbie were finishing off whilst Thomas was in the machine shop going over another job with the turner.

Michael's humming stopped as he became aware of two men entering the workshop. "Hello there," he called out cheerily, "anything I can do for you?"

His friendly greeting died on his lips as he registered the menacing expression on the leading man's face. Both men were of medium height, not much taller than Michael, but of immensely powerful build, and by the look of their clothes, they were not navvies. This was certainly not a friendly visit.

The first man had reached the young Irishman and immediately demanded with a loud, aggressive voice, "Where's Tarelton, laddie," and while the alarmed Michael was trying to make out what he was being asked, the man grabbed the front of his overalls and almost lifted him off his feet whilst roaring in his face, "I asked, where's Tarelton, Mr. Sheehy is not waiting any longer for his money, so where is he?"

Michael was filled with rage but was helpless against the brute's enormous strength. He then remembered Robbie telling him something about the previous foreman, and he yelled at the man holding him, "Get your hands off me, you lunatic, Mr. Tarelton's gone, he does not work here anymore, so just get your hands off me now." At that point, Thomas, who had heard the raised angry voices, came out of the machine shop and ran up to the struggling pair. "Get out of here, man,", he shouted, but was answered by the bully boy swinging Michael round and thrusting him against the foreman.

Thomas staggered backwards, just missing falling into the inspection pit. The second man then joined in, clamping his arm round Thomas and dragging him helplessly towards the doorway. From the machine shop heads were appearing in the doorway leading to the other workshops, but the machinemen were small and rather elderly, which made them hesitant in being involved in the rumpus.

Then the now thoroughly enraged foreman managed to get one arm free and was able to fight back, but could not match the strength of his opponent. Suddenly he was thrown to the ground, landing between the railway lines. For a few moments he lay there unable to get his breath, and then he felt a heavy blow to his face near his eye. Even as he cried out in pain, he heard his attacker yell, then was relieved of his weight as the man toppled sideways away from him.

Standing over the toppled bully boy was the coal heaver, the massive shovel poised ready to administer a second blow, and yelling, "Try any more, man, and I'll lop you, go on, just try it."

Thomas struggled groggily to his feet, blood pouring from his split eyebrow, then went to the aid of his fitter. At the same time the boilermaker appeared from outside carrying a large length of wood in his hands. As he rushed towards the first bully boy still holding on to Michael, Captain Howard's assistant ran down from Thomas's office, and hauled himself on the back of the bull of a man and hooked his arm round his neck. The boilermaker hesitated at hitting somebody, even a bully boy, around his head, and gave the man a mighty blow to his arm. The effect was dramatic: the man simply let go of Michael and, with his face drained of colour, grabbed the vice to stop himself falling to the ground in a faint.

Blood was pouring from Michael's nose and his body felt as if he had been through a crusher, but he still held on to his assailant's arm whilst Ian Blake held on to the other.

Thomas told Robbie to get some rope or thick twine, anything which could be used to tie the attackers up securely.

The fight had gone out of both men; the second man still sat there between the railway lines whimpering. "You didn't have to hit me that hard," he kept saying to the grim-faced coal heaver, who was still holding the shovel ready to strike again at the first sign of renewed aggression, the first one sitting on a box and leaning pasty faced against the bench. With so many men now to deal with the situation, Ian, still a bit weak from his bout of fever, climbed shakily into his trap and urged the pony up the lane towards the town and the police station.

As he left the depot, a third man was being hauled out by two navvies from between the timber stacks where he had been skulking.

Soon after the police arrived, Ian returned, followed by Doctor Mills in his own trap. With him was his anxious-faced daughter Sarah.

Before Sheehy's men were taken away, Doctor Mills examined them. He thought the leader of the gang was probably suffering no more than the effects of the blow on his muscle, whilst the second man did not seem to have suffered any serious injury to his head.

Sarah, meantime, had set to and cleared the blood from around Thomas's eyebrow, and prepared cold compresses for Michael's nose. Robbie, on her orders, had made some hot, sweet tea for the injured pair to ward off shock. She told Thomas that his eyebrow would probably need stitching.

By now, the area in front of the workshops was swarming with people. Apart from the workshop men, there were several navvies and the crane driver all set to join if needed. It had all the appearance of the aftermath of a battle.

Ian Blake was feeling very shaky, and he leaned against the workshop door, his face pallid, and his eyes closed. In a trice Sarah was with him, holding on to him. One of the navvies also dashed forward and helped the girl hold him up whilst somebody got him something to sit on. Sarah was close to tears; she knew that the fever which had laid him low so short a time back had sapped a lot of his reserves, and that he was now in danger of a relapse. She was not a doctor's daughter without knowing something about shock.

The police had departed with the arrested men, and Doctor Mills said that he wanted his patients, three of them now, including Ian, taken to where they could be treated in the warmth. Like his daughter, he was worried about the effects of shock. A little reluctantly, Thomas suggested that they all go up to his hut, although he was worried that the sight of their injuries would upset Beth even more.

As the sorry-looking party made its way up the street, there were people outside every hut. The large number of policemen and the constant movement of pony traps and people through the village had told them that something out of the ordinary had happened. Each of the women were worried that there had been an accident, and one that had involved one of their own menfolk.

Robbie was driving one trap with Sarah holding on to Ian, whilst her father followed in his trap. Thomas and Michael elected to walk to the hut, each holding a pad against their respective injuries.

It was Will who opened the door and his face paled as he caught sight of his father and Michael. Beth was just about to take the first lot of washing out ready to put through the mangle, but at the sight of her husband, she dropped her load back on the draining board and went to him.

In no time at all the injured were seated and Doctor Mills set to putting stitches in Thomas's eyebrow. Victoria brought a bowl of cold water to soak the compresses on Michael's nose, which mercifully seemed to be bleeding less freely. Sarah had begged a blanket off Beth and had wrapped it round Ian. He had begun to regain his colour and was feeling more cheerful. By that time it had become obvious to everyone that he and Sarah were very attached to each other. It had not escaped the notice of the doctor either, but mercifully he did not seem displeased.

Eventually the doctor announced that he had done all he could for the time being, but promised to call the following afternoon and look at his patients. He then told Ian that he advised him to spend a further day in bed before he attempted to do any more work, after which he went back to town. Sarah followed him, driving Ian's trap with the well-wrapped young man beside her.

When everybody had gone, Beth ordered both men to their beds, an order which they were both happy to obey.

During the time in which Beth and Victoria had done the doctor's bidding, providing hot water, clean cloths and such, they had both been too preoccupied to be upset, but now the emergency had passed, reaction set in. They all sat down feeling completely drained, all thoughts of washing abandoned.

Beth suddenly burst out in a low voice, "I hate this place, I really hate it, what with the miserable huts, the mud, the noise of the machines, and now this. I wish we were back in Wroxing."

For a moment there was a stunned silence, then Victoria said, in an equally low voice, "But, Mam, there is nothing to go back to in Wroxing, nothing; you surely…" Her mother interrupted her saying, "I know what you are going to say, girl, but we were managing alright. Oh, I know things could have been better…" Before she could continue, Will said, in a wobbly voice, and very near to tears, "Dad was not alright, coming back wet and looking like a tramp, and still no job, my Dad's better off here," and gulping down his tears, he ran through the back door out of the hut.

"Will," cried his mother, rising to her feet, but Victoria, again showing her newly acquired maturity, put her hand out to stop Beth going after her son, and said quietly, "No, Mam, leave him to come round in his own time."

Beth sat down heavily and wondered anew about her daughter, and listened whilst Victoria quietly reminded her of what they had left behind, including, she said, that horrible Captain Rodgerson. Her daughter concluded sadly, "The only thing I regret, Mam, is that we had to leave Mrs. Rodgerson. I still feel sad about that." At the last sentiment her mother nodded in agreement, and then got up wearily to finish what they could do with the washing. With the upsetting events of the last hour, they had come to a point where to finish what they had set out to do that day would be thwarted through lack of daylight.

In his bunk, poor Michael was in the embarrassing position of hearing what was being said, and not being able to let them know that he was awake; if they realised he had overheard them talking, he knew they would be terribly upset.

So now he knew something of why a family like the Banhams had come to Marshville. He felt immensely sorry for them.

Meanwhile, Will had run blindly out of the hut and across the enclosure to reach the working area behind the workshops. In the whole of his life he had never known of anyone using violence against his father, and today's events had shaken him to the core, then to hear his mother talking about Wroxing like that had upset even more. He could not believe that she had forgotten how terrible it had been to watch his father looking more beaten each day that passed.

Once he had regained control over his emotions, he wandered down towards the workshops; he could not face his mother yet, or for that matter, Victoria.

At one side of the railway line was a raised wooden platform called the coal stage, where the coal was stacked for the use of the locomotives and the steam crane. On the coal stage stood the coal heaver. It was his job to shovel the coal out of the wagons onto the stage.

Johnny, the coal heaver, was talking to a second man and appeared to be demonstrating something by the way he was swinging his shovel. As Will aimlessly approached the two men, Johnny looked round, and espying the boy, asked him, "How is your dad, son?". Before Will could answer, Johnny said, "That ape gave your dad a right nasty clout, but," he added with a chuckle, "I gave him his own back for your dad, I whacked him with this," and swung the shovel around again. "He will have a lump on his head the size of an egg," he concluded gleefully.

For a few moments, the thought of somebody helping his dad lifted Will out of his despondency, and he grinned at Johnny and told him he deserved a medal, then answered the coal heaver's question. "My Dad and Michael are both in bed asleep," he said. "The doctor put some stitches in my Dad's eyebrow."

The man asked him how his mother was, and as he had done before, carried on talking before Will could answer the question. "It's the women I'm sorry for, they 'as to put up with a lot in places like this, they don't have it easy, son." Will nodded his head thoughtfully, then suddenly made up his mind; he was supposed to be helping his mother and here he was, leaving her and Victoria to do everything on their own, so he turned round and walked back to face the music.

Beth and Victoria were hard at work again when Will walked in. He went straight up to his mother and put his arm round her and whispered, "Sorry, Mam." Beth smiled sadly at him and said, "No, Will, it is me who should say sorry." Then she hugged him fiercely. "Now," she said briskly, "let us get back to work, though I think we will only do a bit more today then do the rest tomorrow; with all that has happened today, we are too far behind." Then she said, with a return to her usual manner, "So there will be no wringing out for you today, son, but you can go to Frodsham and collect Peter from the school, it's Frodsham Infants School; if you do that for me, it would be a great help."

Will was quite happy to do that, for he hated washing day when the weather stopped the washing being hung out to dry, and forced them to hang it on the rack inside the house, dripping water over everybody.

Within three quarters of an hour he was back, and by this time, he was ready for his midday meal.

After they had finished their meal, Beth took Peter to one side and quietly told him that his Dad and Michael had been involved in an accident, and that they were in bed having a sleep, so he had to be quiet and not disturb them. By this time both Michael and her husband were fast asleep, so rather than wake them to feed them, she had decided to let them get the benefit of healing rest.

Peter was quite upset, but was eventually pacified, and settled down to do some drawing in one of his father's old notebooks. Once he had calmed down, he then started telling them about his morning at the school, and it emerged that he had made a friend, a little girl, but he had forgotten her name. "But," he added, "she was very pretty." Victoria and her mother exchanged amused glances, and Beth whispered, "I think he will be alright."

Mother and daughter were discussing what to do with the mound of saturated washing; there was nowhere to put it where it would not get soiled whilst waiting for the fresh start on the task the following day. Also Beth had realised that they would not have enough soap to do the whole batch.

After Peter had been settled, Beth turned to her oldest son, and asked him if he would go across to the shop and get another bar of soap. Will was delighted to do so, for he really enjoyed talking to the shopkeeper.

Mr. Hughes also enjoyed having a word with Will, for apart from being a pleasant and intelligent boy, he was also Victoria's brother, and he formed a small link with the girl. Even so, he had to admit to himself sadly, the young woman herself did not seem as perfect as his first impression had led him to believe.

"Good afternoon, Will," said the grocer in reply to his young customer's greeting. "How are your father and Mr. Rourke?" He paused and said quietly, "I heard that they had been attacked and injured this morning." Will answered him and found himself telling the sympathetic shopkeeper how badly his mother had reacted to the latest upset on top of everything else. He obviously did not tell Mr. Hughes all that had occurred in their hut that morning; some things he reasoned, were not for the ears of anyone else, not even those of the kindly grocer.

Mr. Hughes listened to his young customer's outpourings, and could see that the boy was deeply upset by what had happened. Once again he felt a wave of compassion for the Banham family; they were like fish out of water in this rough, hutted village. He decided that the boy needed some words of support and also to know that other people understood what the family were going through.

"You see, Will," he said, "you will all feel very troubled about what has happened today, and indeed what it is like to live in a worker's settlement like Marshville, but this day's trouble is something that has never happened here before, and," he added, hoping he was not being too optimistic, "now that the police have arrested those men, nothing like this will ever happen again."

He then said to Will, who by this time was feeling more cheerful and less alone, "Help out as much as you can at home; being cheerful is as good a lift in the house as helping with the work." He then said to the boy, much as Johnny the coal heaver had said earlier, "You know, Will, the ladies have a hard life as it is; their day's work starts when they arise each morning, and does not finish until they retire to their beds at the end of the day." He continued, "And in the conditions which exist on work sites such as this, there are even more burdens and worries to be borne."

Will had listened very carefully and vowed that from now on he would try his utmost to keep his mother's spirits up. He was also quite pleased that Mr. Hughes had called him by his Christian name and talked to him in an adult way. He thanked the grocer for listening to his troubles, and for his words of advice.

Mr. Hughes had to smile to himself. Here he was, not much older than Will, yet he was giving the boy advice as if he were a older and more experienced man.

He then reverted to his role as a shopkeeper and asked the boy what he had come to the shop for. Will, suddenly feeling rather guilty, told him what it was he needed, and added, "Mam and Victoria were doing the washing before Dad and Michael came in, so everything had to stop. Now they are going to do it tomorrow but with a lot of it still wet and not rinsed, the things are all over the place. You see, Mr. Hughes, we only have one bowl and that's the one we bathe in each night." Then he added mournfully, thinking of the dripping washing everywhere, "I do not know what we are going to do about it."

The shopkeeper suddenly had a thought. "Now, Will, if you are not going to be busy for the rest of the day, perhaps you could help me and earn yourself some money, that is, if your mother can spare you." He looked enquiringly at Will, and the boy replied quite happily, "If my Mam can spare me, Mr. Hughes, I will gladly help you for nothing."

The grocer asked Will to wait for a moment and went into the back of the shop. When he returned, he was carrying a bowl similar to the one which was used in the Banham's hut, and also the bar of soap. "I can gladly lend Mrs. Banham the bowl for tonight, it will help hold the washing until tomorrow, and the job I had in mind is for you to do some deliveries to the houses."

Will thanked him and went back to their hut carrying the bowl and the soap. Within a short while he was back with his mother's thanks and permission to help Mr. Hughes.

The grocer had put two baskets and a sack of vegetables out for delivery, and after telling Will where the first basket was going, he said, with a twinkle in his eye, "The vegetables and the other basket are for Mrs. Garroway; she is suffering from gout at the moment, so it makes it difficult for her to collect her shopping. Mrs. Garroway is a bit fearsome," he added, "but her bark is worse than her bite."

Loaded with a basket, Will happily set off with his first delivery and within ten minutes he was back for Mrs. Garroway's basket and sack. This time he was a bit longer and when he did return, he looked very expressively at Mr. Hughes and rolled his eyes in his usual comical way.

His opening remarks made Mr. Hughes laugh. "Well," said the boy, "I would not like to meet Mrs. Garroway on a dark night, I bet nobody argues with her, and she is so big," he said in an awestruck voice. The large lady had also given him a halfpenny for bringing her shopping. He did not say, however, that there was a rather unpleasant smell in the Garroway hut.

Mr. Hughes let him help tidying up around the storeroom at the rear of the shop, then when he had finished, offered to pay Will for his efforts, but the boy politely refused to accept any money; he had actually enjoyed helping out, it made him feel useful. He said, "If you want any more jobs doing, Mr. Hughes, I am quite willing to do them for you." The grocer then insisted that he took home a fruit cake for the family, which the boy thought was very thoughtful of Mr. Hughes. Little did they know, but it was the start of a friendship which was to last for the rest of their lives.

Just after three o'clock, Sally called on her way back from bringing the boys home from school, and asked Beth how Peter had gone on. When they had chatted for a while, Peter asked if he could be allowed to play with the twins. Sally said she would be happy to have him if Mrs. Banham did not mind him coming over to her own home. Beth thanked her, told Peter to behave himself, and Sally took the boys, and with a wave, said goodbye, and went down to her own hut. It had not escaped both Beth and Victoria's attention that the young woman had referred to her hut as her 'home'.

Later in the afternoon, Captain Howard called at the hut. It was the first time he had visited them since the family had taken up residence and Beth, being extremely conscious of the bareness of the room, felt very embarrassed at the visit. It was not long, however, before he had put her at ease. After expressing his shock at what had happened, he heard about the doctor's visit. He told Beth that he would pay the doctor's bill and any other expenses, such as replacing damaged clothing for both men. It was obvious that the engineer was really angry and upset that such a thing could happen to any of his employees.

He gratefully accepted the offer of a cup of tea and as Victoria put the kettle on the fire, her father came down the stairs. Apart from his damaged eyebrow, he was sporting a fearsome-looking black eye. When Captain Howard caught sight of the injuries, his eyes narrowed in anger. He stood up and held out his hand to Thomas. They shook hands and Captain Howard asked him how he was feeling.

"Well, sir, the truth is I feel a sight better for having a sleep, that's for sure, and," he said, "speaking for myself, I am sure that I will be fit for work tomorrow." He stopped as his employer raised his hand, shaking his head, and said, "Mr. Banham, I do not want you in the workshop until the doctor given a clean bill of health, and that goes for Michael Rourke." Seeing the mulish look settling on his foreman's face, he said quietly, "And that's an order, Thomas."

"Very well, sir, I cannot go against an order, but I would that you allow me to deal with any workshop enquiries if anybody comes up from the 'shops to see me?"

Captain Howard laughed. "You are a stubborn man, Mr. Banham, but I will allow you licence to do that."

After he had been served with his tea the engineer complemented Beth for making the hut so homely. She blushed with pleasure, and thanked him for being so kind as to say so. He rose from his seat and made his leave, promising to call again later the following day.

When he had gone, both Beth and Victoria agreed that Captain Howard was a good employer and a real gentleman. Victoria said wistfully, "I wish Mrs. Rodgerson was Mrs. Howard, it would make me happy and I am sure Mrs. Rodgerson would be happier." Her mother smiled sadly at her matchmaking daughter and said, "While I think you are right, girl, it was not to be and it shall not be as you wish, more's the pity."

The daylight had gone, and Beth sent Will across to bring Peter back. When the little boy came in and caught sight of his father's eye, he burst into tears and rushed over to his mother and clung to her. It took a while before he could be pacified, and a while longer before he could pluck up courage to climb on his father's knee and hug him.

When Clarence came in, he gaped at the sight of Michael's nose and Thomas's eye, and muttered, "I'm sorry, Mr. Banham, Michael, them bad 'uns wants to have an accident on the way to the cells."

It was not long that night before they were all in bed. Nobody was in the mood for talking; the events of the day had been too shocking to dwell upon.

Chapter 14

Looking at a House

Before Beth had stirred from their bed, Thomas had dressed and gone downstairs. When she too went down, she found all three men awaiting their breakfast. The fire, which had been damped down and banked for the night, was now giving out a cheerful glow, the kettle was on and the breakfast dishes were on the table.

She gave her husband a half-hearted scolding for not waking her earlier, but was in truth quite pleased to find everything was in hand, and the room warming up nicely.

Thomas and Michael both told Beth that they felt good enough to go into work, and would have done so had not their employer ordered them not to. Certainly the pair of them behaved much more vigorously, but while Michael's nose looked less swollen, his foreman's eye looked slightly worse.

After they had eaten, Clarence went off to work whilst Thomas and Michael went back to their beds so that Beth could see to her family, then get on with job of finishing the washing.

Dawn had broken when Mrs. Guest called to take Peter to school, and for the first time since Beth and the family had arrived at Frodsham, a weak sun gave promise of a dry day.

Although the air outside was quite cool, the sight of the sun made Beth feel much more optimistic. Later, as the day advanced, a slight breeze prevailed which helped dry everything, the washing and the ground around the huts.

As Mrs. Guest went on her way with the boys, Beth shut the door and turned to Victoria and said, "Right, girl, we will get on with on with the washing again." Then suddenly she noticed that Will had gone back to the table, and was cradling his head in his arms.

"Will, are you all right, son?" Beth asked anxiously. Her son, in a muffled voice, told her that he had one of those sick headaches. Straight away Victoria went to Will and persuaded him to go back to bed. He stood up, swaying and white-faced then allowed his sister to help him upstairs.

Whilst Victoria fussed around with Will upstairs, a knock came on the door and Beth opened it to find a very concerned-looking Mrs. Robbins standing there.

"Oh, Mrs. Banham," she began, "I just had to come in to see you. I did not get back from Moore until late yesterday and Mr. Robbins then told me about what had happened at the workshops." She continued in an apologetic tone, "We both agreed you certainly would not want people troubling you at that time of the night."

Beth welcomed her neighbour inside with a smile, but inwardly, she was resigning herself to yet another stoppage. Normally she would have been glad to see Mrs. Robbins, for she had come to regard her rather slightly built neighbour as a veritable tower of strength. However, with two sick men and one boy on her hands, and a pile of washing still to be done, the last thing she wanted right then was somebody coming in to chat.

Mrs. Robbins said, "How are Mr. Banham and Michael?" and when Beth had told the whole sorry tale, she clucked sympathetically and then said, "I would be happy to help with the washing; between the three of us we could soon get it done. But," she added quietly, "if you and Victoria would rather do it on your own, I quite understand."

A wave of gratitude swept over Beth. She knew quite well that she and her daughter would manage the job themselves, and if the weather continued as it had started, that everything would be washed and dried before darkness fell. Even so, she felt the presence of her stalwart neighbour would be of tremendous help in other less physical ways, and she gratefully accepted the offer.

Suddenly, Mrs. Robbins had a thought, and she said tentatively, "I was just wondering, if Michael and Mr. Banham wished, they could move into next door whilst we do the work." Then she added, "They would not be confined to their rooms and in next door there is plenty of reading matter to occupy them. What do you think of that idea, Mrs. Banham?" she concluded triumphantly.

Beth shook her head admiringly, and again was struck by the real practical help that her neighbour always seemed to offer, and she clapped her hands delightedly.

"I think it is a very good idea, Mrs. Robbins, I will see if Thomas is awake." A few moments later she was back, with her husband following her.

"That is a very kind offer, Mrs. Robbins," Thomas said. "I am quite relieved to be out of my incarceration," he joked. "Are you sure Mr. Robbins will not be in any way put out by our presence?"

For a moment Mrs. Robbins did not answer; she was too shocked by the sight of his injuries. When she did answer, it was in a gentle voice and she said, "My husband is busy in his office today but I am sure he would not object to some male company for a change."

At that moment, Michael poked his head out of the bunk room and echoed Thomas's sentiments. With everyone in agreement with the plan, Mrs. Robbins led the way, and the men moved next door.

When they had gone, Victoria said warmly to her mother, "I do think Mrs. Robbins is an angel, Mam; we are extremely fortunate to have such a kind neighbour," and Beth, nodding her head said, "We couldn't want for a better one, Victoria."

Before they started working, Victoria quietly peeped into the boy's bedroom. Will was fast asleep, so she went back downstairs to get on with her part of the proceedings. In the absence of her brother she had been landed with the job of turning the rollers of the mangling machine. As she worked the handle, she thought wonderingly of the diminutive figure of Mrs. Robbins wrestling with this heavy machine.

When the job was well on its way, the three of them had a break for a few minutes and enjoyed a much needed cup of tea. As they sat there in companionable silence, Beth said hesitantly to her neighbour, "I would be pleased if we were less formal, Mrs. Robbins, people who know me well call me Beth, but of course," she added quickly, "if you prefer to leave things as they are, I quite understand."

Victoria, pleased at her mother's eagerness to make a friend, looked expectantly from one face to another and was rewarded when an expression of pleasure swept across the face of Mrs. Robbins. Their neighbour responded by saying happily, "You know, Beth, I would also be delighted if you were to call me Jessie." Then she turned to Victoria and continued. "You also, Victoria, after all, you are a young woman."

The youngest member of the trio blushed, pleased at being recognised as a woman rather than a girl, but she shook her head, smiling, and told Mrs. Robbins that she was pleased with the compliment, but for the present time she would feel more comfortable if she continued in the formal and more respectful mode of address.

Before the conversation could proceed any further, there came a knock on the door and Victoria sprang to her feet and went over to see who it could be. She had somehow got it into her head that it could possibly be the doctor and she hoped that he would be accompanied by his daughter. She had really taken to Sarah and hoped that she had found a friend of similar age.

Her face was lit up with a welcoming smile as she opened the door, but her smile disappeared immediately when she perceived that the caller was none other than the grocer.

"Good morning, Miss Banham," he said in a pleasant manner. "I called to inquire how Mr. Banham and Mr. Rourke are today, and to offer any help I can give." He could not fail to have noticed her change of expression, and even though he expected nothing more, he still felt a sense of disappointment. Her initial glorious smile had sent an amazing jolt through his whole body. He would have done anything to see that look on her face again, especially if it was meant for him.

Victoria answered very formally, "Good morning, Mr. Hughes, I will bring my mother to the door, excuse me please." Then Beth appeared, very flustered, and acutely conscious of her dampened apron, and invited him in.

The shopkeeper declined courteously, and repeated the words he had spoken to Victoria. Beth explained the situation and what had happened. Mr. Hughes then told her, with nobody calling to collect the day's bread, he had put it to one side for them.

Beth's hand went to her mouth and she cried, "Oh Lor', Mr. Hughes, what with all that is happening, I completely forgot the bread, and the milk too," she cried. She then promised to send her daughter over for everything in a short while. With that the young man went back to the shop. Victoria, who had heard the exchange, was not pleased at all, but she knew that she had to put on a pleasant face or risk another rebuke from her mother.

Without consciously knowing why, she took off her working overdress, then checked her appearance in her bedroom mirror before she sallied forth to do her mother's bidding.

As it was there was no Mr. Hughes at the counter. Instead she was served by the unsmiling Clara. Whether the fact that she had steeled herself to give him her coolest looks to demonstrate that he was wasting his time in ogling her, and he not being there to receive them, had disappointed her was hard to say, but Victoria felt quite deflated.

In the end she had to make two journeys, one with the milk jugs, and the next for bread, sausages and a few other items, and still no sign of the dratted man. Yet there was this inexplicable sense of dissatisfaction. It would have done him good, she thought, to realise that she was not one of those girls without self-respect, who would dally with a married man, even if he were the most handsome man on the earth.

Another thought occurred to her, and she began to worry that Clara, that is Mrs. Hughes, she corrected herself, entertained the idea that she, Victoria, had encouraged the woman's husband to flirt with her and hoped that it was not so.

Suddenly Victoria came to a stop. Was she being vain in thinking that she alone was the object of the man's attention? Perhaps there were others of whom his wife was suspicious. Then again, perhaps the poor young woman was suffering from a health problem. Victoria's soft heart went out to Mrs. Hughes, for whatever the problem really was, the grocer's wife did not look as if she was enjoying life very much.

Victoria made a decision; she would continue behaving towards Mr. Hughes exactly as her mother reminded her she should, but she would act warmer towards his wife. After all, Victoria reminded herself, it would not take any effort on her part to be sympathetic towards the man's wife, for she was really sorry for the young woman. With her mind made up she went happily into the hut.

With her brother laid low by his headache, Victoria realised that it was she who would have to collect Peter from school. The walk did not trouble her, it was the thoughts of having to walk up the lonely lane alone. Still, she could not expect her mother to go, she had enough to do in finishing the washing.

As it turned out, her brother awoke feeling much better, and came downstairs wondering aloud if there was anything to eat. Victoria was so relieved at seeing him more like his usual self that she sat him down and willingly made him some toast and a drink of tea.

Beth also had been concerned about her daughter going into the town on her own, and suggested that brother and sister walk up together seeing that the washing was almost finished, adding that a walk in the fresh air would do Will a world of good.

Just as Will and Victoria left the hut, Robbie the apprentice came galloping up the street towards them. "Hello, Robbie," Will called. "If you have come to see our dad, he is next door with Michael." The panting boy did not attempt to reply; he just acknowledged the greeting with a wave of his hand. Will grinned; he could not say for certain, but the boiler-suited youth, red-faced from his exertions, seemed to have gone even more red when Victoria smiled at him!

Leaving the apprentice knocking at Mr. Robbins's front door, brother and sister set off chatting companionably towards the town. The last time that they had been alone and able to talk freely was on the day when Captain Rodgerson had tried to force himself on Victoria, and they had both missed those sibling conversations. Over the years, Will had been able to talk to his sister about things that mystified or bothered him, and he had always felt better for her advice or even for just letting him express his feelings.

Within a short distance from the village, they had naturally got onto the subject of their mother's state of mind regarding the place in which they were now living. One thing that they both agreed on was that they had to do as much as they could to ease the burden for her, and they also both agreed that Mrs. Robbins was proving over and over again to be a rock for the family.

"The problem is having to live in the hut," said Victoria, and Will nodded, "or to be more exact, the place itself, but even so, I think we could be in a lot worse place than the hut we live in." Again her brother nodded and added, "The trouble is, Victoria, that our dad never seems to have time to go and look round Frodsham for a house."

Victoria nodded glumly and they walked on silently, each with their own thoughts, then Victoria broke the silence by saying slowly, "Do you think we could enquire about houses to let?" Will shrugged his shoulders and said, "Well, I think it is worth a try, though whether anybody with a house to let would talk business with us, I am not so sure." Then he brightened and said, "Well, Mam would be pleased to think that we did at least have a try." With that they decided to try at the Post Office before they went to collect Peter.

Their hopes were dashed almost immediately after they had spoken to the postmistress. She told them that there were few places to be had in Frodsham, but mentioned a family house in Church Street which she thought was up for rent. When her two young enquirers' faces broke into delighted smiles, she shook her head regretfully and said, "I do not think the lady or her husband would rent to your parents if they have anything to do with the navies," then she asked, "you are from Marshville, are you not?"

The deflated pair acknowledged the truth of the lady's observation, but Victoria defended her father by putting the postmistress straight and said, "Our father is not a navvy, he is in charge of an engineering workshop at Marshville."

The postmistress smiled sympathetically but shook her head and said, "I am sure your father must be a very good class of person, but there are many people in the town who are unhappy at the disruption caused by the building of the canal." She hesitated at that point, wondering if she had been unwise to have said so much to these young people. "I think that the local people tend to favour local people." At that point, a customer came up to the counter and the postmistress said, "Do you mind if I serve this lady?" and as they turned to leave the shop she called, "if you wait a few moments, I will give you the address." Victoria then remembered her mother saying that she needed some postage stamps so that she could send letters to the Anderns, Mrs. Rodgerson and Mary, so she was glad that the postmistress had called them back.

After they had obtained the address and the stamps, they walked to the school and waited outside for Peter to come out, and when he did so, they were delighted to see that he was with a small group of friends, and they were all chattering nineteen to the dozen.

"Victoria," said Will, "it looks like that makes two of the family who have settled in at Frodsham." His sister smiled and answered, "I believe we will all settle in eventually, even Mam," but she added in a more serious tone, "That will depend on how soon we find a house here or somewhere near the town."

At that moment Peter noticed them and dashed over to show them off to his new friends. Just as the children were getting over their shyness and starting to tell Victoria and Will about themselves, a stern-faced young woman came over to them, wanting to know who they were. The children instantly became silent, with the exception of Peter, who proudly said, "Miss Bryant, this is my brother Will and my sister Victoria." Then he added shyly, "Miss Bryant is my favourite teacher."

The young teacher's frosty look disappeared and her lips twitched as she tried to suppress a smile. She said to the children, "Now say goodbye to Peter, then go and play." As his friends chimed out their goodbyes, Miss Bryant turned back to Victoria and Will and said with a smile, "With such a charming manner, I would not be in the least bit surprised if this young man became a politician."

Will and Peter were a bit mystified by the remark but Victoria joined in with Miss Bryant's laughter. The teacher then asked them how they were settling in, and when they had covered certain aspects of their new life, Will told her of their hopes regarding renting a house. Miss Bryant frowned and shook her head slightly, then more or less repeated what the postmistress had told them.

Eventually they left to walk Peter home. Victoria had changed her mind about the advisability of calling on the people who were letting the house, and Will agreed that it would be better if their parents did it themselves.

When they reached the hut, Mrs. Robbins was taking the men's midday meal into them whilst Beth was setting out the plates ready for the family's meal. Victoria and her brother could hardly wait to tell their mother about the house. Beth became very enthusiastic and decided that as soon as they had all eaten, she would go next door and tell her husband all about it.

When told, Thomas decided that they would visit the householder as soon as possible, for as he said, his employer had forbidden them from being in the workshop but had not banned them from visiting the town. As it was, Captain Howard called soon after his foreman had learned of the house, and when Thomas mentioned it to him, he promptly suggested that if he, Thomas, felt well enough to walk into town, he should pursue the matter promptly.

With that, Victoria and Mrs. Robbins volunteered to finish what little remained of the washing, so Thomas and Beth dressed in their best and eagerly set off for Frodsham. Peter was obviously tired and his mother had let him go for an afternoon nap. Will, having been told that he was not needed, wandered over to see Mr. Hughes and was promptly put to work, but only on the understanding, that he be paid for it.

It was an odd situation: whilst his parents were delighted with the prospect of having a house in the town, Will was experiencing doubts as to whether he wanted to leave Marshville. For his mother's and Victoria's sake, he hoped that they would be successful, yet he himself had settled in the hutted village. What he had seen of the excavation and all that went with it, he found very exciting. He was not sure that the tame life in Frodsham would suit him; besides, he enjoyed working for Mr. Hughes.

His sister also felt unsettled about it all, but she could not explain why. Like Will she realised that her mother needed to get out of this dreary place and yet at least there was the wonderful Mrs. Robbins, who was such a help to them all. She could not visualise her mother finding such a friendly neighbour in the town, a town where they were finding that so many of the people resented anybody working on the canal contract. Of course, thought Victoria as she finished hanging the last of the washing, she would not have the disagreeable business of having to call at that man's shop again. Even out of the shop it was difficult not to bump into him somehow or other. Yet even that cheery thought did nothing to lift her out of the odd mood she was in.

Mrs. Robbins was also less cheered by the thoughts of her new friend moving. In one way she was pleased that there was a possibility Beth would get the house, for after all it did not necessarily mean that the friendship would end merely by the fact that they would be living some distance away. Making real friends had always been a problem living the sort of life which she and Mr. Robbins had lived all these years, and people like the Banhams were not often met on construction sites.

Over the years she had lived in all types of accommodation, some better, some worse than Marshville. It was a fact though that she had never felt at ease with any of her previous neighbours as she had with the Banham family.

There was plenty of time for Thomas and Beth to get to the town, see about the house and get back before Dr. Mills called, but they were so pleased to have learned that there actually was a house for rent in Frodsham that they managed to get there in just over twenty minutes.

The door was opened by a cheery young woman who, on hearing their business, said, "Oh, you are interested in Granddad's old house, I'll get my mother." With that she swiftly went down the hall and disappeared through a doorway at the end. A prosperous-looking woman, a few years older than the Banhams, appeared and was about to ask them in, then on glancing at Thomas's black eye and his stitches, set herself to conduct her business on the doorstep.

When Thomas enquired about the house, it was patently obvious that the woman did not want them to have it. As he spoke, his Norfolk accent told her that he was not a local and, as such, that made him one of the contractor's men. Her smile disappeared and her mouth tightened. Before Thomas had spoken more than a dozen words the woman suddenly said, "The rent is one pound and five shillings a week and I want four weeks rent in advance." Then she added, "The rent is collected every Friday and I do not allow a tenant to get into arrears."

Beth was so affronted by the woman's attitude that she was stuck for words. Thomas, on the other hand, was more angry than affronted, but when he spoke there was no hint in his manner which showed his true feelings. Instead he said evenly to the woman, "I am sorry to have to have bothered you, Mrs. Dyson, but the terms are much more than I can afford, so I bid you good day." With that he nodded his head to her and tucking his wife's arm in his, he turned and walked back down Church Road. He could feel Beth's hand trembling on his arm, and he himself was seething with rage.

Before they had gone very far down the road, Beth could not contain herself any longer, and said in a fierce undertone, "That horrible woman, I could have slapped her face, how dare she be so rude to perfect strangers." Then she snapped angrily, "She did not want us to have that house, it was as plain as day." In this vein she carried on for quite a distance before she fell silent.

Thomas's anger had abated somewhat, then he recalled what Captain Howard had told him about the reluctance of some Frodsham people to let their houses to the contract employees and he realised that they had just met one of those people.

He was really sorry for his wife; he knew just how much the thoughts of living in a proper house meant to her. His only desire right then was to lift her out of the trough of despondency into which she had fallen. He tried to console her with the assurance that there would be other houses to look at from time to time. However, Beth had now seen a house which she thought was perfect, even though she had not been inside the hall, never mind inside the rest of the house, and it upset her that she could not have it simply because the woman was prejudiced.

It was a pity that they had found out about it, he thought sadly; it was better being only partially happy in ignorance, than being really unhappy and knowing what you cannot have. However, he had realised from the beginning just how troublesome it would be for himself to live away from Marshville; it would have meant that to start his working day, he would have to get up half an hour earlier in order to reach the depot at the proper time. Also he would be half an hour later reaching his home at the end of the day. Another problem that loomed large in his capacity as foreman fitter was the necessity of being quickly available whenever there was a mechanical breakdown.

All these thoughts flashed through his mind but even so, he knew that if another house came up for rent, he would chase after it for Beth's sake.

When they reached their humble abode, they learned that several people had called to see how Thomas and Michael were progressing. These simple thoughtful gestures did go in some way to lift Beth's spirits. As she said later to her family, there was so much kindness shown here in Marshville.

The doctor arrived in his trap at about four o'clock accompanied by his daughter. Whilst he examined both men, Beth put the kettle on for tea. Sarah elected to sit with Victoria on the box which Will and Peter normally used as a seat. Both girls were on the shy side, yet they were finding it so easy to converse with each other. Lately Victoria had longed for somebody whom she could open her heart to. All through her life she had been able to talk things over with her mother, but now there were times when she felt too embarrassed to expose her innermost thoughts to anybody, especially to members of her family.

The examination of the men did not take more than a few minutes and Dr. Mills pronounced both men fit for work, but told Thomas that he would have to wait a few more days before he could have the stitches on his eyebrow removed.

Beth asked the doctor and Sarah if they would share the pot of tea with them, and the offer was accepted, Dr. Mills being especially pleased, for he was intrigued by the Banham family. He, like many others was curious about what circumstances had brought people like them to such a godforsaken place, as he termed it, like this hutted settlement.

He had observed them closely the first time he had been called here, and at the time he had been impressed by the genteel manner in which they conducted themselves. Although he had not been in contact with many of the navvies and other workers from the canal contract, he had on some occasions attended their wives and families. The hard life and the almost nomadic existence was etched on their faces. One noticeable feature, however, that had not escaped his eyes was that he had not seen many undernourished children amongst them.

The faces of these people bore a hard look, the look often associated with people like gypsies, tinkers and others living at the edge of civilised society. He knew, however, that they were mostly decent and honest people with a strong bond of loyalty to their employers and to each other.

It was the absence of this hard look on the faces of the Banham family which told Dr. Mills that they were out of their usual environment.

As a doctor, he had noticed the signs of strain on Mrs. Banham's face, but in spite of that he saw that she was a very attractive woman with the complexion of someone much younger. When she relaxed and smiled, he could see where her daughter had got her beauty from. Even the boy, Will, was blessed with a fine facial bone structure. With that and a fresh, healthy complexion, the boy was just as attractive as the women of the family.

Thomas Banham interested Dr. Mills very much. A good-looking and strongly built man, his easy manner of speech coupled with his moderated Norfolk vowels could easily give anyone less observant than the doctor the impression that the man was an amiable rustic. A few moments in conversation with the man soon dispelled that notion. Later, when they were sitting at the table talking, Dr. Mills was to discover that his patient was a man who cut straight to the core of any discussion, would not be budged from his position when he was sure of his facts, yet was not afraid to admit his ignorance.

What started as a general discussion about the building of the canal and the methods used to accomplish it became a difference of opinion about whether it would actually be finished. On one hand was Dr. Mills, who followed the line of the majority of the Liverpool interests, and declared that the scheme would never be completed. He had heard that there were about seventeen thousand men and boys employed, and also there were hundreds of items of steam-driven machines at work, all using huge amounts of coal for the boilers. He then added that it was the opinion of many knowledgeable people that the promoters of the canal would simply run out of money.

Thomas laughed and replied, "Now, Dr. Mills, that sounds like a quote from either the *Liverpool Courier* or the *Liverpool Daily Post*, and I think it is only natural that they would pour scorn on any scheme which offered their city any competition."

His opponent swiftly riposted, quoting the *Times* newspaper, which loftily expressed the view that a second port was not necessary. To which Thomas replied, "Well, sir, if Manchester had been treated fairly, I would agree with the *Times*, but the decision to build the waterway to Manchester and Salford was taken by hard-headed businessmen because of the greed and arrogance of the Mersey Docks Company and the London and North Western Railway Company."

"Ah yes, Mr. Banham," the doctor countered, "but think of all the investment needed to keep a great port like Liverpool running smoothly, not to mention the costs incurred in running a railway system. Surely even hard-headed businessmen know that an efficient and reliable system of transport cannot be run on the cheap?"

Thomas said quietly, "Do you know how much it costs to carry goods from America to Liverpool, Dr. Mills?" When the medical man shook his head, Thomas quoted, "Six pence per ton for about three thousand miles, and to pass through the Port of Liverpool and to be carried just over thirty-one miles to Manchester costs one shilling and sixpence per ton." He paused and looked quizzically at the doctor, who was looking quite impressed in spite of himself, and continued, "That, by my rough calculation, makes the shorter journey three hundred times more costly per mile per ton than the longer one."

Even the doctor conceded it that was excessive but, not to be beaten, then changed his tack. "Whatever the reasons for building the canal, Mr. Banham, I find it difficult to believe that such a grandiose scheme could be completed. There are so many complicated engineering works to be constructed; has your Mr. Walker enough experience or expertise to tackle them?" he asked, half in jest.

Thomas was not quite sure whether the doctor was doubting the capability of the artisans or whether he was questioning the engineers who had designed the whole scheme, but he was stung enough to reply that the work when completed would stand the test of time.

Michael, who had been listening with a smile of appreciation at his foreman's grasp of the facts, and his adroit handling of the doctor's assertions, also felt his hackles rise. An attack on any of the people working on the scheme was almost like an attack on his own capabilities.

Before Thomas could frame a reply, Michael said to Dr. Mills, "I would say, sir, that there is no shortage of able men involved in the planning or the execution of work, and furthermore the well found and stoutly built masonry of Eastham Locks bears testimony to this." Then he continued, "The size of the locks is well able to take large ocean-going ships; there would no problem on that score, sir."

Dr. Mills held up his hand in a placatory gesture and addressing both men said, "I do apologise, Mr. Banham, Mr. Rourke, it was not my intention to cast doubts on those who work on the construction or any of the tradesmen supporting them; my doubts are more to do with those who have dreamed up the scheme." He halted there as he marshalled his thoughts to put into words, his reasons for doubting the wisdom of the project, without offending the men before him.

When he did speak, he did so in a more serious tone of voice, and he began by saying, "There are several reasons that I will put before you which express my belief that the promoters have bitten off more than they can chew." He held up his hand and with one finger raised he continued, "First is the unknown nature of what will be encountered when the cutting gets deeper; will there be more rock exposed, creating extra expense for it to be removed?" He paused and then said, "That is just one example which I will mention, but there are sure to be other unexpected problems."

Both Thomas and Michael nodded in agreement but stayed silent, allowing the doctor to develop his argument.

Dr. Mills held up a second finger and said, "Then there is Mother Nature, a force that can wreck even the best laid plans of Man." He looked enquiringly at the men and asked them, "Have you seen the river in motion due to the effects of the westerly gales?"

The men shook their heads but still said nothing to interrupt the doctor's dissertation, so he proceeded to tell them about the very large waves which would pound the shore on this side of the river, sometimes causing serious flooding. "Indeed," he said, "there was the breach at Ince in October this year."

The doctor spoke again and observed, "When I saw the line of piling being driven in the river bed from Frodsham Score to Stanlow Point, I could not see how filling in between them with soil to form an embankment would be sufficient to withstand those savage waves, and in that I was proved correct."

Dr. Mills, who obviously knew the local conditions created by the river's moods, was to see some of his prophecies come true. However, it was not so much the tidal section which was to suffer, but mostly the non-tidal inland sections of the River Mersey and the River Irwell.

He then made his third point. "From all accounts," he said quietly, "the scheme has been financed by the cities of Manchester and Salford, helped by most of the surrounding towns, and even by money raised from ordinary working people." He paused and shook his head in admiration at such staunch support, then carried on to reach the crux of his argument.

"The problem as I see it is that when the promoters realise that more money is needed to carry on, there will less eagerness amongst the merchants and ordinary people to risk more of their hard-earned brass in a scheme which would appear to have not been costed out properly from the outset."

Thomas was the first to answer the doctor, and he began by saying slowly, "I can see the sense in all you have said, and we can but hope that your forecast of extreme weather will not be realised, but I am sure that the engineers who have drawn the scheme will have allowed for such conditions." Then he spoke of the man who was in charge of the construction.

"The whole contract," he said, "has been let to one of the most able and," he added as an aside, "the most humane men in this sort of business, a man who was responsible for the building of Dover Harbour, the Severn Railway tunnel, Barry Docks and Penarth Docks."

He asked Dr. Mills if he had been near enough to the works to notice the letters TAW painted on the sides of the railway wagons?

He added, “Those letters stand for Thomas Andrew Walker, a man whom the more I learn about, the more I admire.”

He then proceeded to give his audience, including Michael, the details of how the scheme had been divided into nine sections, which were now altered to eight sections, each with its own engineer. Subcontractors were employed in a specialist capacity. The subcontractor for whom Thomas and Michael worked was Captain Howard.

“So you see, Dr. Mills, the problems or, as you point out, natural disasters would be dealt with by the engineer in charge of the section affected, and would not disturb the other sections.”

Dr. Mills was very impressed by Thomas’s knowledge and said so. Thomas laughed and replied, “I have a confession to make. Until I entered the home of Mr. and Mrs. Robbins earlier today, I had less knowledge of The Manchester Ship Canal scheme than you, sir.” He smiled and added, “Mr. Robbins has a veritable library of booklets, pamphlets and newspaper cuttings, all dealing with the scheme and the main people involved.” He added admiringly, “Mr. Robbins is a very well-read man.” At that point, Michael nodded his head in agreement.

“Well,” said Dr. Mills, laughing, “I must say that I too have learned something today, and I would not begrudge the Canal promoters success in their aims, but,” he added, with a twinkle in his eye, “while I now believe that your cutting will connect Manchester to the sea, I reiterate, that when the well-meaning promoters run out of money, the excavation will not have been cut deep enough to take sea-going vessels.” Then he added magnanimously, “It might be deep enough to accommodate quite large barges.” They all laughed at that, and agreed to disagree.

Dr. Mills rose and shook hands with Thomas and Michael, then turning to Beth, thanked her for the refreshments. Beth blushed with pleasure and was surprised to realise that she had been so interested in the lively discussion just ended, that the feeling of embarrassment at the presence of Dr. Mills and his daughter had quite disappeared. When they had entered the hut the previous day, she had been acutely conscious of the spartan conditions in which the family lived, but the relaxed way with which they shared tea and conversation made their humble surroundings seem less important.

Although Beth still stood in awe of both Dr. Mills and Captain Howard, she was not so bothered now at them visiting as she had been previously.

As the doctor was making arrangements for removing Thomas’s stitches, Peter came downstairs, said hello to his parents and Dr. Mills, then went straight over to Sarah and introduced himself to her. Sarah gave him a hug and within minutes she had heard all about the school and his new friends, the engine and the steam crane which he could see from his bedroom window, and how worried he was about his dad’s eye.

Dr. Mills smiled broadly at Thomas and Beth, and asked them if there were any more children hidden away. They both laughed and Beth said, “Oh no, Peter is our youngest, but by the look of it, the boldest.” Then she said jokingly, “He has only been at Frodsham Infants School two mornings, and already he says he has made a special friend, and it is a little girl!”

When eventually the doctor and his daughter drove out of the village, dusk was well advanced. The family saw them on their way, Peter having kissed Sarah, and stood outside with the others as they waved goodbye.

Beth was especially pleased with the growing friendship between her daughter and Sarah. During the visit, Victoria had regained much of her normal vivacity, and it had been obvious that the older girl had also enjoyed herself.

A short while before Clarence arrived back from his work, Will came in and, after asking what the doctor had said about his father's injury, sat and played a game with Peter. Victoria, noticing how jaunty her brother had been when he had come in, asked him what he had been doing at the grocer's. He told her that they had both been very busy. They had been cleaning much of the shelf space, rearranging things and then stacking the fresh produce. "I enjoy working with Mr. Hughes," Will said. "He tells me so much about the things he stocks." Then he said in a wondering voice, "I never thought there was so much to learn about foods and other things that are sold in the shop."

He turned to his mother and asked, "Do you think it would be alright if I went back after we have had our meal to serve in the shop? Mr. Hughes has got a lot of work to catch up with and he said it would help him a lot if you could spare me for an hour or so." Beth did not object, but she knew that her husband wanted to talk to Will, so she said, "I cannot see that your dad would object to your helping at the shop, but he does want to talk to you about getting a job." Will was delighted; the fact that he was not earning his keep had been weighing heavily on him more and more as time went by.

After the men had eaten, Thomas sat at the table whilst the family had their meal. When they were enjoying a cup of tea, he broached the subject of a job for Will.

He began by explaining to his son that soon after starting at the depot, he had been asking around to ascertain whether any apprentices were needed. Very little had come to light about such jobs, but Robbie the apprentice, being born and bred in Frodsham, had heard of one firm needing a boy to serve his time as a plumber's apprentice.

"You know, Will," said his father, very seriously, "it has been troubling me for a long time now, trying to find you a job which will have good future prospects, and as you know only too well, in Wroxing and the surrounding area, there was no work." He continued in the same vein. "But I say this to you, son, whatever comes along, even if I think it is a good job, if you find that you do not like it after giving it a fair trial, you do not have to suffer in silence." He told Will, "You must not be afraid to talk about things that bother you."

Then changing the subject, he answered Will's earlier question to his mother. He and Beth found Mr. Hughes a very agreeable young man and they were happy enough to let their son work with the man. They told him, however, that he must be back in a reasonable time. With that, Will went across to the shop.

The following two days went by without any news of the plumber's apprenticeship, but on the Friday morning, Robbie told Thomas that the job had gone to a fourteen-year-old local boy, and added that there was no other boy needed. It was a blow to Thomas but he had to agree, the firm was quite right to prefer a boy who would be able to serve his full seven years apprenticeship.

Will was quite upset. He had been really bucked to think he would soon be earning some money for the household; but for the small wage he earned through helping at the shop, he would have become totally fed up. There was also a much deeper reason for wanting a full-time job; his self-respect was suffering. He would have taken any work to be able to hold his head up high. However, when he did get a job, it turned out to be more of a punishment than a pleasure.

Chapter 15

A Christmas to Remember

'In just over two weeks it will be Christmas Day, and I have so little money to buy any of them a gift.' So thought Will as he slumped dejectedly at the table. He desperately wanted to make it a really happy day, particularly for his mother and Victoria.

What he used to call his spends, his father now referred to as an allowance, and normally what he was given was more than enough for his needs. That which he earned at the shop he gave to his mother, and although he wanted her to take it all, Beth insisted that he received part of it back.

Even so, the number of people for whom he wanted to buy a gift had grown in the last few days. Two or three weeks ago it had been had just something for each member of his family, but his mental list now included Michael and Clarence, and also Mr. and Mrs. Robbins Then he had got to know Mr. Hughes, and he would could not leave out Clara. He had a soft spot for the straight-faced young woman, and he thought she liked him in return. She was not really as sad as she looked, it was just her way.

Peter's gift was the easiest one, and was almost ready. It was a toy crane similar to the real one which sometimes could be seen from the bedroom windows at the back of the hut. His dad had been making it whenever he had the odd moment to spare, but the final painting and assembly was to be done by Will.

It was odd really; Will was very adept at making things, in that way he was like his father, and he actually enjoyed putting his skills to good use, but he had no urge to follow in his father's footsteps regarding engineering. In fact he had no fixed idea of what trade he would like to serve an apprenticeship in.

What he wanted was to be able to contribute towards the housekeeping, and at the same time to start saving some money for the future. The present, however, was uppermost in his mind, and he decided that when he got a chance he would speak to Mr. Hughes about ideas for gifts. Obviously he would have to be careful how he approached the subject; he did not want to give even the slightest hint to the shopkeeper that he was planning to give him a gift.

When he next went to the shop he broached the subject and was immediately given one valuable piece of advice. "Do not let the fact that you cannot afford expensive gifts deter you from giving, Will," Mr. Hughes told him. "The old saying 'it is better to give than to receive' has a lot of truth in it," he continued, "but the giving of even the smallest of gifts, when given with love, gives the greatest pleasure to the receiver."

Then he laughed and said, "I know that sounds very much like a sermon, Will, but seriously it is the truth, and if you follow those principles, you will get a lot of enjoyment out of giving."

Will was very impressed by the shopkeeper's almost Biblical-sounding words of wisdom and took heart from them. He then told Mr. Hughes exactly how much he had saved, after which he was presented with several suggestions for modestly priced gifts which would please the ladies. The shopkeeper promised his sometimes-helper that when he had made out his list, then he, Mr. Hughes would get them for him.

That left the problem of what to get for his father. He knew two of his dad's favourite likes, tools and books. However, the cost of any item of those categories would be more than he could afford, and also if he could have afforded such a gift, he would have to consult him if he was not going to duplicate any of them.

Mr. Hughes asked Will, "Does Mr. Banham smoke a pipe?" and added, "A good quality tobacco is much appreciated by a pipe smoker." The boy shook his head and explained that his dad had given up when they found that Peter suffered from asthma. The shopkeeper then suggested that Will consulted his mother about what to give his father and sister. Then he went on to say that it would be wiser if Will and Victoria were to share the cost of buying the gifts as it would give them a much wider choice.

Will was not to know that at the mention of Victoria's name coupled with the giving of gifts, Mr. Hughes was cast down a little. He also would have enjoyed giving a gift to the girl, but knew that with her frosty behaviour towards him, she would most probably send it back, and that would be absolutely humiliating.

It seemed that since the Banham family had arrived in Marshville, he was not enjoying much success with the women around him. Clara was even more short with him than usual, and he decided that if she carried on in the same way, he was going to ask her outright what was troubling her. It could make it very awkward for the family celebrations at Christmas, for he relied on Clara during the festivities.

The following day, Will got word through Robbie of another job in the town, and at half past eight in the morning, he hurried off to Frodsham. He was really buoyed up with hope. Apart from gaining employment, he would possibly be able to afford to make it a really happy Christmas for them all.

The eager boy found the premises easily enough but was shocked by what greeted him. Although he had been told that the place was a battery manufactory, he had not bargained for the awful conditions in which the men were working.

Everywhere were puddles of water, or something he could not put a name to. The benches and the lower part of the walls were covered in a yellow crust, and the tattered working aprons worn by the men were full of holes as though they were rotted. There was also an acrid atmosphere which caught Will's throat even though he was out in the open air of the filthy yard.

Before he had even spoken to anybody in the ramshackle building, Will knew that this was not a good place in which to work, and he made his way out of the yard, glad to be out of the place.

When he got back to their hut, he decided to wash his shoes. He had no idea what the liquid was which he had splashed about in, but he suspected that it was not just water. Later when he recounted his experiences to his father and Michael, they both agreed if it had been water, it probably bore a certain amount of sulphuric acid. He was given a pat on the back for having the sense to wash his shoes right away.

The following day he managed to have a talk with Victoria about Christmas gifts and as it happened his sister had been trying to get Will alone for the same purpose. One thing on which they both agreed was that they should buy their gifts jointly, for as the grocer had said, it would give them a wider choice, and allow them to give their parents something a little more expensive.

When her brother mentioned his talk with Mr. Hughes, her face set slightly, but after he had come out with the man's suggestions, she had grudgingly admitted that she thought that he some good ideas.

Between them they could afford the gifts suggested by the shopkeeper, but Will realised that he would have to earn a few shillings more if they were to buy the other gifts he had in mind.

Victoria remembered the Christmases when Mr. and Mrs. Serle owned Longfields Estate. Reeve House would be decorated and brightly lit, and there was always a servant's party, where Mr. and Mrs. Serle, aided by the butler and the housekeeper, served the meals and gave gifts.

Her thoughts turned to Mrs. Rodgerson having to put up with that evil beast of a husband, and Victoria's heart went out to her late mistress. She hoped that the young Mr. Prentice and his wife would be there, or perhaps Mrs. Rodgerson would go to her parents' house for Christmas.

At least, she thought, here at Marshville, as bad as things were, the Banhams were all together, a close and loving family.

Chapter 16

Captain Rodgerson Brings Matters to a Head

The atmosphere at Reeve House was much more light-hearted with the approach of Christmas, mainly due to the presence of Kate's brother James and his wife, Charlotte. There was also the fact that Captain Howard was away, whilst Cecelia was staying at their parents' house until after the New Year.

There was also a noticeable difference amongst the servants. It was a refreshing change to come across a member of the staff humming a tune whilst they were working, smiling faces were more in evidence and laughter was heard in the servants' hall. Each time Captain Rodgerson and Mrs. Howard were away from Reeve House, the oppressive atmosphere which usually enveloped everyone whilst they were in residence lifted and did not return until one or both of them came back.

After dinner that evening, Charlotte had entertained them with her piano playing and although she was at best no more than competent on the instrument, the three of them were enjoying themselves enormously. Into this happy interlude strode Captain Rodgerson and even the least discerning person would have seen that he was in a foul mood.

Charlotte closed the lid of the piano and joined her husband on the settee. Kate rose and said to her husband, "I will instruct Cook to prepare your dinner, Captain Rodgerson." He ignored her and walked over to the cabinet, from which he brought out a decanter and a goblet. However, before Kate had reached the door of the sitting room, he rasped, "That old fool Rigg let me in, so the kitchen should know by now that I expect my meal to be on the table before too long." His wife answered coolly, "Nevertheless, there are certain specific instructions which I must give to cook, so you must excuse me for a few minutes." This last part was directed at her brother and sister-in-law.

When Kate had left the room, Captain Rodgerson stood with his back towards the fire. Greedily he gulped down his brandy, which caused him to cough and splutter in a most ungentlemanly manner. When he caught his breath he glared at his brother-in-law and asked, "When are you leaving, Prentice?" Just as insolently James answered, "Well, Rodgerson, I was planning to leave tomorrow, but I hear that your carriage is still weary for want of an axle spring, so Mrs. Prentice and I are delaying our departure, then my sister can come with us to our parents' house." He then added easily but pointedly, "I am sure that my springs can just about manage to convey the three of us and our luggage without harm."

Included in his last sally was a subtle allusion to the fact that the estate was showing signs of the lack of the hand of Thomas Banham. To make things even more difficult for the Rodgersons, the local tradesmen were reluctant to take on any work for Captain Rodgerson. This was especially true when it came to the Wroxing village blacksmith, Simon Andern, who would only take on work for the Longfields Estate if the request came from Mrs. Rodgerson herself.

Eventually Kate returned and informed her husband that the table would be ready for him in twenty minutes' time. By the time Rigg the butler came in and announced that dinner was ready to be served, Captain Rodgerson had consumed several more brandies and was in an even more truculent mood. Before the man had eaten half of his meal, he was back in the sitting room, having left the maids in tears and Rigg wishing that the man would choke on his food.

The root cause of Captain Rodgerson's temper was Cecelia. She had accepted an invitation for a theatre outing and an intimate supper with another man, a younger man and a Right Honourable to boot. Captain Rodgerson knew she was a trollop but for long enough he had closed his eyes to her other affaires, secure with the knowledge that in time she would be his again as soon as they had run their course. However, this affaire had all the signs of being a protracted one.

He had left London in a towering rage and then, on his return, to find his supercilious brother-in-law, as he saw him, sprawling comfortably in his house, sent him into a even worse temper. However, one thing he had learned early on in his dealings with James Prentice was to not get involved in a verbal fencing match with the younger man. He always ended a discussion or an argument with him feeling extremely foolish or inadequate.

Captain Rodgerson contented himself with standing in front of the fireplace, blocking the warmth and the comforting sight of the burning coals from the others. His eyes kept sliding over to Charlotte whenever her husband was not looking, giving her a most disagreeable feeling.

'My God,' he thought, 'she is not a patch on Cecelia for looks, but if that fool Prentice were not here I would soon bring her round to my way of thinking.' Then when Kate returned, he switched his attention to her. She was quite aware of his glance but simply ignored him and returned to their earlier conversation.

Her husband's thoughts began to run on new lines. He normally did not give her a second glance, but in the absence of her sister she was better than nothing. Scrawny as a cat he had called her when he was with Cecelia, but now observing Kate, he was seeing her in a new light. 'Why,' he thought, 'she looks very womanly, even her movements are exciting.' He felt his pulse quickening and he thought savagely, 'She is my wife, I own her and she has dodged her duties long enough.'

So his thoughts ran and though he did not realise it, much of it was showing naked on his face. Both James and Charlotte observed Captain Rodgerson's range of expressions and pretty accurately guessed what was in his mind.

Later in their room, a worried James told his wife how bothered he was about his brother-in-law's behaviour. "I know that in everybody's eyes they are man and wife, but I am sure from what we have seen over the years of the man's philanderings, and even more importantly, by Kate's attitude towards the brute, there is no marriage, possibly never has been, whatever the marriage certificate shows."

He paused, then instead of climbing into bed, he went over to the door, opened it a crack, then set himself down in a chair. Charlotte did not need to ask him what he was planning; she also was worried about what Kate's husband would do during the night, so without saying anything, she lowered the light on the lamp. As a woman she did not need to be told that there was no love in her sister-in-law's marriage; she had seen years earlier how much Kate loved Richard Howard. Charlotte also believed that he loved dear Kate, but by the code he lived his life, he would never compromise her or himself by openly admitting it.

In her own room, Kate was in her nightdress and ready for bed, whilst young Mary was putting the day dresses on hangers. Usually it was a time when she would amuse Kate with her chatter, but this night Mary sensed that all was not well, and limited herself to speaking only of immediate concerns.

Suddenly the door was flung open and Captain Rodgerson lurched into the room. Mistress and maid were so startled that for a few moments nothing was said. Then as Kate opened her mouth to remonstrate with him, he turned to Mary and said, "Get out, wench." The maid, her heart starting to pound, bravely stood her ground and answered politely, "I will just finish hanging these dresses straight, sir, then I will leave, sir." She was desperately trying to think of anything she might do to prolong her stay, for she had no intention of leaving her mistress alone with Captain Rodgerson, not with the state he was in.

Before she knew it, he seized her by the arm with such force that she cried out with pain. "I said get out," he roared, then flung her towards the open doorway. The helpless girl hurtled from his grasp but caught her head on the edge of the door and with a cry, dropped to the floor.

Kate, horrified at what had been done to the girl, screamed, "Mary," and went to run to her. Like a madman, her husband grabbed her and threw her onto the bed, tearing at her nightdress. The stitching at first held, causing the neck band to burn into her skin. He was yelling at her hoarsely, spittle flying from his mouth. "I own you woman, I own you, and you will give me my rights," and at the same time he was ripping the nightdress off her.

Her brother had reacted as soon as he heard the first scream, and he raced along the landing to Kate's room. When he saw what was happening, he went for Captain Rodgerson like a crazed bull. Yelling, he dragged him away from her then drove a punch to the man's jaw. All the hate he had for the brute, coupled with the thoughts of the humiliation that his sister had been forced to endure, went into the punch.

Captain Rodgerson hit the floor like a poleaxed beast, and James left him lying there senseless and turned to his hysterical sister. He snatched up her dressing gown and wrapped it round her then pulled her close to him while he tried to calm her down.

Charlotte had followed almost on the heels of her husband and was kneeling by Mary who was weeping quietly.

Another figure appeared in the open doorway; it was Johnson, Captain Rodgerson's man. James was the first to find his voice and asked the man to ring for Mrs. Higson, the housekeeper. "Ah, Johnson, when Mrs. Higson comes, give me a hand to get the Captain back to his room, will you?" he said evenly.

When Johnson had first looked into the room he had wondered just what had happened, then he saw the prone figure of his master and the way Mrs. Rodgerson and Mary were being comforted, and he then realised more or less what heinous deeds had been perpetrated by his employer. He was sickened by the images his imagination conjured up and wondered yet again why he remained working for a man who inflicted such misery on others, especially those who could not fight back.

Johnson was still deeply ashamed at not leaving Captain Rodgerson's employment after the way he had forced the Banham family out of work and home, but now he resolved that on the morrow he would hand in his notice to quit.

He went over to help Mrs. Prentice lift the maid up and get her into a chair. Poor Mary, he thought, she was such a cheerful girl, always helpful and not an ounce of malice in her. Savagely he wished it had been himself that had floored Captain Rodgerson. By the look of the way Mr. Prentice was being careful with his hand, it looked as if he had hurt himself in dealing with the Captain, and his high opinion of Mrs. Rodgerson's brother soared even higher.

Within a few minutes of being summoned, Mrs. Higson came to the room. In her housecoat and slippers, and with her hair enveloped in a voluminous head covering, she nevertheless still retained her air of authority and competence. She placed her candlestick on a table and went straight to Kate. She, like Johnson, had guessed something of what had happened and acted accordingly.

Mrs. Higson was a Cumbrian-born woman who, in her younger days, had worked as a nurse in the Crimean campaign, and there was not much people could teach her about the ways of men. Even so she was still shocked to think that the master of the house could so ill-use a young, pleasant girl like Mary in his temper, and whatever he had done, or attempted to do to Mrs. Rodgerson seemed to have been done with some force. The words in her mind to describe Captain Rodgerson might even shock men in the battlefield; they would certainly shock the Mistress and Mrs. Prentice.

However, none of this showed on her serene countenance as she went from Kate to attend to Mary. From the simple test she gave to the girl, there did not appear to be anything seriously wrong with her, although the large lump at the back of her head looked quite alarming.

In the meantime Johnson had obeyed instructions and had brought in some hot tea in which he added extra sugar. Kate grimaced a little when she tasted it but meekly did as she was told and drank the lot. There was no trouble from Mary; she simply wanted to crawl into her bed with no light to bother her.

Mrs. Higson had taken a look at Captain Rodgerson and was not overly concerned about him. She asked the men whether they could move him out of the room in order that she could see to Mrs. Rodgerson and Mary. "Oh, and by the way, Mr. Johnson, could you arrange for a warming pan for Mary's bed, please."

Johnson answered that he would see to it as soon as Captain Rodgerson was back in his room. He looked at James and asked him, "Excuse me, sir, would you be able to manage the Captain with your hand as it is?" James said dryly, "I do not think we have much choice, we cannot expect Rigg to do this sort of thing at his age; besides," he added thoughtfully, "the fewer people involved in tonight's troubles, the better."

It was an incongruous sight as James, clad in his nightshirt and shoeless, took hold of one of the unconscious man's arms whilst Johnson took the other, and they unceremoniously dragged him along the corridor and back to his own room.

Both men were panting by the time it was done, and James was thankful that the highly polished floor made things easier for them. Once there, Johnson, with the benefit of past experience, heaved Captain Rodgerson up and threw him on the bed.

"Thank you, sir," said Johnson, "I will manage the rest on my own now." After all, he thought, I have done it often enough over the years, "and this is the last time, Captain," he said in a low contemptuous voice as Mr. Prentice left the room.

Coming out of the bedroom ten minutes later, he almost collided with James, who was now fully dressed. It occurred to Johnson that Captain Rodgerson's brother was intending to spend the night on guard in the corridor and as that was also his intention, he did not see the point of both of them losing their sleep.

"Excuse me, sir," he said quietly, "I will be on guard, as you might call it, outside this door for the rest of the night, so if you are happy with arrangement, sir, you might as well retire to your bed."

James considered the man's suggestion, and although he was relieved that Rodgerson was not going to be free to roam, he felt that to calmly take to his bed and leave his sister and her maid unguarded was neglecting his duty. He therefore arranged for him to keep watch until three o clock when Johnson would take over the watch. This plan was agreed on and Johnson locked the Captain's door, then went down to heat a warming pan as requested.

When Kate and the housekeeper were told of the arrangement they were clearly relieved. Mrs. Higson excused herself for a few minutes whilst she went to her own room to get the medicines she needed. James sat on the edge of Kate's bed and held her hands. She was still trembling and at his comforting touch started weeping again.

He held her to him until her tears had stopped, then he said gently, "Why are you still putting up with the brute, Kate? I know, and I am sure that many others know, that there has never been a marriage." When she did not answer, he continued, "You have sufficient grounds for obtaining a divorce, you cannot deny that."

Kate went very still, then making sure that they were alone, said in an anguished voice, "Do you not think that I have longed to be rid of the man?" Still in a low voice she continued, "The grounds for having my marriage annulled are Captain Rodgerson's flagrant affair with, of all people, our sister Cecelia. James, I could not bring myself to embark on a course which would bring so much shame and humiliation to our parents." She then looked up at her brother, her eyes pleading for understanding, and told him, "For that very reason I allowed him to evict the Banhams without putting up a fight, and for that," she sobbed, "I have carried a terrible burden of guilt for months."

James was appalled to think that his dear, gentle sister was trapped in such a heartbreaking situation, but then suddenly he thought of something which could help her.

Some months earlier he had heard a bit of gossip which could possibly give her an extra weapon to use in the event of her petitioning for a divorce.

After a while Kate's sobbing subsided, and her brother said in a thoughtful voice, "You know, little sister, there is no need to even mention Cecelia's name if you did decide to get rid of the fellow. I will present you with another name, and it is Lucinda." He halted at that point, and seeing the puzzled expression which had appeared on Kate's face, laughed softly and continued, "I will not give you her married name, at least not yet, for you might not need to drag her name into the court, but it will suffice to say that her husband has a seat in the House of Lords, and that he is an exceptionally unforgiving man."

The conversation had to end there with the arrival of Mrs. Higson bearing a draught for Kate, a comfrey dressing for James's knuckles and witch hazel for Mary's head.

At first Kate resisted the draught, telling the housekeeper that she wanted to keep her eye on her maid. Eventually, after Mrs. Higson told her that she intended to fulfil that duty herself, she agreed to take it.

After the housekeeper had left the room, James decided to stay with his sister until she fell asleep. Just before Kate drifted off, she suddenly said in a whisper, "James, I have never before been frightened of that man, but I am now." As her brother made to assure her she murmured, "But tomorrow I will face him and give him an ultimatum, yes," she said drowsily, "I will," then James realised that Kate had succumbed to Mrs. Higson's draught and fallen asleep.

For a moment he did not stir; he was too upset by his sister's admission. He too was worried, for what he had witnessed this night had revealed another and more violent side to her husband's character.

Quietly he left the room after first lowering the flame of the lamp, and made his way along the unlit corridor carrying his candlestick.

True to his word, Johnson was seated outside Captain Rodgerson's room, and he was wearing his outdoor clothes and swathed in a blanket. The temperature along the corridor seemed only a few degrees above that outside the house.

"No sign of movement in there, sir," said Johnson in a low voice, "I hardly think the Captain will surface before dawn." Even in the subdued light cast by the candle, James could see the contempt for his master written plain on the man's face.

"Right, Johnson," said James, "I will get my outdoor clothes on and a blanket, then you can get yourself a few hours sleep until three o'clock." The other man nodded and James quietly went to his room to put on extra clothing, and also to set himself up with an oil lamp.

Half an hour after he had taken up his post, Mrs. Higson came along to check on her 'patients' and this she did at hourly intervals. On one of these visits, she brought him a very welcome drink of cocoa. When Johnson took up his duty, she did the same for him. It was certainly needed as the temperature dropped even more as the night wore on.

The following morning the house was buzzing with rumours. One of the maids lighting the downstairs rooms' fires had seen Mrs. Higson twice going upstairs earlier than usual. Then the upstairs maid had been in Mrs. Rodgerson's room to make up the fire, and saw that neither the Mistress or Mary were awake, a fact that had sent her scurrying to see the housekeeper in case there was something wrong with either of them. Also, she reported to the other maids, Mr. Johnson was sitting outside the Master's room looking like he had been there all night. When Mr. Prentice and his wife came down for breakfast, they looked as if they had not slept at all. To top it all, there was also a dressing wrapped around Mr. Prentice's hand. No wonder tongues were wagging.

Eventually Kate appeared at the breakfast table, but Mary was still abed at her mistress's insistence. It was obvious to Rigg and the maids that she was not at all well.

Within a few minutes of her sitting at the table, the sound of angry voices could be heard. There was no doubt whose voice was the loudest. Wearily Kate pushed her food to one side, then suddenly she came to a decision. 'I will put a stop to this,' she thought, 'the fool is making life intolerable for us all.'

By the time she had reached the hall, the shouting had stopped, but coming down the stairs was Johnson, and he was obviously in a very disturbed state.

When he caught sight of her, his face changed, and by the time he had reached the bottom of the stairs, he was already starting to apologise. Kate said, a little impatiently, "Do not apologise for something which is not your fault, Mr. Johnson, Captain Rodgerson should be the one to beg everyone's pardon."

Suddenly the distraught man burst out, "He has dismissed me, ma'am, Captain Rodgerson, and he refuses to pay me my wages," he said angrily. "He said that I was insolent and incompetent, and ma'am," he cried, "I have but a few shillings left to my name."

Kate was immediately sorry for her initial impatience with Johnson and sought to make amends by reassuring him that his wages would be paid to him before he left. She then had a thought. "I suppose that Captain Rodgerson has also refused to give you a reference for your next employer, Mr. Johnson?" she said.

She realised as soon as the words left her lips how foolish the question was, but Johnson showed no surprise at her words, and he answered by telling her simply that there would be no reference provided.

"How much are you owed, Mr. Johnson?" Kate asked him, and when he told her, she became very angry again. "Then you must not have been paid for weeks," she said. He told her. "Nine weeks and two days, ma'am."

"Well, Mr. Johnson," said Kate, "I will give you a reference, and I am sure that Mr. Prentice will also write one out for you when I ask him." Then changing the subject, she asked if he had eaten yet, and when the now much happier man shook his head, she suggested that he had his breakfast before it got any later.

After Johnson had left her, the thoroughly incensed Kate went to her sitting room, where she found James taking his ease with the *Times* newspaper. Charlotte was absent, so her brother was her only listener as she poured out her anger and frustration at yet another instance of Captain Rodgerson's inhuman treatment of those below him.

When she had got it off her chest, she then proceeded to tell her brother just what she had decided to do to rein in her husband's wild, destructive ways.

"What I am about to do will, to some extent, rely on my ability to bluff him, and knowing the man as I do, I know he will be in ignorance of some of the points that I will raise." Then she said, "The only thing I need to carry it off is to know you will be at hand should he turn violent."

Her brother looked alarmed at this and protested, "Now steady on, our Kate, you must not put yourself in danger; the fellow is like a loaded shotgun with a hair trigger." He stopped when his sister shook her head and explained, "He is only brave when he has got the upper hand over an employee or when his temper is fuelled by brandy."

James still looked unconvinced, and Kate explained further. "You will no doubt remember how upset I was when dear Aunt Phoebe bought this estate for us?" James nodded and waited for his sister to continue, and she said, "I found it hard to forgive her for interfering in my affairs when it forced me away from you all, and closer to him." The last part of the sentence was uttered with such loathing that James experienced a rush of sympathy for his unhappy sibling. He hoped fervently that whatever plan she was hatching would succeed and cause the brute to stay away from her. He realised that Kate was speaking again; she had started to describe how the estate was entailed.

"You see, James, for all Aunt Phoebe's romantic notions concerning my marriage, she was nevertheless wise enough about such things as to have a legal document drawn up by our family's solicitor, aided by Sir Henry, which would leave me occupancy of the estate if the marriage failed through no fault on my own part."

At this piece of information her brother sat up and whistled. "Good lord, Kate," he said, "you can pitch the devil out in two shakes of a lamb's tail if you divorce him." Then he subsided as once again his sister shook her head. She said quietly, "I cannot bring myself to instigate divorce proceedings for the same reason that stopped me before, and to destroy the marriage and reputation of this Lady Lucinda, whom I do not know, would be another blow to my self-respect."

James waited to hear what Kate had in mind which might bring Captain Rodgerson to heel and although doubtful of the chances of success of his sister's scheme, he agreed to support her whilst she tackled her husband.

"What I want you to do is this," Kate said. "When Captain Rodgerson comes to see me, you will excuse yourself and leave the room." Then she paused, and added, "Before he comes, make sure the anteroom door to the corridor is unlocked, then open the anteroom door to this room sufficient to be able to hear all that will be said." As an afterthought she said, "I must have a signal word that would summon you to my aid if it were needed."

"Door," said James, "that word would do, it would be very apt."

Kate clapped her hands and told her brother that the signal word would be perfect, then she summoned Rigg.

When the butler answered the bell, he was instructed to ask Captain Rodgerson if he would be so kind as to attend her in her sitting room.

Once Rigg had left the room, Kate's brother jokingly asked her to make sure that if the devil turned nasty, to arrange that the brute would be in a convenient position for James to hit him with his undamaged fist.

At one point during their wait, Charlotte entered the sitting room, but after a very condensed explanation of Kate's scheme, withdrew, announcing her intention of seeing Mrs. Higson to ask whether Mary would be able to have a visitor.

The time dragged on and just when they had come to the conclusion that Captain Rodgerson was ignoring Kate's request, the man walked into the room. James took great satisfaction in noting that the man's jaw was quite swollen. The look of hate he directed at his brother-in-law did nothing to spoil the moment for James.

He languidly rose to his feet and, excusing himself to his sister, he merely nodded to the glowering Captain Rodgerson and left the room, shutting the door firmly behind him.

Almost as soon as the door closed, Captain Rodgerson launched a verbal attack directed at her maid. "I want you to get rid of that insolent wench you call a maid," he said in his usual vicious manner. "I will not stand for any servant being insolent to me, so you had better dismiss her straight away."

Kate was so incensed that for a moment she could not speak, but when she did, it was if a dam had burst; she stormed at her hated husband with all the pent-up anger that had built up over the years.

"Dismiss my maid," she shouted. "Why that young girl is worth ten, nay fifty of you, and as for insolence, there is never insolence from Mary, she was merely doing her job last night, and for you to do what you did to her was nothing short of criminal."

By the way the expression on his face had changed, he obviously did not remember all he had done the night before. There had been a whole gamut of emotions shown as his wife was berating him: bad tempered arrogance, fury at his wife's choice of words, then uncertainty. As for the man himself, he had a horrible feeling that he was now in a very precarious position with regard to the maid.

Kate, quick to notice his change of manner, launched a second offensive on him before he could recover his mental balance. "If that young girl should not recover from the blow to the head," she said in a lower but more intense voice, "I will make it my business to see that you pay the full penalty in law." With a sombre note she added, "If she does not die but lives with her brain affected, you will suffer, I promise you."

Her initial rage had settled now to a cold anger but she was more in control of herself.

She noted with grim satisfaction the fear in his expression; her bluff seemed to be working and it gave her fresh confidence to continue.

Kate carried on before he had rallied his senses. "And as for your despicable behaviour towards me," she said coldly, "that has made me even more determined to shake off the shackles of this sham of a marriage; attempted rape with violence, even against a wife, is frowned upon in the eyes of the law and in society."

At this latest charge, Captain Rodgerson attempted to fight his way out of the situation by shouting her down. "You are my wife, dammit, and I have a right to you, I own you and don't you forget it, woman," he spat. "You hear. I own you."

In the anteroom, James listened with anger and distaste at what was being said, but also he was conscious of the uglier edge in Captain Rodgerson's voice, and he tensed himself ready to spring out should the man turn violent.

Kate, however, felt herself in full control of the situation and was deliberately playing the man before her like a fish on a hook. She let him rage for a few moments longer, just looking at him calmly, then spoke just one word which stopped him in mid rant. "Divorce," she said, clearly. "I have taken legal advice on instigating divorce proceedings, and our family solicitor tells me that I have ample grounds for taking such a course of action, and Sir Henry agrees with him."

For a moment there was silence as Kate's words sank into her husband's brain, then he said in an ugly voice, "If you are so sure of yourself, Madam, why have you not proceeded with your petition?" Gaining confidence at his wife's silence, he said with a sneer, "Or are your grounds for divorce not as strong as you would have me believe, eh?"

Kate remained unruffled at his childish jeering, and answered in the same cool, collected manner as before, saying, "When I approached the matter in the first place, a course of action, I might add, which I took as a direct result of your inhuman treatment of the Banham family…" Here he angrily tried to interrupt, but Kate carried on, disregarding his sneering comments, and said, "I was held back by the shame it would bring to my parents when their own daughter was cited as your mistress."

There was silence, and Captain Rodgerson behaved much as a small boy would when caught in somebody's orchard: he refused to meet his wife's eyes.

"You are a fool, Captain Rodgerson," Kate said contemptuously. "Do you really believe that I did not guess what was going on before my very eyes?" She laughed without humour and continued, "Why, most of the Norfolk society and half the London society know of your affaire and possibly your other liaison."

Kate stopped there to give him a chance to reply, but it was a few moments before he managed to think out a counter riposte. When he did speak he did not attempt to deny any of her accusations, but seizing on the subject of family shame, he said more confidently than he felt, "So, Mrs. Rodgerson, there will be no divorce proceedings, how very sensible of you." Then gaining more confidence by the moment he continued, "How very frustrating for you, my dear, you will just have to carry my name until your parents are no longer here to be shocked." He chuckled at his own wit, but was stopped by the smile that had appeared on his wife's face. Suddenly he had a nasty feeling that there were more unpleasant shocks to come.

"As I said a few moments ago," said Kate, "you are a fool, and an arrogant dishonourable fool at that. You believe that because I am reluctant to bring my family's name into disrepute, I would not enter into divorce proceedings?" She savoured her next thrust, and asked the now wary man sweetly, "Does the name Lucinda mean anything to you, Captain Rodgerson?"

The look of consternation on his face was all Kate needed to know that she was now totally in command of the situation.

"I will not mention her husband's name, sir, but you know as well as I do that he is a very proud man, proud of his seat in the House of Lords and proud of the ancient family name." Her husband did not attempt to comment on her knowledge of his affaire; the bluster had disappeared and he seemed like a trounced fighter wondering where the next blow was coming from, and knowing he could not dodge it.

Kate was in her element; she had all her weapons neatly stacked so that she could reach them as she needed them to cut the man down.

"Most people who know the gentleman are aware that he is an unforgiving man and given to vicious reaction if he is crossed." She then mused aloud, "And he has considerably more power and influence than you have, Captain Rodgerson."

Her husband did not rise to her jibe; he seemed to be pondering over the difficult position he was in, so Kate decided to give him something more to worry about and said, "As I do not personally have the pleasure of a close connection with Lady Lucinda, I would have no qualms in citing her as a co-respondent." Kate silently offered up a prayer to be forgiven for uttering such a lie. She could no more wreck some unknown person's marriage than she could that of a dearest friend.

"So you see, Captain Rodgerson," she continued, "with our marriage annulled you would be out of here with no income to support you." Here, she was interrupted by her very angry but triumphant husband. "Remember, woman, when you became my wife, your property became mine, that is the law of the land, so this estate is mine."

He had bounced back with a vengeance; he thought, 'Mrs. Rodgerson would be out bags and baggage if she continued in her present vein.' Then his new found confidence took another tumble as he beheld her smile, a smile he was beginning to hate and fear.

Kate was speaking again as though he had not interrupted. "Two points I must raise, Captain Rodgerson," she said. "The first one concerns the Act of Eighteen Eighty-Two concerning women's rights regarding property." As she saw the look of incomprehension on her husband's face, it was as she had expected; he was completely unaware that such a piece of legislation existed.

Kate was aware that from the woman's point of view, the Act left much to be desired, but it was enough that women now had some rights.

Whilst she had Captain Rodgerson wrong-footed, Kate decided it was time to let him know just how poor his position was regarding the estate. If he thought that after being divorced he would end up owning a substantial part of it, he was in for a terrible shock. So thought Kate as she prepared to deliver her most devastating broadside.

"Do you know the terms of the gift of Longfields Estate, Captain Rodgerson?" she enquired, still outwardly calm despite her inner turmoil. As she had expected, by the blank but wary look on he gave her, he had no idea that there were any conditions attached to the gift from Aunt Phoebe.

"Well, I will explain in detail the part which will affect you should I obtain a divorce," his wife told him. "When my dear Aunt Phoebe purchased Longfields Estate for us, she did so out of love for me, and a mistaken idea that our marriage would blossom in a place of our own." At this point she shook her head in disbelief at the memory of the time when she realised that she was doomed to spend her life with a man whom she had grown to hate.

Kate steadied her breathing and forced herself to concentrate on giving the facts to the man before her, facts that she hoped would bring him to heel once and forever.

However, she took heart from the way in which her husband was behaving. He had dropped his habitual overbearing manner and was obviously worried about what she was about to reveal, and how his position would be affected.

"The fact that she had a soft spot for you, Captain Rodgerson, did not blind her to the possibility that you might fail me in some way." She looked at her husband straight in his face, and said with feeling, "She was not such a fool after all, for you have proved beyond a doubt that her caution was not misplaced. What Aunt Phoebe insisted upon," said Kate calmly, "was to have three trustees to see that the terms of the gift were observed, and their trusteeship was to span twenty years from the date of ownership, so you see there are many years to go before their duty ends."

Kate knew that she had succeeded in her opening bluff, but what she was about to disclose to him was not a bluff, and she gained a great deal of satisfaction in laying before him the terms which could ultimately ruin him if he did not bow to her own terms.

"There are two major terms which Aunt Phoebe insisted upon," said Kate. "The first is that in the event of the marriage failing due to your actions, and to digress, there is a list specifying what constitutes any such actions on your part, then if such action or actions led to the marriage being annulled, then, sir, the estate would in its entirety become mine and mine alone."

She was braced ready for an explosion of anger, so Kate was not surprised when he jumped to his feet, his face twisted with fury. "The old hag can't do this to me." He spat out, "I'll drag you and your tinpot Trustees through the highest court in the land. I demand that you give me their names, then I will wipe that smug smile off your face. Remember, woman, he who laughs last, laughs best." Captain Rodgerson was beside himself with rage, but mixed with that was fear. He could see himself back where he had come from with hardly any money to his name, and no standing in Society, and the last part was what he had striven for all his adult life.

The state he had got himself in had frightened Kate, and she hoped that her brother had managed to install himself in the anteroom and was ready to come in very quickly if he was needed.

"Well, Captain Rodgerson," said Kate, desperately striving to maintain a steady voice. "You shall certainly have two names but the third trustee is always the most senior member of the firm of solicitors, so that can change over the years." Then she told the apoplectic man pacing up and down, "Sir Henry is one named trustee, the other is Mr. Armitage, who you probably do not know, but I assure can you, Captain Rodgerson, he is a well-respected member of the Church."

Her husband stopped his perambulations at the mention of Sir Henry. For he had already met the man and had found him to be an exceedingly formidable figure indeed. He looked at a man as though he was able to read a man's mind.

Then Kate went in for the coup de grâce. "Captain Rodgerson," she said, quite calmly, "even you could not claim to have made a success out of running this estate. Since you had the bravery to dismiss Thomas Banham," she said sarcastically, "there has been a steady stream of problems with such things as the boundary wall collapse, and no moves to have it repaired, the wind pump failing to work properly, one of the ploughing engines out of service awaiting repairs, whilst the other is waiting for its annual boiler test." Angrily she turned to her husband and said, "These jobs are but a few of those awaiting a decision from you, whilst others such as the carriage spring are not being attended to through lack of the necessary skills."

Her husband interrupted her with a blustering defence of his handling of the estate and said angrily, "That damned blacksmith refuses to do any work for us, he wants a good horsewhipping."

This time it was Kate who cut across the other's words, and she told him to mind his language, at the same time reminding him that she herself had no trouble getting Mr. Andern to accept work from the estate.

"But that is beside the point, Captain Rodgerson," she said. "The Trustees have visited Longfields and have advised me that it will be necessary to employ an agent as soon as possible to stop the rot, and I have agreed that the post be advertised."

Kate braced herself for another bout of bad-tempered invective but was completely taken aback by his reaction. Her husband simply agreed with her, then added smugly, "I said all along that the job was too much for a man of Banham's capabilities. I mean to say, look at the state in which he left this estate."

The sheer effrontery of the man before her took Kate's breath away, and at first it put her off her stride. Then at the thought of the injustices which had been done to the Banham family, a wave of anger swept over her again, threatening to force her to lose control over her temper. She managed to suppress her anger with an enormous effort, for she needed all her concentration to bring the whole plan to a satisfactory conclusion.

"The Trustees," Kate said, "are of the opinion that I am being unduly generous in my assessment of your financial needs, but have agreed that for this year the estate will place a sum of one hundred pounds each month in your account. Also there will be a once only sum of five hundred pounds at the end of this month."

Her husband started to protest at that point, saying, "But I have various other expenses to meet…" before Kate interrupted contemptuously, "You mean paying your creditors, or are there more affaires to be financed?" She ignored his angry bluster and told him quite bluntly, "All creditors will be paid out of your allowance, Captain Rodgerson, from this day on; not a penny more will be paid from either my purse or any other member of my family."

In the anteroom next door James was bracing himself for an explosion of anger from his brother-in-law, but instead he was greeted with a complete silence, so complete that he began to feel alarmed. The problem was that he could not see either his sister or Captain Rodgerson, and if the man had somehow managed to get into a position where he could attack Kate, he could right now be strangling her. Even as he made to rush into the room, Captain Rodgerson's voice reached him.

"So you think you have all the winning cards, do you, madam," he said, savagely. "Well let me tell you this, the game is not over yet. I still might still have some aces to play." At this point he attempted to give a devil-may-care laugh but to Kate and to James, it had more than a little trace of bravado.

Kate had the perfect answer in a flash. "Well, sir, by the number of your creditors I have had to deal with over the years, I would suspect that your aces might not be as useful as you may think." Her gently delivered jibe left him incapable of replying, and before he could think of an answer Kate said briskly, "I think all has been said that is necessary and I will ask you to leave me now."

For a moment James heard no sound, then he heard the thud as the sitting room door was savagely slammed shut. James waited a minute after Captain Rodgerson had left, then slipped out of the anteroom, and crossing over to the sitting room door, locked it in case the furious man returned.

He turned, his face wearing a huge grin, and said enthusiastically, "Little sister, you were magnificent, Sarah Bernhardt could learn…" His voice tailed off as he realised that Kate, far from shaking with laughter, was shaking uncontrollably from what appeared to be an attack of nerves.

Sitting down beside her, he held Kate to him to try and calm her, but she continued rocking and giving out a unnerving moaning sound.

"I'll get Mrs. Higson, Kate," he said worriedly, "then Charlotte will come to you."

He sprang to his feet and went over to the bell rope to summon the housekeeper. When she appeared he left her to comfort his sister whilst he dashed out of the room to get his wife. James told her not to let Mary leave her room until they were sure that Captain Rodgerson had left Longfields; it would not do to spoil Kate's bluff at this stage.

As he was about to enter his and his wife's room, the door of Captain Rodgerson's room was thrown violently open and the man himself came out in a tearing hurry and rushed down the stairs. He was carrying his own bags; Johnson was obviously keeping out of sight until it was time to leave to catch his train.

There was the sound of an ill-tempered outburst, the thud of the front door being slammed, then silence. James went into their room, told Charlotte what had happened, then leaving her to go down to assist Mrs. Higson, hurried away to see if he could get a sight of Kate's husband leaving.

James and Charlotte had been worrying about Kate's nervous state for months, but the way she had acted in her sitting room had convinced him that she needed to be seen by the family physician as a matter of urgency. He decided that as soon as Mrs. Higson agreed for Kate to travel, they would leave for their parents' house.

He was on edge, for he still did not know whether the brute had left the estate, but before he could check any further, Kate came out of her sitting room helped by Charlotte and the housekeeper. As she was helped upstairs she trudged rather than walked, much as an old person would do; there seemed to be no energy in her.

Fear clutched at his heart; had this desperate gamble on Kate's part been too much for her beleaguered brain? He had been amazed at her consummate performance and thought that she was in complete control of the situation, and now this nervous collapse. He prayed that with rest, Kate would soon be her old self.

He realised that there was nothing he could do at this stage, and took on the task of finding out whether the man had finally left the place. He went into the sitting room with the intention of trying to catch a sight of Captain Rodgerson as he set off towards the gate.

Before he had taken up a good position to observe the drive, a knock came at the door and a parlour maid came in. "Mr. Prentice, sir," she said, "Mr. Johnson wondered if he could have a word with you."

James indicated that Captain Rodgerson's late valet should come into the room, and the man, having done so, said in an urgent tone, "I am very sorry to disturb you, sir, but the stable boy has informed me that Captain Rodgerson has taken the trap to the station and taken nobody with him to bring it back." Then he continued, sounding even more apologetic, "I was hoping to catch the twelve forty from Wroxing, sir, and I would willingly walk, but I doubt if I could carry my luggage that far."

James sprang up, stifling a curse in front of the maid who was hovering outside the sitting room doorway, and said to her, "Miss, go and tell the lad to prepare my carriage. Oh, and tell him that I will drive but I want him to be ready to come with me so that he can drive the trap back here."

The excited maid sped away to pass the message on. She was agog with the drama of it all. It was much better than dusting and such!

As soon as the carriage was brought round to the front of the house, Johnson and the stable boy jumped in, and James took the reins and off they went to the railway station.

When they reached the station they found the horse and trap being attended to by two of the station porters. The animal was still in an agitated state and from what the porters told James, the trap had been driven into the yard at a furious pace, giving rise to fears that the thing would overturn. Captain Rodgerson had obviously driven the poor horse hard and it had taken the porters quite a while to calm it down.

Johnson had to get his ticket quickly, so he shook hands with them all and they wished him good luck, and with that he made his way to the ticket office, after which James and the boy checked the horse for any signs of ill treatment. They could see none, but by the sweaty state of the creature's coat, they had no doubt in their minds that Captain Rodgerson had not spared the whip.

James led the way back to Reeve House whilst the stable boy followed on with the trap.

Leaving the boy to see to the horses, James made his way up to Kate's room, only to be turned away as she was sleeping. However, he learned from Charlotte before they went down for their midday meal that there had been further drama after Kate had been put to bed. Her maid Mary had been so upset by everything that she had threatened to stab Captain Rodgerson to death if he attacked her mistress again.

Luckily, Charlotte told him, the only witness to her tearful threat had been Mrs. Higson and herself. The housekeeper had taken Mary in hand, warning her against even talking in that way, never mind doing such a thing. In the end Mary had apologise to both Charlotte and Mrs. Higson, promising not to say anything like that again. Nevertheless, such was her hatred for Captain Rodgerson that in the privacy of her own bedroom she whispered to herself that she would willingly hang if she stopped him from hurting her mistress.

What none of the women realised was that as Mary had cried out her threat, one of the older maids, a woman who found Captain Rodgerson quite exciting, had been listening at the slightly open door. She was more silly than bad, but she was jealous of Mary for being Mrs. Rodgerson's personal maid, and she relished the thought that she alone of the staff knew what had been said.

The next two days Kate did little else but sleep, so it was just one week to go before Christmas Eve when Kate, Charlotte, James and Mary arrived by carriage at her parents' house.

As soon as he could get his parents on their own, James told them of their daughter's state of mind, adding that in his opinion Kate should be seen by the family's physician as soon as possible. He made no mention of her husband's attack, for Kate had sworn them all to silence on the matter.

When the doctor examined her he queried the red wheals on her shoulder and neck, and also the bruises on her body. He knew what his eyes and experience were telling him, but he eventually had to accept her explanation that she had trodden on the hem of her nightdress and fallen on her bathtub. Nevertheless, he stored the evidence in his mind, and if things came to a head sometime in the future, he would be quite willing to testify in court as to the real cause of those injuries. For what little he had observed of Captain Rodgerson had convinced him that the man was the type to inflict pain on persons weaker than himself.

Kate had implored her parents to not let anybody know that she was being treated for a nervous illness; she did not want her husband to have any inkling that she was anything but well and in good spirits. Any sign of weakness on her part would destroy the façade of invincibility she had created for herself.

As it was, she need not have worried, for Captain Rodgerson showed up for the New Year's Day hunt, then went straight back to London, or so he informed everyone.

Cecelia arrived on Christmas Eve and also left after the New Year's Day hunt. As for inquiring after her sister's subdued manner, she did not seem to notice anything unusual, so Kate breathed a sigh of relief and forgave Cecelia for her indifference. The fact that her sister was not at her parents' house when they arrived did not sink in with Kate; she was not in a state to bother about anything at that time. James and Charlotte, however, were quite surprised when they learned that Cecelia had not been there for several weeks.

Altogether, Christmas for Kate was one of the most miserable she had ever spent. A major part of her unhappiness was due to the fact that Richard had written to say that he was unhappily unable to be with them at Christmas or New Year's Day due to his work. Paradoxically, she did not want him to see her the way she was, but she still felt cheated somehow.

—— —— ——

In the hutted village on Frodsham Marsh, the Banhams, their lodgers and their friends, the Robbins's, voted it to be the best Christmas ever.

Clarence had ordered a Christmas tree from Mr. Hughes. He had also obtained lots of bright decorations to dress it with. "Like the rich people have," he told them.

Michael had ordered two very large chickens, as a turkey or a goose would have been too large for the oven. Jessie Robbins cooked one of the chickens whilst Beth cooked the other. She also made a very large Christmas cake and her friend did the puddings.

Thomas surprised the boys and Beth with new bed mattresses; the boys, still having no proper beds, were delighted with them. Beth gave her husband the book, *The Speckled Band*, featuring a fictional detective called Sherlock Holmes. The author, Mr. Conan Doyle, had had his first book featuring the detective published the previous year and Thomas had expressed an interest in it some months back.

A new winter coat for Beth, a new dress for Victoria, a chess set for Will and the toy crane for Peter, just like the one which worked at the back of the hut.

Beth and Jessie, both being first class at dressmaking, had made each of the menfolk a shirt, whilst Beth had designed and made Victoria's dress.

There was Pears soap for the ladies, Fry's milk chocolate and Cadbury's dark chocolate for everyone, shiny coins, nuts and fruit for Peter, and pads and pencils for Clarence, and so much more. Michael was delighted to receive watercolour paints and paper which he had been considering buying in the New Year.

Mr. Hughes was away on Christmas Eve and Christmas Day, so Will and Clara kept the shop open until seven o'clock then shut it until Boxing Day morning.

Victoria was quite puzzled at Mr. Hughes going off and leaving his wife to work in the shop, and she had a vague feeling of dissatisfaction that the man was not there over the two days. As a token of his thanks for their custom, the shopkeeper had given all the hut tenants bunches of holly and mistletoe, and Will had the job of delivering them. Even Victoria conceded that Mr. Hughes was being generous considering that his was the only shop and people had no option but to buy their food and such from him.

Some of the customers gave Will tips, which was very useful with all his buying. When he had finished the last of his deliveries, he returned to the shop and set out his tips with the idea of sharing them with Clara. Her solemn face broke into one of her rare smiles and she hugged him saying, "Will Banham, you are a most kind-hearted and generous boy and I thank you for your offer, but I too have been given tips and I mean to share them with you." In the end they agreed to each keep their own tips.

Beth had asked her husband if he would invite Captain Howard to share their Christmas Eve meal, as they knew that he had been invited to have his Christmas dinner with Ian Blake and his landlady. The engineer was delighted to accept and for a few hours enjoyed a respite from the gloom that had enveloped him at not being able to join Kate at her parents' house.

Christmas Day dinner was another enjoyable day and was made even better when Dr. Mills and Sarah joined them afterwards.

It was only after Captain Howard had received a letter from James after New Year's Day that he learned how ill Kate was. Her letters had not even contained a hint of how depressed she had become. Captain Howard was so worried that he resolved that he would visit her as soon as he possibly could, even if he could only managed a few hours at Reeve House.

Chapter 17

Will Gets a Job

After the euphoria of Christmas, everything went rather flat. Each of them settled back into their humdrum daily tasks, although for Thomas and Michael, their days were rarely humdrum. Apart from the daily workshop tasks, they had to deal with equipment and machinery breakdowns as well as locomotive derailments.

Clarence went back to his work a very happy man. For the first time in his life he had enjoyed Christmas as part of a family. His mind kept conjuring images of what had taken place, and he revelled in the memory of the smiles and complements that greeted his tree.

Although Michael regretted not being able to go home for the holiday, he was realistic about it and admitted to himself that even if he had been able to manage it, he doubted whether he would have enjoyed the bedlam created by his sister's children. Certainly his Christmas here at Marshville had been wonderful, and he could not recall a better one.

Beth had thoroughly enjoyed the holiday; it had lifted her spirits enormously and her heart swelled with love for her husband, who she knew had done so much to help lift her out of the depressed state which she had fallen into.

All the same, she was worried that he might have depleted his savings to achieve this. Beth knew how much he valued the sense of security that came with having money put by.

Thomas himself was ruefully counting the cost of his Christmas spending, not that he regretted a farthing of it. To see the pleasure on the faces of his family had been the only reward he needed.

However, he knew that from now on he would have to put in a lot of hours at work to rebuild his savings. He blessed his employer, who had given instructions that all his employees would receive extra in their Christmas pay packets. In appreciation for the way Thomas had improved the running of the workshops, Captain Howard had told him there would be no further repayments to be made. These related to the loan of money for the train tickets to bring the Banhams to Frodsham.

For Victoria and Will the Christmas festivities had been even better than they had hoped it would be. They had intended that their mother should enjoy herself and on that score they could see that they had been extremely successful.

The frown and the lines of worry on her forehead had rarely been seen over several days. Even now she seemed to smile a lot more. This was especially noticeable when Mrs. Robbins was talking about the different places to be visited when the weather improved.

Will had certainly enjoyed the days when he and Clara had managed the shop whilst Mr. Hughes was away. Clara was very knowledgeable about the things they stocked and he learned a little more each day.

With everything back to normal, there did not seem to be much to do. True, there were the outside jobs around their hut and an occasional errand into Frodsham, but apart from the odd hour or two working for Mr. Hughes, he had nothing else to occupy his mind. Consequently he lapsed back into worrying about his failure to find a job.

Victoria was even more unsettled. For months she had contributed nothing to the household purse and it bothered her terribly. She observed her brother setting off to the shop with something approaching envy. Even though he was only helping out, at least he was able to hand over some money at the end of the day. Another enviable part was that he was involved in something outside the family home.

It would be nice, she mused, to work in the shop, and she thought that with the man's wife being there, she would not be troubled by Mr. Hughes. Actually he seemed to have altered his attitude towards her. Of late there had been no sign of interest at all. Her freezing glance seemed to have put him off. Oddly enough, this did not afford her much pleasure. Even the girl herself could not understand her own contrary feelings.

Two days before New Year's Eve, everything changed for Will. He was told by his father that he could start as a 'points boy' if he wanted to take on the job. Will was jubilant; he was to earn his keep at long last! It did not matter to him that the job had almost no prospects of advancement; it was a job.

Thomas, though, was not at all happy about it, but it was the only opening for a boy that had come along. Reluctantly he had agreed to put his son's name forward but even so, he told Will that if the work was not to his liking, he should say so.

Mr. Robbins gave Will a heavy serge jacket, which was just a bit too large for him, but the boy reasoned that he would eventually grow into it.

Rather than have his father spend more money buying him boots, he elected to go to work in his clogs.

His first shift started at two o'clock in the afternoon of New Year's Day, and the points concerned were at Ince. They controlled the line leading off the 'main line' which let trains descend onto the floor of the cutting.

The 'main line' was the name given to the railway track which went most of the length of the embankment. Another set of points led to a siding which allowed trains to be sidelined to let other trains pass.

Near the points was a roughly made shack for the points boys, and further along the line was a cabin which housed the section railway foreman, and it was to this cabin that Will had been told to report.

The foreman, a man by the name of Clark, was not one whom any sensible person would want to argue with. He was easily six feet tall and broad shouldered, but the most intimidating feature of the man was his cold menacing expression.

"Don't you knock when you want to come in?" were his opening words. "Go out, knock, and wait till I tell you to come in, right?" Will was taken aback by the man's aggressive manner, but was sensible enough to know when to keep his mouth shut. He therefore backed out and closed the door behind him. After a moment or so, he knocked firmly on the rough planked door.

Nothing happened, no answering invitation to enter, and the door remained firmly shut. He waited a minute or more and just as he was about to knock again, he heard the man roar, "Come in, don't stand there wasting my time."

By now Will was extremely nervous. This was the first time in his life that he was being taken on for a job, and he was not sure whether it was normal to be messed about like this or whether, as he suspected, it was just to put him in his place and be shown who was boss.

"My name is Will Banham, sir," said the boy nervously, "and I was told to see Mr. Clark. I am here about the job of points boy."

The big man laughed and said sarcastically to the other men, "Oh yes, we have heard about Mr. Banham of the Frodsham Depot, haven't we?" Only one of the other men laughed in the same manner; the other men gave Will an encouraging grin, and the boy took heart from that.

The big man carried on speaking in the same grating manner and said, "Right, lad, my name is Mr. Clark and I am the railway foreman, and don't you forget it, right?"

"Yes, Mr. Clark," said Will, "I will not forget it," and the man's eyes narrowed, suspecting insolence, but his look was met with such guileless innocence that he just grunted, then told the boy to get down to the signal hut. "The other boy will tell you what to do," he said, then added sharply, "and no loafing about, lad, or you'll feel the back of my hand, now get on with it."

Will did as he was ordered, and on reaching the hut, or shack as he termed it, saw that it was a very crudely made structure obviously knocked together possibly by one of the boys themselves.

There was a boy lounging in the doorway and he looked around as Will approached, and a contemptuous expression appeared on his face. "Oh no," he cried in mock horror, "they were supposed to send another lad for the points and instead they've sent a girl."

Will, whose patience had been sorely tried back at the foreman's cabin, felt his temper rising. He had no option but to take Mr. Clark's nastiness, but he would certainly not put up with it from a boy who looked no older than himself.

Controlling his temper with difficulty, Will said calmly, "Now stop being silly, boy, and just show me what to do and I will get to work."

The other boy's face reddened with anger at being called silly and he came at Will, pushing him violently in the chest. At the second push, Will's head bumped against the side of the shack, and his temper broke loose.

Will swung at him, which totally surprised the lad, and the next moment they were grappling with each other on the ground. Equally matched in size but not in strength, Will had the advantage of being in a temper, so neither was besting the other.

Suddenly the boys were hauled to their feet and an amused Irish voice told them to stop behaving like a couple of 'spalpeens'.

"And would you be wanting Clark's hand round the back of your head, young Al?" he asked as he held them apart. He need not have bothered, for both boys had exhausted their desire to fight. The boy named Al was looking at Will with grudging respect, whilst Will himself was feeling just a trifle ashamed for losing his temper. He felt even worse when he saw the trickle of blood from the other boy's nose.

"Here, use my handkerchief," said Will, "I'm sorry I hit you on the nose," and he thrust the snow-white piece of fabric at Al.

The other boy looked at the handkerchief in dismay and said, "I can't use that, it's clean!" Then he said, "Er, thanks anyway, I'll use me 'and."

In the end Al took up Will's offer and with the aid of plenty of cold water soon had the bleeding stopped.

As they went over to the junction the man said, "I'm Clancy, the fireman on that loco over there, and you will be Mr. Banham's boy, then?" Will nodded, and then as enlightenment dawned said, "You are the man who brought Michael to the Depot, he told us about you."

Clancy was visibly pleased at being remembered, and said, "Tell Michael that Clancy sends his regards."

After he had been shown what to do, Will was urged to say nothing of what he had learned. Clancy winked and said, "He's a good boy is Al, and it would help mend his pride if he shows you how everything works round here." The boy decided that the fireman was a friend, nodded and told him, "My name is Will, Mr. Clancy," and held out his now very grubby had to shake.

Gravely the fireman shook hands and, smiling, said, "Well, I must be saying that it is a pleasure to meet a real gentleman, but," he said, "it's not Mr. it's just Clancy to you, Will."

With that he swung himself up on the waiting locomotive, which was then driven carefully down into the cutting.

As he walked back to the signal shack, Will reflected that at least one of the footplate men was friendly, and he had a feeling that the signal boy would not cause him any more trouble.

When he arrived back at the shack, he was pleasantly surprised to be met with a more affable Al. The lad had made a brew of tea, which was very welcome even if it was a bit strong for Will's taste, and afterwards offered to show him what the job entailed.

Will was instructed what the wooden boards on the post indicated. One position gave a clear road and another position meant 'stop'. The signal board for the main line had been changed to priority now that Clancy and his driver had moved off. Their job that day was to bring out the trains of loaded spoil wagons which had been excavated from the depths of the cutting. Dirt trains, Al called them.

There were also whistle signals from the locomotives to be learned. These told the points boy whether the train needed to proceed along the main line, or main route as some called it. Actually they pronounced the word 'rowt', which puzzled Will.

Other signals indicated whether the driver intended to descend into the cutting or enter the holding or waiting siding.

Other things he learned in the following days included the correct terms when talking about trains. "Never call the driver an engine driver," Al told him seriously. "He is a locomotive driver or for short, a loco driver. You see, Will," he continued, "steam engines drive pumps, mortar mixers, winches and things like that." Then he proceeded to confuse Will by telling him that the drivers often referred to their locomotives as engines.

"Another thing you never ever do is to call the driver a train driver," Al said, wagging his finger. "A train only becomes one when it is made up of wagons or carriages coupled together." The last was delivered in a mock schoolteacher's manner which made Will laugh. Al was showing up as a real comic.

On the first day Al had warned Will of the dangers of getting on the wrong side of 'Clarky', the foreman. "Watch what you say and how you say it, Will," he was told, "and watch out when he cuffs your head, bells will be clanging in your head ten minutes after he's hit you." Then he said, laughing, "You'll soon learn when to duck."

Another day he mentioned the name, 'Black Dog'. "That one is a nasty bit o'goods, Will," he said grimly. "It's a wonder that nobody's topped him before now; at least with Clarky, when he lands out and you dodge him he leaves it at that, but Black Dog and his fireman grabs you and make sure you've been hit."

Will said with a puzzled frown, "Who is Black Dog and why do they call him that, and another thing," he added indignantly, "if he clouted me for no good reason, I would make sure that Mr. Clark was told about it."

That really made the other boy laugh. "Do you think that Clarky or his mates would take any notice of kids like us?" he jeered. "The drivers are the top men to him, and you and me are down there with the navvies." At that he put his thumb pointing downwards to indicate their lowly status.

Then he said more soberly, "You see, Will, Clarky was an express driver for the Great Northern Railway, and even though he ended up in this place," with a sweep of his hand towards the excavation, "he's still a top loco driver and don't you ever forget it." With a knowing look at Will he said, "No one ever asks why he isn't driving for the GNR anymore; nobody asks anyone why they come here to work or why some of them don't give their proper names."

Then he went on to answer Will's other question regarding Black Dog. "Him and his fireman are well known for the bad 'uns they are, but they really know how to get the best out of a loco, and," he said as though pointing out the obvious, "that's all that matters on the 'Cut."

"But why Black Dog?" persisted Will. "Who called him that name?" Al told him, "Everyone calls him that name and when you see him you'll know why." Then he laughed and said, "With all that black hair and his beard he wouldn't look so bad, but then the shape of his nose and mouth makes him look like a dog." Then in a more sombre manner he warned Will, "Don't ever let him hear you call him by that name or you will regret it, I tell you." Al then looked at the other boy's footwear and shaking his head, told him, "You would do better if you wore boots, not clogs, 'cause if he goes for you, you'd better run like stink."

Will was beginning to feel very apprehensive about the man and his fireman working through their particular section, but as the days went by with no sign of them, he began to think that Al was having a bit of fun and trying to make him jumpy.

The work came in rushes depending on the time of day; there were periods when the two boys could sit and have a chat. Al for some reason did not mention his own family much, but was always asking questions about Will's family. He once said wistfully, "Your ma sounds like a real nice lady, Will, and she can't half cook." This last comment was in appreciation of the food which he was given out of Will's snap box.

Each day when Will finished his shift, he would be so tired that it was an effort to stay awake long enough to complete his ablutions. How he longed for a bigger bathtub so that he could stretch out in it and soak in the warm water.

It was true that the boy himself was not unhappy with his lot. However, he wished there was something else he could be doing, but was realistic to see that so far nothing had come up. At least he was in employment and earning a small wage. However, there were times when Will wished he was working in the clean, dry environs of the shop; he really had enjoyed working for Mr. Hughes.

Although his muscles were beginning to ache less, his hands were giving him a lot of pain. The rough handgrips on the points levers were playing havoc with the soft palms, and his fingernails were getting broken and filthy.

Luckily the weather had been fairly mild, so being out of doors all day was not a hardship. In fact to see all the activity around him gave him a lot of pleasure.

Over the new embankment he could see vessels of all types and sizes. Al was quite knowledgeable about them, and taught him about brigs and schooners, and the difference between the Weaver Flats and the Mersey Flats. These last named were shallow draught single-masted sailing vessels suited to their particular river.

Paddleships, tugs towing strings of barges, and all sorts of small boats were quite fascinating to Will. Sometimes he was possessed by a strong yearning to be on one of the ships as it made its way downstream towards Liverpool and the sea beyond.

When Mrs. Serle was alive, she would tell them of other lands far from England, and Will promised himself that one day he too would travel to these places. To see a vessel that could possibly be making such a voyage excited his imagination enormously.

In the excavation below him, hundreds of navvies and others toiled filling wagon after wagon with earth. Also, there were steam-powered excavators of various types. One huge machine was called a Ruston and Proctor, and its bucket with its large teeth could fill a wagon with one scoop. Another was called a Wilson, and though it could not remove as much as the Ruston and Proctor, it had the advantage of being able to move itself on ordinary railway lines. That made it easier to take up a new position much quicker than the larger machine, and with less labour to do so.

Apart from excavators, trains and navvies, there were horses with their drivers, shunting single wagons to be made up into trains. The cutting was seething with activity; it couldn't have been more different than working in the shop.

Chapter 18

Will Gets Another Job

It was the third week in January when Black Dog entered Will's life. He first became aware of the man when a locomotive without a train came rushing along from the direction of Ellesmere Port, and whistled to be put onto the line into the cutting. As usual Will went quickly to the points but even so, he was only just in time to reset them before the loco was entering them.

A black-bearded face glared down at Will as the loco passed him, and the driver roared, "You'll have to be smarter than that, lad, if you want to keep out of trouble." Will had no doubts as to who the driver was, and resolved to be extra quick in responding when that particular locomotive approached.

However, it was to no avail. The man seemed bent on making life difficult for the boy, and when his loco came into the section, Al would try to be on the points before Will, but it was not always possible.

The driver was being more abusive each time he came through, and at one time, when Will almost fell when dashing from one set of points to the other, stopped the loco and jumped down, haranguing the boy, even pushing him in the chest.

Will was at his wit's end. He knew without a doubt that it would only be a matter of time before the man overstepped the mark and attacked him physically. He decided to complain to the railway foreman. Unfortunately for Will, the duty foreman that day was Mr. Clark and he lashed the boy with his tongue, telling him to get back to work or he would feel the back of his hand.

After the worried boy had left the cabin, the mild-looking man sharing the duty with Clark said, "You will have to do something about that man soon, Bill, he's nothing but a bully; one of these days he will go too far and someone will get hurt." Then he added, "We are responsible for the boy's welfare, you know that."

Mr. Clark answered stubbornly, "The 'Dog' is a good driver, we can't replace him as easily as the lad." Then he added defensively, "If the lad can't take it, he can get out, can't he." The other man shook his head and said quietly, "Just like the other lads, Bill?"

As the mistreatment went on, Will gritted his teeth, not wanting his parents to know how bad things were, but wanting someone whom he could confide in.

One morning before he was ready to start on his shift he found he was spilling the whole story to Mr. Hughes in the back room of the shop. His listener was so incensed that he was determined to march down to the Depot there and then, and make Will tell his father everything. The boy begged him not to do anything at all. He felt that he would be seen to be acting like a cry-baby and would be letting his father down.

Eventually Mr. Hughes realised that the boy would not budge from his resolve to weather the bully's treatment, but made him promise to tell his father if the driver or his fireman actually hit him.

After Will had gone the shopkeeper found he could hardly settle to normal business, and it took him the rest of the morning to temper his anger.

Beth had become very concerned about her son. He had become quiet and not inclined to talk about his day as he used to. She asked her husband to try to get Will to tell them what was wrong, but Thomas could no more get his son to divulge what was bothering him than Beth could. Nevertheless, he decided that as soon as he could, he would make it his business to go to Ince.

Before he could carry out his plan, the weather brought everything to a head. Michael had been dispatched to Ellesmere Port with the object of bringing back an excavator bucket for repair, and had taken the breakdown van with its tools and tackle. Will had been given a lift as far as the signal shack. He was delighted to see the gently falling snowflakes clothing everything with a pretty mantle, and for a short time managed to push all thought of Black Dog out of his mind.

It was beautiful snow, the sort beloved by small children and not so small boys! The sort that packed firm to make snowballs and snowmen.

Will waved goodbye to his friend and trudged over to the shack, but it was not Al who greeted him; it was one of the other boys, one whom he did not particularly like.

With a few muttered words of greeting, the boy left the shack and wandered off towards the points controlling entry to the sidings, leaving Will to take the dreaded points for entry into the cutting.

Even as he went along to the points, the beauty of the scene affected him. All the scars of the excavation were hidden, as were the harsh outlines of the machinery, and still the flakes floated silently down.

Soon a loco laboured up the gradient, only just making headway as the wheels lost their grip on the dusting of snow. The texture of the snow was the trouble; the very texture which helped it pack into good snowballs helped it to stay on the lines and pack hard when the wheels ran over it. For Will it was to prove a problem as it packed hard between the points blades, stopping them from closing.

For a while no trains moved out of the cutting, but eventually one started on its way up the gradient, and it consisted of a very long train of loaded wagons.

"He will never get it up in these conditions," said Will aloud to himself, then his blood ran cold, for he saw that it was Black Dog's loco heading the train.

Sure enough it got part way up the bank then stopped as the wheels began to slip. The train then reversed back into the cutting. For a while no traffic moved, but Will saw that some of the navvies had come out of the cutting and had been set to work clearing the snow off the main line.

He turned back as he heard the harsh sound of the loco as it blasted its way up the gradient without the wagons. With only minor slip due to much dropping of sand, the loco made it to the top.

Will breathed a sigh of relief, for he knew that any problems at all encountered by the driver would be blamed on somebody else. The nearest person to be blamed would be himself.

Even before Black Dog had signalled his intentions Will yanked at the points lever to set the loco onto the main line. The blades moved part way across then jammed. Will desperately tried again then realised that the snow had packed hard, stopping further movement.

He let go of the lever and frantically waved his arms and shouted for the man to stop, but as usual Black Dog had opened the regulator and was coming on at speed. Suddenly the driver realised what was going on and applied the brake. With the snow on the line, the loco skidded yards before the wheels gripped, but it was too late. The leading wheels entered the badly set points and dropped between the rails.

By this time the navvies were at work clearing the line, and witnessed the incident and what followed.

Black Dog flung himself down from the footplate and he was in a terrible rage. He came running down the track yelling abuse at the terrified boy, then on reaching him, lashed out, striking Will on his cheekbone and sending him sprawling in the snow.

To the enraged navvies it seemed that the driver was about to start kicking the defenceless boy, and several of them picked up their shovels and charged yelling at Black Dog.

He may have been brave bullying young boys but he had no stomach for a fight with half a dozen shovel-wielding navvies, so he fled back to the loco. Surrounded by the angry men, he and his frightened fireman held them at bay with their own shovels.

At that moment, coming from the direction of Ellesmere Port, the breakdown train, including a wagon carrying the excavator bucket, appeared through the falling snow.

The driver got down to find out what was holding them up and came across the amazing spectacle of the now thoroughly terrified Black Dog on his loco surrounded by a horde of navvies.

By the time he had learned what had happened, Michael had come from the breakdown van, and when he heard it involved Will, he himself was maddened enough to try getting at Black Dog.

Into this angry scene strode Clarky, accompanied by two of his men and a navvy ganger. He was totally disinterested in what had happened to Will; all he was concerned about was protecting his driver and getting the main line cleared.

Michael had gone round to find Will crying, more in mortification that anything else, and sporting an angry red bruise on his cheek which was already swelling.

"Right, Will," he said harshly, "onto the engine, you are not staying here." When the boy protested that he had a job to do, Michael said, "There will be no more movement at all soon, just look at the snow." Then in a more gentle voice he told Will again to get to the breakdown van, get a warm drink down him and keep warm. "Stay there until we put the loco back on the line."

The truth was that the boy was only too glad to be stopped from returning to the job.

With the arrival of the railway foremen and their own ganger, the navvies had backed off from an outright fight, and sullenly gone back to clearing the line.

When the loco was put back onto the line, the breakdown train was shunted into a siding to allow a train of trucks bearing the workers from the Weaver Sluices to pass on its way to Ellesmere Port.

The snow was coming down so thickly that they knew the run back to Frodsham Depot was going to be extremely difficult.

Before they set off, Michael went round to the railway foreman's cabin and told the men in there that he was going to make a complaint to higher authority over the way they had allowed Black Dog to behave.

He knew even as he delivered his message that he was wasting his breath on 'Clarky'. "No wonder they call you the King of the Navvy Crackers," he said bitterly. "You won't do anything until somebody gets maimed or killed by the man."

Eventually the breakdown train arrived back at the Depot. By this time the snow was falling very heavily and looked set to continue.

Michael braced himself for what he had to say to his foreman; he knew that Mr. Banham would want to go back to Ince and settle with Black Dog and 'Clarky'. Michael also knew that if his foreman did so, he would possibly end up being arrested for attacking the men or on an even more serious charge.

As it was luck was on his side, for ensconced in the foreman's office with Mr. Banham was Captain Howard.

Both men looked up as Michael tapped on the door and Captain Howard smiled and invited him in.

Michael decided to go straight to the point and get it over with. He addressed his employer directly and said, "Sir, I have a complaint to make against a railway foreman by the name of Clark, and a driver by the name…" here Michael stopped in confusion, for he did not know the driver's real name!

Patiently his listeners waited, then Michael burst out, "I only know him by his nickname, and that's Black Dog." At that Thomas nodded, for he had heard of the man and something of his reputation.

Captain Howard had obviously never heard the name before, but he told the angry-faced young man to finish his story.

By now Michael was wishing more than ever that it was not he who was about to tell Mr. Banham the facts, but he had to let his foreman know what had happened.

"Well, sir," he said trying not to meet Thomas's eyes, "it's a case of serious bullying by the loco driver and his fireman which has been allowed to go on unchecked by Mr. Clark, and even today when Black Dog resorted to physical violence, Mr. Clark refuses to do anything about it." Then Michael stopped now that he had come to the part he had been dreading.

"Black Dog hit the boy he has been bullying and knocked him to the ground, and only the protection of the navvies saved him from further injuries; the boy," he concluded quietly, "was Will."

With a cry of anger Thomas sprang up, but he was in no position to come out, for his employer was blocking the way.

Michael, already regretting the way in which he had delivered the news, held up his hand and said quickly, "He's alright, Mr. Banham, just a bruise and he is now at home."

Thomas subsided into his seat, but he still wore his anger plain on his face.

Captain Howard, knowing more of his foreman's nature than the man himself realised, interjected a few words of warning and said authoritatively, "By all means, Thomas, go to your son, but for now put those thoughts of vengeance out of your head; such matters are better dealt with when your temper is cooled."

With that he arose and moved out of the office, allowing the set-faced man to get out. Captain Howard said briskly, "I will see you in one hour, Thomas, and we will finish our discussion then."

Turning to the young fitter he said, "Michael, it looks as if the weather is set to cause problems. Would you check with everyone whether they have enough coal and oil to tide them over for at least five days."

Michael said he would do it right away and followed Thomas towards the village. He was worried that his foreman would be hell-bent on punishing the three men responsible for his son's ill treatment. Michael wished he had been able to report the situation in a less dramatic way. Another thing which was bothering him was that he was sure he had interrupted a very important discussion.

As for Thomas seeking vengeance, Captain Howard and Michael need not have bothered themselves trying to think of ways to stop the foreman from going to Ince. The weather did it for them.

It was obvious when they went outside that there would be no movement on the railway, indeed no work done anywhere. The snow was already forming drifts against every building.

Michael struggled round the village following Captain Howard's request regarding coal and oil, and found to his relief that only three huts needed extra.

He saw Johnny the coal heaver, who immediately volunteered to help. Later, when the task had been completed, he called at the Banhams hut, where he found a more composed Thomas sitting with one arm round Will's shoulder, talking quietly to him.

Beth and Victoria showed signs of having wept, and Beth welcomed Michael inside, surprising him with a fierce hug. She told him to get his wet clothes off whilst she made him a drink of cocoa. He was glad then that he had been occupied during the last half hour; it had given the family some privacy in their upset.

Before he and Thomas went back to the Depot, Victoria came over to him and gave him a hug and said softly, "Thank you, Michael, I am glad you were there for Will."

The young Irishman was overwhelmed with emotion. He had grown very fond of the family, but he never thought he would receive a hug from Victoria or from Mrs. Banham, and his heart skipped a couple of beats. All he could manage was a gruff, "Just brought him home, that's all."

As he and Thomas floundered through the deepening snow, they met Clarence and another of the horse drivers. "Got ter go back ter me horse, Mr. Banham," he shouted, "and set 'er up fer the next few days." Thomas nodded then called to him that there would be a hot cocoa drink for him at the hut. Clarence's face lit up, then he and his companion stumbled onwards until they disappeared in the swirling snowflakes.

Grimly Thomas promised himself that he would punish those men whom Michael had named, but he knew that with the atrocious weather he would never make Ince that day.

Even as his thoughts roved over what had happened, he was again beset by feelings of guilt. It was he, the boy's father, who had sent him to that place, amongst those brutes, and all along he had been uneasy about sending him to the job.

He was also angry with Will for not telling him what was going on, but paradoxically he was proud of him for sticking it out so long.

Back at the hut he had sensed the reproach in Beth's attitude and to some extent in Victoria's, and he was even more upset.

On the excavation site there were few trades open for boys. Jobs that were offered were usually very unskilled and poorly paid: working with horses, clearing ashes out of boiler ashpans, fatting wagon axle bearings, or reflooring wagons. All of them were less desirable and more dangerous than the signal and points boy work.

Back in Wroxing he had been given to understand that a boy would eventually be needed to be trained as a millwright. Then, after nearly twelve months, that job did not materialise, and at the time he felt he had let his son down by holding him back whilst they waited in vain. Not that there was much choice of employment in Wroxing.

When Thomas and Michael reached the workshop, Captain Howard told Thomas that they would cut short the discussion and instead work out how many men would be needed to keep the depot going during the present weather conditions.

Those men who lived away from Marshville could go right away before they were completely snowbound. Only those needed to keep the place from freezing up were to stay. In the end the only ones having to work were Thomas, Michael and Jed, the boilermaker.

The following day Mr. Hughes appeared at the shop with two hired mules bringing his supplies of bread and milk. He looked frozen but extremely satisfied that he had not let his customers down.

Will volunteered to take the animals back but help arrived from an unexpected quarter. Clarence said he would do it after he had seen to his horse.

Dafyd Hughes had been furious when he learned of Will's experience, and as soon as he was able he called on the Banhams with a proposition which would, he hoped, keep the boy away from the rougher elements of the contractor's gangs.

He arranged to see Thomas at a time when Will had come to the shop to help out. That way he managed to talk to him and Beth in private about employing their son as a full-time assistant. They had no objection at all; in fact Beth was delighted with his offer. Mr. Hughes assured them that Will would be meticulously trained in all aspects of the trade, and he added that the boy's future prospects would be very good.

When the proposition was put before Will he could not believe his luck. As was mentioned before, he really did enjoy working for Mr. Hughes.

He had often thought of the sort of work he would like to do, but he had not drummed up any enthusiasm for work such as his father did for a living. Even working in wood, which he enjoyed, failed to enthuse him as a full-time occupation. Only one other job had taken his fancy and that was to sail the seas, for he had developed a strong liking for boats.

For two days the snow continued to fall, but less heavily. The third day dawned with a clear blue sky and a pale sun, which lifted everyone's spirits, that is, except those of the children; they knew that a thaw would mean a return to school.

The navvies were set to work clearing the remaining snow, and with the knowledge that the thaw would bring floods to the cutting, extra steam-driven pumps were brought in. The supplies of coal which had been held up were now being delivered.

Even on normal days, hundreds of tons of coal was consumed along the canal excavation. There were several temporary connections to the various railway company's lines by which coal was brought in from all the major coalfields.

A certain amount of this traffic rumbled past Marshville most days. To the people of the village, the noise from the railway never seemed to cease.

Captain Howard knew that he could not hold Thomas back from confronting his son's tormentors forever, and in that respect he sympathised with him. Even so, he hoped that his foreman would not act foolishly and end up in trouble with the law.

Thomas, however, was in control of his temper when he set off for Ince. He had been permitted to be away from the workshop for no more than three hours to settle the affair. What he was unaware of was that on that very morning, the railway foremen, including Clark, had been reprimanded and warned that any further failure on their parts to control their staff would result in the offender being put back on the footplate. Captain Howard had not been idle; whilst the snow stopped everything else, it had not stopped the telegraph from working.

When Thomas entered the locomotive foremen's cabin, he was greeted with the words, "What do you want, I didn't hear you knock." The manner of speaking was insolent and his face as usual cold and contemptuous.

Thomas stood over the man as he lounged in his chair and with his eyes equally cold, he looked at the man for a few moments before speaking.

"You are Clark," he said, "the man who is supposed to oversee the drivers in this section?" The words were said in an unnerving quiet way by Thomas, then he added after he had received no response, "Well, you listen to me. I am Will Banham's father, and I warn you now, give me one chance, and I will make you pay ten times over for what you and your sort did to my son."

After Thomas had finished his warning there was total silence in the cabin. One man leaned forward in anticipation of 'Clarky's' reaction, but there was none. The quietest of the three men smiled to himself. There would be no answering challenge from the railway foreman. The man's size and icy intimidating glare was a carefully developed façade. He was alright at cuffing the heads of the boys, but faced with a man like Banham, he would do nothing. This was the reason why the 'Dog', or Foy, which was the man's real name, was never checked: 'Clarky' was afraid of him.

Then Thomas, in the same cold, level voice asked, "Where is the driver, Black Dog, Clark?" For a moment there was no response from 'Clarky'. Clearly relieved that the focus had shifted from himself, the man growled, "He hasn't reported for work, must be ill or something."

Thomas was filled with chagrin for not being able to confront the driver, but was conscious of the fact that even if he found where the man lived, he would not have enough time to deal with him.

He stood for a moment looking at 'Clarky', then slowly and deliberately turned his back to him and made for the door. However, before he took his leave he swung back to face the silent men and said harshly, "I have yet to settle with your Black, or is it Mad Dog, and you can tell him that, when you see him."

There was a moment's silence after Thomas had left the cabin, then the quieter of the three men laughed and said, "Looks like you've bitten off more than you can chew, eh, 'Clarky'."

"Shut your mouth," growled the foreman, "he doesn't bother me." The previous speaker laughed again and answered, "Well, if he had looked at me the way he looked at you, man, I would be bothered; he didn't look the sort to be bluffing."

Thomas was back at work before noon, and although Michael was on pins to know what had transpired, it was later in the day before he learned the full story of the morning's events.

Two days later the hated loco driver and his odious fireman were back at work, but it was less than two hours before they had pushed a train of wagons into a group of navvies, injuring several, one of them seriously.

By midday both driver and fireman had been arrested and charged with driving furiously and with causing injury to others.

Later that day a train of wagons bearing the returning day shift of navvies paused briefly at Frodsham Depot, and the fireman Clancy hurried across to the workshops to impart the news to Thomas and Michael.

Before February was out, news filtered through which was like balm to those at the depot. Mr. Clark, the railway foreman, had been relieved of his post and was now driver Clark, and as Will was first to note, had been pushed out of his cosy cabin and into the roofless cab of the locomotive. The boy took great satisfaction from that.

Justice seemed to have been served. Sadly for Thomas, he was to carry a burden of guilt for his part in the affair for a long time. It was to be years before he accepted the fact that he was not completely to blame for the events which led to Will's employment problems.

Chapter 19

An Estrangement Between Kate and Richard Seems to be Inevitable

The snowstorm that had affected the western end of the Canal works and altered the course of Will's working life also had an effect on the existence of the Frodsham Depot workshops.

When, on the first day of the storm, Michael had entered the workshop foreman's office, Captain Howard had just been telling Thomas of the very slight possibility that the workshop might be considered for closure!

The promoters, being ever mindful of the difficulties of keeping costs within the original estimate, and the difficulties in raising further monies should they be needed, had concentrated their gaze on all workshops and associated establishments.

If it was considered that work dealt with at Frodsham could be handled by the workshops at Ellesmere Port, some or even all of Frodsham's workshops would be shut down.

Whilst Marshville would continue to exist as worker's accommodation, the Depot would become merely a place where locomotives were supplied with coal and water. The tradesmen who could not be found work at the other workshops would have to be dismissed.

With the thaw and the problem of flooding raising its head, the true value of the workshops at Frodsham was amply demonstrated.

The two pumps that had been brought into the depot for major repair were completed and ready to be installed in the cutting before any of the other establishments were able to supply a single pump. Furthermore, a pump at the Eastham section could not be taken on by the overworked shops at Ellesmere Port and was rushed to Frodsham where it was dealt with in very creditable time.

It was generally agreed that the facility at Frodsham had earned its stripes. It had been a particularly worrying time for Captain Howard, as the ending of his contract with Mr. Walker would put him out of business. Once again he thanked his luck for having Thomas Banham in his employ. As regards his personal affairs, however, he was anything but thankful.

The pleasant dreams involving Kate had been cruelly shattered with the arrival after New Year's Day of a short letter from her. In the disguised language of their usual communications, Kate put it to him that his work meant more to him than she did. Otherwise, she wrote, he would have found the time to visit Reeve House, even if it was only for a few days.

He found it difficult to comprehend how changed was her attitude towards him. He thought that she had understood the difficulties of being involved in such a large and complicated scheme as he was at this time.

In all the years he had known her, her affection had warmed him to her; it was a simple innocent thing which he valued so much. Even those few short months ago when they had realised that their affection for each other was really love, the gentle young girl affection was still evident. What had happened to have changed her? He wondered sadly whether the thirteen years age difference was now proving a barrier.

Whatever the trouble was, he decided that as soon as he could be spared from the depot he would visit Kate, whether Cecelia was at Reeve House or not.

The following day brought a letter from James that explained everything, and after reading it he resolved to see her, even if it was only for an hour.

Although James had given Richard an outline of what had happened that day in her sitting room, he did not give details, including her threat of divorce. He certainly did not mention Kate and Mary's ordeal the night before. What he stressed more than anything was how deeply Kate had descended into a state of melancholia.

He finished his letter by urging Richard to come down to their parents' house as soon as he could manage it, adding, "You are good for Kate; she comes more alive when you are with us."

Captain Howard decided that he would make his way there very soon. Starting from Frodsham by the earliest train he could get, he should be at the Prentice's house by early afternoon. If it all worked out right, he would be back at Frodsham in time to be back at work the following day.

Ian Blake and Thomas were happy to cover for him should anybody of importance come visiting, so two days later he set out on his flying visit.

His plan worked to perfection but he was too late. The previous day Kate, accompanied by her mother and Mary, had left for the South of France. An old friend of Mrs. Prentice's had a villa near Deuville, and had invited them to stay as long as it took to put Kate on the road to health.

Charlotte and James were terribly upset for Richard. They both knew how deeply he cared for Kate, his unusual short but tiring visit had proved that to them, and they assured him that she would be told of his special journey to see her.

It had all been in vain, thought the weary man as he travelled back to Cheshire. If it was at all possible, he was even more worried about Kate than he was before.

When he had learned of the tactics she had used to dispatch her husband, he was amazed, and very proud of her for displaying such ingenuity and courage. He knew, however, that he had not been told the full story. What had occurred that had goaded her to turn on her husband, and why had the man accepted her conditions without any real fight? The whole affair puzzled Richard, as well as giving him more to worry about.

Richard, with due regard to the state of Kate's health, had not expected her to write to him as much as she had before her illness, but he was very disturbed at the length of time it took for her to reply to his letters. What made matters worse was that letters to Mrs. Banham and to Victoria appeared to arrive with much the same regularity as they did in the weeks prior to Christmas.

Thomas Banham, unaware of the dearth of letters from Mrs. Rodgerson to his employer, would usually comment on her health and express the hope that she would soon be well, and Captain Howard would then know that they had again received a letter from Kate.

He regularly received letters from James, and through him he was aware how she was progressing. He also learned that James and Charlotte had taken up long-term residence at Reeve House. This was to ensure that there would be somebody there to keep an eye on things should Captain Rodgerson take advantage of Kate's 'holiday absence' and move back to set up permanent residence. They were sure that if he did come back, he would behave in the same arrogant manner as he had before, and without anybody there to check him, he would make life extremely miserable for everyone.

Richard's own letters to Kate were still affectionate, but had ceased to contain the hidden messages that they had both previously delighted in sending to each other. He felt instinctively and sadly that they were not welcome any more.

It was late March before Kate returned to England. The family's physician was very pleased with the pace of her recovery, but expressed his concern at her intention of moving back to Reeve House. When assured that Mr. James Prentice and his wife were also to reside there for extended periods, the doctor was more at ease with the arrangements. He had grave reservations regarding Mrs. Rodgerson being on her own and at the mercy of Captain Rodgerson.

The first Captain Howard knew of Kate's return to Reeve House was when a letter arrived from his wife informing him that she would be visiting her sister in early April. Her purpose was quite clear; it was to convince her husband that her allowance was inadequate for her needs. The regular and totally unjustified demand was usually dismissed by Captain Howard, as had her earlier one in February. However, this time he decided he would kill two birds with one stone, as it might be said, and pay a visit to Reeve House.

With regard to Cecelia's earlier demand for a meeting, he had suggested, tongue in cheek, that she travel to Chester and stay a few days whilst her financial affairs were discussed. She had been outraged at the suggestion and had refused to come. By the same post a letter arrived from James, urging him to visit them as soon as he was able. He made no mention of his sister, Cecelia, but he did add that he was sure Kate would enjoy a few days of his company. As yet there had been no letter from Kate herself, and Captain Howard was hurt that she had not troubled herself to write to him announcing her return to England.

At that time Ian Blake, Captain Howard's assistant, was away from the site enjoying a holiday with his parents, so there was no chance of a visit to Norfolk for a week or two.

When he was able to make firm arrangements to take some time away from the site, he wrote to both his wife and to Kate suggesting a few days the end of April.

On his arrival he was met by James, who was obviously glad to see him, but before going in to Kate's sitting room he held his brother-in-law back and apologised for having invited another guest at the time when Richard himself was visiting.

"Roderic is one of my oldest friends," he explained. "We were both at the same school, and have remained friends ever since."

Captain Howard laughed and chided James for feeling the need to apologise. "I am quite happy to be here," he said, "and if he is a friend of yours, I am sure that I will enjoy his company."

James patted him on his shoulder and told his brother-in-law that his friend was a widower of just over two years, and was, like James himself, interested in rowing, sailing and fishing.

"Being not too far from the river means that we have been able to indulge in all these pursuits using hired boats," he said with enthusiasm. Then added, "It helps lift his spirits no end."

Captain Howard went to his room to freshen himself and change from his travelling clothes to something more suitable.

On entering Kate's sitting room she came across and welcomed him in, her only sign of affection being a light brush of her lips on his cheek.

"How nice to see you, Richard," she said in an even tone of voice. "It is so good of you to visit us. I know how difficult it is to escape your commitments."

To experience such a barbed comment from Kate on their first meeting in months gave him a severe jolt. He sensed a far deeper anger in her than her letters had indicated. To any other person the comment would have been perfectly innocuous, and so it seemed to the young man who had risen, smiling, at Captain Howard's entrance.

The man was of similar age to his hostess and had such a frank and open countenance that the older man was immediately drawn to him. His friendly smile and firm handshake reinforced the impression of a thoroughly likeable person, and indeed he proved to be just that in the days of Richard's visit.

For Richard Howard, however, what followed gave him another and more painful jolt, for when the introductions were over, Kate, with an uncharacteristically intimate gesture, placed her hand on the younger man's arm and said, "Perhaps you and Captain Howard, er, Richard, could exchange experiences while I make myself ready for dinner." Then, turning to her brother-in-law, she said briskly, "Roderic has travelled extensively in the United States of America, and Canada, and has told us such interesting tales."

What made the moment worse was that the warmth of her smile when addressing Roderic was the same as it had been for himself in previous years, a warmth which on this day was noticeably absent.

That evening at dinner, he found himself more as a listener than a speaker. The conversation was dominated by Kate, Roderic and James, and although Charlotte and James did try to involve Richard in the fast-flowing and, at times, hilarious conversation, he still felt that he was on the outside of the party. Kate was behaving more as a good hostess than a close friend.

Charlotte, when attempting to engage him in conversation, found it difficult to keep it up with all that was going on around them, so it ended up with Richard sitting quietly and trying to appear as if he was enjoying himself.

The following morning he planned that Kate and himself would have a quiet stroll in the garden, where he hoped they could resolve their differences. It was not to be, however, for it transpired that James and Roderic were to indulge in a rowing race and had gone to the river earlier to arrange the hire of two boats. They had taken the trap and Richard, accompanied by the two ladies, was to follow in the carriage bearing the picnic hampers.

Everyone seemed to enjoy themselves except Richard, who felt the odd one out. Whether it showed on his face he was not sure, but at one point, as they watched the two oarsmen battle it out for the third time, he became aware of Charlotte when she linked her arm companionably through his. He felt a rush of affection for her as she smiled up at him.

"Do you indulge yourself in rowing, Richard," she asked. He laughed, and for the first time since he had arrived, he did not feel quite so isolated.

"Yes, Charlotte," he replied, and then with a wry smile added, "but not racing against young bloods like these two."

She felt sorry for her companion with his reference to the age difference between himself and the rest of the party. Charlotte was astute enough to realise what Kate was doing and she had a shrewd idea why she was doing it.

'Oh, Kate,' she thought sadly, 'do not try to punish poor Richard by making him feel jealous. It will not work; it will most likely drive him away.'

Keeping her arm firmly through his, she drew him to where the picnic rugs were laid on the ground and told him, "Well, if you will not demonstrate your prowess with the oars, I hope you are fit enough to eat as much as James and Roderic."

When the hampers were opened he could see what Charlotte meant; there seemed to be enough food to feed a whole rowing club!

Dinner that evening was, if anything, worse than the previous one. For a start, the guest list included the vicar and his wife. Rather than being elderly and staid, they were in fact lively, erudite and young. Even the presence of Cecelia, who had arrived in the late afternoon, failed to make Richard feel anything other than the elder statesman of the party.

Cecelia, on finding a personable young man in the party, employed the full might of her considerable armoury of charms on Roderic, who naturally responded in his usual friendly manner.

It was obvious that this did not suit Kate. She became less lively, but tried to keep everything from going flat by concentrating on the conversation of the vicar and his wife.

To make matters worse, on two occasions Kate addressed Richard as Captain Howard, each time hastily correcting herself and using his Christian name almost as an afterthought.

Charlotte looked at her husband in sad disbelief and he shook his head angrily as he observed the effect it was having on his brother-in-law. Although Richard retained his usual courteous manner, his eyes showed his deep sadness.

When they attempted to draw him into the general conversation, they could see that he had withdrawn into his own private world, and it was obvious that he would not be visiting Reeve House much in the future. Charlotte felt terrible for Richard; she wanted to enfold him in her arms and comfort him. As regards Kate, she wanted to take her to one side and give her a stern talking to.

At first Richard had considered which subjects would be suitable for the light-hearted conversation around the dinner table, but he realised that he had very little to put forward to match the mood of the present conversation. True, he had been invited to a meal with a minor (and very unlikeable) Indian prince, and he had led a tiger hunt to rid a group of villages of a particularly voracious predator which had taken several lives in that year, but somehow he could not match the witty banter of the vicar, and the humorous incidents from Roderic's time in the Americas.

The following day he rose early and took a stroll before breakfast. He wanted to take a last look at the gardens, which had been where he and his newly found love had shared their thoughts. All his hopes had been dashed by Kate's behaviour during the last two days; it had been patently obvious that amongst people of her own age she came more alive. With himself she became, if not unfriendly, certainly more formal. He resolved to make preparations to return to Frodsham as soon as he had breakfasted.

On his return to the house, he was met by his wife, who immediately launched into an imperious demand that he should increase her yearly allowance.

Captain Howard looked at his wife with detached interest as she was speaking. 'Always the same,' he thought, 'endless excuses as she attempts to justify her demands.'

He saw her as if for the first time, elegant and beautiful with a flawless complexion and a figure a woman fifteen years younger would envy. Her eyes were an amazing feature with their lovely shape and colour; they were like deep mysterious pools, something that had attracted him at their very first meeting. Yet now he felt nothing but compassion for Cecelia.

Beyond her beauty, she was nothing but an empty shell. Totally self-centred with not an ounce of thought or consideration for others, and certainly no sympathy for those below her in class. She would, in a few years' time, he thought, be alone and friendless with no aim in life to give her some measure of self-esteem or contentment.

In fact, Richard doubted that his wife would ever be contented.

Against his original intention, he told her that she would get an increased allowance, but even so, it would not be as much as she had been demanding.

During breakfast he told James and Charlotte of his intentions without offering any explanation as to why he was leaving, not that they needed one. James volunteered to take him to the station in the trap as he wanted to have a last word with him before they parted.

Mary, Kate's maid, came in to tell them that her mistress would not be down for a few hours yet. She assured her anxious listeners that Mrs. Rodgerson was not ill, merely tired after a sleepless night. With the doctor's recommendation that when his patient wanted to sleep she must be encouraged to do so, Mrs. Higson had done what was necessary then left her to her slumbers. Mary said she was going to sit and do her sewing close by her mistress's bedroom door.

As Mary left the breakfast room, she gave Captain Howard a shy smile. Somehow it heartened him, as though things were not quite as bad as he was imagining.

Before he left the house, Charlotte surprised him by putting her arms round him and giving him a hug, her eyes brimming with tears. "Come back, Richard, for Kate's sake, and try not to leave it too long." James nodded his agreement with his wife's plea, but thought sadly that his brother-in-law would not be in too big a hurry to visit Reeve House again for a long time.

The two men were just about to set off when, from the direction of the river path, came Roderic. He was obviously surprised to see that Captain Howard was about to leave but was too well mannered to pass comment. He seemed genuinely sorry to see him go, but expressed his pleasure at making his acquaintance. After they had made their farewells, Captain Howard and James went on their way to the station. After a short while, James could contain himself no longer, and burst out, "Look here, Richard, I know how badly Kate has behaved these last couple of days, and I can't blame you for clearing out, but don't give up on her; she has gone through a very bad time since Christmas." Then he said gently, "Charlotte and myself do know how much you mean to each other, so try to be patient with our Kate."

His companion was silent for a few moments, then picking his words carefully, he said, "No, James, I will never give up on Kate; she is most dear to me and has been since she first came into my life." At that point he stopped to consider the phrasing of what he wanted to say without giving away how deeply hurt he was.

"When Kate is more like her old self," he said, "she may feel that our bond of affection is still as strong as ever it was, and with that, I will be content."

His brother-in-law nodded that he understood, but inwardly was sure that Richard would only resume his visits if there was a change of attitude on the side of Kate, or if a situation arose which made it imperative for him to call.

Richard pointed out that the main problem was still the same; he was not free to keep leaving the contract site if and when he wanted to, "And that," he said, "will not alter for the next two years." Then he added, almost as if he was speaking to himself, "That is, if we finish the Canal in the time we have been given."

In an attempt to take Richard's mind off the present miserable business, James asked him how things were progressing on the 'Big Dig', as he was fond of calling it. "What was the name the Opposition call it?, he asked. Richard, gratefully seizing the change of subject, said, "Oh, you mean the Big Ditch," and laughed, then said wryly, "and at the moment it does resemble one." Then he said, "The people working on it refer to it as the cutting, or more often, the 'Cut', and whatever the detractors say, it is progressing very well."

"You know, Richard," James said thoughtfully, "one day I would like to come and see it for myself, you know, combine it with a visit to the Welsh mountains, something I have long wanted to do."

His companion laughed in spite of himself, and said warmly, “James, my dear friend, you could not come to view anything more opposite, large grand edifices of rock, and a muddy trench in the ground.”

Then he said seriously, “You would be very welcome, and if you do get a chance to visit, I would find a most suitable place for you to stay.” They had little to say after that, each man busy with his thoughts.

As the train pulled out of the station, Captain Howard was overwhelmed by such a feeling of sorrow for something precious lost that he felt a lump form in his throat. The presence of another passenger in the compartment forced him to face the window lest his emotion showed, and he stayed in that position for quite a while until the feeling eased.

Once back at Frodsham, he would be able to push the whole sorry business to the back of his mind, and bury himself in his work. That night he would write to Kate, thanking her for having him, and apologising for his early departure. He did not hold out much hope of an early reply, that is, if she even bothered.

Chapter 20

Victoria Obtains a Post In Frodsham

When Will started his job on the construction site, Victoria had been very apprehensive. It was not that she considered him a weakling, far from it; he had been able to stand up for himself very early on in the village school. There were some really rough farm-raised children he had to contend with, and in the first few months of his entry into the classroom, Victoria often had to defend him against them. However, he soon began to fend for himself with the aid of fisticuffs taught to him by John Wilson, one of his father's men at Longfields Estate.

Even so, Will had never been a rough boy, and his sister was well aware that his still-developing physique would be no match for some of the brutish types who occasionally passed through the village. She knew that most of them were perfectly decent men who would treat a young boy kindly, but she was also aware of those whose nature changed when they had consumed strong drink. It was hard, laborious and thirsty work down in the cutting and a great deal of ale was taken with their meals.

As had been shown, her fears for her brother's welfare were not baseless, even though alcohol was not the prime cause.

On the day Will started his job, Victoria was painfully aware that, at eighteen years of age, she too should be working. In fact, to have a job that would take her out of the hut for a few hours would make her feel better.

She had volunteered to take the boys to school and bring them back in the afternoon, something that was much appreciated by her mother and the other women. Sometimes she would manage to have a chat with Miss Bryant, Peter's teacher, which was very pleasant. Occasionally Sally would join her if she had need of something from the shops in the town. On the less enjoyable occasions, Mrs. Guest would walk with her. The lady had little to say and was inclined to be sharp with the boys. Even the normally irrepressible Peter was silenced.

When with Sally, Victoria learned that she and her husband had met in an orphanage, and after being put out to work, they had kept in touch with each other. Fred, her husband, had been trained as a rigger at a boat-building yard and later had landed a job with Captain Howard. Soon after, they had married and lived in a rented room. Until they came to Marshville, they had never lived in a place of their own.

Later, when Victoria related Sally's story to her mother, Beth exclaimed, "So that is why Sally has always referred to the hut as her 'home', now I understand."

There were times when she was busy with her mother, helping Mrs. Robbins with some of her sewing work, but not with the quilts, which was her speciality. Mrs. Robbins was the proud owner of a Singer sewing machine, and taught both Victoria and Beth how to use it. On the days when they were busy with this, they quite enjoyed themselves, even though they both had a lot of difficulty in learning how to work the treadle which powered the machine.

Beth, with her dressmaking skills, was delighted to learn how to operate the machine, and Victoria again thanked their luck at having such a neighbour for taking her mother's mind off her problems.

In the days after the snowstorm and her brother's subsequent misadventure, when Will had left the job of points boy, Victoria felt as if a huge weight had been removed from her shoulders. Like her parents, she had been very upset when she had learned of the treatment that he had been subjected to, and for all her previous hostility towards Mr. Hughes, she was pleased with him for giving her brother a job. Then something happened which further upset all her earlier prejudices against the man.

When Will had been working at the shop for a few weeks, Victoria had gone across to buy a bag of self-raising flour with the aim of doing some baking herself. In the street two young boys were rushing up and down with a handcart that was too big for them to handle.

As she left the shop with her purchases, she stepped off the raised wooden boarding that served as a pavement, but was forced to step back smartly to avoid being hit by the badly steered cart. Unfortunately the heels of her clogs came up against the boards and she ended up sitting down rather ignominiously but with such a force that a sharp pain shot up her spine.

Will did not witness the incident but heard her pained "Oh". He dashed out of the shop and said urgently, "Are you alright, Victoria?" When he got no reply and noticed the whiteness of her face, he realised that she had really hurt herself. Immediately following was Mr. Hughes, and one of the women who had been waiting to be served.

The woman had witnessed Victoria's accident and said, "The lass has hurt that bone at the end of her spine, she will be in a shocked state; better give her a brandy or something." Turning to Will she added, "I know, it happened to me, fair knocked me sick it did."

Will and Mr. Hughes managed to help her to her feet, but then she seemed as though she was about to faint, so the shopkeeper, throwing decorum to the winds, scooped her up and carried her past the goggling customers and into his room at the back of the shop.

In spite of her earlier revulsion of the man, Victoria clung to him, waves of clammy cold sweeping over her, and her breath coming in short gasps. Then she started to wail like a small child. The sound of her crying went through Will like a knife. It took him back to Simon Andern's shed after Captain Rodgerson had attacked her.

Mr. Hughes rapped out to Clara, "Make a hot, sweet drink, will you? I believe that is the right thing for shock."

Gently he held on to her until her crying spasm stopped, he still held onto her when Clara brought the drink and did not let go of her until she had swallowed the liquid and regained her colour.

Will was close to tears himself; the memories of the other incidents were still too sharp in his mind, and it upset him badly to see his sister like this.

As for Victoria, she was curiously contented to stay held close to Mr. Hughes, and it was several moments before she pulled away from him. She was conscious of Clara's anxious face, and hoped that the poor woman would not be offended by her husband's boldness.

Mr. Hughes returned to serve his customers, followed shortly by Clara. Will stayed with his sister until she felt recovered enough to make her way back to their hut. As she was about to leave the shop she thanked the shopkeeper and Clara, assuring them that she would be alright to go home with Will's help. She found it very difficult to look them in the eye and was glad that the shop was busy so that she could make her escape without too much fuss.

Beth made her daughter go to bed with a hot water bottle and Victoria was glad to do so; she felt chilled through to her very bones. As she snuggled down in her bed, her mind's eye returned to Mr. Hughes holding her close and she experienced a guilty but quite delicious sensation course through her body.

Later when Beth peeped into the bedroom, Victoria was fast asleep. She moved quietly so that she could see her daughter's face and was relieved to see that she had regained her normal colour. Just as pleasing was that Victoria had lost the unhappy look which she wore so often.

The following day Thomas was not working, so he was able to attend chapel with the boys whilst Beth stayed at their hut to keep Victoria company. Although feeling much better, her daughter did not relish the walk to and from Frodsham. Victoria also felt shy about meeting Mr. Hughes.

When Will came in from the shop on Monday, he told his sister that both Mr. Hughes and Clara had enquired about her, and added that the shopkeeper had expressed concern at Victoria not attending chapel the day before.

It was two days before she plucked up courage to go to the shop. Mr. Hughes was not at the counter when Victoria walked in, therefore she was served by Clara. The young woman gave a sympathetic smile and asked her how she was feeling. Oddly enough, Victoria had lately found it easier to talk to Clara. The young woman had never showed a trace of distrust or animosity, something that the younger girl had braced herself to expect.

Victoria felt much easier about meeting Mr. Hughes but even so decided to keep her visits to the shop as few as possible.

That night she broached the subject of a job in Frodsham, possibly as a shop assistant. Whilst her parents were not averse to the idea, they had reservations about her having to walk the distance on her own, especially in the dark. When Will mentioned the matter to Mr. Hughes the following morning, the shopkeeper agreed wholeheartedly with Mr. and Mrs. Banham.

Victoria's employment dilemma had still not been resolved when, two weeks later, Mr. Hughes called to see Beth and Victoria about the position of maid to a Mrs. Hilyard. The lady lived in a large elegant house in the town, he told them, and attended the same chapel as they did. The reason why she would shortly be in need of a maid was that the young woman with her at the moment would soon be leaving to get married.

Obviously Beth wanted to discuss the matter with Thomas, but she promised Mr. Hughes that he would have an answer the following day. Victoria herself was nervous yet excited about the idea, but told her mother that she was willing to apply for the position if her father agreed.

Thomas's earlier concerns about the walk to and from the town were largely answered, as the position was for a live-in maid. The only reservation each of them, including Victoria, had was that it could end up with her not being able to come down on a visit should something unforeseen prevent her from doing so.

Mr. Hughes normally called at Mrs. Hilyard's house once a week, therefore he volunteered to act as the messenger for each of them, and on the Wednesday of that week, Victoria, accompanied by her mother, called on the lady at ten o'clock in the morning.

The young woman who opened the door to them introduced herself as Alice, the maid who would soon be leaving. She told them that there were just two maids, the cook and an occasional handyman-cum-gardener.

Alice was a bustling type of person, with a manner totally different to Victoria's calm but efficient way. Before they had entered Mrs. Hilyard's sitting room they had learned that the kitchen maid was only fifteen years of age, and 'was coming on very well', that the cook was a grand person, and that the handyman was awkward and morose but 'devoted to Mrs. Hilyard'.

The interview went very well and both sides were satisfied with the arrangements, after which they were given a tour of the house. Although not as grand as Reeve House, it was elegant with well-proportioned rooms. Alice's room was a reasonable size and had a cheerful, homely air about it. Victoria felt her spirits rise when she peeped in; the thoughts of having to sleep in a poky garret had been bothering her since she learned that she would be living in.

Mrs. Hilyard appeared to be satisfied with Victoria and even Alice seemed contented that she was not leaving her mistress at the mercy of some ill-trained hussy of a girl.

Three weeks later Victoria took up her new position and after the initial upset at leaving her parents, settled in fairly quickly. However, for the first nights Victoria had difficulty falling asleep at night, it was so quiet outside. Having got used to the sounds of machinery and railway activity, which sometimes went on through the night, the silence was unsettling. It was to take weeks before she started to sleep easily.

Sometimes it upset her when thinking of her family, especially her mother, living with all that noise and mess, whilst she, Victoria, was once again living in a quiet, proper house with very little dirt being trailed in from the outside.

Shortly after moving in, Mrs. Hilyard gave her the news that a house in Frodsham would be available for rent in the next week or so, and gave Victoria leave to go down to Marshville and let her parents know of it. After she had given her mother the good news, enjoyed a cup of tea and a piece of her mother's fruit cake, she started out for Frodsham. As she waved goodbye to Beth standing in the doorway of the hut, she decided to call and say hello to Will. Pointing to herself and then to the shop, she indicated that she was popping in for a few moments. Her mother gave a final wave and then disappeared inside.

Victoria was a bit nervous about entering the shop in case Mr. Hughes was on his own, for although they met each Sunday morning at the chapel, there were always several other people present. Under those circumstances she was finding it easier to converse with him, even managing a smile for him when she forgot herself.

On this occasion she was lucky, as Will was working in the front of the shop whilst Mr. Hughes was working in the back room. Her brother's face broke into a pleased smile and he said, "You know, Victoria, I never thought I would say this, but I really miss you." Then he ducked as though dodging a blow from her. Victoria laughed and told him with mock seriousness that she would certainly not miss him the next time he came within reach. Then she told him about the house, but Will, whilst expressing the hope that they would be successful this time and make their mother happy, was not so taken with the idea of moving. When he heard where it was he was even less enthusiastic. Even his sister was unsure if it would be a good move, for the cottage was situated in a place called Five Crosses, and it was further up the hill from the town centre than the house on Church Street that they had looked at some time back. They both thought the same thing but only Will voiced his thoughts. "Long way for Dad to walk each day." Glumly Victoria nodded her agreement. Eventually the girl started on her way back to Mrs. Hilyard's house, rather disappointed at not having a word with Mr. Hughes.

Thomas managed to be away from the workshops long enough to walk up the hill to Five Crosses and enquire after the house. On this occasion there was no hostility from the owner of the house; indeed, he was most friendly and gave them a cup of tea for having walked so far. Unfortunately, by then the house had been let. Even though they had been unlucky, Beth and Thomas were not bitter or downhearted. Meeting a landlord with no animosity towards contractor's men was a refreshing change.

Afterwards Beth confided in Thomas that she was glad they were not moving to Five Crosses; she like Will and Victoria, did not want Thomas to have such a long walk each morning and night.

—— —— ——

Mrs. Hilyard was really pleased that Victoria had come to her. More than anything else, since her husband had died, she wanted a companion. Not simply a maid, but someone whom she could enjoy a conversation with, someone who was interested in more than the trivial things that some of the girls found so important.

Alice had been a good maid and a staunchly loyal person, but her mind seemed to be preoccupied with the mundane day-to-day things of life. Victoria, however, could hold an intelligent conversation on quite a wide range of subjects, but just as importantly for Mrs. Hilyard, she was a good listener. Also, the girl did not try and placate her with meaningless platitudes when she was passing through one of her periods of despondency.

Another quite unexpected side of Victoria was revealed to her one day, something that was to change the lives of both mistress and maid.

The girl had been giving the sitting room a thorough dusting and her final job was to go over the piano with a soft cloth. It was a Steinway upright grand and it was kept in beautiful condition, but as yet Victoria had never heard it played.

Lost in her memories she sat on the stool, her fingers resting on the unopened keyboard cover as though poised to play. Victoria's thoughts were miles away and she was not aware that Mrs. Hilyard had entered the room.

Suddenly her employer spoke and the girl almost upset the stool as she leaped to her feet. "I am sorry, ma'am," she said guiltily, "I just could not help myself, it is such a lovely piano."

Mrs. Hilyard waved her hand to stop Victoria and said, "No, my dear, I am not annoyed with you, I merely asked if you were wishing that you could play the piano."

To her immense surprise Victoria answered shyly, "Oh no, ma'am, I can play. Mrs. Serle, who was mistress of Reeve House before Mrs. Rodgerson, taught both my brother Will and myself." Then she said sadly, "After Mrs. Serle became ill, the piano was never used again."

Mrs. Hilyard was quite astounded; she found herself wondering if there were any other surprises to come from this astonishing maid of hers, and she asked how far she had progressed in her learning.

Victoria answered, "Well, ma'am, I started when I was just eight, and Mrs. Serle said when I was fifteen that one day I would play better than she did, but I do not think that could ever happen. Mrs. Serle," the girl said proudly, "could play any type of music and so wonderfully well."

Mrs. Hilyard looked at her maid and smiled, then said, "Well, Victoria, would you like to play on my late husband's piano? I will leave you for ten minutes whilst you practice."

With that she turned on her heel and left the room, leaving a speechless and breathless Victoria standing in front of the magnificent Steinway. A few moments later there came the first tentative fingerings of the keys

What followed next was the most beautiful rendering of 'Greensleaves' that Mrs. Hilyard had ever heard.

Standing in the hall listening as the last lingering notes died away, the lady of the house was close to tears. Almost as if Victoria realised how the music would affect her mistress, the girl launched into a spirited rendition of 'Hail The Conquering Hero Comes', and by the time Mrs. Hilyard had recovered herself was well into the spirit of the piece.

It was just what was needed, and her mistress looked into the room. Victoria was playing the instrument with her eyes closed, her whole body moving in rhythm with the music. What was more remarkable to Mrs. Hilyard was that there was no sheet music in sight!

Victoria looked up, her eyes shining. "Oh, ma'am," she said happily. "What a beautiful piano. I do believe it is better than the one on which I learned to play."

Mrs. Hilyard smiled her pleasure and replied, "And I do believe that I have never heard it played better." Then she said curiously, "But you do not play to music, were you not taught to read music?"

"Oh yes, ma'am," the girl replied, "but I am lucky in that I can remember most of the melodies after I have played them a few times, and sometimes even if I have only heard it played." Then she giggled and said, "But I have a terrible singing voice," and added, "my mother tells me not to sing in chapel, just move my lips."

Mrs. Hilyard looked down at the upturned face of the happy girl and thought to herself, Dafyd was quite right, she will be good for this house.

From that time on, it became a regular part of Victoria's week to play for her mistress, usually in the evening but on occasions, through the day.

For the first time since her husband had passed away, Mrs. Hilyard felt more inclined to open her house to visitors, but for light-hearted company rather than the more formal visits. With the prospect of an evening enlivened by Victoria's piano playing, she thought that the house would seem less empty and more like a home.

When she approached Victoria on the subject, the girl was not so sure that she could play before a group of strangers, but when her employer suggested laughingly that she could possibly have a screen between her and her audience, she had to laugh in spite of her apprehension. Eventually she succumbed to the idea, especially when Mrs. Hilyard assured her that she was only inviting a small number of her friends, and that she would not be expected to play too many pieces.

The first soirée was on the evening of a dull but dry day in April. There were just six guests invited, but even so Victoria felt very nervous at the thought of having to perform, something she had never had to do in her life before. After the first few chords, however, she surrendered herself to the music. Amongst her favourites was the music of the Strauss family, and by the reception she received after each piece, the gathering also felt the same way about her choice as she did.

By the end of the evening her heart was full of joy, and to see the happiness on the face of Mrs. Hilyard was all she needed to make everything worthwhile. She also knew that she would not be so apprehensive in the future should her employer want to hold another musical evening.

When the excited girl told her family about the piano and later of the musical evening, they were delighted that she was at last able to enjoy the fruits of Mrs. Serle's teachings. As yet only Beth and Will had heard her play, and that was years ago when she was just starting to play her first simple melodies.

At the chapel on the following Sunday, Mrs. Hilyard told Beth all about the event and expressed her wonderment at her daughter's accomplishments.

Mrs. Hilyard would have liked to have Victoria's parents hear their daughter play, but the difficulties arising from their situation with regard to Thomas's job and the feeding of their lodgers precluded them from attending a soirée.

Towards the end of April, Victoria was returning to Mrs. Hilyard's house, after a special visit to her mother, when on the lane she met Clara walking back to Marshville. To Victoria's surprise, the young woman was with a man, and what was quite shocking to the girl was that they were linking arms.

If any sign of Victoria's emotions showed on her face, she did not know, for Clara's face lit up when she saw the girl. Before any greetings could be exchanged, Clara cried happily to Victoria, "Oh, Miss Banham. I have just heard such wonderful news, I am expecting a baby, and you," she added with a smile, "are the first to know." Then she laughed and said, "After my husband, that is."

The man accompanying her grinned at Victoria, then looked at Clara with such an expression of tenderness that left the bemused girl in no doubt as to whom the father of the unborn child was. This man was Clara's husband, not Mr. Hughes!

She was so overwhelmed with the feeling of delight, or was it relief, that she flung her arms around Clara and kissed her on the cheek.

"Oh, Clara." Victoria said joyfully, "how lovely, I am so pleased for you; and when is your baby to be born?"

The young woman, her face a little pink, was touched by the girl's obvious pleasure at her news, and gave her the date. After a few more exchanges they parted, each to continue their journey, Clara and her husband pleased by the reaction of Miss Banham, and Victoria elated but very thoughtful.

The more she thought about the situation with regard to Mr. Hughes, the more foolish she felt. Her actions from the very first time she had come face to face with the man were misguided, and all because she had not taken the trouble to find out the facts. Simply because Clara wore a wedding ring and worked alongside the man, she had made an assumption, and now she knew it had been a false assumption. She cringed inwardly when she recalled her cold and righteous attitude with Mr. Hughes.

"Well," she thought glumly, "I certainly would not blame him if he continued to treat me in the same way." She then said to herself, "But he does not treat me as I have treated him, he has always acted in a most courteous manner." Victoria brought to mind, something she often did, how thoughtful and gentle he had been with her after her painful fall.

For the rest of the week Victoria alternated between despondency and hope. She vowed that from now on she would be just as courteous as he was, for now she wanted more than anything to gain the esteem of Mr. Hughes.

If Victoria was in any way less cheerful than usual, Mrs. Hilyard did not notice it; she was too engrossed in her plan to hold a special soirée for a larger number of people. She also intended that she would have a violinist and a singer. Of all the men who sang in the chapel, one voice stood out, and that was the voice of Dafyd Hughes. The problem was that she had long been aware that for some reason Victoria seemed to dislike the young man. The lady judged that if her maid refused to play the piano for Dafyd, the soirée would be a flop.

Therefore it came as a pleasant surprise when the girl agreed to play, but seemed more concerned as to whether she was good enough to accompany anyone as accomplished as Mr. Hughes than anything else.

When, after the service on the following Sunday, Dafyd was asked if he was willing to entertain her guests, he was only too willing. He had noticed that Miss Banham was less frosty with him of late, and he had actually been on the receiving end of one of her warm smiles, which had played havoc with his emotions.

Mrs. Hilyard had managed to obtain the services of a violinist. The young man was an assistant in one of the shops in Frodsham, and he was quite taken with the idea of playing to a private party. All that was left to do was to get the two men and Victoria together so that they could arrange a mutually agreed selection of music.

On the evening of the soirée, the piano playing of Victoria was received with its usual appreciation, as were the songs of Mr. Hughes. Unfortunately the tunes selected by the violinist were not well received. Though the instrument was played beautifully, the three pieces were slow and sombre.

The hostess, noting the effect on her guests, arranged for the refreshments to be served, and whilst this was being done, had a few words with the crestfallen young man, who was acutely conscious of his failure to please his audience.

"I thought the music I had chosen," he said dispiritedly, "would be suitable for such a respectable gathering, but it seems to have been the wrong choice." Mrs. Hilyard assured him that his playing had been excellent but suggested diplomatically that his remaining pieces be more lively. He thought about it for a few moments, then said, hesitantly, "Well, I could play some lighter, more cheerful music, but it will not be to sheet music."

After the refreshments were finished, Victoria played first, and was followed by a rendition of a Welsh lullaby sung in his native tongue by Mr. Hughes. The audience really enjoyed these pieces, but when the violinist took his place by his music stand, people started to fidget. However, within a few moments of him starting to play, pleased smiles broke out and they began to tap their feet. First he played a Scottish reel, then went on to some sort of gypsy tune. After the performance there was rapturous applause. Like Victoria did on some occasions, he played without music.

It was a magical evening for Victoria. Being so close to Mr. Hughes and in such civilised surroundings exhilarated her more than anything had ever done before. Even the girl herself could not deny that it was more than the fact that they blended together in the music. The only thing that bothered her now that she knew he was not married to Clara was, in fact, whether he was married or promised to another, but how she was to find the true state of affairs she had no idea.

An invitation to one of Mrs. Hilyard's musical evenings was highly prized in the area, but the lady wisely decided that in fairness to Victoria, these events should not be held too often. She was conscious of the danger of turning her into a performing creature, even though the girl herself obviously enjoyed playing. On that score Dafyd Hughes agreed with her.

The young man found himself fiercely protective towards Victoria. It had long been a source of worry to him that she had to walk up to the town by herself when returning to Mrs. Hilyard's house. In fact, sometimes when he caught sight of her leaving her parents' hut, he would ask Will if he would walk with his sister at least to the top of the lane.

Dafyd Hughes, shopkeeper, was by then in no doubt as to his feelings for Victoria Banham; he was in love with the most wonderful girl on the planet!

Chapter 21

Clarence Loses His New Life

It was a beautiful May day, the sky enlivened with fluffy white clouds drifting lazily across acres of blue. The sun was shining, the hedgerows bright with wildflowers, and the sound of birds all tended to make Clarence feel glad to be alive.

He was also pleased with himself for his success in writing his first full sentence the previous evening. Up till that time he had always written what his helpers had told him to write. Peter had made him put down the words, 'the cat sat on the mat', but Clarence's sentence stated that, 'horsis are strong and clever'. He was very proud that he had only made one mistake according to Peter.

On this day he was on his way to the town to get a supply of Strong Black Shag tobacco for MacDonald, the foreman ganger, a task that he was doing quite happily. MacDonald was a big man, tough, and a hard taskmaster but fair. As long as a man got on with his work he was alright, but should a man be caught not pulling his weight, the foreman could be very nasty indeed.

MacDonald was a whisky drinker and when he was drunk everybody steered well clear of him. However, on this particular day he was in genial mood, so Clarence was in his good books.

As Clarence left Marsh Lane and entered Main Street he saw that one side of the street was almost filled by a road train consisting of two traction engines coupled to a many-wheeled trolley bearing a huge Lancashire boiler. On the side of the load were painted the words, DANIEL ADAMSON. DUKINFIELD. MANCHESTER. Behind the trolley were two more traction engines, the smoke from their chimneys drifting gently down the street in the light breeze. The leading traction engine was replenishing its tanks from the water hydrant in the roadway.

Clarence was familiar with the firm and also with the fact that the proprietor, Mr. Daniel Adamson, was a leading advocate in the movement to build a canal connecting the city with the sea.

He edged his way through the people idly watching the procedures and walked towards the tobacconist's shop, which was just beyond the road train, when he became aware that there was somebody close behind him. He glanced round casually and as soon as he did so, he felt as if the blood had frozen in his veins. Behind him was the big Irishman whom he had last seen in the back streets of Manchester!

He could hardly support himself; such was his terrified state that his legs seem to have turned to jelly, and he was shaking like a leaf in a wind.

"Hello, One Eye," said the man with a triumphant grin, "I've been waiting to get hold of you for quite a while now."

At this Clarence nearly collapsed; he could not have been more terrified had he been a rabbit facing a stoat.

The man carried on talking softly, enjoying the effect he was having on his victim. What a stroke of luck, he thought exultantly, and it looked, by One Eye's garb, that he was working on the 'cut', and that was the place where there would be dynamite. He judged that a bit of bluff would work without fail with this quaking specimen.

"Now, One Eye," he said softly, "we've been watching you for months now, and you are just the man to get us what we want, so I'll strike a bargain with you. We'll forget the other matter, that is," he said, grinning menacingly, "if you have ten sticks of dynamite for me tomorrow."

At this, Clarence found his voice and quaveringly tried to tell the Irishman that the dynamite was kept under lock and key, but the big man thrust his face close to Clarence's and ignoring his words said, "Dynamite, One Eye, and I'll pick it up tomorrow when we stop for water." He then said with a kindly smile, "Then you don't have to worry about us anymore, but if you try any tricks…" He left the threat unsaid; he had got the measure of Clarence and he did not have to say more.

Poor Clarence, he felt his new way of living slipping away from him, he was in a terrible state. It took all his power to walk into the shop and ask for MacDonald's tobacco, for he might be scared stiff of the Irishman but the other big rough man was waiting for him down in the cutting, and he could be brutal as well.

Clarence was away from Frodsham as fast as he could, but when he had handed the tobacco over to MacDonald, he was almost in pieces. He knew how impossible it was to get in the explosives building on the Marsh and he had no hope of finding dynamite anywhere else.

The explosives store lying in the area between Runcorn and Ellesmere Port was a strongly built building constructed of brick and perched on brick columns, averting any chance of being affected by floods. There was no steel or iron used in its construction for fear of metal striking metal, causing sparking. Even the locks and keys were made of brass, and were of the strongest type. More to the point, the place was well guarded.

Clarence still had no idea where he was to obtain the explosives from when he went back to the site after his evening meal. He had made an excuse that he was 'going ter see to me horse'. Beth was surprised and rather concerned at her lodger's lack of appetite and remarked to Thomas and Michael about it.

After he had made a show of 'seeing' to the animal for the benefit of any watchers, he decided that he would try MacDonald's cabin on the off chance that the foreman had broken the rules and kept some dynamite in his cupboard. He knew that the man was to attend his eldest son's wedding in Salford the following day, hence his earlier genial mood. It was a much needed stroke of luck. By this time he should be on the Manchester train, so the cabin would be unoccupied.

It was fairly dark in the cutting, the full moon being obscured behind banks of drifting cloud, and Clarence was able to approach the cabin masked by a train of railway wagons. Shaking with fear he crept round to the door, but as he reached it, the moon broke out of the cloud cover and bathed everywhere with a brilliant glow. He bolted into the cabin, only to come up short with a strangled cry of fright.

The strong smell of whisky in the cabin should have told him that the place was not unoccupied, but before he knew it the huge dark form was coming at him cursing like only MacDonald could curse, and Clarence realised that the foreman had not yet left for Salford.

With a speed born of long practice, Clarence was out of the doorway in an instant and was running alongside the wagons. Then he heard a loud crash. Suddenly all was silent; no sounds of pursuit or the roar of MacDonald.

Within ten minutes he was back at the Banhams hut. Thomas was about to make his way up to bed, and after a few words with Clarence, left him to make his ablutions and a last cup of tea before he too went to his bed.

When the still-shaken young man crept into the bunk room, Michael was sound asleep and his soft snoring did not falter as his room-mate quietly climbed into his own bunk.

For a long time he was too agitated to sleep; the sound of MacDonald's suddenly silenced roar was playing on his mind. The old Clarence would have callously shrugged it off, but the new Clarence was bedevilled by images of the drunken foreman lying injured in his cabin and nobody there to help him.

The next thing he knew was Michael urging him to wake up and telling him it was six o'clock. His befuddled mind told him that something important had to be done but it was a few moments before the events of the night before came flooding back. Once again he felt the hopelessness of his position and wished that he could wake up again and find that he had been having a nightmare.

The sounds of movement in the main room told him that the Banhams were up and about.

"I don't feel so good today," Clarence told Michael dolefully. "Another couple of hours in bed might put me right though." Michael clucked his tongue in sympathy and told Clarence that he would let somebody know how he was.

Beth fussed over him and made him have a warm drink, and this made the miserable young man really guilty. He was having to deceive them all and he was ashamed of himself for doing so.

When everyone was away to work, Beth told Clarence that she was taking Peter to school, then was doing some shopping with Mrs. Robbins in the town, so she would not be back for a couple of hours. She was worried that he would need some help whilst she and Mrs. Robbins were out. With a feeling of relief Clarence assured her that he would probably be at work before they were back.

As soon as he saw them pass Mr. Hughes's shop, he pulled out his sack from under his bed and carefully loaded it with his possessions. By this time he had much more to his name than when he had arrived at Marshville over nine months previously.

He had tears in his eyes as he looked at his writing pad and pencils. How everybody had helped him; they had made a tremendous difference to his confidence and to his outlook on life. He would never forget them and he was going to leave before he could show them his gratitude.

When he saw that the street was clear of people, he left the hut and, skirting the shop, he made his way along to the timber field. Eventually he found what he was looking for, a space between the planks where he could hide his sack. He placed some short lengths of wood over his cache then, satisfied that he could easily find it when he came back after dark, he went to his work.

He was given a telling-off by the other horse driver but he could take that; at least he did not have to suffer the wrath of MacDonald. The foreman's name was only mentioned casually in passing, and there was no talk of him being found injured. Clarence began to feel less guilty about leaving him without checking whether the man was not badly hurt.

Even so, he still had to leave the job; the Irishman's friends would soon be on to him when they learned that he had failed to get them what they wanted, and he had heard stories of what the Fenians did to people who crossed them. Perhaps, he thought, even now the big man might be looking for him in Frodsham, and when he, Clarence, did not meet him the man would probably get his confederates on the site to deal with him. His blood ran cold at what they would do.

That night he managed to eat his meal without any difficulty. Now that the die was cast and he knew that he was leaving, the panic had subsided. The worst emotion he had to contend with was sadness. To sit there amongst these people who conducted their lives without quarrelling and swearing, and being thoughtful and kind to each other, was something he had never before experienced. However, he resolved that from that day on he too was going to be like them.

Dusk was approaching when Clarence left the hut for the last time. Again using the excuse that he was seeing to his horse, he let himself out and walked towards the cutting, but instead of descending into it, he walked along the side until he reached the end of the timber stack.

Keeping his eye open for the night watchman, Clarence made his way back to where he had left his sack. Nobody appeared to challenge him, and by the time darkness had fallen he was on his way towards Ellesmere Port.

Like the night before, the moon was playing hide-and-seek with the clouds and there were times when the railway track he was following was only just discernable. In the distance were pools of light where men were still at work. A persistent cold wind was sweeping across from the river but this did not bother Clarence, for he was too steeped in his misery to notice such trifling discomforts. He had not felt so alone in the world since he was a child.

He felt a lump rise in his throat and as his grief gripped him, he howled like a child. Sinking to the ground, he crouched on the railway line and sobbed until he could cry no more. For a while he stayed there with his head cradled in his arms, only to lift it when he had purged the worst of his pain.

Eventually he rose to his feet, wiping the traces of his tears with the back of his sleeve, then set off again.

Presently a locomotive hauling a long train of wagons approached. Clarence stood back to let the train go by. The driver, recognising him from an occasion when he had hauled spoil trains out of the cutting, stopped the train and invited him to enjoy a lift. The kindness went in some small way to lift Clarence's spirits. Even the moon played its part in making him forget his troubles for a few moments as it bathed everything with its brilliance, giving a beauty to everything, even the raw earth of the excavation.

Once at Ellesmere Port, Clarence left the locomotive after thanking the driver and fireman for the lift, then shouldering his sack, he made his way up the road to the railway station. What was ahead of him he did not know, but with his new-found confidence he believed that he would be alright.

Chapter 22

Dafyd Hughes

Mr. Alwyn Bryn Hughes, Dafyd's father, started his working life at twelve years of age in a grocer's shop in Caerwys, North Wales. He was a quick learner and he was interested in the work. He moved to Chester where he met and married Rebecca Eastwood, Becky to most of those who knew her.

By Eighteen Eighty-Seven he owned five shops in the Chester area and dreamed of opening a large shop in the city itself. He also had a twenty-one year old son, Dafyd.

After Dafyd had completed his education, he had a yearning to enter the retail trade. His father insisted that he started from the bottom of the ladder to learn the trade fully. Dafyd was quite happy to do so, but the drawback was that most of his fellow workers treated him differently from the other assistants and the young man was not comfortable with the situation. He simply wanted to be treated as a normal employee.

Everything changed for him after his father read about the building of the canal to Manchester, and followed the saga of the tussle between the promoters and its antagonists with interest. When the Manchester Ship Canal Bill was passed in both Houses of Parliament on the third attempt, he commented on the perseverance of the Manchester men.

However, when he heard that the main contractor, Mr. T. A. Walker, was to provide shops as well as hospitals, schools and rest rooms for his workforce, his interest was really sharpened, and he applied for the chance of setting up a grocery and vegetable shop. Dafyd was really enthusiastic about the idea. The plan was that if his father was successful in his bid, he would stock the shop for the first month or so, then leave the running of it to Dafyd. Eventually the young man was to take over the ordering of everything himself, setting up his local suppliers and, if necessary, employing an assistant.

Dafyd had hoped for a shop at Ellesmere Port, that is, if they were lucky to get one. Therefore he was a little disappointed when they were told that they could have the one at the Frodsham Depot, or Marshville as the hutted village was called.

He was more cheered when his mother told him that her childhood friend had a house in Frodsham, and that she be would happy for him to call on her.

His first few months had been extremely hard. He made several blunders in either ordering too much or not enough and by stocking goods which did not sell. He also had trouble with his first assistant, a local boy, but when Clara came to work for him everything went so much better. He also hated Marshville and was very homesick.

In the summer of the previous year a business acquaintance of his father had attended a garden party at the Christleton home of the Hughes family. Whilst the man and his wife had proved to be pleasant and unassuming, their daughter Julia was a vivacious but very determined girl, and had made it obvious that she was set on becoming close friends with Dafyd. Naturally the unworldly young man, flattered by the attentions of the pretty and graceful girl, had asked her to accompany him on an outing. He then invited her to the tennis club where he played regularly.

Julia did not play tennis nor, it transpired, had she any intention of learning to play, and that was after imploring him to take her there with him. Her conversation with the other people watching was mainly about fashions and clothes generally and expensive possessions. To some of the ladies present she was ill-mannered and shallow, but they would certainly not dream of saying so to Dafyd, who was a popular member,

There were many other instances of her fondness for money, or to be more correct, the spending of it, but it was the criticisms of the things he did for enjoyment that irritated him most. He found that he was defending his singing in the Chapel choir. Even his being a Methodist afforded her some amusement; dull, serious-minded people, she called them. Julia put her foot down firmly against coming on the river with him, pointing out the fact that her dresses would be ruined if they were to be splashed.

Daffyd was very keen on rowing, and also enjoyed walking, sometimes taking a train to North Wales and spending a weekend tramping for miles with his friends. Again, walking was not to the girl's taste, her preferred mode of travel being in a carriage. However, the Hughes family phaeton she considered too staid and old-fashioned. Julia tried to cajole him into buying a smart, brightly painted carriage, but Dafyd could not see the point of buying something that he knew would hardly be used.

Dafyd's mother, whilst at first being charmed by the girl, had very soon come to the conclusion that Julia was primarily interested in the Hughes family fortune, her son being the key to sharing it. Also it had become increasingly obvious that in the presence of Dafyd's father, she was everything a young lady should be, but when he was not there she tended to be polite but not much more to Dafyd's mother. It was this last trait which angered him so much that decided the young man to distance himself from the girl.

He felt that he had had a very narrow escape and it was for this reason that he became suspicious of Victoria's sudden change of attitude towards him. He began to suspect that Mrs. Hilyard had let it slip about his family situation, something he had asked her not to divulge. Of course, he reasoned, it was not beyond the bounds of possibility that the girl had learned of his family from another source, but what was undeniably true in his mind was that he was hopelessly in love with Victoria.

His attitude towards her remained the same, courteous and affable but no more. Only on rare occasions did he let slip his mask of platonic friendship, and those were the times when he had sung and she had played the piano.

Mrs. Hilyard had been quick to notice the change in him during her musical evenings, and she had become concerned for her maid's sake. She had grown very fond of Victoria and did not want her to be let down if Dafyd was only amusing himself, albeit innocently. However, knowing the young man as she did, Mrs. Hilyard had difficulty in convincing herself that he was so insensitive as to play such a cruel game.

The young man himself was always finding other admirable sides to Victoria's nature. When Clarence unaccountably left them, Will had told him how upset the Banham household was. Will's mother and Victoria had wept for the unfortunate young man who had been trying so hard to better himself.

This sympathetic side to the girl's character had made a strong impression on Dafyd, more so because Clarence had never been a prepossessing person in either speech or appearance.

Dafyd's mother had listened to her son's account of the first musical evening with extra interest. It was the first time that he had mentioned the girl who accompanied him on the piano, but she sensed that he was being deliberately neutral about her whilst extolling her wonderful playing. When Mrs. Hughes asked her son if he had met her before, she knew immediately that there was more to the affair when he eventually admitted that she was Will's sister, and that her family lived not more than fifty yards from his shop.

The fact that the father was a contractor's employee caused Dafyd's parents a certain amount of uneasiness. Not that they were prejudiced against people from the working classes; after all, they both came from humble beginnings. It was simply that they saw contractors and other itinerant people as being rootless, almost like gypsies.

Mrs. Hughes wrote to her friend Mrs. Hilyard expressing their uneasiness about his interest in the girl, and asked her to keep an eye on their son.

When Mrs. Hilyard read the letter her feelings were quite mixed. On one hand she sympathised with Rebecca regarding the possibility that her son could end up being trapped into an unsuitable liaison. On the other hand, however, she found herself rearing up in defence of her maid and her parents. Mrs. Hilyard had come to know them as really delightful people and their two sons were also a credit to them.

These and other complimentary observations about the maid and her family were included in a somewhat tart letter, but she then softened it by giving an open invitation to her friend to come and stay with her at a time when she was holding one of her musical evenings

When Mrs. Hughes received the reply to her letter, she was quite surprised at the tone of it but resolved to accept the invitation. After all, she told her husband, it was their son's future happiness she was concerned about, not that of an employee. It was not that she was indifferent to the wellbeing of servants; she had cause enough to be sympathetic to their lot in life.

Therefore, the next time Mrs. Hilyard held a soirée, her friend was invited and she gladly accepted. Mr. Hughes did not accompany her, partly because he was a busy man and also in respect of his son's plea not to let people know that he was anything other than a humble shopkeeper. Dafyd had laughingly suggested that if he was intent on seeing the shop at Marshville, it would be better if he came dressed in poor clothing. That was something his father would not do; his one vanity since he had become better off was to indulge his taste in good suiting, and the thought of dressing poorly did not appeal to him at all!

Mrs. Hughes was met at Frodsham station by Mrs. Hilyard's handyman with the pony trap. Whether it was his passenger's pleasant manner or her inexpensive mode of dress, the man immediately became less surly and engaged in friendly chat with her all the way back to the house.

The front door was opened by a tall, slender girl wearing an anxious expression on her face. However, she was efficient enough and showed the visitor into the front parlour whilst the handyman took the bags up to the landing. Mrs. Hughes smiled and thanked him, at which she was rewarded with a villainous smile and a touch of his cap.

The girl said with an uncertain smile, "I'll go and tell the mistress you are here, Mrs., er, Hughes," then with a quick bob, she almost ran out of the room forgetting to take Mrs. Hughes's coat. "So that is Victoria," said Mrs. Hughes to herself. "Well, she does seem to be trying to please, but surely Dafyd has not fallen for this girl."

Just as she was about to seat herself, her friend hurried into the room. "Becky," cried Mrs. Hilyard, embracing Dafyd's mother, who happily hugged her in return.

Mrs. Hughes answered her and said, "It is good to see you, Florence, after all these months, and it was so good of you to invite me. I am really looking forward to your musical evening."

Her friend clapped her hand and said gaily, "I am sure you will enjoy it, but right now I am sure you will be ready for a cup of tea. Victoria will bring everything to us in a few minutes." Then noticing her friend's coat over the arm of the chair she said resignedly, "Oh, Becky, that girl," and shaking her head placed it over her arm and made for the door.

At that moment Victoria entered the room with a tea trolley carrying the teapot, cups and saucers and a loaded cake stand. She curtsied to Mrs. Hughes and smiled. In those first few moments Dafyd's mother understood why her son was so taken with the girl. She was absolutely beautiful!

When Victoria noticed the coat over her mistress's arm, she quickly said, "If you wish, ma'am, I will take Mrs. Hughes's coat," and she smiled again at the visitor.

The effect of Victoria's smile on Rebecca Hughes was remarkable. She had come to Frodsham resolved to find the true character of the girl and not be deviated from her purpose by winsome looks. Yet here she was, warmly returning the girl's smile in spite of herself. How could she have been so dense as to think that the girl who had let her into the house was capable of rousing such enthusiasm in Dafyd's conversation. This girl, she had to admit, could certainly do that. Victoria positively lit up the room when she smiled. However, she told herself firmly, a winning smile did not give a shallow person any more depth.

That evening at the appointed time Mrs. Hilyard's guests started to arrive and when everyone was present, she introduced Mrs. Hughes to them as her childhood and dearest friend. Victoria had been anxious about what the effect of so many well-dressed people would have on Dafyd's mother. However, she need not have bothered herself. Mrs. Hughes sat and smiled serenely at everyone, looking quite at ease.

The girl could tell that Mr. Hughes was uncomfortable about his mother and her choice of dress, but he too began to relax as he realised that there were no covert glances in her direction, and no signs of anybody discussing her behind their hands. His mother, as was her wont, was very quickly in affable conversation with those around her.

The evening's entertainment was, as usual, well received. A gentleman from the town played the concertina and sang some sea shanties as a light-hearted interlude from Victoria's playing and Dafyd's singing.

For Dafyd's mother it was a revelation. Her son and Victoria were so in tune with each other that it was almost uncanny. She felt her eyes moisten with emotion when Dafyd sang, and she saw something during a particular song directed at her, which gave her a lot to think about. During an unguarded moment on the girl's part, she was looking up at Dafyd with an expression of such sweetness that Mrs. Hughes was convinced that Victoria's admiration for her son was genuine.

It had been a wonderful evening for Dafyd's mother. She had heard her son sing in Chapel and on occasions around the house, but to hear him accompanied by such a gifted piano player and on such a fine instrument moved her ineffably and made her feel so proud.

Later, when they were alone, Mrs. Hilyard said with an amused smile on her face, "Well, Becky, if I were a gambler I would wager that Victoria is not the girl you had imagined her to be." Mrs. Hughes replied slowly. "I have to tell you, Florence, that I am overwhelmed by the girl, and I am having to ask myself, is her demeanour a clever deception or is she as perfect as she appears."

Her friend began to defend her maid, but Mrs. Hughes stopped her with a gesture and said, "I am not saying the girl is a cunning deceiver, indeed, I would say that I have difficulty in believing that she is capable of being devious, but Victoria is like no other girl I have ever met."

Mrs. Hilyard relaxed and told her of an incident involving her maid that painted a different picture of the gentle and cheerful girl, but one of a young woman with a blazing temper.

"We were out shopping," she began, "and at the bottom of High Street where the road starts to climb, you know where I am referring to?" Mrs. Hughes nodded and her friend carried on with her story. "Well, a dray was being pulled by two horses and one of them was having trouble keeping its grip on the sets. The driver was using his whip on the poor creature." She stopped when her friend interjected indignantly, "The brute, he wanted whipping himself." Her friend smiled grimly and told her, "That is what Victoria said and when the poor horse slipped to its knees, she leapt at the man and wrenched the whip out of his hand, and she would have used it on the driver but his mate stopped her." Then Mrs. Hilyard said, "And you know what, Becky, the crowd cheered her, and the driver was forced to leave the animal alone whilst it got to its feet."

Mrs. Hughes was round-eyed as she imagined the scene and said, "What happened after that, Florence, what happened to the horse and what did Victoria do next?"

Her friend said happily, "Well, the constable came over and made the drayman stay there until another horse was fetched; he examined the ill-treated horse then charged the driver with causing injury to the animal."

"But what about Victoria?" said Mrs. Hughes, satisfied that the driver was not getting away with his cruel treatment of the horse. "The policeman," said Mrs. Hilyard, "told her that if she had used the whip on the man, she also would have been facing charges. Then he praised her for her courage and told her to go home and forget all about it." She then concluded by saying quietly, "Victoria took a few days before she was back to her usual self. I have never seen her cry before and I do not want to see her cry like that again."

Mrs. Hughes tried to imagine the girl acting in such a fierce manner and failed; instead of seeing her gripping the whip, all she could see in her mind's eye were those slender fingers caressing the piano keys.

Mrs. Hilyard was speaking again. "Victoria is a charming creature but not everyone warms to her; my handyman can be very surly with her, but she has grown used to him and does not seem to let him bother her." Then she said, shaking her head, "Even my own mother cannot abide her, she thinks that the girl is an upstart and should be put in her proper place."

At that Mrs. Hughes laughed and said, "Well, Florence, that is just what your mother told us when we were younger." Her friend nodded and quoted her mother, saying, "Who do you think you are, girl? What was good enough for your dad and me is good enough for you. Know your station in life."

Both women laughed, albeit a little ruefully, as they reflected on life around Salmons Leap in Chester. The fathers of both women had been salmon fishermen, amongst other things, and life had been hard. The friends had vowed that they would better themselves, which they had done, but it had only served to make Florence's mother more caustic.

The following morning Mrs. Hilyard asked Victoria to sit with her and her friend, and after they had discussed the events of the previous evening, Mrs. Hughes led the conversation around to the Banhams presence in Frodsham. Victoria willingly talked about her family's life at Longfields Estate, and in particular about her and her mother's role in Reeve House under Mr. and Mrs. Serle, but did not mention the new owners.

Mrs. Hughes told the girl that she too had been in service. "I started at twelve years of age as a scullery maid," she said reminiscently, "at Eaton Hall, the Duke of Westminster's place." Then she laughed and said, "It was only about a mile and a half from Salmons Leap, but by the difference in living, it could have been a hundred miles away."

She smiled at the entranced girl and told her, "And do you know, Victoria, in those first few weeks I could not run down that long drive fast enough to get back to that squalid cottage I called home!"

Victoria, who had never experienced that sort of feeling, could not understand, after visiting the cottage near Salmons Leap with her mistress, how anybody could want to hurry back to that place.

Mrs. Hughes went on with her description of life at Eaton Hall for a small, frightened child. However, once she was seen to be a willing worker, she experienced a great deal of kindness and settled in quite happily.

"On my days off," she said, "I would trudge down the drive to Handbridge, that is the area on the other side of the Dee bridge from where Mrs. Hilyard and me was born and bred, and when I got to our cottage my mam would send me straight away to a shop in Chester with a big bundle of coats." She explained to the listening girl, "Mam would get the coats from the shop and sew the linings in to earn a few coppers; a lot of people did what they called 'piece work' at home." Then she said quite soberly, "If the salmon were not running and no other work came Dad's way, we would be out of our cottage and starving within a couple of weeks." Mrs. Hilyard nodded with feeling; she too had known the constant fear of eviction.

Her friend sat back, not seeming to see anything in the room as she looked back to her childhood days. She then turned to Mrs. Hilyard and laughingly asked her if she remembered the first time they had set eyes on the future Mr. Hughes.

Both women laughed and Dafyd's mother said, "There he was in this grocery shop slicing bacon on the machine, then he moved down the counter and he almost disappeared; he was so small that he had to stand on a box to use the bacon slicer!"

The friends set off into further peals of laughter and Mrs. Hilyard giggled, "And then he came out from behind the counter to serve us with broken biscuits that we had come for, and there he was…" At this point the friends rocked with laughter and it was half a minute before they could control themselves to carry on with the tale. "Then there he was," Mrs. Hilyard repeated, "all four foot six of him, all dignified, wearing a man's apron that touched the floor, we nearly split our sides trying not to laugh."

The images that the two friends created had Victoria laughing as much as they were.

After the women had managed to regain control of their mirth, Mrs. Hughes said fondly, "Two years later I suddenly realised that when he walked away from the bacon slicer, he was still at the same height, whilst I was still a little tiddler, but he seemed to like me so I was often going into the shop on some pretence or other."

Mrs. Hilyard said, "And my late husband was at that time his best friend, so later, when Becky, er, Mrs. Hughes started walking out with the young man, we would walk out together; the four of us were almost inseparable those days."

Then Mrs. Hughes said lightly, "Enough about us, what brought your father to Cheshire, Victoria? Your situation seemed to be so very pleasant."

The girl, who a moment ago had been enjoying hearing about her mistress and Mrs. Hughes's childhood, went very quiet and it appeared to the two friends that she was reluctant to talk about that particular part of the family's life. However, once Victoria had hesitantly embarked on the circumstances that caused them to leave Wroxing, the whole miserable story came out and she ended up in tears about her late mistress, Mrs. Rodgerson. "We had to come away and leave her to that beast," she cried in anguish, "he didn't love her, he only loved himself. Oh, how I hate him and after what he tried…" Her voice faltered, and the two stricken women looked on helplessly while Victoria wept.

Mrs. Hilyard moved over to sit alongside the distraught girl and held her until her weeping had stopped.

"Victoria," she said gently, "did this man harm you in any way? If he did you should have spoken out, he should not have gone unpunished." Almost before Mrs. Hilyard had finished Victoria burst out, "But my dad and mam worked there as well, and the cottage went with Dad's job, besides," she said tremulously, "that man did not succeed in harming me, he was thwarted both times." Mrs. Hilyard coaxed the story of both events out of her and continued holding her whilst Victoria wept afresh.

When the girl had recovered, she began to apologise to both women and begged them never to tell anyone about her disclosures. Then she said anxiously to Mrs. Hughes, "Please, ma,am, do not tell Mr. Hughes, I could not bear it if he knew."

The lady looked at her kindly, knowing exactly which Mr. Hughes the girl was referring to, and said, "My dear, Dafyd will only know if the words come from your own lips." With that statement Rebecca Hughes affirmed to herself that she would welcome Victoria as a future daughter-in-law should it ever come to be.

Then Victoria stood up and said, almost whispering to her mistress, "If you want me to leave, ma,am, I will go and get my things and go today."

Mrs. Hilyard almost gaped at her and said angrily, "What on earth are you talking about, girl, why should I want you to go? Just because a man abuses his position and power against you does not make you a sinner." Then she said more kindly, "Now that you have spoken of the matter to us, I hope that you will feel easier in your mind, and for goodness sake, Victoria," she added gently, "stop feeling guilty about it."

With an uncertain smile Victoria excused herself and escaped to her own room. She sat there for a while thinking about all that had been said in the parlour. "It is true," she said to herself, "I am behaving silly being ashamed of what happened, and Mrs. Hilyard is right, I did nothing to invite his attentions and nothing did happen to me."

Victoria busied herself working with Daisy for the rest of the day and was glad to flop into bed that night. However, she may have been tired but in herself was more contented than she had been for a long time; the rebuke from Mrs. Hilyard had served its purpose.

All week she had been looking forward to seeing Dafyd at Chapel, and on the Sunday she took even more pains with her appearance than usual. Although Victoria did not know it, if she had turned up in her normal working garb, she would still have played havoc with the young man's emotions.

After the service, Mrs. Hilyard introduced her friend to the Banham family. Before long, she and Beth were chattering away totally at ease with other. Of course Peter, not to be left out, embarrassed his mother and Victoria by asking Mrs. Hughes if she was coming to see them at their 'hut'. "You can see my vegetables," he said proudly, "me and Clarence are growing carrots and potatoes." Then he said sadly, "Only Clarence has gone now so he won't ever see them."

Beth managed to find her voice and with an agonised glance at Victoria said warningly to her son, "Peter," then Will, seeing the look on his mother's face, quickly ushered his brother away from the group, leaving Beth to apologise for him.

Mrs. Hughes smiled understandingly but passed the little boy's words off saying, "But surely, Mrs. Banham, it shows that you have given him a happy, loving home and he is proud of it." Beth acknowledged the truth of her words, then in a rush said, "Peter may be proud of it but for me and Victoria, it is hardly a place to boast of, though I must admit that right now there is no mud or dust to put up with."

At that moment Dafyd, having spoken to the minister, came over to join them. Mrs. Hilyard, who had been waiting to speak with the minister, excused herself and left them. Mrs. Hughes smiled up at her son and told him, "I am coming to see your shop this afternoon, Dafyd," then added, "and I would really like to see this 'big ditch' that people talk about."

In the presence of the Banhams, Dafyd was cornered. Whatever arguments he might be able to put forward against his mother visiting Marshville, they could hardly be voiced in front of Victoria and her mother. Therefore he had to agree and put on a good face into the bargain. On the other hand, he was proud of what he had achieved with the shop. Also deep down he knew that his mother would not be so thoughtless as to mention his father's shops or their situation in life.

Mrs. Hilyard suggested to Victoria that she should take the rest of the day off and spend it with her family, and the girl was quite happy to comply. Dafyd was to have his midday meal with his mother and Mrs. Hilyard, then afterwards bring his mother down in the trap to Marshville. Will was entrusted with the opening of the shop for the afternoon.

After their meal, Dafyd and his mother set off to the hutted village. Although cool, there was very little wind and as they proceeded along Moorditch Lane, smoke could be seen at various points showing where some steam-driven pieces of machinery were working. Thankfully for the people who lived in Marshville, there were no piledrivers working, so a relative peace reigned.

Dafyd had been explaining various things to his mother concerning the excavation, then during a lull in the conversation she turned to him and said seriously, "Dafyd, how deep are your feelings for Victoria?" When he did not answer immediately, she continued, "I do gain a strong impression that you care for her, and if that is so, I think that you should be perfectly frank with her and tell the girl about our situation." Then she said quietly, "And I do believe that the young lady cares a great deal about you, and what is more, I have grown to like her very much."

For a few moments her son stayed silent, then he said slowly, "I do admire Miss Banham, that I cannot deny, but there is something odd about the way she behaved when the family came here." He looked at his mother and said in a puzzled voice, "Within minutes of her entering the shop she adopted a cold attitude, almost one of dislike, and it was months before she thawed towards me." He then said in the same aggrieved tone, "Then a few weeks ago everything changed, it was if the sun came out. I had seen her smile in a most wonderful way, but never for me." Then he said in a puzzled voice, "Suddenly she became so different, the smile remained on her face even when she looked my way." He then went on thoughtfully, "I cannot help but suspect that somehow the girl has learned that my father is not simply a shopkeeper who is earning just enough to live on. I simply do not understand girls."

His mother laughed at him but not in an unkindly way, and told him, "Your father says that the man who tells you that he understands women is either deluded or a liar, but I can tell you this, Dafyd, we are not so mysterious, we just have our own ways, that is all." Then she added, "Why not ask the girl herself what the reason is for her change of mind? I am sure that Victoria would not be afraid to give you an honest answer."

Her son's reaction was much as she had expected; he was obdurate, he wanted more time to satisfy himself as to the girl's motives. His mother shook her head and said warningly, "Do not procrastinate too long, son, a girl like that will not lack admirers, especially as she is now living in the town where there are many men, and not many girls will wait forever."

Nothing more was said and presently they were entering the street in Marshville. Mrs. Hughes looked around her with interest, and she could see why Mrs. Banham so disliked the place. The black, tar-coated huts and the rough road between certainly looked forbidding, yet here and there were brave splashes of colour where some hut dwellers had planted flowers. There were also at least three small shrubs growing in tubs or boxes. The fact that people were doing something to alleviate the drabness was heartening.

As she alighted from the trap she turned eagerly to look at her son's shop. What a welcoming difference from the dwellings. Under each window were the usual brightly coloured stove enamelled advertising signs. On one a pretty child was depicted with a cup on a tray and was proclaiming the pleasure of drinking Cadbury's Cocoa, whilst a second, more serious one urged everyone to use McDougalls Self-Raising flour. If, however, the ladies were more concerned with cleanliness, a third extolled the virtues of using Pears Soap.

The two windows of the shop displayed just enough of the goods for sale to make them all attractive. Together with the smartly painted signboard above the shop that advised everyone that the grocery and general goods store was owned by Mr. D. Hughes, it was a bright and cheery sight in a drab street.

It took Mrs. Hughes back to when, as a newly married couple, she and her husband had set up shop in Hoole village, which is about half a mile from the centre of Chester. She could still after all these years remember the exciting feeling of adventure.

When she entered her son's shop, Will was behind the counter serving a woman, and he smiled at Mrs. Hughes but stayed attentive to his customer as he had been taught. The woman observed that the rain was holding off, then nodding pleasantly to Dafyd and his mother, left the shop. Mrs. Hughes was given a quick tour of the premises, including her son's cosy living quarters, and expressed her pleasure at what he had achieved with such a small space to play with. Dafyd simply smiled and thanked his mother but deep down he was delighted at being able to show her the results of his labours.

Just as Will was about to suggest that he put a brew on for all of them, Victoria entered the shop. "Good afternoon, Mrs. Hughes, Mr. Hughes," she said, blushing slightly, then added, "and Will." Then, as everyone laughed, she said to Dafyd's mother, "Mam said if you have time to visit, she would be pleased to see you."

Mrs. Hughes looked at her son and, observing his expression, sighed inwardly and thought, 'Oh, son, why don't you talk honestly with the girl?' His whole demeanour had changed when Victoria had walked in; he certainly could not conceal his feelings from his mother.

It was Dafyd who spoke first. He beamed and said, "Well, Mother, if I take you down to see the Canal cutting now, you can call on Mrs. Banham within the next half hour." Then, turning to Victoria, he asked, "Is that alright with you, Miss Banham?" The pink-faced girl replied that it would be perfectly alright, and after Mrs. Hughes had told her that she would be delighted to visit them, excused herself and went back to their hut.

As Dafyd and his mother set off down the street towards the excavation, they met Mrs. Robbins, the two women were introduced, then Dafyd told his mother that Mr. Robbins was doing his bookkeeping for him and it showed that the shop was paying its way. After a few pleasantries, they went on their way whilst Mrs. Robbins carried on to the shop.

Dafyd's mother was simply amazed at the immensity of the cutting. She had not imagined that such a large trench could be made by Man, even if he was aided by the large excavators that, as they watched, were gouging deeper still.

As they walked back to the village, her son pointed out the workshops where Mr. Banham was foreman. Mrs. Hughes said thoughtfully with a sidelong glance at her son, "You know, Dafyd, your father would love to see all this." At that, Dafyd felt even more churlish and he was stuck for something to say, and all he could do was to agree, but added that there were much more interesting sights at Eastham.

When they arrived at the Banhams' hut, Dafyd waited whilst his mother was ushered inside, then crossed over to the shop where Will would make them both a brew.

Beth welcomed her visitor with a pleased smile, and to add to the welcome, Mrs. Hughes was met by the glorious smell of a cake being baked. It transported her back to her childhood, for her mother, although a weary and overworked woman, was a first-class baker, and when she could afford the ingredients, would bake a most delicious fruit cake.

Victoria made herself busy by brewing a pot of tea whilst her mother took their visitor's coat and invited her to sit in Beth's own chair. Peter was under strict orders not to bother Mrs. Hughes and sat on his box-seat with his toy crane on his knees. He was obviously straining at the leash to tell her his news!

Beth said anxiously, "Would you like a piece of fruit cake, Mrs. Hughes? It is my own baking," she said rather unnecessarily in view of the smell coming from the oven.

Almost before she had finished speaking, Dafyd's mother said warmly, "If it tastes as good as it smells, Mrs. Banham, I most certainly would like a piece," and then went on to praise the comfortable homely room they were sitting in.

The place had been transformed since the Tarletons had occupied the hut. The walls had been painted a light colour and the wooden boarded floor was painted all around the edges where no feet were liable to scuff them, whilst on the rest of the floor were home-made rugs. Beth explained that Sally 'With The Twins' made them to earn some extra money. After she had mentioned Sally (with the twins) a second time, Beth laughingly explained that there were two women called Sally, so everyone always tacked on the 'twins' to differentiate between the two.

A well-blacked range with a highly burnished knob and hinges gave off a comforting warmth as well as the mouth-watering smell which pervaded the room.

Three pictures took Mrs. Hughes's attention. One was a painting of her son's shop and was signed 'M. Rourke', whilst a second depicted a half-timbered cottage that she was almost sure that she had seen in Frodsham. The third picture showed a three-masted schooner sailing down river towards the open sea. The last two were good but not quite as good as the first one, and were signed Will Banham.

Mrs. Hughes, who had got up from her chair to look at them, turned as Beth said, "Michael, our lodger, is teaching my boys to paint; he says that Will has a natural talent." Then she added, "Our Peter is getting his own paints soon," and ruffled his hair as he came over and joined them.

Her youngest son, sensing that this was the right moment to speak, said, "Would you like to see my potatoes and carrots, Mrs. Hughes?" and she replied cheerfully before Beth could say anything, "Why, Peter, that is partly why I came to visit. Shall we see them now before the tea is poured?"

In an instant, Peter took her by the hand and led her outside. The vegetables, or those that remained, did indeed look fine and the little boy grinned from ear to ear when their visitor heaped her praises on them. After she had seen the toy crane that his dad and Will had made for him, she was allowed to sit and talk with Beth and Victoria.

She was so interested in all they were telling her about life in Marshville and at the Depot that she was very surprised when Dafyd knocked to remind her of the time. Reluctantly she made herself ready for her return to Mrs. Hilyard's house. She gave them all a big hug and told them how well she had enjoyed her time with them. Dafyd offered to take Victoria back to Mrs. Hilyard's after the girl had enjoyed her evening meal with her family, and he brushed aside her half-hearted protests by saying that it would save Will a long walk to and from the town later.

After their visitor had gone, mother and daughter looked at each other and happily voiced their opinions that Mrs. Hughes was a really nice lady. Peter said sagely that he thought that she knew all about vegetables, an observation which brought a smile to their faces.

As Dafyd and his mother travelled back to town, Mrs. Hughes wisely refrained from mentioning Victoria, but she had no qualms about praising the Banham family. She said to him that they were fine people to know and added that she hoped that they would be counted amongst her friends in the future.

Whilst not being subjected to a lecture about Victoria, his mother's silence on the matter only served to make her disapproval of his stance on the girl seem more eloquent, but he stubbornly refused to be drawn into another discussion about the young lady. As for talking things over with Victoria, her ability to change her attitude towards him so suddenly led him to the conclusion that he could not even be sure of the truth of her answers if he did get her to talk about the reasons for her behaviour.

Even he realised that he was shying away from learning the truth. Nevertheless, one point made by his mother had taken root in his mind and was now growing. Victoria, being at Mrs. Hilyard's house, was indeed more liable to meet eligible men, some of them in business and prosperous, others, whilst not being so prosperous, would be smartly dressed for their occupations, and possibly very attractive to the girl. Few of them would be at all like the men working on the excavation.

Also there were men in the chapel congregation, some of whom Dafyd had already noticed eyeing the girl covertly. One, Jack Yearsly, the clown of the chapel and a very ebullient character, was quite open in his admiration of Victoria, and he did make her laugh when he was acting the fool.

Then there was the older, brooding Mr. Sharples, a man whose wife had left him for another man. He too could often be observed watching the girl, and that man bothered Dafyd very much. There would be others that he was not even aware of, and typical of most idealistic young men in love, he desperately wanted to put himself forward as her protector. Unfortunately that would mean he would have to openly declare his commitment to Victoria, something he was loath to do in his present unhappy state of mind.

Meanwhile Victoria, blissfully unaware of the barrier Dafyd was erecting against her, allowed her love for him to blossom.

Chapter 23

Summer Eighteen Eighty-Nine

Some weeks after Mrs. Hughes had visited her friend in Frodsham, James and Charlotte Prentice had accepted Kate's invitation and moved into Reeve House. Although her health had much improved, Kate was still fearful of having to deal with her husband should he try to assert his marital 'rights'. In fact she was frightened of him, not for herself so much as for Mary. Kate knew he bore her maid a grudge, and she was well aware that he never forgot a grudge.

At one time she had dreamed of having Richard with her, his strong, steady presence there to shield her, but that was in the past, the truth being that he was never by her side when she needed him. He was always far away, at one time in India, and now in Cheshire. Never had there been a time when he was not committed to something that did not require his personal attention, not like James or Rod, who managed their affairs nearer home.

It pained James and Charlotte when Kate was so dismissive of Richard's occupation, but it heartened them when even the slightest hint of criticism of him brought an instant defence from her. Perversely Kate railed against him for not writing very often, ignoring the fact that she rarely wrote more than once a month herself.

With Captain Rodgerson only rarely at Reeve House, Kate saw more visitors than previously, and yet she was lonely. She was thankful for the continued presence of her brother and his wife, and that of James's friend Rod, who along with the vicar and his wife often called. Mary, of course, was her stalwart; without her Kate would have succumbed to melancholia again.

Kate would sometimes wake up from a dream in which she and Richard were friends once more as they were when she was a gangly fourteen-year-old trembling on the brink of womanhood, and realising that it was just a dream, would cry herself back to sleep again.

At Frodsham, Richard, convinced that Kate's love for him had died, also longed for those far-off days when everything seemed so simple. He too would have been happy to settle for their former warm friendship rather than the coolness which had come between them. Those few glorious weeks during which his life was so wonderfully changed were now just a memory, and he was still trying to comprehend how his dreams had been so effectively crushed in such a short time.

He kept his distress hidden and tried to bury himself in his work. However, just when he needed the distraction, the demands on his time had slackened, which left him with too many occasions to brood.

The weather had been very kind to them, and it looked set to continue. Whilst this was a blessing for the contractor, it was also a time when the farmers wanted men badly to help with the harvesting, and were luring the navvies away with the promise of higher wages.

Michael Rourke had asked for a few days off so that he could visit his parents, and was now in Belfast. Thanks to Thomas Banham, the workshops were much more efficient and the apprentices were benefitting from good instruction. Indeed, Robbie was turning out to be a very useful young man. Added to the fact that his physique had developed, he could cope with much heavier and more responsible work. The younger apprentice was also coming along quite well. All in all, everything was running so well that Captain Howard felt that he was not really needed and it left him making work in order to keep his mind occupied.

Beth was increasingly concerned at the pace at which Captain Howard was driving himself. And she sensed that there was a rift between him and Mrs. Rodgerson. Whatever the problem was, it upset her and Victoria to see him looking so unhappy at times.

Dafyd Hughes was also less than his usual cheery self. Just days after his mother had visited, he had finally acknowledged that she was right in what she had told him; he should talk to Victoria about his family's situation. However, he had no idea how he was to approach the matter. To tell the girl outright that his family were well off could appear as boasting and could either indicate to her that he considered his family's position in life to be higher than that of the Banhams, or could be seen as an attempt to attract her to him. It worried Dafyd that if she really was a girl of principle, his revelations would put a barrier between them. However, if she continued to shower him with smiles, he would then be convinced that Victoria was not the one for him.

Meanwhile Victoria, who often met Sarah Mills in the town, would stop for a cup of tea and a cake at the tea shop, and both girls would enjoy sharing confidences. On one such occasion, Victoria was telling her friend how pleasant Mrs. Hughes had been, and mentioned that the family lived in Christleton.

Sarah told Victoria that her father had a friend who lived in the same village and recalled that there was a grocer's shop owned by a Mr. Hughes. She reasoned that it could belong to the father of Mr. Hughes at Marshville

"Mind you," said Sarah, "I do believe that there is a Hughes's shop in Hoole village, but there again, Welsh names are not that uncommon in the Chester area, for after all the city is not that far from the Welsh border."

Victoria attached no significance to what Sarah had told her and the conversation turned to other things, Ian Blake's name featuring several times on Sarah's side.

Mrs. Hilyard had become very exasperated since her friend Becky Hughes had stayed with her. She had become more than ever aware that Dafyd had erected a wall between himself and Victoria even though she, Mrs. Hilyard, was convinced that he cared for the girl deeply. She could see that her maid appeared not to have noticed anything different in his behaviour, and it worried her that Victoria could be heading for an almighty letdown. Altogether she was not pleased with Dafyd Hughes.

Her friend Becky had in the meantime written a warmly worded letter to Beth, telling her how pleased she was to have met her and her family, and hoping that there would be other times when they would meet. Mrs. Hughes finished by extolling the virtues of Victoria, especially her wonderful piano playing.

Beth was delighted to receive the letter; she could hardly wait to tell Thomas when he got in from work. Other than the ones from Mrs. Rodgerson and an occasional one from Ruth Andern, very few letters came to their hut.

During the afternoon she went to the shop, and when the customer Mr. Hughes was serving had left, Beth told him of his mother's letter and how pleased she was to have received it. Before he could frame a reply, another woman entered, closely followed by Will, who had been delivering vegetables to Mrs. Garroway. With somebody else waiting to be served, Beth could not enlarge on the contents of the letter, so after getting what she had come for, she bid Mr. Hughes and Will goodbye and returned happily to the hut.

Mr. Hughes served his next customer in his usual cheerful manner but his thoughts were not so happy. Oh, how he wished that his mother had not become involved; he wanted to sort everything out in his own time and his own way. If he came to the sad conclusion that Victoria was not for him, he did not want his mother to be subject to the bitterness which might follow.

During the afternoon Mrs. Guest brought Peter back from school, and after she had left with her own boy, Peter asked her his usual question. "Has Clarence come back yet, Mam?" Beth felt quite sad; her little boy really did miss their absent lodger. Whilst Peter wandered outside to look at his and Clarence's remaining vegetables, his mother made him a drink.

Later, when the men came in, Beth had a visitor. It was one of the women of the village about a special fruit cake. Beth's reputation for cakes, as well as her dressmaking skills, had become well known. She did not charge a lot but what she did earn was put away, her very own savings!

Thomas was very pleased about Mrs. Hughes's letter; it showed how Beth's circle of friends was widening, and it helped in making her feel settled at Marshville. However, he was still hoping to find a house in the town for them, but so far nothing suitable had come their way, although at the present time, due to the fine weather, conditions were not too bad at the village.

Even so he feared that when the winter set in, it would mean a return to the depression which had settled on her when she first came to the place. With their daughter working for Mrs. Hilyard, it would be very difficult for Beth if things went badly for her. 'At least,' he thought, 'this time she would know that Jessie Robbins was there to help her.'

Towards the end of the week that Michael was away, the workshop dynamo started to give trouble. Thomas had learned much of the mysteries of electric lighting, but the dynamo was still an unknown creature to him. As it turned out, its workings were as much a mystery to Captain Howard. By the Saturday afternoon it finally had to be stopped, and in the workshop, silent now that the slapping of the belts was no longer heard, Thomas and his employer stared glumly at the useless dynamo.

Then through the open doors of the fitting shop, they observed a locomotive coming to a stop, and wonder of wonders! There was Michael, climbing down from the footplate, cheerily thanking the driver and fireman for the lift.

Michael was quite gratified at the enthusiastic reception from both men, and when he learned why they were so relieved to see him, told them that he would start on the problem immediately he had changed into his overalls. Captain Howard insisted he stopped and had his meal before he set to work. Thomas then turned to his employer and said, "Would you care to dine with us, sir? I know that Beth is only too pleased to give you a meal at any time."

Captain Howard was grateful for the offer and accepted. He had resigned himself to sitting in Thomas's office until both men returned. Mrs. Banham, as his foreman had pointed out, was always ready to feed him; she, like Mrs. Joyce, seemed to have taken on the task of mothering him.

Within an hour of returning to the workshops, Michael had found the fault, a problem with the commutator brushes, he told them, and the dynamo was started up. All three men stood grinning at each other as the lights came on, then Captain Howard and Thomas shook Michael's hand, much to his pleasure.

Afterwards, as they stood outside the workshop, the lights having been switched off for the night, the approaching dusk, heralded by the deepening blue of the sky, softened the harsh outlines of the excavation. Down below them there were just a few sights and sounds of activity. The clink of a shovel and the momentary glow from a boiler firehole door as the driver banked it up for the morrow's start, a horse snickered and another horse answered. Together with muted voices, they told of a good day ending peacefully.

Across the top of the embankment they could just make out the outlines of a ship with her navigation lights shining brightly, making her way on the last of the flood tide towards Runcorn Docks.

It was an enchanting time of the day, and of one accord the three men stood without speaking for a few moments, simply drinking in the peace and beauty of the moment.

Michael broke the silence saying in a hushed voice, "You know, sir, Mr. Banham, if you could bottle that, it would make us a fortune." Both men nodded, knowing exactly how he felt.

Captain Howard walked over to his horse and then stopped, turned, and said apologetically, "Thomas, there is no need for both of you to be here tomorrow. I will leave it to you to decide who should have the day off." Then he added, "I will be at the Bear's Paw tomorrow, I have a lot of writing to do."

With that he bade them goodnight and made his way up the village street. They could hear the voices of the people of the village as they acknowledged their employer passing by. He in his turn responded and with the effect of the evening still upon him, reflected that he was at home with these people, he respected them and they returned his respect. There was never a question of having to justify his actions; they knew that he was a man who expected the best from them but gave them his best and was considerate in time of family problems and sickness.

The street was quiet, yet many of the hut dwellers were outside, the women chatting whilst the men sat on the rough forms outside and smoked their pipes. Some of the older children were in groups, laughing and chattering as children do. The lamplight from some of the huts spilled out into the street, making it a homely, welcoming sight. Quiet greetings were called to Thomas and Michael as they strolled homewards, and they both felt a sense of contentment. Altogether, a truly magical end to the day.

Once inside their own hut, Beth insisted that Michael tell them all about his week with his family. "Well," said Michael, "it was not a rest, to be sure; my sister's brood never gave me a moment's peace, the noise was worse than that of the little 'spalpeens' in the street, and they are bad enough." Then he said, after Beth had expressed her sympathy, "I was glad to see Mammy and Da' again though. But," he added ruefully, "my mates were all out with their new mates or courting."

He shook his head sadly, then said in a brighter tone of voice, "I must say that I am glad to be back here though; I missed your cakes, Mrs. Banham." He grinned then ducked as a pleased Beth took a mock swing at him.

Then the conversation turned to things that had occurred whilst Michael was away, and Will said, "Dad, what was that story about those newspaper men who came to visit?"

Thomas chuckled and then said in a more serious tone, "The whole affair could have had tragic consequences, but in the light of how it ended, it was quite funny."

"What happened," he continued, "was a carefully planned trip to show the public how well the Canal was progressing, and there were some unfortunate incidents which could have put a blight on it." Then he concluded, "There was only one coach but owing to the number of reporters that turned up, several open wagons were attached to the train which had been put at their disposal." He started to chuckle again and said to Will and Michael, "Imagine a train-load of men in open wagons, beating each other with their hands, trying to put out the smouldering clothing caused by the sparks from the loco chimney!"

Even Beth could see the funny side to it, although she did say afterwards that she hoped nobody was injured. Thomas told her that nobody got hurt, not even when the loco struck a temporary bridge which brought timbers raining down on the train. "Anyway," said her husband, "they took it in good part and wrote complementary articles on the 'wonders' they had seen."

The following morning Michael volunteered to go into the workshop, giving Thomas a chance to attend Chapel with his family. When they met Victoria and Mrs. Hilyard, Beth and Thomas were given extra-loving hugs by their daughter and they were delighted to see how happy she looked.

Before the service began, Thomas became aware that his daughter was paying more than usual attention to Mr. Hughes. He in turn would glance in her direction but would avoid meeting her eyes. 'Looks like our daughter has an admirer,' he thought, 'and by the looks of things, Victoria is well aware of it.'

He felt a little sad as he contemplated the prospect of losing his little girl to another man. Even so, he was sensible enough to acknowledge that if she did take up with Mr. Hughes, the young man was all that loving parents would want for their daughter. 'Still,' he thought, 'I am running ahead of myself; Victoria may have no serious interest in the young man.'

He felt a gentle nudge from Beth and realised that he was allowing himself to be distracted from the service.

In the press of people at the Chapel door after the service had ended, he lost sight of the young shopkeeper, but noticed that Victoria was eagerly casting her eyes in the direction of the minister. Sure enough, Mr. Hughes with Mrs. Hilyard was listening to the minister whilst he was obviously explaining something to them. After a while, the minister left the couple and moved to the door to have a few words with other members of his congregation before they left the Chapel. However, Mrs. Hilyard and Mr. Hughes appeared to have other matters to discuss, and by what Thomas could see of the lady's face, she was not pleased with Mr. Hughes.

After a few moments Mrs. Hilyard came across and chatted with Beth and Thomas. "I do hope you can come to one of our musical evenings, Mr. Banham, Mrs. Banham, I am sure that you will be as entranced with your daughter's playing as we are." Victoria, whilst trying not to look in the direction of Dafyd Hughes, blushed furiously but echoed her mistress's words, for she dearly loved her parents to hear her.

Then Mrs. Hilyard said, "I am sorry to have to leave you so quickly, but I am having visitors this afternoon and I must be ready for them." Then turning to Victoria she smiled and said, "I will leave you, my dear, to talk with your parents, please be back before half past twelve." With that Mrs. Hilyard made her farewell and left the Chapel.

Almost immediately Mr. Hughes joined them, and studiously avoiding looking too much at Victoria, had a few words with Beth and Thomas. Then, turning to Will as he and Peter came over to join them, said, "Do not rush back to the shop, Will, have your meal first. I am going back now to open up."

Thomas, with his new awareness, noticed the disappointed look on his daughter's face, and also the courteous way that Mr. Hughes addressed everyone including Victoria. 'Hardly the manner of a smitten young man.' Even so, Thomas thought, he is a very likable fellow and if he did take a liking to their daughter, he, Thomas, would not be displeased, nor he thought, would Beth.

If Victoria was disappointed with Dafyd Hughes for not showing much warmth towards her, she did not let it bother her. She was honest enough with herself to know that after her cold shoulder treatment of him, he would naturally be wary of her attempts to make friends. Sadly she was unschooled in the art of courtship; she did not realise that her dramatic change of attitude was a bit too sudden to be easily accepted by the young man.

Dafyd returned to Marshville, cursing his inability to say what was in his mind, or even broach the subject in any way. He had steeled himself to say something after the service but had taken the coward's way out and said nothing. Once again when meeting Victoria after not seeing her for a week, he had been bowled over by how adorable she looked. Perhaps next week he would have thought out a way of approaching the subject of his father's business, but would he have the courage to tell her of his deepest feelings?

Chapter 24

Grief at Marshville But a Ray of Light for Victoria

Beth was just about to enter her front door when she was stopped by the spectacle of a youth running up the street towards the lane. A boy lounging outside his own doorway called out, "What's the matter mate?" The first lad replied, puffing, "Accident, got to get an ambulance van."

Before the ambulance arrived, a group of men came toiling up the street pushing a handcart bearing an unconscious man. By this time many of the women were at their doors, and as the smaller children attempted to come out they were pushed back indoors. The only sound in the quietness of the street was the grating of the cart wheels on the stony ground.

There were no tears shed; the sight of bloodied figures was not unknown to the wives of the contractor's workers, and it was not that they were hard and unfeeling, for they were banded together in their pain for the families of the injured or dead. They were only too aware that the next casualty might be one of their menfolk.

After the ambulance had taken the pitiful burden away, nobody stopped to talk, they simply turned and went back into their huts; life had to carry on whatever happened.

Beth, on the other hand, was not used to the sights of injured or dead passing her door and if she realised what the commotion was all about, she would stay inside until everybody had gone.

The ones that passed through the village were usually local men. Those who were not from the town were normally taken to Ellesmere Port where Mr. Walker had established one of his hospitals.

At least that particular injured man being taken to Frodsham was one of the lucky ones; he was back at work only a few weeks after his accident, unlike the man who, with his family, lived in Marshville.

Thomas had suggested that Beth and Jessie should have a change from the village and Frodsham, and had a suggested a day out somewhere. The two friends had been only too willing, and had gone to Chester on the train. Both women had enjoyed a wonderful day looking in the shops, even making some modest purchases. They had eaten in a pleasant little tea shop which Jessie knew about, and altogether, they were in a very contented frame of mind as they strolled into the hutted village during the late afternoon. However, their feelings of wellbeing were utterly destroyed after they had met Will, who was very upset about something.

"Whatever is the matter, Will?" said Beth urgently, with a sick feeling that something had happened to her husband. Her son replied in a sad voice, "The man at the bottom hut has had a bad accident, Mam, and they have taken his wife to Ellesmere Port to be with him."

Mrs. Robbins's face paled, and she said, "You mean Abel Tasker." Will nodded, but noticing the way that Mrs. Robbins had taken the news, refrained from telling her what had happened. In fact the boy himself knew very little about the accident, for the injured man had been taken from where he had been working at the Weaver Sluices, and had been whisked straight through to Ellesmere Port without stopping at the Frodsham Depot. Rumour had filtered through from the place where the accident had occurred, which said that he had lost a leg when a large piece of equipment had slipped on the scaffolding where he was working, and trapped him.

Beth could see how badly her friend had been affected, and suggested that she came into the Banham hut and have a cup of tea, but Jessie wanted to go to the Taskers' hut to make sure that the youngest children were alright.

"You see, Beth," she explained, "we got to know them when we were in South Wales when Mr. Walker was building Penarth Docks, and although we were never close friends, we were together enough to know that for all his ways, he was a good family man."

She gave herself a little shake then, with a return to her more usual manner, she said briskly, "Well, Beth, Abel might not be hurt too badly, and he might be home before long."

Then she added, "Thanks for the offer of tea, Beth, but I will see if everything is all right at the house before the older two children get home from school."

With that, Jessie hurried down to the Taskers' hut only to find that all the children were at home, their needs being attended to by Sally and another woman.

Relieved that everything was in good hands, she decided that there was no need to stay, but told the other women that she was willing to help if there was anything she could do.

As she stepped out into the street, Sally followed her and said in a low voice, "I have heard that Mr. Tasker is very badly injured, Mrs. Robbins, and that he has lost a leg. I don't think he will be home for a long time to come." Then she said worriedly, "I can't think how they will manage for money."

Whilst Jessie reeled from the bad news, the other part of her mind was thinking of ways in which the people of the village could help until Abel came home. She knew that the man would be offered some sort of work even if he was on crutches, for that was Mr. Walker's way, but the pay would be very low, too low to support the whole family.

However, all this conjecture was to no avail. By nightfall the whole of Marshville was plunged into deep sadness with the news that Abel Tasker had died before he had even reached Ellesmere Port.

On hearing of the death, Beth once again felt the old familiar knot in her stomach. For some time she had managed to subdue the feelings of dread, and now with this grim reminder of the dangers facing those working on the Cut, her fears had been brought to the surface again.

Realising how badly affected Beth was, Thomas quietly explained the difference in the risks attendant with the workshop's type of tasks and the work carried out in the excavation. He pointed out that the dangers were no worse for him and his men than they were at Longfields Estate, and that they were used to working as a team. Also, they did not work under orders from other supervisors; Captain Howard insisted that his men did their work without interference from anybody. He did not mention how badly the men at the workshop had been affected by the terrible screams of the injured man as the train had passed them on the way to Ellesmere Port.

On the day of the funeral, it seemed as if most of the women from the village were there, and surprisingly, other people from the town attended. For Beth, who went with Jessie Robbins, it was a most harrowing experience. Even some of the men, hardened as they were with the life they led, wept without shame.

The following day, a knock came at the door and Beth, on opening it, was surprised and just a little apprehensive to find the large, intimidating figure of Maggie Garroway standing there.

"Sorry to bother you, Mrs. Banham," said the rather insalubrious woman. "We are making a collection to help Mrs. Tasker and her kids; they are going back to Gloucester and we thought that a little extra would tide them over."

Beth was immediately ashamed of her uncharitable thoughts regarding the woman and did not hesitate; she told Mrs. Garroway that when Thomas finished work for the day, she would bring something over to the lady's hut. She was thanked in a most formal way then the woman left. Beth was somehow heartened by the visit; she realised that she had misjudged the woman, and resolved that the next time she would not jump to conclusions so readily.

In the excavation, there was a collection, many of the navvies donating a whole day's pay, something that was not uncommon amongst the tough, hard-living men.

Captain Howard visited the Taskers' hut to express his heartfelt condolences. Later the people learned that not only had he given Mrs. Tasker what was owing to her in wages, but had also made a very handsome donation to her purse. The day that the family left Marshville, everybody came out to wish them luck for the future. Captain Howard had hired a brougham to take them to the station, their belongings having been taken earlier in a Great Western Railway goods cart. It was another image Beth would never forget; the distressing sight of the weeping family bidding farewell to their friends in the village.

Some weeks after the tragedy, Mrs. Hilyard visited her mother in Chester, and as usual her mother was her usual disagreeable self with Victoria. They had brought various items of food with them, and on hearing that her daughter had not included sugar, she had told the girl to make herself useful, and go to the shop in Handbridge and buy a pound bag. Mrs. Hilyard was in the scullery whilst her maid was being sent on her errand, so she did not hear all that was being said, including the name of the shop, which was Hughes.

It was a very thoughtful Victoria who made her way into Handbridge village, and when she arrived at the shop, she studied the name on the board over the window which showed that it belonged to 'B. A. HUGHES AND SON'.

She was served by a boy only slightly younger than herself, and he perked up noticeably when he saw her. A thought came to her as she noticed his extra attention, and after she had made her purchase, she casually said, "Is Mr. Hughes here today?" There came the reply that the girl half expected. "Oh no, miss, he is at one of the other shops. I think he will be at Boughton today." Victoria feigned surprise and said, "I did not realise that Mr. Hughes had more than one shop; when I was talking to Mrs. Hughes some weeks ago she did not mention that there were other shops. How interesting."

The boy, puffed up with his own importance, said grandly, "Oh yes, miss, we have five shops," then leaned forward conspiratorially, and whispered, "and if Mr. Hughes can get a place in the City, he will open a large first-class grocery shop there."

Victoria expressed sufficient wonder to please the boy and he said, "Of course, miss, that is just between me and you."

When Victoria left the shop, it was with mixed feelings. She knew that there was a possibility that the proprietor was not Dafyd's father but she felt instinctively that he was, and also that Mrs. Hilyard was aware of the other shops. If that was so, then she felt hurt that her mistress, Dafyd Hughes, and Mrs. Hughes, she thought sadly, had all conspired to keep her in ignorance. At the same time she was aware of a growing anger. Did they all consider that she and her parents were not important or intelligent enough to talk about such matters?

If Mrs. Hilyard noticed any difference in her maid's manner she did not attach any importance to it, for since the tragedy which had affected a lot of people in the town, Victoria had been very subdued. Her mistress's heart ached for the girl and the families so terribly affected.

For the next few days Victoria did nothing about her suspicions; apart from any other considerations, she had no chance to speak to Dafyd Hughes, that is, until Mrs. Hilyard announced that she was paying for a piano tuner to see to the Chapel piano. Mrs. Day, who usually played the piano, was not going to be able to accompany the singing on the following Sunday and Victoria had been asked if she would help out. On the evening that the piano tuner was able to come, some of the congregation had volunteered to do some cleaning and general tidying up.

Amongst the men was Dafyd Hughes, and he was just as surprised to see Victoria there as she was to see him, but the first thing that struck him was that the girl had dropped her friendly demeanour and had reverted to her previous cold attitude.

When the piano had been tuned to the man's satisfaction, Mrs. Day, who was a fussy sort of person, played a few bars then asked Victoria if she would care to try the instrument. After the girl had played a short piece, Mrs. Day had tut-tutted and reminded her that she needed to practice more often, something which caused Dafyd a great deal of amusement, although he was sensible enough not to show it.

After that Mrs. Day then announced that she was anxious to be away early and made as though to go, but before she went she turned to Victoria and once again said, "Remember, my dear, practice, practice, practice, it is the only way to reach competence." Victoria thanked her, keeping her face straight, and the lady, accompanied by the piano tuner, left the building. After that Victoria went into the back room to wash her hands and, when she had put on her outdoor coat, came out into what seemed to be an empty room. Everybody had left, or so she thought.

Dafyd suddenly appeared and made her jump. All evening he had been plucking up courage to tell Victoria about his family, but with her turning cool to him once more he began to have second thoughts. Then he made up his mind; he was going to get to the bottom of her capricious behaviour.

"Miss Banham," he said in a businesslike tone of voice, "would you be so good as to tell me what it is that caused you to adopt such a cold, almost rude attitude towards me within a few moments of stepping into my shop on your first day in the village." Victoria, completely shocked by the direct and unexpected opening gambit, did not have a word to say for a moment, and the young man, not waiting for her answer, went on, "Then after some months of this treatment, only tempered slightly with the passage of time, you suddenly became more affable, even, if I may say so, friendly." The girl still did not say anything, she was so taken aback by the bluntness of his words, although she was beginning to feel the stirring of anger that had so affected her at Handbridge.

Dafyd said more quietly, "Then tonight you have reverted to your original cold behaviour. Can you put me out of my misery, Miss Banham, and let me know what it is about me that offends you so."

Although Victoria was quite angry with him, she knew that she was in the wrong in the first place, and said rather defensively, "I do agree that my behaviour was unacceptable, and for that I apologise most sincerely, especially," she said, her cheeks turning red, "as I acted purely on an assumption; you see, I thought that Clara was Mrs. Hughes." Dafyd looked at her enquiringly, and she said rather shamefacedly, not looking him in the eye, "I thought you were married." At that she stopped, too embarrassed to go on with her explanation, and Dafyd, looking rather puzzled, decided to let her stew in her own juice; he was determined not to let her off too easily.

"Well, you see," she floundered on, "you looked at me in a way that married men should not look at other girls."

For a moment nobody spoke, then Dafyd said gently, "And what made you change your mind, Miss Banham, did Clara or Will tell you the truth of the matter?" Victoria, now that the difficult part was over, told him about her meeting Clara and her husband and of hearing about the expected child.

Dafyd nodded his understanding and he felt the stirring of hope in his heart. What Victoria had just said cleared up a lot of doubts which had plagued him for months, but still did not clear all of them.

"I see," he said slowly, "but why have you now adopted the same freezing manner towards me? I assure you that I have not married someone else." Immediately he uttered the words Dafyd regretted his attempts at light-hearted levity, for her eyes blazed and she cried out, "Oh, but it's the secrets, the secrets of your family, shared by you, Mrs. Hilyard and, I am sad to say, by your mother."

At the mention of his mother, Dafyd rapped out angrily, "Miss Banham, I would be obliged if you did not drag my mother's name into any difference between me and you."

Victoria gulped at his attack, but was too wound up to let go of her grievances and said, just as angrily, "You and Mrs. Hilyard and, well, everyone know about the Banham family. We are humble working folk and are not ashamed of it, whilst of your family, what do we know?" Then warming to her theme, she cried, "Yes, your family, we know nothing of them," she said. "Oh yes, a father who is a grocer, but with not one shop, not even two shops, but five shops." Victoria, chest heaving, said scathingly, "I suppose you thought the Banham family were not good enough to be privy to your family's situation." As Dafyd attempted to stem the flow, Victoria, well and truly into her stride, shouted, "Well, I do not care for the way you treat me and my family, Mr. Hughes, and once I get out of here, I do not want to see you or Mrs. Hilyard again. I am going straight home." With that she started pulling futilely at the locked Chapel door. Dafyd, thoroughly alarmed at her words, looked across at her and thought sadly, 'What an unholy mess I have made of this. I love this girl so much, but I can see now there is no chance of her ever wanting to return my affections.' He wanted more than anything to hold her to him and let her know how he felt about her.

Dafyd approached her slowly. He was about to put his hands on her shoulders, then he realised that if he did in her present state, the girl might take against him for good.

"My dad and mam have been asking to see my shop at Marshville for a long time," he said quietly. "I have always put them off, but when I started mentioning your name and that of your family, Mam decided to ignore my entreaties, and make a visit." As Victoria became still, his hopes began to rise and he continued, "I asked Mrs. Hilyard never to mention my father's shops, and in a minute I will explain why I took that course of action."

Then he said, "Mrs. Hilyard is one of your staunchest supporters," and added ruefully, "she has been very angry with me for some time now, as is my mam."

Victoria turned round slightly so she was not facing the door, but she would still not face him. Dafyd said quietly, "I will light a lamp and if you would be seated, I will tell you the whole story." Filled with curiosity, the girl slowly went over to a bench and sat down. The nearness of the man, in the chapel lit only by the fading evening light, made Victoria uneasy about her own feelings and she welcomed the lighting of the oil lamp.

Sitting not too close to her, Dafyd said, "A few months before I set up the shop at Marshville, I was introduced to a very attractive young lady, the daughter of a business associate of my father." At the mention of another girl, Victoria's head came up; if he did not have her full attention before, he certainly had it now, and she felt a pang of jealousy, something that was rare for her.

When he reached the part where the girl had treated Mrs. Hughes in such an offhand manner, Victoria gave voice for the first time, and said angrily, "How could she do that, your mam is lovely." He nodded and said ruefully, "I distrusted girls from then onwards."

"That is why I did not want word of my family's situation to be known," he said, and followed that by saying, "I know how much you must dislike me for my thoughtlessness, Victoria, er, Miss Banham, and I offer you my most heartfelt apologies." Then he added earnestly, "I hope that you do not leave Mrs. Hilyard, and I sincerely hope that you will not find anything in my mam's actions which would give you cause to dislike her."

Victoria shook her head and for a few moments there was silence, then she looked at Dafyd and said softly, "Now you have explained everything, your actions do not seem quite so thoughtless, although I do agree with your mam and Mrs. Hilyard that you held your tongue too long." Then as he appeared to protest, she smiled and told him, "And that applies to me also."

She got to her feet and said more composedly than she felt, for she was acutely aware of being in the room alone with a man (and a man she loved), "I must get back to Mrs. Hilyard's house, she will be wondering where I have got to." Then she added, "And I do not hold anything against either Mrs. Hilyard or your mam, I still think she is lovely."

Dafyd Hughes felt amazingly light-hearted as he ushered Victoria out of the Chapel, and he offered her his arm, but to his disappointment, she politely declined to link her arm through his; that was until a drunken man staggered out of the shadows in the street, at which she leaped sideways with a startled squeak towards Dafyd.

From that point on to Mrs. Hilyard's house, she held on to Dafyd's arm, something he had dreamed of for months.

When they reached their destination, Victoria mounted the steps to the front door, and as Daisy opened it to let her friend enter, Dafyd raised his hat, smiled and solemnly said, "Remember, Miss Banham, 'practice, practice, practice'," then with a smile, blithely walked away.

Daisy, glad to see Victoria smiling again, was then taken aback as her friend almost doubled up crying with laughter at Dafyd's leaving sally.

When the mystified Daisy had closed the door, Victoria hugged her and whispered happily, "Oh, Daisy, I think me and Mr. Hughes are proper friends now." Then she sped off to find Mrs. Hilyard. Daisy shook her head in wonderment. "Why," she said to herself, "Victoria and the young man have always been friends," or so she believed. "But still," she smiled, "if it makes Victoria happy, then I am happy too."

Chapter 25

A Month of Tragedy

November Eighteen Eighty-Nine was a month that Kate would remember for the rest of her days. It was also a turning point in her life.

It had started well enough, the mild weather and even one day of warm sunshine lulling the senses into believing that a second Indian Summer had arrived. However, by the sixth day of the month, the temperature had dropped and the early morning mist had reminded everyone that winter was waiting in the wings.

The first part of the month at Reeve House had been happily free of the tensions invariably created by the presence of Captain Rodgerson. During the third week the peaceful ambience was disturbed by the arrival of Captain Howard's wife, which from the servant's point of view was almost as troublesome as the presence of Mrs. Rodgerson's husband.

Cecelia had come with the intention of riding to hounds on the approaching Saturday. To the dismay of everybody except Mrs. Howard, Captain Rodgerson arrived on the Friday afternoon. However, he did seem to be adhering to his wife's terms with regard to his behaviour, but even so it was an uneasy peace which prevailed.

The Hunt gathered outside the House and by the time the stirrup cup had been drunk, the mist had almost cleared. A short while after the Master of the Hounds had set out, the scent was picked up and a view halloo sounded.

Cecelia was usually at the front early on, but on this occasion she was still checking the tightness of the girth strap on her mount. Consequently there were hardly any riders around her when she cleared the second hedge.

As usual she was riding full out and when, out of the corner of her eye, she saw a splash of colour at the estate boundary fence, involuntarily she glanced across and saw that it was a young woman standing on the bottom rail of the fence, watching the riders go by.

That quick glance was the last conscious thing that Cecelia ever did, for her movement caused her to pull on one rein making the horse veer in mid jump.

Almost without sound her horse went down and somersaulted right over.

Miraculously the animal was hardly hurt and with a terrified scream, scrambled to its feet and galloped wildly down the field after the rest of the hunt. When the next rider cleared the hedge he came across Cecelia's unmoving form.

Another rider joined him and when they both dismounted and went to her, they could quite plainly see from the angle of her head that her neck was broken!

The second rider was Dr. Porby, who in spite of his pompous manner was as competent as most doctors, and knew at a glance that there was no hope for Cecelia. "My God," he whispered to his companion, "what a tragedy, what a terrible tragedy."

Meanwhile the girl who had been at the fence, on seeing what had happened, guiltily blaming herself for her part in the accident, had jumped down and quickly run back into the woods. It was the gamekeeper's daughter and she had been hoping to catch the eye of Captain Rodgerson with the Hunt.

Although she did not know how seriously the woman rider was hurt, she thought it was wiser not to be seen, then she could not be blamed whatever happened.

Dr. Porby put a clean kerchief over Cecelia's face and asked the other rider to go back to the house, alert them to the accident and get them to bring something with them on which her body could be conveyed. Also, he told him, at least four men to do the carrying.

The men arrived at the field in very quick time, headed by John Wilson, the foreman. With them they carried a farmyard gate.

Carefully Cecelia's body was lifted onto the gate and the party went back to the house, the men doing the carrying trying not to curse as they stumbled across the tussocky grass.

It seemed that half the household had assembled to witness Cecelia's final return to Reeve House. Kate, with Mary on one side of her and Mrs. Higson on the other, was standing at the bottom of the steps leading to the front entrance. Behind them was Rigg, the butler, whilst behind him were two of the maids. Faces could be seen peeping at some of the windows.

At the end of the house stood some of the male staff and the cook, but there was not a sound, nobody as much as whispered. One of the maids was silently weeping.

Kate quietly indicated that the sweating men should follow her inside to a downstairs room where the body was to be laid. Mrs. Higson had put one of the older maids to the task of preparing a table. She and the housekeeper were to do the laying out after the policeman and Dr. Porby had given them permission to do so.

As the police constable was wheeling his bicycle up the drive, several members of the Hunt arrived with lots of laughter and boisterous behaviour.

One of the riders called out to the officer, who had pulled over to the side of the drive, asking whether he had come to arrest somebody, a sally that gave rise to more mirth amongst the group. The policeman was attempting to let the riders know of the tragedy and to quell the noisy laughter but they were too exuberant to take notice.

He was more successful with the other Hunt members and it was a more sober group which made its way towards the house.

Suddenly there was a roar of anger from one of the first of the riders. It was Captain Rodgerson bellowing at the groom holding the reins. "Don't talk so stupid, man," he yelled at the unfortunate groom, "Mrs. Howard is one of the most alive women in England, she can't be dead." Even as was he venting his anger on the man, he was out of his saddle and bounding up the steps to the house.

The quiet of the room was suddenly shattered as the near-demented figure burst in. Mrs. Higson and the maid were carefully wiping soil off Cecelia's face, whilst Kate, with Mary in attendance, was waiting at one side. Dr. Porby was standing at the end of the table, his eyes showing that he was more concerned with the living than the dead at that moment. Mrs. Rodgerson, who he knew was Mrs. Howards sister, looked as though she would faint at any moment.

"What are you doing to her?" Captain Rodgerson shouted. "Here, you," he continued, "why are you standing there like a dummy, why don't you do something to bring her round. You are supposed to be a doctor."

Suddenly the voice of Mrs. Higson rang out. In stentorian tones she halted the man in a trice.

"Stop that, Captain Rodgerson," she ordered, "this is a room of tragedy. How dare you behave in such a disgraceful manner?" Then turning to one of the Captain's companions who had come to a stop outside the door, she asked him, or more correctly, ordered him, to take the man, get him a brandy, and stop him coming into the room until everything had been done for Mrs. Howard.

Kate was nearly at the end of her reserves and, after giving Mrs. Higson a grateful look, said, "Yes, Mr. Rowland, would you stay with Captain Rodgerson until he has calmed down." Mr. Rowland nodded and, giving her a look of sympathy, turned to her husband and led him from the room.

Dr. Porby greeted the constable who, on entering the room, had removed his helmet. "Would you excuse me for a moment, Bob," he said. "I will just see to Mrs. Rodgerson and then I will be back: broken neck," he concluded in a low voice.

"Now, Mrs. Rodgerson," he said gently to Kate, "I want you to let young Mary here to get you a hot sweet cup of tea and I hope you will have a rest whilst we get on with things here."

Kate felt guilty at the doctor's solicitous manner to her. She had never had much time for him and his pompous ways, nor had she any faith in him as a doctor, yet here he was, doing what was needed with kindness and without fuss.

He received a tired smile, then saw her ushered out of the room by a really worried Mary. "I will come to you later, Mrs. Rodgerson," he called, "and I will prepare a draught for you."

It did not take long for the full facts to be given to the constable, who agreed with Dr. Porby that there seemed to be no doubt that it was an accidental death, but said that he wanted to see the horse and examine the saddle for any sign of damage which could have caused the rider to be thrown. Also, his superiors would want him to see the area where the accident had occurred.

Meanwhile, in Kate's sitting room, Mary was trying to talk her mistress into having a lie down, but Kate had set her mind to occupy herself and take her thoughts off her sister's death. There were telegrams to be sent and arrangements to be made to take Cecelia's body to their parents' home, for Kate wanted her sister to be buried in the family burial plot. She was also worried about the possibility that there would be an inquest.

"I will start by composing a telegram to Captain Howard," said Kate, "then I will send one to my parents."

Later, in the privacy of her room, Kate whispered to herself, "Why could it not have been Captain Rodgerson who had broken his neck instead of my sister?" She knew she was wrong in wishing death on anybody, but she could not bring herself to beg forgiveness. Later she had reason to regret wishing death on somebody else.

—— —— ——

At the time when the telegram was delivered to the Bear's Paw, Captain Howard was attending a meeting with the engineer over the Latchford section. Consequently it was late in the morning on the following day when he became aware of the tragedy.

Although there were strong reasons why his presence was required at the depot, a sympathetic Mr. Jones, the engineer, agreed that in the circumstances, he must go to Norfolk as a matter of urgency. With Ian Blake standing in for him and Thomas Banham overseeing the workshops, he felt that everything was in capable hands. Mr. Jones was certainly happy enough with his arrangements.

The only problem was that Captain Howard himself was feeling close to exhaustion. In fact Ian Blake had confessed to Sarah that he was very worried about his employer's state of health.

Late Monday afternoon saw Billy Timms setting Captain Howard down at Reeve House. It was James who met him, explaining that Kate had been laid up in bed with what Dr. Porby suspected as influenza.

When Captain Howard heard the news, he was filled with dread. Whilst serving in the army he had seen all too often how badly people were affected when the illness swept through the barracks. Deaths were not uncommon.

As he walked into the sitting room he was greeted by Mr. and Mrs. Prentice who had come to Reeve House to be with Kate. He was terribly sorry for them, for even though they had no illusions about Cecelia, she was their flesh and blood.

Afterwards, in an attempt to take their minds off the tragedy, they asked about the Canal and he tried to bring them up to date with the progress being made. Eventually his weariness overcame him and he excused himself and went up for an early night in bed.

After he had gone to his room, the rest of the party stayed for a while, thankfully free of the presence of Captain Rodgerson. The conversation naturally turned to the condition of poor Kate and also Richard. Mrs. Prentice senior expressed the opinion that her daughter was not suffering from influenza, but from some other less dangerous fever. Then she added that she was really concerned about her son-in-law, and believed that he was more than tired, and gave her opinion that he was a sick man. Eventually the gathering broke up and they all went to their beds.

When Richard had retired for the night he fell into a deep sleep and took a lot of awakening the following morning. James and Charlotte, like Ian, were extremely concerned about him.

Richard was relieved to find that due to Captain Rodgerson not being at Reeve House, there was no shortage of seats in the carriages taking them to the Prentices estate. When they arrived at the Prentices' house, Richard awoke to find that he had slept the whole journey and apologised for his rudeness, only to be told that as soon as they had eaten, he was free to take to his bed and stay there for the rest of the day if he wished to.

He roused himself sufficiently to manage dinner, then, excusing himself again, went back to his bed.

Early the following morning, Mary came to see Kate's mother and told her that her mistress seemed a little better when she awoke, and that Mrs. Rodgerson had insisted that she was well enough to attend the funeral. Her parents had warned Kate that if they considered that she was still suffering from the fever which had laid her low, then they would insist that she stay at home.

Captain Rodgerson turned up at the house in good time before the cortège set off for the cemetery, and he was accompanied by one of his fellow ex-officers. Kate's husband had been drinking but it did not show in his walk and he gave no trouble throughout the service. However, as soon as the funeral was over, he and his companion went away without informing anybody about their intentions. The family were quite relieved about them leaving, and the atmosphere lightened considerably.

For Captain Howard the funeral was an unreal experience. He did not feel deep grief; it was if Cecelia was an acquaintance who had died. As people came up to him to offer their commiserations, he felt as though he was playing a part. Others were more affected than himself, particularly Captain Rodgerson and also young Rod, James's friend. Back at the house, Mr. Prentice drew Captain Howard to one side and said bluntly, "Richard, you look all in. You simply must see a doctor when you get back to Cheshire, you are obviously driving yourself far too hard." Then he said kindly, "We are all worried about you. Do take care of yourself, there's a good fellow." Captain Howard knew his father-in-law was right; for months he had been driving himself in an attempt to block out Kate's rejection. However, he was wondering whether his present low state was actually a return of the fever that had laid him low in India, something that had returned from time to time.

He promised that he would get to a doctor as soon as he could after he had returned to Frodsham, but as they were speaking, a telegram boy knocked on the door with a telegram for Captain Howard.

There were a few looks of dismay as it was handed to Richard, and their fears were confirmed he when read it and told them resignedly, "I am sorry, I must leave for Frodsham as soon as possible!"

Seeing their looks of consternation, he explained, "It concerns Mr. Walker, the main contractor," he said sadly. "He died yesterday." Then he added quietly, "And there is no doubt about it, he will be almost impossible to replace, and also, being the gentleman he was, he will be mourned by everyone."

Those in his vicinity made the usual sympathetic noises, as people do when somebody unknown to them dies, but James and Mr. Prentice, who had been following Richard's accounts and stories of the Canal construction and knew how much he admired Mr. Walker, felt a sense of empathy for him.

"I will say goodbye to the ladies," said Richard but then Charlotte came over at that moment to tell them that Kate had been ordered to bed by her mother and had gone gladly.

Richard felt flattened. Once again he had planned to speak to Kate and clear the air properly, and if the outcome was not how he would have wished it, then at least he would know how he stood in Kate's eyes. Now the longed-for chance had slipped away, and once again a deep gloom settled over him.

Half an hour later he was seated in James's carriage on his way to the station. Normally he would have commented on the carriage, a gleaming ruby-red and black affair, one of Aunt Phoebe's last purchases, but on this day, however, he felt totally out of sorts with life and all he wanted to do was get back to Frodsham and have a long sleep.

James recognised his brother-in-law's mood, or to be more precise, his state, and forbore to make conversation during their journey, but at the station platform he gently urged him to get a good doctor as soon as he could. "Otherwise," he said quietly, "you will be going the same way as Kate, and none of us want to see you in that state."

After that they parted with a handshake, and James made his way back to his parents' house.

He reflected on the morning's events: Kate struggling to contain her sorrow, Captain Rodgerson obviously trying to do the same thing, and Richard unsuccessfully trying to be alone long enough to speak to Kate. Then there was the rather sinister behaviour of Rodgerson .

As the family moved away from the grave, James had seen Kate's husband looking across at his wife with an expression of pure malice and dislike, and a short time later, just before his sister had left them to go upstairs, he bore a triumphant smirk. Soon after, he and his companion had left, and there appeared to be an air of determination about Captain Rodgerson that had not been in evidence for many months.

James felt very uneasy and was convinced that the man was up to some mischief that could harm his sister.

——— ——— ———

Meanwhile, Captain Howard was fighting the urge to settle back and doze. To stop himself from doing so, he kept the window of the carriage open, but when two other people came into the compartment, he was forced to close it. The very fact that he reached Frodsham without falling asleep and missing any of his connecting trains was a miracle in itself.

At the Bear's Paw he gave instructions that he must be roused by seven o'clock, then after taking his medicine, he retired to bed. When he was roused the following morning, he was pleased to find that although he was still tired, the feeling of illness had left him, and he enjoyed his breakfast for the first time in days.

Before eight o'clock, Jacob Morris was shown in, and handed his employer a letter. The contents informed him that a meeting between the section engineers, the contractors, certain sub-contractors, and a committee of Manchester Corporation Councillors was to be held in Manchester. The meeting was to open at ten o'clock that very morning!

A few minutes past eight, his foreman had left to return to the Depot, and Captain Howard quickly made ready for his journey to Manchester.

On the same train were several others, including the engineers, Mr. Jones and Mr. Manisty. For Captain Howard that was a relief, for he had convinced himself that he would be the last to arrive and even worse, the only late arrival.

In fact they were in good time for the start of the meeting, which was addressed first by Councillor Bosdin Leech, then by Mr. Leader Williams, the Chief Engineer of the scheme.

Mr. Bosdin Leech was no stranger to Captain Howard, for they had met more than once when the Council members had visited the section during their periodic tours of inspection. Indeed, in his room at the hotel, he had a photograph of the workshops presented to him by the Councillor, who himself was an amateur photographer of some skill.

The main reason for the meeting was to explain the position with regard to the equipment and other items which were now under the control of the late Mr. Walker's executors. For Captain Howard, apart from tools owned by individuals, that applied to most of the machines and equipment at the Frodsham Depot.

The question of whom the executors would appoint to run the late contractor's business was yet to be answered.

On the second day after the Manchester meeting, Captain Howard was on his way to Ellesmere Port, leaving an unfinished letter to Kate in his room. He was hoping to see Mr. Manisty to check on a piece of equipment that at the time was in the fitting shop at Frodsham Depot.

Beyond the Ince section was the Gowy Siphon, a pair of very large-diameter pipes which channelled the River Gowy under the canal cutting to discharge into the River Mersey. He intended to stop and look at the siphon as a matter of interest, but as he neared it, he felt waves of cold sweep over him and realised that if he did not dismount, he was in danger of falling off the horse.

No sooner had his feet touched the ground than an attack of dizziness assailed him and he attempted to stay upright by grabbing hold of the saddle, but he missed and crumpled to the ground in an unconscious heap.

For a while there was nobody in view to help him, but after ten minutes or so, two navvies, who had noticed that he had failed to rise after his collapse, climbed out of the cutting to see if he needed help.

They were not skilled in any way that would help deal with him, and as they were debating whether to go down and find somebody with the right knowledge, one of the men espied a train coming towards them from the Frodsham direction.

As the train neared the group by the side of the track, the loco driver brought it to a stop. It was quickly decided that the unconscious man should be taken to

Ellesmere Port where the ambulance could come right up to the train and get him to hospital. By then several other men had joined the group which made it easier to lift Captain Howard onto an empty wagon.

At Ellesmere Port an ambulance van was sent for, the unconscious man breathing badly and his face a very poor colour causing those who had accompanied him to fear the worst.

One of the horse drivers had taken the Captain's horse in hand promising to look after it until the animal could be restored to its owner.

—— —— ——

Looking back to the day of Cecelia's funeral, and around the time Captain Howard was arriving at Frodsham, Kate was awaking from a sound sleep. She was feeling better than she had been for days, and she was hungry.

In those first few moments she was not thinking of the horror of Cecelia's death or the funeral, she simply felt much more like her old self.

Then she caught sight of her maid's face as the girl came in from preparing her bath. "Whatever is the matter, Mary?" she said quickly. "Are you unwell?"

Mary replied with a rush, "Oh no, ma'am, it's Captain Howard, he's gone, he got a telegram, to do with his work, I think."

The girl was close to tears; she had hoped that her mistress and Captain Howard would make up their differences, for she was convinced that Mrs. Rodgerson would get better if they were friends again.

Kate felt completely deflated; she had set her mind on mending some of the damage she had done to their friendship. That was the least that she could expect, for she now doubted that Richard would feel love for her.

When Mary had mentioned the reason for his departure, she had almost said, "Oh yes, his work," but stopped herself just in time. When she had eventually recognised the reason for her foolish treatment of Richard, she had resolved never again to let his commitment to his work come between them.

Kate had berated herself for ignoring the realities of life outside her cosseted sphere. Apart from the importance of his role in a great scheme, he was responsible for the livelihoods of many and their families, and that included the Banham family.

Thinking about her late employees and dear friends, she had been swept by a wave of shame; for was it not her who had begged Richard to help them? He had honoured his promise and given Thomas a job and found shelter for the family. These deeds she had pushed to the back of her mind.

Kate had become thoroughly disgusted with herself, and Cecelia's funeral had presented her in a rather grim fashion with a chance to try and put matters right with him. She reflected drearily that he might not wish to come to Reeve House ever again, and when he did visit Norfolk again, and she was sure that he would, he could go directly to her parents' home; she knew how much he cared for them, and they for him. He would not want to break the ties that held them together.

With a heavy heart she went down to join the family for dinner, but her appetite had deserted her. When her mother told her the reason why Richard had been forced to leave them and return to Frodsham, Kate had been even more stricken. She had heard him more than once express his admiration for Mr. Walker and she knew that he would be truly saddened by the man's death.

When Kate mentioned that she had been looking forward to having a word with Richard, a glance passed between James and Charlotte, and he said easily, "Well, I am sure that he would be glad of a letter from you, Kate."

She was not sure that she could commit her thoughts to paper. It would be most unfortunate if the letter was read by the wrong person, so she decided to put off writing for a day or so until she had thought out how to phrase the letter. She had still not written it by the time she was ready to return to Wroxing.

James and Charlotte were hoping to go back with her but to Kate's great disappointment, her brother had some business to attend to, so he had to put off their return for a few more days.

However, James put his carriage at her disposal with one of his father's men to drive it. On their arrival at Reeve House, Kate and Mary were dismayed to find that Captain Rodgerson had returned that morning. To make matters worse, the man had regained some of his old arrogance. Although he was still controlling his temper with everybody, it was obvious that he was riding cock-a-hoop about something!

Once or twice he had looked at Kate with an expression of malicious triumph on his face. Again she felt that old familiar sick feeling in her stomach and wondered whether he had learned something which he thought could overturn the terms laid down by Great-Aunt Phoebe. Kate did not believe for a moment that he could do anything to change things, but her illness had left her feeling vulnerable, and she felt in dread of the man. 'Oh, James,' she thought miserably, 'how I wish you could have come back with us.'

Mary was also subjected to his malevolent glances and she had become really frightened. His attack on her and her mistress nearly one year ago had left an enduring impression etched on her memory, and all she could think of was to arm herself with something to protect them both if he should try anything again.

As it was, the rest of the day and the following morning passed without incident, but even so, Mary, unknown to her mistress, had got a small knife wrapped in a handkerchief tucked in her apron pocket.

As soon as he had eaten, Captain Rodgerson rode off in the direction taken by the Hunt the day of Cecelia's death. He was certain that Cecelia's mount could not have fallen accidentally. He wanted to examine the area where she had died in the hope that he would find some evidence which would lead to somebody being punished for her death.

In a life dedicated to putting his own interests before anybody else's, he had never concerned himself whether he liked a person, man or woman, as long as they served his purpose. His actual purpose, or to be more accurate, his hunger, was to be part of the upper classes, a hunger born of being close to them but never being part of them.

His childhood as a son of an impoverished clergyman in Ireland had been an unhappy one. In truth it was more the fault in his nature than anything else. He had been a cruel child and when at first he had been allowed to play with the children of the local landowner, his cruel streak had shown up on several occasions. Eventually his father had been asked to not allow him to come into their grounds again. He had grown up always on the outside looking in, but never joining in.

As a youth he had sworn that, one day, he too would be part of that elevated society, and when he became involved with Cecelia, he had seen his chance to obtain a toe-hold. By sheer chance he had met Kate, and saw her as the first rung on his ladder of ambition. An entry into the Norfolk society was as good a start as any, so he wooed her and won.

The fact that he despised women did not deter him from using them to further his aims, and he certainly did not think in terms of love or affection. However, when Cecelia began her affair with a younger man the previous year, he had been consumed with jealousy.

Although he was driven by envy of others in a more exalted position than himself, he had never before experienced such jealousy over a mere woman.

So unused was he to such a sensation that it was quite a while before he would even admit that he had actually grown to love Cecelia. That is why he now wanted more than anything to make somebody suffer for her death.

Running through his thoughts of vengeance was the anticipation of how he would humble his wife when he had put his new information into good use. 'My God,' he thought savagely, 'I'll make her suffer for the way she played me for a fool.'

Only lately he had learned that the Women's Property Act was not all she had pretended it to be, and he hated her for perpetrating such a plausible bluff on him.

Then there was the note he had found in his room informing him that his wife was 'carrying on' with that stuffed shirt, Captain Howard. The very thought of it filled Gavin Rodgerson with glee. Another weapon in his counter-attack.

Eagerly the man dismounted at the scene of the tragedy, and examined everything to see if there was anything that would show if a trip rope had been used or perhaps a horse-scaring device of some sort. A sudden idea sent him to the temporary fence which formed the estate boundary. He examined the rails for signs of any rope fibres or anything else suspicious, but could see nothing at all to excite his attention.

He then decided to look at the tree trunks on the other side of the fence to see if there was any bruising on the bark.

No sooner had he dropped down after scaling the fence than a burly figure stepped out from the shelter of the trees. It was that of the gamekeeper, George Huddersley, and as usual with the man, he was carrying his shotgun broken across his arm. For a moment neither man spoke, but the mutual dislike hung thick in the air. In the past the man had been more than willing to be of assistance, especially with regard to Thomas Banham, but he, Captain Rodgerson, despised and disliked the man intensely.

George Huddersley was in just as foul a mood as the trespasser and when he did speak, he went straight to the point. "My girl is bearing a child," he rasped, "and she says it's yours."

In the woods behind the gamekeeper was Graham, Thomas Banham's friend, who was now only the assistant to Huddersley, and he could hear everything that was being said, yet he dare not show himself to the gamekeeper, for he was only just checking for snares, a job he was supposed to have done the previous day.

When Captain Rodgerson recovered from the shock of George Huddersley's words, he threw back his head, roared with laughter and said jeeringly, "Have you tried asking most of the red-blooded men in Wroxing, Huddersley, if any of them is the brat's father, eh?"

The gamekeeper's face flushed to an even deeper hue with anger, and he roared, "What are you trying to say about my girl, mister? She might not live in a grand house and wear fancy clothes, but she is not a slut like some I could mention." As he shouted, he snapped shut the shotgun, for he knew of the vicious temper of the man facing him.

"Well, Huddersdley," the Captain sneered, "no doubt you know how loose some of the women are at your level, but I doubt that you would be familiar enough with the ladies of the superior class." Back came the answer from the enraged gamekeeper, and he spat out, "The ladies, you say, mister, the superior class, like that trollop Mrs. Howard."

Crouching behind the undergrowth, Graham was aghast at what he was hearing. 'Whatever is Huddersley saying,' he thought, 'he will be out of a job before the day is over for what he has just said.'

Even as these thoughts were going through his head, he saw the Captain launch himself with an animal howl at the gamekeeper, his riding crop raised to strike the man's face.

Huddersley instinctively dodged back to avoid the blow, and stumbled on the tree root which caused him to hit the trunk of the tree with the butt of the gun. There was a deafening roar as the gun went off, and before the horrified gaze of both gamekeepers, Captain Rodgerson fell backwards with a mess of blood and cloth on what was left of his chest.

Just a few seconds passed with nobody moving, but to Graham it seemed as if he was staring at the ghastly tableau for minutes. Then slowly, George Huddersley pushed himself upright and putting down his shotgun, looked at it as if he had never seen it before. He turned his desperate gaze on the man he had just killed, and approached the still form, gazing at the face, still twisted into a snarl, as if hoping that the man was not dead after all.

Suddenly the gamekeeper spun round and with an unnerving noise in his throat, made as if to rush away. He then stopped, snatched up his gun and made his escape.

Graham was trembling so badly that he could hardly straighten himself up, but he forced himself to examine the body for signs of life. He knew even before he had checked for a pulse that Captain Rodgerson was dead, but he was then satisfied that nothing could be done for the man.

He decided that before he reported the accident, he needed a strong drink to steady his nerves.

Meanwhile, two fields away, John Wilson, aided by two labourers, was working on a sagging gate as instructed by the new Agent. On hearing the sound of a shotgun, one of the men remarked casually, "That's Huddersley's gun; bit close, isn't he?"

Almost at once they saw the riderless horse clear the hedge at the far end of the field. On seeing the men, the animal swerved and went to the boundary wall, swerving round again then coming to a stop, shaking its head in agitation.

"That's Captain Rodgerson's horse," said John. "I bet he has dismounted for some reason and the shot has frightened it."

As the men approached the horse, they could see that it was in a very agitated state, the whites of its eyes showing. Carefully John took the reins, all the time speaking gently to the creature. Gradually it calmed down somewhat, so the foreman and one of the labourers held it while the other man examined the harness. Everything appeared to be in order. John and the first man led the horse back in the direction it had come from and it gave no trouble, but as soon as they neared the gate close to the temporary boundary fence, the animal became very alarmed and tried to shy away from it.

"We will have to move her away from here," the foreman said. "Something is upsetting her; just take a look by the fence." As soon as the man reached the fence he called out, "No wonder the poor creature's jumpy, the owner is here, and," he added callously, "he won't be raising hell around here anymore, he's as dead as a doornail."

He then peered closer and said excitedly, "And it looks like he's been murdered!"

John Wilson saw immediately the implications of the sound of the shotgun, and when he sent one of the men to fetch the doctor and the constable, he warned him not to mention the sound of the shot or Huddersley. He reasoned that if the policeman asked questions about anything that they saw or heard before the finding of the body, then they would have to answer truthfully, but John did not want to bring the gamekeeper's name into it if it was not necessary.

Dr. Porby and Bob Freely, the constable, arrived together and as all present expected, quickly came to the conclusion that a murder had been committed, but more ominously for George Huddersley, the constable wanted to speak to the gamekeeper as soon as possible.

It was decided that the shocking news be imparted to Mrs. Rodgerson by Constable Freely, with Dr. Porby in close attendance. John Wilson and the men would bring the body back to the village as soon as the place where the death had occurred had been thoroughly examined by the police. As the light was already fading, the examination was somewhat rushed, leaving the constable out of temper at being unable to do his job properly.

Kate, on hearing of her husband's death and the suspicion of murder, astounded Constable Freely and alarmed Dr. Porby by covering her face with her hands and crying, "Oh God forgive me."

For a moment the two men could think of nothing to say, the policeman feeling very uncomfortable. He liked and respected Mrs. Rodgerson but after what she had just said, it seemed that he had a duty to question her as to the meaning of her outburst.

Dr. Porby, on the other hand, was conscious of his standing in the eyes of the lady. Before the death of Mrs. Howard, he had never been called to Reeve House in any capacity, never mind as an invited guest. He certainly did not want to jeopardise his chance of keeping such a contact with the people of the House in the future.

Then Kate's hands fell from her face, and she squared her shoulders and asked the constable, "Is there any chance that it could have been an accident or," her voice faltered, and then she continued quietly, "could it have been suicide?"

Bob Freely felt as if he had been holding his breath for too long, and said with a feeling of thankfulness, "Well, ma'am, an accident, or a suicide, possibly, that is, if we could have found a gun nearby, and up to now we haven't found one anywhere." Then he said, "Is there a likelihood that Captain Rodgerson took a gun with him, ma'am?"

At that Kate said thoughtfully, "If he did, Constable Freely, there would be an empty space in the gun cabinet; if you would care to follow me, we can check the cabinet now."

A glance through the glass doors of the locked cabinet showed that no guns were missing, but the constable was a thorough man and he wanted to check that none of the guns had been fired recently.

The small pouch that had been removed from the body held several keys, one which fitted the cabinet. As soon as the guns were checked, it was obvious that none of them had been used for some time.

A second key unlocked the drawer of Captain Rodgerson's desk, in which another key for the gun cabinet was found. Even before the keys were accounted for, Constable Freely had reached the conclusion that Mrs. Rodgerson did not have any involvement in her husband's killing.

"There will have to be a formal identification of the body, ma'am," said the policeman. "And I would say for certain that there will have to be a coroner's inquest."

At Constable Freely's words, Kate's heart quailed and once again she cried to herself for Richard to be with her in her time of need, but this time she did not feel bitter; knowing that he could not possibly be there, she had finally come to accept his situation.

When the constable and the doctor had gone, Kate set about organising everything. There was a new air of purpose about her that made Mary's heart sing. It was if they had all been struggling in a bog and now they had finally managed to pull themselves out of it. Mary had no conscience about her vengeful thoughts; she hated the man and was glad he was dead. In her own room, she removed the knife from her apron pocket, unwrapped it, and put it back in the drawer. Then she broke down and wept her cleansing tears.

Downstairs, Kate and Mrs. Higson were discussing the arrangements for the funeral when they were allowed to go ahead with it. The housekeeper had willingly agreed to accompany Kate to identify the body, for they were both in the same mind: they did not want Mary to have anything to do with that side of it.

Afterwards Kate sat down to compose the telegrams. She was having the greatest difficulty in writing the words down; it was if a numbness had come over her brain, and she was struggling not to break down. Then through the door came her brother. Then she did start to cry, but they were tears of relief. He held her close until the weeping had stopped, then in a more practical manner he said, "Now come on, our Kate, let's have a cup of tea and then I will offer you my services, heart and soul, and we will soon have everything sorted out." He then went on to say that they had met Dr. Porby on their way, and from him they had heard about the tragedy.

One of the first things that James did was to send telegrams to their parents and to Richard.

Meanwhile, when Dr. Porby opened his bag after he had eaten his evening meal, he found a note tucked inside which was clearly intended for the police. It read, 'That Mary said she would stab Captain Rodgerson to death. Just before last Christmas it was.' The note was unsigned and the letters were poorly formed, but the meaning was correct.

He was intrigued and decided to take it to Bob Freely right away, and when he entered the cottage, he handed the note to the constable and watched his reaction with interest. In the event he was disappointed, for Bob simply shook his head and said testily, "Women, trying to incriminate someone they have a grudge against."

The doctor looked at him in amazement and asked, "How do you know that, Bob, from just reading a note?" The constable grinned at him and said, "Oh, you know, Dr. Porby, clever detection," then explained his reasoning.

"In that house, apart from Mr. Rigg, the butler, they are all women, the only Mary I know there is Mrs. Rodgerson's maid, and thirdly, only one woman was crying when news got out." Then he shook his head and repeated what he had said after reading the note, "Dratted woman, she was probably a bit sweet on the late Captain."

Then he said slowly, "Well, he wasn't stabbed was he, he was shot, and that," he pointed to a shotgun propped in the corner of the room, "is the weapon that killed him." Before the doctor could say anything, Constable Freely said heavily, "And the man that killed Captain Rodgerson has left just before you came."

Dr. Porby raised his eyebrows in astonishment and said, "Well, Bob, you obviously have your reasons for taking such a bold step, and I must say I am curious as to why you let him go." Then he said, "Am I allowed to ask who the killer is?"

"George Huddersley," said the policeman, and picking up the shotgun, he broke it to see if there were any cartridges in it, then carefully laid it on the table. The doctor was still shaking his head at the revelations when Bob reached for an old-fashioned magnifying glass and, turning to his companion, said, "Well, Dr. Porby, you are just the man I need, an impartial witness."

With that he examined the butt of the gun through the glass. Then, with a satisfied grunt, he observed, "There, Doctor, this bears out part of what Huddersley said; here, have a look and tell me what you see."

Dr. Porby peered through the glass and said, "It looks like lichen, and something else driven into the slots of the screws. I would not like to say what that is, Bob."

Constable Freely told him. "Tomorrow I am going to look at the scene of the crime, that is, if a crime has taken place, and if that man is telling me the truth, and I believe that he is, then the stuff in those screw slots will match the bark of the tree I am going to examine." Then he said, "I would be obliged, Doctor, if you will be a witness of what I find tomorrow." To which the doctor readily agreed, for he had never had the excitement of being involved in a crime investigation before.

The following day, in answer to Constable Freely's message, an Inspector arrived on the train from Norwich. The first thing he did before he had interviewed George Huddersley, was to charge him with the murder of Captain Rodgerson. In vain did the constable point out that the position of the bruise of the tree indicated that the man was telling the truth, and that it did seem as though the death was indeed a tragic accident. Even the matching remnants of bark lodged in the screw slots of the butt plate failed to deflect the Inspector.

When the news got out, it spread like wildfire through the village. It soon reached the ears of Graham, the assistant gamekeeper, and he brushed aside his wife's entreaty to stay away from the police, and turned up at Bob Freely's cottage declaring himself as the only witness. For all the anger that was turned on him by the Inspector, he would not change a word of his story.

Eventually the Inspector very reluctantly accepted his story, especially when he learned that Graham had very strong reasons for disliking Huddersley; consequently the accused man was freed. After Huddersley had left, the Inspector turned his anger on Graham, telling him that he had wasted police time by not reporting the accident right in the beginning, and told him that he was lucky that he was not being charged.

As the relieved Graham came out into the street, Huddersley met him and said, "I owe you my neck, Graham, and I won't forget that." Then he continued, "I don't have much time for you, never will, but you are a good man and I hope you get the head gamekeeper's job, 'cause I am leaving Wroxing."

With those words he turned and walked away. His daughter, who had been standing in the street, ran over to Graham and flung her arms round him and sobbed, "Dad's right on one thing, Graham, you are a good man and a brave man as well." Then she ran after her father and the assistant gamekeeper found himself having his hand shaken by some of the villagers.

Word reached Reeve House before the police came to report their findings, and Kate said fervently to Charlotte, "Thank the Lord for that, the thoughts of somebody being hanged for an accidental death was something I couldn't bear to think about."

——— ——— ———

By a series of misunderstandings, the people at Frodsham Depot failed to learn that their employer was missing until two days after the collapse that put him in hospital. The reason that they were not too alarmed at his absence was due to fact that at the time, Captain Howard had been attending so many meetings that the normal routine of his days had been put to one side. Even so, it was unusual for their employer to not tell Thomas and Ian Blake about his movements.

Thomas was curious about the situation and resolved to find out if anybody knew of his whereabouts. Beth, however, was extremely worried; she, like many others, had been quite upset at Captain Howard's manner and appearance when he had returned, and to now find that nobody seemed to know where he was bothered her even more.

Meanwhile, at the Bear's Paw, a telegram had been delivered for Captain Howard. The landlord gave it to the maid who cleaned the room, and she put it in a position such that it could instantly be noticed by their lodger when he entered. Unfortunately the telegram was not propped up and it slid down, and was lying amongst other papers. Consequently, when the landlord put his head through the door to see if Captain Howard had returned, he did not realise that the telegram was still lying there unread.

The next day the landlord managed to buttonhole Ian Blake in the street and express his concern about his missing lodger. Ian immediately checked with Thomas and Mr. Robbins, but it was Dr. Mills who provided them with the first hint of where he might be.

As a matter of course, since the incident of the smallpox case at the Norton settlement, in which there had been one fatality, all suspicious cases of sickness were reported to the medical officers along the Canal.

Dr. Mills had been told of the man who had ended up in hospital at Ellesmere Port, a man with good quality clothing but unfortunately with nothing on him which would tell them his identity.

When Ian proposed to visit the unknown man at the hospital, Sarah begged him to let her go with him. They took a train to Ellesmere Port, but on asking at the hospital whether they could see the man, they were denied access as he was in isolation and still unconscious. However, when they were shown his clothes, they were able to confirm that the man was indeed Captain Howard.

Ian gave them such details that he knew about his employer, which were sparse, but he did recall that Captain Howard had suffered an attack of some sort of fever whilst in India. He also told of their concerns about him overworking himself.

Although the doctor was pleased to receive the information, he stressed that the patient would have to remain in isolation for at least three more days before they were satisfied that he was clear of any contagious infection. He also stressed that they should keep quiet about the possibility of the man having smallpox.

At least they now knew where Captain Howard was, and although they were naturally worried about him, Ian was convinced that his employer was simply suffering from exhaustion.

Returning to Frodsham, Ian lost no time in informing everybody about his findings. He also resolved to write to his employer's sister-in-law, but with his extra work burden, he had to leave his letter-writing to the following day. Beth had also decided to write to Mrs. Rodgerson.

By then, Ian Blake was feeling the strain of coping with Captain Howard's work as well as his own. However, the engineer over the section had been informed of the situation, and soon the burden was being shared.

He was returning to his lodgings when one of the maids from the Bear's Paw ran over to him and breathlessly told him that they had found the telegram for Captain Howard.

The first task on the following day, which was a Saturday, was to visit his employer and give him the telegram. Captain Howard was still in isolation but was awake and very much better. On this occasion Ian had gone to the hospital unaccompanied. Whilst not allowed to give the telegram to the patient, respecting the confidentiality of the message, he opened it and without looking at it, pressed it up against the glass pane so that the quarantined man could read it.

On reading the telegram, Captain Howard looked grim, then after a few moments, mimed that Ian should read it himself. As usual for a telegram, the words were meagre but to the point. It read, 'CAPT RODGERSON DEAD. JAMES'.

Ian looked in askance at his employer; he knew that his sister-in-law was named Mrs. Rodgerson, so he assumed that the dead man was her husband. He was surprised to note that his employer looked concerned and thoughtful, rather than sad. Obviously the man Rodgerson was not a dear friend.

With the telegram delivered, Ian left Captain Howard and went to speak with the duty doctor, who told him that his employer would be out of isolation within the next two days, so it was a very relieved Ian Blake who returned to Frodsham.

Tuesday afternoon saw Captain Howard leaving hospital accompanied by Sarah Mills and Ian. He was glad of the offer of a room at Mrs. Joyce's for a few days whilst he made a complete recovery; the thought of moving back to his room at the Bear's Paw whilst he was still feeling shaky did not fill him with enthusiasm. Whilst he had no grumble with the landlord or the maids, the hotel was a busy one and he would not expect to be looked after if he fell ill again. The arrangement pleased the landlord, who was relieved that he would not have to look after an invalid.

In the Banhams' hut at Marshville, Peter was sitting at the top of the stairs thinking about the things that small boys find so important, such as whether to ask his mother if he could play out with the twins, or whether to stay in and draw a picture of the crane that worked at the back of the hut. He had the idea that if he drew it, he would get Michael to help him to paint the drawing.

Then he heard his mother mention Captain Howard's name. Victoria was spending her day off with them and that is why Peter was unsure whether to go out to play. He was loath to miss any time with her, for since she had gone to work at Mrs. Hilyard's he did miss her a lot.

His mother said to Victoria, "I'm worried to death about Captain Howard; he has not looked well for months and he hardly ever looks happy." Her daughter nodded in agreement and said, sadly, "The only times I have seen him at ease and smiling is when he shares a meal with us. I really think that he has fallen out with Mrs.Rodgerson..Then she burst out, unaware of the young pair of ears on the stairs, "I wish Mrs Rodgerson was here, at Frodsham, I mean. Captain Howard was a different man when they were in the same room, well, they were both more alive; he really does light up when they are together," she added.

Beth looked at her daughter fondly and said, "You and your dreams of our Captain and the mistress being married; even now they are both bereaved I doubt such a thing will ever happen." She stopped as a knock came at the door, and Peter took advantage of the distraction to steal back to his room.

He liked Captain Howard, he was kind and had been a soldier so he must be brave as well. The thought that he was sad because Mrs. Rodgerson was not here bothered him. His dad was happy and so was Michael, and Will was happy working for Mr. Hughes, who did not seem sad either. Peter thought his mam was sometimes happy, especially when Victoria was at home, or when his mam was with Mrs. Robbins. He thought Victoria was very happy. He loved his sister more than anything else in the whole world and he would not like to see her sad.

Whilst his puzzled thoughts went round in his head, he worked away at the drawing of his crane and by the time his mother called him down for a drink of milk, it was almost finished. The dusk was settling over everything anyway, so he was forced to give up drawing for the day.

That night before he went to sleep, he had an idea how he could help to make Captain Howard happy again. He would write a letter to Mrs. Rodgerson!

He knew what to do, he had seen his mother writing letters, so all he had to do after writing his was to get an envelope and a stamp. Will would be able to get him both, but Peter was wise enough to realise that his brother would want to know why he wanted them. Eventually he decided to ask Will for one item only, and with that, he asked his mother could he go across to the shop to see his brother. Beth smiled and said he could but warned him not to mither Will or Mr. Hughes if they were busy.

When he entered the shop his brother was serving and Mr. Hughes was just putting his order book back on the shelf, so Peter leaned on the counter, prepared to wait until Will came to him.

Mr. Hughes smiled and said, "Hello, young man, can we help you?" Peter did not know what excuse he could use to put the grocer off, but before he could stop himself he blurted out, "I just wanted a stamp, Mr. Hughes, one that you put on letters."

The young man raised his eyebrows in surprise and said, "Well, Peter, we are not a post office, but I do have some stamps for my own use. But whatever would you want a stamp for?"

The blushing boy said in a tiny voice, "I don't have any, Mr. Hughes, I've never had any stamps of my own." His tone of voice was so sad that the grocer was hard put not to burst out laughing, but instead he said solemnly, "Peter, that is a shame, but if it would make you happy, I will let you have two Penny Blacks." With that he tore the stamps off the sheet and, to Peter's joy, dropped them in an envelope, and handed it to him. "There you are, Peter, two stamps of your very own."

Will, who had finished serving his customer, was looking at his young brother suspiciously, but Peter returned his look with such an expression of innocence that Will was convinced that the little lad was up to something that their mother knew nothing about.

"Thank you so much, Mr. Hughes," cried Peter. "I will pay for them, and the envelope when I have some money."

"That is all right young man," said Mr. Hughes, gravely. "I am pleased to oblige, they are a gift."

Peter waved to both of them then dashed back to their hut, and when he had gone, the shopkeeper burst out laughing and said to his assistant, "I wonder what scheme is going through your brother's head at the moment, Will. He is a rum one."

Back at the hut, Peter nonchalantly made his way up to the bedroom, and hid his precious envelope.

Eventually he managed to write his letter, but addressing his envelope caused him a lot of pencil chewing before he decided how to name the person he was sending it to. He could not spell Rodgerson, so he wrote, 'To Miss Rog'. Then crossed that out and put, 'Miss Kate. Reeve House, Rocsin, Norfolk'. The final step was just as difficult, how to put it in the post box.

The following day Beth was walking the boys to school accompanied by one of the women from the village, and as they chatted, Peter contrived, with the help of the twins, to drop behind sufficiently to push his missive into the post box. He was only just in time, for alerted by the mischievous giggling of the twins, his mother swung round and told him to walk in front so that she could keep an eye on them.

Peter secretly hugged himself; all he had to do now was to wait and see if his letter would make Captain Howard happy again.

Chapter 26

Kate Visits Frodsham

Reeve House was a house of mourning and yet the truth was that in a guilty way, there was an air of buoyancy about people. It was if everyone sensed that the bad times were over and life was going to be better in the future.

Kate and James were obviously affected more than the staff or even Charlotte, but they were also sad rather than sorrowful, Cecelia had never been one to inspire love in her family, but the natural pain of losing a sibling left them in low spirits. Mercifully the inquest on Captain Rodgerson's death had been held before too much time had passed, and the verdict of accidental killing satisfied most people, and the funeral had taken place the following day.

The funeral had saddened Kate more than she had expected. It had been the paucity of mourners which affected her the most, for apart from Charlotte, James and herself, there had been only one other. He was the fellow officer of Captain Rodgerson who had appeared at Cecelia's funeral.

The melancholy sight of the man throwing a handful of earth onto the coffin, then silently walking away without a backward glance, upset Kate more than she thought possible.

Later, when the vicar had gone, Charlotte said quietly, "When that man paid his respects at the grave, I nearly broke down with the poignancy of it all." James nodded and said soberly, "Fancy leaving this life with just one mourner to send you on your way." The fact that James did not see themselves as real mourners was not lost on his listeners.

Kate wished more than anything that Richard could have been there, but since she had learned of his illness and stay in hospital she had been beside herself with worry over him, and it had forced her to face up to the reality of his situation.

Their parents had not been able to attend because Mrs. Prentice had succumbed to the same malaise that had affected Kate at Cecelia's funeral. Albert, their older brother, had simply refused to come, for as he had told them bluntly, he did not consider the fellow worth mourning over.

The following morning Mary brought her mistress's mail to her room. Peter's letter stood out from the others; as Rigg had pointed out to Mary, it was either from a child or from somebody with an unpractised hand. Kate's immediate thought that it was a child's hand that had penned it, and she was puzzled but rather intrigued, and opened it first.

Dear Mr ~~Bo~~ Kate.

Captain Howard is better now but
he has bin poorly and he always looks
sad. Please come to ~~F~~ Frodsham it is
easy on ~~that~~ the traine, if you ascat
the station they will tel you. Mam and
Victoria wory ~~abu~~ about Captain Howard
and Victoria says he lites up when you
come in the room.

from Peter Banham with love.

Victoria and Mam likes you very ~~love~~ much
Will likes you as well and so dose Dad.
it is not a ~~gud~~ good letter but I only hav one peese
of paper. love Peter.

Her eyes spilled over with tears at the little boy's simple message, and she whispered to herself, "Oh, Peter, out of the mouths of babes…" She did not complete the quotation, but touched the letter with her lips, then carefully put it away in her escritoire. In the drawer was every letter she had ever received from Richard, the first when she was a gauche young girl. Peter's letter was placed with them.

At breakfast Kate calmly told her brother that she had decided to travel to Cheshire and visit Richard. James sat there open-mouthed in astonishment, then as Charlotte took her seat at the table, grinned and said cheerfully, "Now that, Kate, is the most sensible thing you have said for a long time." Charlotte laughed and chimed in saying, "Watch out, Kate, he will be offering to carry your bags next." To which Kate replied hopefully, "Would you both like to accompany me? I would certainly feel more confident if you did so."

James immediately accepted. He was so pleased that his sister appeared to want to settle her differences with his favourite brother-in-law. As he confided later to his wife, a contented Kate enjoying her former close friendship with Richard was so much more preferable to the forlorn creature that she had become. Also he was very interested in the Canal scheme, and to see it at this stage before it was filled with water would allow him to see the full majesty of the construction.

The major consideration was obviously accommodation. Kate racked her brains about how to find lodgings without letting anyone know she was coming. Regretfully she ended up having to confide in Victoria, for of all the people involved, the girl was more often in Frodsham than Beth or Thomas, therefore Victoria would probably know more about hotels and boarding houses than her parents.

When Victoria received Kate's letter she was both ecstatic and overwhelmed by the responsibility that had been thrust upon her. In the end she asked Mrs. Hilyard her opinion of the hostelries in the town. Her mistress very quickly dismissed certain of them but told her maid that finding decent rooms in Frodsham at this time would be difficult anyway. Of course there was Miss Yard's boarding house, but she seemed to only take in long-term lodgers.

Then she took the girl's breath away by telling her that her former employer and her party were welcome to stay with her, but she warned Victoria that it would mean more work for her and Daisy. The other girl was so excited at having visitors that Victoria said laughingly they might be royalty coming to see them.

Victoria wrote her letter the same day, then she and Daisy set to under the direction of Mrs. Hilyard to open up the unused rooms. Fires were lit to warm and air the beds, fresh bedding was brought out, and everywhere was dusted and polished. Daisy had heard so much about Mrs. Rodgerson that she had her in mind as someone akin to a princess, dignified but beautiful.

The difficult part was keeping the visit secret. The day she would normally meet Sarah Mills had to be cancelled as she was so busy. Actually, that was fortunate, for Victoria was sure that she would forget herself and let slip about the visit.

She knew that her friend would not divulge anything to Ian, but Victoria decided that the ones who already knew about it were the only people who needed to know.

However, during the week of frantic preparations it came to her that if Mrs. Rodgerson took it in her head to visit the Banhams, her mother would not be pleased if the hut was not spick and span on the day. With that in mind she let her mother know, on the understanding that nobody else found out, particularly Captain Howard and definitely not Peter!

On the Saturday, the rain which had plagued them for several days had stopped, and by the time that Kate's party arrived at Frodsham, the streets were quite dry.

Victoria was obviously the best person to meet the train and by good luck, only the second train from Chester brought the visitors.

The first sight of Mrs. Rodgerson gave Victoria quite a shock. She looked so pale and thin. However, there was no mistaking the pleasure which lit up her face when she realised that the poised, elegant young woman greeting her was her former maid.

"Victoria," she cried as she ran forward. "How wonderful you look." Then as the tears started to flow, she put her arms around the girl and hugged her fiercely.

Victoria's initial shock at Mrs. Rodgerson's appearance gave way to an almost motherly urge to protect her and she hugged her tightly in return. She made a vow then that whatever it took, she would make sure that her late mistress and Captain Howard would meet in as private a place as she could manage to arrange for them. Victoria had no idea how that could be managed but she was sure that something would come to her.

Kate then told her that she had reverted to her maiden name and now was to be addressed as Miss Prentice. "I would be pleased, Victoria, if you and your family addressed me as Miss Kate." Then, still holding the girl's hand, she went back to her party. Charlotte greeted her warmly and offered a cheek to be kissed, whilst James bowed slightly and touched his hat.

When it came to Mary, she became very unsure at how to greet the elegant Victoria, but her friend had no such inhibitions; she hugged her friend tightly with a cry of delight.

Then, turning to Mr. James, Victoria said, "The house is less than fifteen minutes walk, sir, but if you wish, there is a carriage for hire in the station yard."

The driver, a rather surly-looking man, looked at the party and then at the luggage and started complaining about his springs, but Victoria cut him short and told him, "That is all right, my friend and myself will walk, which leaves just three people and the bags, and I am sure your springs will survive the short distance to Mrs. Hilyard's house. You do know where that is?" she queried.

James's eyebrows rose; the former maid had put the ill-mannered driver in his place without batting an eye. 'Good for her,' he thought with a grin, as without another word the driver opened the carriage doors and helped the ladies in.

Victoria and Mary arrived at the house arm in arm, having talked without stopping all the way there. Most of the bags had been taken in by the handyman, so the two girls helped with the rest of them. Mary was introduced to Mrs. Hilyard, after which Daisy took Mary up to her room where an extra bed had been moved in. Daisy, however, had been disappointed when she first glimpsed Victoria's late mistress; she was not a bit like her friend had described her, Mrs. Rodgerson was so thin and pale.

Meanwhile Victoria went to help Cook with the refreshments for the guests, James having performed the introductions in his usual inimitable way. Mrs. Hilyard could be heard laughing delightedly at something he was telling her. The anxious girl felt that everything was going to be alright; she had been on tenterhooks ever since Mrs. Hilyard had offered to accommodate Miss Kate and her party.

The following morning all four visitors accompanied Mrs. Hilyard and Victoria to Chapel. The Prentices were of a different religious persuasion but they were not averse to worshipping in another's church. Victoria was delighted to see that her father was there with the family. To her mind it suggested that the workshops were not busy today, and that meant that Captain Howard would probably be at Mrs. Joyce's. An idea came to her and she decided that after the service she would put it into practice.

It was quite an emotional meeting; Beth and Kate clung to each other and wept. Even Thomas was affected, as was Will, but Peter was beaming from ear to ear. Kate gave him special hug which pleased him immensely.

Later, as they stood talking at the Chapel, Victoria asked if she could be excused then hurried down the street to Mrs. Joyce's house. When the lady herself saw who it was at the door, she immediately asked her in, for Victoria had called on other occasions with Sarah Mills.

Victoria enquired whether Captain Howard was at home, but was told that he would not be back from church for another half hour yet. Quickly the girl explained what she wanted to do, and Mrs. Joyce, delighted to be helping in a reunion, told her that her sitting room would be kept unoccupied.

Excitedly Victoria hurried back to the Chapel, and could see by the enquiring glances directed her way by her parents that they were uncomfortable at her absence. She apologised but asked the company, who were by now very curious about what was going on, if they would excuse Miss Kate for a short while. A lot of bemused glances were exchanged, but the pink-faced girl had got the bit between her teeth by then and was not to be deflected.

Drawing Kate to one side, Victoria said quietly, "Would you come with me, ma'am? Captain Howard will be home shortly, and Mrs. Joyce has invited you to use her sitting room."

Kate looked at Victoria in such a startled way that for a moment the girl thought fearfully that she had overstepped the mark. Then suddenly she was rewarded with a loving smile and Kate said, "I will excuse myself to the others, then you can take me there."

As they walked along Main Street, her late mistress linked Victoria's arm and the girl felt the trembling of the other woman. She realised that Miss Kate was in a more nervous state than she herself was!

Within a short time they were in Mrs. Joyce's sitting room, and after introductions had been effected, Victoria left Kate, whilst the warm-hearted lady of the house bustled out to make a warm drink for her visitor.

The apprehensive visitor had hardly taken a few sips of her drink before Captain Howard entered the room. The look he bestowed upon Kate was reward enough for Mrs. Joyce, and as she went back to the kitchen, she decided that her temporary lodger would not want his cup of tea for a while.

In the sitting room there was a moment's silence, then before Richard had recovered from his surprise, the nervous woman said in an unsteady voice, "I must first of all let you know that I am to be known as Miss Kate Prentice; the other hateful name that I have borne so long is now in the past." Then she said in a rush, "Oh, Richard, I am here to see if we can at least be friends again. I simply cannot bear to think of the damage I have done to something that has always been so precious and sustaining to me."

The appeal in her eyes was so powerful that it was all Richard could do to stop himself from going to her and taking her in his arms, but he refrained, knowing how delicate the situation was.

Keeping his voice as steady as he could, Richard said, "I would be glad and proud to have such a friendship with you, Kate. I too would have difficulty enjoying life without the bond we have shared for so many years." Then, as the first glimmer of hope appeared in her eyes, he continued, "Nevertheless, I feel that you must be told one truth: throughout the years, and especially this last terrible year of your illness, I have always loved you and always will."

Kate's eyes filled with tears, she gulped and said in a tremulous voice, "But, Richard, how can you still feel love for me when I have acted so badly towards you?" Her voice wobbled and the tears fell unchecked. This time Richard did not hesitate; he went to Kate and held her as she wept her tears of joy.

After a while he went to the kitchen and told Mrs. Joyce that he would escort Miss Prentice back to Mrs. Hilyard's house, then return in good time for his midday meal. Seeing the anxious look of enquiry on her face, he smiled and said, "Thank you, Mrs. Joyce," and surprised the lady by giving her a hug. He did not have to tell her more; she could see by his whole demeanour that something wonderful had occurred in her sitting room.

Richard, with Kate on his arm, walked slowly towards Mrs. Hilyard's house, both of them reluctant to arrive too soon. The lightness in their steps was as nothing compared to the lightness in their hearts.

When they arrived at the house, it was Victoria who let them in, a jubilant Victoria, as she had been peeping out of the window on and off for over twenty minutes, and what she had just seen told her that her intervention had not been in vain.

Indeed, after the front door closed, Kate put her arms round her and whispered, "Oh, Victoria, as always, you know just what to do. I will always bless you for this day." Poor Victoria, she had a struggle not to burst out crying, she was so full of happiness for Miss Kate. And there was another problem; she knew that she would have the greatest difficulty not to use the name Rodgerson after so long, but having been asked to call her former mistress Miss Prentice, or more preferably, Miss Kate, Victoria was quite happy to comply.

She almost danced back to the other girls, who had been on pins to know what had happened, and Daisy had later confessed that Miss Kate did now look lovely even if she was a bit thin.

The following day it had been arranged that the party would visit the excavation site near Frodsham Depot, then afterwards have a meal with Beth.

Their first sight of Marshville had silenced them all. The blackened collection of dwellings repelled them as it had done Beth and Victoria one year ago. Although there were more plants and shrubs now, the time of the year had seen the flowers die away and the resultant straggly vegetation looked sad and neglected. They were all glad to reach the works area.

Whilst looking down on the activity in the cutting, the women were silenced by the sight of so many workers, many knee deep in water, shovelling the spoil into the railway wagons. Conditions were bad, and the intermittent rain, which seemed to have intensified since Mr. Walker had died, was forcing the contractors to use the pumps more often. In places the ground was a quagmire, and even James was silenced.

The sight and sounds of men and machines toiling seemingly without stop had affected them profoundly. Charlotte voiced the thoughts of them all when she said sombrely, "It is like watching slaves working, almost as though their lives depended on how much they do."

Richard agreed with her and said, "Well, their lives might not depend on their efforts, but certainly their livelihoods do. They do get paid at a rate above that of a farm labourer. But a ten-hour shift at that pace is not for the weak or faint-hearted of men."

Each way they looked, the deepening trench stretched seemingly endlessly into the mist-shrouded distance.

As Mary said later as she was describing the scene to Victoria and Daisy, "It was awful, there were these machines tearing away at the earth with all the smoke and steam, but the worse bit was the hundreds of men digging out, then throwing the earth into the wagons." Then she added angrily, "And you know what, they didn't have a chance to rest, 'cause as soon as the wagons were full they took them away and put in another load of wagons for them to fill." She shuddered and said dramatically, "Miss Charlotte says it is like slave labour, and that is just how it seemed to me!"

James especially enjoyed the workshops, but it was the electric lights that impressed the ladies most of all, and Charlotte smiled as she observed the thoughtful look on her husband's face as he examined the dynamo. Michael lifted their spirits with his infectious smile and good humour, whilst Thomas impressed them all with his knowledge about everything. After seeing the cutting, the workshops seemed like an oasis of order and calm.

With adequate warning from Victoria the Banhams' hut was transformed. The place had been scrubbed to within an inch of its life. Jessie Robbins had lent Beth some good rugs, and what with a warming fire in the grate and the glow of the oil lamps dispelling the gloom of the day, the effect was really welcoming.

Knowing that there would be a full dinner awaiting her visitors when they sat down the coming evening at Mrs. Hilyard's house, Beth had prepared something light, but warming, and had excelled herself. One thing was noticeable: Beth was not a servant anymore, she was a woman entertaining guests in her own home, a subtlety that was not lost on them, and they warmed to her all the more for that. One significant fact that emerged from the visit was that Beth felt less ashamed of her situation than previously.

Before they returned to the town, they visited the shop and were introduced to Dafyd Hughes. Kate had yet to learn of the strong attachment between the shopkeeper and Victoria, but she was most impressed with the young man. Will was as pleased as Punch to see them. Altogether it was a most enjoyable and interesting visit, that is, with the exception of the women; the sights they had witnessed in the cutting had made a very uncomfortable impression on them.

Even though they had all found the hutted village terribly depressing, once they had shared a meal with Beth, they were heartened to see that she was coping with the conditions and, in fact, looked remarkably well. Afterwards Charlotte remarked how homely the hut was and Kate replied, "I am more at ease in my mind now that I have seen where and how they live; it did seem homely, I must say, but even so, I pray that soon they will be able to rent a house in the town, for I think that is what keeps Beth's spirits up."

Tuesday was an atrocious day which made them glad to be indoors. The sporadic rain only ceased as dusk approached. Kate had been invited to an evening meal at Mrs. Joyce's. Sarah and Dr. Mills had also been invited and it quite soon became obvious to Kate that Sarah and Ian Blake, whom she was meeting for the first time, were very close.

She found, as Richard had done on his first visit, that Mrs. Joyce was very good company. Richard recalled that visit and his thoughts at the time, that Kate would have enjoyed it as he had done. Their hostess, with her warm heart affected by the sight of Richard and Kate's happiness, felt that she could not be happier herself.

Before Kate fell asleep that night she reflected on all she had seen that day and the people who surrounded her dear Richard. Very few had any real wealth, in fact most of them had no wealth, yet they had all been so interesting and so friendly. She felt that if she could be part of that, she would be quite contented.

As Dr. Mills had rather optimistically forecast the previous evening, Wednesday dawned bright but cool with no sign of rain. James had mentioned that he would like to see the walled city of Chester. Kate, unable to see Richard that day, decided to join her brother and her sister-in-law, so they arose early and took a train into the city. Mary had looked rather weary, so her mistress told her to stay at the house and rest, an order that the girl was only too pleased to comply with.

Armed with the knowledge gleaned from Beth and Jessie, both women knew where the best shops and teashops were, whilst James had his mind set on seeing the River Dee first. He really enjoyed the waterside and, even on such a cool day, took pleasure in walking by the river. Later, after a pleasant meal in a tearoom with a glowing fire burning in the grate, they set themselves to walk the full length of the City walls. As the air was turning colder, they completed their hike, and returned to the railway station and back to Frodsham. In spite of the cool weather they had thoroughly enjoyed themselves and agreed that Chester was a delightful city, and vowed that they would visit again in the future, but only when the weather was much warmer!

Market day started dry and Main Street was thronged with people. Mrs. Hilyard let everybody know that she was having a look round the stalls. Charlotte expressed an interest in going, so Kate and Mary decided to go with her.

James had taken it into his head that he would like to climb to the top of the hill which formed a backdrop to the town. Mrs. Hilyard looked doubtful about walking such a distance with the uncertain weather. However, he was quite determined and when the ladies made their way to the market, James, suitably garbed, went with them, then following his hostess's instructions, he turned into Church Street and started his increasingly stiff climb. Eventually he gained the top and was rewarded with a splendid view towards the River Mersey dotted with various vessels, both sail and steam. Before he had been there for a few minutes, the rain started and he was forced to hurry back to the town.

When he arrived back at the house, he found that he had missed the midday meal. However, after he had changed into drier clothing, he was served with a hot bowl of soup with large chunks of crusty bread. "It was worth coming back late for," he said contentedly to Daisy, who had waited on him.

That evening, Mrs. Hilyard had arranged an intimate soirée for her guests. Without any intervention on Victoria's part, and much to everyone's pleasure, she had invited Captain Howard.

Dafyd arrived before they were all seated, and he had brought with him the sheet music of the songs he intended to sing. The guests were seated but a few minutes when, to their amazement, a blushing Victoria took her place at the piano.

She started the proceedings with two short light-hearted pieces which brought forth a great deal of appreciative applause. Daisy covertly watched the expressions on the faces of the listeners, and she was not disappointed at the way her friend's playing affected them. The look on Mary's face was especially rewarding, her jaw dropped in amazement. Miss Kate started by looking at her former maid with pleased surprise, then as the music filled the room, her expression changed to awe then to absolute delight.

Dafyd then followed with two of Mr. Stephen Foster's songs, 'Beautiful Dreamer' and 'Camptown Races'. For the latter songs he invited them to join in, which they did with gusto, that is, with the exception of Victoria!

Eventually Daisy received a signal from Mrs. Hilyard and went out of the room to bring in the refreshments. Mary jumped up and went after her to help. For Victoria there was no chance to help with the serving; she was hugged and kissed by Kate and Charlotte, and congratulated by the men. Her head was in a whirl with all the attention that she was receiving. Dafyd, who got his share of appreciation, looked on happily, a contented smile on his face. He was so proud of his loved one's gift.

After the refreshments came what can only be described as a musical romp. Dafyd had noticed that James had a good tenor voice and asked him whether he would like to sing himself. James was up like a shot. He sang another Stephen Foster song, 'The Old Folks At Home', which some people called 'Swanee'. A sad song, it brought tears to the eye, but then he and Dafyd sang a duet which caused more tears to flow, but they were tears of hilarity.

The song was from Mr. Gilbert and Mr. Sullivan's 'Pirates Of Penzance', and was 'We Are The Bold Gendarme'. The spectacle of James and Dafyd rocking on their heels and bobbing up and down reduced everybody to helpless laughter. Poor Victoria, she had a terrible job keeping playing, it was so funny.

Richard and Kate had not laughed so wholeheartedly in years, and it was a most significant sign to the others that the healing process had started for both of them.

Friday was their last day at Frodsham and Richard had arranged for them to visit the site at Eastham Locks. The party took a train to Eastham, then hired a coach down to the locks area. Unfortunately, on arrival they were stopped by two policemen and told that they would have to wait as an important party was at that moment visiting the locks.

Richard introduced himself to the sergeant and was about to ask whom the personages were, then he caught sight of the most illustrious of them. It was Lord

Egerton of Tatton, another strong supporter of the Manchester Ship Canal scheme. Both he and Mr. Daniel Adamson firmly believed that it would be built, differing only in how the money was to be raised to make it possible.

Lord Egerton considered that the best way to raise money was to approach the City, and in fact the Rothschilds and Barings banks eventually provided most of the millions that were needed. Mr. Adamson, however, preferred that Manchester money from businesses and from the local people would make it truly a Manchester effort, a People's canal in fact.

The inspecting party moved off the locks and to their awaiting carriages. As they passed Richard's party, Lord Egerton and the other men tipped their hats to the ladies, but one of the men raised his hand to Richard, as if to acknowledge his presence.

James looked enquiringly at Richard, who said, "That is Mr. Manisty, whom I have told you about; he is well thought of by everybody and particularly by his men." Then he turned to them and pointed to the hill lying between the canal cutting and the River Mersey. "That is Mount Manisty, the navvy's tribute to him." He went on to explain about the spoil deposits which had grown and grown until they resembled a small mountain.

After Lord Egerton's party had gone, Richard escorted his group onto the lock area. James was particularly interested in the enormously tall lock gates which opened outwards towards the river instead of inwards like the majority of the gates. Richard explained that they were there to hold back the exceptionally high tides when they were higher than the normal height of the canal waters. They were all amazed at the depth of the riverwards channel leading to these massive entrance gates, a depth approaching sixty feet. "The tide in this part of the country can rise about thirty feet," said Richard, "and with a twenty-six foot depth for the largest vessels, there must be enough water over the lock sill within four hours before and after high tide." Then he added, "Of course, vessels with a shallow enough draught will be able to enter or leave at any state of the tide."

Charlotte exclaimed when they were looking at the stonework of the lock piers. "Why they look so beautifully made that it seems a shame to let them be hidden under the water?.

Mary and to some extent Kate felt quite nervous when looking over the edge, but James had no such fears. Everything held so much interest for him. The earth dam which was holding back the waters of the Mersey from the excavation claimed his attention, and he questioned his brother-in-law as to how it was to be removed when the canal was ready to hold water.

"When the tide is low," said Richard, "the navvies will remove as much soil as they can, and by the way there will be scores of men working at top speed to do so, then when there is enough water to float a dredger, it will eat away at the remaining soil until it clears a navigable channel."

Charlotte lifted her eyes and gazed out onto the river. She gave a shudder and said sombrely, "How forbidding it looks, so grey and just a little frightening." Mary, who had been thinking exactly the same thing, nodded in agreement. The mist shrouding the far shore, the long lazy swell of the waters reflecting the grey sky, did indeed look uninviting, even menacing.

"You are quite right, Charlotte," replied Richard. "It is not a good day to appreciate the beauties of Eastham Locks, but I can assure you that on a clear, bright day, summer or winter, when the far shore, that is the Lancashire side of the river, is plain to see, it is a very exhilarating view."

After explaining something of the workings of the locks he asked them, with a twinkle in his eye, if they were ready for a hot drink. With no objectors he led them into the boiler room of the Cornish Pumping Engine. They were quite surprised to see a clean table and forms with clean covers set out. "For our distinguished visitors," said Richard with a laugh, "and now for us."

A grinning elderly man in clean overalls was just placing the large cups he had just washed onto the table.

"Morning Captain Howard, ladies, sir," he said. "Is it a look around the engine house you will be wanting or would you be ready for a brew of tea?" Richard laughed with him and answered, "Good morning, Joe, you are right on both counts, but I am sure everybody would enjoy a cup of tea first before we look at your beloved engine."

At first the women were apprehensive about having tea in the gloomy boilerhouse, and when Joe filled a blackened metal canister with water, then thrust it into the glowing furnace of the boiler on a long metal bar, they were not so sure that a drink in this place was what they wanted.

Within seconds the canister was removed from the fire and Joe deftly poured the boiling water into a large spotlessly clean teapot. He had noticed their worried looks and grinned, saying, "Lord Egerton always tells me that I make the finest pot of tea ever."

After the first tentative sips, Kate said warmly, "And he is right Mr., er… Joe." Certainly nobody refused a second cup.

It was obvious that the men looking after the boiler and the engine were proud of their charges, for every piece of brasswork gleamed and the paintwork was kept spick and span.

James was very interested in the engine. The huge overhead beams, rocking silently and ponderously with each stroke, and the gentle sigh of exhausting steam, gave it an air of unstoppable power. Again, as she had been with the steam excavators, brave-hearted Mary was rather fearful of the machine. They were told by the proud Joe, "Works night and day, she does, and shifts enough water on each stroke to fill half a dozen bathtubs."

Afterwards the party went to the end of the locks to see the progress in the cutting itself. They were told that Mr. Manisty believed that, with luck, they would be finished in this section in about eighteen months from that time.

Later, whilst having their midday meal at the Eastham Ferry Hotel, Kate commented on how many cheerful, even enthusiastic people they had met on the site. Richard agreed but added, "Certainly those whom you have met do, in the main, enjoy what they have to do, but there are many more, particularly the navvies, who given the chance to work elsewhere for the same wages, would leave immediately." He continued, "However, while they are here, when the weather is kinder, they are quite cheerful and work with a will."

Saturday morning and the party were up and ready early for their return to Norfolk. Kate and Richard had managed to make their goodbyes in private, so the fact that he could not be at the station to speed them on their journey did not trouble Kate unduly. She knew now that she was secure in his love for her. Kate was truly happy, and now that she had seen with her own eyes the work that claimed so much of his time, she was content to share Richard with his Manchester Ship Canal.

With the exception of Thomas, the Banham family were at the station and although tears were shed, they were tears of happiness for all they had enjoyed during their visit. When the train drew out of the station, those on board knew that they would visit Cheshire again and in the not too distant future.

It was very quiet in Mrs. Hilyard's house, but the lady herself was contented with the part she had played in bringing happiness to those people, and she now thought of them warmly as friends.

Peter Banham was very pleased with himself for what he had done. Miss Kate had hugged him tight and whispered, "Our secret, Peter," and although she had cried, he knew that he had made her happy again. And Captain Howard did not look sad now either.

Will, who had witnessed the fuss Miss Kate had twice made of his young brother, had started to wonder about Peter's need of a stamp. Surely he had not written to Miss Kate? Then as quick as the thought came to him he dismissed it. Even Peter would not be as bold as that!

Chapter 27

A Testing Time for the Canal Builders

Following the happy events of the previous week, the days leading up to Christmas were, for Captain Howard and the Banham family, filled with an extra feeling of cheerful anticipation. Even the worsening weather conditions could not dampen their optimism. As for Beth, she was still basking in the praise heaped upon her by her visitors for the meal that she had conjured up for them. For a while she had even forgotten that she was living in a hut in a dreary-looking contractor's settlement.

In those first few minutes after Miss Kate came through the door, Beth had been upset to see how pale and thin her former employer had become. However, once the initial awkwardness had evaporated, thanks mainly to Mr. James's easy manner, they all relaxed and Kate became quite animated. When Captain Howard's name was brought into the conversation, Kate's features took on a much healthier colour and Beth was comforted that Miss Kate still possessed the same sparkle

Beth smiled to herself when she recalled her daughter's contention that Miss Kate would be happier with Captain Howard. 'Well,' she thought, 'they are both free to remarry now if they wish, but life being what it is, they will probably go on as before, remaining as just affectionate friends.'

One habit that Beth was trying desperately to get out of was the unconscious use of her late employer's married name. After referring to her as Mrs. Rodgerson for so long, it was an effort to remember to address her now as Miss Kate.

The visit did Beth a power of good, and it gave a different perspective to her life in Marshville. She was a lot less conscious of the place's shortcomings.

Captain Howard had arranged for a carriage to come to the village before the afternoon was too advanced so that the party could be taken back to Mrs. Hilyard's house whilst there was still light, but before they started on their way back, Kate wanted to call in at the shop to see Will.

It was a quiet time of the day at the shop, so they were able to talk without being in the way of customers. Will was really pleased to see Miss Kate (as he understood he must now address her) for he had always liked her. They had already been introduced to Mr. Hughes, and the young man had come as yet another surprise to them, insomuch as he was well spoken and obviously of good education. Many of their preconceived notions about the type of people on such a site were being upset, and for the Banham family's sake, they found that very heartening; they certainly were not living amongst a bunch of savages!

Dafyd Hughes had enjoyed their surprise visit and especially the later musical evening. Weeks after Miss Kate's party had left Frodsham he would recall some particular moment at that happy event. Also he had seen another side of Victoria, a poised young woman at ease amongst people of that level of society, and she was in turn treated, if not as a complete equal, certainly not simply as a servant.

Several times in the last few weeks Dafyd had almost plucked up courage to ask her if she would walk out with him, but at the last moment he had lost his nerve and drawn back, and that evening he vowed that he would take the plunge very soon.

He himself found Miss Kate's brother very easy to get along with. During their conversation James had mentioned his stroll by the River Dee, and when Dafyd told him that he was a member of the Grosvenor Rowing Club, the talk became very animated. Dafyd ended up by inviting him to visit the club with him the next time that James came to Cheshire.

For Captain Howard the visit had changed much of his thinking. For the first time since he set up his workshop at Frodsham he was seriously considering renting a house for the remaining time he was at the Depot. It would give Kate and members of her family somewhere to stay if they came to Cheshire again, and he was sure that Kate would, even if nobody else wanted to visit. However, knowing the difficulties encountered by other people, including the Banhams, he was not confident of finding a house.

Also, and most importantly, he had decided that after allowing a decent period of mourning, he would ask Kate for her hand in marriage. In the meantime he would make inquires about a house and he knew just the right person to ask. With his far-flung round of patients, Dr. Mills was a mine of information about all that was happening in and around the town.

Christmas Day was enjoyed by them all. Victoria was able to spend most of her day with her family, but sadly for her, Dafyd was not at Marshville; he too was spending his day with his family. Captain Howard had enjoyed his Christmas dinner with Mrs. Joyce, Ian, Sarah and Dr. Mills. On Boxing Day he was invited to join the Banhams. It had been one of the best Christmases he had passed for many a year. His personal life certainly looked brighter than it had done for a long time.

A flurry of letters had descended on Frodsham from Kate, Mary, and James and Charlotte. Mrs. Hilyard and particularly Daisy were delighted to receive theirs. Wisely, Kate had not sent Peter a letter, although she had been tempted to, but she had sent her love both to him and Will in her letter to Beth.

Richard Howard had been overwhelmed when he received his letter from Kate. It was her first ever love letter to him, and he read it again and again, marvelling at the tender passages she had written. He was still getting used to the reality that he had not lost her love after all.

But for Thomas and Michael, New Year's Eve was not so jolly, for as most of the inhabitants of Marshville were snug in their huts celebrating, they were both perched precariously on top of the main water storage tank which supplied Frodsham Depot and the village.

During the dying days of the year, the temperature had plummeted and the ground had become rock hard. Braziers had been placed at several points to prevent freezing of pipes and water valves, but although they had prevented the water in the tank from freezing, they had failed to stop the huge float valve from icing up.

With the aid of cotton waste soaked in paraffin wrapped around the valve and set alight, they were struggling to get it free. When the float arm suddenly crashed down, it caught Michael's finger, almost taking the end off.

Thomas, seeing the way the young fitter was clinging onto the ladder, immediately decided to abandon the job until he had made sure that he was alright.

When Michael recovered from his momentary nausea, he was helped to the ground and escorted back to their hut. Thomas assured him that he himself was not doing anything further than drawing a brazier closer to the incoming water pipes now that the water was flowing into the tank once more. Then he too would be returning to the warmth of the hut. It had been a near thing for Michael's finger, and in fact it was to be months before it completely healed.

This episode set the pattern for the next few weeks. The ground was so hard that even using picks, a navvy was hard stretched to fill one wagon each day. The large powerful Ruston & Proctor excavators were not much more effective, the buckets having to be swung time and time again to break through the rock hard surface of the soil. As a consequence, the navvies were earning very little money by their back-breaking efforts and with the weather changing for the worst so soon after the death of Mr. Walker, morale had got very low. The more vociferous element of the workforce was calling for better treatment, better wages, and shorter working hours. Strike talk was in the air.

Apart from the problems caused by the weather, there was also a major problem in that the executors of the late Mr. Walker were showing their shortcomings in supervising the work and in their lack of sensitivity towards the mood of the employees.

When the thaw came, there were whole sections that were turned into dangerous quagmires. Railway tracks in the cutting became unstable, resulting in very few trains of loaded wagons being removed. A large number of men had to be laid off, which stoked up the fires of resentment further. But in the sections away from the tidal reach of the River Mersey, even more trouble came as torrential rain, which came on the heels of the thaw, swept the hills surrounding Manchester, causing the rivers Irwell, Bollin and Mersey, and their tributaries, to swell to many times their normal size. These rivers, which crossed and re-crossed the cutting many times, were held back by earth dams. With the constant rain softening the dams, some of them gave way, resulting in several sections of the cutting being flooded. It was April before the water was pumped out using a great many pumps working day and night. This disaster led to more men having to be laid off.

At Frodsham Depot the work increased for a while as they struggled to cope with the number of pumps and other equipment which was sent to them from other beleaguered workshops.

The cutting between Warrington and Eastham was largely unaffected by the floods and was at that time progressing at a reasonable rate. Even so, optimism had fallen and it was clear that the completion date for the scheme overall would have to be put back.

Meanwhile, as this disastrous tale was unfolding, at Frodsham and Marshville events were shaping of a less gloomy nature. Dafyd had finally summoned enough courage to ask Victoria if she would do him the honour of walking out with him, and there was no doubt in the girl's mind: she was ecstatic. However, the young man, ever conscious of the conventions, asked permission from her parents before he and Victoria could be seen walking out together in public.

Both Thomas and Beth were of the same mind; from the first weeks after their arrival they had come to regard him as a thoroughly decent, hard-working young man and they were very pleased to give their approval. Thomas had the same feelings of sadness as many fathers do at the knowledge that his precious daughter was preparing to fly the nest, but he was glad that it was Dafyd Hughes she had given her heart to.

Around that time, Captain Howard, who was by then back in his rooms at the Bear's Paw, was told by the landlord about a house in Church Street that was shortly to be let for rent. Two previous houses had proved to be totally unsuitable but the latest one appeared to be promising. Unfortunately, it had just three bedrooms and a small room which, in Captain Howard's opinion, was little more than a box room, and he had set his mind on a house with four bedrooms. However, such was the scarcity of houses in and around Frodsham that he decided to lower his sights and arranged to see it.

When he had first learned about the house, his thoughts went to the problems that the Banhams had encountered in their search for a house, and knowing how much Beth wanted a house, he felt a little guilty at having a choice of places to rent. When he raised the matter with them, they were touched at his concern, but told him that the sort of house that he was able to consider was well beyond their means, and wished him good luck with the one he had found.

Captain Howard wrote immediately to Kate, and told her that he had paid one month's rental on it. He explained that he wanted to give her somewhere to stay when she next visited Frodsham.

Kate's reply surprised and delighted him. She told him that she would visit him in the next two weeks. However, she was in a dilemma. Mrs. Hilyard had kindly offered to put her and her party up on future visits. What was particularly embarrassing was that the lady would not take recompense for their last stay. Whilst Mrs. Hilyard was obviously not a woman of limited means, Kate, by comparison, was a wealthy woman, and she did not want to take advantage of the lady's generosity.

That awkward matter was solved when Captain Howard learned that Mrs. Hilyard was soon to spend at least two weeks at the home of the Hughes family at Christleton whilst some rooms were being decorated at her own house. Victoria was also going with her.

For those particular weeks Captain Howard arranged for Kate and Mary to have the best rooms at The Queen's Head Hotel in Frodsham. During the month of March, Kate had seen the house, liked it and had helped Richard with the choice of wallpaper, carpets and furnishings. She had interviewed the lady who had been employed as cook for the former tenants, and employed a girl as a maid. Kate had also talked with Beth and Jessie Robbins about the making up of the curtains, and the two friends had jumped at the chance of doing the job.

On the afternoon of the last day of their visit, Kate had let Mary off to see Daisy, who was still at Mrs. Hilyard's house. Richard, seizing the chance to talk with Kate whilst they were alone, hesitantly broached the subject of marriage.

Whilst he now had no difficulty in expressing his love for her, he felt constrained by his respect for the conventions regarding the period of mourning that had to be observed. "Perhaps if we allow twelve months to pass," he said hopefully. "Or would sometime next year be more respectful."

Kate looked at him lovingly, thrilled by this, his first mention of marriage, but shook her head decisively. "No, Richard, not one year and certainly not next year." Looking away from him Kate said quietly, "My disastrous marriage lasted from the moment when I signed the Marriage Certificate and ended before eleven o'clock that night." She continued, her voice hardening, "The man who was supposed to be my husband, under the influence of drink, showed his true self, disgusting me, my family and guests by behaving in a most lecherous manner with, well, another woman." She could not bring herself to say that the woman was Richard's late wife, her own sister.

Then she turned to face him and said evenly, "I awoke the next morning, and the marriage bed held only myself." Then seeing the appalled look on Richard's face she added, "And I have woken up each morning since to the same empty bed, and blessed my maker for my happy escape."

Richard found his voice and said equally quietly, "So are you telling me, Kate, that you do not want marriage, that you would not want to share a bed, not with anybody?"

Kate looked at him sweetly and answered, "Oh no, Richard, I do not mean that. Over the years, the loving affection that earlier I held for you changed into a much deeper love; it was you who occupied my thoughts each night." Then she touched his lips with her fingers when he seemed as if he was about to say something, and she said with feeling, "I do not care about the conventions that have ruled my life so long, conventions that have stopped me from doing what was right, especially," she said bitterly, "for the Banhams."

Then in an almost pleading tone she said, "I do not want to wait a year, or even half a year; please, Richard, cannot we be married soon?"

Richard, his heart full of joy, reached for Kate and drawing her close to him, said huskily, "Oh, my dear lovely Kate, I would marry you in one hour from now if it were possible. It is just that I am still waking each morning struggling to grasp the fact that you really love me." Laying his cheek against hers, he said softly, "Marriage to you my dear, which I have dreamed of for years, seemed like a callow youth's dream." He stopped as the woman in his arms started to whimper, then, still clinging to him, she broke down, noisily crying. Holding her tight, he stroked her hair until her weeping had stopped.

Still snuffling, Kate said shakily, "I do not know why I did that, for I am not upset, I am very happy, but, oh, Richard, you must think that I am silly fool behaving in such a way."

"In all the years that I have known you, Miss Prentice," said Richard tenderly, "I have never thought of you as a 'silly fool', and I see no reason to change my opinion of you now."

As the afternoon wore on, they sat close together on the only seat in that empty house, a decorator's plank set on two soap boxes, and oblivious to everything else, talked animatedly of their future together.

Later, as the lamplighter was doing his round in the town, Kate and Richard walked slowly arm in arm back to The Queen's Head. They were still floating on clouds of euphoria, Kate having got her way on her wish for an early wedding. May was the month that had been decided upon, and she wanted to marry in Frodsham with just her immediate family and a few friends. For Richard it would mean no family members at all as his only relatives were just two elderly aunts and some cousins whom he had not seen in years.

Kate did not want anybody to know about their plans until she had spoken to her parents, after which James and Charlotte would be told; therefore when they met Sarah and Dr. Mills in Main Street, she had the greatest difficulty in suppressing the urge to tell them her wonderful news.

Whilst Dr. Mills expressed his pleasure at meeting Miss Prentice and Captain Howard once more, Sarah watched, smiling and observing the expressions on the faces of the two people opposite them. Although she was the youngest person present, she was, in some respects, better at reading people's emotions than the others, and had more than an inkling of what was going to happen. However, Sarah imagined that if she was right, and a wedding did occur, it would probably take place in Norfolk, which saddened her, for after her rather unfortunate first meeting with Captain Howard, she had grown to like and respect him very much. She would have loved to have been present when he wedded Miss Kate.

When Kate reached her room, she again had the same difficulty in hiding her exciting news from Mary, although in fact her maid was only too aware that something was going on by the extra sparkle in her mistress's eyes. It was moments such as these that made the age difference between her and Captain Howard seem as of no importance, and Mary thought then that it would not surprise her if they did marry when the time was right.

Captain Howard was to dine with them later, but Mary had also been invited to eat with Mrs. Hilyard's cook and Daisy, but that depended upon whether Miss Kate needed her. Naturally her mistress was delighted that she and Richard were to dine alone on her last night of the visit, so she let Mary go with her blessing.

It was arranged that Captain Howard called at Mrs. Hilyard's house before ten o'clock to escort Mary back to the hotel, so Kate decided to join him, anxious not to lose her last chance to walk with her future husband before she returned to Norfolk.

The following morning Richard managed to be at the station to see them off, but this time there were tears, it is true, but no sadness, Kate buoyed up with the knowledge that in the not too distant future, she would be returning to make a home for herself and Richard.

Mary's mind was in turmoil. If, as she suspected, Miss Kate did marry Captain Howard, in what way would the new arrangement affect her? She hoped that her mistress would want her to stay on as her maid. Although the girl's family lived near Wroxing and she had friends at Reeve House, she felt quite at home in Frodsham, especially as Victoria and her family were there. Also she liked Daisy and got on well with Sarah Mills. Whatever happened she was sure that Miss Kate would visit Reeve House from time to time and when she did, Mary could see her family.

There was no mistaking Kate's parents' delight at their daughter's news, and they were in agreement with her that she should marry when she and Richard were ready and not when other people thought it was seemly. However, due to Mr. Prentice's business commitments, a May wedding began to look unlikely. When her older brother Albert was informed, he was also in the same difficult position, so the wedding date was put back to June.

James and Charlotte were jubilant when Kate told them, and when they learned the date, James, after consulting with his wife, decided to combine the event with a visit to North Wales and the Snowdon Mountain Range.

When Beth received Kate's letter, she was the only one who was surprised at its contents, but was nevertheless delighted. Whilst she was happy with the news, Beth was rather troubled when she read that Miss Kate was asking Victoria and Mary to be her bridal attendants.

Even though Beth, when in service as a maid to Mrs. Serle, had occupied a position almost like that of an unofficial ward, she had never considered herself as anything other than an employee. And the very idea of having servants as bridal attendants, even if one of them happened to be her own lovely daughter, upset Beth's ideas of what was correct in the eyes of the upper class.

Even so she could not resist thinking how she would dress the two attendants if it was left to her. That night before she fell asleep, she told Thomas about her ideas and he did not see them as anything but admirable, so the following day Beth set to and came up with a rough design which she sketched on the back of an envelope. That night Michael drew her design on a better piece of paper then lightly painted it in the colours she had suggested. She knew what colours would suit Miss Kate, and she had thought up something which would complement the bridal gown. Of course, if Miss Kate had other colours in mind then she, Beth, would have to alter her ideas to suit even if she disagreed with Miss Kate's choice. Still, she thought, Miss Kate might not want Beth interfering with her plans, she might have a complete scheme planned out and might resent her former cook having the temerity to even think of making suggestions. With the letter already on its way, Beth grew cold as she thought of what she had done.

Mary was in the same mind as Beth and immediately started worrying about what people would say about somebody of her class playing such an important part of the ceremony amongst the upper-class Prentice family. And she was miserably conscious that she would not appear as elegant as Victoria.

Kate realised that something was bothering her maid and asked her sympathetically if she was feeling alright. At that Mary started sobbing and for a while could not tell her mistress what was troubling her.

When it all spilled out, Kate shook her head and said, "Mary, you silly goose, I am no different from any other woman who is marrying the man she loves, and I want my close family and close friends around me when I do so." She gave Mary a quick hug, then went over to her escritoire and came back with Beth's letter, which also contained the sketch of the proposed dresses for the bridal attendants.

Before Kate let Mary see the sketch she said briskly, "Now, Mary, next week I go to see my dressmaker in Norwich, and you will accompany me. Whilst there, we will get all new clothes and linen for you and," and she added, "you need not worry about not showing up well alongside Victoria." She continued seriously, "You know, Mary, you are a very pretty girl, and as for being slightly smaller, we will get shoes with slightly higher heels." Then before Mary could frame a reply, Kate showed her Beth's sketches.

Despite her reservations, at the sight of Beth's creation Mary felt a quickening of interest. Even from such a small sketch she could see herself looking very elegant, and she became less apprehensive about her role in the wedding.

The visit to Norwich was really enjoyable for both mistress and maid. Kate had not enjoyed a visit to the city so much for many a year.

A few days before the wedding, her family started to arrive at Frodsham. Kate was already established at Mrs. Hilyard's house and had been for almost a month. James and Charlotte came to stay on the Friday afternoon. Mr. and Mrs. Prentice had been invited to stay with Mrs. Joyce, whilst Kate's brother Albert and his wife were staying at the Queen's Head Hotel. Their eldest son was at public school and their younger children had been left in the care of their nanny.

Mrs. Albert Prentice had not been happy at having to travel so far north from London. She had a fixed idea, gleaned from earlier travel writers and from ladies in her social circle, that the northern countryside was bleak, with what seemed like a preponderance of bogs, and populated by dour uncultured people. Therefore it came as a pleasant surprise to pass through lush countryside with its occasional gently rounded hills. The town of Frodsham also pleased her, as did the soft Cheshire vowels of the inhabitants. Albert did not make the mistake of taking her anywhere near the Canal works, even though he was curious about the scheme.

During the time that Mary had been at Mrs. Hilyard's, she and Victoria had been down at Beth's hut to have their dresses fitted. The third time Kate went with them, and when the girls put the finished dresses on, she clapped her hands together, her eyes shining. "Oh, Beth, they look wonderful," she cried delightedly.

A proud Beth smiled at her enthusiasm and thought, 'Miss Kate is just like the two girls, she could almost be the same age'. The years had fallen off her since her first visit to Frodsham in the winter.

Mary had hardly said a word, she just kept looking down at her dress and smoothing the material as it fell over her hips. The image, or as much as she could see of herself in Beth's wall mirror, showed her as she had never imagined herself to look, so slim yet so shapely, and she knew that alongside Victoria she would not appear so dowdy after all.

Dafyd had offered the use of his trap to convey them and their parcels back to Mrs. Hilyard's house, and Will acted as driver. It was then Will and Peter's turn to be fitted with new suits and shoes. For these they had to go to the tailor and shoe shops in Frodsham. Whilst Will would rather have not been involved in the ceremony, for he was rather a shy boy, Peter was only too pleased to be part of it. To be invited to be her pageboy, even if it meant that Miss Kate wanted him to wear a cravat, pleased him a lot, especially as he was getting a new suit and shoes.

Back at Mrs. Hilyard's house, the dresses had to be tried on once more, but with the advantage of them being able to see themselves in the full-length mirrors of their hostess's bedroom. Mary's fears were completely banished. Standing alongside Victoria and wearing the slightly higher-heeled shoes, she felt no qualms about being a bridal attendant.

Daisy, who had sat watching them as they glided up and down the room practicing their stately walk, said wistfully, "I wonder if I will ever be asked to be an attendant to the bride."

Victoria felt a rush of sympathy for the girl and said cheerfully, "Of course you will, Daisy, you and Mary must be my attendants when I get…" Her voice faltered and she went quite pink as she realised what she had said. To make her even more embarrassed, Daisy's face lit up and she said happily, "Oh, Victoria, would you really ask me?" then with a worried expression she continued, "But what if Mr. Hughes doesn't want me at your wedding?"

The silence that followed Daisy's words was broken when Mrs. Hilyard said comfortably, "Well, Victoria, has given you her word, so whatever happens, I am sure that you will not be disappointed."

Kate smiled at the girls and said, "Well, I do think that we have presumed on Mrs. Hilyard's patience for long enough, so it is time, girls, that we came down to earth and return to our own rooms, and," she added cheerfully, "change back into your normal clothes."

Victoria, her face still flaming, was glad to escape from the room, followed by Mary, who was desperately trying to stop herself from giggling. Daisy, blithely unaware of the effect of her words, followed happily and went down to the kitchen.

On the day of the wedding the weather looked very promising, but those who knew the area predicted that there would be showers before the end of the afternoon. Captain Howard, however, had obtained a number of umbrellas and had passed the responsibility of dealing with them onto Will.

A carriage had been sent down to Marshville to bring the Banham family, Mrs. Robbins and Dafyd to Frodsham, where they were to board the coach which had been hired to take the guests up to the parish church. When the coach set off, it was followed by the carriage taking the two bride's attendants and Peter the pageboy, whilst a second carriage followed carrying a radiant Kate and her proud father.

Frodsham Main Street had witnessed many brides on their way to the church and it was only natural that heads turned as the carriages swept by. Whether it was the two charming young bridal attendants or the small dignified figure of the pageboy, so smart with his cravat, which caused it, but people started to wave. When Kate and her father came by, some of them called out "Good luck," and a few of the men raised their hats. The warmth of these salutations from perfect strangers filled Kate with an almost familial feeling which she was to remember for many a year hence.

At the church there were several people from Marshville and even some men from the excavation gangs, such was the esteem in which Captain Howard was held.

Inside the church Beth was on edge as to whether her dresses were to be complementary to Miss Kate's gown, but as soon as the bride walked down the aisle, followed by Victoria and Mary, she saw with relief that everything had worked out just right.

By cleverly designing the bridal gown to be complemented by the attendant's dresses and adopting the same colours, Miss Kate's dressmaker had produced a beautiful creation. Whereas Beth had suggested a cream-coloured material with trimmings of apricot for the attendant's dresses, Kate's gown was in an apricot colour with cream trimmings.

No longer was Kate the pale colourless creature of her first visit to Frodsham; she had filled out and was now a comely and much younger woman, her face aglow with happiness.

Captain Howard was having great difficulty in keeping his eyes off her. His bride was little better; those who did see her face could hardly miss the loving glance which she bestowed on the handsome soldierly figure she was to marry.

Little did anybody present realise that the brave Captain was inwardly shaking with nerves. That morning he had been unable to manage more than a few mouthfuls of his breakfast, he was so wound up.

Another victim of nerves was Mary. She later confessed to Victoria and Daisy that her legs were trembling so much that she thought the whole congregation must have heard her knees knocking!

A photographer had been hired and he and his assistant had set up two large cameras. Each of them were anxiously eyeing the weather and ready at an instant's notice to drape the waterproof sheets over their equipment should they be needed. Will had already taken the precaution of distributing the umbrellas in readiness. Also the drivers had put up the hoods on the carriages.

By an amazing piece of luck, the last photographic plates had been carefully put away when the first spots of rain were felt. There was a rush for the carriages, whilst those unfortunate people who would have to walk were given umbrellas.

As it turned out, the rain was light and of short duration so most of them arrived at the house to enjoy the wedding breakfast relatively dry.

The cook at Captain Howard's (and now Mrs. Kate Howard's) house would never claim to do anything other than plain meals. Certainly she did not prepare dishes such as would be served at Reeve House, but what meals she did make were well cooked and very tasty. Extra help had been hired so there were no long waits between courses. Kate had been worried about the arrangements but she relaxed as the meal proceeded; she could see that all was going well.

A chance remark by Sarah Mills concerning her father's knowledge of opera led to him being seated next to Albert Prentice's rather starchy wife, who herself was an opera lover. The lady found herself enjoying an argument about her favourite operas, but Dr. Mills's gentle humour robbed their differences of any sting.

Although the rain shower could have spoiled the day for Richard and Kate, it did no such thing. In fact it could have snowed and they would still have been gloriously happy except for the knowledge that their honeymoon would be over by the Tuesday evening, as a meeting of engineers and agents was to be held at the Bear's Paw on the following Wednesday morning. However, whilst Kate was naturally disappointed, she had arrived at a frame of mind where she accepted that this sort of occurrence was part of her husband's job.

One other disappointment was the absence of Michael Rourke. He had volunteered to carry on with urgent repairs to a locomotive which at that moment was in the workshops at Frodsham Depot. Thomas himself was to hurry back to the workshop as soon as he had joined in and toasted the happy couple. The moment he was back at the Depot, he would be donning his working clothes and joining Michael and Robbie to finish the job. It was to be six o'clock the following morning before the locomotive was ready to be steamed up. Michael and Robbie were sent to their beds whilst Thomas completed the steam trial before he handed the locomotive over to the railway foreman in the afternoon. He too then went off to his bed.

At the time when Thomas was returning to the Depot, Richard and Kate were preparing to leave Frodsham for their three days at Llandudno. The house would then be used by her parents, and also by Albert and his wife. James and Charlotte were staying with Mrs. Hilyard. Mary was also staying until her mistress returned.

Monday saw the Prentices paying a short visit to Chester, then returning for one more night at Frodsham before leaving for home. Whilst Albert's wife was glad to be going home to her beloved London, she was first to admit that she had completely changed her mind about the countryside and the people of the North, and what is more, she averred that she would be happy to visit Cheshire again in the future.

James and Charlotte, however, were not returning to Norfolk for at least another week, and instead said their goodbyes to the family on Chester station and caught a train to Caernarfon from where they planned to tour the Welsh mountain region.

The last evening of their stay was to be a musical one and apart from the remaining Prentices, Mrs. Hilyard had invited Dr. Mills, Sarah, Ian Blake and Mrs. Joyce.

The family had heard all about James's performance of 'We Are The Bold Gendarme', and were disappointed that he would not be there to repeat it for them. Nevertheless, they enjoyed the evening. As usual for those who had known Victoria previously as a lady's maid to Kate, her piano playing came as a complete surprise, drawing expressions of appreciation from everybody. Even so, as Mary commented later, in contrast to previous musical evenings, the Prentices, especially Albert's wife, still treated Victoria as a servant, although not in a way as to cause any real offence to the girl.

Dafyd came in for his share of appreciation but nobody was more enthusiastic than Albert's wife. With her love and knowledge of music, she held him in conversation for much of the refreshment period.

Later, Daisy joked mischievously to Victoria, "I think Mr. Hughes has got an admirer," then, turning to Mary she giggled and added, "I was waiting for her to ask me if we would wrap him up so that she could take him home." At that all three girls went into fits of laughter.

Downstairs, Mrs. Hilyard, on hearing the muted sounds of hilarity coming from upstairs, smiled to herself. How thankful she was for the happiness which Victoria had brought to the house since she had been taken into her service. 'And how many more friends have I made through the girl,' she thought contentedly.

After breakfast on the Tuesday, Mrs. Hilyard loaned Mary the use of the trap, driven by the handyman, to take her and her bags up to the Howard's house on Church Street so that she would be ready to greet her mistress and her husband when they arrived back from Llandudno.

When Kate had allocated the rooms, Mary had tentatively asked for the room which Captain Howard had labelled little more than a box room. Her mistress had thought that it was too small, but Mary liked the cosiness of the room, as well as the view from the window of the Overton Hills, and eventually she was allowed her choice.

It was almost four o'clock when a carriage from the railway station brought the Howards home. Mary was really glad to see them, and her mistress gave her a hug, obviously glad to see Mary. Kate was bubbling over with enthusiasm about Llandudno, the freshness of the air, the brightness of the light and the sparkling sea, and it was clear that she and Captain Howard had fallen in love with the little Welsh town lying between the huge rocky outcrops of Great Orme and Little Orme.

Later, when all the excitement had subsided, Kate went over Mary's duties with her. Captain Howard indicated that he would be employing a stable hand, and handyman. Also he would be purchasing a pony and trap for his wife's convenience. Altogether it was a happy ending to an eventful day. It was a very contented Mary who slipped into her bed that night.

The engineer's meeting was due to start at ten o'clock on the Wednesday morning, and when Captain Howard arrived he found that Mr. Congreve and Mr. Hunter were there before him. After a short time, Mr. Manisty and Mr. Jones arrived. There was a lot of back slapping and congratulations before they settled down to discussing the reasons that had brought them to the meeting.

Following the problems created by the winter's bad weather, progress had been slowed, but at the time of the meeting the work had made great strides. Unfortunately, the seasonal poaching of labour by the farmers, combined with the labour unrest, had affected certain sections, and these were not advancing as well as had been planned. To add to the company's woes, some of the more active strikers had, under the influence of drink, been damaging equipment and buildings. A new and potentially more dangerous concern was the threat of arson.

Each depot had a large timber storage field, and the only barrier to an attack by the strikers was a night watchman, and these men were usually the ones known as Walker's Splinters or Walker's Fragments. These were the names given to men who had been incapacitated by injury on the construction site. The late Mr. Walker did not simply cast these workers to one side after they had been crippled; he had kept them on in a capacity that was within their capabilities.

That was the problem; they were not in a fit state to resist a mob of men determined to do damage. Hubert Congreve had taken the step of employing extra and more able-bodied men and he suggested that the extra cost in wages was worth it rather than lose enormous amounts of expensive material. The others agreed and Captain Howard was given permission to employ at least one more man for Frodsham Depot.

Once all matters had been dealt with, the meeting broke up and they went in for their meal. Afterwards Captain Howard rode down to the depot to have a word with Thomas and the other foremen.

Some days after the meeting, Jacob Morrison approached Captain Howard about the extra night watchman. With him was a large amiable young man. He had been a navvy and was recovering from an injury to his hand in which the sinews had been damaged, resulting in a partial loss of grip in that hand.

The man, whose real name nobody knew, was known to the other men as 'Arthur the Teacher', due to his habit of explaining everything in great detail. As their present watchman was also named Arthur, the new man was henceforth simply called 'Teacher'. Captain Howard took him on and the man, being particularly easy to work with, continued working at Frodsham Depot until his hand healed.

At the shop, Dafyd was getting more concerned about Will's growing interest in all things connected with the sea. The boy had long been interested in boats, but it seemed to the shopkeeper that Will appeared, from his conversation, to be increasingly hankering after a more adventurous life, and the life would be that of a sailor.

By this time Dafyd often enjoyed a meal with the Banham family. Beth did not like to think of him eating on his own at the shop, and since he and Victoria had started walking out (that is when they got the chance), she had got into the habit of inviting him to their hut to eat with them. One such evening, at a time when Will was serving in the shop, Dafyd broached the subject and spoke plainly of his disquiet on the matter to Will's parents.

It came as no surprise to Thomas and Beth, but they had no idea that it was quite so serious an interest. Beth was particularly worried as some of her distant relatives were fishermen and sailed out of Lowestoft. Over the years they had lost a few of their menfolk at sea. Beth was terrified of the sea and when Dafyd raised the matter, she felt an overwhelming sense of dread at the thought of one of her sons being tempted into the life of a sailor. All that she could pray for was that it was just daydreaming on Will's part.

However, during the summer, something came about which tested both Will's abilities and his loyalty to Dafyd Hughes. All thoughts of the sea left Will's mind.

—— —— ——

It was early Monday morning and Will was just finishing his breakfast prior to starting work. A knock came at the door and when Beth opened it, there stood two of the village women.

"Sorry to bother you, Mrs. Banham," said the older of the women, "but the shop is closed and there are no lights on. Does your Will know if the shop is going to be open this morning?" Will, hearing what was said, went to the door and told them, "I will get the key and see if Mr. Hughes is alright."

Dafyd had gone to spend a weekend with his parents, as he did once in a while, and he should have returned on the Sunday evening. Will experienced no feelings of alarm, merely curiosity as to why Dafyd had not risen earlier.

On checking the back room of the shop, it was obvious that nobody had slept there overnight. Will immediately shut the shop and told the women, and there were a good number of them by this time, that he would have to go to town for the bread and milk, and concern himself with the mystery of the missing shopkeeper after he had made the shop ready for business.

As he was about to leave with the pony and trap, Clara came up and offered to look after the shop whilst he was away. Giving Clara a grateful look, he handed her the key then started on his way.

Both the dairyman and the baker allowed the boy to take his order without paying on the nail, at which he expressed his gratitude and promised to pay them the next morning at the latest. Hopefully, he thought, everything will be back to normal by then.

Back at Marshville, he and Clara worked like demons to serve their anxious customers, whose husbands needed to be fed and off to work before seven o'clock. As the flow of customers slowed, Mrs. Robbins came in and offered to help out, which allowed Clara to go back to her baby, who during the emergency had been watched over by one of the girls of the village. By that time Will was feeling just a bit ragged and quite a lot hungry.

Just after nine o'clock, a large smartly dressed young man entered the shop, and it was quite plain that he was in a bad temper. Wrinkling his nose as though detecting a particularly offensive smell he said, "What sort of a midden tip is this, the place is nothing more than a slum." Then catching sight of Will as he came out of the back room he growled, "Here, boy, get my bags and bring them inside." As the startled Will hesitated, the man said bad-temperedly, "And get a move on, boy, I'm the manager here while young Mr. Hughes is away." Then he added, "You will address me as Mister Jowet and don't forget it."

Then, swinging away from the indignant Will, he said briskly, "Right, boy, let me check the till." Fixing the angry boy with his eyes he said insultingly, "I hope you haven't taken advantage of your employer's absence, laddie, because if I find you have, I..." At this point he was interrupted by the cold tones of Mrs, Robbins, who had been listening to the bad-tempered harangue with mounting fury, and said, "Will Banham is completely trustworthy."

Mr. Jowet put on his false smile and genially asked her if she was an employee of the shop, and when he received the answer said, "Then, madam, if you have completed your business, I bid you good day."

Mrs. Robbins was absolutely furious, but keeping her voice calm, told the offensive Jowet, "I will leave but I tell you this, young man, every word of this conversation will reach the ears of Mr. Hughes when he comes back." With that she swept out of the shop.

As she went out into the street, Mr. Jowet said scornfully, "When or if Mr. Hughes comes back." As Will heard those words, his anger was replaced by fear at what could be wrong with Dafyd. "What has happened, what is wrong with Mr. Hughes?" he cried

Mr. Jowet shrugged his shoulders and replied, "I don't know, some sort of food poisoning, something like that, anyway, he is in the infirmary," then realising that he was being questioned by a mere boy said testily, "Whatever it is, it is no business of yours, boy, and I will remind you again, you address me as Mr. Jowet. Now get this floor swept, it is a disgrace."

Will was fuming and had great difficulty in keeping his temper, but overriding everything was the sick feeling about Mr. Hughes. He wondered whether there would be a letter from Dafyd's parents; he was sure that they would not want the Banham family kept in the dark about their son's troubles. Poor Victoria, he thought, she will be frantic when she finds out that Dafyd is ill.

A short time after Mrs. Robbins had exchanged words with Mr. Jowet, a telegram arrived at the Banhams' hut. It read, 'Mr. Hughes ill Stop Manager coming Stop'.

It was brought over for Will to see by his very angry mother, who let Jowet know her mind about his insinuations regarding her son, for Jessie Robbins had wasted no time in letting her friend know what had been said at the shop.

For the sake of Dafyd and their customers, Will was doggedly determined to carry on working at the shop, but it was very hard to take the sneers and insults which seemed to be the man's method of asserting his authority. During the day there had been several instances where Mr. Jowet managed to upset customers with his high-handed attitude. Then he decided that the prices charged were too low.

"Mr. Hughes," he said disbelievingly, "has not grasped the simple tenet that as this is the only shop for over a mile of this place, then people will pay the extra if it saves them a good walk; that is sound business boy, remember that." After that he added three farthings to the price of a pint of milk, and half a penny to a loaf. Other goods were similarly raised in price. In vain did Will protest that these prices were well over what Mr. Hughes judged as reasonable for the people of the village, comments which brought forth more temper from Jowet.

During the evening there were several angry exchanges and even poor Will got the rough edge of some people's tongues.

The following morning, Will once again had to go for the bread and milk, but this time the manager came with him to see if he could beat the suppliers down in price. In that endeavour he singularly failed, and the boy had to stand there miserably witnessing the goodwill so carefully built up by Mr. Hughes disappear within minutes.

Back at the shop the angry Mr. Jowet turned his temper on his first customer, and as it happened it was Mrs. Garroway. Will derived a great deal of pleasure as the man was made to look a fool by the incensed woman. The boy had never seen or heard her in full flow before and he had never heard such language from a woman before either! Mrs. Garroway simply ignored Jowet's demand for extra money for what she had bought, plonked down the money at the old prices and pushed her way out of the shop.

When Sally (with the twins) came to pay for her purchases, the manager, still smarting after his defeat at the hands of the enormous Mrs. Garroway, was particularly nasty and almost brought the young woman to tears.

Will, seething at her treatment, said in a voice loud enough for all in the shop to hear, "Don't worry, Sally, I have been taking a note of all those who have been overcharged," then he added, "I am sure that Mr. Hughes will reimburse everybody when he returns."

The Banham temper, held in check for so long, was only just being controlled and as the livid Jowet turned on Will, the boy shouted, "You are not fit to run a shop, the goodwill between Mr. Hughes and the people who live here is being destroyed by your attempts to make a name for yourself." As he was shouting he had untied the strings of his apron and he threw it over the counter towards the raging manager. Then as a murmur of approval came from those in the shop, he flung himself through the door!

When he went into their hut he was surprised to find that his mother was not there. After a while, during which he had made and drunk several cups of tea and let his anger subside, he went next door, where he learned from Mr. Robbins that his mother and Jessie had gone to Frodsham to post a letter and pay somebody a visit.

Later, when his mother came in, she told him that she had written a letter to Dafyd's father informing him of the problems that the temporary manager was making for the people of the village and for the shop. Also she expressed their great concern at his son's ill health.

After posting the letter, Beth and Jessie had called on Mrs. Hilyard. They learned that she had earlier that day received a letter from Mrs. Hughes telling her the news concerning Dafyd. Victoria was still very upset, but her mistress had promised the girl that when Mrs. Hughes let them know that her son was home from the infirmary, she would pay a visit to Christleton and Victoria would accompany her.

When they heard of the situation at the shop and how Will was being treated, Victoria became even more upset and was only slightly less so when her mother told her about the letter that she had just posted to Dafyd's father.

The answer to Beth's letter came in the form of Mr. Hughes in person. During the morning of the following day he arrived at Marshville by carriage. After he had spent twenty minutes at the shop, he crossed over to the Banhams' hut and presented himself to Beth with the request to talk to Will. After accepting a welcome cup of tea (and a piece of Beth's fruit cake), Mr. Hughes questioned her son about what had happened whilst his son was absent.

Since the day before, after his temper had cooled, Will had been beset by feelings of guilt about walking out of the shop and leaving the man Jowet without help. Several times he had almost gone back and offered to continue working for the man, but he knew quite well that he would not have changed; Jowet was too arrogant to alter his attitude.

Will found himself making excuses for the manager, but the boy was not an accomplished deceiver and Mr. Hughes had not become a successful businessman without being able to learn the truth from what was left unsaid.

Looking first at Will and then at Beth, he put forward his proposals for the running of the shop until his son returned. "What is obvious," he said, "is that the shop is vital for those who live here, and yet I cannot but think that Mr. Jowet is not the man to be in charge. Therefore," he continued, "I am proposing that you, Will, should manage it, with help of course, but only opening for so many hours each day."

Will was astounded, but Beth was apprehensive. Mr. Hughes was quite aware of the effect that he had created and was quick to assure them that if Will did take on the task, he would in no way be responsible for any problems with the shop.

"You see, young man," Mr. Hughes said smiling, "my son has a very high regard for you and your family, and I must say Mrs. Banham, the more members of your family I meet, the more I agree with him."

Although Beth became quite flustered at the compliment, she was also very pleased and proud that her family should be held in such high esteem.

Then Mr. Hughes asked Will if the young woman Clara, whom he knew worked for his son, would help, and also if any other person would be considered suitable. He then offered to send somebody down to Marshville on occasions to make sure that the stock was replenished. At that, Will made his mind up: he would try his best to not let everybody down (but if only he could have got out of the early morning run to Frodsham).

When it was all settled, Mr. Hughes and the decidedly less dapper Mr. Jowet left the village at just after two o'clock, and Will took over. A short while after, Clara arrived, pushing her perambulator with her baby inside, luckily fast asleep.

The first thing they did was to check everything to see that all was in order. The till drawer held enough money to tide Will over for the next day's dairy and bakery purchases. He had his fingers crossed that there would be no difficulties with those people. A note in the drawer, signed by Jowet and Mr. Hughes, confirmed the amount of money that had been left for him as a float.

Will then sat down and made out three cards: the first informing customers of the hours that the shop would be open whilst Mr. Hughes was away, the second concerning the overcharging of customers by Jowet. His third card was to hang in the window if he was on his own and needed to leave the shop unattended for short periods. As Mr. Hughes pointed out delicately, there would be moments when he was on his own that he would have to leave the counter unattended.

His dreaded early morning task turned out to be easier than he had imagined. Both the people at the dairy and at the bakery were sympathetic and helpful, although they had a few choice words to describe Jowet.

Jessie Robbins came in to help when he got back and Will, after overcoming his nervousness, actually began to enjoy himself, especially as most of the customers heaped praise on him for standing up to the bullying manager.

Clara replaced Mrs. Robbins, who then went back to her husband and made him his breakfast. Soon after, Will followed suit to get his breakfast. Then it was back to the shop until half past nine, then closing until eleven. They closed again at one o'clock and opened once more at four, staying open until eight in the evening. And that set the pattern of their working day. On most afternoons Will would try and get an hour or more of sleep, for he was certainly being affected by the extra early morning start. Thomas was proud of how well his son was bearing the responsibility of the shop, but was keeping an eye on Will's wellbeing.

Two days after Jowet's departure, another of Mr. Hughes's employees turned up to check whether anything was needed. When he had finished at the shop, he went over to see Beth and gave her a letter from Mr. Hughes. Beth gave the man his midday meal, which he much appreciated. He then left to arrange a delivery for the shop.

They learned from the letter that Dafyd was now home and sending his blessings for their efforts on his behalf. Mrs. Hilyard also received the news and told the anxious Victoria that they would visit Christleton the following day.

At first when they were shown into the room where Dafyd was resting, Victoria amazed herself by not bursting into tears. The sight of his face, so grey and drawn, almost destroyed her self-imposed control. Instead she gave him a shy uncertain smile, and was rewarded with such a loving smile in return that before she realised the social gaffe she was committing, she crossed over to his chair and knelt down by his side.

Mrs. Hilyard bit her lip and glanced at her friend, but was immediately reassured by the understanding smile on Becky's face. "Dafyd, dear," his mother said brightly, "would you excuse us for a short while?" Then turning to Mrs. Hilyard she said, "I have something I want to show you."

With that the two friends left the room, then Mrs. Hilyard was surprised to see Becky dabbing her eyes with her handkerchief. "Oh, Florence," she sobbed, "we thought that we were going to lose him, and now to see him smiling like that again." Then she said shakily, "Do bring her again whenever you can manage, Florence. I am sure that Victoria will do him more good than any medicine."

Her friend, who had also been very shaken by Dafyd's appearance, disguised her feelings with a show of cheerfulness, and said brightly, "Well, Becky, if that is what it takes to make Dafyd better, then I suppose that I must bring Victoria here more often." Then she gave her friend a hug and before they knew it, they were both comforting each other.

True to her word, Mrs. Hilyard rearranged some of her usual arrangements and every other day, she and Victoria visited the Hughes's house.

Whether the girl's presence speeded Dafyd's recovery is not certain, but within two weeks he was back at Marshville. However, for the first week after his return, Will insisted on bringing the milk and bread, allowing his employer an easier start to the day. Also, Mrs. Robbins helped by preparing Dafyd a good breakfast. As she explained to Beth, Mr. Robbins did not have to be at the workshop before seven o'clock as Thomas and Michael had to do, so a slightly later breakfast did not trouble him.

One of the first things that Dafyd was eager to do when he got back to Marshville was to reward those who had helped him during his illness.

Clara was given her wages at twice her normal rate and also a well-stocked hamper of special foods. Beth and Jessie Robins were presented with a hamper as well. Although Will protested that he had done only what had to be done, Dafyd insisted that he was amply rewarded. As Will had told those who were being overcharged, they were reimbursed.

The episode had boosted Will's confidence and his standing in the eyes of everyone, but it had left him very jaded, and after Dafyd once again took over the reins, he was really unsettled. More than anything else he wanted to be out in the open air, and once again he was torn between the job he was doing (which most of the time, he did enjoy) and the exciting prospect of going to sea. Ever since the family had moved to Marshville the sight of the different types of craft had stirred in him feelings he had never experienced before.

Dafyd was aware of Will's restlessness and it troubled him, but he had a pressing concern of his own and he was pondering how he was to go about settling it.

One early evening, Michael called at the shop for a quarter-pound of aniseed balls and mentioned that he was going back to the workshop to finish a rush job. That meant that Mr. and Mrs. Banham would be alone, so it presented Dafyd with a good opportunity to do what he wanted to do. Taking off his apron he asked Will if he would mind the shop, and after a nod from his assistant, he dashed over to the Banham hut. After about ten minutes he came out with a happy smile on his face, and disappeared into the back room of the shop, emerging washed and changed into his suit ready to go out.

Will stared at him open-mouthed, but then seeing the look on his employer's face knew that it was something to do with Victoria.

"Do you mind, Will?" Dafyd said. "I want to make a quick visit to Mrs. Hilyard's house, and if you could look after the shop for half an hour, I would be really grateful." Will nodded his head, smiling. 'So I am right,' he thought, 'he is going to see Victoria.' He was still smiling when the pony and trap set off for Frodsham.

Daisy opened the door to Dafyd, then took him in to Mrs. Hilyard's sitting room. After he had told her what his errand was for, Mrs. Hilyard took him across the hall to another room and told him to wait there. A few moments later, Victoria came into the room, an anxious look on her face.

Less than a quarter of an hour later, Victoria rushed into Mrs. Hilyard's sitting room and flung her arms around her mistress and sobbed, "Dafyd has asked me to become betrothed to him."

Mrs. Hilyard was very affected by the girl's announcement. She had known Dafyd since the day he was born, and with no children of her own, he had always occupied a special place in her heart. Victoria had also become dear to her, and to see them both betrothed to each other gave her great happiness, and she patted herself on the back for being instrumental in bringing them together.

Daisy was delighted; her wish to become a bridal attendant looked like being realised. She wondered if Mrs. Banham would make a dress for her. When she had seen what Mary and Victoria looked like in their dresses, she had been filled with longing to look as wonderful as they did.

Kate and Mary were also delighted but not surprised (unlike Captain Howard, who had merely noticed two very likable young people at ease in each other's company but had seen nothing significant in that!)

The Banham family were particularly pleased, none more so than Peter, whose first thoughts were whether his sister would soon want a pageboy. As he said quite sensibly, "If they leave it too late, my new suit and shoes will be too small for me." Unfortunately for Peter's way of thinking, he was to have several sizes of suits and shoes before he became a pageboy a second time.

Mrs. Hilyard allowed Victoria an extra day off so that she and Dafyd could visit Chester to choose a betrothal token. Although Dafyd wanted to give Victoria something expensive, the girl preferred a less ostentatious token, and ended up with a simple diamond ring, and she still considered it enormously expensive.

Afterwards they went to Christleton to see Dafyd's parents, who were so proud of acquiring such a lovely future daughter-in-law. Mr. Hughes then took his son into his study and gave him a man-to-man talk and warned him not to do anything silly which would cause the girl harm.

—— —— ——

One evening, Michael arrived with a morsel of information concerning a temporary job on a seagoing ship.

An overheard snatch of conversation between some navvies and the travelling 'drinks man' concerned the man's son, who was a deckhand on one of the stone-carrying ships that plied between the Stone Jetty at Eastham and the Isle of Anglesey.

Michael approached the man and learned that his son needed some time off to attend to some business of his own, but had to find a temporary replacement so that the vessel would not be left short-handed.

The 'drinks man' plied his trade with two containers hung from a yoke, and the woman with him carried the milk and sugar. Their hot-water boiler was carried on a handcart and was heated with a coke fire. Michael obtained the man's address and promised that he would let him know whether or not he had found somebody for the job.

When Beth heard Michael's news, her stomach went into knots, but Thomas told her it was better that Will learned as soon as possible whether the life of a seaman suited him.

"You know, Beth, girl," he said cheerfully, "if he has to try his luck as a sailor, he might as well do it at this time of the year, when the weather is more settled and also do it on a coastal vessel for a short trip." Beth could see the strength of his argument but still hoped that Will would not want to go.

However, her hopes were dashed when her son decided that his father was talking sound sense, and made his mind up to call on the 'drinks man' to see if the position was still open.

Dafyd was resigned to the fact that he could possibly lose his apprentice, but like Thomas, he thought that it was better that the boy found out for himself whether a life at sea suited him.

One late afternoon Will managed to get to Helsby Junction with the help of a friendly locomotive driver. After a long trudge, he reached the cottage where Mr. Parks, the 'drinks man', lived. It was at the bottom of a Robin Hood Lane.

The cottage woodwork looked as though a few coats of paint would not go amiss, but the drabness of the place was alleviated by the riot of colour from the profusion of flowers in the garden.

His knock brought a girl to the door and Will's heart gave a mighty lurch in his ribcage. She was simply the most beautiful girl he had ever met, 'well, after Victoria,' he added to himself. With her dark hair and sun-blessed skin, she affected him like no other girl ever had before.

When he stammered out his business, she went back into the cottage. She returned and invited him inside. Mr. Parks was a short, comical-looking man with an amazing luxuriant drooping moustache. When he spoke, however, there was nothing comical about his voice: it was deep and authoritative. And he was very well spoken.

"Lucy, my child," said the lugubrious Mr. Parks. "Make a fresh cup of tea for our visitor."

The girl immediately went into the scullery and the sounds of crockery being set out reached the boy's ears.

'Child indeed,' he thought, then realised that Mr. Parks was addressing him. "I beg your pardon, sir," he said, and the man smiled for a brief moment before his features settled back into their former sad mould.

Will was questioned about his desire to go to sea and was warned about the danger and discomfort, the isolation and the drifting apart from family and friends. The melancholy tone and the dreariness of the picture he was painting of the sailor's life unsettled Will quite a lot, but the occasional glimpse of Lucy's face stopped him from feeling too miserable, and he vowed that whatever happened, he would definitely see the girl again.

Eventually Will left the cottage and the exciting Lucy. It was dark when he reached Marshville and he hoped the colour of his face did not show up in the lamplight in their hut, at the point in his narrative when he mentioned the girl.

When the message reached Will telling him when to join the vessel, it simply read, 'Join schooner *Sisters Three* at Eastham Stone Jetty 5.30 am Monday!'

Chapter 28

Will Goes to Sea

When Thomas learned the time that his son was to join the schooner, he knew that Will had no chance of getting a locomotive ride to Eastham at that early hour. He and Michael were pondering the possibilities when Captain Howard came into the workshop. He was just in time to hear the last part of the conversation and made a suggestion of his own.

"If your son took a train down to Eastham Locks on the afternoon of the Sunday, he could probably stay in the Cornish Engine boiler house overnight." Then he said, "If you like the idea, Thomas, I could give Will a note for Joe the boiler man; I am sure he would be most obliging in finding him a bed for the night." He explained that the boiler house was manned day and night, and that there were some roughly made cots in a little corner of the building.

Dafyd, like Beth, was resigned to the fact that Will was finally going to do what he had hankered after for so long. Ever since the boy had come to Marshville he had taken an interest in ships. They both knew that Thomas was right, and accepted that whatever the outcome, it was Will's choice.

Victoria was really upset as, surprisingly, was Clara. The young woman had grown fond of the boy and did not like to dwell on the stories she had heard of the grisly 'initiation' ceremonies carried out by older sailors. Like everyone else who knew him, she saw him as a fine and courageous boy, but a gentle and sensitive one. She did not think he was cut out to be a seaman.

After Chapel on the Sunday, Will set out to join the vessel with his spare clothing in one bag and a supply of food in another. He managed to get a ride to Ellesmere Port but found that no trains or locomotives were going to Eastham. Just as he had decided that he would have no option but to walk, a train of wagons loaded with coal came into view. Putting his bags down, he waved to see if it would stop.

He was really fortunate: the fireman on the loco was Al, his former 'points boy' friend. The driver listened with amusement as the two lads vied with each other to tell all that had happened to themselves since the incident at Ince.

When Will told them why he was going to Eastham, both Al and the driver said, but in different words, "Rather you than me." Even so, the eager boy's enthusiasm was not dampened. Indeed, he felt a thrill of excitement after they had passed Mount Manisty, and saw the broad expanse of the Mersey before them.

Will shook hands with the driver and Al, then as they prepared to exchange the empty wagons for full ones, he walked into the boiler house to see Joe the boiler man. In that he was disappointed, for the man was not there, but his mate

Sid gave the note a cursory glance, and said in a friendly manner, "Oh, Captain Howard, well, that's all right, son, just put your stuff on one of the cots. Joe will be here later." Then he said, "Will, did you say your name was? Now then, Will, I'll be putting a brew on in about ten minutes, so if you want to look round the engine house, now's your chance." With that he went back to oiling the engine bearings.

After Will had seen the engine and pump, he strolled outside and viewed the locks, now nearing completion. Seeing the size of the lock chambers made him realise how large the vessels would be that they could accommodate.

Later, after he had enjoyed a drink with Sid, he strolled down to the Stone Jetty to see if the schooner was there. As he came in sight of the jetty he was disappointed to see what he thought was a ketch moored alongside. He scanned the river to see if a schooner was moored offshore, but apart from a tug forging its way towards Liverpool, there was nothing.

Feeling rather disturbed he continued along the shore until he got close enough to read the name on the stern of the vessel. It came as a shock to discover that the small sailing ship was not a ketch but a two-masted schooner and her name was *The Sisters Three*! He had expected something much bigger, and his first thought was to pick up his bags and make his way back to Marshville. However, he had said that he would take the place of Mr. Parks's son, so he had to stick to his promise.

As he approached the vessel, he called out to let the crew know that he was there. After several minutes of trying with no success, he went back to the boiler house. When he got there he found that Joe had returned. "Hello, lad, you find your ship then?" Joe said, and added cheerfully, "Give my regards to Captain Howard when you see him next. I hear he's got married now, good luck to him." Changing the subject he asked Will if he had seen Captain Skil yet. "Hard man to work with," he said, "but as a seaman, they don't come any better."

Will was not feeling happy at all. He was wondering what sort of a mess he had got himself into. With all his worrying he was surprised that, when woken by Joe, he had slept soundly through the night.

The Cornish steam pump was quietly working as they sat and enjoyed their breakfast. It had been prepared by Joe, and consisted of bacon and eggs washed down with cups of sweet tea. In spite of his apprehension about the forthcoming voyage, he still left an empty plate!

When he was ready to join the schooner, he shook hands with the two boiler men, shouldered his bags and trudged over to the stone-handling jetty.

He could see the lit stern navigation light from the locks, so he knew that the crew were awake. He stepped aboard and called out. A head popped out of the companionway and a voice told him to come below.

The smell of frying bacon met him, and even though he had only just had a breakfast, he could not resist accepting a bacon sandwich, which was thrust in his hand by the man who was doing the cooking. The galley was cosy and warm, but they didn't dwell; they were back on deck before he had eaten his sandwich, and Jim, which was the man's name, 'showed him the ropes', literally.

“Only we don’t call ’em ropes,” he said. “Them as holds the masts up are called stays and shrouds, right, and them as hoists the sails up are called halyards, right.” Then he dashed over to where the ropes were neatly coiled. “These are the sheets,” he said and then with a grin continued, “’cause they control the sails, sheets of canvas, right. Mainsheets, mainsails,” he chanted, “jib sheets, jib sails, that’s them at the bow, right.”

He then finished by telling Will about those securing the vessel to the jetty, referring to them as warps. Moving to the centre of the deck, facing forward, he recited, “Looking ahead is the bow, looking behind is the stern, to my right is starboard, and to my left is port, right.” Finally he ended his instruction by saying, “Step ahead is going for’ard, stepping to the stern is going aft, right. Now you are a trained deckhand,” he concluded with a grin.

Then he turned to the amused Will and told him seriously, “Captain Skil is a tough man but he is fair. When he says move, you move quick, right, and don’t loiter, ’allus keep yourself busy.” Then he added, “You call him sir until he lets you call him skipper. Oh, and another thing, he likes a tidy ship, right.”

Another man joined them and his name was Abe. He just nodded and winked at Will before going forward to make ready to hoist the jib sails. Soon after the jib sails were hoisted. Jim told Will that it would not be long before slack high water, and that was when they would cast off and head downriver.

Captain Skil arrived on deck, looking rather bad-tempered as he always was after a evening’s drinking, and Will, mindful of what Jim had told him, ‘jumped to it’ as soon as the man bellowed an order. In spite of the skipper’s rough state, there was nothing wrong with the way he took the schooner away from the jetty.

Then they were gliding quietly through the smooth water towards the sea, and Will for the first time in his life experienced the thrill of sailing.

By the time they were passing Liverpool’s waterfront, *The Sisters Three* was moving quite fast. Jim told him that they were picking up the ebb tide which would help them well out to sea.

The schooner was meeting an increasing swell which brought an occasional dash of spray over the bow. Will was feeling just a trifle uncomfortable and beginning to regret that last bacon sandwich!

“Winds veering,” shouted Jim. “Looks like it will be a long passage.” No sooner had he spoken than the cry came, “Ready about,” then “Lee ho,” and there was a sudden burst of activity on the schooner as she ‘went about’. The rattle of blocks, the swinging booms and the crack of the sails as they filled in their new setting should have brought excitement to Will, but he was feeling too queasy to note anything. He was ‘jumping to it’ as he had been told to do, but it was more of a ‘stumbling to it’ in reality. He felt dreadful.

As *The Sisters Three* plunged and bucked towards the Welsh coast, with Hilbre Island on the port beam, Will gave up his bacon sandwich, aye, and everything he had eaten for days, or so it seemed!

Captain Skil roared at him, “Get that mess cleaned up, lad, I won’t have my ship dirtied by any weak-bellied landlubber.” As he was shouting, Will had a long-handled mop thrust in his hand whilst Jim was dangling a bucket on a rope into the sea.

Swilling and mopping occupied the boy for quite a while as fresh bouts of sickness engulfed him. The only thing he wanted to do was to lie down and forget the ship, the world, everything. His head felt like it was splitting in two with pain, and still the skipper had him mopping the deck and doing all kinds of useless tasks. What the boy did not realise was that he was being deliberately kept busy to combat the sickness.

At one point Jim pointed over towards a beautiful silvery strip of coast which was backed by sandhills, and said, "Prestatyn, nice place that." The name rang a bell in the boy's mind. It was where the Chapel had gone on a day out by train (and Peter had come back in borrowed clothes). He had fallen in every pool of water he could find!

Other places that were pointed out to him meant nothing at all to him until Jim pointed to a little town nestling in the lee of a great rocky outcrop. "Llandudno," he was informed and he remembered that it was the town where Captain and Mrs. Howard had gone after their wedding.

He was constantly beset by bouts of shivering despite the warmth of the day, and Abe brought out a heavy woollen jersey which smelled a bit, but was nevertheless very welcome to the boy.

By then the island they were heading for was in view and Will was beginning to feel the stirring of hope that the voyage would soon be at an end. *The Sisters Three* had been forced to tack several times and consequently they were in danger of missing the high tide necessary to enter the harbour at Traeth Bychan, their eventual destination.

Several vessels had been sighted since they had left the Mersey, but one particular ship held his attention. It was a fine paddle steamer with twin funnels and it surged past on its way to the Menai Straits, that is, the wide channel which separates the Isle of Anglesey from mainland Wales.

As it disappeared behind Puffin Island, Abe told Will that the vessel was the *Bonnie Princess* and was owned by the Liverpool, Llandudno and Welsh Steamboat Company. It was on its regular run between Liverpool and Menai Bridge.

Not long after, *The Sisters Three* was approaching Red Wharf Bay and in particular, Traeth Bychan, but they were too late to attempt an entry into the harbour, so were forced to drop anchor and wait until the tide turned. As Jim explained to a much more alert Will, "Even though we are not loaded, we still have too much draught to get near the harbour; the beach shelves for a long way out."

A smell of food from the galley made Will realise how hungry he was now that the seasickness had left him. Even so, he longed for the moment when he could set foot on firm ground again.

He was given a plate of what Abe said was 'Lob Scouse', but what he knew as stew.

"If you take it below," Jim said, "don't leave a scrap, it only encourages the rats and the cockroaches."

At that the boy decided that as it was a fine warm night, he would sleep on deck; the thought of vermin crawling over him as he slept revolted him. He dragged his blankets from his bunk and snuggled down for the night fully dressed.

He awoke, but it was still night and the sky was a carpet of stars. As he lay staring upwards he became aware of somebody smoking a pipe. He realised that it was Captain Skil.

"That's a beautiful sight, lad," said the man in a quiet voice. "I never tire of it." Will nodded in agreement, but said nothing as the skipper was still talking. "Do you know, lad, that for hundreds, nay thousands of years, seafarers all over the world have steered and worked out their position by the same stars."

The boy knew something about astral navigation but wisely did not say so, and Captain Skil talked about the advantages enjoyed by modern sailors over their ancient counterparts.

"With the modern compass, the sextant and the chronometer," he said, "we can now find our position to within a few miles anywhere in the world."

"See that star, lad," he said, pointing with the stem of his pipe. "That's the Pole star, Polaris; though it is not exactly true North, it is near enough for an experienced sailor to give general direction." Then he said, warming to his theme, "The way to find Polaris is to look for the Big Dipper, see there," he pointed, "and take the star on the rim of the bowl of the Dipper, that's Dubhe, and the star at the bottom edge of the bowl, that's Merak, strike a line through those two, take it up from the bowl and at five times the distance the line will cross Polaris." The boy was interested, but thought to himself, 'I'll never remember all that!'

"You know, lad," Captain Skil continued, "of all the thousands of stars in the heavens, only about a hundred and seventy are of any use to a navigator, but really, I only use about fifteen or so of them." He went on to explain about the galaxies, the Plough, Pegasus, Cassiopeia and Orion. Will was given the names of stars he had never even heard of: Aldebaran, Betelgeuse and Benetnasch. He was quite glad that he had kept quiet about his limited knowledge of the heavens!

Early the next morning he was awakened by Abe, who told him to 'shake a leg' as they were about to weigh anchor and move to the harbour. Dawn was breaking and the tide was still rising. Soon *The Sisters Three* was slowly making her way shorewards. Then she swung to starboard and Will could see a narrow entrance between rough stone walls and he was amazed to think that a vessel of their beam could squeeze through.

Without any fuss the schooner slipped inside the tiny harbour, Jim and Abe with boathooks at the ready, whilst Will stood by to catch the rope thrown from the quay. Before many minutes had passed they were moored, one warp fore and one aft with a third along the full length of the schooner, which Jim told Will was a 'spring' to allow for the rise and fall of the tide.

No sooner was the vessel secured than Abe and Will were hard at it removing the hatch covers, whilst Jim went to below to make their breakfasts.

By the time they had eaten, the men working the derrick had started work and loading commenced. The rough-dressed stone blocks were swung aboard and stowed in the hold. As each layer was laid, wedges were knocked in to stop the cargo shifting when they were under way.

Will's soft hands were soon cut and bleeding, his nails broken and ragged. He wondered if they would ever be right again. Both Jim and Abe tried to give the boy the easier jobs, but he could not avoid hurting his hands. They had already suffered on the previous day, for he had thrown himself into the work of hoisting and trimming the sails on their outward voyage.

The harbour was supplied with the stone blocks carried on an endless cable system hung from gantries, and this contraption ran right along the beach under the face of the cliff from where much of the stone was coming. Several times a horn sounded, followed by explosions as the rock face was blasted.

Just as he was wondering how much more punishment his hands could take, Will was told by the skipper to come out of the hold. The man was obviously in a bad temper and he sent the boy to clean his hands and wait while Jim came to see to them. Captain Skil then strode along the quay and returned, followed by two men who leaped into the hold and started working alongside Abe and Jim. He then saw to Will's hands himself with a touch as gentle as any woman's. A yellowish ointment was smeared on his palms and cloths wrapped around them. The skipper did not say much, only to tell the boy, much to his relief, not to get involved with the stowage again.

After that it was Will's job to make drinks for them all every so often, and heat up the 'lob scouse' for their meals.

Whilst they were loading, two brigs had entered the bay and taken to the ground when the tide went out. Horse-drawn carts were clustered around them. The cargo was coal, some of which was taken to the square lime-kiln nestling in the low cliff at the head of the beach.

Abe told Will that the cliffs were of limestone, but other stone used on the Canal construction was the much harder granite which came from Penryn in Cornwall.

By noon the following day *The Sisters Three* was almost fully loaded, but Captain Skil told them they would be leaving at high tide on Thursday morning. During the Wednesday morning the skipper again showed the gentler side to his nature. He told Will to come with him and gave the lad a bag to carry. Whatever was in it was fairly light so it gave the boy no trouble. The skipper himself carried a large bag which seemed very heavy.

The narrow lane leading away from the harbour was quite steep in places and even the skipper was puffing a bit when they reached the road at the top. They crossed over the road and entered another narrow lane which climbed again until it entered a small village. "Marianglas," said Captain Skil tersely.

He stopped at a low whitewashed cottage and his knock was answered by a small and very old woman whose face lit up when she saw who her visitors were.

When they entered, both of them had to stoop to avoid banging their heads on the lintel. The floor was flagged and one wall was taken up with a large inglenook fireplace, but the actual fire grate was not very big and held only a small fire. Everything was clean and well looked after, but it all spoke of poverty.

Captain Skil smiled broadly at the woman, whom he addressed as Mrs. Williams. She smiled back at him and patted his arm, speaking in a mixture of Welsh and English which the skipper seemed to understand. He spoke to her and she turned to Will, obviously concerned, and looked towards his hands, shaking her head. She told the boy to take a seat, and then she put the copper kettle onto the fire.

Meanwhile Captain Skil had part-emptied his sack into a blackleaded box by the fireplace. It was coal he had brought to Mrs. Williams. The rest of the coal was taken through the cottage to some other storage.

They all sat at the table and the man opened the bag which Will had carried. It contained packets of tea and sugar. Mrs. Williams smiled affectionately at Captain Skil and, turning to Will, she said softly, "He is a good man, God bless him," and she patted the skipper's arm again.

Eventually they bid goodbye to the smiling Welsh lady and made their way back to the harbour, where the loading was almost complete.

Although Will would still not care to get on the wrong side of Captain Skil, his respect and liking for the man increased as he got to know him better.

Later, Jim told the boy that the skipper's father and Mr. Williams had served at sea together for many years when they were younger, and Captain Skil had known Mrs. Williams since he was a small boy. His father had died of a fever, whilst his friend had sailed one day in a well-found ship and, along with the rest of the crew, was never seen again.

From that sad tale Jim and Abe moved on to tales of shipwrecks that had occurred around Anglesey. They spoke of the clipper *The Royal Charter* which had sailed all the way from Australia only to be wrecked on the rocks near Moelfre, just a short distance round the coast from Traeth Bychan. "Eighteen Fifty-nine," said Abe.

"Over four hundred and fifty lives were lost, including women and children," he said sombrely. "Only fifty saved, and the good people of Moelfre did what they could, but had to watch all the others drown." It was hardly the most encouraging subject to instil enthusiasm into a boy who already was dreading the return journey to Eastham!

Will's outward voyage had imprinted itself on his mind (and his stomach), but by then he had settled to the fact that he would have to endure the ordeal, knowing that it would be over by the end of the following day. However, after hearing about the wrecks and sudden storms which had occurred around Anglesey's rocky coast, his fragile optimism deserted him.

That night he elected to sleep on deck again, but sleep eluded him, and when the others came up to make ready for leaving, he was still awake and feeling jaded. Remembering the consequences of eating too much fried food before leaving Eastham, the boy ate just a small amount of porridge.

Just before the tide turned from high water slack, Captain Skil slid *The Sisters Three* out of the harbour, passing close by the collier brigs, and heading out to sea. The headland on the opposite side of the bay was a hazy mass, the sun's warmth not being enough to dispel the sea mist.

Will had been full of admiration at the way the schooner was handled. Very few commands, and no apparent hurry, yet soon the vessel was bowling along under full canvas.

Even though he was tired, the start to their homeward trip had again aroused in Will the thrill of sailing. The heavily laden vessel heeled just a few degrees and cut through the calm waters with a gentle chuckling sound.

Within ten minutes of leaving Traeth Bychan, the idyllic episode had ended. Abe, Jim and Will had been brushing the deck of the last pieces of stone and dust from the loading, and Will was just about to start using the mop when a barely perceptible rolling motion began to affect *The Sisters Three.*

Abe, seeing the anxious look on Will's face, said laconically, "Beam sea," and continued brushing as he spoke. Within a short space of time the schooner was rolling gently through an arc of about fifteen degrees.

Poor Will, his earlier optimism disappearing, staggered to the bulwark and was violently sick. As he valiantly attempted to get back to his task, he was assailed by a vertiginous attack and sank to his knees, unable to stand upright.

He was pulled to his feet by Jim, who almost dragged him to the hatch cover and laid him down. His head felt like it was splitting and he was frightened to open his eyes for fear of bringing on another attack. A blanket was thrown over him and he was left, his arms covering his face. The glare of the sunlight had been sending stabs of pain through his head.

The conditions and the sea state were perfect: a light swell and a steady wind. On a broad reach, *The Sisters Three* bounded along at her best with just the lightest of spray occasionally flying over the bow. Conway River, Great Orme and the seaside towns, all linked by a chain of silvery beaches and the light-coloured rock of the Welsh coast, all were passed in their turn. A sparkling sea, a warm sun and a blue sky, everything that Will had dreamed about, but which he was then sadly missing, for the exhausted boy was fast asleep!

Seaward there were several ships, sail and steam, some heading away from Liverpool and the North-West ports, some making their way towards places like Parkgate, Mostyn and Connah's Quay on the River Dee. Apart from those heading for the northern Lancashire ports, the rest were bound for Liverpool and the other Mersey ports.

Once again the Anglesey-bound paddle steamer *Bonnie Princess* passed them, this time close enough to see the passengers on deck, some of them waving. Jim and Abe were not too blasé to wave back. Later another twin-funnelled paddle steamship, the *Cobra* surged past heading in the same direction.

It was a perfect run and the schooner was in good time to take advantage of the rising tide that helped her up the Mersey. Will awoke as they were passing Bromborough, and hoisted himself shakily and guiltily to his feet. Jim grinned at him, then without a word went below, reappearing minutes later with a mug of tea for the boy.

Will could hardly meet the man's eye, he felt so ashamed of himself. Abe, observing the boy's hangdog expression, said cheerfully, "Don't worry, lad, it happens to us all at some time, you've 'nought' to be upset about."

After they had made everything ready for the unloading, Will gathered his bags and prepared to leave the vessel. Captain Skil had not berated him or treated him with disdain but even so it did nothing to stop him feeling ashamed of himself.

As he approached the skipper, he was greeted with an understanding smile, and was kindly upbraided, "Don't look so down-hearted, lad, many seamen get affected on the first two days back at sea." However, Will was not reassured and said in a guilty voice, "But I have let you down, sir, I have not been much use to you at all." The skipper brushed his protests at one side and said, "Now look here, lad, you never refused to carry out an order, you did everything without a grumble even when you were tearing your hands to pieces, and we did not expect you to even start on that job." Then he said in a kindly tone, "You are a good lad, Will Banham, but you are not cut out for a life at sea."

He then said briskly, "I owe you sixteen shillings and sixpence, but to show you that I was glad to have you with us, here is eighteen shillings. Oh, and by the way, lad," he added with a grin, "you are from Marshville, right?" and as Will nodded, he said, "That ointment for your hands, you can get some more off Maggie Garroway, she makes the stuff!"

Will was quite surprised, although he had heard that she made up medicines from plants, and it explained the peculiar smells that came from her hut and pervaded her person.

It was time to be going if he was going to be home before it got too dark, so he shook hands with them all and climbed onto the jetty. Immediately he experienced a most peculiar sensation. The solid landing felt as if it was moving, and Will grabbed for a bollard to steady himself. He looked back at the vessel he had just left and saw that the three men were grinning. "Aye lad," called Jim, "you'll have to get your 'land legs' back, be all right tomorrow."

The boy laughed with them, waved and made his way unsteadily towards the locks. He looked back once at the schooner and thought, 'She is not a bad vessel, *The Sisters Three*.' His first disparaging thoughts had been replaced by something approaching affection, and certainly respect.

Joe was at the boiler house when Will arrived there and after hearing the boy's account of his ignominious voyage, sympathised with him, then, changing the subject, told him that his timing was very good as the coal train was due shortly.

Clancy and Bill were manning the loco and they said that if the swingbridge at Ellesmere Port was not turned against them to favour shipping entering or leaving the port, the boy might manage to get a ride on the coal train up to Frodsham Depot.

At the 'Port', Will watched in frustration as several vessels left the docks, for the light was fading and he had no idea what he would do if he missed the coal train.

In the event, there was not the slightest trouble in catching the train. He did not recognise either driver or fireman but they were quite agreeable for him to ride on the footplate with them. It was dark when Will thanked them and climbed down at Frodsham Depot. "Home," he said aloud, and how very glad he was to be back.

In the workshop Michael was talking to the younger apprentice. On seeing Will his face split into a smile and he was about to say something when he caught sight of the wrappings around the boy's hands. Then Thomas joined them and gave his son a hug, but at the same time asking him what he had done to his hands. Will explained about the two missing men whilst they were loading the stone and defending Captain Skil said, "He made me come out then went for the men, and afterwards he saw to my hands." Then he grinned and said, "And do you know, the ointment he used on them was made by Mrs. Garroway."

Thomas shook his head and said suddenly, "Look boy, go and put your mam's mind at rest, she has been on edge for days." He did not press his son for details or ask him if he had enjoyed his experience; he knew that the boy would tell them soon enough what he had decided.

Will walked into the hut and before he could put his bags down he was engulfed by his mother and Victoria. They hugged him and kissed him, both of them crying. Whilst he was pleased to see them, he felt with embarrassment that he had not earned such an emotional welcome. Then there were fresh tears as they undid the wrappings on his hands. Beth was furious that he should have been used so badly.

The boy was thoroughly upset and he hugged them both in return, saying in a rather thick voice, "I'm sorry, Mam, Victoria, for worrying you, but you will be glad to know that the sea is not for me."

Beth sat down at the table, her head in her hands and cried with relief. Will crouched down beside her and held her for a few moments, then said dramatically, "And I will tell you this, Mam, I am going to enjoy the water, the water in my bath, that is." Then he wrinkled his nose at himself.

His mother sprang up and said, laughing through her relieved tears, "I knew there was something smelling but I didn't know what it was, now get out of my way while I get the water hot." Victoria said softly to her brother, "Go over to Dafyd, he has been worrying about you, Will." Her brother did as he was told, glad to be seeing somebody who would not be weeping over him, and he was eager to tell his employer all the details of his adventure, or to be more honest, his misadventure.

Dafyd was pleased to see him and let Will tell the story in his own time, only nodding his approval when the boy said how much he enjoyed what he had seen of Anglesey.

Eventually Will told him about his acceptance that he would never be a seaman, and what was more important to the shopkeeper, the boy did not seem to have any regrets, although he did say that he still loved boats.

"Perhaps one day I will have a small sailing boat of my own," Will said hopefully, but added quickly, "but only for the river or maybe just off the beach a little way."

Later, after he had revelled in the tub of warm water and enjoyed his evening meal, he went across to the shop for the last half hour whilst Dafyd took Victoria back in the pony trap to Mrs. Hilyard's house.

The following morning Clara came in, and her affectionate welcome, coupled with her concern at the state of his hands, made him feel even more embarrassed at his poor showing on the schooner. Clara brushed aside his protestations and told him, "My man said you wouldn't get him on the sea for twenty gold sovereigns."

For the next week Peter was his constant companion. Although his younger brother was developing quite an independent streak, he had felt Will's absence very strongly. Will did not mind so much but in truth he was trying to find time to visit Helsby. His thoughts had been full of Lucy, the 'drinks man's' daughter, and he was hoping to meet her again to see if he had aroused any interest in her.

His chance came a week later when Dafyd mentioned that Clara had asked him if she could do a few extra hours work. She wanted to buy something for her baby.

Will seized the chance and suggested that he give up the odd Sunday afternoon and let Clara work. The young woman was pleased as she could be, and Dafyd was satisfied with the arrangement.

After his midday meal the following Sunday, Will, in his best suit, strolled nonchalantly to the railway station where he took a train to Helsby. He walked down Robin Hood Lane, but his knock on the door of the cottage failed to arouse anybody.

Eventually he gave up and walked back to the station. He suddenly decided to check whether there were any trains ready to go down to the Canal site, and if there were he would beg a ride. He caught a glimpse of a plum-coloured shawl on somebody disappearing round the end of a line of wagons. Lucy wore a shawl of that colour, for he remembered every little detail about her from their first meeting. He was surprised but thought nothing odd about it, as Lucy and her father worked along the Canal cutting every day selling their drinks.

He hurried his pace to catch up with her, only to stop short when he realised that she had a man with her. Even in the few moments he saw them together, he could see her response to the man's embrace that was not that of an innocent young lady.

It was a measure of the depths of his feelings for the girl that he felt angrier with himself than Lucy. 'You fool,' he told himself savagely, 'she has never given you real reason to make you feel that she was interested in you, Will Banham.' Even so, he was close to tears to see his dreams crushed in such a way.

During August, Captain Howard suggested to Kate that they must visit his home, Milford House. Not many miles from Winchester, Milford Estate had been in the Howard family for several generations. Kate, in the past, had often wanted to visit Richard's home, although Cecelia had been very dismissive of its attractions, which of course did nothing at all to stifle her sister's curiosity.

Towards the middle of September, Captain Howard decided that as the work was not too pressing, and while the fine weather was still holding, they would make a visit. Mary became quite excited about it but, as she explained to Victoria and Daisy, she wondered what her future place would be amongst the present staff at the house.

The visit, which could only be for four days, came at the closing days of the month. Whether it was the beautiful balmy days or the totally different appearance of the Hampshire countryside is not certain, but Kate fell in love with Milford without any urging from her husband.

Whereas Reeve House was of brick and flint, the rear wings being oak-framed infilled with flint, Milford House was built of a light golden-coloured stone. The rather plain south-facing front had been made more impressive at some time with the addition of a classical-looking portico supported on two columns.

The gardens surrounding the house were well maintained, and spread out a long way at one side, reaching down to the River Itchen which marked one boundary of the estate.

After they had washed off the dust of their travels and had some light refreshment, Captain Howard introduced Kate to the servants, the staff consisting of Mr. and Mrs. Carrington, the butler and the housekeeper, Mrs. Baines, the cook, and just three housemaids and a scullery maid. Richard explained to his wife that one upstairs maid had left to get married, and was to be replaced as soon as a suitable girl was found.

The outside staff consisted of a head gardener, two under-gardeners and a stable hand. Later Mary found the image of the fair-haired, freckle-faced under-gardener, the one named Jem, repeatedly intruding into her thoughts.

There were fewer bedrooms than at Reeve House, but Kate knew that they were ample for the number of visitors that they were likely to receive. She was delighted at how tastefully the main rooms were furnished, although certain of them would need decorating in the near future. Richard's parents had collected many fine pieces of furniture and under the dust sheets everything was clean and polished.

"I must say, Richard," remarked Kate, "your people have looked after everything wonderfully well whilst you are away, it is all to their credit." Her husband smiled mischievously and looking past her said, "Well, Mrs. Howard, why not tell them so yourself." Kate spun round, her face coloured, for rising up from behind the grand piano was Mrs. Carrington and one of the maids.

It was difficult to say whose face was the most red, Kate's or the housekeeper's, the latter apologising for startling the mistress. She explained that they were replacing all the floor covers now that Captain and Mrs. Howard were soon to leave.

Kate was quick to put the housekeeper at her ease. "Oh no, Mrs. Carrington," she exclaimed. "Pray do not apologise, there is no need, and I meant what I said, Captain Howard is indeed well served. Milford House is a credit to your endeavours."

It was the most fortuitous happening, for in no time at all, the rest of the staff were informed by the housekeeper and the maid that Mrs. Howard was a real 'lady!'

One major point that weighed heavily for Kate in favour of Milford House was that it had never been tainted by the presence of her late husband. Another point was that she was not bound to live there as she had been by Aunt Phoebe's misguided generosity. Even on those occasions when she had been blessed with the light-hearted company of James and Charlotte, or the deep pleasure of a visit from Richard, she had never felt that she was playing hostess in her own home.

Dear understanding Richard had already promised her that he would reside in any house that she felt was truly her own home.

All too soon they were on their way back to Frodsham, each in their own way glad to be returning to their normal routines and friends, although the memory of a smiling young gardener made a certain young lady wish they could have stayed longer.

Kate was glad to be going home for all the pleasure of seeing Richard's family home. After reaching their house and after they had recovered from their journey, she wandered from room to room as if to reassure herself that everything was as she liked it. With a sigh of contentment she settled down and talked over their visit with her husband before they retired for the night.

When Mary got the chance to see Victoria, she was full of Milford and its charms. She was happier now that she had met the other servants; she felt that there would be no difficulty in settling in.

Later, when Daisy had heard everything from Victoria, she seemed rather unhappy that Mary might soon be gone from Frodsham. Victoria, sensing the problem, assured her that Captain Howard had to stay until the Canal was completed, and that, as far as she could make out, was supposed to be by the end of the year 'Ninety-one'. That would give them over a year of Mary's company. Actually it was to be much more than that, but at that time very few people were aware of how badly the various misfortunes visited upon the Company had affected the progress.

With the settlement of the wages dispute, and helped by the weather, progress had been good, although the Company realised that more capital had to be raised if the scheme was to come to fruition.

By late October the weather had deteriorated as would be expected, but by November there was considerable anxiety, especially at the eastern end of the Canal, for the rainy weather had set in with a vengeance. Their worst fears were borne out when after days of torrential rain, on the seventh of November, the rivers breached the embankments and flooded over fifteen miles of the cutting, from Trafford Park near Manchester to Latchford near Warrington!

As on the previous breach, temporary road bridges were smashed aside by the debris carried by the rushing floodwaters. There was little to be seen of the buildings and equipment drowned in the depths of the cutting.

Once more by a miracle, nobody was drowned or injured. Whole trains were underwater, the driver and fireman of the locomotive *Lancaster* managing to scramble clear before it was engulfed by the roaring wave of water.

Again it caused a great deal of hardship for the men as thousands of them had to be laid off, and the mood of optimism was cruelly dashed.

Chapter 29

Comedy and A Betrayal

With all the problems and news of disastrous floods, it is hard to imagine anybody working on the Canal scheme looking forward to Christmas and its jollities. But as with human beings generally, the opportunity to enjoy a respite from the ills that were dogging the Manchester Ship Canal Company was eagerly seized upon, and at Marshville there was a noticeable air of anticipation, especially amongst the young ones.

Dafyd had set up a Christmas club which allowed his customers to put a few pence away each week to buy special extras they wanted. He also ordered certain items, mostly edible, in bright tins and packages that he would sell at cost. As he laughingly explained to Will, it might not be profitable and might enrage a certain Mr. Jowet, but anything that would make Christmas special for his customers was good business to him.

Kate and Richard were spending Christmas at Reeve House with her family, then whilst her husband was returning to Frodsham, Kate and her family were spending the New Year at her parents' home.

Since her visit to Milford, Kate had been toying with the idea of letting Longfields go to James and Charlotte. They certainly enjoyed staying at Reeve House. For James particularly, the nearness of the river made the estate especially attractive.

Thomas Banham and Michael managed to spend Christmas and New Year's day without being called out to frozen water-tank valves or burst pipes and were thankful for that. However, that is not to say there were no problems with the icy conditions for others. Progress in the cutting was once more slowed due to the state of the earth to be excavated.

Dafyd had managed to spend a few days at home with his parents over Christmas, but the three of them spent the Saturday at Mrs. Hilyard's house. Also invited was the Banham family.

Of all the unfortunate things to have happened, Victoria was prevented from playing the piano for her parents by the fact that she had inadvertently touched a hot pan and raised painful blisters on two of her fingers. The poor girl had been looking forward to the occasion for so long that she was naturally very upset, and she was also sorry that she was letting Mrs. Hilyard down on the evening.

As it was, Dafyd's father played the piano reasonably well and had a good voice, so the party was not a disaster. A good meal and an evening singing together (Victoria of course abstaining) made it a very enjoyable occasion.

For the Manchester Ship Canal Company, the festive season was not a time of rejoicing. At the flooded eastern end of the Canal, the water was constantly freezing up causing the dozens of pumps to become ineffective. So that masonry work could proceed, sections around lock and bridge works were temporarily dammed and drained.

However, the difficulties experienced with the executors of the late Mr. Walker had been settled with the payment of four hundred thousand pounds in respect of machinery and equipment, which meant that the Manchester Ship Canal Company were then solely responsible for the completion of the scheme.

One evening Michael came in with a huge grin on his face. "You know the trouble on the Marsh when those drunken Irish lads got fighting," he said. "Well, with so many having their bones and heads broken, the polis' have had another go at finding that still."

The problem had stemmed from a very crude sort of potato alcohol called poteen which was being made somewhere on the Marsh and sold at a shebeen, an illegal drinking den. Several times the police had attempted to raid the shebeen, for they had a very good idea where it was, in that they were frustrated by the number of lookouts posted when the still or the shebeen was in use.

Michael told the story with great satisfaction. He had also known men and some women in Ireland who had been physically and mentally ruined through the effects of poteen, and he hated the makers of the poison like he hated the Devil.

"The polis'," he said, "gathered together dozens of officers and hired a furniture pantechnicon, loaded them in a quiet place, then with the Inspector and two sergeants dressed in furniture removal men's aprons doing the driving, set out down the lane through the Marsh." Michael paused for a moment then said, "I would have loved to have been there; the polis' were nearly up to the place when the wheels got stuck in the mud, and some navvies came up and put their shoulders to the wheels to help them get moving." Then he chuckled and said, "The lookouts abandoned their posts and joined in so the pantechnicon was able to reach the lodging house, that is where the still was hidden," Michael explained.

Beth felt sorry for the men who had helped to push the vehicle out of the mud, but Michael put her mind at rest by telling her that as soon as the police poured out of the pantechnicon, the other men were off over the Marsh, leaping ditches like startled hares!

"No, Mrs. Banham," he said. "They wanted the main men who worked the still, and they got them."

It appeared that police surrounded the place whilst other officers charged inside. Several men were attempting to cover the still, which at that moment was continuing to produce poteen, and another man was caught kicking a bucketful of the stuff over onto the dirt floor. By chance the bucket went over and sloshed the poteen into the man's boots. Quick as a flash, two policemen held him firm whilst a third yanked his poteen-soaked boot and sock off his foot, put them in a bucket and took them away as evidence.

The still was dismantled and taken away. The old man and the women who worked at the lodging house were left to keep the place open for those who had beds there. Altogether it was a feather in the cap for the Inspector, who had so long tried to put a stop to the problem.

During one Sunday afternoon in March Thomas and Beth were alone in the hut, Will being at the shop and Peter playing with the twins in their hut. Thomas had just been reading the news-sheet, *Ship Canal News*, and he was commenting on the difficulties posed for the scheme by the floods at the eastern end of the Canal. He was startled when Beth burst out, "Oh, Thomas, that is all I hear, floods, disasters and more money needed, it's just like Dr. Mills said." Then she broke down weeping and Thomas, very disturbed, went round to her side and attempted to comfort her. It was a while before he could get her to say why the news was upsetting her so badly.

"Don't you see, Thomas?" she cried. "The whole thing will never get finished and we will be trapped here forever with the mud and dirt in this black, miserable place. Oh, Thomas, will we never get away?"

Even as he sat beside her, his arms around her shoulders, her husband guiltily admitted to himself that he had not noticed that Beth was once again slipping back into a depressed state. He too was conscious of a growing anxiety about their situation but for different reasons. How much longer would the work at Frodsham Depot last and where would they go when they had to leave Marshville?

Most of the people involved with the section between Eastham and Runcorn were confident that their part of the scheme would be completed by the closing months of 'Ninety-One', and that of course would lead to the major part of the workers being paid off. And that would probably include those employed at Frodsham Depot.

Thomas had not mentioned any of this to Beth, as he had foolishly thought that she had settled down quite well to living in Marshville. Now he was aware of how she really felt, he decided to tell her about their future situation without giving too much importance to the fact that he would then be looking for work.

He explained everything to Beth and reminded her that the main problem in finding a house in the town was the objection of the townspeople to the contractor's workers. Therefore, he reasoned, with the departure of thousands of men from the Canal site, there would be less objection to letting houses to those few who remained to work in the area.

Whilst Beth felt some stirrings of hope, she was not fooled one jot by her husband's casual mention of, "When I get a job," and "When we rent a house here in Frodsham."

When she voiced her thoughts, Thomas answered in his usual optimistic way and said, "You cannot argue with me, Beth, when I say that we are now better known in the town, that there are people at the Chapel who we can count on as friends and others who are friendly towards us."

Seeing the frown on his wife's face, Thomas said with a smile, "Surely, girl, you must admit the people in the town are kindly disposed towards you. Why, only a few days ago Jessie remarked on how pleasant and respectful the shopkeepers were to you both."

Beth smiled, planted a kiss on her husband's cheek, then rose to get on with what she had been doing before her outburst. She felt rather more cheerful now that they had talked about their future at Marshville. She had no idea Thomas's work at the depot would soon be over and they would be free to move away from Marshville. Nevertheless, she knew that their present situation was a lot less frightening than the uncertainties that lay ahead.

Beth's words had left a strong impression on Thomas's mind, and a little later he was looking out of the window and seeing the street as she would see it. He was mulling over the problem of what he could do to change things when Peter came dashing in. The boy came up short, then offered his father a scrap of paper on which he had been crayoning trees, or what he told Thomas was trees. "Can I put my trees on the wall of our bedroom, Dad," Peter asked. "I like these colours, they will make our room look nice."

His father ruffled his son's hair and said smiling, "Well, son, if your mother says it is all right, then I don't mind." Even as he was speaking an idea came into his mind on how to at least attempt to make the outside of the hut look brighter. Obviously there was little to be done with tar-coated walls, but Peter's drawing had given an idea of how they could change the appearance of the hut.

The moment he could talk with Will and Michael without Beth or Peter overhearing, he outlined his plan. Both were enthusiastic and so the following day Thomas approached Captain Howard about buying some wide boards, two feet long.

When his employer heard what the boards were for he said, "Just cut the boards and you can have them without charge." After that there followed a few days when every moment they had free was spent shaping, chamfering, sanding and painting the boards. After they were prepared, Will, Michael and Thomas decorated them with bright, colourful designs.

The success of the idea was evident once they had been fastened on either side of the doorway for all to see. Whereas Michael and Thomas had painted flowers on their boards, Will had covered his with colourful strong geometrical patterns. Dafyd and Mr. and Mrs. Robbins were given two boards each, and after Beth had made her choice, the rest were put up for sale at a very modest price.

Within one day all the boards were sold, and Will elected to fasten them to the huts of those who wanted them on show. The difference in the appearance of the street and the attitude of the hut dwellers was amazing. There were certainly more smiling faces than there had been for weeks. Also it started a fashion. Other painted panels of different shapes and sizes appeared with various designs on them. One of the men who came from Scotland had painted a very striking cross of St. Andrew. Some were not very well executed but the colourful panels were a source of pride to those who had created them.

Beth, knowing without being told why they had been done, loved them all, and Captain Howard was very impressed with the display; later, as he recounted what had been done to Kate, he said, "I am constantly being surprised at Thomas's imaginative ideas." It seemed to him that Marshville was developing a character all of its own thanks to his foreman.

—— —— ——

A Thursday morning and Beth was fed up, not depressed, simply out of sorts with everything. She and Jessie Robbins had been planning a day trip and a walk round Chester when their arrangements had to be put back a few days, then again by a few more days, and here they were in the second week and still no sign that they would get their day out.

Both Thomas and Ted Robbins had agreed that their respective wives needed a break from their duties at home, but a rush of work for both men kept their noses to the grindstone well and truly until late evening, and the women did not like to leave their husbands to fend for themselves after their long day at work.

Then there was the dratted weather, Beth fumed; after some weeks of mild dry days, the rain had now arrived heavy enough to create a small river down the street, turning the soil back to mud. Only yesterday evening Jessie had suggested a visit to Frodsham market seeing that they were denied their treat to Chester, and now look at the dratted rain.

So Beth's thoughts ran as she banged about the oft dusted rooms, vigorously attacking anything that did not have a shine on it, when suddenly she heard a raised voice bellowing outside at someone. All Beth could see was Mrs. Garroway, fists raised in a threatening manner, her huge bulk hiding whoever it was she was haranguing. Usually Beth did not open the door to strangers, for there were many dubious characters visiting the community from time to time, some trying to sell things, others begging, and others who were simply looking for lodgings.

One of Mrs. Garroway's less objectionable traits was that she made a very effective guard dog!

For some reason Beth sensed that there was nobody out there to be afraid of and she decided to open the door a crack. As she did so she was in time to see a shabby, diminutive figure of a woman backing away from her aggressor, holding her hands up as though to ward off a blow.

"Get away from my door, you filthy vagabond, on yer way, we don't want your sort 'ere." Beth could hear the words quite plainly now but could not hear anything from the woman who was stumbling away from Mrs. Garroway, who, on seeing Beth peeping out of her doorway, shouted, "Don't let 'er near yer, it's one of them thievin' tinkers."

As the pathetic figure slowly moved nearer, Beth then noticed that the woman was limping badly; both her feet were obviously giving her a great deal of pain. The woman looked up, her lips barely moving, but only a whispered "please," reached Beth, the huge beseeching eyes telling her that this was no threatening tinker, but a poor defenceless soul in need of help.

Her door was fully open and before she stopped to consider what trouble she was inviting in on herself, Beth beckoned the girl, for she did not look like a grown woman, towards her.

Dressed in a coat that was too large for her, a man's cap and boots, and a mud-splashed skirt hitched up to clear the puddles of more mud, the girl did indeed look like a vagabond. Beth thought, 'No wonder the poor creature is limping': the boots were falling to pieces and were held together with string and bits of wire.

Beth ignored the bellowing of Mrs. Garroway, exhorting her to "send the vagabond on her way", and helped the now weeping girl into the hut. "Come in, my pet, and let's get you warm and dry." Still the shivering girl could only whisper the words, "Oh, please." When Beth, her maternal instincts in full flight, gently removed the saturated jacket from the girl, she simply let her take it, swaying on her feet as though she was holding herself upright by willpower.

She was led unresisting to a chair, though the pain from her feet caused her to wince as she moved, but before she was seated, she pulled out a crumpled and rather damp piece of paper, and handed it to Beth. "I'm looking for my husband," she whispered, then sagged forward in a faint.

Beth, now thoroughly alarmed, just managed to catch her before the girl hit the floor, easing her down before dashing out of the room to get something to cushion her head. As she was carefully putting the cushion under the girl's head, she heard a faint knock on the door, the familiar sound of her neighbour, Jessie, and not the banging din of the, thankfully rare, visit of the Garroway woman.

The ever watchful Jessie had come in to help, and to Beth's relief was equal to the occasion. Bolting the door and pulling the curtains, she told her friend, "Get her out of those wet things and into something dry before the men come in, she will need a warm drink inside her quickly."

Beth quickly put the kettle on the fire and set the pot for tea before going back to help unclothe the unconscious girl. As they proceeded with their task, Beth told Jessie what she had heard, for the soft, almost whispered voice told her she was Scottish. "Why, the poor thing looks younger than our Victoria and she is wed at that."

When the girl regained consciousness, she found herself wrapped in a nightgown and a blanket, ensconced in Thomas's chair. Her feet were resting on a stool and Jessie was dressing them, whilst Beth, her eyes wet with tears, was kneeling on the other side of her holding the jar of ointment.

The girl's eyes opened wide in alarm. "My clothes," she said in a shaky tone, "where are my clothes?" and she made as though to get her feet off the stool, but Beth and Jessie were too quick for her and made the girl sit back again.

"Your clothes are going to be washed and made ready for you, my girl," said Beth, "and before anything else, you are going to have some food, a hot drink and then off to bed; your story can wait until tomorrow." Before the bemused girl could answer there came a knock on the door and Peter's plaintive voice reached them, telling his mother that it was 'raining toads and frogs' outside.

Wiping her eyes first, Beth opened the door, letting Peter in, then waved to the woman with her children who had just accompanied her son on his way home from school.

Peter had rushed into the room talking nine to the dozen when he espied the 'patient' in his dad's chair. He came to an abrupt stop, gazing at the blanket-clad figure with his mouth open. The effect on the girl was also quite unexpected. A lovely smile came on her face and she said softly, "Hello, wee mannie, home from school, come and tell me all about it," and Peter did as she asked.

As the two amused women moved over towards the sink they could hear him telling her his name and the girl telling him that her name was Jeannie.

As Beth poured out a cup of tea for Jeannie, her friend said quietly, "If you have one of the men bring her next door, I will have a bed ready for the lass, for I know that you could not possibly fit her in here," then as a thought struck her, she added, "Mind you, if Michael moved next door for the night, Jeannie would not have to be exposed to the rain again."

This was agreed upon, then Beth said that she would rig up the sheets in the room to allow the girl to bathe herself. Beth gave Jeanie a cup of tea, which the tired girl took gratefully, swallowing it as though she had not had a drink all day, which Beth thought was probably so. The sweet smile of gratitude she received melted Beth's heart and she hugged the blanket-clad girl, and Jeannie clung to her, weeping afresh. Peter was then upset and kept patting her arm.

"Now, Jeannie," said Beth forcing herself to be brisk and businesslike, "Mrs. Robbins and me are setting things up so that you can have a good wash, then after you have eaten you will be ready for bed, which we are now making up for you."

Afterwards, bathed and fed, Jeannie fell asleep, whilst Peter was shooed away and the women set to sorting out some clean bedding, the tired girl only opening her eyes at the sound of men's voices.

When the men came in, accompanied by Will (who actually considered himself a man), it was quite comical for the women to observe the different expressions on their faces. Thomas managed to carry off his surprise as though it was a normal occurrence to come in from work and find a pretty girl wrapped in a blanket occupying his favourite chair. Will became very shy at seeing a very attractive girl in his home; he did see Victoria, but then she was his sister, so that was different.

Michael was for once stuck for words. The sight of Jeannie affected him like no other girl ever had done before. True, back in Ireland he was as good as any boy at the art of flirting without getting tied to any girl, but until that day no girl had ever made him feel the way he did at that moment.

The look on his face was not lost on Beth or Jessie, but although both women felt a surge of sympathy for the young Irishman, Beth experienced a clutch of fear that Michael might become entangled with the wife of another man. Her cheerful lodger was almost like a son to her and, unless she read the signs wrong, to Thomas as well. As a 'stand-in Mammy', as Michael referred to her, Beth felt that she had to look after him.

Jessie looked meaningfully at Beth as they bustled forward to get everything organised, but it was Beth who took the lead by explaining everything to her husband and at the same time making sure that Michael knew that there was a line drawn that he must not cross.

Michael was stunned; this lovely girl, married! His spirits plummeted; she looked so young, so in need of protection, yet was married to a man who had left her alone to fend for herself. His anger boiled up at the man who could do such a thing.

He realised with a start that Mrs. Robbins was addressing him and apologised. When he grasped the fact that for tonight at least he would be giving up his bed for Jeannie, he was spurred into a flurry of action. He was so pleased that it was him who would be helping her have a good night's sleep. Dashing into his room, he started to straighten the blankets, trying to make it seem more cosy, then looked round in despair. Nothing was right in the room for Jeannie; it was a man's room. How could he make it appear more welcoming? Beth's voice came from behind him. "Don't worry about the bedclothes, Michael," she said briskly. "Just take everything off and carry it into Mrs. Robbins's hut; she has gone in to get the room ready for you." She went on in a gentler voice, "I am putting all clean bedding on the bed so all you need to do for me is to take your bedding into Mrs. Robbins's hut. Oh yes, and any other things that you will need for tomorrow." She looked at the forlorn figure of Michael and patted his arm and said, "It will only be for tonight, boy, and meanwhile I do not want her waking up once she is asleep, so make sure you have everything you need." Michael nodded and started bundling up his bedding. He would come back as quickly as he could for a change of clothes ready for the morrow, and also his shaving tackle. He wanted to look as smart as he could the next time Jeannie clapped eyes on him.

When all was ready, Beth and Jessie carefully helped the girl to her feet. Although it was obviously very painful for Jeannie, the bandages swathed round her feet made it bearable for her to move into the bedroom. After removing the blanket, the ladies put the exhausted girl to bed, but before she settled back she reached out and kissed the hands which had helped her. Then to their consternation, she whimpered, "Oh, when will I see my bairn again, I miss my wee Flora so much." Jeannie was so tired she could hardly enunciate her words, but her meaning was clear enough to the two thunderstruck women. Jessie Robbins was the first to recover her voice, and gently helping the weeping girl lay her head on her pillow, said, "Now, lassie, we will soon have you back home, so don't you fret. Now just get your sleep and you will be able to face things much better tomorrow." Before they had blown out the candle they could see that Jeannie had fallen asleep.

Around the table Thomas and Will had been discussing the girl and her troubles. Whilst Thomas was affected by the affair, his son was furious, but managing to keep his voice low he raged, "How can any man leave his young wife and not let her know how or where he is? He must write home some time to send her money to live on." Then he said, "How can anybody leave a girl like Jeannie without any protection?"

His father said quietly, "Well, son, any normal decent person would wonder at such heartlessness but it happens too many times; it is not the first time that a wife or another family member has turned up on the 'cut' looking for some man who had stopped sending them word of how they were faring." Thomas paused for a moment then went on, "You see, Will, their families want to know if their absent son, father or husband is all right, it is not always the money." At this point Will burst out in a low fierce voice and said, "But she does not look much older than me."

Before his father could reply, the door opened. Michael was back and, noticing Thomas's chair empty of Jeannie, came straight to the table. At that moment Beth and Jessie came out of the bedroom, gently closing the door behind them. Beth was wiping the tears from her eyes and even the imperturbable Jessie was under some sort of emotion. Beth burst out in a low voice, "Jeannie is mother to a baby girl, and she is in torment about the child."

For a moment the group around the table were speechless, then Thomas said, "Well, that is even more reason for us to find the man." He went on, "Once we know his name, where exactly he was supposed to be working, and what his trade is, we will find him, and if we do not, the word will go out." He added with a wry grin, "As we have said many times before, news travels fast round here."

It was not a very good night for Michael: whilst next door Jeannie slept the deep sleep of the exhausted, he tossed and turned for hours, the image of the Scots girl's huge eyes imprinted on his brain. Savagely he reshaped his pillow and tried every position to get comfortable but it was hours before he slept. His mind would keep returning to the girl and the fact that she was another man's wife and the mother of his child. Michael would have loved to be the one who would bring back her husband, earning her gratitude and maybe a loving friendship. Then he thought that if he did find the absent husband, he would probably want to give the man a good hiding!

Then his thoughts took another turn: he wondered what the little girl looked like. He could visualise little Flora, as Beth had told them she was called, growing up just like Jeannie. Then he would get depressed again, reminding himself that the girl would go back to her child, never to be seen by any of them again. And so his thoughts ranged on until, at nearly three o'clock, tiredness conquered him and he slept.

Awakened early by Mr. Robbins, he dragged himself out of bed with an aching head to match his aching heart. There was no time to worry about personal discomfort, for he had to be down at the workshops for seven o'clock.

Washed and breakfasted, he was only a few minutes later than Thomas at the depot. The rain had eased but it was still a dreary-looking day, matching Michael's mood exactly. The job for the day was a hydraulic test on a steam-crane boiler, a job which they all detested at the best of times, but as it had to be done outside the workshop, the weather made it even less attractive.

The first words out of Michael's mouth, spoken in a casual manner which did not fool Thomas at all, was to enquire how the young lady was. Of course Thomas had as much idea as his young fitter, for the girl had been in a sound sleep when he left the hut and he thought she would probably want to sleep a lot longer. From what Beth had told him regarding the poor girl's feet, he was convinced that she had been walking for many days. He passed on what little knowledge he had, then seeing the upset look deepen on the younger man's face, he suggested that he should spend the rest of the morning making enquiries.

"Start by having a word with Mr. Morrison," he said, "and then talk to the loco drivers." Thomas paused, frowning, then burst out, "The only thing we have to go on is that he is a Scotsman and possibly near your age; we don't even know that for certain, we certainly do not know his name or his trade." He scratched his head in frustration. "Just ask around about someone who has gone missing. I leave it to you, Michael." Then he grinned at the young Irishman and said, "Well, it will keep you out of mischief, so I will see you about midday." With that he went back to the steam crane.

Michael was off like a shot from a gun, his spirits lifted at the thoughts of some action, even if it was like going blindfold into a dark alley.

It was a few minutes after twelve o'clock when he returned and had very little to show for the amount of distance he had covered, mostly walking. He had met two Scots, one a crane driver, the other an excavator driver, both nearer to fifty years of age than to twenty. But he had learned that a young Scot had been part of a gang whose job it was to set up the excavators when they had to be moved to a new position.

Unfortunately, nobody seemed to have any idea where he was now. Even if Michael had known his surname it would not have made the task of finding him any easier due to the shyness of many concerning their names.

Before he did his ablutions or changed into clean clothes, Michael told Jeannie what he had discovered. He felt unreasonably that he had failed her. Jeannie said nothing for a moment, then looked up and said quietly, "Michael, his name is Fergal Patrick, and I am sorry you have had to do so much, and I thank you very much." Then she said, "I have written to my mam and Mrs. Banham has posted it for me." She smiled at him and said, "My mam will be glad to know that I am amongst friends."

Michael would have stood listening to her all evening, but decided that it was time to tear himself away and clean himself up.

Peter had decided to be her servant whilst he was at home and the others hardly had a chance to do anything for her, which was galling particularly for Will and Michael, both of whom found her fascinating.

The following day brought a surprising visitor. On opening the door after hearing a knock, Beth was not pleased to find Mrs. Garroway standing there.

Without any preamble, Mrs. Garroway said, "I was wrong to say what I did to the girl, Mrs. Banham." She then thrust a covered jar towards Beth and said, "My own ointment, good for her feet, your boy Will knows how good it is." Then she nodded and trudged away without waiting for an answer. Beth called after her, thanking her, but the woman merely raised her hand without turning and carried on down the street.

Another visitor called the following day. It was Dr. Mills and he had come to see Jeannie. The girl became very agitated and said worriedly, "But I can't afford a doctor, I've got no money, sir."

Dr. Mills said gravely, "Now that is very serious, young lady, a doctor must have payment to keep in practice. But I will barter with you: I look at your feet and in exchange you will tell me what a 'clootie dumpling' is." For a moment Jeannie and Beth stared at him, then the girl burst out laughing.

Beth was delighted to hear the peals of laughter from her invalid lodger, but she was also completely mystified by the doctor's reference to the strange-sounding dumpling.

When Jeannie had recovered, she wiped her eyes and said, "Why, Dr. Mills, it is suet and flour, eggs, carrots and sultanas. Oh, and breadcrumbs, syrup, cinnamon and nutmeg." Then she said, "Some people do it different, but that is what me and my mam put in it. Oh, and apple and ginger," she finished, smiling impishly.

Beth said, laughing, "I think it would be a good idea, Dr. Mills if Jeannie wrote the recipe down on a piece of paper, or better still, on two pieces of paper, for I quite like the sound of 'clootie dumpling'."

Later, after seeing to the soles of Jeannie's feet, he told her that Mrs. Garroway's ointment was helping, but added that the girl was not to do any real walking or wear shoes until he was satisfied that they were healed sufficiently to bear her weight. He stayed chatting for a while over a cup of tea, then took his leave, promising to come back in a few days time.

Three days after Jeannie had written to her mother, the girl received a reply. In it her mother thanked the Almighty for sending her to a house of angels. Flora was missing her but was well enough in health. There was still no news of Fergal.

Jeannie wept afresh for her little girl but recovered herself a lot quicker than she had been doing. She was determined that as soon as her feet healed sufficiently to wear shoes she was going home. She asked Michael if he could mend her boots enough to let her use them, but the young man threw the offending footwear to the back of his workbench and made a promise to himself that Jeannie would have the best boots that he could afford when she could get into Frodsham.

On hearing about Jeannie, Kate was so moved by her story that she came down to Marshville in her pony trap and spent an hour at the hut talking to the girl. Later she and Richard came to the conclusion that Jeannie was being helped very adequately by the people around her, but when the time came for her return home, they would ensure that she would be able to afford the train home at the very least.

Not everybody was so sympathetic to the girl. Mrs. Guest and another woman were of the opinion that she was not much of a mother, walking out on her child and expecting others to pay for her selfishness.

In the shop, Will, mindful of what Dafyd had drummed into him regarding arguing with customers, kept his mouth shut with great difficulty. How he longed to defend her.

It was a few days before Jeannie told them how she had got to Marshville. With little money to spare at home, her mother had given her what she could afford, and that was only sufficient to buy her the cheapest ticket to reach Preston in Lancashire. The rest of the journey was mostly on foot with just the occasional ride with a kindly carter. But she ended up on the wrong side of the River Mersey.

She was then directed to the Runcorn-Widnes ferry and by an act of kindness by an old man, her fare was paid and she was rowed across to Runcorn. Another act of kindness by a lady gave her a cup of tea and some bread and jam. The lady also got her some wire and bound the soles back on her boots. She did not dwell on the horror of lying exhausted under hedges or snuggling into the straw of hayricks, praying that no rats would crawl over her.

Her story horrified them all and made them all the more thankful that they were in a position to help her.

When the second letter came from Jeannie's mother, it contained another letter, which was from Fergal Patrick.

Jeannie was still for a moment, then without a word handed her husband's letter to Beth. The message was that he had met another woman and would not be coming back to Scotland. The rest was a meaningless attempt to apologise for what he had done and was lost on the girl.

Beth was thunderstruck; of all things, she had not expected this. She looked down at Jeannie's bowed head, unable at that moment to say anything that would help.

The girl looked up, her eyes glistening with tears that did not fall, her face looking more her true age. "We were too young," she said in a low voice, "and a girl grows up when she has a baby, but a boy does not always become a man." Then she looked away and told Beth, "I am not surprised really; when I had Flora, he changed towards me, and the excuse that he wanted to come down here to make things better for us did not ring true at all."

Jeannie rose to her feet and moved towards the bedroom. "I will have a lie down if you don't mind, Mrs. Banham," she said in an expressionless voice.

Beth felt anguished at not being able to comfort Jeannie, but she knew that the ones that the girl wanted to be comforted by were many miles away.

She sat at the table, willing herself not to go to the girl, and wishing that Jessie was here with her. How long she sat there she did not know, but a slight sound behind her brought Beth to her feet. Jeannie was just coming into the room, and without a moment's thought Beth went over to the girl and wrapped her arms around her. Jeannie did not resist and clung onto the older woman, sobbing. Beth felt better herself now that she was being of use to the girl.

After a few moments she got Jeannie to sit at the table then she brought her a bowl of warm water and a towel. "I don't want the men to come in and catch you like this. They might think I am being cruel to you," Beth said, trying to ease the situation. Jeannie answered in the same vein, saying, "Then I won't tell on you."

Later, when everyone was at home, the girl seemed to be much brighter than she had been since she arrived. When they had all eaten, she thanked the men for their efforts in trying to find Fergal, waiting until Peter had gone to bed to tell them what her husband had written. Although Beth was concerned that the ordeal of telling the tale might distress Jeannie, she need not have worried: the girl was quite composed.

"So you see," she said, "there is no need for me to bother you any longer; as soon as Dr. Mills says my feet can be walked on, I will get back to my wee Flora and my mam." At the last part of the sentence her voice wobbled a bit but she did not break down.

Michael stood up and announced that he would be off. He explained that he was a bit tired, then turning to Jeannie, he said, "You will be well shod before you go home, Jeannie, I promise." With that he said goodnight and left the hut.

Jeannie stared at the door after he had left, then turned anxiously to Beth, who, seeing that the girl thought she had done something to upset him, told her that Michael often went early to bed, but inwardly she sighed to herself, 'poor

Michael.' Then she thought, 'Poor Jeannie, I do believe she feels as much for Michael as he does for her.'

Dr. Mills arrived shortly before midday and pronounced that the new skin on the soles of Jeannie's feet was almost ready to bear her weight. "But I will let you have some special white cotton socks to go over the dressings."

Later the four girls arrived crammed into Dr. Mills's trap. On Sarah's knees was a carpet bag. With a lot of squeals of laughter they tumbled out of the trap, and whilst Sarah put the nosebag onto the horse, Victoria, Daisy and Mary went to the door of the Banham hut.

Once inside they gathered around Jeannie to show her what they had brought. Just after they had started lifting the first item out of the bag, Will barged in to see them. As one they told him that boys were not allowed, Sarah and Mary catching hold of two cushions to beat him with. Beth told them to only hit him lightly as they were her best cushions, or better still, use a broom.

Laughing, Will retorted, "Well, I only came to see what the noise was; it sounded like a parrot cage at the zoo." Then he ducked and left the room, still laughing.

Jeannie looked in bewilderment at what was handed to her. New undergarments, stockings, the white cotton socks from Dr. Mills, and two child's frocks.

As the tears trickled down Jeannie's cheeks, Victoria said quickly, "Daisy bought the little dresses." Sarah, the practical one, seeing how weepy they were all getting, adopted a brisk tone and said, "Now, Jeannie, I will show you how these socks fasten; if they are not done right, they will be uncomfortable."

Daisy and Mary both started telling her something at the same time, then Mary stopped and let the other girl tell her about the carpet bag, which was a well made one. "Mrs. Hilyard says she will not use it again, so if it is any use to you, Jeannie, you can have it."

Jeannie hugged them all tearfully and promised that she would write each of them a letter when she got back home. Then Beth told them she was making a drink and that there was a fresh farmhouse cake to be eaten, but only if they behaved themselves.

Later, Beth and Jeannie were sitting contentedly sewing. The sun was shining through the open door, and the fresh spring air scented the room. Jeannie was wearing one of Jessie Robbins's dresses, their sizes being almost the same. She was mending her undergarments, whilst Beth was putting the final touches to one of the dresses which she was making for the girl. She was determined that Jeannie would not go home without good clothes. Also, everybody in their hut had put a little money into a pot to make sure that she did not go away penniless. Captain Howard and Kate, Dafyd and the Robbins's had contributed.

As the conversation proceeded, Beth noticed with sadness how often Michael's name was almost casually mentioned by the girl. Beth hoped that they would not be hurt when Jeannie left them, for she was very fond of both her and Michael.

Dafyd heard that Jeannie needed to go into town for shoes, so he suggested that during the morning Will took her there in the trap. The girl was touched at his kindness, but was worried about having to walk around the shops to find something suitable. However, when they got to the town, she did not even have to walk a single yard. She was accompanied by Beth and Mrs. Robbins, whilst Will walked the pony.

They were lucky when, having stopped at the first shop which was recommended by Jessie, the owner of the shop, a large middle-aged woman, came out to Jeannie. She and Jessie carried a selection of shoes and boots. The lady had been asked not to bring out anything but the best quality footwear she stocked: that was Michael's orders.

The ones that Jeannie found the most comfortable were lace-up boots of a supple leather. Beth and Jessie knew that Michael would be pleased at the girl's choice. Obviously they had to be of a slightly larger size than she normally wore to accommodate the dressings, and Beth was pleased that she had not used up all the money that Michael had given her.

Two Scotsmen came to the hut, one carrying a cap containing coins of all denominations. They said that all Scots should come to the aid of Scots in times of trouble, although they did admit grudgingly that some Englishmen had helped. The bigger of the two was an excavator driver and he had known Fergal Patrick. An offer of refreshment was politely refused as they had to get back to work, but they were happy with a kiss from the tearful Jeannie.

Dafyd had also been given money for 'the poor young Scots girl'. Therefore, with the money that he had contributed, he knew when he had changed all the loose coins into notes that Jeannie would have enough to support herself and her little girl for a few weeks should she fail to find work when she was home. As well as subscribing to the fund, he had made up two small parcels, one for Jeannie containing soaps and lotions, the other for Flora and Jeannie with chocolate and an assortment of sweets.

The night before the Scots girl went home, Peter became very upset, only placated when she promised to write him a personal letter. He cried later and sobbed to his mother that everyone he got to like went away. He still had not forgotten Clarence.

Jeannie wanted to thank Mrs. Garroway for the ointment and she managed to walk over to her hut without much difficulty. The flustered woman was taken aback, but was very pleased when the girl came to see her. Jeannie promised to write to her as soon as she could once she was home. 'Really,' she thought to herself, 'I'll be writing the letters that I have promised for weeks.'

Beth and Jessie knew that the awful coat that Jeannie had arrived in was fit for nothing but burning, yet the girl had no other coat to wear. A visit to a second-hand stall on the market had been fruitless. Jessie looked at herself in the mirror and said to her husband, "Well, Ted, I still like this coat of mine, but I have to admit the truth of my eyes, it is too tight on me now."

Her husband just smiled and said, "Well, Jessie love, it will be more use to young Jeannie than to you, so you might as well let her have it, anyway." He added, "You can always have a new coat for your birthday. I think I can afford it."

Without more ado, Jessie dashed next door to try the coat on Jeannie. She pushed aside her regrets when she saw it on the girl and the wonderful effect it had on her. When Michael saw Jeannie dressed for going home, he hardly said anything. Since she had come into his life he had become uncharacteristically quiet. Also, in the young Irishman's presence, Jeannie became very shy, and it bothered Thomas and Beth, for they could see nothing but heartbreak ahead for both of them.

At six o'clock the following morning, as Captain Howard had promised, a cab arrived to take Jeannie to the station. Michael asked Thomas's permission to see her on her way. Thomas was in complete sympathy with his young fitter and gladly let him start work later.

Beth and Jessie accompanied the girl and Jeannie held on to Beth's arm all the way to the station. Now that the moment had come for her to leave them, she was fairly composed. She did shed a few tears when Dafyd gave her the two parcels. She kissed him and Will, the boy himself fighting back the tears which threatened.

At the station the three of them stayed until the train came in, then after giving Jeannie a quick hug, Beth and Jessie hurried away and left Michael to see the girl into her carriage.

Left alone Jeannie burst into tears, and pulled the young man to her and begged him to reply to her letter when she wrote to him. For those few moments whilst they held on to each other and kissed, it seemed to Michael that nothing else mattered. No words of love had passed between them, yet they both knew that the future held a promise of something wonderful.

The train had been gone for over a minute before Michael felt that he could face Mrs. Banham and Mrs. Robbins. He wiped his eyes, squared his shoulders and strode out of the station to the waiting cab. To the surprise of both women, he kissed them on the cheek, and they were relieved to see that he was smiling just as he used to do before Jeannie came.

Chapter 30

An Historic Day So Soon Overshadowed by Tragedy

The eighteenth of June, Eighteen Ninety-One, was an historic day, for the first planned watering of a Canal section commenced. Although the Company tried to keep the event quiet, there were hundreds of spectators lining the embankment to witness the occasion. By early July, after the river channel approaching the locks had been dredged, the first ship entered the section through Eastham Locks. The vessel was Mr. Samuel Platt's steam yacht, *Norseman*.

Whilst the opening of Eastham Locks was of tremendous significance to all who were involved in the Manchester Ship Canal, the effect was as nothing to Michael compared with the arrival of a letter from Jeannie.

Within a week of her return to Scotland, there had been a positive flurry of letters to Frodsham and Marshville. Beth and Thomas, Will, Peter, Dafyd, and Jessie and Ted Robbins all received the grateful thanks of the girl. Dafyd also received a letter addressed to 'The Angels of Marshville', which he put on show in the shop.

Mrs. Garroway came into the shop clutching her letter. It appeared that she could not read or write, so she had come to ask Will if he could read it out to her. If Jeannie herself had been present to witness the expression of pleasure on Mrs. Garroway's face, it would have been reward enough for the girl.

Captain Howard and Kate, Mrs. Hilyard, Dr. Mills and each of the four girls received letters. A letter also arrived addressed to 'Mr. Donal, Excavator Driver, and all the Angels of the Cut'. And also there was a letter for Michael, which he had so anxiously waited for.

Jeannie confessed in her second letter to Michael that her fingers had got very stiff from writing; she said she had not written so many words since she had left school.

She had been very fortunate, for a few days after returning home, she had started work at the millinery shop where she formerly worked. She assured everybody that the kindly proprietor made sure that she was not on her feet for too long. She promised that she would send a likeness of Flora when she had one taken. Michael did as he had promised; he replied to her as soon as he was able to.

For a long time their letters contained no more than the news of what the other was doing, but as time went by, they poured their hearts out to each other.

Michael went into Frodsham looking very smart, with the intention of having a photograph taken; Jeannie had requested a 'likeness' to show her mother and the little girl just how handsome he was!

Whilst Michael was weaving his dreams of a life with Jeannie, Mr. Manisty the Engineer in charge of the Eastham-Ellesmere Port section, had more down-to-earth matters on his mind: the closing of the Gap at Ellesmere Port.

The Gap had been a thorn in the side of the Company from the start of the construction. It had to be left clear to allow shipping to enter or leave Ellesmere Port docks, and it split the Canal cutting between Eastham Locks and the River Weaver into two sections.

Ellesmere Port, formerly Whitby Locks, was the River Mersey connection for the Ellesmere Canal of the Shropshire Union Railway and Canal Company. Obviously that company had insisted on safeguarding its navigational rights with penalties against the Ship Canal Company if access to the port was interfered with. The reason for closing the Gap was to allow the earth dam between it and the Eastham section to be cut away, making it possible for shipping to come to Ellesmere Port through the locks. This would be of tremendous benefit to the port as it would give shipping many more hours of each tide to enter and leave the Canal and would give a constant water level in the docks, thus eliminating the need for lock gates at the docks entrance.

Prior to the opening of Eastham Locks, Mr. Manisty had employed about three thousand men working round the clock to complete the section, and at the time he was ready to close the Gap, many of the navvies had been put to work on the eleven-mile section to the River Weaver. Others were now about to build the dam which would close the Gap.

As the entrance through Ellesmere Port lock was subject to the state of the tide, there were many hours between the tides when there was no shipping movement.

The engineers had planned to block the Gap during the hours when the tide was low enough to expose the foreshore.

Thomas Banham was in the area by the fact that he had brought a locomotive to the workshop at Ellesmere Port to have the boiler lifted out, Frodsham Depot having no lifting gear capable of handling such weight. With him on the loco was Captain Howard, who had been invited by Mr. Manisty to witness the Gap closure.

By the time they arrived, several train-loads of boulder clay and stone had been tipped and other trains were waiting in line to tip more loads onto the makeshift dam. Then disaster struck. The leading locomotive came off the line and completely blocked any further railway movement.

Thomas, of course, being used to dealing with derailed locomotives and wagons, knew that by the time the derailment had been dealt with, the tide would be licking at the dam. He felt profoundly sorry for the frustrated engineers and the navvies. His mood was not helped by the jeers and catcalls of some of the onlookers. It aggravated him to hear this sort of ill-mannered humour, especially as the new entrance to the docks would bring so many benefits to the town.

Their doubts as to whether the dam would hold were borne out when the tide simply thrust the boulders and clay aside, leaving the Gap unusable for any vessels. The first one was the Liverpool Packet, and the vessel failed to dock at

Ellesmere Port for the first time in fifty-three years! This incurred a penalty to the Company of three hundred pounds each day of stoppage.

The following day's work was just as unsuccessful, and it was to be two more days before the Gap was finally no more. There was jubilation amongst the men who had brought it about, and even the most vociferous of the Canal's detractors were forced to admit the advantages that had been gained by the docks and the town.

Two days later, on the eighteenth of July, the mood of euphoria had changed to one of grief, for one of the worst accidents of the Canal's construction period occurred near Ince.

For Will the news was to have a particularly bad effect. It had been busy at the shop during the morning but after midday few customers were coming in. Outside they could hear the sounds of children playing and the excited barking of a dog. Suddenly the shop filled up with four little girls and, unusually for them, they were all trying to talk at the same time.

Their ages ranged from about eleven years to six years, and they were sisters. The one who usually had the most to say was the second oldest at ten years of age (as she had told them on her last birthday), but she was having the greatest difficulty in saying what she wanted to say above the clamour of the others.

Dafyd and Will really enjoyed the antics of the girls; if they were not racing about with hoops, they were galloping along between two ropes as a team of horses with a driver, or taking it in turns to push each other up and down in their father's wheelbarrow.

But as the words came tumbling out, Dafyd and Will's smiles were wiped off their faces. "Now then, children, one at a time," said the shopkeeper, then pointing to the eldest sister he said, "You tell the tale."

For a moment, unaccustomed to the role which had been thrust upon her, she hesitated, then in a rush said, "Some trains have fallen in the Cut on top of lots of navies."

Will could not speak for a moment; his time on the railway had made him only too aware of how accidents happened, but if the tale was true, then there would be many dead and injured as a consequence. Sadly, they were later to learn that the girls were indeed telling the truth.

Although the full details were not known, everyone learned that two locomotives propelling a train of wagons were turned onto a disused line which terminated at the edge of the cutting. Below, a large number of navvies were working at the base of the slopes. Ten men, including those on the locomotives, were killed and dozens terribly injured. Both locos were destroyed.

The points boy was arrested but the police later released him without charge. If the persons responsible for the track had removed the points controlling entry into the redundant spur line, the accident could not have occurred. However, such was the rush to complete the section, many things were left to be dealt with at a later date. What was significant to Will, and was to have a profound effect on him, was that the points involved were those where the boy had spent such a miserable two months in the early part of the previous year.

Following the accident the people of Marshville grieved as if they had lost friends and yet nobody knew any of those involved. It was simply that they were part of a fellowship. The worst affected was Will. He became noticeably quieter, to such an extent that some of the customers at the shop commented on it to Dafyd.

However, worse was to come. Will started having nightmares, waking up shouting in terror.

The first time it happened Thomas and Beth came awake hearing his anguished shouting and Peter's screams. They found Will sitting up on the mattress sobbing, whilst their youngest son was backed against the wall, crying hysterically.

Beth seized Peter and held him close until he subsided into weeping. Thomas held onto Will, who had gone to his knees, his head in his hands. He said in a broken voice, "I've killed them, I've killed them."

Downstairs, Michael had bounded out of bed and was standing at the foot of the stairs clad in his nightshirt. When he heard the voices of Thomas and Beth he decided that the best thing he could do to help was to make a warm drink for everyone; he was sure that there would be no further for sleep any of them for a while.

After Will had recovered somewhat, he told them that he had dreamed that he was manning the points and had put the train through onto the disused spur line. As the train rolled over the edge into the cutting, his friend Al, who was on the second loco, just smiled at him as he went to his death.

Next door Mr. and Mrs. Robbins, awakened by the noise, came out into the street to see what was wrong, but when everything went quiet but the lamps stayed lit in the Banhams' hut, they decided not to interfere until their help was sought.

Eventually all was quiet and they went back to their beds, but Thomas insisted that Will slept in Victoria's room. After Will had explained to Peter that he had been dreaming and given him a hug, the little boy had quickly gone back to sleep.

It was not easy for the rest of them. Beth blessed Michael for his brew of tea, but neither she nor Thomas slept much for the rest of the night. Will was very contrite the next day and apologised to them all. Peter seemed none the worse for it, but told his brother sternly not to wake him up again.

Dafyd felt really sorry for his assistant; he realised then how badly the accident was affecting the boy.

That night it was just as bad, but Peter did not come fully awake and soon went back to sleep after Beth had been in to see him.

Thomas talked about the problem the following morning with Captain Howard and Michael. The engineer suggested a talk with Dr. Mills, possibly obtaining a sleeping draught. Then Michael spoke up. "Do you mind if I talk to Will, Mr. Banham?" he said hesitantly. "You see, when I was about ten years of age, I suffered a lot from nightmares, and I learned a method of stopping them." Then he laughed and said sheepishly, "It was a little girl who shared my desk at school who told me what to do."

Although Thomas was quite prepared to let Michael talk to his son, he thought that they might be needing Dr. Mills before long.

That evening Michael asked Will to walk down to the workshop with him so that they could talk. The young Irishman told him of a silly dream that he started having as a child, which turned into a terrible nightmare.

He began by telling the boy about one of his teachers, who loved reading German fairy stories out to the class. "Some of them were really frightening," he said, "and we loved them, but one of them must have stuck in my mind, for I started to dream about this little old lady with a Gladstone bag." He gave a shiver and said, "Even thinking of her brings it all back. She would knock on the door and when I answered, she would whisper to me and I would lean forward, then as quick as a flash she brought out her scissors and cut off my ears."

Michael saw the beginnings of a smile on Will's face and took heart from it. "Oh, it is all right you smiling, young Banham," he said sternly, "but it was upsetting for a ten-year-old to wake up with no ears.

"But," he continued, "my little school friend told me to treat the nightmare like a play, one written by my brain, and change the end of the story." He then said to Will, who had been hanging onto every word, "What I did was to lie in bed, close my eyes, then make the dream come into my mind, and when it came to the part where the old lady opened the bag, I made my mammy come from behind me, snatch the scissors and the bag, and order the woman to go away and never come to this house again." Then he said triumphantly, "And do you know, Will, after a few nights, I was never bothered by her again."

The boy cried out, "But that was your imagination; this has happened, this is real." Michael shook his head gently and told the unhappy boy, "No, Will, the accident was real, but your imagination has written the dream, so you write your own version tonight; you write that you have chained the points lever and the train cannot enter the spur line."

Will shook his head, unwilling to believe that the idea would work, and then whispered, "It is as though Al is dead and trying to tell me so." Roughly Michael broke in on Will's anguished words and said, "Oh no, Will, Al is on the train but he is swearing at you for not letting them through."

Michael's urgent tone reached Will and for a moment, he could actually see his friend yelling swear words at him, and he gave a wry smile. That night, Will cried out just once then continued sleeping. His father stood by his bed for a while watching the peaceful face of his son. 'Perhaps Michael has helped him,' Thomas thought, 'let us hope so for the lad's sake.'

The following night there was hardly a sound from the boy, and his parents blessed Michael for his 'cure'.

The final part of Will's recovery came two days later when Al walked into the shop! With scant regard for his pristine white apron, the boy flung himself at the grimy overalled Al and hugged him, much to the young fireman's embarrassment. Dafyd looked on at the reunion with a smile. If he was right in his thinking, this moment would mark an end to any recurrence of Will's torment.

After introducing his friend to Dafyd, Will asked if he could go over to let his mother meet Al, and his employer was only too glad to let him go. Al protested half-heartedly that he was not dressed for meeting ladies, and also that the driver was only stopping for a minute, but really he had long wanted to meet Will's family.

Nevertheless, he was hauled into the hut, whereupon Beth, on hearing who he was, hugged him saying, "Oh, Al, we have been so worried about you."

Will's family was as unlike his own as it was possible to be, and yet Al, for the first time he could recall, had been greeted in much the same manner when his mother had learned of the fatal accident. She had certainly never cried over him and his dad before as he could recall.

Will and Beth learned that Clancy, Bill and others Will had got to know were not amongst the dead, and also that the police had not charged the points boy. Beth even managed to worm out of the boy that his name was short for Alistair, but in spite of Will and his mother saying that they liked the name, he swore them to secrecy on the matter.

Eventually Al went back to the loco, happily carrying several pieces of fruit cake to placate the driver. Will then changed his apron for a clean one and washed his hands before returning to the shop in a very much more settled state of mind.

From then on, Captain Howard and Thomas would say that without Michael's intervention, it would have taken Will a lot longer to rid himself of his nightmare. Thomas solemnly bestowed on him the honorary title of 'Doctor Rourke'.

Even though nobody in Marshville knew any of the deceased, on the day of the funeral most people wore black or black arm bands. The dead were buried in the churchyard of St. James The Great in the village of Ince. Railwaymen, stonemasons, navvies and engineers rubbed shoulders with the villagers and the families of those who had died, all united in grief.

The sombre mood that had descended on Marshville persisted longer than usual. The women were beset with worry, only relaxing when their menfolk returned unharmed each night. It was against this tense and gloomy background that Kate came visiting in her pony trap.

Jessie was showing Beth some material she had bought on Frodsham market when Kate arrived, and as usual when in her late cook's company with somebody else present, she spoke more formally when referring to her husband.

"Good morning, Beth, Mrs. Robbins," she said gaily. "Captain Howard and I have received some wonderful news from Reeve House. Charlotte has been blessed with a baby boy, and we were relieved to hear that both mother and child are very well."

Even as she finished telling them her news, tears had started to fall. Beth put her arms around Kate, glad to be there for her former mistress to turn to in a moment like this. For weeks they had all been worrying about James's wife and the unborn child, and she knew that the thankful tears were what Thomas referred to as 'a woman's safety valve'.

Meanwhile Jessie had put the kettle to boil, and later, after they had enjoyed a refreshing drink, Kate told them her other happy news.

"My dear Mary has received a letter from one of the men in my husband's employ," she said, smiling impishly. "He is one of the under-gardeners and is a most cheerful, engaging young man." She went on to explain that Jem, his full name being Jeremy, had written to Captain Howard and herself requesting permission to write to her maid, and of course they were only too happy to grant him his wish.

"Obviously he is quite at liberty to correspond with Mary whatever our thoughts on the matter are, but still it shows at least that he has good manners."

Beth, who was very fond of Mary, said, "Well, I am sure he is a suitable person, Miss Kate, for I don't think you would approve of Mary being involved with the young man if you had any doubts about him."

Kate smiled and replied, "Captain Howard certainly thinks highly of Jem, he is a fine-looking boy, fair-haired and with an engaging freckle face." Then she added with a giggle, "It does not surprise me that my dear Mary is all of a flutter."

Before Kate left, she made her customary visit to see Will and Dafyd, then afterwards made her way back to Frodsham, where she intended to give the news to Mrs. Hilyard and to Mrs. Joyce.

After their visitor had gone, Jessie turned to her friend and said, "That is just what we needed, Beth, a cheerful piece of news to take us out of this misery which surrounds us." Beth nodded and answered thoughtfully, "You are right, Jessie, it is a good thing to be reminded that whatever happens, life goes on, and I say bless the child for that."

Chapter 31

Saltport

With the opening of the entry section of the Canal, those working on the section up to the River Weaver knew that for them, the work was nearly at an end. For those working at the Frodsham Depot the future prospects regarding their employment were not so clear-cut.

Also, for the families at Marshville, there was the gloomy certainty that they would soon be having to move, but as yet not knowing where their menfolk's work would take them next, or even if there was work for them at all. However, it was not just those at Marshville and the Depot who were facing the coming months with trepidation.

Victoria had long been aware that the time was nearing when the workshops and the facilities of Frodsham Depot would probably be redundant and she was beset by worries about her parents and their future. Even if her father did find a job locally, there was the vexing problem of finding a house, and she knew without being told that he would not go back to Wroxing. Her thoughts turned to Dafyd. The shop would certainly have to close and he would go back to Chester and rejoin his father's business. Will would also be joining the Hughes family business if Dafyd had his way. Where did it leave her? she wondered. She loved the man so much and Victoria knew that he felt just as strongly about herself, yet since their engagement he had never said how long it would be before they would marry.

The young man himself had given the future a great deal of thought these last few months. How much longer could the shop continue to exist when the people of Marshville started to move out of the 'village'? Of particular concern to him, was where would Victoria's parents go? Perhaps Captain Howard had already made plans which included the Banham family, but he was sure that they would have discussed any future prospects between themselves, and as yet he had heard nothing from Will on the subject.

Although he had not attempted to rush Victoria about setting a date for their marriage, he was anxious to do so soon. It would mean that her future at least would be assured. Also, if Will agreed to come to Chester and join the Hughes grocery business, he, Dafyd, would be of help to two members of the Banham family. He just wished he could do more for them.

Will was aware that Dafyd was sure that he would be an asset to their family business and he did not have any objection to his employer's suggestion, for he had taken to the trade like a duck to water. Facing facts, he could not see the shop staying open for many more weeks after the completion of their immediate section of the Canal. Like Dafyd and Victoria, he was worried sick about his parents' situation, for he thought that it was quite probable that Frodsham Depot would be shut down in the near future.

For Beth, it was a time when her dearest wish, that of getting away from Marshville, was to be granted, yet she was now frightened of what hardship the closure of the Depot would bring to her and Thomas. She wondered whether there would be any jobs thereabouts for a man with her husband's skills. Just as serious, she thought, would there be any Frodsham landlord willing to let a house to them, knowing that they were former Marshville dwellers? More than ever she wished that they were in a house that did not depend on her husband's employment.

There was no doubt in Michael's mind: he knew what he was going to do. If or when the workshops were closed, he would move to be near Jeannie. He had all the confidence of the young and all the recklessness of the lovelorn.

Jessie Robbins already had her future planned out. She was determined to open a shop and she wanted one in Frodsham. Her husband Ted was quite happy to fall in with her ambitions; he himself had tired of moving around from one place to another and had decided that he would look for a job as a bookkeeper in the town or within travelling distance of the town.

Most of those living in Marshville were inured to moving from one contract to another, and whilst the prospect of moving was not welcome, it was accepted as part of their lives. Some of those not connected with the workshops had already been promised jobs elsewhere, but for the others, it was an uneasy period whilst they waited to hear what the next few months would bring.

Captain Howard had decided when he and Kate married he would finish with the business of contracting. After all, he had kept himself busy for years simply to take his mind off Kate when she was his sister-in-law. He was very happy to settle in any place that his dear wife chose. His main concern was that he would leave his workers, especially Thomas Banham, with no prospects and nowhere to live. That is, unless the family stayed on at the hut whilst his foreman looked for a job. Somehow he did not think Beth would enjoy that, especially as he could see Dafyd Hughes's shop closing down. Meanwhile, he would see what he could do on Thomas's behalf to find him another position.

Kate was happy enough to be wherever her husband would be and when his work was finished here at Frodsham, she was quite prepared to settle at his family home at Milford if that is what Richard wanted. And she had decided that soon she would talk with James and Charlotte about them taking Longfields permanently. No money would be involved for, as she said to her husband, it was not her money that had paid for the estate.

Richard had talked to her some weeks ago about the imminent completion of the Ellesmere Port-River Weaver section of the Canal and the probability of leaving Frodsham in a few months' time. On hearing that it would mean the closure of Frodsham Depot, Kate had immediately begun to concern herself with the possible plight of the Banham family. She was only too aware of the difficulties they had encountered trying to find a house locally, and the thoughts of them being left homeless and Thomas without work for a second time upset her very much. As before, she hoped that Richard would be able to help them.

Sarah Mills was also aware of what the finishing of the section would mean for Ian Blake. He would be moving away from Frodsham and onto another job. She could never bring herself to voice the depths of her feelings for Ian, not even to her friend Victoria. The friendship between her and Ian flourished due to a shared love of certain writers and composers, to the appreciation of the countryside and a lively interest in people and events. But he had never shown by deed or words that he was hoping to share a future with her. Her father, a perceptive man, felt helpless in a case like this; he too was surprised that young Blake had not announced his intentions to date.

The possibility that he would have to move from Frodsham troubled Ian Blake a great deal. He had thought long and hard about whether to leave Captain Howard's employ when they were finished with the Depot, and find a job that did not depend on where the next contract would take him. The truth was, he would dearly like to marry Sarah and settle down, possibly in Frodsham, but although they got along famously, he was not sure that her feelings for him were any more than just platonic.

He had come to the conclusion that he must very soon risk rejection and ask her to marry him. If she did not reject him, he would tender his resignation to Captain Howard when the work at the Depot was over.

Even as the various persons were worrying about the effects of the canal works being completed, a scheme was being prepared that would allay everyone's fears.

A meeting was held in August at the Bear's Paw between the engineers and certain contractors to discuss the creation of a new port, which was to be situated near the confluence of the River Weaver and the Canal. Captain Howard and Ian Blake were amongst those at the meeting.

It had been decided that in the first year, as shipping would only be able to come as far as the embankment separating the mouth of the Weaver and the River Mersey, a new set of jetties needed to be constructed.

The decision to build the new 'port' was prompted by the necessity to close Runcorn Docks for an extended period at some time in the coming months. Runcorn Docks was where the Duke of Bridgewater's canal connected with the River Mersey. A considerable amount of trade passed through the docks, and as they and the Bridgewater canal belonged to the Manchester Ship Canal Company, the revenue from the port of Runcorn would be badly missed by the money-strapped company when the port was closed.

Obviously, when the embankment and locks between the river and Runcorn were being constructed there would be no shipping movement possible, and it was proposed that the traffic be diverted through the River Weaver, hence the need for a new port facility.

The new jetties being proposed would have to be built quickly and a decision was reached that they would be made of timber to speed up construction.

Captain Howard was asked if he would undertake to keep Frodsham Depot working beyond the term of his contract, as there had to be at least two locomotives and three cranes in use. There were also other pieces of equipment to be maintained, and in all it would necessitate keeping the workshop running.

He agreed, but with the proviso that the Company should take over the Depot and the workshop after the Canal was completed.

Two days after the meeting, he was in a position to be able to tell the men at the Depot and workshop that the Company had agreed to his suggestion regarding the Depot and that they would take responsibility for the running of it after he, Captain Howard, had left. The following morning he addressed the men and told them about the new port and the subsequent need to keep the depot and workshop open for a few more years.

It was as if a collective sigh of relief went through the assembled group, for apart from Michael and two of the machinists, the men had no idea what employment would be for them at the end of Captain Howard's contract. They all knew by then that he would be giving up the business, so it was a case of finding another contractor who would employ them or leave the contract business and look for other work. The two elderly machinists were actually looking forward to retiring before too long anyway, so they were not really concerned about the closure of the workshops.

As for poor Michael, he had set his heart on moving to Scotland and finding a job near to Jeannie, and the unexpected news had left him in a quandary as to what he should do.

Ellesmere Port and the entrance to the River Weaver were being cleared of equipment and temporary buildings. The piledrivers were being moved up beyond Frodsham Depot and were being set up on both sides of the cutting. In the cutting itself, all railway tracks had been removed, but sitting on one side was a dredger. This had been brought to the site in parts and assembled ready to be floated when the section was watered. There were several of these vessels along the length of the Canal.

The Dutch fascine workers were laying the osier mats on the slopes and spreading the soil which would afterwards be sown with grass seed.

Very soon the construction of the jetties got under way. Train-loads of huge timber piles were delivered and the piledrivers, the 'Long Toms', were soon driving the piles into the sides of the cutting. The noise could be heard and felt in Marshville, even though the huts were about half a mile away from the jetties, and it started at first light, sometimes not finishing until well after dusk.

Beth and Jessie tried to console themselves with the thought that at least it was bringing more work for the men at the Depot, but some days, especially when the wind was in the east, the noise made them thankful for the necessity of spending time shopping in Frodsham.

Observing the number of timber-trains passing the workshops, with no sign of stone, bricks or cement, Thomas commented thoughtfully, "It looks to be something of a structure meant to last but a short time only." To which Michael replied, "I would certainly agree with you there, Mr. Banham, but the Canal is being built by money from Manchester and the surrounding towns to bring goods to those places, so I suppose they would not want too much of it going elsewhere."

Thomas nodded his agreement and concluded, "So it would seem that once the whole of the Canal is completed, the work will die out at this port and we at the Depot will not be needed. It makes you wonder how long this place," sweeping his hand, indicating the workshops, "will be kept going." Both men were silent, each with his own thoughts. Michael did not want to leave his foreman short-handed, yet he was anxious to move nearer to Jeannie and the new port was stopping him from going.

Thomas estimated that the Canal would be completed and taking ships to Manchester by the year 'Ninety-Two', which gave him and Beth another sixteen months or so before he would be out again looking for work.

With regard to Michael, he had seen how the news of the extension to the life of the Depot had subdued the young Irishman, and knowing why, he sympathised with him. After talking with Captain Howard about his thoughts on the matter, their employer suggested that Michael had some time away from Frodsham, and paid the young lady a visit.

Later that day Thomas spoke to his fitter, mentioning Captain Howard's suggestion and began by saying, "We are not so busy at the moment, Michael, but once the new port is being used, it is probable that there will be plenty of work for us."

Michael just nodded his head; he knew that his foreman was leading up to something, but was happily surprised when Thomas said, "Michael, Captain Howard and I think it is an ideal time for you to take a few days off, and I am sure that Jeannie would be able to find lodgings for you if you should have a mind to visit Glasgow." Then he added with a grin, "If the dynamo breaks down, I can always send you a telegram."

The younger man's face was a study; whatever he was expecting to hear, it was not that. Then a joyous smile swept his face and he said enthusiastically, "I will write a letter to Jeannie tonight and let her know that I am coming." He held out his hand and said, "Thanks, Mr. Banham."

Afterwards he was so buoyed up and so like his old self that even the blacksmith, on hearing him singing, popped his head around the workshop door and jokingly complained about the terrible noise coming from the fitting shop!

When Thomas told Beth about their lodger's proposed holiday, she was worried that he might be in for a disappointment when meeting Jeannie on her home ground. Whilst he agreed with her, he observed that even though the girl arrived dirty and in rags, and taking into account that she had endured a terrible journey, he was inclined to think that she would never be like that normally. "In Jeannie's favour," he pointed out, "you, Jessie, and all the girls had no misgivings about her, and I am sure that you would have noticed if the girl was not as decent as she might have been." Beth nodded her head at that.

"Anyway," he added, "if Michael finds that the girl is not all he imagines her to be, then sad as it will be, it is better that he finds out soon rather than too late."

As it turned out, the visit was a success. Michael returned after a week away and was full of tales concerning Jeannie, Flora and Jeannie's mother, who, he said, treated him like a king. The little girl, Flora, had been very wary of him at first, but as the days went by, she had got used to him. He did not make too much fuss of her, although he would have loved to have had her climb on his knee, but he reasoned that if she got too fond of him on the first visit, Flora would have been very upset when he left them.

Jeannie was just as lovely as he remembered her and he had made his mind up: he would certainly be settling in Scotland when he was finished at Frodsham Depot.

It was Victoria's day off, and as the weather was so beautiful, Dafyd suggested having a picnic and inviting Sarah Mills and Ian Blake to accompany them. Sarah immediately volunteered the use of her father's pony and trap, for she knew that he would be away visiting his friends on that day. Having the trap meant that they could go further afield, and in the end they chose to go to a place that Sarah had been with her father when she was younger.

The picnic spot was alongside the River Weaver and was a really pretty, secluded place. There were no commercial vessels moving on the river that day, just one man wearing a straw boater rowing in a leisurely fashion.

Later, after they had rested following a pleasant meal, pleasant, that is, except for the attentions of the wasps, Dafyd hoisted himself to his feet and proposed a short walk along the river bank to settle their stomachs.

"Do you mind if we don't come with you, Dafyd?" said Ian in a rather diffident manner. "There is something I would like to discuss with Sarah." Then, turning to the startled girl, he added anxiously, "That is, if you have no objection, my dear?" Sarah shook her head wordlessly; she wondered if he was about to tell her that he would be leaving Frodsham soon or something of the like.

Victoria saw things differently than her friend, and rose to her feet saying, "Right, Mr. Hughes, we will enjoy the wonders of nature for half an hour. Which way are we going?" With a little wave at the others, they strolled leisurely towards the next lock.

Once their friends had left them, Sarah faced Ian, her composed features belying the turmoil in her mind. Ian, though uneasy about the outcome of what he had to say, nevertheless was certain of the way Sarah would prefer to be addressed on such a serious matter. She would appreciate plain words with no doubts as to their meaning.

"Sarah," he began gently, "for a long time now I have enjoyed your company and the benefits of your conversation, and I do not want to lose that. I can see only one way of continuing to enjoy those pleasures, and that is to hope, no, pray, that you would consent to be my wife." Even as he said it, he realised how cold and businesslike his proposal had sounded.

For a few moments there was silence between them, and Ian thought miserably that Sarah was thinking of how to word a refusal without hurting his feelings, when suddenly she answered simply, "Yes, Ian."

The stunned young man thought for a moment that Sarah had not understood what he was proposing and said a little uncertainly, "Er, did you mean that you will marry me, Sarah?" She nodded her head gravely and answered, "Yes, Ian. However, you mention that you enjoy my company and conversation, which is very complimentary, but you did not mention love or even affection, the ingredients that a woman prefers in a marriage."

With a shout of delight Ian leapt to his feet and cried, "Oh Sarah, how dense I am! Love, affection, for you I have those aplenty, and if it pleases you, dear Sarah," he said in a more serious tone, "I will say to you that I love you, Sarah Mills, much more than I can say in simple terms."

As Victoria and Dafyd came in sight of their picnic spot, the girl held the young man back and whispered, "Hold back for a few minutes, Dafyd, I think it is not the right moment to intrude."

Dafyd glanced at his fiancée and said with a smile, "The right moment, Victoria. We usually wait for the right moment to make important pronouncements, to show by some token what we feel or think." Then he grinned and said mischievously, "Do you think my raising the question of when we are to marry is important?"

Victoria, entering into the spirit of the game pretended to seriously consider the question, then replied breathlessly. "Well, I suppose there are plenty of instances when the moment was the wrong one, such as, er, well when you had just eaten something which disagreed with your stomach, or perhaps," she said impishly, "when you are standing near a pigsty feeding the animals, or even if you had bent down to pick up a farthing and then lost a golden guinea."

"How imaginative you are, my love," said Dafyd with a broad smile. "But I believe that today the scent from the fields and flowers could not be sweeter, and we have eaten and suffered no ill-effects, and I promise you, my love, should a farthing appear before my very eyes, I will conceal it with my foot."

Victoria dropped her playful pose and said earnestly, "And if I agree that this is the right moment to discuss when we might marry, had you a date in mind, Dafyd Hughes?"

Equally serious, he spoke about the reasons why he had held back on the matter. "Some months ago, Victoria, I was convinced that by the end of this year, Frodsham Depot would be closed, Marshville would hardly be home for more than three or four families, and the shop would be unable to earn enough to stay open." Then he said quietly, "That was the time I planned to concentrate on our future, but the truth is that I could not see us blithely going ahead with our plans when your family were facing so much uncertainty."

He put his arms around her shoulders and said sombrely, "How many times this year have we worried about the fate of your mam and dad when the Depot closes, and now, at a stroke, they are not out of home and your dad still has a job." Then he added, "Whilst I am naturally pleased and relieved, I was hoping to be finished with the shop soon, and free to marry you, set up our own home, and now I have to keep the shop open for goodness knows how long."

Victoria kissed him on the cheek and said, "That is another side of you that I love, Dafyd, your consideration for others, but harking back to our affairs, now that those difficulties have been resolved, is there anything to stop us from marrying in June next year?" Dafyd kissed her properly and answered lovingly, "Nothing at all, my love."

Before they walked back to their friends, Victoria said quietly, "We will not say anything to Sarah and Ian because I do believe that they may have something important to tell us, and I want this afternoon to be special for them."

When they reached the picnic spot, Sarah was putting everything back in the baskets and Ian was feeding bits of apple to the pony. With a patently assumed nonchalance Ian said to Sarah, "Shall I tell them our news, dear, or do you want the pleasure of telling them yourself?" Sarah nodded, then in an unnaturally bright sort of voice said, "Ian has asked me if I would be his wife and I have said yes."

Victoria flung herself down alongside her friend with a cry of joy, hugged her and at that, Sarah's precarious hold on her emotions disappeared and she wept on Victoria's shoulder.

Dafyd was quite affected and, turning to Ian, held out his hand and congratulated him. Unfortunately Ian was still holding the remains of the apple, and Dafyd ended up with bits of the fruit between his fingers. The pony promptly nuzzled between the two men and nearly chomped on their hands!

The tear-wet faces of the two girls turned to the astounding spectacle of the two men waving their hands about whilst the pony, seemingly thinking that this was a new playful way of being fed, ambled after them braying loudly.

Sarah and Victoria dissolved into helpless laughter and it was a few minutes before everybody was able to talk without bursting into fits of giggling. Later, when the men were escorting the girls home, it was fervently agreed that it had been the happiest picnic any of them had ever been on.

The following week was a not so satisfactory for Beth. One afternoon, Mrs. Guest brought the boys back from school and as she came to Peter's front door Beth met her to thank her as she usually did, only to be handed a note from the school. Mrs. Guest was not the nicest woman in the village and she gave Beth a false sympathetic smile but with just a hint of malice in her eyes. It was not the first note that had been sent from the school regarding Peter, and his mother was seething that this was the second one delivered by Mrs. Guest.

Her youngest son stood near the table with the usual penitent expression on his face whilst he waited for the note to be read and the lecture that always followed. Beth already knew of his daydreaming in class, of his reputation as the class comic and his innocent utterances on subjects not normally spoken of, subjects that reduced those around him to guilty sniggers or embarrassment, dependent on the age or status of his listeners.

"Oh, Peter," groaned his mother. "Not privies again, why must you keep bringing those into your conversation? I have told you many times before, it is not nice to mention the subject in polite company."

"But, Mam, it wasn't me who started it," said Peter desperately. "It was Goff Bolton and I didn't mention, you know, privies, it was him, he said we didn't have them, he said we live like savages and go behind bushes and, well, you know."

Beth went cold and closed her eyes in distaste, then opening them she said grimly, "They do not sound a very nice lot of children in your class, Peter, but why did Miss Bryant send me this?" and held up the note. Her son said, wriggling uncomfortably, "Well, Mam, Miss Bryant heard me tell Goff Bolton that the, you know, were kept very clean and were emptied every week by Lavender Joe."

He stopped at his mother's gasp. "Now, Peter," she said angrily, "I have told you once before, only coarse people give them that name, they are night soil men if you have to mention them, and I DO NOT want you to mention those things again, do you understand, son?" Peter nodded his head miserably, but he still could not see why grown-ups had so many daft rules about what you could say and what you could not say.

Later that night when Peter was in bed asleep, the men had difficulty stopping themselves from bursting into laughter. "That Peter of yours," said Michael, wiping the tears from his eyes, "has a mind of his own, or should I say, he has a questioning mind, and if I am right it will stand him in good stead in the future."

"Well, Michael," said Beth doubtfully, "maybe you are right, I don't know. I find myself worrying what he will come out with next, especially when we are at Chapel."

Thomas laughed and said, "I am inclined to agree with Michael, but the boy is still young, he will eventually learn the rules." Then he added, "Our Peter is what the Navy men refer to as a 'loose cannon', and I think that I prefer him that way."

By September the piledriving was almost finished and much of the jetty decking was in place. Within days the water was lapping around the feet of the piles and two weeks later the whole seven-mile section from the River Weaver along to Ellesmere Port was filled to the working level. This meant that the first ten and a half miles of the Canal was completed.

It was a wonderful sight for all those who had worked on the construction, and also for the crowds of visitors who flocked to see it. The number of people coming through the 'village' increased enormously, much to the displeasure of those who lived there.

Dafyd, however much sympathy he had for the Marshville dwellers, was pleased at the way his profits soared, and several times Will was sent up to Frodsham to buy extra milk, bread and cakes as well as other edible items.

The Twenty-Eighth of September was an historic date for the Manchester Ship Canal Company and for the people of Marshville, for on that day the steamship *Fanny*, carrying the Company directors, arrived from Liverpool for an inspection of the new port. Very few were aware of the planned visit; consequently there were not many people around to witness the event.

From that date onwards vessels carrying cargo began to arrive, the first being the barque *Lancashire* with fifteen hundred tons of pitch pine, from Mobile, Alabama. That was in late October, and on the Tenth of November the first foreign-owned vessel, the Norwegian ship *Deodata*, arrived carrying a further cargo of timber.

The first auction of timber was turned into a fiasco when the Liverpool merchants simply turned their backs to the auctioneer and refused to bid. However, their pointed gesture did them no good at all. The Company set up another auction and advertised that the timber would be split up into smaller lots. By the end of the day every stand of timber was sold, heralding the end of the

Liverpool monopoly. From that day on, there was no further trouble in selling the timber.

On the Thirteenth of November, *Hellen*, a vessel of four thousand tons, docked. Most of the ships using the port were by then taking cargoes outward, salt, coal, and pottery being the main bulk of this traffic. The new port had attracted the unofficial name of 'Saltport'.

By the end of the year, a very satisfying number of ships were calling at the new port. Unfortunately for the Company, just as was in the case of the shipping traffic up to Ellesmere Port, no tolls could be charged. However, port and other associated fees earned the Company much-needed revenue.

Chapter 32

Sarah Mills Acts Out of Character, and a Wedding Takes Place

To the many visitors who came to view the Canal, it would appear that the scheme was then completed. Indeed, the sight of the tall, graceful barques with sails furled, or the strings of Weaver and Mersey flats being towed by sturdy tugs, and the steamships passing towards or away from the new port, tended to reinforce that impression.

Even some of the denizens of Marshville seemed to have come to a state of mind that the worst part of the task was done. But the most optimistic of them could not blind themselves to the fact that on the other side of the earth dam near the mouth of the River Weaver, thousands of men and the machines were still toiling to construct the section skirting Runcorn.

Before the end of the year, floods once again halted parts of the upper sections of the cutting, but this time they were not quite as extensive as on previous occasions. However, on the financial side, yet again there was call for more money, and it was answered by Manchester Corporation when a further two million pounds was pledged.

Michael and the Banhams were reminded of the predictions of Dr. Mills and wondered if he was going to be proved right after all. One thing by then was certain: the completion date for the whole scheme was moving further away each day.

Christmas and New Year in Marshville at the close of Eighteen Ninety-One was a relatively peaceful time compared with the same period of previous years. The workshop men were especially thankful for that. Gone was the frantic rush to deal with the urgent repairs and breakdowns. Such jobs did come to the Depot but were not so pressing.

Michael managed to visit his parents, but again was glad to be back to Marshville, worn out after a hectic family gathering.

Beth and Thomas had to watch what they spent at Christmas, knowing that the following year would bring the extra expense of Victoria and Dafyd's wedding. Their savings had been steadily growing with all the overtime and night call-outs Thomas had worked, and after their near state of destitution, they never wanted to be in that situation again. Therefore, as delighted they were at Victoria's approaching wedding, they were naturally worried about how much they could afford to spend.

Dafyd's parents were as aware of the situation as were the Banhams, and arranged to call on them at Marshville to talk it over. Thomas, who had not had the pleasure of meeting them before, was instantly taken with Alwyn and Rebecca Hughes, and found his reservations about sharing the costs of the wedding being put to one side. By the time the Hughes's were ready to leave, they had come to an arrangement whereby the cost of the carriages and photographer was to be borne by Dafyd's parents, and the rest was to be borne by Thomas and Beth.

Another very welcome gesture by Mr. Hughes was the offer of obtaining the materials for the dresses at a lot lower price than Beth could have managed. She had lately come to the conclusion that the dream design of a wedding gown for her only daughter would not be possible due to the cost, but with Mr. Hughes's help, Beth believed that she could manage to do it as she had planned after all.

When she did make the bridal gown, such was her quest for perfection that it took the same length of time to make as it did for the bridal attendants' dresses, and there were four of those!

The fourth bridal attendant was to be Bronwen Hughes, Dafyd's cousin, which caused something of a problem for Beth. To solve the difficulty of taking the girl's measurements, Dafyd was to bring her back with him after he had been to visit his parents, and she was to stay with Mrs. Hilyard. As well as visiting Beth, the girl would be able to meet the other girls and get to know them.

Victoria and Dafyd were also busy. With their limited time they were hard pressed to find a few hours in which they could search for a house to live when they were married. With the problems of renting houses in the town, and the limited space in the cupboard-like room at the back of the shop, they came to the sad conclusion that Victoria would be better off staying on with Mrs. Hilyard, leaving Dafyd (with his exceptionally early starting time) living at the shop. It was the early-morning start which put paid to their renting rooms at a cottage on High Street. The owners were not prepared to put up with Dafyd waking them at that time in the morning. Also Victoria and Dafyd did not like the idea of sharing the kitchen and dining room with the owners.

The alternative was for Dafyd to give up the shop and the two of them to move to Christleton where Dafyd's parents had made some rooms ready for their son and his bride. After the unfortunate experience involving the aggressive Mr. Jowet and his eagerness to profit from the situation at Marshville, Dafyd was loath to inflict such a burden on those who lived there, and Victoria wholeheartedly agreed with him, and with regard to living apart, it would only be for a short time; after all, she reasoned, the Canal would be completed sometime in the near future. As it turned out, the girl was being very optimistic; on a scheme as difficult as this, a lot could go wrong, and so it was to prove.

Although Dafyd blessed the shop for being the means whereby he met Victoria, he was now finding that it was something of a millstone around his neck.

One Sunday afternoon they were taking advantage of the dry, bright weather and having a walk along the canal embankment. The sun was out, the sky was a washed blue but the cool breeze which prevailed did not encourage people to merely stroll. There were a good number of walkers that day; the embankment on the Frodsham side of the Manchester Ship Canal had become quite a favourite place for a promenade in spite of the railway tracks and rough uneven ground

After a while, they came across one of the drinks sellers accompanied by a young woman. As they came level with the couple, the girl, who at that moment was putting milk into a customer's cup, smiled at Dafyd, then briefly at Victoria. Dafyd touched the brim of his bowler hat and returned the girl's smile before walking on. They had walked but a few yards when Victoria said with a mock serious tone, "Well, Mr. Hughes, pray who is that girl who smiled so familiarly at you?" Replying in a similar vein Dafyd said, "Well that, my sweet, is Lucy Parks, and now you have seen her, I will have to confess." At that point he paused to create an effect, then facing the startled Victoria he continued, "You see, my dear, the girl has developed a habit of coming into the shop for sugar, milk and other supplies and, well you know how it is." Again he stopped, but by now Dafyd could see that Victoria was looking at him quite seriously and he judged that his banter might not seem so humorous to her, so he finished quickly by saying, "And you see, my true love, I believe she has taken a shine to your brother."

"Will?" exclaimed Victoria in surprise, and Dafyd laughed, and said, "Yes, Will, surely you can see what a catch your brother is. He is a fine young man, and I would have thought that even you, his sister, could see how handsome he would appear to other young ladies."

"Oh yes," said Victoria thoughtfully, "Will is a fine boy and I know he is handsome, and a lot more than that, he is gentle but he is brave." Then she said soberly, "And I love him, and I do not want him to be hurt by the wrong sort of girl."

Dafyd looked at her quizzically and as if in reply to his unspoken thoughts, Victoria asked him, "Do you think I am acting as though the Banham family are too good for the girl Lucy?" Then before Dafyd could answer she added, "She has a lovely face and such beautiful eyes, but I feel that she is wrong for Will."

Her fiancé laughed at her last observation and said, "Those beautiful eyes have been displayed to full effect on your brother at the shop and I can assure you, my love, Will appeared completely unaffected."

In that, Dafyd was very much in error, for the first sight of Lucy when she entered the shop had affected his assistant dramatically. He felt as though his heart would burst through his chest, and when she turned those wonderful eyes on him he went weak at the knees.

It was only by making a supreme effort that he appeared cool and unaffected by the girl. Even as he was passing through this welter of emotions, the image of Lucy clinging to the other man at Helsby sidings insisted on intruded into his brain as it had done many times since. The boy ruefully knew that she was not for him, despite the fact that she drew him like a magnet draws iron.

Poor Will: he was in the grip of emotions he had never experienced before and he hovered between the urge to get to know her more, to convince himself that Lucy was seriously taken with him, or whether to consider that he was just another conquest and forget her. At the back of his mind, though, he was sure that the last part was the truth.

If his mother had not been so involved in the preparations for the wedding, she might have noticed that her son was not his usual self, but Beth's main preoccupation at that time was the design and making of Victoria's wedding dress. Once she had arrived at an idea for something that her daughter would be happy with, she then would put her mind to the design for the bridal attendants' dresses and the materials to be used.

Beth blessed Dafyd's father for offering to get the materials much cheaper, for she was now making the sleeves of Victoria's gown in fine lace, something she had set her heart on doing.

One useful piece of information came out of Lucy's visits: word of a house for rent in Helsby. In an attempt to engage Will in conversation, she told him that her father had considered moving to a better house, but when he learned the amount the landlady was asking for the rent he decided not to bother going to see it. Before Lucy left the shop, Will had obtained the address to pass on to his parents. Dafyd, in view of his eagerness to have a house for Victoria and himself, was generous enough to let the Banhams have the first chance to see it.

When Beth realised where it was, she was disappointed. With it being over two miles away from Marshville, like some of the others they had gone to see, it was a long way for her husband to walk every morning and back again each night, but Thomas insisted that at least they would have a look at it as soon as he could get some time off from his work.

They decided to take the train to Helsby from Frodsham and that part of the journey took only a few minutes. A short walk led them to the lane on which the house was situated. The weather had been quite dull when they started out, but the threatened rain had held off, something they were thankful for. Both Thomas and Beth were rather disappointed at the neglected state of the place; as they approached the front door, the sun broke through, bathing the house in sunlight, but even with the sunshine on it, the place did not look very inviting.

The smiling woman who opened the door to them looked well dressed and clean, but there was an odd sickly smell in the hall. Thomas recognised the smell from a lodging house he had stayed in for a short while when he worked in London. Sure enough, as they entered one room, the source of the smell was plain to see. The warming sun's rays on the curtains showed several bed bugs crawling towards the shaded parts of the curtains! Beth abandoned any pretence of polite behaviour: she just wanted to get out of the house as fast as she could.

"Now then, my dear," said the house owner. "They do you no harm; they never bothered my other tenants, I'm sure." But her cheerful, if less accurate observation had no effect on Beth, who was backing out of the room in horror.

Thomas looked at the beaming woman in disgust. "Why, this house is not fit to live in," he said coldly. "I would advise you to get something done about it. We certainly will not be taking on the tenancy." Then he wheeled round and followed his wife out into the fresh, clean air.

As they went back to the station, Beth was in a hurry and she kept brushing her hand over her skirts. "Ugh," she said, grimacing. "That house was horrible, and that woman smiling as though everything was just right, as though it was normal to have those things crawling all over."

After leaving Frodsham station they hurried towards Marsh Lane, and then Beth said something which pleasantly surprised her husband. She said, "I will be glad to get home to wash and change into fresh, clean clothes. I feel as though the things are crawling all over me." Although Thomas did not say anything at the time, he was really pleased to hear Beth use the term 'home' when referring to the hut at Marshville, for she had never called it home before.

Soon after that unsettling episode, a much more cheerful event took place. A concert was to be held in the Victoria Room on Chapel Lane, and it was held to raise some money towards repairs to the Chapel. The tone was to be happy, tuneful, and even rib-tickling (in the best of taste of course). As expected with amateur performers interested in taking part, singers were in the majority and the musicians mostly played piano. To bring variety to the concert, people not belonging to the Chapel were allowed to join in.

The start of the concert could have been marred by the last-minute withdrawal of the man who was to act as Master of Ceremonies, but his place being taken by a fellow Chapel member, Mr. Deakin. The last named gentleman, an official with the Frodsham Gas Works, had a reputation of having never been known to smile; in fact, going further than that, he frowned upon others who had the temerity to smile in Chapel. As it was, with some of the more problematical of the acts, he was later seen as the ideal Master of Ceremonies.

Victoria had been asked to open the proceedings with two pieces, the first being a cheerful polka, the second a waltz, both by Johan Strauss. It was a very lively start to the evening and the audience obviously enjoyed the tunes and the playing.

In the audience were the other members of the Banham family and, amazingly, it was the first time that any of them had heard her play properly. Thomas and Beth were so overcome with emotion at Victoria's playing that they both sat there with tears in their eyes. Thomas had to restrain himself from turning to those around him and telling them that the wonderful piano player was their daughter.

Will was just as affected; he sat there his eyes glued proudly on his sister. Even Peter, although a little bored with most of the performers, was proud of his big sister Victoria.

The first act to follow Victoria was a large lady who was accompanied by her own pianist. She sang a tragic song of betrayed love with so much dramatic posturing that the message in the lyrics was lost. Her habit of gazing upwards to the roof rafters whilst holding her hands to her breast, and lamenting the mistake of 'trusting her heart to the wayward son of the squire', at first caused a few chuckles, but then led to outright laughter from the less inhibited members of the audience. Her dramatic finale, with her head down, eyes closed, and hands clasped in supplication, was excruciating. No sooner had her voice, throbbing with emotion, died away, than Mr. Deakin was there thanking her and quickly leading her off the platform. She was followed by her incompetent pianist, who loudly complained of the disgraceful condition of the piano, ignoring the fact that not many minutes before, Victoria had produced perfect notes on the same instrument.

There was a ripple of laughter when the Master of Ceremonies introduced the next act. Two brothers, both of them under fourteen years of age, one towering over the other, were to play some tunes on mouth organs.

The tallest boy, his face brick red with shyness, had to be almost pulled onto the platform by his younger brother. It was then that Mr. Deakin showed the other side of his nature. He gently talked to the boys and ended up by allowing the older of the brothers to face away from the audience whilst they played!

The sympathetic murmur of laughter from those present died completely when the boys played, for they were very accomplished players for their age. Each tune they played was greeted with enthusiastic clapping, and at the end of their turn, whether it was their youth or simply that they had chosen cheerful, foot-tapping tunes and played them well, but they earned rapturous applause. Both boys, beaming from ear to ear, were thanked by Mr. Deakin before they left the platform.

Mrs. Tanner, singer of the more respectable of the music hall songs, managed to slip in a third song before a wrathful Master of Ceremonies hauled her off. This was particularly embarrassing for Victoria, as she had only been given sheet music for the first two songs and she had to follow the third tune at a delayed pace. The woman's coquettish style in her first song earned her good applause, but her second song brought her only polite clapping of hands. When she started on her third song, there was an audible groan of exasperation.

When Mr. Deakin had dismissed Mrs. Tanner, he immediately brought on a gentleman who performed card tricks and some sleight of hand, The fact that he was very good at it was lost on most of his audience as his voice could not be heard beyond the first three rows of seats, and the tricks themselves could not be seen by the people nearer the back of the room.

After a respectable round of applause, the next act was introduced. The man, a labourer working for Frodsham Council, was a strongly built, craggy-faced individual, but with a wonderful bass voice. Such was the power and quality of his voice that many of those listening felt the hairs on their necks bristle. When he finished each of his two songs, he stood there, buttons on his waistcoat straining, and beamed hugely at the rapturous applause. Mr. Deakin actually shook him by the hand before he left the platform.

The interval was greeted with enthusiasm and one of the first to reach the refreshment table was Peter, who, with one of his school friends, managed to beg extra cake, which they declared made them glad to have come!

His family were surrounded by their friends and some of the Marshville folk, all of them come to congratulate Victoria on her playing, so Dafyd and Will made it their business to get the refreshments for the family as they could see that they would have difficulty breaking away from their well-wishers.

As in the first half of the concert, Victoria opened the second part with two pieces, which were received well enough if not rapturously, then Mr. Deakin brought on a violinist. It was John Tinker who had played previously at Mrs. Hilyard's soirée. Mrs. Hilyard had stressed to him the importance of keeping the audience happy by playing the livelier tunes of his repertoire, and he gave them three Hungarian gipsy-inspired tunes by Liszt. The Master of Ceremonies nodded his approval but did not smile, even when the audience applauded loudly, nor did he smile when he announced that the ladies and gentlemen of the Chapel would sing a selection of songs by Mr. Gilbert and Mr. Sullivan. They were to be accompanied by Miss Victoria Banham, who was also a member of the Chapel congregation.

Dafyd had worked hard every moment he could spare to drill his band of singers. Apart from the good voices, the proven popularity of the work was enough to guarantee that his efforts would be rewarded. The audience loved it. They swayed to the gentler melodies and laughed uproariously at the comical verses sung by the men. Most of those present had never experienced a proper performance of the work of Gilbert and Sullivan, and for those people, far from it being just a local amateur concert, it became a special event.

Dafyd had only one regret, that the big man with the wonderful bass voice was not a member of the Chapel! He would have loved to have him sing with them that night.

Ian Blake had invited Mrs. Joyce, Dr. Mills and Sarah to the concert. Afterwards they were chatting with Captain and Kate Howard, and whilst they all said how much they had enjoyed the concert, Kate said, "It was wonderful, I agree, but my abiding memory of Gilbert and Sullivan will always be Mr. Hughes and my brother James singing 'We Are The Bold Gendarmes'. Charlotte and I nearly split our sides laughing."

A few days after the concert, Dafyd's cousin Bronwen came to Frodsham, and the following day Dafyd took the girl to see Beth. Luckily her measurements were the same as Mary's, which meant that the making of the dress could be accomplished whilst Bronwen was still at Mrs. Hilyard's.

The girl visited the shop and Will took to her immediately. He found her a real 'good sort', as he said afterwards, and he enjoyed her way of playfully poking fun at Dafyd and himself. Of course, he did not know what was going on in the lively, dark-eyed, Welsh girl's mind, which was probably as well, for Bronwen had decided that Will was the one for her, and she was a very determined young lady!

When Dafyd had arrived, having escorted Bronwen from Chester, Victoria had taken to her at first sight. On meeting Mrs. Hilyard, the girl had flung her arms around her neck in an enthusiastic hug and addressed her as Aunt Florence.

But for Victoria, things changed when Dafyd was leaving to make his way back to Marshville. Before he left, Bronwen flung her arms around him and kissed him soundly, promising him that she would be down to see him the following day.

A bolt of jealousy went through Victoria, mixed with a feeling of witnessing something special whilst being no part of it. She suddenly felt very unsure of herself. It was not the first time that she had felt that way; she was so wound up about everything to do with the wedding lately that she sometimes felt close to tears.

On the afternoon of the following day, Dafyd had brought Bronwen back from her dress fitting, the vivacious girl bubbling over about her outing. The dress, she declared, was so stylish, so beautiful, and she loved Mrs. Banham, she was so lovely.

Victoria found difficulty joining in the happy chatter and excused herself to attend to her work. Afterwards, when Daisy was recounting some bits of the conversation, she archly remarked, "Bronwen seems to be very smitten with your brother," Victoria experienced a strong feeling of antipathy towards Dafyd's cousin. It was so foreign to her nature that she was quite uncomfortable with herself, but the girl felt as though Bronwen was claiming more and more of the people whom she, Victoria, saw as her own.

Tuesday was the day of the final fitting of the girls' dresses. Mary's dress had been finished and tried on a few days previously, so Sarah took Daisy and Bronwen to Marshville in the trap for their fitting. Everything went well, and before they set off back to town they called in to see Dafyd and Will. Actually, it was Daisy's doing. She wanted Bronwen to meet Will again, for she was very romantic at heart and she liked them both.

The Welsh girl was surprisingly quiet; even her cousin wondered why she was not her usual ebullient self. Will welcomed the girls with a wide smile, but was quite disappointed by Bronwen's muted responses to his good-humoured chatter.

When Daisy and Bronwen got back to the house, Victoria was in her room supposedly doing some mending to her clothes, but in fact she was just sitting there feeling very depressed and ashamed of herself. She wished that she could turn the clock back and start again with Bronwen. She felt very much alone at that moment.

A tap came at the door and she was surprised to see the Welsh girl herself standing there.

Bronwen did not wait to be invited into the room; she simply entered and shut the door behind her. "I will not waste words," the girl said quietly. "I realise that you do not like me, though I do not understand why, but I want to tell you this: I have known my cousin Dafyd all my life, and I love him very much." Then she moved to stand near the bed and continued, "He has always been my prince and I his princess, at least Dafyd said I could be until he found a real one." She gave a wan smile at her childhood memory and said, "So I made him promise that I would be a flower maiden or even a bridal attendant when he did get married, and he said that he would keep to that promise." Then, without looking at Victoria's face, she said, "Well, he told me that he had found his princess and I was to be one of her bridal attendants as he had promised all those years ago." Still not looking at the other girl, she continued, "I will be your attendant for my cousin's sake, and for your mam's sake, for she has made me a lovely dress and I like her very much."

Bronwen was determined not to cry, and she went on, straining to keep her voice steady. "Once you are married I will not trouble you again. I will stay away from Christleton, and that would mean that I will not see much of Dafyd, and also I will not see your brother again, and I am not ashamed to tell you this," she said, her voice quivering in spite of her determination not to show how upset she was. "I like Will very much, very much indeed."

But it was not Bronwen who broke down and cried, it was Victoria, and she wept those pent up tears with total abandon.

Her visitor stood for a moment unsure of what to do. Here was the beautiful but cold young woman who had acted so aloof with her, crying like a hurt child. Tentatively she approached her cousin's fiancée and gently placed a hand on her shoulder. For a moment Victoria did not do anything but weep, then she reached up and covered Bronwen's hand with her own.

After a while she looked up, her face wet with tears, and said shakily, "Oh, Bronwen, I am so ashamed of myself. How could I have been so cruel to act towards you as I have done?" Then she pleaded, "Can you find it in your heart to forgive me?"

A feeling of joy swept over the Welsh girl, and she replied, half laughing, half crying, "Forgive you?" she cried. "I am just so glad that we can at least have another try at being friends." Then she said, with a return to her impish manner, "That way I can still see your brother now and again." But then she added anxiously, "You do not mind me talking to him, do you, Victoria?" And the other girl, thinking of the girls of Marshville who sometimes came to the shop simply to talk with him, said slowly, "No, Bronwen, I do not object," then, thinking about the rather dangerous Lucy, she said more positively, "I do not object to you getting to know Will better at all, but be warned, Bronwen, he does seem rather immune to girls who try to flirt with him." Then she said quietly, "You see, just as you love Dafyd, I too love my brother and would not want him trifled with; he is too fine a boy for treatment of that kind." To which Bronwen, her eyes shining, nodded vehemently and said, "I agree with you wholeheartedly about that Victoria, and I will fight the others off." That really broke the ice between them and Victoria found herself laughing along with the other girl.

Bronwen made as if to leave, still uncertain whether any sign of affection on her part would offend Dafyd's fiancée, but Victoria came to her and gave her a hug. It was all that was needed; Bronwen then had her little weep.

The following morning Victoria asked Mrs. Hilyard if she could accompany Bronwen to the station, and her employer was only too glad to say yes. She also had been puzzled and rather surprised at Victoria's attitude towards Dafyd's young cousin, so she was relieved to see the girls on such friendly terms again.

Wedding or no wedding, there were still other things to be attended to, and one morning Victoria was hurrying along Main Street to pick up a dress which had been altered for Mrs. Hilyard, when she saw Dr. Mills and Sarah on the other side of the street, so she waved and crossed over to speak to them.

After the usual exchange of news, Victoria mentioned that Daisy would possibly be walking out with a young man, a railway worker. When the man's name was mentioned, Dr. Mills stiffened and said abruptly, "Tell the young lady she would be better keeping well away from that fellow; he is not fit company for any woman, especially a decent girl like Daisy."

The two girls exchanged worried glances. The same thoughts went through their minds: how could they possibly talk the girl out of seeing the man, her first real suitor? Apart from anything else, it was possible that Daisy would resent their interference, but on the other hand, if she did take their warning seriously, it would be bound to upset her badly.

Daisy was so excited about the young man, her first beau, that Victoria did not have the heart to tell her what Dr. Mills had said. But she did suggest, gently, that she should not let the affair develop too fast until she knew more about Noah Dixon, which was the young man's name.

When Victoria learned from Daisy that she was spending her day off with the young man and that he was taking her on a surprise outing, she began to agonise about what might happen, and where he would be taking Daisy. The problem was that when one of Mrs. Hilyard's maids was having her day off, obviously the other had to be on duty, and that left Victoria unable to keep an eye on Daisy, that was, if she could think of a way of achieving such a thing.

The worried girl managed to get a note to Sarah, letting her know of the proposed day out and the time when Daisy would be leaving Mrs. Hilyard's house. Also, Victoria learned that as a railway employee Noah Dixon was entitled to cheap railway travel, which suggested that they would probably be taking the train somewhere. Daisy was not happy with train travel. Her own parents lived near Hatchmere in Delamere Forest and she only visited them twice a year, as it was not a straightforward journey to make by train. Knowing Daisy, Victoria foresaw that, with her fragile confidence, if she found the man's companionship unpleasant, the girl would be totally dependent on him to get her home.

But it was the normally staid, common-sense Sarah who decided that she would do something about the matter, and planned to follow the couple on the day.

Noah Dixon was taking Daisy to Chester, but far from walking round seeing the usual visitor attractions, the young man went round to several beerhouses and tried to get the girl to enter with him. In that he was unsuccessful, and at the final beerhouse he left her outside in the street. This put her in a very vulnerable situation, and sure enough, Sarah's worst fears were realised when, to her horror, a well-dressed man accosted Daisy and caused her to back away in terror.

At that point the outraged Sarah darted across the street, took Daisy by the arm and led her away from the place. Over a meal and a drink of tea, the relieved Daisy told her friend that Dixon had been trying to get her to join him in a 'private' room at the beerhouse, and also that he had borrowed money from her, first a shilling and then a florin. As that was all the money she had brought with her, she was unable to leave Chester without the man's help.

Afterwards, Sarah and Daisy took a cab to the railway station and made their way back to Frodsham, and that left Sarah almost penniless as well.

When Dr. Mills heard what his daughter had done he was furious at her for putting herself in such a risky position, and in telling her so, he reduced her to tears. But then, with his housekeeper standing up for Sarah, he hugged her affectionately and told her that even if he did not approve of how she had gone about the business, he was very impressed by her tenacity and her courage. His daughter clung to him for a few moments, then said, "I do not know what came over me, Father, but the thoughts of dear Daisy at the mercy of that beast was more than I could bear." Dr. Mills then insisted that he paid for her adventurous outing, for deep down he was rather tickled at the antics his daughter had got up to!

A few days later, Daisy was in Main Street on an errand for Mrs. Hilyard when Noah Dixon came swaggering along the pavement and, for a moment the girl froze. Then the memories of her humiliation roused her temper, and she stopped in his path and said in a loud voice so that passers-by could hear, "You borrowed a florin and a shilling of me, Noah Dixon, and I want it back." He looked at her with a cocky grin and said jeeringly, "What are you going to do about it, Daisy, wrestle me for it? I wouldn't mind that."

Just then a voice came from behind him saying, "I think you owe the young lady an apology, mister." The speaker was, by the look of his apron, a shopkeeper or an assistant, and at first Daisy did not recognise him. Then it came to her: he was the violinist who had played at Mrs. Hilyard's soirée and also at the concert.

When Dixon spun round to face the man with the apron, he started to grin, and said mockingly, "Oh yeah, a knight in a shining apron; well you can just get back amongst your cheeses and bacon, sonny."

But the 'knight' did not go back in the shop; he stood his ground and repeated, "I said you owe the young lady an apology, Dixon. Oh yes, I know you," he continued. "The school bully. Well, we are not little boys any longer, so act grown-up and apologise."

Suddenly Noah Dixon's face lost the cocky expression. He had just recognised the other man, and he knew from painful experience how effective John Tinker's fists were, so adopting a casual air he said, "Well, if you must know, I was just teasing Daisy." Then he delved into his pocket, fished out some coins and handed the girl her three shillings and said, "Sorry about that, Daisy, just slipped my mind, alright," and with that he sauntered away.

The girl blinked in astonishment. What was it about the young shop assistant that had put Noah Dixon to shame? She saw only a pleasant man of no particular distinction before her, and now that the grim expression had left his face, he looked quite harmless. Suddenly she was overcome with shyness and she could only mumble her thanks.

"That's alright, miss," said the young man with a smile. "It was the least I could do." Then he followed on by saying, "You are with Mrs. Hilyard; I remember you at the soirée and also at the concert. My name is John Tinker by the way."

The girl managed a smile and said quickly, before the young man went back into the shop, "I'll have to go, Mr. Tinker, or Mrs. Hilyard will be wondering where I've got to." She smiled shyly, but as she turned away she said, "My name is Daisy," and fled leaving the smiling John Tinker to go back to his 'cheeses and his bacon'.

Suddenly, or so it seemed to the anxiety-ridden Victoria, the wedding day arrived, and at least two of her worries disappeared. The weather, which had played cat and mouse with her all week, was absolutely perfect, and her wedding gown was perfect. Her mother, who was helping her to dress, was in tears of happiness at the sight of her daughter looking so beautiful, so regal.

Even the task of getting everyone to the Chapel, a job that had fallen to Will, who was also best man, was accomplished without a hitch. The shop had been shut at eight o'clock for the rest of the day, and with Dafyd preparing himself at Mrs. Hilyard's house, he had left the job of taking the contingent from Marshville into Frodsham to Will.

Mr. Robbins, Michael and Peter (who once again was a pageboy) were the first to be taken to the Chapel. By the time Will got back with the pony trap, the carriage taking Victoria and her father was manoeuvring in the lane, ready to get as close to the hut as possible.

Jessie Robbins and Beth were the last to be taken, after which Will could leave the trap near the Chapel and prepare himself for his duty. The boy was very conscious of the honour of being best man, and he was rather nervous, but managed not to show it.

When Thomas was handing Victoria into the carriage, he felt her trembling, and to calm her he said lightly, "Chin up, nearly there, girl."

The street through Marshville was unnaturally quiet, most of the women and the older girls having walked to the town earlier. Amongst those who were still there to see Victoria on her way was Mrs. Garroway, and she beamed at them and wished the girl much luck and a lot of happiness. Victoria was exceptionally touched by the words of the well-wishers and was in danger of bursting into tears.

Meanwhile, in Main Street outside the Chapel, the onlookers were asking each other who the bride and groom were. The sight of the carriage bearing four bridal attendants and a pageboy caused them to come to the conclusion that the people involved must be from one of the more important of the town's families. Certainly, to see such beautifully styled and matched dresses pointed to that conclusion.

However, when the bride arrived, one woman exclaimed, "Why, that is one of Mrs. Hilyard's maids, well I never; mind you she is a very well-mannered girl." Then one of the other women joined in and said, "I believe her family live in one of those huts on the Marsh, but I hear that they are quite respectable." "Well, just fancy," said the first speaker!

Beth was sharing the front row of seats with Jessie and Ted Robbins, and when she looked around the chapel, she was amazed at how many people were there. She recognised some of the women from Marshville and gave them a wave of her hand when they looked her way.

Captain Howard and Mrs. Howard were sharing the seats behind her with Dr. Mills. Michael had still to take his seat. The first row of seats on the other side were unoccupied and awaiting the arrival of Mr. and Mrs. Hughes, Mr. Hughes's brother and his wife (Bronwen's parents), and the girl's brother. Even as Beth looked across, the Hughes family party entered the Chapel and took their seats. Rebecca Hughes gave her a delighted smile which warmed her heart. Dafyd's mother always had that effect on Beth; she was such a warm-hearted woman.

On the next row of seats was Mrs. Hilyard, then Ian Blake's landlady, Mrs. Joyce, and two other ladies whom Beth did not recognise. Ian Blake had agreed to act as usher, so he was at that moment probably outside the Chapel. Beth felt a rush of affection for all these people, many from that place she had hated so much when she had first come here, and whom she could now count on as friends and neighbours.

When Dafyd and Will came in and took their places, Beth was so proud of her son. He matched the bridegroom in bearing and appearance. The hired suit he wore belied the fact that he lived in the huts of Marshville and was the son of a Canal contractor's employee.

The minister spoke to the congregation, then the harmonium gave out a hymn tune which brought a softly voiced response from those of the congregation who were familiar with it. Beth had heard the same hymn sung at a wedding once before and, as on that occasion, it provoked in her a powerful feeling of communal love. The emotion that went through her almost broke through her defences, for she had been determined to not greet her daughter through a cascade of tears. But when she saw Thomas, so proudly escorting Victoria as they slowly approached the minister, her resolve was forgotten. Her face might be wreathed in a smile but the loving tears flowed without check.

Dafyd had worn an anxious look when he had come to take his place, he appeared quite nervous, but he became a different man when he set his eyes on Victoria. Those who could see his face were deeply affected by the look of love which transformed his features. It told them that this was indeed a love match, but the effect on his bride-to-be was simply to leave her breathless.

The bridal attendants drew a lot of admiring glances and comments, but not everyone was happy about them. A small number of the more conservative members of the congregation were not in favour of such ostentation, even though the dresses themselves were of a deceptively simple design and were not immodest in any way. Beth, however, heard none of the criticisms and felt a warm glow of contentment at how well the girls looked wearing the results of her imagination and her fingers.

When Thomas took his place beside Beth and watched the ceremony, he was engulfed by a mixture of emotions, a pride in his daughter and the realisation that his little girl was about to become a wife, and had difficulty swallowing the lump in his throat.

Captain Howard felt privileged to be part of the occasion, and honoured to be considered by the Banham family as more than just an employer. He glanced down at his smiling wife, so enraptured by the sight of her dear Victoria as a bride, and then she looked up at him. The look of love on her face was for him as well as Victoria, and he marvelled for the thousandth time that Kate was his.

The ceremony was over, the register signed and the newly married couple, arms linked, made their way between their friends and well-wishers, answering smiles with beatific smiles of their own.

Outside the Chapel everyone gathered to bestow their best wishes on the radiant couple. The photographer had set up his camera tripod in the road in order that he could get a full group in the picture. He was relieved to see that the road had been swept of animal droppings the day before, for sometimes after cattle had been driven through the town, the mess was really unpleasant.

The people of Marshville hung back as the newly-weds were receiving their congratulations, but then Victoria took Dafyd's arm and went over to join them. Dafyd asked them if they would care to join him and his wife for a photograph. At first some of them were not inclined to be photographed as they felt that their clothes did not do justice to the occasion, but after an entreaty by Victoria, first one then another decided that they would join the happy couple. The daughters of the women were only too ready to be in the picture! The photographer was asked if he would take their picture first, as some of them were anxious to do their shopping and return to the village.

Whilst the arrangements for the photography were being made, the grocer's assistant, John Tinker, was walking towards the wedding party carrying a basket of groceries for an old lady whose cottage was quite close to the Chapel.

His eyes were taken by a laughing group of girls, obviously the bridal attendants, when one of them turned towards him and he saw that it was Daisy, Mrs. Hilyard's maid.

He had seen her many times when she had been on some errand in the town for her mistress, and the other day when she had been troubled by Noah Dixon, but apart from the time when he had seen her at the concert, it was unusual to see her laughing so joyously.

John Tinker found himself smiling broadly at such a light-hearted spectacle, and he decided that Daisy really did seem a nice girl, in fact, wearing that dress also showed what a pretty girl she was.

Then he saw the bride and her husband. "Why, it is Mrs. Hilyard's other maid," he said to himself, and for a moment he envied those people in the wedding party. The beautiful girls, the happy chatter, and the consciousness of being part of something special, how he would have liked to be one of that group of happy people. He was just about to turn away when Daisy saw him and gave him a wave, then she spoke to one of the other girls and the next moment they both hurried towards him.

He recognised the second girl as Dr. Mills's daughter, and it was she who spoke to him. "Mr. Tinker?" Sarah said, and the young man, taking his hat off, nodded enquiringly. "I would like to thank you, Mr. Tinker," Sarah continued, "for coming to Daisy's aid last week, it was most kind of you."

John Tinker beamed and was about to answer, when Daisy's name was called. She looked around and with a delighted cry rushed over to where a grinning man and a smiling woman were standing. "Mam, Dad," she cried and hugged them both in turn.

"My, our Daisy is looking very fetching," said her father cheerfully, whilst her mother simply put her arms around the girl, her eyes shining with pride, and said, "We missed your last wedding but we were not going to miss this one, and seeing you like this, I am so glad we came."

Whilst her father stood there smiling and Daisy and her mother discussed the dress, Mrs. Hilyard joined them. After saying hello to Daisy's parents, she told the girl that she was wanted outside the Chapel. Kissing her parents again, Daisy hurried back to join the group. Mrs. Hilyard turned to Daisy's parents and said,

"Mr. Lloyd, would you and Mrs. Lloyd care to have something to eat with us before you leave for home?"

"That is kind of you, Mrs. Hilyard," said the man, "but we will not have time to accept your offer. We still haven't finished shopping, and there is a ton of stuff that I need from the ironmongers for a start." With that, they said goodbye, the couple walking up the street to where their cart was standing, and Mrs. Hilyard to rejoin the wedding group.

John Tinker, on witnessing Daisy's meeting with her parents, was visited by a curious feeling of pleasure, almost tenderness, for the girl's sake. She did not seem quite so alone as he had thought.

The young man was buoyed up and did not feel quite as envious at not being part of the wedding group, and he returned to the shop in a very cheerful state of mind. His opinion of Daisy climbed even higher, and for her to be a friend of Miss Mills reinforced his impression that she was indeed a decent girl.

Shortly after that, the carriages started taking the bride and groom, the parents and the bridal attendants to Mrs. Hilyard's house where, in the garden, the rest of the photographs were to be taken. Afterwards the wedding breakfast was partaken of. The meal had been prepared by Mrs. Hilyard's cook, who rivalled Beth in some of her dishes, but the cake had been made and decorated by Beth of course, for Cook admitted that cakes of that grandeur were not her speciality.

The speeches were kept short but were no less heartfelt for all that, for the newly-weds were catching a train soon afterwards, which would take them on the first part of their journey to Windermere, in the Lake District. The presentation of gifts to Victoria and Dafyd was left until the week after they had returned. Two of the girls were particularly disappointed. Mary had purchased a plain tablecloth of good quality and Daisy had embroidered it. They had been so looking forward to the look on Victoria's face when she received it.

From the bride and groom, both Mrs. Hughes and Beth were each presented with a silver brooch, whilst the bridal attendants were given a silver pendant, the drop being in the form of a single letter denoting their Christian name. Daisy gazed at her letter 'Dee', and her eyes filled. She had never, in all her life, owned anything at all made from silver, and she thought it was beautiful.

When the time came for Victoria and Dafyd to leave, everyone came out of the house to send them on their way. The carriage was to take them to the station where, without any fuss, they would board the train and start on their new life together. Victoria was particularly thankful for that; she could not have coped with an emotional send-off on the station platform.

After the carriages had disappeared from view, the party went back into the house, where Mrs. Hilyard ushered them into her sitting room. Daisy went into the dining room to help Cook and was promptly chased out again. Mr. Hughes had persuaded Mrs. Hilyard to let him pay for the temporary employment of two women helpers seeing that both maids were otherwise engaged!

Rebecca Hughes was creating gales of laughter as she recalled the near disaster of her and Alwyn's wedding. Her narrative encouraged others to tell similar tales and Mrs. Hilyard was pleased to see everyone relaxed and so at ease with each other.

Later, light refreshments were served, and afterwards the four girls ended up in the hall trying to learn the waltz. Peter was standing disconsolately by his mother's chair, whilst Bronwen's brother sat on the floor looking very fed up.

Kate, observing these things, asked the assembled guests if they would excuse her while she showed the girls the correct way to dance the waltz. Mrs. Hilyard immediately suggested that they use the other room.

It started with Kate and the four girls, but then Ian, Will, Peter and Bronwen's brother were roped in. There was a lot of self-conscious giggling at first, but as they started to master the steps, things got more serious. The two young boys then began to get a little giddy, and Bronwen decided that they would be less troublesome running their energy off in the garden, so she took them outside.

Will, who considered that Bronwen was being almost monopolised by Peter, felt rather left out of everything. He experienced such a strong pang of jealousy as to make him feel ashamed of himself. Kate had seen the direction of his glance and the set of his normally pleasant face, and came to the conclusion that the boy was more than a little interested in the impish Bronwen!

In the other room the party had formed into two groups, the men at one end and the ladies at the other. Dr. Mills had asked Richard Howard how the Canal was progressing, and he, Thomas, and Michael were answering many of the questions, but it was Ted Robbins, with his 'library' of newssheets and pamphlets, who was able to explain the financial problems which continued to bedevil the Company. Costs had risen by almost three million pounds over the original estimate, but luckily the determination of the promoters ensured that their calls for more money continued to be answered.

Even whilst contributing to the lively conversation with the other women, Mrs. Hilyard was happily aware of the men's conversation and she breathed a sigh of relief to see how well they were all getting on with each other.

Although she knew that there would still be occasions in the future when she would find herself mourning her late husband, she had the optimistic conviction that the house would never again feel quite so empty. Since the advent of Victoria into her life, she had widened her circle of acquaintances, some of whom she could now count on as friends, and she had regained contact with people who were not ship owners, shipping merchants and others from the same business world. The people in her house that day were diverse in their occupations and interests, and were equally diverse in their financial status and social standing, but Florence Hilyard blessed Victoria and Dafyd for introducing her to this world and making her feel part of it.

When the time came for the respective Hughes families to leave, everyone else made themselves ready to depart. The four girls changed into their normal dresses, but Mrs. Hilyard insisted that Daisy did not metamorphose into a housemaid until the last of the guests had gone!

Before the Hughes contingent left to catch their train, Bronwen, now dressed for travelling, came up to the set-faced Will and said, "Well, there you are, with a face like a wet weekend." Then before the incensed boy could reply, she continued, "If you are going to be like that, I will not bother to answer your letter when I am home."

Will frowned and said without warmth, "I have not sent you a letter." To which Bronwen replied jauntily, "No, silly, the one you are going to send to me!" Then, realising that the boy was not acting any warmer towards her, she said anxiously, "You are going to write to me, aren't you, Will?"

The boy felt his bad mood evaporate in an instant, and he shook his head and thought, 'How can anybody continue being grumpy with a girl like Bronwen?' His usual sunny smile returned to his face and he said, much in the same vein as the girl, "Well, if that is an order I suppose I must, but Bronwen, you must give me your address first." And the girl delved into her coat pocket and drew out a small piece of paper which she then handed to the surprised boy.

It had been a good day and everybody had enjoyed themselves (with the exception of Mrs. Hilyard's handyman, who resented all those people who had tramped all over 'his' garden!). Peter, however, had enjoyed himself too well: the amount he had eaten exceeded that which he had partaken of at Miss Kate and Captain Howard's wedding! His stomach felt quite overfull, but he had enough sense not to complain to his mother and went to bed regretting his greediness.

The four girls had all enjoyed the day because of their shared role in the proceedings, but each had their own memories of the day to cherish. Daisy had seen her parents and John Tinker, and had been seen by them wearing her wonderful dress. Then there was the lovely silver pendant given to her by Victoria and Dafyd. When she went to bed that night, her cup of happiness was brimming.

For Mary, the day was even better, for the reason that she had received another letter from Jem at Milford that very morning, and she marvelled that a girl like her should get such tender-worded missives, for the girl still had difficulty seeing herself as others saw her.

It had been a memorable day for Sarah, for she had danced with Ian, albeit rather clumsily at first as they both learned the steps, but eventually they found themselves moving together in unison, giving her the fanciful notion that in the years to come, they would move through life together in the same harmonious way.

Will went to bed early that night, for he had to be up early to get the bread and milk from Frodsham in time for the shop opening at seven o'clock. But he was contented now that he knew that he and Bronwen were still friends and it pleased him a great deal, for he did enjoy the easy way he could talk with her.

As usual, when he went to his bed his mind conjured up the image of Lucy Parks, and he wondered, as he had done many times, if he had misjudged her or whether she was really as flighty and worldly as he imagined her to be. Often he wished that he could talk about it to somebody sympathetic to his dilemma. Then before he fell asleep, the ideal solution came to him: he would write to Bronwen and ask her advice.

About the same time, the Welsh girl had Will in her thoughts, and knowing nothing of Lucy, was complacently congratulating herself that with a little persuasion from her, he would soon see that she was the right girl for him.

Chapter 33

Frodsham Depot Survives Whilst Saltport Thrives, But Runcorn Struggles

Will was so busy the following week that he had no time to write to Bronwen, and he felt a little guilty. Even if he had time to spare, with his early morning start to the day and his late finish he was too tired to think of what to put in the letter, except of course his decision to ask her advice on how to approach Lucy about the matters that troubled him.

In the shop, Clara as always was a blessing. In fact, Will confessed to her face that he considered it was she who actually managed the place and he was not grumbling about that! Whilst Clara was pleased with the compliment, she was quick to assure him that she was alright when he or Dafyd was there to bolster her confidence, but would not dream of doing anything other than serve the customers whilst either of them was absent.

During the week some of the village girls came in to see Will, using the excuse that they were enquiring about the wedding photograph which included themselves. The young man was well aware of their motives, but whilst keeping them at arm's length, he did it without injuring their feelings.

It was a bad week for the town of Runcorn. To construct the locks and separating embankment obviously blocked the approach to the docks, effectively closing them down. As most of the town's working population was dependent on employment through shipping, many were facing destitution.

At the same time, members of the Salt Union paid a visit to the infant port on the Canal and named it officially Saltport. The Chairman ceremoniously 'launched' the port by breaking a bottle of champagne on a jetty mooring bollard. The event was witnessed by Peter and the twins, who were peeping round the warehouse.

They swiftly conveyed the news to the people of Marshville and promptly earned a telling off for playing where they shouldn't have been!

The inevitable and sad results of the closure of Runcorn Docks manifested itself the week after Victoria and Dafyd returned from the Lake District. Several men came looking for work, in some cases having tramped the road from Runcorn. It was a blessing for some that they were given jobs as dockworkers, and they were fortunate enough to find lodgings at Marshville. Later, two of the huts vacated by those who had moved away to work on other contracts became occupied by Runcorn families.

Victoria and Dafyd had fallen under the spell of the Lake District, even though they had endured two days of rain. Dafyd, with his love of walking, was well equipped, but his wife was not, so he bought her a good stout pair of walking shoes and heavier outer clothes for walking through brambles and thick vegetation.

Whilst everyone was glad to see them back, Will was particularly pleased to relinquish his early morning duties. He also had time to write his first letter to Bronwen, and as he had intended, he put down his thoughts on the problems posed by his uncertainty over Lucy's unsettling behaviour.

He did write about his everyday life, but that one part of his letter concerning Lucy was enough to dominate the contents for Bronwen. However, she answered quickly and gave her opinion in a diplomatic way (albeit through gritted teeth!) She was quite disturbed that the boy should even consider looking at another girl after being in her (Bronwen's) company for a few hours!

Will's second letter did nothing to placate her, but his third one forced her to come to the humiliating conclusion that he did not think of her in a romantic way at all. Her reply to that letter simply stated, 'Will Banham, do not write to me again, write to Lucy Parks,' and she did not even bother to sign it!

Will was very taken aback, he could not believe how badly he had misjudged the girl. His first impression of her was of someone with a good sense of humour, perceptive and sympathetic. An intelligent girl and one a man could feel at ease with.

At first he wondered if the note (he hardly considered it to be a letter) to be some sort of a joke, but by whom? Bronwen had only one brother. And the wording of the missive was the work of someone older. But after comparing the handwriting with that in her previous letters, he came to the conclusion that the writer was indeed Bronwen. He felt so angry and humiliated that he could not bring himself to mention the matter to anyone else, especially Dafyd.

A few weeks passed and by then he had simmered down, and he sometimes wished that he was still corresponding with the girl, for try as he may, despite the unhappy affair with the last letter, he still saw her as a lively, personable character.

One afternoon when he and Dafyd were alone, his brother-in-law said casually, "Will, have you and my cousin fallen out with each other, or more to the point, have you written something that you know has offended her?"

Since the time when Victoria and Dafyd had set their wedding date, Dafyd had asked Will to call him by his Christian name, and not address him as Mr. Hughes. Although the boy had found it strange at first, by this time he had got used to calling his employer Dafyd when no customers were present. But now it seemed as if a small gulf had opened up between them and he felt unable to treat him as a friend and brother-in-law.

Will flushed and said in an aggrieved tone, "I have not put anything offensive in my letters; it was Bronwen who suddenly turned funny with me, and I am really disappointed with her."

Dafyd looked at Will, arched his eyebrows expressively, and said quietly but definitely, "Bronwen does not 'turn funny', as you phrase it, without just cause, and if she does fall out with someone, they are left in no doubt as to the reason."

Then he added, "My aunt is worried about Bronwen's lack of spirit. You saw what she was like both times she was here, and that is how she usually behaves."

Will said nothing; he had an uneasy feeling that he must have written something to upset the girl, but for the life of him he could not think what it could be. With his kindly nature it upset him to think that the effervescent Bronwen with her mischievous grin should be unhappy, especially if it was he who had caused her to be so.

Dafyd broke in on the boy's thoughts and said curiously, "Why did you write to Bronwen? I know that you got on well from first meeting her, but you must have liked her exceptionally to want to keep in touch." Will burst out before his brother-in-law had finished speaking and said, "But it was Bronwen who wanted me to write to her. I had not even considered sending her a letter."

His employer looked at him in surprise, then said, "Do you not see, Will. Girls like Bronwen do not casually ask boys to write to them; she obviously has taken a strong liking to you, so even an innocent phrase from you could take on a more significant meaning to her."

The boy flushed at that, and he recalled with embarrassment some of the things he had written concerning Lucy Parks. If Dafyd was correct in his thinking, it was no wonder that Bronwen had decided that he was not worth bothering about.

Will gnawed his lip in indecision. Bronwen had told him not to write again, but the only way he could put things right was to write to her and apologise, this time making no mention of Lucy. Even if the girl was still annoyed with him, he was sure that she would read it and not simply throw it to the back of the fire. The only difficulty, as he saw it, was to not encourage the girl to think of him as her 'young man'. Dafyd did not press him any further; he merely nodded when his brother-in-law told him of his intentions.

Over a week went by after he had written, and to Will's chagrin, there had been no reply from the girl. Then, when a letter did come, it was couched in very formal language. His soft heart flinched as he visualised Bronwen still nursing her hurt feelings.

He had mentioned the three other girls (he hoped that he was not being unwise bringing them into his letter). He told her how they were all keeping and about Daisy, who was then walking out with John Tinker, a young man who was a good violinist. But he had the sense not to mention Lucy's name!

Actually, something of a barrier had come between Will and Lucy Parks, and it had appeared after the boy noticed that she had a habit of treating Clara in an offhand manner, and that made Will feel very uncomfortable, as he had a high regard for his fellow assistant. Another side of Miss Parks showed when she was in the shop whilst Clara's little boy was there, something that occurred from time to time. Jimsy, as they called him, was a happy little fellow and was at the stage where he would toddle about quite well. However, like all children, he could get quite cranky when he was tired. Will was very adept at pacifying him when he was in that mood.

One afternoon Dafyd had gone to Frodsham station to pick up some parcels and Clara was helping out behind the counter. Jimsy was playing in a cardboard box, and Will had taken a basket of vegetables for one of the women who had bought a large order.

Returning to the shop, he was just outside the door when he heard the crying of the toddler and the unmistakable voice of Lucy Parks, but she was speaking to Clara in a tone that Will had never heard her use before. She was berating Clara for not doing something about that 'skriking kid', as Lucy put it.

Will entered the shop and, without saying anything, he picked Jimsy up and soothed him. Immediately Lucy's voice became quite soft, and she smiled at Will and said, "Well you seem to have the magic touch, don't you? Poor little lad, he's probably tired."

"He is," said Will shortly. "Clara should have been home ages ago but we have been too busy." Then, turning to Clara, he said, "Mr. Hughes has just arrived back, so if you want to get away, we will be alright now."

The young woman behind the counter had continued making up Lucy's order without being flustered by the girl's attitude, but her eyes showed her dislike, and she nodded without speaking. Lucy might be many things but she was not slow-minded, and she realised that Will had probably heard some if not all of her bad-tempered outburst, so as soon as her order was paid for, she gave a little grimace at the boy and left the shop.

Neither Clara or Will commented on the girl's behaviour, but they both knew that Lucy Parks had shot her bolt as far as the boy was concerned, and Clara breathed a sigh of relief, for she had watched with alarm Will's infatuation with the awful Lucy.

When Dafyd recounted the episode and how it had affected her brother, Victoria had also been very relieved, for she had been extremely worried when she had heard that Will had become besotted with the girl.

The next time Will wrote to Bronwen, he broke his promise and commented on Lucy's ill-tempered treatment of Clara, and it was like balm to the Welsh girl's senses. However, she was astute enough not to condemn the other girl's behaviour, hoping to impress on him just how high-minded she was!

Will, however, was still writing as a friend and nothing more, so Bronwen subtly introduced a young man whom she referred to as Ifan. Not every letter contained news of the young man, but even so, after a few weeks, Will was finding it very irksome to learn of his latest humorous sayings and activities. He thought them unfunny and uninteresting. One thing that Will would not admit even to himself was that he was getting jealous of the man. However, what Bronwen failed to mention was that Ifan was her best friend's young man and the things he said were not to her but to her friend Glenys!

Victoria was disappointed that her brother did not appear to be any more interested in Bronwen now that Lucy Parks no longer had him in thrall. Still, as she had told the young Welsh girl before the wedding, her brother did seem rather immune to girls that flirted with him, and Bronwen had been just a little too obvious in the beginning.

In Marshville the sound of children's voices disturbed the peace of a drowsy warm day. Because of a smell of gas inside and around the school, the council had been forced to close it and send the children home whilst the problem was traced and repaired. The closure of the school was to be a blessing in disguise for the Banham family.

Late September had brought a spell of gloriously sunny weather and Captain Howard was discussing the work which during the week had occupied Thomas and Michael until late each day. Their employer suddenly changed the subject and said to his foreman, "Thomas, I want you to take some time off, have a holiday; you have certainly earned a rest, and I do know that you are the only man at the Depot who has not taken any time off since you came here." Then before Thomas could frame a reply, his employer said with a smile, "I am sure that Beth would be glad of a change of scenery, and I can certainly recommend Llandudno."

Thomas pursed his lips and thought for a moment before replying, then, thanking Captain Howard for his thoughtfulness, he explained the reason for his hesitancy. "You see, sir, Victoria's wedding took my savings right down again, not as far as they had been, but I really am determined to build up my capital again; a holiday would just about floor me sir."

His employer nodded sympathetically, but assured Thomas that he and Michael were to be paid extra in recognition of their efforts of late. "And," he added, "I fully intend that you shall not lose a single day's pay if you take a week's holiday." He smiled and said, "It is a good offer, Thomas, and for Beth's sake I urge you to consider the matter." Thomas thanked Captain Howard again and told him that he would talk it over with Beth.

That evening they sat round the table discussing the offer, when Dafyd, who had just shared a meal with them, said earnestly, "Mam and Dad have said often enough that they would be pleased to have you stay with them if you got a chance to make a visit; certainly there is plenty of room in the house." Then he added quietly, "They really would like you to visit them. Besides," he said, brightening up, "whilst that gas leak at Peter's school keeps it closed, he would not have to play truant to be off school if you decide to have a few days at Christleton. would he?"

Beth looked at Thomas and he could tell that she was very taken with the idea. However, like her husband, she would not even dream of foisting herself on anybody, especially as it was some time ago since Dafyd's parents had issued the invitation. So for the time being, the matter was left to lie.

But Dafyd did not let it lie; he wrote to his parents asking them to repeat their invitation, for as he said to Will, the Gas Company might manage to repair the faulty gas-pipe joint sooner than expected. His parents promptly did as he had asked and invited the Banhams for a week's stay with them.

Thomas knew when he was beaten, so he accepted the invitation (with some trepidation) and informed Captain Howard of his intentions. Oddly enough, although Thomas was swayed by his consideration for Beth and Peter, they were the ones who then raised objections, but it was to no avail. The following Sunday, after Chapel, they were on their way to Chester.

They were met at Chester station by Mr. Hughes with the phaeton, and in no time at all arrived at the village of Christleton. The Hughes family home was a modern brick-built house surrounded by a large garden. It was slightly bigger than their friend Florence Hilyard's house, but still a great deal smaller than Reeve House. There appeared to be no shortage of servants and from their demeanour they gave the visitors the feeling that it was a happy home.

Within a remarkably short time, any awkwardness felt by Beth and Thomas was dispelled by Alwyn Hughes. One of the traits that Thomas liked about Dafyd's father was that he was a good listener as well as an entertaining raconteur, and seemed to have a thirst for knowledge about everything. At one point, after Thomas had answered his questions about the workings of a dynamo (Thomas thanked Michael for being able to do so!), Mr. Hughes said slowly, "You know, Thomas boy, I envy you: such a varied experience, such a wealth of knowledge."

His guest looked at him in astonishment and said incredulously, "You, Alwyn, envy me? How can you say that with all you have achieved and all that you have made of your life." His host looked pleased at Thomas's observations and said, "Well, yes, I am proud of my business, but I will confess to you, I have always liked the idea of taking bits of metal or wood and making something out of them, something that works."

Then he said, a little diffidently, "I have a small workshop, not a proper one, just a place in which to do a bit of woodwork." When his companion looked at him with fresh interest he said hopefully, "Would you like to see it, Thomas? I know that it is not as interesting as the place that you work in but I enjoy being in there."

Thomas laughed and said enthusiastically, "Why, Alwyn, woodwork is one of my greatest passions. I can't tell you how much pleasure I get from the feel of a well-finished piece of wood." His host grinned happily and said, "Right, I think you will find my workshop to your taste." With that he led the way down the garden and introduced Thomas to his 'small' workshop.

For a start it was not so small, and it was wonderfully equipped. A treadle-powered wood-turning lathe, a hand-powered bench drill and a spacious bench with racks of gleaming chisels of every sort. There was also a wealth of other tools, all oiled and lovingly cared for. Thomas was entranced; he had never seen such a well-equipped and orderly woodworking shop in his life, and he said so to the proud Alwyn. Later, after he had been shown some of his host's work, Thomas's admiration grew enormously. It also established another bond between the two men.

After the weeks of fine weather, there was a change overnight and the following day it did not encourage them to go out and risk a soaking, and it was just as well, for in the afternoon they were surprised to observe a cab draw up and discharge Victoria, Will and Dafyd!

Everybody was delighted to see them, but Thomas and Beth were both worried that something had gone wrong at Marshville. But there were no problems, and they had left the shop in capable hands for a few days. It transpired that Jessie Robbins and Clara had come up with the idea that if they ran the shop, Dafyd and Victoria could have a few days away with the family. Then Clara had volunteered her husband Tom to bring the bread and milk each morning, which meant that Will could also enjoy a few days away. Dafyd had not been too keen on the idea at first, but eventually warmed to it, and insisted that they should all be paid a proper wage for their pains. When Mrs. Hilyard had been approached about Victoria taking some leave, she had given her blessing and told them to enjoy themselves for a few days, so all three had played truant!

Whether it was the spontaneous way that the visit came about or just the joy of all being together, but that evening was one of the happiest they had enjoyed for a long time. Alwyn, like his son, had a good voice, and with Victoria playing the piano father and son sang several duets. Alwyn then organised them and coaxed them all (with the exception of Victoria) into trying harmony singing.

The next day dawned sunny and with the slightest of breezes, so it was decided that they would go into the city and enjoy the sights. For the ladies there was the pleasure of gazing into shop windows even if they were not buying! Dafyd's father was due to visit one of his shops, so he needed to use the phaeton, but there was a wagonette in the village which could be hired, so the rest of them went in that. Returning later would be easy: there were plenty of carriages in the city centre for hire, and Dafyd knew that after a few hours trailing round, they would not be pleased to have a two and a half mile walk to get home.

Chester, with its Roman name of Deva, was a wondrous place for the Banhams. The bustling streets, the impressive cathedral, the ancient city walls and the wealth of medieval buildings; there was so much to see that there was not enough time in one day to appreciate it all.

The most amazing part of all was the Rows. These consisted of ornately decorated, half-timbered buildings which stretched from Chestergate around the corner and marched down Bridge Street. An outstanding feature of the Rows was the covered galleries lined with shops. Below the galleries were yet more shops at street level, and in some cases, below street level. Above the galleries rose several stories of rooms where possibly the owners lived. The same galleried buildings lined Watergate, Eastgate and parts of Northgate.

It was not the first time that Beth and Victoria had visited Chester but they still found it charming and exciting. Will and Thomas were more interested in the wonderful buildings and the architecture than the shops, although Thomas did find a most marvellous tool shop!

During the afternoon they were back in the Rows. Peter had earlier seen, of all things, a miniature set of step-ladders, and he had mentioned them so many times that eventually Victoria told him that she would treat him. Peter almost ran back to the little toy shop!

Mrs. Hughes, Beth and Thomas were still inside the shop with Peter, whilst Victoria had rejoined Will and Dafyd on the gallery. They were trying to make the important decision of which tearoom they were to go in before they made their way back home, when a familiar Welsh voice reached their ears. It was Dafyd's aunt and with her was Bronwen.

There were cries of surprised delight from both parties and a lot of hugs, except between Will and Bronwen. The truth was that the girl was a little shy of Will; she saw him differently on meeting him this time. When she had first met him, in her confident way she had decided that he was the one for her without having the slightest idea of what sort of a boy he was; she knew nothing at all about his interests or tastes. All she knew was that he worked in the shop with cousin Dafyd and not much else.

However, since corresponding with him, over the months Bronwen had learned a lot about Will, especially as regards the depth of feeling he was capable of (thanks to Lucy Parks!). But more than ever she believed he saw her merely as a friend and nothing more. Ruefully, she reflected, by mentioning Ifan's name, instead of making him jealous, she possibly could have succeeded in causing Will to step back like a true gentleman in order to not create difficulties between her and her 'young man'. But Bronwen did so want Will to be her real young man.

Whilst all this was going through the girl's mind, her mother had other concerns on hers, and after the enthusiastic reunion, she whispered to her sister-in-law, "Becky, we could do with finding a tearoom with a ladies' room." To which her sister-in-law said, "I know just the place," then turning to the others, she announced that the tearoom round the corner was where they were heading for. It was an order and, delicately, nobody questioned it!

In the tearoom, once everyone was gathered together, there was a lively exchange of news, much of it naturally concerning the Hughes family, and during this time Peter stayed close to Bronwen, claiming her attention so effectively that Will hardly managed more than to ask the girl how she was keeping.

Though Will found Bronwen subtly different in some way, he could not explain what that difference was. In the few months since he had last seen her, she had taken on a new quality and in doing so had left behind some of her exuberance, or so it seemed to the boy. Whilst he hoped that he was wrong about that, he was fascinated by the new, rather enigmatic Bronwen.

Later, when they had all enjoyed a light afternoon tea, Bronwen's mother regretfully told them that they would have to make their way to the station, as to catch a later train would mean a mile walk to Caerwys in pitch-black darkness.

Accordingly, Dafyd went into Eastgate and secured two cabs, saying that they would see them off at the station before making their own way back to Christleton. Rebecca Hughes, Bronwen and her mother climbed into one cab, and before anything was said, Peter joined them. Dafyd exchanged amused glances with Victoria, then helped her and Beth into the second cab. However, whilst being amused by Peter's eagerness to be with the girl, Victoria had observed Will's face and felt sorry for him. In the general exchange of news and happy conversation in the tearoom, she had noticed that her brother and Bronwen hardly said a word to each other. It bothered her a great deal, for on the few occasions she had been in the company of the girl (except for the one incident which she would rather forget), she had grown to like Bronwen. True, the girl was still young, but in a couple of years' time, Victoria could well imagine that she would be a real beauty, but more importantly, an intelligent beauty.

The train was not yet at the platform when they reached the station, but within a few minutes it arrived and quickly they found an empty compartment. Will was standing there rather disconsolately whilst everybody exchanged hugs and kisses, then he found himself with Bronwen.

For a moment he was stuck for something to say, then desperately seizing the first thing that came into his mind said, "And how is Ifan these days,

Bronwen?" It was just the opening that the girl needed to alter the course of their faltering friendship, and she replied airily, "Oh, Glenys's young man. He is not a telegraph boy any longer, he has been promoted and now has a postman's job." Then she added meaningfully for good measure, "Glenys is hoping that next year they will have an 'understanding'. She will be old enough by then."

As the astounded young man, with a wakening feeling of joy spreading through him, searched for something to say in answer to the revelation, Bronwen's mother called to the girl, telling her to board the train. Almost before he knew it, Bronwen reached up and kissed his cheek, then said, "Keep on writing to me, Will," and with that she climbed into the carriage. A whistle was blown, a flag waved and the train moved out of the station. Will, so much happier now, was not sure, but he thought that Bronwen had tears in her eyes as she leaned out of the window to wave them out of sight

Victoria had observed this quiet tableau with interest, and the return of Bronwen's impish grin gave her as much pleasure as her brother's answering smile. As they walked out of the station to find a carriage, she linked Will's arm companionably and by the way he pressed her arm, she knew that he was his happy self again.

The next day Mrs. Hughes needed to be at the house, so the Banham family and Dafyd once again went into the city with the intention of visiting the cathedral, walking the city walls, and seeing the river. Also Dafyd wanted to show them round the clubhouse of the Grosvenor Rowing Club.

On the water there were two single sculls out practicing, and Beth found it rather frightening to think of her son-in-law risking his life in such a fragile, slender craft. She would have had an attack of the vapours if she had known that Will was planning to take up rowing if he did stay with the Hughes's family business and moved to Chester!

The 'truants' were returning to Frodsham after their evening meal, but before dinner Dafyd took them on a short tour of the village. At the southern end of the lane was a humpbacked bridge spanning a canal, which he told them was the same 'Shroppie' which went through the city and ended up at Ellesmere Port and the Manchester Ship Canal. As they were gazing down from the bridge, a horse towing two narrowboats passed through on their way to the city.

Beth and her youngest son had never seen a narrowboat before. The colourful scenes and the intricate pattern of roses painted on the sides of the cabins added a charm to the boats, but the watchers, Beth in particular, found it hard to imagine how a whole family could live in such tiny cabins. Later, when they were back in Marshville and she was recounting their experiences to Jessie, she found that it was the cramped living quarters which had impressed itself most strongly on her mind.

Before the family had gone to Christleton, Thomas had been quite worried that by staying at the Hughes's house with its fine furnishings, Beth might be cast down, but although she did revel in the comfort afforded by such fine furniture, she was not affected too much. As Beth pointed out to her husband later, when she was at Reeve House with its even finer furniture and furnishings, each night she would return to their own cottage with no thoughts of comparing the two abodes. She never felt that their home was in any way inferior to that of the Big House. She was also very proud of her own furniture, as it had all been made by Thomas, which to Beth made every piece very special! Besides, there was the fact that whilst the Banhams were staying at Christleton, they saw that Becky and Alwyn Hughes treated their house as a real home and not as a showplace. Beth comforted herself as she always did with the thought that when they got a house of their own, she would have her precious furniture and dearly loved things around her once more.

At the end of their stay Beth and Thomas were ready to go home. They were not too reluctant, for they knew that such comfortable living amongst the dust-free, carpeted surroundings of the Hughes home was not their lot at this time of their lives. They were sensible enough to know that the sooner they were back in Marshville, the quicker they would settle to those spartan conditions again.

On a lighter note, on the first day of their stay, Beth had taken Peter to one side and impressed on him the advisability of not saying anything to anybody about the new 'privy'! She had learned that Mr. Hughes, always eager to embrace any new device, had decided that whilst he was having a (rather obtrusive) central heating system installed, they would have the latest type of water closet put in. Peter was fascinated by the marvellous flushing mechanism, and eventually his mother had been forced to limit his visits to the 'little room'!

The visit to Christleton came to an end, and by the exhortations of both Rebecca and Alwyn Hughes to come again, Thomas and Beth were convinced that the open invitation was genuinely expressed. They had most certainly been made to feel at home.

Dafyd's mother hugged Beth and said, "Do you mind if I come to see you the next time I stay at Florence's?" Thomas was very glad to see that his wife did not hesitate for one second before she answered, "I would love to see you Becky' in fact, I would be most disappointed if you could not come to see me." In that short exchange there had been no sign that Beth was ashamed of her humble abode. The change in his wife's attitude towards the hut was remarkable and heartening to Thomas.

On meeting Captain Howard on his return to work, Thomas gratefully thanked his employer for insisting that he took the holiday; he had not realised how badly he needed the respite from his work, even though the pace of it had, by then, settled to a less frantic tempo than previously.

Some days after their return, an incident occurred which, whilst at the time was quite upsetting, later was seen as offering new hope for Peter's future health as regards his asthma.

The weather had been hot and dry for days, and on that particular day, a gang of boys had chased Peter, the twins and their friends down the lane to Marshville. Peter had ended up at the rear of Mrs. Garroway's hut struggling to breathe, and when Mrs. Garroway saw the state he was in, she fetched one of her 'remedies' and wetted a cloth with the stuff, and clamped the cloth over his mouth and nose. Miraculously, or so it seemed to the boy, within seconds he felt an enormous relief, and after ten minutes was breathing naturally!

Afterwards, when Beth came round to thank Mrs. Garroway, the woman looked rather puzzled after she had heard that Peter was prone to asthma, and she told Beth that she did not think he suffered from that ailment. In her opinion he was suffering from something that her people (gypsies) called, and uttered an almost unpronounceable word. She then said the stuff she had administered to Peter was always used. Then she nearly made Beth choke with horror when she said, quite seriously, "'Course it's usually horses that are treated with it, Mrs. Banham!" However, needless to say, after seeing the way it had worked on Peter, Beth was only too pleased to purchase a bottle of the odd smelling 'elixir'.

Christmas Eighteen Ninety-Two was one that most of them would remember with no pleasure, for many of them at Marshville and some of them in Frodsham went down with a form of influenza. Michael was one of the fortunate ones, as he had gone to visit his parents for a few days. It was months before those who had been affected began to shake off the effects of the illness.

At the end of March, Captain Howard and Kate managed to visit his house at Milford, although the weather was bitterly cold. Mary had been both ecstatic and fearful at the thoughts of meeting Jem once more, but she need not have worried; he too had been longing to see her again. Then during the summer Kate and Mary had gone to Wroxing for two weeks and on the second week Richard had joined them at Reeve House, and they were able to visit her parents. James and Charlotte were in fine fettle and were proud as Punch to show off baby Charles.

Another chance in September allowed them a second visit to Milford and Mary began walking out with Jem. That was only after Captain Howard had talked man to man with his under-gardener concerning Mary.

The summer months saw Daisy and John Tinker engaged, and although Mrs. Hilyard realised that possibly she could soon lose her younger maid to marriage, she was quite contented with Daisy's choice. Prior to them getting engaged, John Tinker had gone with Daisy to see her parents. Being accompanied by her young man, the train journey to Chester followed by another train ride to Hatchmere in Delamere Forest held no terrors for the girl.

Her parents were no strangers to John. Over the years, when they had needed to call in the shop on their occasional visits to Frodsham, they had seen him develop from a shy diminutive boy into a tall, confident, young man, and were more than happy to welcome him into the family.

The long-distance friendship, for all that it seemed to be, between Will and Bronwen was not advancing at all, thanks to the obstacles put in the way of the two young people seeing each other. Her father considered his daughter too young to be thinking about boys, even though he had formed a good opinion of Will at Victoria's wedding. Also, she was training to be a telegraphist and was showing promise at the job, and he did not want her to be distracted from what she was doing.

Dafyd was not convinced by his uncle's reasoning; he saw him wanting to keep Bronwen at Caerwys, and if she did find someone whom she felt serious about enough to marry, then he wanted him to be a local man. Another excuse was that he would not let her meet anybody without a chaperone. Dafyd could see his point of view about that, but to provide a chaperone would be easily arranged.

Will knew nothing of these family matters. All he knew was that the girl had a habit of coming into his mind on more and more occasions; he had even dreamed of her, but they were rather sad episodes, and in them she always smiled at him but walked away, leaving him feeling frustrated. All he wanted to do was to be with her and share their thoughts and feelings for each other.

July saw a change in the population of Marshville again. With the opening of Runcorn Docks, most of the Runcorn dock workers returned to their home town. However, within weeks of the huts being vacated, many of them were occupied again as other men came looking for work on the jetties of Saltport, in some cases bringing their families with them. Ted Robbins had been given the task of letting the huts and collecting the rents. Other people not connected with the Canal Company were allowed to rent a small number of the huts; it was preferable to seeing them uninhabited and neglected. However, those who had lived there over the years found it all very unsettling. They felt that they did not belong anymore. Johnny, the coal heaver, was not worried about the changes to the village, and made it clear that he would stay as long as the place was still being used.

As was to be expected, after July some of the shipping that had been calling at Saltport reverted to docking at Runcorn, but the transhipment of salt and other commodities from the Weaver Navigation continued. Also the coal tips, mainly used for the bunkering of steam ships were still busy, so to those who lived in Marshville, the dirty, noisy coal trains passing the end of the street were still a part of their daily lives.

The wedding of Ian Blake and Sarah Mills, planned to take place in late summer, had been put off at Sarah's suggestion. Ian's father had been taken ill with a serious complaint and it had been a very difficult few months with Ian travelling back and forward to his parents' home. With Mr. Blake senior on the mend, a new date was to be decided upon, but it was to be sometime in the following year.

About this time Dafyd had a serious talk with Will about eventually joining the Hughes family firm, which of course meant that he would have to travel into Chester each day or come to live at Christleton. Of course, his decision would depend on the situation his parents were left in when the Canal was completed. As it was, Dafyd had made him the offer and he was left with plenty of time to make up his mind, as by that time it was obvious that the completion date for the Canal was still a long way off.

Even so, the completion of the Canal was now taken as an inescapable fact by the scheme's opponents, and a panic had set in as they tried to think up ways to blunt the impact of it on the fortunes of their particular businesses. Suggestions such as building more cotton mills in Liverpool were outweighed by easier moves to lower the port and other charges, which in turn led to the furious response, that if the port authorities had not kept their charges high in the first place, the building of the 'Big Ditch' would never have been mooted. The railway companies had already introduced lower charges on goods. But for all the harsh and derisive words that had been printed against the canal scheme, some newspapers were big enough to admit their error and praised the tenacity and courage of their Manchester opponents.

Late autumn brought mixed weather and, on occasions, thick fog, the bane of the ships' pilots, but even the better days tended to be grey and dreary. It was on such a day, the Seventh of December, that the ferry, *Snowdrop*, with the Canal directors on board, quietly left the landing stage at Liverpool and made its way to Eastham Locks and the start of the first full length passage along the Canal.

No word had been released about the trip, and although *Snowdrop* passed Frodsham Depot at about nine o'clock that morning when the men were working, very few witnessed the event. Even those who were lucky enough to see the vessel steam past were not aware of the significance of the event, or who the group of well-wrapped gentlemen passengers were. But by the time the vessel was nearing Manchester, news had got out and crowds were beginning to form on the embankments.

On arriving at Pomona Docks, Manchester, the party aboard *Snowdrop* was greeted by hundreds of excited people crowded (rather frighteningly) right up to the edge of the quaysides. After just over six difficult and, at times, heartbreaking years, the Manchester Ship Canal was seen to be completed!

Of course, there were still formalities to be attended to. The Councils of both Salford and Manchester had to certify the new facility as fit to be a port, which then involved the setting up of a Customs and Excise office, but those were mere details to the ordinary man in the street. There was an air of euphoria everywhere!

Naturally, when the people of Marshville learned of the successful first passage, they were delighted, but chagrined that they had not witnessed it. However, in the Banham household, on hearing the news, they were more subdued. Long ago Michael had spoken of his intention of seeing the Canal finished before leaving them, after which he intended to move to Glasgow so that he could be nearer to Jeannie, and the little ferry's trip had confirmed that it was indeed completed, so now it was just a matter of time when the young Irishman was gone for good.

After living together in the same hut for so long, the Banhams considered Michael to be part of the family. He had been an immense support for Beth in those miserable early months after her arrival at the 'village'; his cheerful presence and understanding manner had lifted her spirits time and time again. He was like another son to Beth and Thomas, but the whole family were dreading the day when he went out of their lives.

Whilst on the subject of families, there was the usual problem with newly married couples as to which set of parents would be the first to enjoy their company over the Christmas meal. To Alwyn Hughes there was only one answer: his son and his-daughter-in-law must spend Christmas Day with Victoria's family.

His gesture stemmed from the conviction that Thomas would soon be looking for another job and probably somewhere else to live, so a dinner together in their own home would lift the spirits of the Banham family. Therefore, Victoria and Dafyd spent Christmas Eve at Christleton, joining Mrs. Hilyard, who had accepted her friend's invitation to stay with them over the festive season. The following day the young couple returned to Marshville, where they joined the rest of the Banham family over Christmas dinner.

Despite their sadness at the imminent departure of Michael, and the anxieties about their future, Thomas and Beth felt their spirits rise as the year drew to a close. Indeed, it was not to be wondered at, for word had gone round that a great many vessels were rumoured to be gathering ready to traverse the Manchester Ship Canal!

However, with regard to Michael, when word spread of the planned celebration to take place on New Year's Day, which included the flotilla of ships passing Frodsham Depot, he decided to postpone his departure until after the event. Therefore, he spent Christmas with his family in Belfast and returned to Marshville on New Year's Eve. When he got back to the 'village', his stomach was just about recovered, as the crossing had been quite rough and Michael had never been so glad to be back on dry land!

New Year's Day, Eighteen Ninety-Four, and from first light on that dull morning, the ships started coming up the Canal. There were vessels from the diminutive tugs, carrying but a few passengers, to the largest ferries, carrying hundreds. At the head of the flotilla was Mr. Samuel Platt's steam yacht *Norseman*, a brave and cheerful sight on a gloomy day.

By mid-morning the embankment was massed with people cheering each ship as it sailed past. Near the workshop, one of the men had hoisted a large Union Flag, and a rather faded string of bunting had been draped between the huts. Dafyd's shop was doing a very brisk trade, whilst on the embankment Mr. Parks and Lucy, together with other 'drinks sellers', were busy with people wanting hot drinks, for it was a cold, miserable day for a celebration. But it did not seem to dampen the spirits of those who were there.

Captain Howard and Kate, having spent Christmas in Norfolk, were back in time to come down early to Marshville. Beth was pleased to see them and was glad of some help from Mary in making up the food for all her visitors. Mrs. Hilyard did not decide to come down until later and regretted the delay, for the lanes were crowded with people, carriages and traps. The police were there to make sure that the lanes were not completely blocked, but there was no major trouble; most people were in a good mood.

When Mrs. Hilyard, accompanied by Victoria and Daisy, did manage to get near to the Canal, she was surprised to see a face she recognised from the time when her husband was alive and had his office in Liverpool. The person had been the part owner and a superb chef of a high-class chophouse in the business area. She could not remember all the details of how his business had failed, but she did know that his partner, a man called Dufay, had mishandled the financial side of things. He had then disappeared, leaving his partner to shoulder the blame and carry the stigma of being declared bankrupt. And there, reduced to selling drinks from a cart, was the chef, Mr. Parks. She also recalled that the man's wife had run off with Dufay. Perhaps, she mused, Mr. Parks had been lucky to be rid of her!

The incident left Mrs. Hilyard very sad, for Mr. Parks had always been the perfect gentleman and well thought of as a man and as a chef. That such a man should fall so far through no fault of his own upset her badly.

When Dr. Mills and Sarah accompanied by Mrs. Joyce, did manage to get there, many of the ships had passed through and the crowd was thinning slightly.

Due to the fact that the ships were having to enter the Canal through the locks at Eastham, and only so many could be accommodated at a time, every so often there was a break in the line of vessels passing the Depot. The persons with the telescopes became very popular, as they were able to shout out when another cluster of ships were on their way!

In all, seventy-six vessels entered the Canal, but because of the delays as they passed through the locks at Latchford, Irlam, Barton and, finally, Mode Wheel, many failed to travel the whole journey that first day and were forced to moor up for the night where they could, and sail into the docks at Manchester and Salford the following day. Crowds lined the banks for much of the way, cheering each vessel.

However, it was not a time of celebration for everyone. People going about their everyday business at various points along the new waterway found it very frustrating to join the queues of carts and wagons as they were being constantly stopped whilst the bridges were swung to allow each batch of ships to pass through. Not everybody was happy that day, some cursing the coming of the 'Cut'!

At Marshville on the third day of the year, many tears were shed in the Banham hut as Michael said farewell to them all. They had known long enough that it was inevitable he would one day take leave of them, but it did not make it any easier now that time had come. Beth clung to him and wept, and Peter was just as affected, whilst Michael attempted to lighten the mood by making jokes and acting flippantly, but he too ended up in tears.

Thomas and Will accompanied him to the station in Dafyd's trap, and he carried several parcels of gifts for Jeannie and Flora from everyone. Everything that needed to be said had been said at the hut, so they simply wished him a safe journey and told him they would look forward to seeing him again even if they had to wait a long time to do so.

What should have been a hopeful, happy start to the year was the opposite for some of them. Ian Blake had been dashing back and forth to his parents' home as his father still had not fully recovered from his illness. And for his fiancée Sarah, she had not had such a dreary Christmas for a long time. Apart from an invite for herself and Dr. Mills to share Christmas dinner with Mrs. Joyce, she had resigned herself to a lonely few days until Ian returned. Then she met Victoria whom she thought would be at Christleton, and her spirits lifted. A visit with her father to witness part of the flotilla of ships, then a visit to the Banhams' hut cheered her immensely. When Ian returned to Frodsham with the news that his father was now on the mend, Sarah's happiness was complete. The worrying fact that Ian might not hold his job for much longer did not trouble her as it had been doing. Sarah felt more hopeful about the new year.

Chapter 34

Leaving Marshville. Getting a House at Last

For all the rough-and-ready men and women who made up the population of Marshville, there had always been a warmth amongst the 'villagers', born of the shared experience of hard work and basic living conditions. When the Banham family arrived at the village, they were seen as 'different' to the rest of them, but after a while they were accepted and treated with the same spirit of camaraderie.

But as families moved away when their menfolk went on to other contracts that camaraderie began to decline. It became noticeable at the time when Sally (the one without the twins!) and her husband left, followed soon after by the family with the troupe of four girls. Whereas before that time, when meeting on the street, people tended to stop and exchange a few words, the newer people simply nodded and passed by.

Christmas, New Year and the cavalcade of ships had the effect of bringing the villagers together for a while and lifted everybody's spirits, but after Michael left, Marshville seemed a duller, less cheerful place. Prior to that, Jacob Morrison had decided to retire and move to Warrington where his sister lived, and later, in February, Sally (with the twins) went to live at Runcorn when her husband obtained a job in a boatyard. The heart seemed to have gone from Marshville.

Not everyone was bothered by this. Johnny, the coal heaver, and one of the crane drivers appeared to be oblivious to the changed mood of the village or to the declining position of Saltport, and were determined to stay on as though everything was the same as it always had been.

Jessie and Ted Robbins were certainly aware of the problems that were building up for the little port and the Depot, and observed the change in people's attitude, but were not making any moves to leave. The fact was that they were hoping to rent a shop in Frodsham and settle in the town, and they were prepared to wait until one was available. On top of the job of collecting the rents for the huts, Ted Robbins dealt with the wages of the men working at the Depot and Saltport. He also had to be present as a witness on payday when the cashiers came from Ellesmere Port. Apart from his Company duties, through the good offices of Dr. Mills he had built up a small but growing clientele in and around the town for his bookkeeping services. Therefore he and Jessie were in a good position to wait until a shop came along to realise Jessie's dream.

At the workshops Michael's absence was keenly felt, but it was as a person, not so much as a fitter, because by then the amount of work had lessened. Also Robbie was now fully time-served and the younger apprentice was not far off from being out of his time. Thomas was proud of the two young men, and the fact that he and Michael had been able to pass their skills on to the pair of them.

But the job itself did not hold the same attraction for him as it had done previously. He missed the urgency that formerly added spice to his working day, and he regretted that most of the work coming to the workshop rarely required the skills that the men could offer. Much of it was of a level that even a tradesman of average skills could deal with. As a consequence he was not enjoying working at the Depot as he had in the earlier times. By the end of February he had decided to look for another job. Robbie, being a local man, had started making enquiries about vacancies in the area for his foreman.

However, Robbie's enquiries did not bring news of any jobs, which was not surprising as Frodsham was not blessed (or cursed, depending on whom one spoke to!) with many industries which required men with engineering skills, and when jobs of that nature did occur, local men were usually considered first.

Thomas's chances of finding employment were little improved even though the Banham family had a good standing in the eyes of many people in the town. Apart from their good name with members of the Chapel congregation, others were influenced by the family's friendships with persons as elevated as Dr. Mills and his daughter, Mrs. Hilyard, and Captain and Mrs. Howard.

About this time, Will again spoke to his parents about Dafyd's earlier offer of a job with the Hughes family firm. When he raised the matter he said seriously, "What bothers me is that I would be leaving whilst you would still be without a proper house, and you, Dad, could be facing an uncertain future at the Depot." He added miserably, "I feel as if I would be abandoning you if I left."

His mother hugged him and said cheerfully, "Now don't you fret, our Will, we will be alright. I don't want to see you go, but that is just plain selfishness on a mother's part; what you need to do is what is best for you, boy."

At this point his father broke in and agreed with Beth, but reminded his son of how things were before they came to Marshville. "When we were at Wroxing there seemed to be no prospects for your future, but here in Cheshire you have been offered a wonderful opportunity and I say to you, son, that unless you have no wish to go to Chester, then seize the chance without a second thought." Then he smiled broadly and told his son, "Your mam is right, Will, we will be alright, and remember this, if it does not turn out as you would have it, you are not obliged to stick with it, you can always walk away and look for something else." He then said seriously, "Dafyd would be disappointed, but I doubt that he would want to hold you if he knew that your heart was not in it."

Beth nodded her agreement and said, "Whatever you do, Will, we are not that far away from you anyway." Little did Beth know, but a few months later they would not be at Marshville, but somewhere even further away from Chester!

The following day Dafyd received his answer and later wrote to his family that Will would be joining them at Christleton. Will also wrote to Bronwen giving her the same news, which made the girl very happy indeed, for the young man of her dreams would be within just one train journey away from her instead of two.

Spring arrived with only slightly warmer weather than that they had endured since November the previous year, but there did not seem to be any more warmth in the 'village'.

At Saltport there was a flurry of activity for the workshop men when a loaded coal wagon became derailed in one of the tips. The coal tips were mechanical structures which allowed a complete railway wagon to be tipped, depositing its load directly into the ship's hold or bunkers, and these were the bane of Thomas's working life, and a major reason why he had become dissatisfied with the job. Dirty work, heavy work, he was used to that, but the coal dust at the tips seemed to get everywhere and clogged his lungs. He disliked them more than anything else he had to deal with.

The problem resulted in emergency call-out and meant working all through the night to put it back into operation again. But even this call on Thomas's skill and ingenuity failed to raise his enthusiasm for what he was doing. That he did not comment on the job and the fact that he very rarely mentioned what he had done during his day told Beth that he seemed to have lost the zest for the job.

She had been worried about him for some time and one Sunday, when Will was at the shop and Peter was out playing, Beth asked him outright what was troubling him. Thomas was only too glad to unburden himself and began by telling her that he would have spoken earlier but he did not want to worry her, at which Beth had replied, "Oh, Thomas boy, I do worry about things, but I am not about to break down with it all. After what we have gone through these last few years, it will take a lot to get me in that state again." Then she smiled and told him, "I am a lot stronger now, you know."

Thomas grinned fondly at his wife and, reaching across the table, he took her hand and answered, "Yes, girl, stronger, but not harder." Then he said sombrely, "We have seen the effect that years on contract work has on people; it is stamped on their faces, and I did not want that to happen to you, my love." Then Thomas said very seriously, "That is another reason why I feel we should get away from here."

Then he said very slowly, "I believe that we should move away before we are forced to, and," he added half jokingly, "before I get much older: at forty-seven years of age I am getting to a point where no employer will take me on."

Beth broke in and said forcibly, "But you are a strong, healthy man, Thomas Banham, and your skills would be a boon to any firm." Her husband smiled ruefully and answered, "Unfortunately for me, you are not an employer, girl." He stood up and looked out of the window on to the dreary 'street' and said to his wife, "The work at the depot is no longer to my taste, Beth, and besides, if I am any judge, none of us will be needed in a few years time. Saltport is very slowly losing traffic. I just cannot see any future here for us."

Then, in a change of mood, he said briskly to the silent Beth, "I have asked Robbie to keep his ears open for any hint of a suitable job, and if there is anything, we will try again to find a house." At that Beth said quietly, "But, Thomas, in all these years we have still not found one. Will things be any better these days?"

"Well," said her husband, "I don't know, and that brings me to the crux of the matter. If I cannot find a job in or near Frodsham and if we don't find a house, we will have to look elsewhere, and that could mean moving to Runcorn or, perhaps, Warrington."

"Oh, Thomas," Beth burst out, her voice trembling, "that would mean we would be even further from Victoria when she moves to Chester, and Will as well now that he has accepted Dafyd's offer. We would hardly see either of them."

"Now, Beth," said her husband soothingly, "both towns are but a short distance away from Chester. Another ten or twenty minutes on the train would not be so bad, would it, and Jessie too, would still be only a short distance away." It all came as an unpleasant shock to Beth, for she had blithely allowed herself to dream of settling in Frodsham.

However, she was not alone in observing Thomas's ennui with his work. Captain Howard had also noticed his disenchantment with concern. For some time he and Kate had discussed how they could ensure that the Banhams were settled before they, the Howards, moved to Hampshire. They both carried a burden of responsibility for the Banhams' situation. Kate, in particular, was still feeling guilty (and would do for some years) for not acting more forcibly with her late husband on that dreadful day.

When Captain Howard eventually broached the subject, Thomas was somewhat embarrassed and rather guilty, but he owned up that the type of jobs the workshop was dealing with of late gave him little or no pleasure at all.

The future of Saltport and the Depot was raised by Captain Howard, who told his foreman quite bluntly that in his opinion the facility would cease to be used in a few years' time. At the present time more and more of the cargoes previously handled at Saltport were being dealt with at Salford and Manchester docks, and coal was being routed in much larger quantities at the massive coaling basin at Partington.

He then told Thomas about his enquiries and his lack of success, finally coming to the chance of a job at Barton. When he explained that Barton Installation, to give it the full title, was just over six miles from Manchester, Thomas made his mind up immediately: the job was not for him. Neither Beth nor himself would want to be so far from Victoria, Will and Dafyd. However, other factors eventually persuaded them to think differently.

Thomas learned that a Superintendent was to be appointed for Saltport and more pertinently to the foreman, he would be over Frodsham Depot and the workshops. That the gentleman was not an engineer or a tradesman of any sort bothered Thomas a lot even before he had set eyes on the man.

A further unsettling factor was the news contained in two letters that he and Beth had received. Beth's letter was from Sally (with the twins) in which she wrote that her husband had settled in quite well at the 'Sprinch', the local name for the boatyard, but due to the stomach-churning smells from a nearby tannery, they had been looking for another house but with little success. She wrote that though poor quality houses were sometimes to be had, better quality houses were very hard to come by.

The second letter was from Jacob Morrison, who had been in regular touch with Thomas, and he had generously spent a lot of time walking round Warrington looking for houses for the Banhams and enquiring after jobs for Thomas. The results made depressing reading.

Like many places along the route of the Canal, with the scheme completed many of the workers, rather than dispersing to where they had come from, had settled in the areas where they had worked, resulting in a glut of labour and a corresponding demand for houses

Jacob hardly needed to point out that this applied to Warrington like everywhere else.

Finally, nearer to home, Peter had become very subdued since the twins had moved away. Whilst his parents were fully aware of his upset about them leaving and tried to soften the blow by giving him more of their time, they did not know that there was another, much uglier problem that Peter was having to endure.

The first they knew about it was during a conversation between his father and Will concerning Captain Howard's news, and without realising that his son was there, Thomas mentioned the job at Barton. Peter came fully into the room and said fervently, "Let's go there, Dad, then Goff Bolton's gang can't get me."

There was a moment's silence, then his father said sharply, "What is this, son, and who is Goff Bolton?" Hesitantly at first, Peter had told them everything, and it was a relief for him to get the whole business off his chest, and when he had told them what had been happening, the family were seething.

Goff Bolton, a boy in Peter's class, had long been jealous of his popularity at school. The boy and some of his like-minded companions had taken to harassing him, but had never got beyond the name-calling and jeering stage due to Peter having the twins and other boys around him when he had made his way home from school.

But now that the twins were gone and the other boys were too scared to face Goff Bolton's gang, Peter had been chased several times, as he had been when he ended up outside Mrs. Garroway's hut struggling for breath. The gang had become increasingly bold, subjecting Peter to a bit of manhandling at times. Recently they had taken to waiting for him in Marsh Lane to torment him.

"Why didn't you tell us about it?" cried Beth. "I could have stopped it in no time if I had known." His father, who understood his son quite well, said, "There is nothing cowardly or childish about telling your parents about such things, Peter. You are a brave lad but you cannot do much to defend yourself when you are outnumbered; you need help sometimes."

Will broke in and said fiercely, "I'll tackle them tomorrow, Peter. Don't worry. They have got to be shown that you are not on your own." At that Thomas nodded, but said quietly, "We will all go, son. If me and your mam are in Main Street and watch what they do when you are coming home, you, Will, could be stationed in Marsh Lane so that we can trap them and put a stop to their games."

Peter was still worried, but he felt buoyed up with the thoughts that he now had reinforcements. He was treated to extra hugs from his mother and just as pleasing was the bar of chocolate from Dafyd!

The following afternoon Beth and Thomas were standing outside the Chapel, pretending to read a notice, when six or seven grinning boys ran past, their boots clattering on the pavement as they headed for Marsh Lane. Ominously, some of them were carrying sticks, whilst others had something hidden under their jackets.

Then Peter came into view, completely alone and very nervous. Thomas said quietly, "Once you get into Marsh Lane, son, slow down to a dawdle, and we will not be far behind you." Their youngest son nodded, then walked on.

The plan worked to perfection. Goff Bolton had got the lads to form a passageway so that Peter was to be forced to pass between them, and to add a bit more fear, they were tapping the sticks together threateningly. Catching sight of Peter coming towards them, the Bolton boy began calling out, "Jungle music for a savage," and the others cackled and joined in by bawling, "Banny the Savage."

Will had experienced difficulty finding enough cover to conceal himself, and he ended up along the lane near the brickfield, and when he saw that he was needed, he had to dash in order to corner the boys before they managed to escape. One lad who tried was roughly dragged back by his collar. Will was in a ferocious temper, having witnessed the fear on his younger brother's face as he slowly approached the braying mob.

Some of the boys had tried to escape into the town, but when confronted by their victim's angry parents, their triumphant expressions were replaced by those of frightened small boys, and as one they threw down the sticks.

Thomas had impressed on Beth and Will that it would be more effective if he alone did the talking, and although both his wife and his oldest son were boiling with rage, they stayed silent but grim-faced. In no time at all, he had learned the names of the bullies and where they lived, in the process reducing the cowardly Bolton boy to a blubbering jelly. The boys were then marched single-file back to the school, where Peter's shocked teacher took them in to see the headmaster. Whilst Thomas was sure that the culprits would be dealt with properly, including being made to pay back money taken by threats from some of the other children, he left with a strong conviction that the headmaster resented the Banham family's methods of dealing with the problem.

The family were quiet as they made their way back to Marshville. Rather than feeling jubilant at the way that they had dealt with the matter, the adults wondered whether they had created further problems for Peter. Even the boy himself could see the possibility that some members of the gang would make life difficult for him in other ways.

On reaching their hut, Peter showed little inclination to play out with the other children, so Will suggested he helped in the shop until his evening meal. The unsettled boy brightened at that and went with his brother to 'help'.

Beth made a pot of tea for herself and Thomas, but as she set the cups down onto the table she started to weep. In an instant Thomas was with her and she clung to him until her tears stopped.

"Now, Beth," said her husband soothingly, "Peter's troubles are now in the open and we can deal with them. Don't worry, my love, we will not let it get that serious in future." Almost before Thomas had finished speaking Beth said miserably, "But, Thomas, it happened here in Frodsham; it will never be the same again, and I had fallen in love with the town, and now it's all spoiled."

Her husband tried to console her by telling her that such things happened in every town, village or hamlet, and that they had to be faced up to just as they had been that day, but it was to no avail. Thomas tried to reassure her and said, "We will make sure that Peter is not left without protection from now on." He continued, "There must be someone with him going to school and returning home, and, Beth," he said quietly, "you will surely find that the town is not such an unfriendly place as it seems on this day." Beth nodded, but she was not any happier; the town she had fallen in love with was not the same anymore. She felt betrayed by Frodsham.

From that day on, Peter was always accompanied to school, but, on his insistence, not within sight of the place. In the afternoon he would be met on Main Street, and although he made a show of not wanting to be chaperoned, secretly he was very glad of the service!

The following week there occurred something which gave rise to further feelings of anxiety in Beth, and she spoke of it to her husband and Will.

On the Monday of that week, she met Peter, and not long after entering Marsh Lane they came upon two youths aimlessly shuffling about in the roadway. At first Beth thought it was a bit odd but no more than that, but when the same thing happened on the Tuesday afternoon, she felt the stirrings of fear, although the youths had not acted in any way threateningly towards them. It was more what they did not do that worried her. They did not speak, nor did they seem to have a purpose for being there: they were simply loitering.

The following day Will made it his business to meet Peter and on that occasion there was only one youth in the lane, but on seeing Will, he made as though to walk back towards Main Street, but still no nod of the head or greeting. Peter had no idea who they were, but was convinced that they were the older brothers of one of Goff Bolton's gang, and he was very much afraid.

The same week, the new Saltport Superintendent made his appearance. His name was Mr. Truscot and he was introduced to the men by Captain Howard who, with the man's arrival, ceased to have any jurisdiction over Frodsham Depot. In appearance he was the completely opposite of Captain Howard. A man below medium height and portly in build, he was hardly a commanding figure, but he demonstrated his steely qualities the following day when Captain Howard was not at the Depot.

Apart from those at the Depot he had already earmarked as unnecessary, the man let Thomas know that two journeyman fitters and one foreman fitter was one employee too many. He also considered that a foreman over such a small number of tradesmen was an expensive extravagance; a charge hand would be sufficient in his opinion.

The man's meaning was quite clear. Thomas would have to accept a reduction in position along with a reduction in wages, and make the unhappy choice as to whether Robbie should go, or whether the apprentice (soon to become a journeyman) would be sacked.

Another and even greater shock was that the man, as Superintendent, was entitled to one of the two largest huts in Marshville, as his rooms at the Bear's Paw were only a temporary arrangement. It was a matter of no concern to Mr. Truscot whether the Banham family moved to a smaller hut or whether it was Ted and Jessie Robbins who had to move, but he did not say whom he would displace. It angered Thomas, for it seemed that he had been put into a position where any unpleasant choices that had to be to be made would be made by him.

Not surprisingly, when the Banhams talked to Jessie and Ted that evening, their neighbours were very angry at Mr. Truscot's calm assertion that he could, and would, take possession of one of their abodes without any consideration for the distress he would cause. Beth had never seen their friends so furious, even Ted, who had not been made aware of the Superintendent's intentions, was blazing.

But the question of who should move to the smaller hut remained unasked, and surprisingly it was Beth who settled the matter when she turned to her husband saying in a very determined voice, "Well, Thomas, I think we should look at that job for you at Barton."

Whilst everyone was taken aback by Beth's dramatic change of subject, Thomas experienced a surge of hope. Certainly there were sacrifices to be made, but he would not have the unpleasant task of sacking one of his lads, and there would be no need for Jessie and Ted to leave their hut. And he knew from the new man's attitude that he held Thomas, or for that matter, anybody at the Depot in no great esteem, and their future looked to be less than comfortable. Neither Jessie nor Ted was happy with the idea of losing their neighbours, or even more upsettingly, their friends, but they could see that such a move was almost inevitable.

When Captain Howard was informed of their decision and the reasons behind it, he was at once angry at the man Truscot's actions and attitude, but glad that the Banhams would be moving to Barton, for he believed Thomas would have a better chance at that away from Marshville. Even so, Captain Howard felt that he could not simply do nothing about Truscot's cavalier way of dealing with the workers at the Depot and resolved to talk to someone when he visited Manchester in a few days' time. He and Kate had been fortunate in being invited to attend the official opening of the Canal by Her Majesty Queen Victoria on the Twenty-Third of May.

The ceremony was to be held in the main turning basin between Salford Docks and Trafford Wharf, and because they were not to be in the main pavilion, Captain Howard did not manage to meet the person with whom he had intended to voice his complaints about Mr. Truscot.

Knowing that they would be in an open-air compound with many other guests, Kate had wisely not chosen too delicate an ensemble, and afterwards she was thankful for her decision. People were there in their thousands, and even in the railed-off enclosure, it was a crush.

The Admiralty had sent two gunboats, *HMS Seagull* and *HMS Speedy*, and for the occasion, Her Majesty was to carry out her engagement on board the Admiralty steam yacht, *Enchantress*.

The whole of Manchester and Salford were en-fête, streets were decorated with flags and bunting, bringing colour and brightness to a rather dull day. An arch of fire escape ladders had been erected and decorated by the fire brigade, and other decorated set pieces had been erected to celebrate the historic day.

But when the Queen arrived to board the *Enchantress*, Kate felt exceptionally sorry for her. As Kate said afterwards when she described the scene, "Her Majesty did not look at all as if she noticed anything, in fact," Kate said sympathetically, "She simply appeared as a tired old lady, anxious to have it all done with and be allowed to be on her way."

The ceremony began with a short cruise by the *Enchantress* towards Mode Wheel Locks, then after a button was pressed, the lock gates swung open and symbolically the steam yacht *Norseman* proudly entered the 'Pool', which was surrounded by the cheering multitude. From the adjacent Manchester Racecourse, a twenty-one gun salute thundered out, causing Kate and most others to almost leap out of their skins!

Then came the ceremony where the Lord Mayor of Manchester and the Mayor of Salford were both knighted. After a short while, Her Majesty came ashore, boarded her carriage and was driven back to London Road Station where the royal train was waiting to whisk Queen Victoria on her way to Scotland.

Meanwhile, at Marshville many of those living and working there were under the impression that Queen Victoria was to sail up the Canal to declare it open, and were disappointed to witness the Admiralty vessels pass by, with no signs of Royalty aboard.

However, the Banham family were more concerned with their own coming visit to Barton, and thanks to the sympathetic perception of Mrs. Hilyard and Dafyd, both Victoria and Will were to accompany their parents. In truth they were all excited about what they would find when they reached their destination, but Will paradoxically felt as if he was the one who was moving away from his family at a time when they needed support.

After alighting at Patricroft Station, they walked to Barton and were pleasantly surprised to find how soon they were there. They were also surprised at the warm welcome they received from the Installation Superintendent and his staff. Whether it was due to being faced with two very attractive ladies, but whatever the reason, the men showed a friendly face towards Thomas which put him completely at ease.

The family were quite impressed by both the swingbridge and the aqueduct, the latter being exceptionally busy with barges and narrowboats working along the Bridgewater Canal as they passed over the Manchester Ship Canal. When a large ship approached, they were fascinated to witness the turning of the road bridge, and the aqueduct, still holding water, allowing the steamship *Venango* to pass through on her way to Manchester.

Beth, whilst being just as entertained as the others, was more interested in seeing the house they would probably be offered. However, although untenanted at the time, workmen were busy installing water and gas supplies. Even so, Beth felt a stirring of interest, for it was roomy and in a good position. The house was situated on Peel Green Road, which in fact was little more than a country lane, and there were a scattering of thatched cottages further along from the house that they were viewing.

After they had partaken of a light meal, armed with directions they walked the short distance along Barton Lane to the school. St. Andrews was an imposing building, opened only the previous year.

There was some slight difficulty at first, but after Peter had been given a small series of tests involving reading, writing and arithmetic, the headmaster was impressed enough to promise his parents that there would be a place for Peter should the family move to Barton.

On leaving the school, they walked the short distance to the centre of Eccles, and were fortunate in that it was market day. Beth took a liking to the town immediately and was sure that she would probably settle to the place.

A short ride on the horse-drawn tram to Patricroft, then it was back on the train to Frodsham. They were all heartened by what they had seen that day, and coupled with the fact that the railway journey time was not too protracted, the move to Barton did not seem so much like being exiled. Peter, of course, could hardly contain his eagerness to leave Frodsham.

In Will's next letter to Bronwen, he poured out his troubled thoughts on his parents' probable move, and the girl, her heart so full of love for the English boy she so rarely saw, wished she could be with him to give him comfort.

The following morning Captain Howard visited the workshop to enquire how Thomas had fared at Barton. He was happy to learn that his one-time foreman had decided to accept the job offered and was writing to the Barton Superintendent that very evening.

At the same time Captain Howard issued an invitation on behalf of Kate and himself for Thomas and his family to attend a farewell meal at their house in Church Street. Afterwards he proceeded to the shop to issue the same invitation to Dafyd and Victoria. He had already issued invitations to Mrs. Joyce, Dr. Mills and Sarah. His last call was on Mrs. Hilyard, and he told her that Daisy must come too.

Beth was in a flutter when her husband gave her the news during his midday meal, but Thomas calmed her down and told her to have a talk with Jessie Robbins, as she and Ted were also invited. Both women were tremendously excited at the prospect of dressing their best, and they made the most of it.

Captain Howard sent a carriage down to Marshville for them and, together with Dafyd's pony trap, none of them had need to walk the distance.

As an occasion to say farewell to their hosts and Mary, everybody was expecting it to be a sombre affair, but that was not the way it turned out to be. Kate and Richard Howard disguised their feelings of sadness very well, and their guests found themselves less upset than they had anticipated, but it was Dr. Mills with his infectious smile and gentle wit that lifted everybody's spirits. They all responded gladly to the cheerful mood, and their hosts found to their relief that they were really enjoying themselves. The food was simple but tasty and Cook had made a splendid cake, which Beth declared was better than the ones that she herself baked!

However, as expected, the leave-taking was rather emotional, with the four girls very affected, and Mary in particular, as she would soon be over two hundred miles away from the others. She wailed, "I will never see you all again, never, and you will all still be able to see each other." Kate entered the room and said gently, "Now, Mary, there is no saying that we will not visit Cheshire again, and we would not do so without looking in on our friends."

The Banhams were the last to leave, and Kate's control over her emotions was taxed to the limit. She clung to Beth and Victoria with a fierceness which almost undid their defences, and for the first time both mother and daughter realised that between the Banhams and the Howards, there really was no class barrier.

Two days later, Captain Howard, Kate and Mary were gone from Frodsham, and the house on Church Street was ready to receive Ian Blake.

Thomas received a letter confirming the job and the house was his, and he then made arrangements for the move to Barton. He wrote to Simon Andern asking for him to arrange for the furniture he was storing in his shed to be sent to Patricroft Station, Eccles. The cost of the carriage had been worked out and Thomas sent the money to the smith after Simon had replied to his letter, promising to do as he had been asked. The furniture was to be delivered to the house at Barton on Tuesday the Sixteenth of June. They planned for Will to 'camp' in the house ready to receive it, and for his parents and Peter to come the following day with just their personal bags.

Dafyd was having his own problems in quitting Marshville. He had been approached by Clara and her husband Jim with a view to taking on the shop when Dafyd left, and although they could not afford to buy the stock, they hoped to come to some arrangement which would allow them to pay over a period.

As far as Dafyd and his father were concerned, they were quite happy to help the couple to start up business for, after all, there was not a huge stock at the shop and Dafyd felt that he owed Clara a lot for helping him over the first few months of his time at Marshville.

As they were settling the final details in the shop one day, Mr. Truscot walked in with a very proprietary manner and demanded to view the shop as the Company's representative. He then asked what rent was being paid for the use of the building, and when he heard what the figure was, tutted and said that the figure would have to be raised, quoting a figure that was so much higher than that which Dafyd had been paying that Clara's fist went to her mouth in shock. She saw her dream of running a shop disappear in an instant, and she could have wept. At first Dafyd was as shocked as Clara, then he was swept with a feeling of anger but before he could even express his outrage, Clara's husband spoke, and said, shrugging his shoulders ruefully, "Well, sir, I doubt if we could make a profit if the rent was so much." Then turning to Dafyd he said sadly, "It seems that you will have do as you proposed, close the shop, Mr. Hughes and clear your stock, but I am sure that my wife will stay with you till you close for good."

Dafyd looked at Jim, and seeing his bland unsmiling face suddenly realised what the man was doing: his air of disappointment was a bluff. Clara was unsure what was going on, especially as Dafyd gave her an almost imperceptible wink.

For a moment Truscot said nothing but his face had changed, then abruptly he said, "Well, of course, a shop must make a profit. I will go and have a word with Robbins, he deals with the rents."

As soon as the Superintendent was seen to enter the Robbins's hut, Jim said contemptuously, "It was good to see that smirk wiped off that toad's face, and him trying to put the blame on Mr. Robbins." Then Clara said worriedly, "But, Jim, if he puts the rent up we won't be able to take the shop on, will we?" Her husband laughed and said, "Love, do you see that slimepot, begging your pardon, Mr. Hughes, walking up to town each morning to get his milk and bread? Well I can't, and what's more, if he brings a wife here, she won't thank him for closing the only shop in the village."

A short time later, Ted Robbins came across and he was in grim mood. "Dafyd," he said, "don't take any notice of what that puffed-up fool says. In fact, I am writing to Head Office in Spring Gardens to explain how things are here in Marshville, and how much trade has been lost for this shop since the navvies have gone." Then, before he turned to leave the shop, he added, "That man was trying to claim credit for winning a few more shillings a week for the Company, as though the Chief Cashier would even notice it." As he left the shop he said, "I will write today; we will soon put a stop to his antics."

Two days after the episode, Dafyd and Victoria moved to Christleton, and Clara saw her dream come true. She and her husband were now the shopkeepers in Marshville.

The business of leaving Marshville was just as upsetting for Beth and Thomas as they had imagined it would be, but they were really surprised and very moved to find that the village still had a heart. People they had never seen before, never mind those they had seen but had not spoken to, came up to them and wished them well in their move. Mrs. Garroway had struggled up to their hut (her gout was troubling her again) and presented Beth with a bottle of her medicine for Peter's chest and some ointment. "Just in case, Mrs. Banham," was what she said.

Jessie had been more emotional than any of them had ever seen her before. She and Beth had sworn tearfully that they would never lose touch with each other, whatever happened.

As the train drew out of Frodsham station, only Peter was in a happy mood. To him it was the beginning of an adventure; for Thomas and Beth it was if they were in the grip of a current which was sweeping them further away from their family and friends.

Chapter 35

The Barton Years

Once they had arrived at Patricroft Station, their spirits revived a little. It was a beautiful day, and of the few people they met as they walked to Barton, most of them nodded a greeting and some smiled. The family found it quaint at first when they heard some greet them with the phrase, "How do?" but eventually Thomas worked out that what they were saying was, "How do you do?"

Beth found it very comforting and by the time they reached the house on Peel Green Road, she was quite cheerful. The door was open and as they entered they were confronted by a roughly dressed man wearing a grubby flat cap and no jacket. His waistcoat looked as if he had spilled more than one dinner down the front of it, but he had a friendly manner and they found themselves smiling at him. "How do?" he said warmly. "You must be Will's mam and dad. I'm Cyril, I'm helping t'lad wit furniture."

As the family looked back at him a bit uncertainly, Will appeared, grinning all over his face. He hugged his parents and ruffled Peter's hair, then said, "Cyril has been a great help. We have got most of the furniture where I think it should go but we can always move things round if you want it different." Then he added, "Kettle's on the fire, Mam," and, turning to his helper he said, "Are you ready for a cup of tea, Cyril?"

The man grinned, but declined, addressing them all, saying something which sounded like, "Th'ole lady'ul be mashin a brew, so I'll geet ome." With that, he touched the kneb of his cap to Beth and went out of the house. His was a broad Lancashire accent and, as they were to learn when they got to know him better, one of the easier accents to understand, especially after they had heard other people from the towns north of Eccles.

Once they were left to themselves and their initial greetings were over, Beth went to freshen herself whilst Will put everything out for a cup of tea. Peter had already staked a claim on a particular chair and was almost bouncing about in it with excitement.

When Beth came in she looked radiant. "Oh, Thomas," she cried. "To run my hands over my own familiar furniture again, I can't tell you how happy it makes me." Then she said firmly, "Mind you, Thomas, I'll have to give it plenty of elbow grease to get it back as I like it."

That first day was a happy one, and Thomas felt the first stirrings of optimism for their future lives at Barton.

Weekend brought Victoria and Dafyd with a letter from Rebecca Hughes and two parcels from Alwyn Hughes. The largest parcel was a large box of candles with a note inside asking Thomas not to buy any candles in future, and the second parcel contained a pair of beautiful brass candlesticks as a housewarming gift. Dafyd explained that his father bought thousands of candles each year and obtained them at a very much lower price than Thomas could possibly buy them.

It was a lovely surprise and Beth's eyes filled with tears at the thoughtfulness of Dafyd's parents. The promise of supplying candles was a Godsend, for no longer were they given candles, lamp oil and coal as they had been at Marshville, and with Thomas's wages being lower, any help to keep down the household expenditure was very welcome.

The whole area around Barton Bridge excited Dafyd's interest, and the house with its long garden sweeping down towards the canal, and the open vista stretching westward towards Barton Locks, he found very exhilarating.

On the first Sunday after Chapel they were amazed to observe the throngs of people crowded on and around the bridge. They soon realised that it was the place where people came dressed in their best to stroll, to see this wondrous new Canal and, with luck, witness a ship passing through. Later they were to hear that the place was sometimes referred to as the 'Monkey Run', where boys and girls would parade to attract each others' attention!

The first attendance of the Chapel had left the family with the impression that the congregation were a stiff unbending lot, very much like Mr. Deakin at the Bourne Methodist Chapel, but as time went by they found that the people were just as friendly as those at Frodsham.

There were quite a lot of Welsh people in the congregation, families whose menfolk had worked on the Canal construction and had settled in the area. For some time Beth felt very much an outsider when she came to the Chapel on days when there was work to be done, but gradually, over the months, she became accepted. Her cake-making and baking skills were once again the key to entering the ladies' group who were the backbone of fund-raising and other events. The trick was, as Beth knew only too well, to recognise which of the ladies was metaphorically speaking, the 'Queen Bee', and to not tread on her toes!

Peter settled in at St. Andrews School the first day, with his classmates, especially the girls, being fascinated by his different and rather attractive accent and his amiable ways. His mother breathed a sigh of relief when he arrived home full of enthusiasm for the school, the pupils and the teachers. But on the afternoon of the second day her son walked in with a shiner of a black eye, bruises on his face, scraped knuckles and blood on his shirt. He also sported a happy, if lopsided grin, and before his shocked mother could utter a word said, "Hey, Mam, I've made a friend today, he's great and his name is Eddie."

Beth found her voice and cried, "But, Peter, who has done this to you, and what are the teachers doing letting it happen?" As she was speaking she was taking off his coat, and then she made him take his shirt off whilst she got a bowl of water and something to bathe his wounds. She shut him up for a moment whilst she attended to him, then asked him again, her temper rising, "Well?" she said grimly. "Who did this to you? I want to know their names, and tomorrow I will see the headmaster."

At that her son looked alarmed and said anxiously, “Aw, Mam, don’t do that, he will get into trouble, and anyway he won’t do it again, ’cause I gave him as good as I got.”

“I don’t care,” cried Beth. “Who is the lad? I’ll give him a piece of my mind tomorrow.” Then Peter looked at her and pleaded, “Don’t go to school, Mam, everyone will think I am a cry baby ’cause I’ve had a fight with the ‘cock of the school’.” Then his face broke into a smile and he said smugly, “Well, he was ‘cock of the school’. I think me and Eddie will have to share the title now.”

Beth looked at Peter and said faintly, “Did you say Eddie? He is not the Eddie you say is now your friend?” Peter laughed and said, “Course he is, Mam, and with Eddie as my best friend, nobody will bully me, we are the best in the school!”

Afterwards, as Beth soaked his bloodstained shirt in cold water, she felt as if a weight had been lifted from her shoulders. Peter would be alright; he had done it the hard way but she did not think she would worry so much about him from that moment on. Later, when Thomas heard the story from Beth, he came to the same conclusion as his wife, and he laughed, saying, “Well girl, if that is what his friend did to him, I hope Peter does not make any enemies.”

Thomas had a good talk with his son and warned him not to start throwing his weight around and get a name of being a bully himself, then he gave Peter a sixpenny coin and told him to buy some toffees and share them with Eddie.

Their youngest son might have more fights over the years he was at St, Andrews School, and he and Eddie might be no strangers to the teacher’s cane, but his time at the school was a happy one, and he came out at fourteen years of age, a credit to his parents and his teachers. He and Eddie were to remain friends, always trying to be better than each other, a fact that worked as a goad to Eddie and made him work much harder at his lessons than he had ever done before.

Eddie came from a very rough family and lived in Timothy Street, a bad slum in the centre of Eccles. He never took Peter to his home, but he was often at the Banham house, where he soaked in everything he saw and heard, for he had decided that their way of life was going to be his in the future. He idolised Beth and was awed by Thomas, and they in turn grew very fond of the boy.

However, Beth and Thomas were happily in ignorance of the scrapes that the two best friends got into. Eddie taught Peter to swim (in the Bridgewater Canal!). Many were the times that they would get out of the water only just in time to dodge the lumps of coal thrown at them by the irate boatmen. Sometimes they would gather up these same pieces of coal, and Eddie would take it home!

They also managed to evade capture by the gamekeepers in the grounds of Sir Humphrey de Trafford’s estate, which lay on the opposite side of the Manchester Ship Canal from Barton. They never did any damage; both boys liked to watch the deer and it was more of an adventure than anything else. Nevertheless, Peter’s parents would have had a fit if they had known what he was up to at times.

Eddie once brought his sister to see them, and whilst the boy was always welcome at the Banham house, the girl was not. She was sly, greedy and with no manners to speak of. Her eyes were everywhere and Beth was careful not to leave her in any room on her own. She could neither trust nor like the girl, however hard she tried. Therefore it was ironic that some years later, the girl was responsible for bringing the Banham family a great deal of happiness.

Eventually Eddie stopped bringing his sister, much to Beth's relief, and it was another four or more years when she appeared at the house again.

They had been at Barton about six months when Thomas took Beth to the premises of Mr. Stephen Shawcross, the auctioneer. He was also the purveyor of sewing machines. Beth was in ecstasy: a sewing machine of her own! Beth never thought that she would ever have one, they were so expensive. That evening after they had finished their meal, Beth spent her time learning everything about it until she was forced to retire for the night.

Her husband knew that, as before, Beth was not settling as easily as he and Peter had done, so he had bought the machine to occupy her mind and in that he certainly succeeded. He was surprised and delighted by the difference it made to her life. Apart from giving Beth a lot of enjoyment, it helped her earn money towards the train fares when she visited Victoria, Dafyd and Will at Christleton, and their friends at Frodsham.

Thomas had settled in at Barton Installation quite quickly. The Superintendent, who lived at the first house in Peel Green Road, was an equable man with the gift of getting the best out of the machinery and the men who worked under him. Also, like Marshville, the workplace was only a few minutes' walk from the house.

The machinery was, of course, all new, and this meant that it was simply maintenance that occupied his days, but some of the equipment on the aqueduct was occasionally damaged, especially the closing water gates at each end of the 'tank', as people were apt to call the swinging aqueduct. He was also called upon to do a night shift on occasions, though not too many as they had one man who preferred to work regular nights.

When he had a Saturday afternoon and Sunday free, the three of them would visit Christleton, staying overnight, and it was a pleasure to see how happy Victoria was and how well their eldest son was doing. Will had worked for a while at each of the shops and gained as much experience on how to work with people as he had with the grocery business. Naturally, he was not received kindly at first; the suspicion that he was eventually to usurp somebody's place created barriers between him and more senior shop workers. However, his sunny nature and willingness to work and learn was gradually winning most of them over.

A year after the Banhams had left Marshville, Ted and Jessie Robbins managed to get a small shop with living accommodation in Frodsham, and opened it selling haberdashery. Jessie was also offering her services as a seamstress. Beth was not normally an envious person, after all, she knew it was a sin, but she allowed herself to feel just a little envious at her friend's good fortune. Unfortunately, the shop had just one bedroom which meant that when Beth, or she and Thomas, paid a visit, they could not be put up for the night.

About that time they received a letter from Michael and Jeannie, informing them that they were to marry. Everyone was delighted, for nothing could please them more than to see both of them find happiness.

Almost two years after the move to Barton, Beth and Thomas had one of their weekend visits from their daughter and son-in-law. By their demeanour Beth knew instinctively what she and Thomas were about to learn, and she was quite correct. Victoria was pregnant, and she and Dafyd were overjoyed.

After mother and daughter had had a weep and the men had shook hands, everyone showed how pleased they were for the young couple, but Beth, like most mothers, had begun to worry about being so far from her daughter at a time when she needed her.

Peter was really pleased; he liked the thought of a little playmate to look after, and Victoria was too touched by his delight to remind him that by the time the baby was old enough to play, Peter would be getting on for thirteen years of age and no longer wanting to play games.

As time went by, Beth became less on edge about it all, especially as Mr. Hughes had by then decided to have one of the new exciting telephones installed at the house, and the Barton Superintendent, whose house also had a telephone, promised that in an emergency, Beth would be able to talk to her daughter. Barton Installation, of course, was connected by telephone to the Company's offices, but the use of it was subject to strict regulations, and Thomas was not so sanguine as to see his superiors smiling on him if he were to use the device on business other than the work matters.

Becky Hughes, on a weekend visit to Barton, told them that they would be most welcome to stay at Christleton any time they wished, and Beth did take up the offer on a few occasions, getting quite brave and travelling unaccompanied on the train to Chester.

It was on one of those visits, two weeks before the baby, or babies (nobody seemed to be very sure) was due, when Elizabeth Rebecca and Megan Jane made their appearance.

The arrival of the twins caught everyone by surprise and it was a local woman who sometimes attended the poorer women in the village that attended to Victoria, the Hughes's family physician not being available at the critical time.

Dafyd rushed home sick with worry and promptly wept when he was confronted by Victoria smiling tiredly, and holding their two little girls.

Beth and Becky clung to each other and shed tears of relief for Victoria and the safe delivery of her babies. Thomas received the message from his Superintendent, who promptly suggested that as they were not too busy, Thomas should get himself off to Chester as soon as possible. When he arrived at Christleton, he was met by Alwyn Hughes, who almost crushed the breath out of him with a hug. Alwyn was, if nothing else, a very demonstrative man.

After everyone had been informed of the event, Victoria and Dafyd received several letters of congratulation, including one from Kate and Captain Howard, and also, to their pleased surprise, a letter from James and Charlotte Prentice.

Mrs. Hilyard asked her friend Becky if she minded her visiting to see the twins, and was promptly told off for even thinking of asking. Becky told her she should know by now that she was more than welcome to come as she was almost family anyway! The tart answer gave Mrs. Hilyard a lovely feeling.

Will let the excitement of the arrival of the twins subside, then when Bronwen and her parents came on a visit to Christleton, he asked the girl's father for permission to become engaged to their daughter. Even though Bronwen was nineteen years of age, her father realised that in eighteen months time she would be able to please herself, so he gave his consent, but with poor grace. Bronwen's mother, who was not as possessive as her husband, was quite pleased that her daughter was to be promised to such a kind and personable young man.

Following on from that event was Daisy's wedding to John Tinker. Again, like the Blakes, the couple decided to make it a quiet affair, but even so, they did invite a good number of guests. It was held in the village of Hatchmere, which was close to where Daisy grew up. Most of her friends managed to attend, but Captain Howard, Kate and Mary had not been invited simply because Daisy (and John agreed with her) did not believe that she could expect somebody of such social class to attend the wedding of a mere maid, although she would have loved to have had Mary with them. However, for the happy couple it was a wonderful day, and Daisy's parents were very proud of their daughter and were delighted that so many of her well-to-do friends had consented to attend.

Daisy was staying on with Mrs. Hilyard and was training the 'new girl' (she had been there since Victoria had left) and would say sometimes, "She is coming on quite well," in the same propriety way as her mistress, an echo of when she, Daisy, was learning her craft!

When the Banhams had arrived at Barton, all the houses were tenanted, the men all being employed by the Company. The very end house on the row was occupied by a couple of around thirty years of age, and Thomas understood that the man worked at Barton locks. He and his wife were both fine-looking people and seemed to be very jolly, but their jollity could be a bit wearing, especially when heard through the bedroom window very late at night.

Both of them enjoyed the theatre, or rather the music hall, and attended shows every week at a theatre in Salford. By their uninhibited laughter and loud voices on these occasions, they also enjoyed a drink or two as well.

The state of affairs continued to everyone's annoyance until the couple received an official warning from Head Office about the nuisance they were creating. After that the noisy revelry very rarely occurred, but there was a lot of talk about drinking bouts in their own house.

However, they did not cause any bother with the other tenants and when everyone heard that the woman was expecting a child, people began to be more tolerant towards the couple, and hoped that they would settle down to a more responsible way of life. But within a year of the child being born, the parents shocked everyone by acting in a way that made them seem quite indifferent to the child, a lovely little girl, that is, when her face was clean. She did not show signs of being ill-treated, but she rarely looked properly dressed or clean.

The neighbours were scandalised, especially as the mother of the child sometimes appeared to be affected by drink. Some of the women surreptitiously took the child into their houses and gave her a wash and something to eat. The mother of the little girl did not seem to be bothered that her child was not within her sight.

About that time Peter and Eddie, both now fourteen years of age, had left school and started work. Peter had been lucky to get an apprenticeship at the newly established works of Mr. Lawrence Gardner and Sons at the Barton Hall works in Patricroft. The firm were makers of, amongst other things, oil and gas engines.

Eddie also started as an apprentice at James Nasmyth's Bridgewater Foundry, makers of machinery and steam locomotives. His workplace was also in Patricroft, and although the two boys were only seeing each other on some nights and at weekends, they still remained firm friends, each trying to better the other.

Eddie scoffed at the idea that oil engines would ever amount to more than a noisy, smelly contraption for powering things like cement mixers and the like. Peter was just as vehement that steam engines would be finished in about ten years' time.

They had both joined Eccles Lacrosse Club and vied with each other as to which of them would be the best player. In that, it was Eddie who became the most fearless and feared player, whilst Peter developed into a very dependable defence man.

One Saturday afternoon, the two friends set out along the canal bank towards Barton Locks. They were aware that Eddie's sister Ada and her friend were shadowing them. Ada's friend had taken a shine to Eddie, and his sister had fallen in with her friend's plan to follow the boys wherever they went. There was a slight mist about that afternoon and the girls lost sight of their quarry. The area still contained meandering sections of the old River Irwell course, cut through when the Canal was constructed, and some of these were filled with stagnant water, the sides being quite steep and muddy.

As the girls threaded their way through these dangerous sections, vainly trying to catch sight of the boys, they heard the sound of a child crying. On one of the sloping sides of the old river section was a little girl clinging to tussocks of grass, her little legs futilely scrabbling as she tried to push her way away from the water.

Whatever faults Ada had, and they were many, she was not a coward and where little children were concerned, there was nothing she would not do to shield them from hurt. Her own younger siblings had a lot to thank her for.

Without any hesitation, Ada carefully let herself down the slope, all the time talking soothingly to the whimpering child, and on reaching her, grasped her wrist and hauled her slowly to safety. When they were out of danger, Ada hugged the sobbing child to her and said to her friend, "See here, Josie, we will have to take her somewhere and get her seen to." Then a thought occurred to her and she said, "I know, we will take her to Mrs. Banham, Peter's mam, she will know what to do." By then her friend Josie was getting chilled and had lost interest in following a couple of 'daft lads', and was quite willing to go anywhere that was less inviting.

When Beth answered the knock on the door, she did not recognise either of the two muddied girls, but she recognised the child. "Oh, Emily," she cried. "Where have you been to get into that state?" Then, remembering her manners, she told the girls to come in, automatically asked them to wipe their feet, then, realising how ungracious she seemed, asked them if they would like a warm drink. Both girls showed no signs of being offended by her shortness of manner and nodded enthusiastically.

Whilst waiting for the kettle to boil, Beth dragged the galvanised bath into the kitchen and prepared a bath for Emily. Ada helped to undress the child and then suddenly burst out, "Emily's got nits, Mrs. Banham." It was true, the little girl was so dirty and her undergarments, such as there was of them, were so filthy and ragged that it was a wonder the poor child did not have lice on her body as well.

As the girls sat drinking their tea Beth and prepared the bath, Ada shyly asked if she could bathe the child: "I'm used to bathing little 'uns' at home." Beth, who by this time had recognised Eddie's sister, answered gratefully and said, "Thank you, Ada, that would help, I want to give these clothes a good wash before she wears them again."

She turned her back before the girls could see how upset she was. Apart from the smell, the child's undergarments were not far short of being rags; there were so many tears in them, and repairs so badly done, that they were only fit for throwing away.

Ada had put Emily in the bath, then let the child finish her drink of milk before bathing her. From the sounds behind her, Beth could tell that the child was loving being in the water, and the way that the two girls were talking to her was heart-warming; they were different girls now that they were doing something useful.

As Beth hung the wet clothes in front of the fire to dry, she came to a decision. She would make the child some new undergarments whether her mother objected to her interference or not, and perhaps she might find enough material to make Emily a dress as well.

Ada attempted to comb Emily's tangled hair to drag out the head lice and to a certain extent managed to make the child less neglected, but Beth realised that she would have to get a fine-toothed comb to do a thorough job of it.

Afterwards the little girl, wrapped up in a blanket, fell asleep in Thomas's chair, and Ada, anxious to help, took on the task of stitching Emily's undergarments, by then a light shade of grey rather than the darker shade that they were before Beth washed them.

Beth brewed them all another cup of tea and cut the girls a slice of cake each. Then she and Josie attempted to make the boots belonging to the girls look more presentable before they went home. It seemed to Beth that neither of the girls that were familiar with boot polish and brushes!

Then, just before the girls were about to leave, Beth got them to stand on a stool whilst she brushed down the hem of their skirts. The mud had dried and the girls were terrified at what their mothers would do to them if they arrived home in such a dishevelled state. Whilst she was cleaning Ada's skirt, she looked up at the girl and her heart jolted in her: there was a look of something poignant, longing? affection? Beth did not know, but she felt guilty at her previous uncharitable thought about Ada. Just as quickly as the look had appeared, it was gone, but in that moment Beth had glimpsed an ordinary young girl, desperate to escape from the life she had to lead, a life where there was little room for affection.

As they were about to leave, Beth gave them each a sixpenny piece, at which their eyes grew round with pleasure, then, as an afterthought, she dipped into her precious store of best soaps and gave each of them a cake of Pears soap. Again that fleeting look appeared in Ada's eyes, then she and Josie hurried away in the direction of Barton Lane and home.

After the girls had gone, Beth checked that Emily's clothes were completely dry and ready for the child when it was time to take her home. Emily still slumbered on, and Beth looked down at her and felt a lump form in her throat. Even with her hair only partly untangled, she looked like a little angel with her long dark eyelashes and her golden hair. Earlier, Josie and Ada had remarked enviously at the child's lovely blue eyes.

When Emily awoke, the smile on her face was like a sunburst to Beth, and she lifted her up and gave her a hug. When the child was dressed, Beth made her a warm drink of milk, then reluctantly took her home.

Mrs. Smith, Emily's mother, did not seem in the least bit bothered as to where her daughter had been, and only tutted when she heard what had happened to the child, but did manage to say, "Ta, Mrs. Banham," and that was that.

Beth came away angry and depressed, but as she told her husband later, she was not standing back and doing nothing in the future; she was determined that Emily would have somebody to see to her. From that time on, there was always someone to keep an eye on the child. What is more, people helped in other ways: a piece of material to make a frock, a toy or a picture book. Beth was extremely grateful for anything that would help Emily have some kind of normal life.

However, one day a neighbour called and angrily informed Beth that she had seen Mrs. Smith at a second-hand clothes stall on the market, and she was selling the child's clothes. Dresses made from the material that she had given to Beth were two of the items.

Beth was as angry as her neighbour, but she cautioned against confronting Mrs. Smith, fearing that if the woman took it into her head to stop Emily visiting the other houses, the child would be the one to suffer. But she assured her neighbour that in future, Emily would not return to her own home in any new clothes; she would always be dressed in the garments she was wearing when she arrived.

Victoria was as appalled as anyone else when the child first came to Beth's notice, and she took it on herself to keep Emily supplied with undergarments. The child was more or less the same size as her own two. Jessie Robbins visited on one occasion and met the child, with the result that the next time she and Beth saw each other, Jessie was able to hand over several day-to-day smock dresses that she had made. In the room that was normally used by Victoria and Dafyd when they visited, several drawers held clothing just for Emily.

The child's father did come round sometimes to apologise for the trouble that Emily was causing them, thanking the neighbours for helping out when his wife was 'ill', as he put it. When asked if Emily could stop overnight with the Banhams should circumstances dictate it, he did not hesitate in granting permission; indeed, he seemed only too glad for that to happen. Likewise, an overnight stay with the Banhams at Christleton brought no objection from Mr. Smith, for there was no doubt now, Mrs. Smith was rarely sober.

The following year after Ada and Josie had brought Emily to Beth, Ada left school and was put to work in the cotton mill. She really wanted to go into service; her occasional contact with Beth had left her with the conviction that if she did work in one of the 'posh' houses, then she too would be like Peter's mother.

Alas, the poor girl was terrified at some of the tasks that younger and smaller workers had to do in the mill, and when she was ordered to crawl under a loom to do one process, she was so frightened that she had to be hauled out by the other girls. Ada lost her job, with the result that when she got home her father gave her a sound thrashing. In the middle of the punishment of Ada, Eddie walked in the room and promptly laid into his father.

Eddie was a big lad when he left school, and in the short time he had worked in the railway workshops he had broadened out and developed more muscle, with the result that he bested his brutal father, and got him to promise that he would never hit Ada or anyone else in the house again. Eddie felt terrible afterwards, but knew that it was something that had needed to be done for a long time.

Soon after, Ada was working as a scullery maid in one of the large houses in Ellesmere Park, a gated and guarded estate on the northern boundary of Eccles. She had realised her dream, and now had a bed she did not have to share with others, and a garret room at the top of the house, and she loved it!

Not long after that, Eddie went into lodgings with a lady called Mrs. Blood, who had a house on Peel Green Road, a quarter of a mile from where the Banhams lived. However, he did not abandon his family altogether, and he was pleased to see that his father was keeping his word regarding physical punishment.

Whilst a ray of hope had settled on his family in Timothy Street, and with Ada settled in a job she loved, Eddie should have been content, but his friend Peter was being more of a know-all than ever, and what upset Eddie more than anything was his friend's attitude towards his own father.

Eddie had a very high regard for Thomas, both as a man and as an engineer. To see his best friend airing his new-found knowledge to his father was, at first, rather comical, for Eddie realised that Mr. Banham had made it his business to learn about oil and gas engines, and was equal to his son in that side of engineering. As time went on, however, Eddie began to get annoyed at Peter's assertiveness, and was upset that his friend's father was so often drawn into a pointless and heated argument, with the result that the Banham house was no longer a pleasant place to visit.

Beth was seriously disturbed at the growing tendency of her son to argue with his father, and to be so contradictory at times. Thomas dismissed her worries about their son's attitude, saying that Peter was no worse than most boys as they entered manhood; flexing their muscles, Thomas called it. Even so, sometimes Beth stepped in and put a stop to the argument when she could see that things were getting too heated, and her husband getting angry.

Despite what Thomas had said to his wife, he was hurt and rather bewildered by his son's dismissive attitude towards him and his engineering knowledge, but he was beginning to have difficulty in hiding his irritation with the boy. He was also worried that his son would drive a wedge between himself and those he worked with and, his friend, Eddie. Peter really was becoming a self-opinionated boor.

When the family came to visit, they had become increasingly worried about the situation and were not slow to let their younger brother know how they felt, but it did not alter the situation much. Peter could not see how thoughtless he was being and how his father was being affected.

When Emily was three years old, a series of events took place which completely and tragically changed her life, and at the same time caused Peter to stop acting so awkwardly towards his father, as he too was overtaken with worry for his little friend.

It all started on a late November morning with a thick fog blanketing everything. Nothing could be seen from the house of the Ship Canal, never mind the church on the far side. It was obvious that no ships would be moving that day, for even the warning lamps on the bridge and the aqueduct were invisible until a person was within feet of them.

The first intimation that something was wrong was when the muffled sound of screaming came to people's ears. Eventually the women realised that the terrible noise was coming from the Smith's house.

A shaken man in the uniform of a Company lockkeeper stood outside the house, and at the sight of the women said in a relieved voice, "Perhaps one of you could see to Mrs. Smith, send for the doctor or something. I've just had the job of telling her that Jack Smith has gone into the 'Cut'." Then he added, recovering a bit, "We can't find him and I don't think we will now."

It was the beginning of a nightmare period, and one which led to Emily's future being put in the balance.

After the doctor and officials from the Company had visited Mrs. Smith, she locked her door and refused to see anybody. In vain did the neighbours try to get in the house; even when they offered to do the shopping for her, the door remained firmly closed.

Luckily, at the time of Mr. Smith's disappearance, Emily had been with Beth, so it was simply a matter of holding her there until her mother started to face the world.

A few days later, one of the neighbours came to Beth, and by the woman's agitated state, it was obvious that something else was badly wrong. It emerged that the woman had smelt gas and after a while she decided that it was coming from Mrs. Smith's house. She had tried the back door, found it unlocked and walked in to find her neighbour's body crouched with her head partly in the open gas oven.

After the police and the doctor had investigated the tragedy, it was decided that the loss of her husband and the fact that she was deemed to be dependent on alcohol had caused her to take her own life whilst the balance of her mind was disturbed. Before she could be buried, her husband's bloated body surfaced by the sluices at Irlam Locks. A week later husband and wife were lowered into the same grave, and Emily was an orphan.

The nightmare became worse for the Banhams when a lady named Mrs. Jones and a gentleman by the name of Mr. Tingle called from the Board of Guardians on behalf of Emily Smith.

The family were shocked to the core and Beth felt sick with anxiety about what was about to happen to the child. Although Mrs. Jones seemed sympathetic to Beth's plea that Emily was left with them, she explained quite gently that the Board had to ensure that the child went to a good home, and preferably to someone she was related to. The next few weeks were agony for the Banhams as they all waited in dread to hear that a relative had been found. Meanwhile, Emily stayed quite happily with them, helping herself unwittingly by charming the members of the Board with her obvious pleasure at being with the Banhams.

The Board received such glowing testimonials about the family, including letters from the Superintendent, the neighbours, and from members of the Chapel. They also received two letters, one from Miss Kate and one from Captain Howard as previous employers.

Eventually, to their relief and great joy, the Banham family were granted custody of the child, and they then took steps to make it completely legal. They learned that a relative had been found, the sister of Mrs. Smith, and she lived in Lincolnshire. But she had declined to take the child. Whilst Beth and Thomas were disgusted by the heartlessness of the woman, they blessed her for giving them a chance to keep Emily.

It seemed that the relief of keeping Emily had freed Peter from his temporary truce with his father and he once again became the bumptious boor that he had been before. Eddie still came to the house but not so much as he had done at one time. He too was finding Peter a lot less pleasure to be with. Peter would call at Mrs. Blood's house and she would always make him welcome, for she was fond of both friends, but if they got arguing too seriously, she would put a stop to it very quickly.

Although Thomas could and did halt Peter's diatribe on 'modern' engineering methods quite easily, he did not enjoy scoring off his son. Eddie was there on one such occasion when his friend (he was still loyal to Peter, although it was a strain sometimes) was holding forth about a casting process that was being used. His father was listening as though interested, when suddenly he interjected in an innocent tone and said, "Oh yes, it is a first-class method, and to think that the ancient Egyptians used it thousands of years ago."

Eddie laughed outright at the way that Mr. Banham had taken the wind out of Peter's sails, and as his friend's face showed his chagrin said, "Put that in your pipe and smoke it, Peter Banham." Then, observing the stubborn look returning to his friend's face, he jumped up and said briskly, "Come on, lad, let's get off to the club, otherwise we'll get no practice today."

Victoria and Will talked more than once to their younger brother about the unhappiness he was creating, and Peter was genuinely surprised to hear that they thought he was the cause of it. They scolded him for trying to prove that he was as good as his father and told him, "You don't have to prove a thing to Dad. He says that you are a natural engineer, you just have to gain experience."

Peter was thrilled to think that his father had such a high opinion of him and resolved to not argue so much in the future. But one evening their difference of opinion became a full-scale row, with father and son angrily facing each other across the table. Into this ugly exchange came Emily, clad in her nightdress, and she went for Peter, pummelling him with her little fists and shouting, "Don't shout at my Dad, Peter," she cried. "I don't like it, stop it, stop it," then she rushed to Beth, sobbing.

It was too much for Beth, and she berated her husband and her son for upsetting the poor child. Shamefaced, they both sat down, and as Beth soothed the weeping little girl, Peter told her he was sorry. He felt thoroughly wretched and miserable, for he was at last recognising that he was to blame for most of the problem.

From that time onwards, he moderated his attitude, even when Emily was not present. He also realised that his father was not happy at his work any longer, and he was aware of the reasons for this.

Some months previously, the Superintendent had been promoted and the man who had replaced him was creating a lot of unhappiness at Barton Installation. The man was a very experienced hydraulics engineer and certainly knew about machinery, but he had no skill in handling men. As a consequence, the fitter who preferred to work at night had left, creating a situation where the other fitters were forced to work more night shifts.

Apart from that, there were other problems caused by the man, and it had got to such a pitch that Thomas and some of the other men were considering following the night fitter's example and look for another job. The problem for Thomas was that if he did manage to find suitable employment, he would have to give up the Company house. There were, of course, the new Company workshops at Mode Wheel, Weaste, and when Thomas had visited the place, he had been very impressed with the buildings and the up-to-date machinery that had been installed. However, when he had made enquiries, he learned that no other skilled men were required.

On a happier note, some months previous to the upsets at Barton, Will married Bronwen at her home village of Caerwys. Her parents were not poor, but they could not afford a lavish wedding, so it was a quiet affair with the guests being mostly family and a few friends. Bronwen, however, got her own way about bridal attendants, with Victoria as matron of honour and two of her friends as attendants. For all her father's opposition to his daughter marrying, he did his best to make it a happy occasion, and in that he succeeded. The couple went to live at Christleton whilst they found a little house in Chester, and within a few weeks they were successful, and they were now living at the village of Goole.

Some months later, Peter had met the niece of Mrs. Blood, Eddie's landlady. The girl's name was Lilian, and the young man was totally smitten. She was not beautiful like Victoria, but she was extremely attractive. Her dark hair, steady grey eyes and her calm, confident manner affected him like no other girl he had ever met (and Peter had met quite a few).

Although Lilian was similarly attracted to Peter, it was a while before she consented to walk out with him. She worked in the office at Gardners, and had heard that the young man was quite clever, but was inclined to be a bit of a show-off. However, the girl could see beyond Peter's bumptiousness and knew that eventually he would grow out of it (with a little help from herself, of course!).

Beth breathed a sigh of relief when Lilian showed a serious interest in her son, for some of the girls who had called on Peter in the past had given her and Thomas some misgivings, but the girl seemed to her like the answer to a mother's prayer.

Lilian was at the Banhams' house when Victoria came visiting one day in May. At first Victoria felt a little constrained in the girl's presence, but the twins had no such inhibitions when Emily introduced them to 'her friend' Lilian; they went to her and wanted to hug and kiss her.

When the girl commented that Peter had told her of his sister's piano playing, Victoria found herself engaged in a lively conversation about their favourite music, and she learned that Lilian played violin with a small string orchestra in Eccles.

Then Victoria told her parents in private what the main purpose of the visit was for. She wanted them to know that she was expecting another baby, and that it was due in late January or early February the following year.

On hearing the news, Beth promptly burst into tears, and even as she hugged her daughter she began to worry as before about everything. She still had not got used to the fact that, for Victoria, money was not a major problem, her mind carrying memories of the hardship that babies brought to people on poor incomes. Victoria laughed and said, "Dafyd and I are very pleased about it, but this time we hope that the baby will be a boy, and, Mam, I am feeling very well, so do not worry about me." Whilst Thomas also hoped for a grandson, more than anything he wanted Victoria to be alright.

The previous year, on the twenty-second of January, Queen Victoria had died. Dafyd and Victoria were considering naming the child after the late queen if the baby was a girl, but in the event that name was not appropriate.

Meanwhile, the three little girls had been excitedly telling Lilian about their respective schools, for being of a similar age, Emily, Rebecca and Jane, as the twins were now referred to, had started in the infants' class at school within days of each other, so they had much to talk about.

When a ship passed the bottom of the garden, the three girls (and Lilian) would rush down to wave to the captain. Usually Emily received an answering wave from members of the crew, but if she did get a wave from the bridge, she would always say that the captain had waved to her!

On the Seventh of February, Nineteen Hundred and Two, the infant Thomas, or to give him his full title, Alwyn Dafyd Thomas, was born. As Victoria playfully told her husband, "Well, he would take his time in coming; after all, he is a boy, and you know how lazy they are."

Everyone was pleased as could be, especially the girls, for they now had a little boy to spoil. The adult members of both families, as pleased as they were about it, were especially relieved that mother and child were both well.

One Sunday some months later, Thomas and Beth, accompanied by Emily, Peter and Lilian, were paying a visit to Jessie and Ted Robbins. They had all enjoyed a picnic on Overton Hills and were sitting around chatting contentedly when Ted Robbins said, "Tell them about Mrs. Dyson's house, Jessie." His wife said, "Well, it cannot be of much interest to you, Beth, but Mrs. Dyson died some months back." She paused then said, "The point is that her daughter now owns both houses and she is talking of letting one of them out for rent; in fact, Beth, the very one that you had set your mind on, what was it, twelve, thirteen years ago?" Thomas said, "That is a nice house, Jessie," and turning to his wife he added, "You were really taken with it, weren't you, Beth?" She smiled and answered, "Oh yes, I fell in love with the house and I sometimes wonder that if we had managed to get it, whether we would ever have left Frodsham." Then she added thoughtfully, "Mind you, it was the best thing that could have happened for our Peter, he has landed on his feet with a good trade," and smiling at Lilian she said, "He has met you, Lilian, my dear." Then turning to look at Emily, who was sitting by the girl watching her as she sketched the view over the town, she said lovingly, "And we have Emily."

Lilian answered and remarked, "Yes, and look what I have been landed with, a lazy, good-for-nothing who sleeps instead of enjoying the lovely view." She was interrupted when the 'good-for-nothing' said, without opening his eyes, "I am not asleep, girl, I do know what is going on." Then opening his eyes, he propped himself up on one elbow and said seriously to his father, "Why don't you move back here, Dad? We all know that you are not happy at Barton."

For a moment there was silence, then both Beth and Thomas made as if to speak. Beth gestured for her husband to continue, and he said slowly, "But, Peter, you still have two years left of your apprenticeship to serve; we could not expect you to abandon that."

He was interrupted quietly by his son, who said, "No, Dad, not me, I would stay at Barton. I am more of an Eccles lad now, my friends are there, my work, my sport and most importantly, Lilian." He looked seriously at the girl and said, "I would not leave Barton if there was nothing else but Lilian to stay for." The girl's face had gone quite pink and Beth thought, 'Why, she is quite beautiful. I have never seen her like this before.' Beth dragged her attention back to what Peter was saying, and he looked at his parents and said, "I could visit you at weekends, the train is so handy, it would be no trouble at all."

Then Thomas said, "I don't want to leave Barton without you, boy, your mam and myself would worry about you too much," and at that Beth nodded her head decisively. Peter smiled fondly at his parents and said, "I don't deserve your affection for the headstrong and thoughtless way that I have behaved, but I really mean what I say. I would be pleased to see you both happy again, and I think that you would be happier coming back here."

"Anyway," he continued, "I could stay at Lilian's aunt's house. Mrs. Blood has said many a time that should you throw me out, she would be glad to put me up, if it was only to give you some peace." Everyone laughed at that and they wondered whether the lady was serious when she had told him that, but then, if he was determined to live in Barton, they were sure that he would find rooms somewhere; he was a very determined and independent young man.

Even whilst they were talking, Thomas was reflecting on how things worked out. Only that morning, not long after they had arrived at Frodsham, he had met Robbie in Main Street, and after they had exchanged news, the young man, now married and working for the Weaver Navigation Company, had mentioned that a fitter was needed at the Gas Works, and that the maintenance engineer at Kydd & Kydd, the jam makers, was due for retirement and the firm would shortly be needing a replacement. Thomas had laughed ruefully at the thought that at one time when he had been trying to find work in the area, there was nothing to be had, and now there was a possibility of two jobs to choose from. A few hours prior to the picnic Thomas had entertained no more than a passing interest, but now, after what Peter had said, a germ of an idea had taken root in his mind.

Later, as they strolled down Church Street towards the Robbins's shop, Thomas suddenly took it into his head to speak with Mrs. Quinn, the late Mrs. Dyson's daughter, about the house she was considering renting out. To say that Beth was surprised was to put it mildly, but she followed her husband up the path to the house without protest, her hopes rising.

When the woman opened the door she smiled at Jessie, whom she knew from frequenting the shop, but she also recognised Beth and Thomas, even though thirteen years had passed, and gave them a surprised look.

Mrs. Quinn's house was much as Beth recognised it and a wave of longing swept over her, and she tried to stifle it, knowing that she had little chance of having it.

The woman was apologetic when she disclosed how much she was asking for rent. "We cannot manage to keep the house in good order for less," she explained. "There are jobs to be done which will cost us more than we can afford, and in fact my husband and myself were considering selling it to help pay for the work to be done on this one."

Thomas took no more than a few seconds to decide. "We will take it, Mrs. Quinn," he said quickly, "but it will be a couple of weeks before we move can in, so if that is alright by you, I will put down four weeks' rent in advance." Beth could hardly believe what she was hearing, but what she was hearing was music to her ears, and whilst she did not know how they were to manage the rent, she felt as reckless as her husband at that moment.

Afterwards they walked to the Robbins's shop. Will turned to his father, grinned, and said, "Good for you, Dad, though I must say you have taken me by surprise," and his father answered, "Boy, I have taken myself by surprise," he said ruefully!

They were all very quiet during the journey home, which in Emily's case was not surprising. She lay fast asleep along the seat, her golden hair fanned out across Beth's lap. Beth was dreaming of all she would do with the house, and what she would do to help out with the money. A jubilant Jessie had told her that she would welcome some help with the sewing work at the shop.

Lilian leaned back contentedly with Peter's arm around her, whilst Thomas stared blindly out of the window, his thoughts on the course he had just embarked upon. He was not having second thoughts, he was having much more than that! What if he could not get a job, and what if he could not afford the rent? Even so, he had not burned his boats completely; any change of plan in the next few weeks would simply involve the loss of four weeks' rent, and although he could ill afford it out of his slender savings, it had been worth it to see how Beth's face had lit up at the prospect of moving to Frodsham.

Peter and Lilian had promised to help with the move and with any work that needed doing to the house, and he was sure that Will would also want to help.

A day later Thomas posted a letter addressed to Messers. Kydd & Kydd enquiring about the position regarding the maintenance engineer's job. At the weekend he received a reply thanking him for his interest but informing him that the position would not be vacant for some weeks yet. However, he was invited to attend an interview and was given a choice of three dates.

The result was an interview at Frodsham two weeks after he had first written, and when he attended he was dismayed to come face to face with the unsmiling Mr. Deakin from the Chapel and formerly an official of Frodsham Gasworks. However, nobody could have been more surprised than Thomas at the affable tone of the proceedings; the man actually smiled several times! Then when Thomas was offered the job he thought that he must have met a different Mr. Deakin, possibly his twin brother. But whatever, Thomas was given a starting date six weeks from the day of the interview.

When Thomas handed in his notice to leave, he was gratified when the Superintendent expressed his regret at losing such a good man, and when his superior offered his best wishes for his new position, Thomas felt rather guilty for his uncharitable thoughts about the man over the last few years.

Peter's assertion that Mrs. Blood would take him in proved correct; to have the two boys, and best friends at that, as regular boarders, suited her very well. He moved in with her a week before his parents' and Emily moved to Frodsham.

The leave-taking from their friends at the Chapel and their neighbours was sad but nowhere as upsetting as it had been on their move from Marshville eight years ago. On this occasion they both felt a sense of going home, and when the LNWR cart came to take their furniture and goods to the railway goods yard, they were quite buoyed up. All they then had to do was to walk to Patricroft Station and catch the train that would take them to Frodsham. Emily, however, did have one regret: there would be no ships passing the bottom of their garden at the new house!

Chapter 36

Return to Frodsham

Settling in at the house on Church Street took on an almost dreamlike quality. Beth was still having difficulty in accepting the fact that they were at last back in Frodsham, the town she had fallen in love with so many years ago. And to be in the house she had also fallen in love with was even more wonderful. To have Thomas at home, busy but happy, took her back to the earlier days of their marriage when he had put the old cottage to rights.

Thomas himself had recovered much of his former enthusiasm, and in fact was considering, amongst other things, making three doll's houses, one each for Victoria's girls and one for Emily. Also he planned to make a tug boat for Victoria's little boy when he was a bit older.

Beth tried not to worry about the amount of rent they were paying each week, but she had a sublime confidence that her husband would not let the house go now that they had got it. To help out with the rent and housekeeping she had worked with Jessie a few times and thoroughly enjoyed herself on each occasion. Her friend had two orders for her special quilts to fulfil, and having Beth to help freed her from the shop and the dress alterations that formed an important part of her business.

Emily had very quickly settled down and was looking forward to starting school, and happily she had already made friends with two of the children in the nearby houses.

Will and Bronwen came on the second weekend, and whilst the weather was dry, Thomas and his son managed, with the aid of borrowed ladders, to put right the loose slates and ridge tiles on the roofs of both houses, thus saving Mr. and Mrs. Quinn a considerable amount of money. The damage had been caused during the very high winds of the previous winter and the quotes for having the work done had been worrying the couple, who themselves, did not have a large income. That repair, and others which Thomas, helped by his sons, eventually dealt with, persuaded the lady to grant the Banhams several rent-free weeks, and later, a reduction in their rent.

Thomas was looking forward to starting his job at Kydd & Kydd's jam works with some trepidation, for he had never before worked amongst females, and he had been warned humorously to watch out for himself, especially amongst the older women! As it was, it turned out alright, although he was somewhat shocked by the way that a small number of them acted when men were around.

He was extremely thankful to be free of the Barton night shifts; however, he did work late on occasions to put some piece of equipment right in order that it would not interfere with the following day's production. There was also the added bonus of a fine view over the town and the River Mersey in the distance from the windows of his workshop and office.

He and Beth enjoyed meeting old friends at the Chapel; it was if they had never been away. Even Mr. Deakin seemed to smile more readily!

One Sunday afternoon when Will and Bronwen were visiting, they all walked down to Marshville and what they saw depressed them. The shop, which held so many memories, was empty and boarded up, as were many of the huts. The two larger huts once housing their family and the Robbins's were occupied and indeed looked quite well cared for. Some of the other huts were also occupied but most of them were shabby and in a poor state.

Then Will spotted Mrs. Garroway and they went over to speak with her. She was obviously pleased to see them and told them that she was still making her ointments and medicines, a fact that was evident by the odd smell that always clung to her! Little Emily was overwhelmed by this monstrous figure in her voluminous skirts, and hid behind Beth, who laughed it off, saying that the little one was shy.

Afterwards they visited the jetties of Saltport, now merely a ghost of its former self. No moored vessels alongside, no railway connection and only one steam crane, and that looked as if it had been abandoned. Captain Howard had been quite right in his forecast: the little port had served the purpose it had been built for, and was no longer needed.

As they were walking back through the hutted village, Mrs. Garroway stopped them and asked about the rest of the Banham family, then she told them that Sally (with the grown-up twins) was hoping that she would soon be able to move to the village of Barnton now that her husband had got a job with the Weaver Navigation Company. Beth had already learned that Clara and her husband and Jimsy had moved to Ellesmere Port; Clara was running a shop not far away from the docks where her husband worked.

By this time they had been visited by most of their friends from the town, and one of the most pleasing was that of Dr. Mills, accompanied by Mrs. Joyce, Ian's former landlady. They were, by then, firm friends and were often seen together at events in the town, and it pleased Sarah that her father was not always alone and she liked Mrs. Joyce very much.

Ian and Sarah had called soon after the Banhams had moved in, and they had offered their assistance should help be needed. Mrs. Hilyard did not visit until she was invited formally, but once she had been assured that she would be most welcome, she had visited two or three times afterwards.

Daisy and John Tinker had called and from them the Banhams learned of a most heartening tale concerning Mr. Parks, the drinks man, and his daughter Lucy (now married).

It seemed that Mrs. Hilyard, after learning of Mr. Parks's situation, had set to and enlisted the help of her late husband's shipping friends, and between them they had helped Mr. Parks to start up again in the restaurant business. As before, it was a chophouse and was situated in Liverpool's shipping business area. Lucy was dealing with the financial side of it and apparently they had made a success of it.

Beth and Thomas were very moved by Mrs. Hilyard's kindness and pleased for Mr. Parks and his family. As Beth said to her husband, "Mrs. Hilyard had demonstrated true Christian spirit in a most practical way rather than merely talking goodness."

Jessie had spoken of her desire to have a larger shop, one with two bedrooms. Her idea was to have the second bedroom as a workroom with a large table for the marking out and cutting of the materials when she was making her quilts. Now that Beth was working with her, she could see that such an arrangement would help her friend with her dressmaking.

Some weeks after the move to Frodsham, Beth was confronted one morning with the upsetting spectacle of heaps of partly burned thatch and debris on the pavement in front of some cottages. The roofs of the dwellings, West Bank Cottages, had been destroyed by the fire and although the wall facing the street was still standing, it looked doubtful whether the building could be put right again.

The effect on Jessie was very marked. She became fearful of the roof over her shop, for that also was thatch, and she decided that the next shop, when one became available, would have a slate or tiled roof. She also had Ted place buckets of water at various points in case they too had a fire.

However, Jessie was not able to find another property for some time, but when she did, it was in no small way thanks to help from Thomas and Beth, and in a way that none of them would have previously dreamed possible.

The weekend following the fire, Thomas, Beth and Emily went to Christleton to attend the christening of Victoria and Dafyd's little boy, Alwyn Dafyd Thomas. It was a wonderful family gathering, with Will and Bronwen, and her parents. Peter and Lilian had also managed to get there, the first time the girl had met Dafyd's parents, and at first she was rather overwhelmed by Mr. Hughes, but by the end of the day he had charmed her over.

Peter told his parents the news concerning Eddie's family. His father had been ill for some months and had died in March. On a happier note, the Corporation had decided to demolish Timothy Street and had built houses in Patricroft to house those who had been displaced. Just prior to Peter visiting Christleton, he and Eddie had helped move the family into the new house in Lewis Street, a wonderful house and neighbourhood compared with the grim Timothy Street. Peter was especially pleased to inform his mother that Eddie had become quite proud of his sister, Ada, and to say that the girl had told him that she 'wanted to be like Mrs. Banham'. Peter told his mother that Ada was 'quite the lady now'.

The conversation veered to Peter's sporting life, for he was now a participant of many of the games played by the Gardners teams. Victoria and Will had both become members of the tennis club where Dafyd belonged, Will being an enthusiastic and competitive player, whilst his sister preferred a more relaxed game. Will had also become a member of the Grosvenor Rowing Club and was, like Dafyd, a very competitive oar.

Lilian professed a desire to have a picnic on the river sometime, so it was decided that if the weather was fine the next time they visited, they would all go, hiring several boats to accommodate them.

One evening some weeks after the christening, Thomas arrived home after working late, and he could see that Beth was in a scarcely concealed state of agitation. Once Emily had been put to bed, Beth pushed a letter across the table and burst out, "It's from Sleaford in Lincolnshire; that is where that sister of Mrs. Smith lived, and it looks official and I've been frantic with worry all day about it." Then looking perilously close to tears, she continued, "They can't take Emily off us, can they?"

For a few moments Thomas allowed Beth's anguished pleas to upset his normal balanced approach, and without considering whether the letter might concern something else, he grimly replied, "She is ours legally Beth, and she would have to apply to the court to try and get her away from us."

But instead of allaying Beth's fears, the mention of the word 'court' only served to exacerbate them, and she cried, "But, Thomas, we love her, that woman didn't and she would not take her, so how can she want her now if she didn't love her then?"

Thomas shushed her and said quietly, "Now calm yourself, girl, we don't want to wake the child, and the sooner I read what it is she wants, the sooner we can plan what we have to do about it."

Beth gazed in an agony of anticipation as her husband opened the official-looking letter and for a few moments there was silence in the room. Then Thomas's face became transformed, but in a way that did not tell Beth whether the contents were better or worse than they had feared. He simply looked astounded.

After a moment his wife spoke, her voice filled with dread. "Thomas, what does it say, is it from that woman or from a lawyer, please, Thomas tell me, does she want Emily?"

Thomas pushed the worrisome missive across the table and said in a tone of wonderment, "Here, girl, read this; it concerns me, not our little girl."

Tremulously Beth began to read the words that had so affected her husband. It was indeed a solicitor's letter, but the contents were not concerning Emily, as her husband had told her, nor was it anything that would cause them worry or give them trouble.

The solicitor had been trying to trace him for some months to inform him of the death of Thomas Richmal Banham, cousin of the late Lionel Banham, the father of Thomas Banham, with the object of ascertaining whether he, Thomas Banham, was the real son of the aforementioned Lionel Banham.

He was asked to reply and if he was the Thomas Banham mentioned, then would he send proof of his identity, and procure persons of good standing to vouch for the veracity of his statement.

Beth's face was a study and her husband had to laugh, his previous fears about Emily having been swept to one side, and that to him was more important than news that he had inherited a gold watch or some such thing from his deceased relative.

Then Beth laughed in return and said rather shamefacedly, "Oh, Thomas, I was so silly, jumping to conclusions like that, and now that we know that it does not concern our chick, I want to pop in and see if she's alright." Thomas nodded his head understandingly; he knew how she felt. The dread which had gripped them had been lifted and they were both a little euphoric.

When Thomas showed the letter to Dr. Mills the following day, his friend said with a twinkle in his eyes and just a touch of heavy humour, "I hope that you will still talk to me, Thomas, when you find that you have inherited a country estate. Mind you," he added, "Lincolnshire is a long way from here. I doubt if you could make your voice reach Frodsham from there even if you shouted." Both men laughed, and Dr. Mills promised that he would write to the solicitor and suggested that he countersigned Thomas's answering letter.

That evening Thomas wrote a letter to Captain and Mrs. Howard requesting that they provide proof of identity. Some days later he received a reply which informed him that two letters, one from him and one from Miss Kate as his earlier employer, had been sent to the solicitor. He also received their congratulations and their hopes that his legacy would be to his great advantage.

Thomas had to smile at the last bit, for his memories of his father's cousin did not conjure up an image of a prosperous landed gentleman. Uncle Richmal, as he was usually called, was a man very similar to Thomas's father, not too well dressed and with the same air of gentle optimism, and Thomas remembered wryly where that optimism had led his father financially.

After the flurry of letter writing, Thomas and Beth got on with the more important things in life, in Thomas's case, the making of the doll's houses for the twins and a wheeled tug boat in readiness for when baby Thomas was old enough to play with such toys.

A further piece of news was that Bronwen was pregnant and the child was expected to arrive in March the following year. When Beth heard the news she acted just as if the girl was her own flesh and blood: she started worrying. However, after a visit to Hoole, and seeing for herself the blooming, cheerful Bronwen, she settled down in anticipation for another grandchild.

A second letter from the Sleaford solicitor informed Thomas that the communications from Dr. Mills and Captain Howards and Mrs. Katherine Howard had been deemed sound enough to prove that he, Thomas Banham, was the same Thomas Banham named in the Last Will and Testament of the late Thomas Richmal Banham. It went on to give details of what was due to him and ended up by offering his congratulations and best wishes for the future. The letter ended by informing him that a banker's draft would be sent to him as soon as the necessary arrangements had been made.

When Thomas read the letter, he could hardly believe what he was reading, and in a voice that was little more than a croak he said to his wife, "Here, girl, read this." Beth's eyes opened wide with shock and she said shakily, "Thomas, this must be a joke, surely this can't be meant for you." Her husband shook his head in disbelief and stretched out his hand and took back the letter.

Once again he read the contents, but the words remained unchanged. Mr. Thomas Richmal Banham had died the previous Christmas and had had left an estate which amounted to a sum which, when divided up as instructed, gave Thomas Banham the sum of Three Thousand, Seven Hundred and Sixty-nine Pounds, Seven Shillings, and Four Pence.

For some reason Thomas could not explain, his eyes kept landing on the very welcome sum of Sixty-nine Pounds, Seven Shillings and Four Pence! His brain seemed to reject the fact that he now had over three thousand seven hundred pounds to his name.

For some moments it was as if they both had been holding their breath, then they both started off at the same time, excitedly talking of what this fortune would mean to them. Thomas nearly choked when Beth said with all seriousness, "Well, we won't have to worry about the rent, will we?" He had decided that the rent was a matter that would not bother them in the future if he had his own way, and accordingly he approached their landlords the following day with a view to buying the house. The Quinns were only too willing to sell, and a week later the house belonged to Thomas and Beth!

Only then, when everything was settled, did Thomas let the family know of his good fortune. He invited them to Church Street and while they were all together, he gave them the news and presented Victoria, Will and Peter with four hundred pounds apiece to help them buy a house.

They were all astounded and a babble of voices broke out. But Victoria shook her head and said quietly, "I don't want the money, Dad, I think that Will and Peter deserve it more than I do." Dafyd added his words on the matter and said, "We thank you from the bottom of our hearts, Mr. Banham, but I agree with Victoria wholeheartedly."

Thomas shook his head and told them, "Each of our children get the same, and if you want to set up a bank account for each of your children as we are doing for Emily, then that is alright with me." Victoria smiled and gave her father a hug, and Dafyd shook him by the hand and thanked him on behalf of their children.

Amidst the excited and joyful chatter, Beth noticed that Lilian had sat to one side, almost as if she had withdrawn from the rest of the family. Before Beth could go over to the girl, Peter went to Lilian and started softly talking to her. Then the girl put her arms around Peter's neck and a lovely smile lit up her face. Peter then took her hand and she arose and came to Beth and Thomas.

"Mam, Dad," said their son, "I have asked Lilian if we could be engaged and she has said yes, so when I see her parents, I am going to ask their blessing."

Quietly as he had spoken, he was overheard and before Peter and Lilian knew it, they were surrounded by the others offering their congratulations, hugs and kisses. Then tears flowed as they do on such wonderfully happy occasions!

——— ——— ———

If the family were astounded, or amazed and even delighted, there were no words to describe Thomas and Beth's emotions. They seemed to exist in an unreal dreamlike state, and it had not sunk in that they were of independent means. Thomas had no intentions of giving up his job, and neither had Beth.

Jessie, without knowing exactly how much money her friend had come into, was delighted that the future for the Banhams looked more secure, and her face was wreathed in smiles of happiness for the rest of the day

A few days later, Beth was talking to one of the parents of a little girl who was starting school at the same time as Emily. They had seen Beth often enough in Jessie's shop and they casually mentioned that a slightly larger shop on the same side of Main Street was being put up for rent soon, and they thought that it would be much better suited to Mrs. Robbins's business.

Beth could hardly wait to tell her friend the news, and an idea was forming in her mind as to how she and Thomas could help. When Jessie heard about the other shop, she put up her board which told would-be customers that she would be 'Back in Five Minutes', and they hurried across the road to view it from the other side. The premises were situated diagonally across from the Bear's Paw, and Jessie wanted to make sure that it had a slate roof. Once that detail had been established to Jessie's satisfaction, they crossed back again and strolled past the shop making mental notes.

Jessie was very taken with the place, but worried herself as to how much it would cost to make it suitable for their purpose. However, she had obviously made up her mind that the shop was just what she wanted.

That evening Beth talked her idea over with Thomas and he was enthusiastic about it, with the result that on the following morning, when talking to Jessie, Beth suggested that she and Thomas put two hundred pounds towards making the shop suitable for the work they were engaged in. Any left over after the work had been completed would be kept as a 'float' in case anything untoward occurred.

Jessie was not inclined to take any money from the Banhams; she said that they had been through enough hard times and she thought that their windfall should be used for their own and their family's good. However, a meeting involving Ted Robbins and Thomas as well as the two women resulted in Jessie tearfully accepting the offer, and now all that was wanted was for the other shopkeeper to announce that he was quitting the business, and they could make a bid to take over the shop.

The following week Emily started school and she settled in quite quickly. She made some friends on her first day and one of them, Emily earnestly told her mam, came from a very large family, so she did not have many nice clothes. She wondered if any of the clothes that she had grown too big for could be given to her new friend.

Beth knew that there were several dresses and other items that were indeed too small for their little girl, but she gave Emily a word of warning. "We must be careful how we make the offer, Emily; some people do not like charity, so I suggest that we talk to the teacher first, and see what she has to say."

Emily was an intelligent child and could see quite plainly what her mam was meaning, so Beth approached the teacher the next day about the matter. Emily's teacher was pleased with the offer, but told Beth that the school already had a scheme to give the less well-off children better clothing. However, she told her, some of the girls objected to wearing clothes that they had previously seen being worn by somebody else. In Emily's case nobody had ever seen her wear the dresses that Beth was donating, so there would be no problem in handing them out to other girls. The teacher promised Beth that Emily's friend would certainly receive her share. When Emily heard what had been decided, she was quite satisfied.

When things had settled down after the allotment of money to the family had been concluded, Thomas turned his attention to their own needs. He left it to Beth to choose the carpeting which was needed throughout the house, but unknown to his wife he had made enquiries about having a water flush privy installed, for he knew how much she was taken with those at Rebecca and Alwyn's house.

He had made arrangements for the installation of a telephone, although he was aware that Beth would avoid using the instrument if she could, and for himself, he was looking to buy one of the new metal smoothing planes he so coveted since he had first clapped eyes on one!

The house was being made spick and span in readiness of visitors, for Captain Howard and Miss Kate were coming to Chester soon and had promised to call before they went on to North Wales. Also Michael, Jeannie, Flora and Fraser were coming in the late autumn if they could manage it. Thomas had laughingly warned Emily not to stand still for too long. as she would be in danger of being polished as well, so for a day or so, the child had made a game of it and skipped out of the way each time Beth appeared with a duster in her hand!

One afternoon, Beth was returning to the shop with a bag of shopping when she became aware of a couple walking towards her, the man looking vaguely familiar. For a moment Beth was unsure whether she was correct in her thinking, but when she saw the dark area around the man's eye and saw the grin of recognition on his face, she knew who it was.

"Clarence," she cried delightedly, and putting her shopping down she hugged him. "How good it is to see you," she said. "We have never stopped wondering what could have happened to you."

For it was indeed Clarence, 'One Eye', as he had been cruelly nicknamed in his native Manchester, but such a different person. Gone was the diffident, almost shifty manner; instead he looked taller, more confident and he held a person's gaze without looking away as he formerly did. It warmed Beth's heart to see him like this, for she still felt guilty at her initial antipathy on first meeting Clarence.

He introduced her to the dark-haired young woman as his wife, Gwyneth, who smiled broadly at Beth and said in a strong Welsh accent, "He has always talked about how you changed his life, Mrs. Banham, he will never forget you all."

Then Clarence embarked on an explanation of why he had left in such a hurry, and he held nothing back. "Gwyneth knows everything about me, Mrs. Banham, and she made me send the ten shillings back that I stole from my mam."

Beth, seeing that there was much more to be said, "I'll tell you what we can do, let us step off the street and have a talk round a cup of tea and a piece of cake in the shop." At that Gwyneth laughed and said, "That is another thing that Clarence has never forgotten, your lovely fruit cake; he is always getting me to make fruit cakes."

When they entered the shop, Jessie was sorting out the button box (a job which usually kept Emily happy for hours) and she stared at Clarence in amazement before giving him a hug.

Afterwards, sitting round the table, Clarence explained what had happened after he had left the Canal site, and he told them how he had ended up in North Wales.

"I was walking down a lane away from Chester," he said, "when I came to a road gang, and they had a tar boiler and it was on fire. In the shaft the horse had started to panic and to make it difficult for the men to free it, the burning tar stopped them from reaching the horse." He stopped, and then said soberly, "I couldn't just stand there and see the horse being burned and before I knew it, I was uncoupling the poor beast and leading it away from the fire." He then told his enthralled listeners about being taken on by the gang and working with them until they reached Queens Ferry, and the Welsh border.

By then he could see the hills of North Wales and he wanted to be amongst them, so he said goodbye to the road gang and, with a little more money in his pocket, set off walking again. A few days later he joined up with another road gang which paid him just a few shillings to look after the horses. One morning they were working near Holywell when one of the men clumsily backed the heavy tipping cart into a farmer's dry stone wall and sent it tumbling. Clarence volunteered to rebuild it whilst the others carried on with their work. He had managed to rebuild most of it when he became aware that he was being watched.

It was the farmer in person, and he spoke English with a very strong Welsh accent. But for all that, Clarence began to understand that what he had done was satisfactory to the man. Mr. Rowlands, for that was the farmer's name, spoke to Clarence on the second day and asked him if he would like to work for him for a short while. The wages offered were low but they were better than the few shillings he was then earning, so he quit the road gang and started working for the farmer.

The few weeks' work turned into months and then years, and when Mr. Rowlands received news that his son, serving in the British army, had died from an insect bite in South Africa, Clarence stayed on permanently. He had grown very fond of Mr. Rowlands, and was glad to be by the man's side after his son had gone.

The farmer could not read or write, and usually went to his neighbour's cottage where their daughter would read his letters for him and, when a reply was needed, write it for him. And that is where Clarence met Gwyneth. Before long the girl had taken on the task of teaching him to read and write.

At first her parents had no liking for this shifty-looking Englishman, but as time went on they saw a difference in him, and they noted his kindness to Mr. Rowlands, and his gentleness when talking to Gwyneth and her mother.

After he had been at the farm for about six years, Clarence married Gwyneth with the blessing of her parents and the girl came to live at the farm. Mr. Rowlands now enjoyed the company of two people he looked upon as a son and a daughter-in-law.

Clarence concluded his story by telling them proudly that they had a son, Rowland Owen, and that he was now six years old. He was that day staying with his grandparents.

Then he asked about the family and when he was told that none of them had ever forgotten him, he looked really pleased. He also asked them to pass on his thanks to Michael, when they next wrote to him, for the help he had given him with his writing.

Gwyneth explained that she had long wanted to see the place where his life had changed so much, so they had made a special journey to Marshville and she found it very depressing, not at all like she had pictured it. However, she told them a little self-consciously, now that she had met and talked to Beth and Jessie, she could see why he had been so happy in that grim place.

Eventually, after refusing to stay for a meal, Clarence and Gwyneth took their leave and after an affectionate hug off both women, made their way to the railway station. They were both happier after meeting some friendly faces, and now knew that they could visit Frodsham in the future and be sure of a welcome. Gwyneth was particularly contented, for after meeting the two ladies, she was pleased that such decent people were there to give him some sort of a home life in that terrible village, although she found it hard to imagine such nice women living in those huts.

——— ——— ———

It was one of those days in September when people started talking of an Indian Summer. Beth had gone shopping with Victoria and Jessie Robbins, leaving Thomas looking after the children and their friends. He was stretched out in a deckchair with a straw boater tipped over his face and keeping one eye on the children as they ran around the garden making those terrible noises that indicated that they were enjoying themselves.

Then Beth walked in and kissed him on the cheek before sitting down in the other deckchair. She said, “I will make a pot of tea in a few minutes, Thomas,” then asked him, “How have the children behaved, they haven’t given you any trouble, Thomas?” Her husband pursed his lips and said equably, “Oh no, just had to pull two of them out of the apple tree, but otherwise, no trouble.”

Beth shook her head and said ruefully, “Boys, they are all the same,” only to be interrupted by Thomas, who told her, “No, girl, it was Emily and one of the other girls.”

Beth grimaced and said, “I hope she is not going to turn into a hoyden.” Thomas said smiling, “Like Victoria was at the same age? Well, love, look at her now.”

They were both more contented than they had been for many years. As Beth would sometimes remind her husband, “None of this would have come about if you hadn’t lost your temper that day with Captain Rodgerson.” Thomas would nod in agreement, setting how much they had lost against how much they had gained, but even so he vowed: never again would one bout of bad temper be allowed to dictate their futures.

Thomas intended to continue working at Kydd's Jam Works, for the simple reason that he enjoyed his job. Even though he and Beth no longer had any money troubles, and now that they owned the house they were living in (something that they would never have dreamed of in previous years). Thomas still saw himself as an ordinary working man.

Of course, life was not without its problems, one which was particularly upsetting to Beth was the remnants of ill-feeling from a dwindling number of those who had been angered by the drunken antics of some contractor's employees.

Thomas had experience a whiff of this animosity, but on very rare occasions, however, an encounter with one of Frodsham's most vociferous opponents of the Manchester Ship Canal showed him that Thomas, amongst others who has settled in the town, were still held in contempt by those with bitter memories.

"I know you, mister," the man said, without attempting to disguise his dislike. "You were one of them 'as come here to work on that there Ditch."

Thomas refused to be drawn into an argument and answered placidly, "You are quite right, my friend. I am one of the people of the Cut and I am proud to have been part of it."